JOHN MCNICHOL

WHERE THE
RED SANDS FLY

THE YOUNG CHESTERTON CHRONICLES
BOOK 3

HILLSIDE EDUCATION

Cover art and design by Grayson Bowling
Book Design by Mary Jo Loboda

ISBN: 978-1-955402-24-8

The Young Chesterton Chronicles, Book 3, Where the Red Sands Fly, is a work of fiction.
All incidents and dialogue and all characters with the exception of some well-known
historical and public figures are products of the author's imagination and are not to be
construed as real. Where real-life historical or public figures appear, the situations, incidents
and dialogues concerning those persons are entirely fictional and are not intended to depict
actual events or to change the entirely fictional nature of the work. In all other respects, any
resemblance to persons living or dead is entirely coincidental.

Hillside Education
475 Bidwell Hill Road
Lake Ariel, PA 18436
www.hillsideeducation.com

At the end of my thousand year journey
To the land where the Red Sands Fly,
I saw a wood nub in the ground
And I stopped from passing by.
I dug and it became a cross
Buried deep so long ago,
I dug more and't became a dome
To hold the faith I couldn't show.
I dug and dug, and found a church
House of bread in house of gold
A faith I'd lost was finally found
And old was young and young was old.
An ancient wrong now put to right
I sit, and stare and cry
At wonder, romance, and love so fair
In the land where the Red Sands Fly.

Noah J. Clemon

For Our Lady of the Red Sands Shrine in Tamil Nandu, India.

Prologue

"The free man owns himself. He can damage himself with either eating or drinking; he can ruin himself with gambling. If he does he is certainly a damn fool, and he might possibly be a damned soul; but if he may not, he is not a free man any more than a dog."

– Broadcast talk, June 11, 1935

1892 A.D.
MARS.

The sun hung in the pink-orange sky, scorching the ground with the same splendor as it had for millions of years. The red dust of the mountains and valley floor soaked up the sun's rays with the same patience it had displayed for eons, lying quiet and unmoving. Very occasionally, a breeze tugged at the dirt.

And so it had been for the first few billion years of the valley's existence. For this was Mars, a world ancient, dry and dying. For the last few decades, though, the valley had been home to a colony of humans. Consequently, it had seen a fairly regular ebb and flow of human and Martian traffic once the colony's outlying settlement had been built.

The settlement was, indeed, small by almost any standard. It was a humble outcropping of square-topped, one-and-two story buildings that had sprouted and struggled to bloom in the harsh light of the Martian sun and the cold night of the double moon. It went on to hold its place in the unforgiving red desert with the tenacity of a dead man's grip, becoming the kind of hardscrabble place where folks kept to themselves so long as rents were paid and pepperbox pistols stayed in their holsters.

Too far from the larger settlement to be truly noticed and too poor to be a threat to anyone's power, the settlement had never even had a real name for any length of time. The territory surrounding it changed hands every year or two, which meant it was renamed after some historical figure from whatever country owned their valley at the time. Currently held by either the Germans or the Americans (no one quite remembered which), it was called VonSteubenBurgh, after some general or other. And it was in the largest building in this small colony town that the man known as the Gardener stood at the window and watched the red sands swirl beautiful, delicate patterns.

The Gardener thought about his own school days—especially of the football games in the public school green of the field. What he wouldn't give right now to look out a window and see green instead of red sand for a change . . .

"Two-pair, sixes and sevens!"

The voice behind crowed in victory, high-pitched and filled with triumph as it yanked him out of his thoughts.

"Three of a kind," another voice drawled, followed by the quiet *tap!* of the playing cards hitting the tabletop. Coins jingled as the winner dragged the pile of coins from table's center.

Curses sounded from the first voice, then chuckles from the second. It had gone back and forth like this for the past few hours, and for two days before that. The Gardener had dropped out of the game an hour into the first day in their new home, which had been two hours after he and his associates had murdered the previous owner and moved in.

The Clerk had worried aloud the first day about others in town discovering their crime, his hand trembling as he'd slapped down card after card with his screechy voice. The Gardener and the Reader had done their best to quiet him without smacking him. Soon, after a few threats and a little actual violence on the Gardener's part, they'd silenced the Clerk and set up Jimmy in the basement with his paraphernalia. The previous unpleasantness soon forgotten, the card game had started and hadn't stopped since.

"Gardener," the Clerk said, frustration seeping through his highborn accent, "will you please check on our guest downstairs, and discern how long he's going to remain there?"

"Hopefully," the Reader said, "he'll take just enough time for me to take the rest've your flash, my dear *claaaark!*"

The Clerk swore under his breath and readied himself for the next hand. The Gardener turned without a sound and stepped down into the basement.

He pushed open the creaking wooden door and stepped into another world. The basement still had its thick, red brick walls and dry smell, but the racks of food and other goods had long been replaced by a series of machines. He stepped quietly down the short stairwell, watched one machine do its job for a few minutes until he tired of it, and then he turned to the next one. One hissed like a sleeping dragon, while another drew pictures with dotted ink spots on a rolling piece of parchment, the ink drying instantly from another machine blasting warm air on it. The next machine tapped, sliced and punched holes in the papers until they were the size of regular pages, and still another clicked and clucked like an unhappy schoolteacher as it slapped paper after paper into a neat pile, promptly gluing and stitching each page to the previous one, then attaching a green, woven-board book cover to each pile of pages once it reached one-hundred sheets. The books, twenty-something of them so far, were stacked neatly in the corner by another mechanical arm that moved and acted without tiring or erring in any way that the Gardener could see.

And in the center of the whirling, chattering, smoking mayhem sat a man at a table. He wore dark pants and a black vest and a bowler hat. His shirt had been a clean white when he'd begun the work a week ago, but now the armpits were yellow and the cuffs were dark with ink, dirt, and soot.

In the middle of the table was a small device that held a tiny cardboard disk in the center of it. Wires and tubes that seemed more like veins and arteries of a living being sprouted from the disk-holder and connected it to every other machine in the basement.

The man in the bowler hat seemed to take no notice of the Gardener as he entered, gingerly stepping around machines and over wires. The bowler hat man remained crouched at his desk, pouring over papers, rolling dice, making feverish scribbles on other papers, and scurrying to one machine and then another.

The Gardener gave a wary look at the ink-dipping machine. Seeing a machine draw a picture without the aid of human hands always left him feeling a bit unsettled for reasons he could never quite articulate.

"How goes the work, Jimmy?" the Gardener said, trying to sound casual.

"Is this important, mate?" Jimmy snapped, tipping back his bowler hat with a hand still clad in a black fingerless glove. " 'Cause if it ain't, I want you to go. I'm almost finished an' I don't want to make a mistake."

"Just checking on your progress, Jimmy, that's all. You need anything?"

"You to be quiet is all for now. You can stay, but don't touch anything, see?"

"You're the boss in here, Jimmy," the Gardener said. Suddenly warm from the machine's exhaust, he rolled up the sleeves of his own work shirt and watched Jimmy toil at the long workbench. After a minute or two, he snuck a peek at the picture that the ink machine was making with thousands of rapidly tapped black dots—*stipplograph* was what Jimmy had called it. The building it was drawing was intricately designed, with five towers and a courtyard.

The Gardener had been in one of the ancient Martian cities once already. The place had smelled of death and old dirt, and the gooseflesh on his arms hadn't stopped sprouting for a week. He hoped yet again that he wouldn't have to go back and look for the place Jimmy was drawing. After they'd gotten what they needed and killed Jimmy, of course.

"A practical question," Jimmy said, removing the jeweler's monocle from his eye and looking at his visitor. "What happened to that little red-headed chicken what used to give me my flash for working for you blokes?"

"The redhead? We called her the Actress. She was delayed, Jimmy. She's someplace else for now. We needed you up here, safe from prying eyes."

"Huh." Jimmy said. The Gardener got a little worried about that, too. When Jimmy spoke, the Gardener couldn't read anything into it at all. No annoyance, no resentment, nothing. Jimmy was totally unreadable. And that made the Gardener more nervous than a dozen Tesla rifles pointed at his face.

Nervous enough that the Gardener's hand instinctively crept to the small revolver he kept in the pocket of his denim workpants. Experience had taught him that a man who couldn't be read could be very, very dangerous.

"So, Jimmy, how much longer 'til you're done here, then?"

He tried to keep his voice light, quiet enough that it wouldn't startle Jimmy out of his work, but loud enough to be heard over the hiss of the steam and gears of the machines.

4

"Well," Jimmy said, leaning backward in his chair and cracking the muscles of his lower back. "I must say [grunt!] that this is without a doubt the most pressin' assignment you lot've ever given me! I took a look at just one little disk wit'a few of them new, circular punchcards innit, an' blimey if it ain't got more info innit than the biggest book in a bishop's library."

"Yes. Well, Jimmy . . ." the Gardener said, dropping his guard. It was the last mistake he'd ever made.

Jimmy pulled something from his back waistband and flung it at the Gardener's face. The Gardener first felt the splash as the world went black, then felt his eyes begin to sizzle and burn a half-second before he heard them. He screamed with an exquisite level of truly ferocious pain. He covered his eyes with his hands, trying to rub the poisoned acid out, even as it dissolved both his eyes and fingertips.

"'Scuse, gov," Jimmy said with a casual air, as if he were on his way to get a cup of coffee. While the Gardener sank to his knees and howled over his ruined eyes, Jimmy reached out with a gloved hand and helped himself to the maimed agent's pistol and took an ambush position at the bottom of the stairs as he heard the footsteps above.

****

After it was over and the three agents' bodies lay cooling in the basement, Jimmy stood on a hill near the little town and looked down at the squat, red-and-brown brick buildings that were crowded near the crossroads.

He almost had to chuckle. They hadn't expected Jimmy to be as good as he was, or expected the kind of savage resourcefulness found in a man born and raised in the East End slums. In truth, Jimmy hadn't killed very often in his life. But there was always a kind of twisted satisfaction to seeing the look of surprise on their faces right before he took their lives. Jimmy felt no remorse for his recent acts, since he'd figured out in the first day or so the men who'd hired him had no intention of paying him for anything once they'd gotten what they'd wanted.

There'd only been a little money on the agents themselves, and some squirreled away in the house in the usual places people hid things. Far less than he'd been promised, but enough to get him to the British colony-city of Syrtis Major. Perhaps after that he could grease enough palms to get back to Earth. Then maybe back to his old apartment in the Rookery, if it were still available.

Jimmy had an odd twinge in his belly. He'd done many things to survive in his life of twenty-five years, but killing *three* people in *one* day was a new thing for Jimmy, no matter how bad the people actually were.

Yes, three bodies, he thought as he hefted the sizable backpack full of papers onto his shoulders. Three bodies and a few stacks of papers. Papers so important that powerful men would kill him to keep their contents secret once he'd deciphered and cataloged the whole mess. Jimmy had always had good instincts for survival, and his instincts had told him his life was in jeopardy the day he started the job. Well, no more! Someone would probably pay a pretty penny indeed for the papers he had in his pack. He might be a rich man indeed, if he played his cards right.

Jimmy was still thinking this as the slimy, wet tentacle wrapped around his throat, cutting off his air and making him gasp as it shoved him forward and down onto all fours.

"Hello, James," said a voice behind him.

Jimmy recognized the voice, even though he'd only heard it once before. And what he remembered made him wet himself with fear for the first time in his adult life.

"It's been a while, hasn't it, James?" the voice said as Jimmy's world started to turn dark at the edges. "Don't worry, now. Not much longer."

As Jimmy lost consciousness, his hands gradually beat with less and less strength against the tentacle wrapped around his neck. His body went slack, and the pack slid off his shoulders.

The tentacle slipped around the pack, sliding it up and onto the back of its new owner with hardly a whisper.

"It's good to be back," he said with a voice filled with elegance and gravel. "Now, to prepare for Gilbert."

Chapter 1

"An inconvenience is only an adventure wrongly considered; an adventure is an inconvenience rightly considered."

– *"On Running After One's Hat," All Things Considered*

1892 A.D.
EARTH, ENGLAND.

Gilbert looked carefully at the piece of paper in his hand, and then up at the transport rocket ship designed to move a hundred people to and from Mars in relative ease and comfort. It looked like a huge dart made of brass and iron, capped on the end and riddled with rivets and thick-glassed portholes. Smoke and steam hissed around his feet. The noise mixed with screams of upset children, harried travelers, and loud mechanics complaining about each other's shoddy work.

"All aboard!" a man roared from a nearby podium. "Leaving from Dock Seven for the British colony on Syrtis Major! All aboard! All passengers must be secured for a full hour prior to launch! Please proceed . . ."

Gilbert looked down at the satchel between his feet. In a world of constant change, his satchel seemed to be the one thing he could keep track of and control. He scooped it up and slung it over his shoulder, not worrying about whether or not it would wrinkle his suit jacket. *Gonna be on that oversized cigar for a good while*, he thought as he sauntered toward the dock, *so I'm not gonna worry about my clothes so much. Don't know why chief Eddy had me dress up for this, anyway. Not like I'm gonna wear a suit in a desert!*

The sound of cymbals playing nearby interrupted his thoughts about his newspaper's chief editor.

Gilbert had to chuckle. The beggars and minstrels plied their trade at the interplanetary docks, just as they did at the shipyards and airship docks on the coast. In the interests of national secrecy, the docks to Mars had been built over a decade ago on a few isolated islands a good hundred miles from the British coastline. Their existence had become public knowledge months ago, and the number of poor people flooding to see the interplanetary etherships and rich people racing to take trips on them had almost doubled every few weeks. But for Gilbert the most curious oddities had been the junky little mirth-makers who'd traveled from big cities like London to perform for stray coins from wealthy traveler and poor onlooker alike.

Gilbert looked up and saw a juggler. He was busily keeping a knife, ball, and a regularly bitten apple in the air, while hitting a series of musical instruments with his hands and feet. Gilbert was almost tempted to stop and watch, but another call from the man with the megaphone jolted him back, and he began striding to the departures platform even quicker than before. Although Gilbert wanted to watch the show, he knew he'd be a year away from reaching his destination if he missed his ship's departure.

He walked closer to the docks, staying in the middle of the crowd that was headed for the lineup. Once in line, he waited for the better part of an hour as the crowd thinned to a single file and people were herded toward the ship by a combination of guards and velvet ropes.

Gilbert looked up at the enormous craft he was about to board. How had they kept this a secret for so many years from the public? The thing was much larger than any building in his memory. Then he remembered: the few folks who'd tried to blow the whistle on this operation had been ridiculed in the press for their 'wild' stories. Journalists who tried to reveal the existence of colonies on Mars found their stories scooped by 'yellow' journalist papers of ill repute.

The shrill screech of a tin whistle pinched his ear. A young boy with a uniform and a pillbox hat was bicycling on one of the many paved paths leading to the launchpads, flashing his identification pass to the armed guards who half-heartedly stood to block him. "Telegram!" he called, "Telegram for Gilbert Chesterton!"

"Here!" called Gilbert. This was getting a tad annoying! No one had tried to contact him for any reason at all for the better part of a month. But now, just as he was trying to board the ship, a telegram? From whom?

"Here you go, gov," the boy said, stopping his bike by Gilbert and pulling out a clipboard. "Sign 'ere, please an' thank you."

Gilbert took the pencil that was attached to the board by a string, signed his name and looked at the envelope. "From whom?" he asked.

"No idea, m'lord," the boy said, packing away the clipboard and swinging his leg over the bicycle seat. "Got a few more o' these to get to their new owners. 'Ave a good trip!"

The boy rode off, calling another name down the line. Gilbert turned the envelope over in his hands a few times, wondering if he should open it now or after he got on board the ship.

He looked up again. The ship looked even more huge as he neared it, an enormous construction of wood, iron, glass and steel. After the British government had admitted to the world the existence of its colonies on Mars the previous year, several private shipbuilding companies had immediately set about building the world's next generation of space-faring vessels.

Gilbert looked carefully at the hull of the ship he'd be on. The name *Elbereth* was written on it in giant letters, three stories high. He remembered how he had once been scheduled to sail on another ship. Just as large, but built for the ocean, it had been touted as unsinkable. Right up until it hit an iceberg on its maiden voyage. Pure luck had saved him from making the trip on that boat.

Or . . . had it been luck alone?

"Excuse me. Did he say you were Gilbert Chesterton?"

Gilbert turned around, his sealed telegram still in hand.

A rather large woman, perhaps forty years old, was staring at him through a pair of spectacles. Age spots sprouted across her face, and her smile showed teeth that could have used a great deal of straightening.

Gilbert tried to smile back, then sent up a prayer to Almighty God that this woman wasn't going to be an annoying fan of his work. Worse, an annoying fan who would be following him around for the next two months as they travelled through space to the Martian colonies.

"Yes," he said, smiling while he cringed inside.

"How wonderful!" she said. "Then you're friends with Herbert G. Wells! I am a great aficionado of his work, if not his *greatest* admirer! Do you know why he hasn't put out any more books as of late?"

Gilbert kept his smile frozen in place as he made yet another note to himself: It could always be worse. Always. However bad he thought a trip could be, there really was no depth to which the company could sink to make things even worse, including a fellow traveler being a fan of the work of Gilbert's former best friend, who'd shot Gilbert in the chest last year.

Chapter 2

"Women have a thirst for order and beauty as for something physical; there is a strange female power of hating ugliness and waste as good men can only hate sin and bad men virtue."

– *"Bleak House," Appreciations and Criticisms*

Frances Blogg had always been taught to be a sensible girl. But, as with most young women, she found it easier to be sensible at certain times than at others. Being sensible when the Archbishop of Canterbury or the Prime Minister came to dine was relatively easy. Being sensible when father or mother began talking about politics, business, or the Americans was even easier, since there was only one American in the universe whose actions actually interested her.

But when *that* American wrote her a letter? Or when *that* American managed to evade her father's security team long enough to sing to her outside her room? Or *that* American fired a love note attached to an arrow through her open window? Under such circumstances, sensibility for Frances Blogg was as unattainable as Napoleon's conquest of Russia.

And when one of the servants delivered a letter to her on a tray, stating it was from a certain Mister Gilbert Chesterton, Frances completely ignored the odd look on the servant's face and very *in*sensibly tore the letter open in front of the serving girl.

The address to her was typed, for a change. Dear Gilbert usually wrote in his very distinctive penmanship style, but it most certainly was *his* name on the return portion of the envelope!

"Oh, Mara!" Frances said to her maid, eagerly smelling the letter. "Well, he didn't spray it with his cologne this time. Still, isn't it exciting? Perhaps he's ready at last! Do you know how often I've dreamed of opening such a letter? One where he says not only how much he loves me, but that he's truly ready to wed? That his family affairs are in order now and we can be one forever? Do you know how often I've dreamt of such a letter, Mara?"

11

"At least once a week, m'lady," the serving girl said with a tired voice. She was a few years older than Frances, and her eyes rolled as Frances looked with a dreamy expression out the window at the forest of roofs and towers of London beneath her family mansion's bedroom window, all the while holding the letter to her bosom.

"Oh, Mara!" Frances said after a minute or two, "I can't bear to read it. Please, please, Mara, will you?"

Mara sighed. She'd been asked to do this the last few times Gilbert had gotten a letter past the trousered apes at the front door. "M'lady," Mara said with a resigned air, already holding out her right hand. "I really don't think it's me place to . . ."

"Oh, Mara!" Frances cut her off, pirouetting and slapping the letter into her palm, "who else has proven so trustworthy to me? More so than even my own sisters! Mara, please do!"

Mara took the letter, folding her fingers over it slowly. "I'll do it, m'lady, but if I may warn ye, guard yeself. A man don't wonna a woman so much when he knows 'e has her heart all locked up. Mark me words."

"Oh, Mara! You don't know Gilbert! He's the sun, moon and stars! He's the only boy who's written poetry to me! And he can make a living on his own skills besides! Now that I've told that stuffy fool Fortescue Williamson that there's not an icicle's chance in the heart of the sun that he'll ever have me, the way is clear for Gilbert and I to . . ."

She stopped. She'd been dancing a waltz, reels and a few other dances typically reserved for weddings with Gilbert as her imaginary partner. Mara had sighed again and pulled the letter from the opened envelope as she'd done several times before. She unfolded the paper and, after a quizzical-faced few seconds, stared at the paper with wide eyes.

As Frances watched, the older girl quickly folded up the letter and turned to go.

"Mara? Mara!" Frances first spoke, and then yelled; unconsciously falling into the commanding voice used for disobedient servants she'd heard her mother use time and again in their house.

Mara stopped, her eyes squeezed shut at the sound of Frances' sharp tone. She turned to face her, her long-fingered hand still clutching the folded paper in her hand.

"M'lady," she said, "you don't wanna see this. There's been some kind've mistake, a terrible one. Please don't make me . . ."

"Mara," Frances said in an icy voice, "you will immediately surrender that paper to me, or face consequences for your willfulness."

Mara paused, looking at Frances with eyes that were filled with pity and formality. "Yes m'lady," Mara said, straightening her back and holding out the paper to her.

Frances snatched it, ignoring Mara and unfolding the letter. . .

Oh—

She inhaled, holding back a sob and covering her throat with her free hand. The letter shook.

Mara covered her eyes with her hand. "Will you be . . . needing me at all, m'lady?"

"No," Frances said, willing her voice to remain even as she kept her eyes from Mara's. "Thank you, Mara. You may go now. And I . . . I hope you can forgive me for being . . . harsh with you a moment ago."

Mara's own eyes were red. "Of course, m'lady. Of . . . of course." After she left, Frances folded the letter shut. She walked around the room slowly, unfolded it again, scrunched her eyes shut, and crushed the letter into a crinkly ball. After she finished stomping on it, she ran to the opposite end of her spacious room and tore open the door to her main closet, the one that was larger than most apartments found in the East End.

After rummaging about inside it for the better part of fifteen minutes, she emerged looking composed, focused, well dressed in her best morning clothes, and with an expression fit to kill anything that got in her way. She scooped up the paper she'd tried so hard to grind out of existence a few minutes before, unfolded it, and tucked it into a safe place in the folds of her dress. In another five minutes she was downstairs and ready to step into one of the fleet of hansom cabs her family had on standby.

"Where to, m'lady?" asked Grissom, the driver.

"The offices of the *London Times*, Grissom, where *Gilbert* works. Get me there in less than ten minutes and I'll pass you a five pound note."

"Yes *madam!*" he said happily, waiting until she was secure inside the cab then cracking the whip on his horses.

Chapter 3

"The true soldier fights not because he hates what is in front of him, but because he loves what is behind him."

— *Illustrated London News, Jan. 14, 1911*

1892 A.D.
MARS.

The young soldier stood on the flat stone of the fort's wall, his crossed arms resting on his bent knee while his body leaned forward with a defiant air. He glared at the red sea of sand beneath him with the sun at his back. The wind tousled his brown hair while the pink-orange sun warmed him through his red tunic. His eyes were a fierce, piercing blue, and as his gaze passed from the dune sea to more rocky terrain, he focused on the horizon as if daring it to produce an enemy for him to fight.

On the ground below, the men busied themselves in preparation. Soldiers with red tunics like his own wheeled cannons into place, then poured in black powder. Others assembled and loaded rifles, all the while roaring, swearing, and hooting at each other to both build up spirits and convince themselves they would survive to see the next sunrise.

"Sergeant Belloc!"

The voice below him had a high, nasal ring to it. Hearing it made him want to stuff the voice's owner into a very dark hole with a grenade and a large quantity of fire.

"Yes, sir!" he said, rising and readying himself for the next torrent of unearned abuse.

"Sergeant Belloc, report to me at once! Front and center!"

He stood at the officer's order, cracked his back, and walked along the top of the wall to the nearest ladder. His easy pace was a marked contrast to the hustle of the men beside and around him. One soldier sidestepped slightly but noticeably when their paths crossed. Another man, carrying a barrel of powder, settled for giving a slight but perceptible nod at the sight of the young sergeant. The action nearly made him fall with his load, but Belloc stopped, righted him, and sent him on his way with a straight-faced slap on the soldier's back.

"Sergeant Belloc! Did you not hear me?"

He slid down the ladder from the top of the fort wall, took a few more easy-paced steps, then stopped at attention in front of the officer. Belloc was close enough that he could see the captain's bars on his uniform gleaming in the pink Martian sun, now halfway down to the horizon. The captain's face was young, not yet thirty, but his face was white and his nose looked about to bleed from several large veins pulsing with fear and anger.

Young Sergeant Belloc, age twenty-two, stood now in front of his Captain.

"Sergeant Hilaire Belloc reporting for duty, Captain," he said, saluting by bringing his hand up and down in a slow arc.

"SERGEANT!" the captain screamed, pacing around Belloc while he spoke, screeching without pattern or plan, "*We*, are at *war* here! Are you aware of that?"

"Yes, sir!" Belloc's eyes were still focused forward, careful to make no eye contact at all with his superior.

"Then perhaps you can tell me just *what* you were doing up on that wall, while the rest of us are preparing for the attack we've been told to expect! Have you ever seen a Thark up close, Sergeant?"

"Yes, sir!"

"Right! Well . . . What do they look like, then?"

"Green sir," Belloc answered crisply. "Eight feet tall on average, with green skin, large, bulbous eyes, four arms, and tusks where men would have canine teeth. They also display a curious level of resistance to most forms of melee attacks, showing far more deference and respect to those capable of close-quarter fighting. Furthermore . . ."

"That's enough, *Belloc*! When I want a history lesson, I'll send for one of my old tutors at Eton! Now, if you know so much about 'em, then why, I ask, why were you staring at the sky and the sand?"

"Looking for signs of the enemy, sir. Stealth and self-preservation are not their strong suits, and their warbands tend to announce themselves with significant clouds of dust on the horizon."

"Oh, really, Belloc? Is that so? Well, if that's the case, then why worry about when they're going to come knocking? Do you think that by staring at the sand, that they'll be more likely to disappear when you ask 'em to?"

"No, sir."

"Maybe you think they'll leave if we put a spot of tea out for them?"

"No, sir."

"Oh? Really? Well, then, perhaps you'll tell *me*, your *Captain*, just why you think looking out there will help more than getting to work *in here*?"

The Captain was now close to Hilaire's ear, shrieking loud as he could. Hilaire could smell what brand of tea the Captain had drunk that morning, and roughly how much laudanum had been mixed in with it.

"I was going to tell the cannons what range to fire at, sir. I was also awaiting the Maxim gun to be delivered to my post on the wall."

The Captain seemed taken aback. The men around him had fallen silent too; with scowls on their faces and disdain in their eyes, they had paused to watch him yell at Hilaire.

"We . . . We have a Maxim gun in the fort?"

"Yes, sir!"

The captain paused at Belloc's reply. "Well, that's something nice to hear, isn't it? YOU MIGHT HAVE TOLD ME SOONER, BELLOC! Now, all of you, back to work immediately! Fit those cannons! Bolt those Maxims down! Move those . . . *things* to their proper place! And get ready to mow those ugly green blighters down! Lieutenant!"

"Sir!" A short man with glasses appeared at the captain's arm, as if by magic.

"My tea. Bring me my tea, extra *hot*, to my quarters. Sergeant Belloc, see that I am notified the minute this conflict has reached its conclusion!"

"Yes, sir!"

"Dismissed!"

Sergeant Hilaire Belloc found the ladder and climbed again to the top of the wall. Two other soldiers were quickly tightening the final bolts of the base of the gun into the pre-drilled holes in the rim of the stone wall of the fort.

"We're all set then?" Belloc said, testing out the gun, loading the belt of bullets and checking the precious water supply that kept the gun from overheating.

"We're all good 'ere, Sergeant Belloc!"

"Right! Wait a moment." He first checked the pistol in his holster. A standard six-shot. Not a pepperbox like the Captain sported in his quarters—quarters that were bolted safely shut with walls four-feet thick.

It'd have to do.

Next, he pulled out a collapsible telescope from his pocket and scanned the horizon.

It took only a few seconds to spot the clouds of dust, and the small green shapes moving around inside them. He snapped shut the telescope and turned to face the inside of the fort.

"Men!" he roared, his voice carrying above the sounds of tinkering, loading, and grunting.

At the sound of his voice, they all stopped to listen.

"Men!" he repeated, "I've spotted them, and they'll be here within the hour. If the scouts are right, we've got ourselves quite a job today. And that job is staying alive and convincing these overgrown green bags of phlegm that they're better off finding easier prey than members of the English army!"

The men cheered, many raising their rifles in a salute!

"Men," Belloc continued once they'd quieted, "we're outnumbered four to one today. They're bigger than us and they can shrug off a sword the way we did a schoolmaster's cane in school. But we've got two things they don't!"

He paused, letting that sink in.

"First, we're *all* scared. Every one of us. It's proof you have backbone— we may be softer on the outside than those greenskins, but we're a hundred times tougher in the middle! And those four-armed walruses are *just the opposite!* Crack their shells, and their insides flow like eggs!"

More cheers! Followed quickly by obedient silence.

"Second, lads," Belloc continued, "we're from tough stock— every one of us! Our ancestors," he continued, walking along the rim of the wall, his drawn pistol still in his right hand, "our ancestors in England brought the word of God to the heathens of the Isles and the rest of Europe. They changed the whole world, when Satan himself was against them. And they did it with the Bible in one hand, and the sword in the other. Well, God's word is the same today as it was then. But the sword," he here cocked his pistol and raised it high in the air, "has been *updated!*"

18

More cheers! More rifles raised and loaded! But no bullets were fired. They'd all been in battle enough to know how precious a loaded round could be.

"And one more thing, lads!" he spoke while they still cheered, "whatever happens! Whatever they think to throw at us! Always remember that we have the Maxim guns, and *they do not!* Private Budd, start that powder run! Lads, let's crush some bugs!"

As the men roared their approval, Captain Fortescue James Tiberius Vespasian Williamson stirred more drops of laudanum into his already heavily drugged tea. The sound of the men cheering barely registered through the thick stone walls of his quarters, specifically designed to protect officers and their most valued staff from unwanted intrusions like the one they were now threatened with.

"Beastly habit they have, shouting like that," he said. He sipped loudly. Then at the next roar up top, he gulped the entire cup. "Just hot 'nough. Just . . ." His voice grew more sluggish with each second, and he dropped to sleep in his bed, still wearing his uniform, just as the first clashes of steel with flesh and the screams of battle and death rang out above him. He couldn't hear the clacking sound of the Maxim gun as the entire, bloody battle grew fierce.

Chapter 4

"When we step into the family, by the act of being born, we do step into a world which is incalculable, into a world which has its own strange laws, into a world which could do without us, into a world we have not made. In other words, when we step into the family we step into a fairy-tale."

– "On Certain Modern Writers and the Institution of the Family," Heretics

1892 A.D.
Earth. England.

Gilbert sat in his easy chair, strapped in and waiting for the launch. Mars.

Gilbert thought again about just how crazy this was. The last time he was in the air, he was a prisoner in a zeppelin on the way to a floating city in America. Now he wouldn't just be in the air, but in the cold, empty reaches of space itself. Traveling to a red pinprick of light in the sky that mankind had stared at since humans had begun looking higher than the top of the nearest tree.

His hand crept to his jacket pocket. He took out the two pictures inside. One was of a young girl, about Gilbert's age but maybe older, who had his jawline and eyes. The other was a younger boy about thirteen, who had Gilbert's smile and forehead—even his hairstyle.

Cecil and Beatrice, Gilbert thought. There was a letter inside, too. He took it out, unfolded it, and read the untidy hand script.

They are Cecil and Beatrice, your younger brother and older sister.

They are with me here on Mars.

Would you like to meet them?

Come and see us. We have things to finish.

Your Servant,
The Doctor.

The Doctor, a cold-hearted, amoral, evil man. A man who had taken much from Gilbert and who knew just what button to push to make Gilbert jump all the way to Mars.

A button marked *Family*.

Gilbert really had no memory of younger siblings. He remembered younger children in the home. In particular, since seeing Beatrice's picture he'd remembered the image of a little girl falling off a toy horse of some kind, hurting her head in the process. Other than that there was nothing. It was as if he had a blank space in his head each time he tried to think about the girl in the picture. Gilbert had learned that his mother had made some of his memories disappear when he was seven. Had she done so on other occasions? Perhaps with these siblings?

He remembered something else now. There was another time his mother had been very, very tired for a period of several months, seeing no one and putting on a great deal of weight. She had gotten her strength back but been very sad for months after. A Minnesota farm wife rarely talked about the source of her sadness, and Gilbert forgot about it once she seemed to rebound.

Cecil and Beatrice, he thought again.

Chief Eddy at *The Times* had known something was up when Gilbert requested the assignment.

"You've just got back from Rome, Chesterton," he'd said, "and you want me to pay for you to take *another* trip?"

"You didn't pay for the Rome trip, Chief," Gilbert had answered, "and you know that the only folks you can get to ride in one of those giant tin cans are new guys who have something to prove. Or maybe have a death wish."

"You're not a new reporter, Gilbert," the Chief had said quietly. "You've proved your worth many times over. Do you have a death wish, then?"

"No," Gilbert said. "Life is God's greatest gift, and I've no desire to throw it away."

"What, then?" the Chief asked, looking straight at the young reporter. Gilbert knew his boss was trying to find something in Gilbert's face that would give some insight into his motivations.

But Gilbert had no intention of giving away his reasons for his trip. Not until he'd saved his siblings. "Chief, you told me once never to bring my personal problems in to work. Remember that? Well, I'm not saying I've got a problem. But I *do* have a few things in my life that could be fixed with a trip to the Martian colonies, and you need someone who's good at his job to go there. I think we can help each other this way. If you can see your way to letting me go there, that is."

Chief Eddy looked at Gilbert with a steady air. "Every time I think I've got you mapped, sewed up, and packaged, Chesterton," he said, "you manage to throw me a cutter. Can you tell me exactly what it is that has you so eager to see Mars?"

"Would you believe the desire to see a new, uncharted land?"

"It's been charted for over a decade, Gilbert, even though the public's only been aware of it for the last year. Try again."

"What about a desire to go into the desert to live as a hermit?"

"I've seen your girlfriend, Chesterton. The only way you'd run to a desert is if she were going with you. So, I don't buy that one either."

"What if I told you I'm going to seek the lost treasure of the Martians, marry a beautiful, red-skinned princess of Mars, and live as their king in a palace hewn out of mountain stone?"

"I *could* believe you'd be after that. But I don't think that's it, at least not this time. Well, Gilbert. Your reasons are your own. I know you can do the work, but it'll take you out of circulation for at least six months. Are you sure you're willing to do that?"

"Yes, sir."

"Then away you go. Fanny on the first floor has the tickets— you'll be leaving within the week. Sooner if a spot opens up. Can you close down your affairs in that space of time?"

"Without too much trouble. If you can keep my pay routed to my landlady, I'll at least have a place to come back to when I return. So, it's a done deal, then? I'm off to Mars?"

Chief Eddy looked at Gilbert over the large arms of his considerably thick moustache. "Gilbert," he said quietly, "I don't generally pry into other people's affairs, especially those of my reporters. But in your case, I'd just like to know if all . . . Well, I recall how happy you were whenever you received a letter from that little lady friend of yours. You two look quite lovely together, you know, even if she is a tad older than you are."

"I make up for it by being quite a bit taller than she is."

"Gilbert, I am serious. When you get to be my age, well," he stood from his chair and looked out the window of his office at the soot-encrusted skyline and streets of London. "The few times I've seen you two together, well . . . Running off to Mars, Gilbert, being gone for half a year . . . It's like . . . like hair growing."

Gilbert paused. "Hair, Chief?"

"If you're with someone every day, Gilbert, the little changes you undergo, you change *together*," he said, now facing Gilbert and holding two index fingers of his opposite hands together, curling them around each other, "like two branches of ivy that grow and intertwine. Their hair may change, growing a quarter inch a week, and you don't really notice it, since, after all, who has time to watch some else's hair grow?

"But at your age, if you two are apart for a long time, if you haven't seen someone for a very, very long time, Gilbert, when you finally do see them, you might say in surprise, 'My dear, how long your hair has grown!' They've changed. But since you weren't there, you didn't grow *together*, like ivy. You'll be more like two tree branches that grew further and further *apart*."

At the last comment, the Chief uncurled his fingers and pointed them in opposite directions. The Chief's voice drifted; he was no longer looking at Gilbert. The Chief suddenly seemed far away, lost in memory. After a few seconds he blinked, straightened his back, set his shoulders, and turned to fully face Gilbert with his hands behind his back. "Well, lad," he said, his usual gruffness returned, "I can't afford having you be distracted on the job, now, can I? Not when this fine newspaper is paying your way to the stars. Will you find yourself distracted while there?"

"Chief," Gilbert said, "your concern means a lot to me. But you need to know that I'm fine. Frances and I, well, I do love her, and she loves me. But I have things to do before I'm ready to get married to anyone, much less someone as fine as she is. So, we're waiting. And we've got to both keep in mind that maybe, maybe not getting married at all," he breathed in and clenched one hand just a little, "well, that maybe that's for the best instead."

At that, the Chief *did* smile. "You've come a long way since you first walked through that office door, young Chesterton. You know that? Now, is there anything else you need from me?"

"Nothing I can think of, Chief."

"Then leave my office! You think I'm paying you to sit and chat? There's a world of stories out there that need to be told!"

"Right, Chief!" Gilbert jumped up, smiling, then headed out the door. Today he'd seen a side of Chief Eddy he'd never take advantage of, but never forget either.

After meeting with the Chief, Gilbert spent the next week securing every piece of his life that might come loose without him in the next six months. He'd been so busy he'd barely had time to squeeze in a goodbye moment for Frances. She'd been on some kind of holiday herself in the countryside and had only returned the night before he was to leave for Mars.

Gilbert had lobbed a few pebbles at her window, and he'd brought a love poem he'd written earlier in the day. In seconds the back door was unlocked by one of the kitchen boys, a lad who'd become infatuated with one of the scullery maids. Gilbert gave the poem to the boy to use for his own beloved, and soon Gilbert was inside the kitchen of the Blogg house, sitting across the table from Frances.

Even with her hair disheveled, she looked beautiful dressed in a sleeping gown, slippers, and a dark night robe. They'd talked for the better part of an hour while holding hands and sitting at the rough wooden table. To them, though, it seemed like only a few minutes. When her sympathetic maid Mara had dropped by to warn them that they might be discovered, they'd held one another for a few seconds and said their goodbyes.

"Until the sun stops setting, dear one," she said, giving him a peck on the cheek. He'd gulped with surprise, then returned her kiss.

Sitting now in his chair on the rocket, Gilbert touched his cheek. She'd given him the kiss last night, and the sensation still lingered as he sat, waiting for the launch. He stretched, said a short prayer, and was just about to slice open the telegram envelope when an announcement sounded through the pipes in the speaker system.

"Your attention please! Your attention, please! We will soon be raised to a vertical position in preparation for our launch to Mars. Please fasten yourselves into your seats and secure all loose articles."

Gilbert checked his belts. Two of them criss-crossed his shoulders and body, and one went around his waist. He was glad the passenger section of the ship was a series of single-file rows of plush chairs. This trip would be nerve-wracking enough, flying millions of miles in a glorified tin can to the red planet, but it would be even more difficult to keep his mind from snapping if he were squished and packed like a traveler in a stagecoach back home in America.

He looked for a moment out of the porthole-shaped window. The passengers had long since filed onto the ship in neat rows, and the entertainers had gone. Now, workers outside wearing brass goggles and fireproof robes scurried back and forth shouting at each other over the sound of the massive industrial equipment, looking like monks in a vast, technological cathedral. Cranes with huge, two-pronged claws groaned and sighed with blasts of steam as they swung in slow arcs toward the *Elbereth*. Gilbert was more than a little in awe. For most of his life, the largest machine he'd ever seen was a farm harvester that could do a day's work of many men in under an hour. But in the last couple of years he'd seen armored Zeppelins, giant walking tripod tanks, and even a floating city. The *Elbereth* was a little different, though. It was not only as huge as the *Titanic*, but so big that even its helper-machines were of jaw-dropping size.

The crane's claw, fully fifty feet wide when extended tip to tip, swung out of Gilbert's field of vision as it passed over the roof of the ship. A few more seconds, and he felt and heard the loud clank! as the pincers closed over the roof.

Firmly in the grip of the helper-crane, the ship rose in an arc to a forty-five degree diagonal angle. Gilbert heard a number of the passengers gasp, with *oohs* and *ahhs* sounding up and down the well-lit, carpeted corridor of passengers.

What would they do if someone couldn't handle this? Gilbert thought. What would they do if someone got claustrophobic when they were a good thousand miles in the air?

When they were tilted at just above forty-five degrees, the crane stopped. Gilbert heard several complaining voices wafting up and down the passenger corridor.

"Ladies and gentlemen," the now familiar voice said through the speaker pipes, "we are in the midst of some difficulties with regard to our mechanical devices. The issue should be rectified shortly. Thank you in advance for your patience and co-operation."

Well, not like we're going to leave in a huff and take the train, Gilbert thought. He'd heard of situations like this, though. One fellow who'd claimed he'd made the Mars trip said his ship had been locked nearly upright for a good half-hour before they'd fixed the problem and gotten on their way.

He heard a crinkle in his pocket as he shifted his position, then saw the corner of the telegram poking out of his pocket.

Well, why not?

He slid the message paper out of the envelope. He unfolded it and began reading.

After one line, his eyes softened.

Two lines, and his eyes narrowed.

Three lines, and his eyes widened in panic.

"No," he whispered, his hand tightening and crumpling the paper. "No ... no ... There must be a ... no!"

He hit the release button on each of his belts, which popped off and retracted obediently into the seat.

"Seat forty-seven!" the voice boomed out over the speaker pipes as soon as he'd undone his belts, "This is a message for seat number forty-seven! Our instruments indicate you have removed your restraints! Return immediately to your seat and replace your belts! You will be in danger if you do not do so!"

Gilbert only half listened to the carping noise above him. He stood shakily on the tilted floor and started a hesitant, jumping walk down to the door at the end of the passenger corridor.

"Passenger forty-seven! If you do not return to your seat, we will be forced to dispatch security officers!"

Yeah, right. Gilbert thought. On a vessel like this, the kind of fellows used for security were hired for looking both cultured and threatening, rather than having any actual ability that made them dangerous. The only kinds of security guards he'd ever felt a serious need to tread lightly around were the kind of trousered apes that Frances' father would hire to keep people like Gilbert away from Frances and her sisters.

Frances!

He had to get off this ship!

The door at the end of the corridor was in sight. "Third Class" proclaimed a pair of neatly stenciled words on the door at eye level.

Third class?

The Chief had bought him *third* class tickets?

The door in front of him popped open.

Two men with close-shaved heads stood behind it, wearing red leather tunics with shiny buttons and black trim. Their expressions were both annoyed with and focused upon him.

Uh-oh.

"Sir, you need to return to your—," began the larger one.

Gilbert didn't wait for the lead man to finish his sentence. He turned and ran the other way, trying hard to clomp up the tilted aisle, ignoring the angry and surprised comments of the other passengers as he passed them.

Gilbert didn't care. His brain burned with the three sentences in the letter he'd just read, and his entire being was focused on a single goal of getting off the *Elbereth*. His brother, sister, and the Doctor could wait until he'd straightened things out. Six months on Mars no longer seemed a grand adventure; reading the letter made a trip to Mars a short road to tragedy, and he wasn't going to accept that without a fight!

Ten, fifteen, twenty steps up the hill that the flat aisle way had become. He could hear two heavy sets of feet clomping behind him in heavy black boots. The door at the other end of the corridor was in sight and twenty, fifteen, five feet away and . . .

It opened in front of him. Two more guards with shaved heads and unhappy faces.

Oops.

Chapter 5

"For fear of the newspapers politicians are dull, and at last they are too dull even for the newspapers."

– *"On the Cryptic and the Elliptic,"* All Things Considered

" . . . and why was he assigned this article, exactly, Mister Edwards?"

"Miss Blogg, I told you, just as I suspect he told you. He received it because he specifically *requested* this assignment. I've no clue why and even less interest."

Frances held the older man's gaze with a straight face.

"You are aware of who my father is, Mister Edwards?" she said, without a trace of a threat in her voice.

"I am," answered Chief Eddy. "I am also aware that since this paper was recently bought by one of his competitors, your father has no power over me or any other reporter in this building. So please don't try to intimidate me. People more experienced than yourself have tried and failed miserably."

"Perhaps I need to clarify the nature of my inquiry, Mister Edwards," Frances said carefully. "I know exactly why he *really* chose to go to Mars. However, knowing his *particular* assignment would make him easier to find, should I need to follow him there."

"Miss, I sincerely hope you aren't thinking of follow—,"

"What I think or plan is *not* your concern, Mister Edwards," she said, maintaining her perfect poise. "And while my father no longer owns a controlling interest in this paper, he plays Whist, Cribbage, and Bridge with your publisher on the third Wednesday of every month at the Diogenes Club on Fleet Street, just past . . ."

"I know where the club resides, Miss Blogg," Chief Eddy said, several beads of sweat suddenly visible on his forehead. "The location of Olympus Island and the Star docks are common knowledge now, and I can only recommend that you try your luck there next. Protocol requires I not reveal the specific travelling plans of a reporter to anyone, so as to ensure their safety. Please understand that I . . ." he made a furtive look over his shoulder, as if he was worried an ear might sprout out of the wall. "I really, truly, cannot think of anything to say that could help you. Furthermore," without a sound, he grabbed a small piece of paper and a pencil stub and scribbled out a few lines after making sure she was watching him. "Furthermore, I can truthfully say that I have absolute confidence in Gilbert's ability to carry out his assignment safely, and that if he is left to his own devices, he will perform admirably for this office."

He slid the paper into her hands, widening his eyes while making eye contact with her.

She took the folded slip, making it disappear into her sleeve like a stage magician.

"Thank you for your assistance, Mister Edwardson," she said, standing. "While I am sorry you could not assist me, I can see Gilbert's praise of you as a chief editor was not misplaced, nor was his loyalty toward you and the *London Times*."

They exchanged a few more pleasantries as she left, careful to ignore the reporters in the office that had obviously been listening in on the conversation.

Once back in the coach, she wondered what to do next.

"Miss Blogg?" said her driver, "where to next?"

"The Star docks, Grissom. Be there in under ten minutes, and it'll be another five pounds for you."

Grissom didn't answer, instead leaning back and cracking his whip with a yell. As the coach sprang forward, Frances braced herself, and Grissom thought of several nice things he'd been promising to buy his wife for the last few years. A few more trips like this, and he'd be a rich man!

Frances unfolded the paper Mister Edwards had given her in his office: It read, "OLYMPUS ISLAND, STAR DOCKS—THE *Elbereth*!"

What on Earth was an *Elbereth*? Nevermind that now. She'd been given another lead, and she would make the most of it!

If *Elbereth* was another girl . . . Perhaps she was the one who— Her eyes rested on her waist pocket where the terrible letter lay. No matter. If that were the case, Frances would rise above and be mature. She would wish Gilbert well on the path he had chosen, he and his new love.

Right after giving him a piece of her mind for breaking her heart.

Chapter 6

"Then fell, as falls a battle-tower,
On smashed and struggling spears.
Cast down from some unconquered town
That, rushing earthward, carries down
Loads of live men of all renown—
Archers and engineers."

–The Ballad of the White Horse

"Please stop struggling, sir. We are professionals, and you will not succeed."

"Look," Gilbert said, trying to struggle free from the two very large sets of hands that held him firmly in his seat, while the third guard strapped him in securely, "guys, I've gotta get off this boat! There's been a huge mistake and—"

"Right, look, mate," said the largest of the guards, clearly frustrated and not interested in niceties. "You need to hold still," he said, waving his fist under Gilbert's nose and slipping from high English into a lower-class cockney accent. "You're at the bottom of the heap 'ere, not important like them tossers up in First Class. We see at least 'aff a dozen of you lot get all scared like before launch and try to run off the ship. An' when that 'appens, it's all got to be 'please an' thank you' while some rich, fat-arsed bloke is screaming for his mum. Now, after the last 'un we had to get back in place, I have a rather overpowering desire to smack someone's gob. If I knock you senseless, me mates 'ere will be only too happy to say it was a terrible accident. Issat wot you want?"

He made this speech to Gilbert with his face no more than an inch from Gilbert's nose. When the guard was done, Gilbert was just about to respond when he heard a *click*, followed by a sound like a winding clock. He looked down and saw one of the other guards twisting some kind of small key in the lock of the belt that held him.

"Done, an' done," he said. The two guards who'd been holding Gilbert's arms to the chair released his arms, while the third stood up.

"But you don't understand!" Gilbert said, as they half-slid and half-walked down the aisle, "It's not that I'm scared! I've got to get a message to Frances Blogg! I've got to talk to her now, or this might never get straightened out! Please!"

If they heard him, the guards gave no sign. They slid out through the door as Gilbert clawed at the belts which held him in place, punching desperately at the buttons which had opened at his touch before but now were locked in place.

He pounded his fist on the armrest. Why did this have to happen *now* of all times? Why did this have to happen to *him*, of all people? Hadn't he suffered enough?

He reached into his pocket again and pulled out the paper, looking it over for some sign that he was mistaken, or that it had gone to the wrong person. He was so focused on it that he hardly noticed when the ship suddenly lurched, continuing its arc up into a vertical position pointing straight at the sky. When it stopped, Gilbert was lying on his back looking upward, and tears of frustration had sprung up in his eyes.

"You have had an injustice befall you?"

Gilbert looked at the passenger next to him—a small man with an East Indian complexion and accent. "Please don't take this the wrong way," Gilbert said, "But I want a conversation right now about as much as a hole drilled in my head."

"It is funny you should mention that. I am going to a Church on Mars that was begun under such circumstances. Here,"

He opened a pamphlet, and the words "Our Lady of the Red Sands" was written in pretty calligraphic letters on the front.

"I'm already Catholic," Gilbert said.

"Then you should pay us a visit. The original in India was unearthed recently, after being buried underground for many years."

"I'm not—"

"The Church in India was said to be founded by Saint Thomas himself, but much later whole village was buried under red sand, as punishment for a widow's cruel martyrdom. But the church was discovered and unearthed only a hundred years ago."

"Maybe it shoulda stayed buried. How was she martyred?"

"An evil king found she was a Catholic, and ordered holes to be drilled in her head and set on fire."

Gilbert was quiet for a moment. "That's how my heart feels right now."

****

"I'll need a ticket for the ferry," she said, digging into her purse past multiple paper bills to find a few coins.

"To the island?" said the man in the booth.

Frances tried very hard not to sound sarcastic. "Yes. I have to stop a ship from taking off. One for the ferry, please."

The man paused, long-unused parts of his brain gearing to life after being dulled by months and years of simple labor. "No one's ever tried to get to the island when the ship's about to leave," he said slowly. "You sure about this, Miss?"

"As certain as I've been about anything."

A price was quoted, money changed hands, and a piece of paper passed across the till. Frances had started to run across the wooden dock, the tapping of her shoes sounding very loud on the nearly deserted dock when she heard the rumble.

It was a sound she'd never heard before—the noise of something so large that it could shake the ground. She steadied herself, and when she looked up she saw a glowing fireball rising into the air several miles away, leaving a long, bright, tapering smoke trail behind as it ascended to the clouds.

****

Gilbert gripped the armrests as the *Elbereth* rose, the small fellow in the seat beside him silent and saying prayers behind closed eyes. The ascent had begun smoothly. The ship was using some of those glowing rocks that had held aloft the floating city he'd visited a few months back, so the amount of force needed to break the bonds of gravity wasn't the kind that could crush you against a wall. But the ship still needed to steer, and the kind of power needed to point a giant hunk of wood and metal at a particular point in the air would be far, far greater than needed to steer a water-bound craft of the same size.

He'd been warned about this prior to boarding, how the force of the engines propelling them would push him uncomfortably into his seat, how his ears would feel full for some reason as they did when he flew on the Zeppelin to the city in the clouds and the only way to cure it would be to work his jaws again and again.

But the discomfort from the restraining belts and the launch itself paled in comparison to the aching upset in his heart. The telegram from Frances had utterly dashed his hopes to make the trip a holiday of sorts, adventurously looking for his long-lost brother and sister while taking on the Doctor to ensure their safety.

No. As the *Elbereth* rose into the air, his eyes glanced down at the scrap of now crumpled paper in his hand and the typewritten words in the center of it.

GILBERT. HAVE THOUGHT THINGS OVER
AFTER OUR TALK. COULDN'T TELL YOU THEN,
BUT OUR LIVES ARE ON DIFFERENT PATHS
SO PLEASE FORGET ME , & FIND SOMEONE ELSE.
I HAVE.
FRANCES

I have? I *have*? She'd found someone *else*? Who? When? While he was in Rome? She'd seemed herself when he'd visited her last night.

Could Frances be that fickle? Could a girl so religious be so cruel? Cruel and uncaring enough to end things with a *telegram*?

The *Elbereth* was higher in the air, now. Wisps of cloud sped by his round window, barely visible through the thick glass. Though he now faced the sky, in minutes he caught glimpses of the sea below, islands in the sea, and even tiny buildings winking in and out on patches of green behind the white wisps of cloud cover.

He wouldn't be able to get back. He would be two months reaching Mars, at least. He'd be on the planet itself for who knows how long, and then at least *another* two months returning.

There would be no chance to talk to Frances face to face for at least half a *year*. He wept, his tears sliding out of the far corners of his eyes. They fell down the aisle back toward Earth and against the door of the passenger section.

****

It took an hour or so before the *Elbereth* stopped rising directly into the atmosphere and leveled off.

Several decks above Gilbert, a different class of passengers enjoyed a very different experience of takeoff. They had cushier chairs and less uncomfortable safety belts, and soon more polite attendants also served them better food. These and other amenities set them apart from Gilbert and the general rabble several floors below.

Soon the passengers felt free to talk to one another across aisle ways. As always, there were two who bonded with each other better than most, and they began talking loudly enough that the entire floor could hear their conversation.

"Rum thing, you know," one man said, a fellow in his forties nursing a paunch and a balding head. "I'm being sent to Mars to try and drum up a spot of business for the company. See if we can get the money-lending industry going in earnest on the red planet."

"Perhaps we could help each other, then," said the man beside him, similarly paunchy but with a full head of dark hair and sideburns. "I've got a similar assignment—to see if I can open a branch textile plant there. A lot of folks are seeing it as the new frontier now, and they're going to need clothes even in the terra-formed regions."

"The wot?"

"*Terra-formed.* It's a word they've been bandying about lately. It seems those mollusks planned to turn whole swaths of Mars into earth-like areas that would serve as farms for our kind. Now that they're largely gone, we still have the regions they converted. Grass, trees, the lot. All there and fit for settling, trading, and farming."

"Well, at least they won't be farming us."

They chuckled.

"Don't be so sure of that."

The voice had come from the row to the side. Something in his voice stilled their conversation, and they turned to look. It was a youth with dark brown hair, dressed in a dark longcoat and wearing gloves.

The businessmen paused, then chuckled some more. "Young man," one of them said, "does your mother know you're travelling such a great distance alone?"

The young man stared at them for a moment, then looked off into space with a bored expression. The two businessmen began another conversation, ignoring the young man and virtually all the other passengers on the ship. After a while, the young man unfolded a letter from his pocket, written in the same typewritten script as Gilbert's telegram:

ALL IS MOVING FORWARD. PROCEED TO THE
RED PLANET. THE DOCTOR IS TO BE REMOVED
FROM HIS POST WITH ALL AVAILABLE SPEED.
AWAIT FURTHER INSTRUCTIONS ONCE YOU
HAVE COMPLETED YOUR LATEST ASSIGNMENT.

The letter was unsigned, as all his mail was these days. He folded it again and put it back into his breast pocket, beside a pair of stylish looking goggles. Anyone who bothered to look a little closer at the outside of the folded paper would only see the addressee on the back:

HERBERT GEORGE WELLS
WRITER IN RESIDENCE, CHRISTCHURCH COLLEGE

Chapter 7

*"If we walk down the street, taking all the jurymen who have not
formed opinions and leaving all the jurymen who have formed
opinions, it seems highly probable that we shall only succeed
in taking all the stupid jurymen and leaving all the thoughtful
ones."*

–All Things Considered

1892 A.D.
MARS.

The room was large. Large enough to accommodate the half-dozen
men who sat on one side of the long table facing Sergeant Belloc. The
only light in the room came from the setting sun as its pink rays streamed
in through the closed glass window.

The table was covered in a red tablecloth, which was held in place
by various official-looking weights and emblems. The seated men wore
uniforms, and all looked visibly annoyed or uncomfortable.

Belloc stood at attention in front of the seated officers, awaiting his
next order. One of his epaulets was askew, and the buttons on his tunic
were shiny, but one-off in their pairing on his chest.

Captain Williamson sat in one of the nearby chairs, facing the table in
full uniform, looking far more official and competent than he had just a
few days before in the fort with Belloc. He took a sip of water and placed
the now half-full glass back on the table.

The man in the center of the table stood, straightened his red tunic,
and tapped a bell on the table three times with a small wooden wand.

At the sound of the bell, all in the room stood. Captain Fortescue
Williamson stood more slowly than others, moving as if it caused him
great pain.

"This court is now in session," the older man said, his voice as crisp and sharp as the ironed lines on his tunic's sleeves. "May almighty God look down upon us and enlighten our minds, may His blessings be upon us and . . ." he turned to a portrait on the wall, "God save the King."

"God save the King," they all said, Belloc's voice carrying over the rest. The officers all sat. Captain Williamson mumbled under his breath and sat slowly.

"Sergeant Hilaire Belloc," said the older man who'd led the prayer, "are you aware of the charges you are currently facing?"

"Sir, I am aware I face charges. But I'm not aware of which ones."

"You weren't told, then?"

"Sir, I was rousted from sleep not a quarter hour ago. The charges may have been mentioned, but they were not made clear as I rushed to this site in order to avoid penalties for tardiness."

"Yes or no will do, Sergeant," said one of the men on the left side of the table facing Belloc. Captain Williamson smiled in his seat.

Belloc hesitated. "No, Sir," he said quietly.

"I will reiterate the charges," the older man at the center said, giving an annoyed look to his colleague. "Sergeant Belloc, you are charged with insubordination, cowardice and . . ." he moved one, then two sheets to the back of the stack of papers in his hand. "Well, a host of other charges in relation to the attack of the Tharks on Fort St. Henry. How do you answer?"

"Not guilty on all counts, Sir."

"You may now, according to the protocol of this court, give an account for yourself."

"Sir," Belloc continued, still standing at attention and facing forward as he spoke. "When the Tharks attacked, as per Captain Williamson's orders, I had the men readied in their positions. When the attack commenced, the men were in a state of combat readiness. Prior to the attack, the Captain retreated to his quarters. . ."

"That is a lie," the Captain said, still seated but visibly angered. "You will have your opportunity to speak, Captain Williamson," said the central officer. "Proceed, Sergeant."

"The Captain," continued Belloc, his voice taking on a new edge, "secured himself in his quarters. Said quarters have four-foot thick walls and a double-bolted door."

"Another lie!" The Captain bellowed as the eyes of the seven officers at the table swiveled to look at him. "I was in command of that fort at all times and leading the men to their victory!"

"And his tea," Belloc continued.

"Liar!"

"Laced with laudanum."

"I'll have your worthless, common head dripping on a spike outside my family estate!" shouted Williamson, rising suddenly from his seat, his eyes bulging and his head bobbing in place.

"Captain Williamson," said the inquest's leader, "please be seated. You've made your complaint—"

"Has he ever done otherwise?" muttered another man at the long table.

"I heard that! My father is going to hear about it, too!"

"Captain," said the oldest man at the table, "your father is a several month journey from here. I'd strongly advise you to remember that fact."

"Brigadier Brackenbury, you insolent old goat! Have you any idea what—"

"Bailiff," said the older man, the small remaining wisps of red-stranded hair turning brighter among the white as his face colored with anger, "remove the Captain from these proceedings, please."

A very large man in a red tunic with three stripes on the upper arm had been standing quietly at the door. He now walked over to Williamson, giving a small, straight-faced wink to Belloc as he passed. "Let's go, Captain," he said, "Brigadier Brackenbury's orders."

"Lay a hand on me," Williamson said, glowering, "and I'll have you transferred to . . . to . . ."

"Mars, sir?" the Sergeant-Bailiff said with an innocent air.

Huffing, puffing, and blustering threats, Williamson left the inquest room on his own, slamming the door behind him. The bailiff shrugged his shoulders and returned to his post.

After a few seconds, the inquest continued.

"You were saying, Sergeant Belloc?" said the Brigadier at the table.

"Sir," Belloc said, coming to attention again and speaking while looking directly forward. "The Tharks attacked in force, at least double the number we faced at the battle of Syrtis Lapis. We fought back three waves of enemy attack, and I saw not a single coward among our men, despite our being outnumbered at least four to one."

"How, then, did your forces survive, Sergeant? Aside from a cut on your forehead and a flesh wound or two, you and nearly ten-percent of your men appear to be in tip-top shape!" The last question had an unfriendly tone, and had come from a Major at the end of the table. Belloc resisted the urge to look at the single red-and-gold crown on his epaulet and scratch it to see if any Williamson money would fall out.

"Sir, with all due respect, most of my forces *didn't* survive. As I stated in my initial report, seven of every ten of my men under my command that day now lays buried in Martian soil. Those casualties are closer to ninety-*five* percent if you include the wounded. We would *all* be fertilizing the soil if it hadn't been for that sniper."

"Sniper?" the Brigadier said, leaning in. His pale fingers gripped the ends of his pen a little more firmly, but even Belloc could see how tense the older man became, despite only being able to look at him out of the corner of his eye.

"Yes, sir," said Belloc. "During the battle I was distracted for a moment by a fellow soldier's pleas for aid. I lined up his attacker in my sights, pulled the trigger, and saw one of his Thark assailant's four hands disappear in a green and red mist.

"The creature howled with rage and pain, clutching his stump while the Thark next to him nearly doubled over with laughter. They do that, you know. It's part of their culture to laugh hysterically when another creature is in pain."

"We are aware of the proclivities of the natives, Sergeant. Pray continue."

"I watched further to make sure my soldier had managed to escape to the nearest bit of cover. I was turning to do the same when something very, very heavy and solid caught me upside the head.

"I blinked, and suddenly found myself flat on my back, staring at the sky with a high-pitched whine in my left ear. A Thark stood over me. He blocked out the sun, but I could still see each of his four arms held a bladed weapon with decorated hilts. His eyes were clear as green glass and filled with hate, and the skinny mandibles in his mouth were flicking in and out, like a dog licking his chops before a favorite meal.

"I reached for my pistol, though I knew I was done for. My rifle had jammed, and my holster was empty, as I'd apparently dropped my pistol when I'd been struck. I was screaming at the monster and saying a prayer to St. Michael when the Thark's forehead exploded.

"It soiled my uniform quite badly. I sincerely doubt they'll ever get the smell out of it, but at that point I didn't much care. I jumped to my feet and told the men to pull back, but by that point two more Tharks had fallen in the same way. Someone was manning the hills behind us, sir. And they were using a long-range rifle to great effect. In the next minute that sniper took down over a dozen Thark brutes, saving the lives of at least as many men. We regrouped and retook the wall they'd breached. Once we had control of the Maxim gun they'd overrun earlier, we made short work of the stragglers. When the last of them had got out of range, I took my spyglass and swept the field and hills, looking for our benefactor."

"Were you successful, Sergeant?"

"Partially, sir. I did see someone in the hills nursing a rifle."

"And?"

"It was a woman, sir."

The room was silent. "A woman, Sergeant Belloc?"

"Yes, sir. It was undoubtedly a woman, wearing a long skirt and puffed sleeves while carrying a long-barreled rifle, possibly a Lee-Enfield, though I can't be certain. Though she was a couple of hundred yards off, my spyglass could see her red hair bobbing in the breeze."

"Indeed," said the Brigadier.

After the inquest had officially ended and the other officers were gone, Belloc followed his next order and reported to the Brigadier's office. When Belloc arrived, the Brigadier looked him up and down. "Relax, Sergeant, and take a seat," he said. Belloc sat.

The Brigadier was an older man. Now that he was again calm, his hair had reverted to a shock of short, neatly clipped white strands with barely discernible red roots, along with a pair of very alert blue eyes. He sat as well, opened a drawer at his desk, and pulled out and opened a small cigar case. "Would you like a smoke?"

"Yes, sir," Belloc said, careful not to sound too eager. He reached over, pulled one from the case and lit it with the match the Brigadier offered a second later. Belloc shook the match to extinguish it as he'd seen his father do when he'd lit his Indian cigars at the Sunday brunch table after Mass.

"Sergeant, do you have any questions for me?" The Brigadier said, leaning back in his chair and lacing his fingers behind his head. His jacket was unbuttoned, exposing a paunch that was slight compared to that of many of the other officers in the colony.

Belloc thought as he puffed, then he took the cigarette out of his mouth. "Permission to speak freely, Sir?" The Brigadier nodded. Belloc took a deep breath, then spoke. "With all due respect, Sir," Belloc said, "what is all this about? I led a group of men to victory over immense odds, and possibly saved one of our cities from a major attack by hostile natives. And I did so while my commander hid under the bed. Yet *I'm* brought up on the charges my commander should be facing.

"Moreover, a few minutes ago I received my new orders. I've been reassigned to a patrol boat! Gone from defending forts to steering glorified airborne rowboats on milk runs across the desert! The men who survived with me are scattered around the colony, yet 'Captain' Williamson goes back to a new fort with another comfy bed, a crate of whiskey, and a box of cigars. He also gets a platoon of new soldiers who haven't a clue that they're in far more danger with him in charge of their lives than they ever would be under attack from the Tharks."

"Sergeant, could you tell me why you and the men have such contempt for the Captain?"

"I could indeed, Sir. My first day under his command, he led us on a simple foot patrol around the city. It was my first week here, his second. We were dune-whacked by a few brigands and had to fight our way back. I kept waiting for him to give an order but he froze. Two men *died*, Sir, waiting for orders that never came. Instead I yelled for the men to get to take cover, and Williamson followed *me*."

"And then?"

"He screamed like a little girl the whole time. I had to stop several of the men from pushing him out in the open so the dunewhackers could use him for target practice. We settled for having him curl up in a fetal position and jamming his cap low enough that it covered his ears. His face was far enough in the sand that most of his screams were muffled. After I made a few shots on the brigands, they decided to move on to easier prey and headed North toward that French outpost."

"Hilaire," the Brigadier said. A good sign—officers didn't often use first names of their subordinates. "Do you know why the-ah-, uh, *Captain* is here to begin with?"

"I've got an idea or two, sir. He's tried to swagger like a soldier since he got here, but he moves and talks like a rich fop. I'd guess his daddy sent him here to punish him for something."

The Brigadier stood and walked to face the window with his hands folded behind his back. He waited a very long minute before speaking.

"You're right about Williamson, Hilaire, in that his father purchased him a commission and specifically requested he be sent out here to the colonies. There was trouble of some stripe or another over a journalist. I don't know whether he wanted to toughen up his son or he just found him too much an embarrassment, and I've not a whit of motivation to find out.

"But Captain Williamson's father *does* have an arm long enough to reach throughout Britain, which means he can reach here as well. People who have gotten between that *Captain* and Daddy's goals for him either disappear or turn up cold in an alley.

"Hence, Hilaire, your reassignment. It was *my* decision that you would serve on a small, Aphid-class vessel, patrolling the East side of the Dune Sea outside of Syrtis Major. It's a Cavorite powered, well-armed gunboat. It moves quickly and is rather difficult to track or corner in a maze of ships and ports. More important, a patrol assignment keeps you out of the city for weeks at a time. Even when you return, you'll be back only for a day or two before shipping out again. And during *any* time in port, you'll be either on the ship or the very, very safe and monitored confines of a fort. Are we clear? Hopefully, after a year or so, Williamson will have made other enemies and I'll be able to put you back on real duty."

Hilaire stifled a curse. *A year?* He breathed, exhaled, and nodded his head. "Understood, Sir. Though, for the record, while I appreciate your efforts to protect me, I'd humbly suggest that my surviving a Thark onslaught would show I'm quite capable of taking care of myself. Further ..."

"That is all, Sergeant Belloc," the Brigadier said as he turned to face the young soldier. Hilaire stood, snapping to attention with his arms at his sides and his eyes once again facing forward.

"Dismissed," said the Brigadier. Hilaire turned on his heel and left the office. He had two places on his mind as he walked past the secretary's desk, but he forgot about both of them when he saw Captain Williamson, a mite older than Hilaire in years but much younger in the things that truly counted in life—sitting outside the Brigadier's office with his Captain's hat in his lap.

Hilaire gave the Captain a blank-faced salute, which Williamson returned without moving from his seat.

Now, Hilaire thought, remembering, *first to the chapel to give thanks for what happened, then to the bar to forget what happened.*

Over the next few hours before he shipped out, Sergeant Hilaire Belloc tried very hard *not* to think about Williamson getting chewed into tiny, cowardly little pieces by ferocious Martian predator beasts. If he indulged in that little fantasy too much, he might have to go to confession afterward.

Chapter 8

"Precisely because our political speeches are meant to be reported, they are not worth reporting. Precisely because they are carefully designed to be read, nobody reads them."

– All Things Considered

1892 A.D.
OUTER SPACE. EN ROUTE TO MARS.

Gilbert was angry.

No, he thought, anger was too simple an adjective. There was no way that a simple, two-syllable word like *anger* would be able to encompass the boiling, seething resentment that had sprouted in his heart, growing tendrils and tentacles in his soul over the next several weeks of travel.

Worse, the thought of being so callously thrown over by Frances after all he'd been through for her? *That* brought even *more* rage and anguish into his heart and head every time he thought about it.

And he had a little over two months to nurse his wound, trapped in a tin-and-wooden box hurtling through the ether faster than literally any man had dreamed travel to be possible. Each second brought him farther away from Frances, along with any chance at discussion or resolution.

Worst of all was the lack of distractions on board. Well, distractions interesting enough to take his mind off his troubles, anyway.

The East-Indian fellow who talked to him at the beginning of the trip had sequestered himself in his room virtually all day, every day. Gilbert had wanted to argue theology with him, but the fellow instead would only smile at Gilbert when they passed in the hallways but offer no more communication whatsoever. Gilbert also tried joining a few of the card games held nearly every night in the recreation room of the steerage class passengers. Then he tried exercise in the gamesmen's room that was barely bigger than his Ma's kitchen back home in Minnesota.

But nothing seemed to work. He couldn't focus on the card games, even once he could understand the bizarre rules some of them employed (*"that card is only wild, chap,"* one player had said, *"if we're in a month whose name contains an 'r'"*). As for the gamesroom, a rather large-muscled fellow seemed to inhabit the small exercise room for a majority of each day. And no one felt completely comfortable asking him to share the weights.

Gilbert tried many times to write, both in his small, cramped room and the small library for the people of his travelling class. But all his attempts were fruitless. Be it a letter to Frances, an article about space travel, even a few stuttering attempts at poetry, nothing could pull him out of his foul mood. He fretted and sighed. At least fifteen times a day a vision jumped into his head of Frances in a beautiful wedding dress alongside the fop Edward Williamson. Last year, in fact, Gilbert had learned that when the two were children, Williamson had been betrothed to Frances by their business-partner parents. Williamson, now some kind of Army or Navy officer, had hired a few thugs back then to work over Gilbert and convince him to bow out. The plan had failed spectacularly, but since Williamson's father had a reputation for making people in his way disappear . . .

Disappear . . .

Something in Gilbert's head grabbed the word and wouldn't let go.

Disappear.

Dear God, Gilbert thought, *why did you let this happen? Why has Frances really rejected me? Does she no longer love me, or is she being pressured by Williamson, or someone else? Things looked like they were finally going my way. Why have You let us be split apart like this?*

****

1892 A.D.
OUTER SPACE. EN ROUTE TO MARS.

Frances stared out the window now that her ship was aloft. Liftoff and flying weren't nearly the traumatic experiences she'd thought they would be, despite the heavy rumbling everywhere from the ship's sizable engines. She'd been assured that the small globe of Cavorite in the hold would keep the ship in the air safely so long as it remained charged with electricity. Even so, the vessel still needed huge engines once it broke free of Earth's gravity to steer to its destination on Mars.

She wondered if there had been any cases thus far where the electrical charge had failed, causing the ship to drop to Earth like a giant rock. She tried not to think of a ship full of screaming passengers, knowing their end was near and preparing to meet God . . .

She shook her head to clear the horrifying image, and she thought of other things instead.

Once she'd gotten to the island and seen Gilbert's ship launch, she'd sent a telegram home, explaining the situation to them as best she could. She then used her family's punchcard number to secure a horrifically expensive, last-minute place on the next ship leaving for Mars.

Gilbert, she thought, *I've no idea if you've truly betrayed me. I thought you a gallant young man, worth any other ten young men I know. Whether I was right or wrong, I must know the truth.*

She looked around at those with her. Her ship, the *Eddas*, was not a large vessel like Gilbert's. Whereas the *Elbereth* had been built to be the planet-faring equivalent of a luxury ocean liner, the *Eddas* was much smaller, with fewer accessories. It also had the kind of passengers that Frances wasn't used to seeing on a long holiday. Rather than well-dressed and festive-minded bankers and businessmen and their families, many of those on board looked shifty, shabby, and furtive, taking the trip for reasons impolite to enquire about.

Frances sighed again. It was going to be a long trip of several months. She'd brought no real luggage from home, and so had purchased a host of items in the shops on the island just after she'd bought her ticket. Among them were a few random books. Perhaps she could get away with reading them only a few times each before she grew too bored.

The ship had risen steadily for several hours before escaping the gravity and atmosphere of Earth. Francis had *oohed* and *ahhed* out the window like everyone else at the view of the Earth's curve, but after a time had grown bored with even that. When the electric lights had come on in the passenger areas and they'd been told they could move about, she'd retreated to her tiny personal cabin and pulled out the first book she could find.

She'd not given herself any time on purpose to choose a particular book, worried that she might waste hours and have nothing in the end. While still in the shop, she'd pointed to a shelf of books, which the willing shopkeeper had happily boxed up after he'd run her number through his punchcard reader.

After a short while, the hard wooden chair in her cabin grew uncomfortable, and she returned to her cushioned travelling seat.

She'd settled in and had been enjoying her read for several minutes when it started.

" 'Ello, miss," said a voice near her. She didn't know the man's name, but the tone told her all she needed to know about the man himself.

She looked up over the corners of her book. "May I help you?" she asked, using a tone both polite and firm. The man standing over her had a few days' worth of scruff on his chin, wore clothes a shade too small, and reeked of cheap scent.

"I was just er, wonderin' Miss, seein' as how we're going to be neighbors for the next few months an' all—"

His eye seemed to take notice of her book's cover. Underneath the title of *Pugilism Illustrated* was a photo of a man on the cover with a handlebar mustache who stood wearing an undershirt and boxer shorts, his fists raised and a cocky look on his face.

Frances waited while the man stared at the cover for a very long ten seconds. "Never mind, miss," he said after the pause, "there's been a mistake."

"As you wish," Frances said, returning to her book. She pretended to be deeply immersed in the book she'd bought on boxing. After a few minutes she became *truly* interested, and she spent the next few hours far more pleasantly than she thought she would.

Chapter 9

"Because a girl should have long hair, she should have clean hair; because she should have clean hair, she should not have an unclean home; because she should not have an unclean home, she should have a free and leisured mother; because she should have a free mother, she should not have an usurious landlord; because there should not be a usurious landlord, there should be a redistribution of property; because there should be a redistribution of property, there shall be a revolution."

– *"Conclusion," What's Wrong with the World*

1892 A.D.
MARS. BRITISH COLONY OF SYRTIS MAJOR.

When the alarm clock sang its morning twang, Beatrice hit the button to shut it off and looked up at the ceiling. The dream she'd had of her old house in the green hills and gables of Eastern Canada was already fading. By the time she'd gotten to the washroom to begin her day, the dream was gone and she was plotting out the rest of the day for both her and her little brother, Cecil.

She looked in the mirror at her own face. She was in her early twenties; still young. The few who bothered to comment to her on her looks told her that. But her eyes looked older than her age, and she felt older than she looked. She'd only been on Mars for a little over a year, but life here hadn't matched what she'd been led to expect.

Still, she thought as she finished washing her face, life here had its benefits. If only she could get Cecil to buckle down with his schoolwork . . .

She was just about to call out to him when she paused in drying her face.

She smelled bacon cooking. Tea was brewing, too.

Something was very, very wrong.

She left the tiny washroom and walked to the kitchen.

Their house was more of a cabin, really. The downstairs was more of a basement cut into the side of a hill. It was here that Beatrice and her brother typically ate their meals, played chess, and had their evening talks; it was also where Cecil slept in a bed behind a drawn curtain.

Cecil had apparently risen with the sun's pink rays and begun preparing breakfast. Beatrice had been in the fog of the newly awakened, so she hadn't noticed him at first. A small feast was laid out on the table. Bacon, toast, coffee, even fruit juice had been arranged with loving precision.

"Beatrice!" Cecil said happily, "Isn't it a wonderful morning?"

She looked at him with narrowed eyes. "What's your game, Cecil," she said. "What do you want?"

"What?" he answered, looking hurt. "What? I can't believe you'd stoop to such levels as to accuse me of ulterior motives! I only wanted to do something nice for my loving sister, who has cared for me this past year since we had to travel to—"

"Cecil, every sweet action you've performed over the past *thirteen* years might as well have had a price tag. Now, what did you do? Are you in another spot of trouble you need me to bail you out of?"

"Well, now that you mention it—"

"Cecil, get your books and head to school. After that, get to your job, get paid, and bring the money home. Our rent is due tomorrow."

"Yes, well, about that . . ."

She looked at him from behind crossed arms. Her steady eye grew colder each second.

"I . . . the money's due tomorrow, yes," he said, barely controlling his stammer, "and he's going to pay me today, yes. But, well . . ."

"Well what?"

"I seem to have incurred a few debts this past week."

Beatrice closed her eyes and inhaled slowly. "How much this time, Cecil?"

"It was a sure bet, Bea. Really, it was. I thought we had it for sure!"

"How much?"

"Well, if you want to put a price on what I've learned from the whole experience . . ."

As if by magic, Beatrice produced a wooden spoon and stood between her brother and the doorway. "What did I tell you would happen if you went gambling again, dear brother?"

"I . . ." he said. His eyes darted back and forth—he seemed ready to flinch, duck, bob, and weave to avoid the most to-be-feared kitchen utensil on two worlds.

A knock sounded at the door. A half-dozen rapid raps, followed by a pause and then a few more knocks.

"You wait *right there*," she said, waving the spoon for emphasis, "I'm not done with you by a long shot!"

Cecil looked at her and nodded, his bottom lip quivering and his eyes filling with tears.

As soon as Beatrice turned to answer the door, he wiped his eyes, stopped quivering his lower lip, and raced up the stairs without a sound.

Beatrice heard him escape as his foot slipped on the last step at the top of the stairs; it was too late to grab him. Whatever was she going to *do* with this child?

The rapping at the door entered its third and likely final round. Weighing the risks of giving chase to her annoying brother or answering the door, she decided to let Cecil escape for now. She could deal with him later. And would she ever!

She opened the door. The man who stood in the doorway was tall, with thick black unkempt hair on his head and a pair of ropy whiskers on his face. The right arm of his coat had been folded up and sewn shut. His top hat and black longcoat had once been stately looking on Earth, but on Mars nothing in the way of clothing looked nice for very long. Wind, the hardscrabble life, and red dirt fine as talcum reduced every piece of finery from Earth into shabbiness in a matter of months.

"Why, Doctor!" she said with genuine pleasure, "what a happy surprise! Please, do come in!"

The Doctor smiled and stepped across the threshold. "Delighted to, my dear," he said with a voice smooth as oil. Unlike his filthy coat, his manners were always immaculate.

****

By the time the Doctor had crossed into the house, Cecil had climbed out his window and onto the window-frame. Crouching like a cat, he sprang like an acrobat into the air. While still in the air, he pulled his legs back and up, landing in a crouch with hardly a sound.

Pleased with himself, he stood straight and dusted the red dirt from his pants. Though that crazy Doctor had gotten them the house they lived in, Cecil had never quite trusted him.

Off, then, to work. Well, school first. Draw letters, pictures, read, find ways to annoy the teacher, but not so much that he'd get into trouble again. Then, once dismissed, the real workday for Cecil began at the White Sloat Tavern.

He trudged off down the red-dirt street, dodging crimson piles of sludge where someone had spilled water near a pump outside the courthouse. The last time he'd come to school with muddy shoes he'd gotten a switch across the back of his hands, and he couldn't risk serious trouble today. Not with his sister already on the alert.

"Hello, dirt rat," a voice growled behind him.

Cecil felt his insides go cold, but shoved away the feeling. He took off running without even looking behind him, flying far and fast enough that he couldn't stop when a leg popped out of an alleyway and tripped him as he rounded a corner.

Cecil went down, his face smacking hard into the dirt track left by a wagon wheel. He was glad he always did his schoolwork quickly and well, since it meant he could leave his books in his desk each day. Traveling light was essential in the line of work he was growing into, never more so than when rivals decided to give chase! He sprang to his feet barely a second after his fall, but the heavy hand on his shoulder held him fast.

"Leaving so soon, mate?" said a cockney-accented voice as thick fingers dug into his shoulder. "Ye'd hurt me feelings if ye did that, ye know."

"Kevin," yelled Cecil, "I'll hurt more'n yer feelings if you don't get that meat hook out've my shoulder! Help! *Fire!*"

There were a number of people walking in the streets, but none looked at Cecil longer than a second. One man even smiled, giving a knowing nod to the large boy who'd tripped Cecil and now held his shoulder in a grip tighter than a metalworker's vise.

"Oh, my little dirt rat," he cooed, looking at Cecil as a half-dozen other boys wearing brown caps surrounded them, each one as big or bigger than Cecil, "don't ye know that lyin's a sin? A terrible, awful sin at that. Worse than just abou' anything, I'd say. Besides, you've picked too many pockets 'ere to have any hope of help from anyone. Now, on to business."

"I got no business with you!"

"Oh, but you *do*, dirt rat! You owe me money, and that's a bad bit o' business indeed! Bring 'im in the alley, boys! Let's show this dirt rat what happens when you don't pay up to the Brown Hat gang!"

As they hauled him to the alleyway, Cecil looked at the bully who stood smirking at him. Cecil had done most of his growing up in Eastern Canada, and living there had exposed him to many bullies and louts like Kevin O'Brien and his Brown Hat gang. While the lessons had often been quite painful, by the time he and Beatrice had moved to the colonies Cecil had learned how and when to fight, run and escape better than many soldiers facing their first combat.

This situation, for example, called first for a quick analysis. Cecil had a captor gripping each arm, and a gang controlled by a bullying leader. Two quick twitches told him the weaker thug held his left arm. Spinning his arm like a pinwheel, Cecil's left arm was free in a second. In the same movement he dropped to his knees, spun right and punched his other assailant in the groin. The hands holding his right arm melted away like ghosts.

Ignoring the screams of outrage around him, Cecil tucked into a ball and rolled away from the group. He sprang to his feet and ran like a desert wind down the street, trying hard to ignore the noises behind as the gang gave chase.

Cecil knew he'd be caught in a long race. Kevin O'Brien and his squad of Brown Hat toadies were tough to ignore. Most of them had longer legs, and all of them were too scared of Kevin to give up the chase.

Cecil's advantage lay in his knowledge of the neighborhood. In the next minute he leaped over one fence and through a hole in another. At one of the largest houses in Syrtis Major, Cecil shimmied up a drainpipe, over a rooftop, and across a clothesline, all the while taking extra care not to knock down the laundry of Brigadier Brackenbury's family. The Brigadier's kind mother was elderly but spry, and she had bandaged more than one of his knees after one of his misadventures. Escape was his first priority, but he didn't want to make any extra work for anyone who'd been good to him.

Up to one roof and across another, the Brown Hats lost a member or two to a fall or similar stupidity each time Cecil dodged a new obstacle. Soon it was only Kevin left—older and bigger, but stupider and now without any friends.

"I'll rip ya a new ear 'ole, you an' yer dollymop of a sister!" Cecil heard Kevin yell behind him. Cecil wanted to turn and fight at that one, but he kept moving. Revenge could wait!

Now Cecil jumped on the McCarthy family's house. It had a lopsided roof that dropped down at a steep angle once you got over the peak.

Cecil hopped over the peak and then found a hand-hold where one of the shingles used to be, flattening himself against the wall of the sheer drop while hanging on with the fingertips of both hands.

Kevin O'Brien, blind with rage, launched himself over the roof peak with a triumphant *whoop!*

Which turned to a scream of fear and surprise as fell off the side. He slid down the sheer side of the roof's unexpectedly steep incline before hitting the ground below, splattering in a pile of grungy refuse and interrupting the morning meal of several stray dogs.

"I'll get you for this, dirt rat!" Kevin screamed after he realized the kind of slime his angry little adventure had covered him in. "I'll get you!"

Cecil didn't wait, but he laughed instead as he scampered to another rooftop. "And Kevin," he shouted over his shoulder, "the Brown Hats is *the* stupidest name for a gang *ever!*"

Kevin's impotent and incoherent rage in the garbage pile below warmed Cecil's heart as he leaped off the McCarthy's gutter and back onto the roof of the Brackenbury home.

Off to school now, he thought. True, Kevin O'Brien and his band of toadies would very likely "get" him one day for this little transgression. But right now, he would savor this moment as if it was the sweetest piece of Turkish delight.

****

"But of course, Doctor! I'm *quite* open to obtaining a new position!"

Beatrice was nothing if not efficient. She'd grown up having to make sure her younger sibling towed the line and everything else stayed shipshape. As such, when the Doctor dropped by for an unexpected visit, it was a small matter for her to put on some tea and put out the few items to be had in their pantry onto a wooden serving tray. While he was too old to be a serious prospect for marriage to Beatrice, he had been nothing but kind and generous to them since their arrival, and that merited a great deal of graciousness.

Still wearing his dark longcoat, he sat at the table drinking tea with

54

his left hand from one of the least-cracked cups in the house. He smiled, dark whiskers pulling back to reveal perfectly white teeth in a smile both happy and genuine.

"My dear Beatrice," he said, "I am so very glad to hear that! I had been terribly concerned that your current state of affairs would render you unavailable."

"Doctor," said Beatrice, sitting with her best poise, "while the local barrister is a kind employer, I fear that the salary of a maid is not sufficient to command the style of living I'd hoped to raise my brother in. My own level of education suggests that I would be better suited to the position you describe.

"After all," she continued, "to be the assistant to an archaeologist sounds most exciting! To say nothing of the opportunity it would provide young Cecil! Imagine, having the chance to examine an ancient Martian city!"

"I am quite glad that you feel that way, dear, dear girl. More glad, I think, than you could possibly imagine." He paused for a moment, then sipped his tea and continued. "Helping you and your brother has been something of a happy project of mine as of late, one I delight in pursuing."

"Doctor, I don't wish to embarrass you, but Cecil and I are very, very grateful for the help you have provided us. We were lured here with the promise of lucrative employment opportunities for me and free education for young Cecil, and sadly all those promises came to naught. If you hadn't happened to be here on that day that we landed, well, we may very well have been destitute."

"Did you ever find out what happened to the man you were supposed to meet, dear Beatrice?"

"No, in truth. After our parents passed away in Newfoundland, a recruiter for the colonies came through Labrador. The farm was difficult to run on our own. Nigh impossible, actually, for a girl of my age and a boy of twelve, and we had to give our farm back to the bank. After that we had no prospects and neighbors were wearying of giving us charity.

"And then the recruiter offered us a smaller plot of land to work and a house to live in, and well, it seemed a dream come true. When we arrived here, though, the man who was supposed to meet us was nowhere to be found, his office nonexistent. We're thankful for your generosity, of course. But living in this part of the city has had its challenges. Now with the chance to work in the open air as an archeologist's assistant and bring Cecil out from this . . . this . . . Well, he's a good boy, Doctor, but—" Her eyes reddened and she tried to find the words.

The Doctor stood, placing his cup on the table in the awkward quiet. "My dear, dear Beatrice. You have suffered much. Sadly, if things were different, we might, well . . ." he stood and moved behind her, placing his left hand on her shoulder. Beatrice tensed up the smallest amount at his touch.

"Well, enough of that," he said, removing his hand and holding the trim of his vest as he moved back in front of Beatrice again. "You and your brother are wonderful people who deserve better than the hand that has been dealt you. How could I do otherwise? If you are willing to accept the position of archeologist's assistant, please be in the city square tomorrow at dawn."

"Thank you again, Doctor, for your recommendation."

"It wasn't only my recommendation that procured you this position, dear girl. My associate has had his eye on you for some time now. Be of good cheer. He's left an advance on your first week's salary as a token of his esteem." He smiled and dug into his pocket. His hand passed over the table and seemed to shimmer as a pile of coins spilled out of his hand and onto the table with tinkling sounds. Still smiling, he doffed his hat and left.

Beatrice looked at the money. Silver! *British* silver! Metal was so rare here that virtually everything was made of stone, brick, or local plant life. *Tonight*, she thought, tonight all those prayers she'd been offering up would be answered. No more would she have to clean others' homes in the day and play chess games with well-to-do older men for shillings in the evenings. There must be at least a dozen pounds' worth of silver on the table! Here on Mars, its value would be ten times their value on Earth. Money like this could be used to return to Earth or relocate here to better dwellings with better schools for Cecil.

She put the tea things away and went back to the washroom, getting ready for the rest of the day. She'd be late for her first cleaning job with the town physician, but no real matter. The town physician was a kind lady. Like Beatrice, she had been raised as a farmer's daughter, which gave Beatrice a certain leeway when she made mistakes.

Chapter 10

"That is the whole strength of our Christian civilization, that it does fight with its own weapons and not with other people's."

—All Things Considered.

1892 A.D.
SPACE. HALFWAY FROM EARTH TO MARS

When the alarm sounded, Gilbert woke from his dream and looked around. The large horn-shaped protrusion into his room was talking in a loud voice, saying words he could only vaguely understand.

... SECURELY FASTENED. REPEATING: WE ARE ENCOUNTERING AN UNEXPECTED OBSTACLE IN THE FORM OF A METEOR SWARM. THERE IS NO NEED TO PANIC, BUT WE WILL HAVE TO BEGIN OUR DECELERATION EARLY. PLEASE MOVE IN AN ORDERLY FASHION TO THE CHAIRS YOU SAT IN WHEN WE DISEMBARKED FROM EARTH. STRAP YOURSELF SECURELY. YOU WILL EXPERIENCE WEGHTLESSNESS FOR A TIME, BUT PLEASE RESIST THE TEMPTATION TO FLOAT FREE. YOU WILL LIKELY SUSTAIN SERIOUS INJURY ONCE WE RETURN TO A STATE OF GRAVITY IF YOU ARE NOT SECURELY FASTENED. REPEATING ...

Gilbert was groggy and unhappy as he half-stumbled in his nightshirt to the row of chairs where he'd been strapped in at their departure. His sleep-fog faded when he saw the faces of the stewards, who checked the safety restraints on the passengers with calm voices, but grim faces and eyes wide with fear.

"We're going to die!" moaned a man over and over again two seats back. "We're going to die!"

"Could you then, please," quipped a prim, slim woman in her fifties, "allow us the privilege of dying *quietly*?"

A sound echoed throughout the dimly lit room, very much like rocks being thrown against a metal wall.

"No need to panic, ladies and gentleman!" shouted one of the stewards, his face still pale with fear, the edge in his voice peeking through the calm words, "this is nothing more than a storm you might encounter while driving in a coach at night. The ship was built to withstand . . ."

Three *pings* sounded against the hull outside, followed by a *bang*! That sounded like a gunshot. Gilbert wished he'd brought his rosary in his pocket instead of packing it away. He fumbled his way through a muddled prayer in his head instead.

But something very odd happened when Gilbert tried to pray.

He couldn't.

Not the way he had before, anyway.

Something had changed in the weeks he'd spent brooding over Frances' telegram. Something had shifted in his head and heart. Now, when he prayed, instead of talking to God, he felt like he was shouting in darkness.

And just before the lights in the ship went out completely, he wondered if Frances was happy. What was she doing right now? Likely having dinner at a posh restaurant in the West End of London, with Fortescue Williamson.

Or some other *rich boy*.

****

Frances sat down with her tray of food in the small meeting room that had been converted to a cafeteria. She stared at the bowl and the almost unrecognizable brown lumps of food and the pasty white gravy it sat in. She'd been raised in a home where gourmet meals were a thing of regularity, but she was also raised to believe in virtue and a willingness to keep a stiff-upper-lip when things were going poorly and nothing could be done to change that. She moved her book to the side, breathed through her mouth to block the smell, and had just dipped her spoon into the mess, when Edward sat beside her with his own tray.

Edward looked to be in his late twenties, had fingerless gloves and a scruffy, three weeks' growth of spiky black beard. He'd given no last name when he'd introduced himself a few days before, and he looked like the kind of man mothers warned their children to avoid. " 'Ello, Frances," he said, smelling his own food with gusto, "and 'ow's the pretty one this evening, then?"

"I am doing quite well, thank you," she said, keeping her voice quiet and focusing on her food.

"You know, m'lady," he said, his mouth full after shoveling several noisy spoonfuls into it, "I do think I've got you figured out at last. You're not just playing 'ard to get. You genuinely aren't int'rested in my attentions. Issat right?"

"Truly, you have a knack for the interpretation of body language, Edward. Is there anything else?"

"Well, yes, as a matter of fact. Y'see, we'll be on this tin can for the next four weeks before we arrive on Mars. I'll start me new life, and you'll do whatever it is you're going there to do, and we may never see one another again. But, in fact, there's a decent chance we may not make it there at all, you know. All it takes is a rock the size of an apple, and *boom*, there's a hole big enough to let all our air out, an' we're dead in space up 'ere, never to be seen by our loved ones or anyone else again."

"You also have a talent for unique dinner conversation, Edward. Are you aware of that?"

"Didn't mean to upset, of course. Whatcha readin' now?"

She held up the book until the cover was visible.

"Nick...Nick-oh..." he said, trying to read the title.

"*Nicholai Tesla and You*," she finished for him. "It's a book about the practical applications of electricity."

"Wot, to light the house?"

"Among other things," she answered, shoveling another spoonful of stew into her mouth.

"Well m'lady," he said, "I'd suggest that you're hiding yourself far too much in that little cabin o' yours, reading. The only time I've seen you outside of your room is wiv' one of your books, an' even then, you'd only go to the exercise room, look at a picture ye've tucked in between the pages, hit the punching bag a few times, and go back behind your door again. Tell me, love," he moved in closer. Frances could see frayed threads poking out from the collar of his cheap blue suit jacket, along with a number of unattractive hairs growing out of his nostrils, "what's it you're hiding from?"

Frances paused, years of training in etiquette fighting her instincts of the moment. "I have just remembered something," she said, "it is, unfortunately, time for me to write my fiancée his nightly letter. If you will excuse me," she said, rising to go.

"Now, love," Edward said, grabbing her hand and looking hard into her eyes, "Whoever your man is, it's a long way off to anywhere on Earth or Mars. 'E need never know what happens on board a ship like this. Don't you—"

"Unhand me, Edward," she said quietly.

"I should think you really *need* a man's hand on you, don't you think?"

"Edward, I want to leave."

"I think you need to stay, love. I've made a little arrangement with the porters. I give them a bit o' flash from my pocket an' they look the other way when I want a bit of pleasurable company. And on this trip, dear, it's gonna be y—"

Edward never got to finish his thought. Frances dropped her tray on the floor and bunched her hand into a fist, her thumb pushing her middle knuckle out into what her book on boxing called a "hoodlum's point."

Considering it was the first punch she'd ever thrown in her life, and with her left hand at that, Frances could be forgiven for missing Edward's nose the first time. And the second.

But the third punch connected, hitting his nose so hard that Edward's initial chuckles at her fighting attempts turned to howls of pain, surprise, and anger.

He then saw his blood on Frances' knuckle.

"Bloody 'ELL!" he roared, releasing her and covering his injured nose with both his hands. "If that's how you treat a man who *likes* ye, it's no wonder *your* man ran off to Mars to get away!"

The small dining hall was very silent, but the twenty or so people inside it looking at Frances with expressions ranging from shock and awe to beaming admiration.

"A word of advice regarding women, Edward," Frances said, her voice surprisingly even as she shook her left hand, "none of us like to be grabbed. Not one. Sometimes we may pretend otherwise, but only if we see ourselves without options. Today, you tried it on a woman *with* options. Good day to you. Porter!" she continued, raising her voice, "I fear there's been an accident! I have dropped my tray."

She scooped up her book and walked back to the cabins, her feet making loud *tap-tap-taps* down the hall. Once her face was no longer visible to the other passengers, she let loose the tiniest of sobs. When behind her cabin door, she locked it and cried into her thin pillow with all her heart, careful to keep her voice quiet as the tears flowed.

After a few minutes, she suddenly sat up and grabbed the book titled *Pugilism Illustrated*. Knowing it was the worst thing she could do but unable to stop, she pulled the dreaded piece of paper from between the book's pages and unfolded it. Her face held the kind of horror a young child might have while pulling at a painful scab.

The sheet that Mara, her maid, had looked at a month ago and tried to hide from Frances was a picture drawn from a *stipplograph*, a series of ink dots drawn by needles to copy a picture snapped on film.

Stipplographed pictures ranged in quality, from unrecognizable blurs to sharply drawn near-photographs. This one was the finest quality Frances had ever seen, using not only extremely tiny dots to make its picture, but even various shades of *colored* ink in the process.

Frances' romantic life with Gilbert had not been the picturesque, Jane-Austen-romance novel she and every other girl hoped for. Gilbert had been away on assignment as often as he'd been in London. Many of his declarations of love had been in the form of long letters and beautiful poetry. Though her father never openly disapproved and mother seemed to actually like Gilbert half the time, many of their meetings had had to be furtive as she snuck away from her watchful bodyguards for a few stolen minutes with her beloved.

And now . . .

The stipplograph stared up at her. Two faces were drawn on the stippled sheet, and one of them could only be Gilbert's.

Last year, when she and Gilbert were still sorting out their feelings for each other, they'd met in a floating dance hall in Munich at the World's Fair. The party had literally been crashed by a quartet of pilots with flying machines and mechanized guns strapped to their backs. One of them, a woman with locks of red hair flying out from beneath her leather airman's cowl, had called Gilbert's name and saved him from being killed.

And now, staring up at her from the paper in Frances' hands was a picture of Gilbert and a beautiful, red-haired girl.

Gilbert's eyes were closed in ecstasy.

Worse, he and the red-headed girl were locked in a kiss. A passionate, deep, *open-mouthed* kiss.

The kind they'd agreed was best reserved for married people.

Frances' mind reeled again as she folded up the paper and shoved it back into the book.

She'd find her answers on Mars, one way or another!

She made sure her door was locked, then she dressed for bed and settled in with yet another of the random books she'd grabbed. *One-Thousand-And-One Ways to Survive in The Desert* was the title. It would either be fascinating, or just the thing to put her into a good, deep sleep.

The book began to do its work, bringing on sleep as it educated her. And as she slipped into the land of dreams, her last thoughts were of Gilbert.

What was the truth? What was to be done? Whatever the truth was, Frances knew that before the adventure was over, she'd unseal a tin of comeuppance on someone.

Chapter 11

"It almost looks as if the advisers, and even the officials, of the German Army had become infected in some degree with the false and feeble doctrine that might is right. As this doctrine is invariably preached by physical weaklings like Nietzsche it is a very serious thing even to entertain the supposition that it is affecting men who have really to do military work."

–All Things Considered

1892 A.D.
MARS. BRITISH COLONY OF SYRTIS MAJOR.

"Belloc!" roared the Lieutenant. Belloc looked at him for a split second before facing forward again.

"Yes, Sir!" Belloc shouted back, coming to attention.

"Belloc," yelled the Lieutenant between hiccups, "I will be engaging in a meeting for the next two hours with my superiors. I am placing you in command of the *Red Locust* during my absence. In the event I am unable to break away from my, er, *duties*, I expect you to ensure this vessel begins its mission on schedule. Is that clear?"

"Yes, Sir!" Belloc shouted back, trying hard to ignore the men behind the Lieutenant, who were busy miming pouring bottle after bottle of liquid down their throats and staggering away without a sound.

"Hmm, yes," said Lieutenant Walford, the wax in his handlebar moustache shining brighter than usual. He tucked his riding crop under his arm, turned on his heel, and walked down the gangplank. "Bridge!" shouted Belloc as the ship's commander left. All the men on board snapped to attention and held it for a count of three.

After the silent three-count, and a few more seconds to make sure the Lieutenant was out of hearing range, every one of the eleven men on the deck burst out laughing.

Belloc ran a hand through his dark hair and smiled. When this assignment was finished, he'd either be back in a fort or on a ship to Earth. *Life could certainly be worse*, he thought, as the sight of the green lights and orange flame of a liner coming down slowly for a landing caught his eye.

"That's the *Elbereth*," said Coleman, a lanky sailor who was known for doing the best imitations of the Lieutenant.

"Right," said Belloc, shielding his eyes from the sun and looking at the green glow as it descended from the pink-orange sky. "Lads, I've been left in command of this boat, and I mean for you to know it! Crew! Form up on deck!"

His last five words were shouted loud enough that the crew below deck ran at full speed to the upper deck, falling into a line order they'd gotten very familiar with over time.

"Right!" said Belloc, his voice crisp and clear enough that he had no real need to raise it, "crew, right, *dress!*"

"One, *one* two three," said thirteen young men in unison, stepping forward on their left foot, "*arms* two three," they said, looking to the left and raising their left arms to the shoulders on the men on their left, "shuffle!"

With the last word, they shuffled their feet until each man's left fist just touched the shoulder of the man to their left. They were now perfectly in line and exactly one arm's length from each other, their bodies facing forward while their heads were turned to the left.

"Crew," said Belloc, stalking down the deck of the ship with a scowl on his face, "eyes, *right!*"

"One!" they shouted, snapping their arms down and facing their eyes forward.

"Right, lads. The Lieutenant's off this boat, and from what I've been told, he intends to stay off until they run out of *duties* for him to drink up in the Officer's Club. I've been told to ship out on our patrol on time, and that means having the crew present and ready. Let's see who's on time, and who's going to be swabbing the deck with their tongues today! Trimsman!"

Coleman, all traces of humor and silliness evaporated, raised his chin. "Coleman, Sergeant!" he barked, his eyes facing forward.

"Helmsman!" Belloc shouted, his voice carrying across the docks to the uninterested drunks at the nearby bar. "Lamb, Sergeant!" shouted an airman with a large Adam's apple.

"Don't get yourself sacrificed, Lamb. You've only one life, and you're not allowed to lose it without my permission. Gunners, Light cannon!"

"Arias, Sergeant!" shouted a dark-skinned man.

"Barnes, Sergeant!" said the large man next to him.

"Do your jobs well, lads, and I'll forget one of you is named after a heretic so evil Father Christmas punched him in the face while he was preaching. Rotating Cannon, *Starboard!*"

"Danaher, Sergeant!"

"Rotating Cannon, *Port!*"

"Zeppieri, Sergeant!"

"Where are you from, Zeppieri? And don't say Wales, because I'll know you're lying!"

"My family is from Italy, Sir. We came over to England for business during the Renaissance and never left."

"Mess up on *my* boat, Zeppieri, and I'll make you wish they did. Savvy?"

"Yes Sergeant!"

Belloc looked at the young men, and snuck a glance at the names on the paper in front of him.

"Rotating Cannon, *Rear!*"

"Friesner, Sergeant!"

"Port and Starboard Machine Guns!"

"Fyfe, Sergeant!"

"Luno, Sergeant!"

"Engineering! Stokers!" Belloc shouted, happy he'd nearly reached the end of names.

"Darcy, Sergeant!"

"Thomasvery, Sergeant!"

"Aspenall, Sergeant!"

"Lookout!" said Belloc, drawing out the last name on his duty roster.

"Budd, Sergeant!"

Belloc looked confidently at the men who'd sworn to serve and die, if need be, under his command.

"Right, lads! Listen closely, because I never say things twice. We're set to take off in *exactly* one and one-half hours. A ship from Earth just landed. Anyone not on duty can head into town and see if any of the new locals are worth, um, *greeting*."

The men whistled. Thomasvery stood and made a pair of vertical, wavy lines in the air from the height of his head to his waist.

"But," Belloc said, his face serious, "any man who's scheduled to ship out with me in the Captain's chair had better be on board, shipshape and ready to sail, or you worthless wogs will have *me* to deal with."

Silence.

Belloc smiled. "Right! Off you go!"

Six men laughed, whooped, and jumped like schoolchildren released from class on the first day of summer. Heedless of the warning they'd just been given, they tore down the gangplank and the dock to the dusty street, then along the street toward the other side of the small town.

Belloc chuckled. Whatever state their virtue was in, Belloc could be virtually certain it would remain intact. Running to the arriving ship would burn up some excess energy, and although the men had their minds on girls all the time, virtually every woman who'd arrived on the last few ships had either been married, grossly unattractive, or a nun.

Still, for males that age, hope sprang eternal. With a small smile on his face, he watched the young soldiers run into town. A few more seconds, though, and his face clouded, his smile disappearing with a sad sigh of regret that could have belonged to a man twenty years older.

"Right!" he said, shouting to the remaining three sailors on board, each of whom was engaged in a task on the vessel, "we've a skeleton crew and no Lieutenant. But that just means I'm in charge, and we're going to keep this miserable boat ship-shape before launch or my name isn't Sergeant Hilaire Belloc! Did you pathetic wogs get that?"

"Yes, Sergeant!" they all shouted without pausing in their work.

Chapter 12

"My correspondent, who is evidently an intelligent man, is very angry with me indeed. He uses the strongest language. He says I remind him of a brother of his: which seems to open an abyss or vista of infamy."

–All Things Considered

1892 A.D.
MARS. BRITISH COLONY OF SYRTIS MAJOR.

The sun's pink rays shoved through the drawn yellow curtains and tried hard to light the room. The young man, who looked to be barely into his twentieth year, leaned forward in his chair with his elbows on the table. He pushed a long lock of wheat-colored hair out of the way of his bright, blue eyes to get a better look at the map he'd unrolled. His dark hair was getting longer and he needed a shave. The fuzzy stubble got more uncomfortable on his face and neck every hour, but he wanted to translate the ancient wording on the old, leathery parchment in front of him.

"Are you enjoying yourself, Ambrose?" his companion asked, sitting cross-legged on the floor, trying to look relaxed.

"John," started the younger man, not taking his eyes from the map. His voice sounded young by years yet old by experience and knowledge. "First, you *know* I don't like that name. I much prefer the Welsh version of my name, *Emrys* rather than the Roman *Ambrose*. And I prefer my *given* Old Welsh name of Æsalon to either of…"

"*Ass*-alon, Ambrose?" John said with a smile and a twinkle in his eye.

"Really, John? Really? You've the command of the armies of the red planet at your disposal, haven't appeared to age past thirty in *Dagda* knows how many years, and you're going to sit there and make a posterian double-entendre of a noble name older than the name of Caesar?"

"Are you saying you prefer Ambrose to *Assalon*? Spit it out, boy! We

67

haven't got all day, you know!"

He looked at John for a second more and sighed. "Debating the point with you would be an exemplary exercise in pointlessness itself. Back to our *original* discussion: Second," he paused for a stretch. "I've studied languages and virtually everything else about the ancient world since before you were . . . well, since before most of your *relatives* were born, at any rate. And I can't do that effectively with you sitting here all skittish. Might I suggest you try the roof? You'd spot unwelcome guests far more effectively there than from in here."

John smiled, his trimmed black mustache pulling back as he grinned, then yawned wide enough to swallow a ship.

"Well, *Ambrose*," he said stretching then leaping with a sudden movement from a cross-legged position to a standing one, "I do believe you make an uncharacteristically good point. I further believe that I shall take another look at those amateurish oafs from the Special Branch whom I spotted eating breakfast earlier in the café. Ta-ta!"

He left through the door that led to the back room, and Emrys sighed with relief. He tucked a long strand of white hair behind his ear and turned back to his parchment.

Ten seconds later he heard the small *shhhunk* of the window frame to the alley slide open, followed by the quiet scuff of John's agile-booted feet leaping from the window ledge.

Emrys chuckled. John Carter at least twice the age of any other man walking the city's streets, but he didn't look a day over thirty. Despite his years, much of the time he acted like a good-hearted, rambunctious schoolboy who'd barely gotten out of short pants.

Unless, of course, those he loved or was loyal to were threatened in some way. Then John tended to solve problems with a sword or two. Sometimes the violence stopped further violence. But sometimes...

"Well, best not to think of that now," Emrys muttered, as he leaned forward to gaze at the squiggles and crude drawings of mountains on the parchment.

*****

The *Elbereth* moved slowly as it descended, engines-first, down through the thin Martian atmosphere. Leaning back again while strapped to his seat, Gilbert felt the strengthening pull of gravity as they neared the Red planet.

"Please remain strapped in your seats," called the megaphone through the pipe-network. "When we reach a full stop, do not disembark until the ship has come to a full rest in the horizontal position. Thank you in advance for your cooperation."

Gilbert looked out the thick-glass of the porthole as the sky turned from black with cold glowing stars to light pink with twinkles set in the heavens, and then to pink with an orange tint. Even after the cold dark of space for the past eight weeks, the change in color and altitude outside the porthole made Gilbert feel queasy inside.

Gilbert felt heavier and heavier as the ship descended. Back when the ship turned around at midpoint of the journey in the field of asteroids, the passengers had to switch cabins to the other side of the ship to avoid having to fly the rest of the journey with their beds on the ceiling. There had to be a more efficient way to get a job like this done!

As the rumble of the steering jets got louder in the thicker air and the hum of the Cavorite grew quieter, Gilbert thought more of the reason he'd angled to get the Mars job in the first place.

He'd wanted to see his siblings.

He had *family* here: a brother and sister he'd never known existed. And even though he knew the Doctor was a filthy, evil man, he'd never *directly* lied to Gilbert about anything. Even though this was obviously a trap, Gilbert knew that this was the only way to see them.

But something had been chewing at the edges of Gilbert's mind and soul since he'd woken up this morning.

He'd done the *wrong* thing before. And done it for what seemed like the best of reasons.

He'd run from Father Brown's canonization in Rome out of fear of the powerful Williamson family, whom he'd crossed by falling in love with Frances.

He'd run all the way to America and had been swallowed up by a floating city. His adventure had ended with his best friend Herb switching sides and shooting Gilbert in the ribs. *Ouch.*

After that, Gilbert had done the *right* thing. He'd gone back to Rome and righted things, testified to Father Brown's sanctity, and done a host of other things. He'd *fixed* things. And when he'd heard his brother and sister were in trouble, he'd rushed to help.

He'd done the *right* thing, but he'd been burned anyway.

If I'm going to get hurt, no matter what choice I make, why be good? At least being evil is easier.

He stored away the thought for later.

****

When the ship landed pointing to the heavens, a giant crane and claw identical to the one that had lifted the ship upright on Earth gripped the *Elbereth* at the enormous brackets on her hull and slowly lowered her into a horizontal position. Another half-hour and the highest of three doors in the ship's side had opened with a creak of hinges and blasts of steam. Dutiful porters wheeled a long metal staircase to the opening, and the first class passengers left through the now open doorway.

Herb Wells was the first to step from the highest doorway.

He carried no bags. He'd been promised a small crew of lackeys on this mission, and he knew they'd find and carry his luggage.

Herbert had also dressed in clothes both functional and the height of fashion on the red planet. He had a pair of dark goggles strapped to his head, their dark lenses capable of both protecting his sight from even the toughest sandstorm and hiding his eyes from all onlookers. He also wore a sporty looking vest and trousers, along with a black longcoat, good for keeping the fine, dusty red dirt away from skin and personal equipment, and doubled as a heat-absorbent blanket on cold evenings or windy treks across the desert.

He stepped down the stairwell that had been wheeled up to the door of the ship, his thick-soled desert boots making steady, hollow clanking noises on the metal stairway as he descended. At the bottom he met up with the two who'd been waiting for him for the last few hours.

"Good afternoon, Cleaner," said the older, larger man, his waxed moustache catching a glint off the sun. "Did you have a good trip?"

"Yes," answered Herb. "You must be the Painter and the Driver. Are we all ready, then?"

It was the Driver's turn to speak up, and he did so after a small, barely visible glance toward the Painter, who then nodded his head.

"Yes. Quite ready," he said, pointing to a nearby floater. "We've got the location of the event, and orders to bring you there."

"Let's get to it then, shall we?" They obeyed Herb, striding to the baggage pile while Herb strode to the parked floater.

****

70

John Carter had looked down from his rooftop perch as the agents of the Special Branch left the café and began walking to the docks. A number of locals in the street gave each other subtle glances as the agents passed them.

And John knew what that meant: the locals already knew the agents didn't belong. More important, if the agents disappeared, no one would worry or cause a fuss.

Good, thought John. *Maybe someone will do my work for me, and I won't have to get my sword or dagger dirty.* Dried blood was surprisingly difficult to scrub out of the nooks and crannies in his hilt, and Martian-Redman blood much more so than Thark blood.

John considered leaping from the rooftop to one only twenty feet away, but he opted against it. Instead, his eyelids narrowed as he gazed toward the docks where the ship had just landed.

As the passengers disembarked, John watched the agents walk back with a *youth* leading them.

This was new—the boy who seemed in charge of them couldn't have twenty summers under his belt.

John whistled low. Either the kid was some kind of prodigy, or the talent pool for agents was getting mighty shallow. Where most folks from the Special Branch at least *tried* to blend in, whoever had dressed this kid hadn't done anything more than read stories about Mars in the nickel novels. Black longcoats and brass goggles? Here, folks often dressed in plain brown, tinted a dark crimson by the omnipresent Martian dirt and sand. The agents of the Special Branch were slipping up more and more lately. In a Martian colony, the wise man tried to blend in and disappear. Dressing all in black here may intimidate folks on Earth, but here in Syrtis Major it was a sure-fire way to draw unwanted attention.

John watched the three of them for a few more minutes, noting facial expressions and subtle signals of body language. In another minute he could tell that the lad dressed in black *thought* he was in charge, but that the other two were only putting up with him.

As they left the street, Carter further noted the cheap hotel they holed up in. If they followed the same pattern as the other Special Branch agents he'd dispatched lately, the young fellow would unpack, take in a little tour of the town, and then get down to business.

Maybe they'd actually go to the location of their latest scheme, and Emrys could stop looking at old papers all day in their garret. If they could just put an end to this little operation the Special Branch had been working on for the past few months, he could finally go back to his wife and son across the desert . . .

****

A half-hour later, the mid-class passengers disembarked from the ship through their doorway.

An hour after *that*, the *lowest* door on the rocket opened wide. An older porter pushed a rickety wooden staircase with squeaky wheels over to it, and the passengers began walking outside with a restrained excitement.

When the door opened and the hot, fresh air wafted in, Gilbert inhaled a deep breath through his nose. The Martian air smelled like sand, grit, and the bottom of a cave. But it was still better than the metallic smell of the stored air he'd breathed for the past nine weeks, and that made him suck in several deep breaths.

And then he left the ship and actually *saw* Mars.

It all looked familiar at first—much like one of the miner villages he'd seen back in England. The town had rows and rows of two-story houses pushed together like the middle section of a giant accordion. But the hot sun felt exactly like what he'd thought a desert would be like: beating down like a summer day at the beach, but without the cool feel of evaporated water in the air. The sky wasn't the familiar blue he'd been dreaming about in his cabin, and he couldn't see a single cloud in the pink-orange vista over his head and all around him.

The people milling about the docks below were dressed much like the denizens of London. But unlike a London shipyard, there were few people embracing loved ones as the passengers disembarked. Gilbert had learned in conversations with his fellow passengers that most people didn't come to Mars willingly. Most came either for business or to make a fresh start after one too many poor decisions back on Earth.

I wonder if deciding to come here will be another one of my poor decisions, Gilbert thought as he trudged to the wooden dock with the other passengers. His feet now on the ground, he saw the remaining members of the third-class travel group file past as they left the docking area. Where ought he to go from here? Was there a hotel, or a customs office or something?

He needn't have worried. All the passengers moved through a squat brown building on their way out from the shipyard. The building had a sign out front, declaring it with stylized letters to be "His Majesty's Travel Authority." Once inside, Gilbert talked to a bored looking porter wearing the same red-leather uniform that many of the crew on board his ship had worn. The porter confirmed who Gilbert was and checked his name off the passenger manifest without any other questions or so much as a passport check. *No wonder the line moved quickly*, Gilbert thought as he carried his satchel over his back, striding out of the building. *I guess they don't care who you are on Mars.*

Once in the dusty street, one hand at his shoulder under his satchel strap, the other shielding his eyes from the midday sun, he felt much like he thought a pioneer would feel in the American Old West. True, this was British territory. And it still looked like a British mining town. But although he didn't hear a single American accent in the crowd, it made him think of the frontier towns as they'd been described in the Nickel Novels he'd loved reading when he was little. There were unpaved streets, horses pulling wagons to and fro, men and women dressed in attempts at finery mingling with others in poorer, workman's clothes. Stores advertised dry goods, hardware, and other sundries. Had he not known better, Gilbert would have thought this was Dodge City.

"Need a place to stay, my friend?"

Gilbert looked to his right. A lad about thirteen stood near his elbow. He wore a white cap over his head and a pair of brass goggles to ward of the sun, along with a white, collared shirt that was clean but wrinkled. He also had a red bandana unfolded and wrapped around his face, protecting his nose and mouth from stray dust. This was a lad who spent much of his time outside. Suspenders held up his brown tweed pants, and he had the thick, brown boots many people wore to keep out the chalky, fine red dust that seemed to be everywhere.

Gilbert squinted. He'd have to get a set of those goggles, pronto!

"Sure do!" he said to the lad. "You know a place where a man could find a bed?"

"You bet! Lemme guess," the boy said, holding his chin and making a big show of looking Gilbert up and down. The boy's accent wasn't British, but not exactly American either. "You look like a fellow who's used to spartan accommodations," the boy said. "For you, home'll just be a place to sleep, little more. Not here to live fancy, only to do a job, right?"

Gilbert smiled. He'd dealt with street urchins before, but the kid had a high level of what New Yorkers called moxie. "You got it right, kid. No price too small. You got a place in mind for a guy like me?"

"By all means! Follow me!"

Gilbert did just that, following the lad after slinging his satchel over his back.

This must be the main street of the town, Gilbert realized. Most people meandered about in British garb, and some wore brass goggles, bandana masks, or longcoats to keep off the dust and sand. Gilbert wished he could walk slowly and take in the sights. Around the corner came a group of men with bright red skin and dark hair, dressed only in loincloths and boots. Behind the men were three red-skinned women swathed in long red dresses that covered them from neck to ankle. Gilbert had heard that native Martian women normally wore next to nothing, but by law they had to be fully clothed before they could enter most Earth-owned settlements.

Gilbert's new friend walked ahead, striding forward like a soldier on parade while Gilbert sauntered behind. Suddenly, a huge creature the size of a Clydesdale horse moseyed down the dusty street. It looked like a cross between a large green lizard and a dinosaur, but no one else seemed to think the sight an unusual one. An older Martian red man pulled the creature's bridle as it towed a covered cart of goods even larger than the lizard itself, and two red men and a woman rode on its green, scaly back.

"How far up is this place?" Gilbert asked, trying to shield his face. The wind kept picking up and dropping without warning, first blasting sand in his face and ears and then dying down without a trace. It was like getting stung by an annoying horsefly back home, one you couldn't swat or flick away. Gilbert made a mental note to get a set of goggles *and* a bandana the first chance he got!

"Jus' down the street—not far!" the young boy called over his shoulder. Gilbert kept walking, savoring the breaths of fresh air, and walking on dirt instead of the hard deck of a ship. Even if the air and dirt were of an alien world millions of miles from home, there was something about being back out in the open that made him feel more alive than he had in a long time.

A few more steps, and he realized something else: he wasn't in anguish over Frances for the first time in months.

"You got a telegraph office 'round here?" he called ahead. The boy was a good dozen feet ahead of him now, and Gilbert had to stretch his neck a bit to keep sight of him amid the thickening crowds.

"Yep," the boy said, still a few steps ahead, "but they charge you a pretty penny to send any kind of message back to Earth. It's way cheaper to just write a letter and post it. Here we are!"

Gilbert looked up. The building looked like all the rest in town: squat and made of brick and some kind of local fibrous plant that didn't quite look like wood. Then Gilbert looked again. No, he realized. The place looked even *worse* than the other squat buildings in the port town. Perhaps it was the crudely drawn sign that advertised it as "MABELS ROOMIN HOWS." Or maybe it was the unswept tracks of red dust and dirt that trailed in and out of the front door, and all over the front stoop and the sidewalk besides.

Gilbert followed the boy and entered. The place looked even dumpier *inside*. It wasn't just the look of the place; it was the *smell*. The smell of cheap beer drying in a hot room wafted out from the open door. Did he really want to sleep above a saloon for the night?

His distaste must have shown on his face. The boy was back at Gilbert's elbow in a second. "I know it don't look nice," he said, "but it's safe for your things. And they've never had a fight in the place yet. Not a *real* bad one, anyway."

"Nothing else in town, huh?" Gilbert asked.

"Not if you're as poor as your shoes say you are, mister."

Gilbert looked down at his cheap loafers. The kid was sharp indeed! He'd have to show the lad the picture of his siblings right away after he secured a room and dumped his satchel.

"C'mon in!" the kid said, "I'll introduce you to Mabel. She's a nice lady, and she'll give you a discount if you're a friend of mine!"

"And you get the difference, right?" Gilbert said. The kid answered with a little wink behind his goggles, and then he ducked further into the tavern. Gilbert followed and found himself liking him, in spite of his little game.

Inside past the doorway it was dark and cool, cutting off the midday sun like a cave in the desert. A long, polished mirror shimmered in front of Gilbert like a mirage while his eyes adjusted to the change in light. He could hear muted hums and mutterings as card games, conversations, and clinking glasses sounded around him in a dull whirl.

"This way," the boy said to Gilbert, leading him through the murk of the hotel's bottom floor.

"Um," Gilbert said, struggling to keep up amid the crowd, smoke, and muted noise, "just what's your name, anyway, kid?"

The boy mumbled something under his breath, but as he was facing away from Gilbert he lost the boy's name in the din of the bar. As they passed some men playing cards, Gilbert heard several chuckles that made the hairs on his neck prickle for no apparent reason, and he turned to see what had caused them.

The older men had stopped their card game to look at him. Several had smiles on their faces.

"Something funny?" Gilbert asked. He wasn't sure if it would be a good idea to take any kind of stand this early in his stay. But he had the feeling he was the butt of a joke and he didn't like it one bit.

"Young lad," said the oldest man, his white beard bobbing over his expensive-looking waistcoat, "Would you mind bringing out your billfold?"

"My billfold's gonna stay right where it's supposed to—" Gilbert stopped midsentence as his hand reached for the place in his back pocket where his wallet usually rested.

It was gone.

Gilbert's insides turned to ice water. His surprise and fear must have showed on his face, because the rest of the table in front of him started laughing even harder.

"Looks like little Cecil just put another notch on his belt, didn't 'e?" said another card player, streaks of red dust matted into his workman's coat and his salt-and-pepper hair.

Gilbert paused again.

"Cecil *Chesterton*?" he asked.

"Well, we don't exactly know his last name, lad." chortled the oldest man again, wiping the tears from his eyes. "But we *do* know you just fell for one of his classic ruses, dear boy! It's how he collects enough rent money every month to keep he and his sister Beatrice from being evicted! If I had a pound sterling for every mark like you he's led in here or the White Sloat tavern down the way, and then robbed them while distracted by the noise? Well—."

"Where'd he go?"

"Oh, he's halfway home now, lad," said the old man, pointing eastward. "You might find your wallet in an alley, but your money is quite gone!"

"I don't care about the money! That kid is my brother!" Gilbert tore down the hallway in the direction the old man had pointed, ignoring the laughter behind him while mumbling under his breath the same word over and over again:

"Stupid, stupid, *stupid!*"

76

Chapter 13

"I do not believe there is any harm whatever in reading about murders; rather, if anything, good; for the thought of death operates very powerfully with the poor in the creation of brotherhood and a sense of human dignity."

–All Things Considered

Herb hated working for the Special Branch, and had so from the first day. But the rewards for completed assignments and believing he was making a better world silenced his conscience and his intellect. Silenced them so well, in fact, that now he found himself embracing beliefs he once would have laughed at: good and evil were petty concepts, ignored by all superior people. All religions were essentially the same. Your worth came from how much you contributed to the powerful.

Oddly enough, knowing that everyday people would have laughed at his new philosophies made him disdain the common man even more, even though if asked he would have professed a love of the human race.

He was musing on this when he saw Gilbert in the dusty, red-rimmed street of Syrtis Major, running toward Herb through the crowded street.

"Stop," Herb said to the men carrying his things beside him, looking at Gilbert. The two men on either side of Herb, dressed in the light brown common clothes of the area stopped. The Painter was already feeling bored, hoping he'd soon receive an order to kill this pretentious young fool he'd picked up not three-quarters of an hour ago, while the Driver was thinking about a girl he'd seen in one of the taverns the week before.

"What's wrong?" the Painter said quietly, noting the object of Herb's gaze.

"That's Gilbert Chesterton," Herb said.

"That's quite interesting," the Driver said, thoughts of girls forgotten.

"Yes," the Painter added, giving Herb a sidelong glance, "Didn't *you* shoot him just last year, Cleaner?"

****

Another sight made John Carter focus on the street, a mini-show so animated it made him stop thinking about his Martian wife's smooth, red skin.

Cecil was at it again.

He'd found a mark, likely another young, naive fool new to the red planet. Sure enough, a minute or two after they'd entered, Cecil had leaped out of a side window with a wallet clutched in his hand, and the tall, skinny rube had burst out of the front door. "Cecil!" he'd yelled, looking for the boy who'd lifted his money right out of his pockets as he'd done to so many other newcomers.

But, John noted, there was something just a little different in this victim's face than he usually saw on Cecil's marks. There was always anger, but on this fellow's face there was also a kind of anguish, as if he'd missed a big opportunity.

Odd, John thought. He must be wrong. Would anyone come all the way from Earth just to meet a little cutpurse?

John stared a bit more intently, not just at the tall fellow with the glasses looking for Cecil, but at the other three fellows from the Special Branch who'd just emerged from the hotel down the same street. John had been in countless fights and battles on both Mars and Earth, and they'd left him with a keen sense of timing for knowing when life was about to be threatened.

He waited, looking to see how this new chapter played out. What wonderful fortune today that he decided to stretch his legs and do a little scouting run!

He was rewarded when he saw the lone, tall rube lock eyes with the new young agent dressed in black. Even two stories up and with a crowd of disinterested people milling between them, John could sense the tension, fear, and anger exchanged between the two.

****

Although Gilbert was still chasing after young Cecil, his eyes locked with Herb's when the two old friends were barely thirty feet from each other.

Herb felt rush of remorse, which turned instantly to a white-hot stab of anger.

And Herb's anger turned to a cool understanding. Gilbert having

78

survived was bad enough. But there would be no hope for *Herb's* survival, much less his advancement, if Gilbert rose to enough prominence to get the attention of the Special Branch.

He'd have to fix that. Now.

"Scrag him," Herb whispered quietly. The words sprang to his lips, coming from a part of him that had adapted to ordering and doing terrible things in the name of humanity.

"Right," said the Painter, already realizing how his own life was in jeopardy. Herb had erred in letting Gilbert live, and now there'd be a need to clean up the witnesses afterward.

The Driver didn't think at all, but only acted, running forward to Gilbert while already reaching for his silenced pepperbox pistol.

Gilbert turned and ran.

****

When the dark-clothed boy motioned to his toadies and the tall boy ran off from them, John Carter, one-time Confederate war hero and now Warlord of Mars, knew it was time to act. After all, not only was an innocent in trouble, there was also the opportunity to dispatch some agents of the Special Branch!

Having seen chases exactly like this between people who were angered, upset, or owed each other money, John knew the route the tall boy was most likely to take. Leaping from rooftop to rooftop, he arrived at an alley Gilbert was destined to run through in perhaps thirty seconds; John looked it up and down and appraised the spot for its strategic value.

Hmm. Nope. Too narrow. He might have trouble defending the boy if things got dicey. He knocked down a number of trash barrels to discourage him from running here, then leapt back up to the roof in a single bound and began hopping to the next spot. He hadn't had a truly decent fight in weeks, months maybe. Perhaps a strategically placed pile of sloat droppings would spice things up a bit . . .

****

Gilbert ran, having seen in Herb's eyes the same steely coldness he'd seen the day Herb had shot him. But on that day, Herb had shown at least a twisted modicum of concern for Gilbert, a willingness to risk himself so that he and Gilbert could live.

But this time, Gilbert first saw recognition in Herb's eyes, then cool anger. Herb said something to the two men at his left and right. By the time

79

they started after him, Gilbert had already turned to run.

Thoughts and memories whipped through Gilbert's head now as he ran from the two men who'd flanked Herb. He ran without plan or thought, tearing down the street and dodging in between people with the red dirt of Mars dusted on their clothes and caked in the creases of their skin. Hardly anyone looked up, the tired looks on their faces hardly changing as he jumped, bobbed, and weaved in between them, and two men older than Gilbert ran behind, one with a drawn pistol in his hand.

It wasn't the first time someone had come after Gilbert through a set of city streets. When a cowboy detective with a mechanical leg had chased him through New York a year ago, he'd been able to take advantage of a city whose streets and buildings had been paved, torn, and remade several times over. Nooks, crannies, and a hundred other places abounded in any older city to run, dodge, and hide.

But here things were different. Though many people lined the streets, the settlement's buildings were side-by-side and nearly all alike. There were barely any alleyways that Gilbert could see. Syrtis Major was too new a place to afford hidden shelters to him.

He almost ran into a narrow alleyway, but then he went back onto the main street when he saw the way blocked by garbage cans and other refuse. No time to climb over trash! He settled for running alongside the front porches of the brick buildings lining the street, hoping to find an open door or some other nook or cranny he could duck into.

Gilbert risked a look back. When he'd been a cross-country runner, he'd been told time and again that the greatest error was to look back at the opponents behind you. This time though, it was good that he did. His pursuer had dropped to one knee, aiming one of the eight barrels of his pepperbox pistol right at Gilbert!

The pistol popped with the sound of a firecracker. Gilbert felt a breeze on his right cheek and heard the whine of a bullet as it missed him by inches. Gilbert jumped forward and ran without thinking. He finally found an alley between a house and a restaurant, one where the smell of dirt, trash, and dried waste was even more pungent than it had been in the last, blocked alley. He ran ten steps when his right foot slipped on something. He pitched forward, his face smacking on the ground and jamming a pile of red dust into his mouth.

Gilbert had already started scrambling to his feet when he heard the thump of booted feet behind him.

Chapter 14

"We owe to each other a terrible and tragic loyalty. If we catch sharks for food, let them be killed most mercifully; let any one who likes love the sharks, and pet the sharks, and tie ribbons round their necks and give them sugar and teach them to dance. But if once a man suggests that a shark is to be valued against a sailor...then I would court-martial the man—he is a traitor to the ship."

—GKC, All Things Considered

A ship is a thing of beauty, Hilaire thought, as he watched the giant liner touch down, the glowing green globes attached to the engines gradually going dark as it neared the landing pad. While he preferred walking to sailing or flying, he'd give just about anything to be at the helm of a ship like that, one that traversed the space between the worlds.

But, he told himself, *I do have a job to do.* And thus far it hadn't involved flying a giant metal-and-wooden box through the air from the Earth to Mars.

Sighing, he looked over the men who'd followed him. In earlier times he'd fought and bled alongside them. They'd follow him to the gates of Hell and back, if only because patrols he led always came home.

Well, the *survivors* came home, anyway.

"Right, lads," he said, now that the men had returned. "You all came back so soon, I can tell there weren't any faces pretty enough to be worth your time. Now we'll get on our latest milk run. With a bit of luck we might see a stray sloat or two running around this time."

"Sergeant?" one of the men asked, the fellow from Wales named Danaher.

"Yes?"

" 'Ow long 'til we get to pop some more Tharks?"

"Not all of them need poppin', Danaher. Just the ones that're trying to kill us. And most aren't smart enough to drive a flyer. Set your mind at ease, lads. Seeing the *Elbereth* land over there is the single greatest bit of excitement we'll have for the next week or so, unless there's a bit of gambling on my boat."

The men smiled. Gambling was highly illegal while on duty. As such, the men and officers engaged in it at every opportunity.

Sergeant Hilaire Belloc began a crisp, military walk down the deck of the *Locust*. The lieutenant allegedly in charge of the ship hadn't been fully sober for weeks, and Belloc as second in command was fine with being left in charge of the flight.

Yes, he thought. *Hopefully, a boring flight.*

****

"About a week, wouldn't you say lass?" the man said to Frances, leaning back against the bar.

Frances looked at him with a blank expression.

For all his attempts at understatement, this fellow still might as well have been trying to telegraph his intentions with a foghorn. After the required few minutes of polite conversation, he was now leaning back with his elbows on the exercise bar, just near enough to her to make her a shade uncomfortable.

What had he just said again? Oh, yes. "Yes," she answered, keeping an eye on his hands with her peripheral vision, "about a week until we land. It's quite exciting."

"An' what might you think could happen between now and, uh, then, Miss . . . ?" he asked, letting his little finger dawdle over the skin on her left hand.

"Please don't do that," she said, her voice even and controlled, even as his touch made her skin crawl.

"Aww, but Miss. It's been a while since I've had any pleasurable company. Could you see our way to. . ."

"No," she said, and stood up.

He grabbed her wrist.

She grabbed *his* wrist with her other hand and spun in place, twisting his arm with a jerk and a meaty crack.

A nearby table of men and women cheered, while at another table a

82

group of men dressed as shabbily as Frances' latest victim spat and swore, digging into their pockets for money and coins.

" 'E didn't last 'arf so long as the last one," grumbled a greasy-looking man at the table with a thick black beard.

"At this rate, we'll run out of young men with unbroken arms before we touch the first grain of red soil," said one of the older men at the winner's table with a chuckle as coins poured into his hands.

His laughter stopped, though, when the shadow appeared over him. He looked up and saw Frances standing over him, her hands folded politely in front of her. "Good afternoon, Mister Jaggers," she said, "I have come to complete the terms of our arrangement."

"Yes, of course, young lady," he said, his voice letting out a small note of fear. The girl could go from a wave of human destruction to pure and proper again in a matter of seconds, and Jaggers had learned to respect that.

He put several coins into her hand. She counted them, then held out her hand a second time with a slightly wider smile on her face. Her new benefactor straightened his slightly shabby top hat, then pretended to look abashed and upset with himself as he searched the pockets of his grey suit jacket and found more coins and counted out the correct amount.

"Apology accepted, Mister Jaggers," Frances said as she counted the money. Pocketing it, she walked back to her cabin with a small spring in her step.

"Wass' she want money for? She's dressed like her daddy's *made* of tin!" said the woman next to Jaggers.

"He is," he answered, "on *Earth*. Unfortunately, she just found out a few days ago about how worthless the English pound is on Mars. She could've brought a thousand of her father's paper pounds with her, and it wouldn't have bought her a week of the kind of life she had back in London."

"The poor thing."

"No, not at all. That's the lovely part of a colony, lass, highborn or lowlife, we're *all* poor as church mice when we step off the ships. And once she realized that, my offer to broker a few wagers on how long her suitors would last against her seemed far more acceptable."

"Quite the practical lass, then. Where'd she learn to fight?"

"Books. That's all she brought with her besides the clothes on her back—a long stack of books. Isn't that the saddest thing you ever heard of? Not to mention what the sun there does to their—"

Frances had already shut their conversation from her mind. Counting up her money, she entered her cabin, knelt at the edge of her bed, said her prayers and undressed for sleep.

But sleep didn't come easy, even after she was under the covers and counted sheep. A week more and she'd be on Mars, she thought as she stared at the ceiling. A week! Then she would see her Gilbert and find out exactly what the meaning of that picture was.

At the start of this journey, she was ready to believe any explanation he'd give, forgive any transgression, and accept him back under almost any terms he'd name. But her time on the ship had altered her thinking in a number of areas. She was not ready to do damage to Gilbert, even if he *had* indeed betrayed her trust. But she was strong enough, she knew, not to marry a man who could not be faithful during courtship.

She sighed. Despite what she'd learned about pugilism on this journey, she wasn't actually ready to *harm* Gilbert at all. The biography she'd read on Teresa of Avila had confirmed that much in her—that true love wanted what was best for the beloved. If it were best for Gilbert to be with someone else, or if he had to do a spot of growing up before thinking about marriage, then she'd accept it and wait either for Gilbert to be ready or for someone even better to come along, whichever came first.

But as for that *redheaded* girl? The one who'd dropped out of the sky and (if the picture in her dress pocket told the truth) kissed *her* man? She was another story. If Frances's suspicions were confirmed, Frances would need only five minutes with her new skills to turn that crimson-headed hussy into her own personal jousting dummy.

Satisfied, Frances gave up on sleep for now and propped herself up with her latest book. *Prometheus Unchained* declared the title in large letters, its subtitle in slightly smaller letters below: *The Practical Use and Applications of Steam Powered Personal Weaponry of the Peculiarly Electrical Variety.*

Chapter 15

W hen Gilbert fell in the alley, he stared for only one second at the red
dust mixed with some brown rocks likely from his home shores.

Then a pair of high boots with leather straps crisscrossing the legs
high as the knee had stomped in front of him, shoulder width apart.

Gilbert looked up. The man wearing the boots also wore what looked
like red underpants and a black belt, along with another set of leather
straps in the form of an X across his chest. He wore nothing else that
Gilbert could see; it was the kind of outfit that would have gotten a man
arrested for indecent exposure back in Minnesota.

The man's pencil-thin mustache rode atop the smirk on his face as he
looked at something behind Gilbert and drew a sword and a long dagger
from his belt in each hand with hardly a whisper.

"I don't know who you are," said a voice of one of Gilbert's pursuers
behind him as he pulled the hammer back on his pistol with a *click*, "but
I've got business with this skinny little blighter that you don't want any
part of. Now clear off!"

"Really?" said the man, his smile so wide Gilbert could hear it in his
voice as he stepped over Gilbert and closer to the man with the gun. "And
just how, good sir, would you know what I want?" The stranger's Southern
twang was so thick Gilbert could place the state. Virginia, perhaps?

Gilbert turned over. His scantily dressed rescuer faced the younger of
the two men.

"Based on that outfit?" said the younger man, his feet steady but his
gun and English accented voice wavering just a little, "I'd guess you
want to impress young ladies from a dying race with skin the color of

85

sunburned apples. Last chance, Yank."

"Sir! I am appalled! With your training, you ought to know that men from my region of the Five Americas do *not* refer to ourselves as Yankees! In fact, if you were to look at a decent map of the Confederate States of America, such as the one here—"

Gilbert saw him point to a spot on the ground with the tip of his sword, taking another step toward the younger man with the gun. The young man looked away from Gilbert and the man between them for a split second, following the sword tip as it pointed at the ground.

But that split second was everything.

Before Gilbert knew what had happened, the young man with the gun let out a sharp gasp. Gilbert looked, hardly daring to move lest he draw attention to himself and get a bullet or a sword thrust into his back, or both.

The younger man's gun arm had a red stream flowing down his suit. At the top of the red streak poked out the hilt of the rescuer's long dagger, its blade invisible, buried in the younger man's bicep.

Gilbert looked back. The swordsman was already in motion, twisting with the quiet, deadly efficiency of a baseball player getting ready to hit a home run. The sword, perhaps four feet long at the blade, curved a deadly arc in the air above them in the narrow alleyway and came down hard on the wounded agent's shoulder joint.

The agent's gasp became a scream in less than a second.

Gilbert's jaw dropped. He was no stranger to violence, but not immune to something like *this*! The sword had bit into the agent's arm like an axe biting into a thick cord of wood. Gilbert's rescuer turned to look at Gilbert, the rescuer's hands still on the hilt of his sword as he freed it from the screaming agent's shoulder.

"Better run, young fellow," he said. "This one has at least two friends I've seen, and even John Carter of Mars can't fight in more than one place at a time."

Gilbert could hold his own in a fistfight, but he wasn't foolish enough to try and hold his ground when he had only his fists and everyone else had blades or guns. He rose and ran further down the alley, his mind racing even faster.

He'd been saved by *John Carter* himself! John Carter, the Warlord of Mars!

He left the other end of the alleyway and bumped into a robed, red skinned woman and a half-dozen red-skinned men dressed in the same, odd outfits made of leather straps and boots that Carter had worn. "Er . . . excuse me!" he said awkwardly, looking for a moment at the Martian woman's pretty dark eyes.

With a force of will he turned and kept running. After a few more minutes, the street was filled with hawkers at makeshift tables, each shouting and trying to get Gilbert to look, taste, or touch their wares. Their shouting mixed with the chanting of some of the more religious-looking red-skinned Martians, who were clapping finger-sized symbols and carrying small censers burning pungent-smelling incense.

Gilbert dodged more red-skinned Martians and pink-skinned Englishmen and women. At one point he slammed into a very large Englishman wearing a red tunic and the white, dome-shaped hat of a soldier and commander. Gilbert began to back away and apologize immediately. A roar from behind startled him, and he was almost stomped by a giant, lumbering gray dinosaur of a pack animal. It was much bigger than the lizard he'd seen before, and it was ridden by one of the shrouded local women and led by another of the red-skinned men.

The streets might make a good place to get lost in, but they were also a place to get into trouble! Aside of the obvious danger of being crushed by pack animals, if the agent that Carter had just taken down did indeed have friends, there wouldn't be a better place to slide in close to Gilbert and put a knife between his ribs than a crowded market street.

Better to find a building, someplace to hole up in for a little while until he and everything else around him calmed down.

He looked around, trying to avoid being jostled by the milling crowds. In a second he saw a dilapidated doorway, the door itself sagging open on one hinge. Gilbert, no longer in a mood to be polite, shoved his way toward it and made his way inside.

****

"Right!" roared Belloc as the steam boiler powered up and the turbine began chuffing and humming. "Cast off!"

"Casting off, Sergeant!" Lamb yelled back over the din of the engine, as he unwound complicated knots and threw the thick, heavy ropes over to the dockside.

"Crew secure!"

They all shouted as one: "Yes, Sergeant!"

"Helmsman!"

"Yes, Sergeant!"

"Ship, rise!"

Belloc and the men felt the smallest twinge from the deck beneath their feet as the Cavorite rocks implanted in the hull glowed dully with electric energy sent to them by the steam-powered turbine engine.

The ship rose from the ground and hovered a dozen feet from the ground below. Belloc knew that if he measured it with a yardstick, the distance would be a dozen feet exactly, as per the Navy requirements for patrol boats that had cast off but not yet sailed forth.

"Raise to thirty feet, Helmsman!"

"Aye aye, Sergeant! Raising to thirty feet!" The green rock glowed brighter as the ship rose eighteen more feet, high enough to clear most of the building roofs in the town.

"Helmsman, hoist sails!" Belloc said, leaning on the railed, chest high wall that surrounded the deck as the ship rose even higher.

"Aye aye, Sergeant!"

The sails unfurled like the wings of a giant swan. Belloc's chest always swelled with pride at this point. Men had wished to fly for as long as they could see the sky. And out in the desert, far from the prying eyes of gossips, assassins, or chief petty officers, Belloc loved to stand on the prow of the ship, plant one foot high on the rail set at chest height, and look at the wide expanse of the Martian horizon like a sea captain of old. Only instead of the sea, he saw a vast, red desert vista, literally above the cares of the world.

True, there was and always would be protocol to follow. Sails would need to be furled, safety regulations followed, and the like. And one of those regulations first involved flying twice around the city to ensure there were no obvious visible threats from within.

"Engine room!"

"Aye, Sergeant Belloc!" The voice came from under the deck, almost directly below his feet.

"Increase to quarter speed!"

"Aye, Sergeant!"

"Helmsman! Twice around the city, then head due North."

"Aye aye, Sergeant!"

Now filled with coal, the boiler below the deck chuffed and sent more electricity to the Cavorite, the anti-gravity wonder rock developed by a Belgian scientist years ago and now a staple of British flying ships throughout His Majesty's Armed Forces. The ship rose higher, while on the deck the helmsman moved a series of levers with the practiced instinct of a professional, steering the ship with the wind, trapping the air currents in the delicate yet tightly woven sails, which propelled the ship forward.

Yes, thought Belloc, fighting to keep down the gnawing feeling in his gut that something difficult was going to hit during this trip. *Yes, I will make sure that this will be a safe, boring trip without any adventure.* An adventure was "an inconvenience rightly considered," or so said that American writer whose works he'd been following. But Belloc, who'd had his share of adventure both on Earth and Mars, begged to differ. Virtually every adventure he'd had was the result of poor planning by his superiors, and no amount of consideration changed that.

As they gently curved around the colony, Belloc surveyed the city from his high perch. Much of the colony of Syrtis Major was actually built in the central square of a former *Martian* city. Long deserted by its makers, at its height it had had a population of millions of red-skinned Martians. Now, the tallest buildings were unsafe, crumbling shells of their former selves, large broken spires on the outer areas of the colony that still gleamed in the light while the safer, squat, two-story British buildings made of red-dust bricks filled the former city's center.

Hilaire inhaled the dusty air with a happy sigh. The city was still a thing of beauty, even if the first British city on Mars had made the dubious choice of settling in the middle of a lost city. While he still had a love for the countryside, seeing the sights and smells of a bustling place always appealed to Hilaire, particularly at the end of each month when the Red Martians began flooding the place with their wares and money.

As their patrol boat rose higher, he thought he espied a disturbance in the flow of road traffic in the North end. People along the major artery of the city's life and commerce usually moved in a predictable pattern. But something was causing them to bob, jostle, and jump in a way that suggested a chase was underway.

Hilaire frowned a bit. He could ignore it or give a look as part of his patrol. While part of him wanted to get the necessary twice-around city survey over and done with, leaving a loose end like this would gnaw at him for the rest of the trip if he didn't resolve it.

Most likely it was little dirt rat Cecil lifting some newcomer's wallet again. If it was, nabbing the boy again wouldn't take too long and they could be on their way.

He gave the order and the boat swung around, chuffing and throwing small clouds of soot into the air. As they dropped in altitude, Hilaire noted the usual things one saw this time of day at mid-week: merchants hawking their wares, buyers milling about the streets, some leather-strapped Red Martian men and at least one shrouded Red woman leading a huge, docile grey gasshant beast laden with goods.

By the time he arrived at the street, the disturbance had apparently resolved itself. Cecil was a clever lad. He could argue his way out of a tripod's tentacle. But . . .

Hilaire left the thought unfinished. He spotted something that made his eyes narrow. He pulled out the telescope from his belt and looked at a rooftop about an eighth of a mile to the northwest.

On the roof stood a white Earth man, dressed in the garb of a Red Martian. And he had a sword and dagger drawn.

"Carter," Hilaire Belloc grumbled. True, all who'd fought alongside him had vouched for his integrity and skill on the battlefield. But in Hilaire's experience, John Carter was the kind of fellow who would appear somewhere, bring utter chaos in his wake, and then leave with a flourish while others cleaned up his mess.

"Cut to one-eighth speed," Belloc barked to his crew, "and start a slow curve around the corner of George and Henry Street."

"Aye, aye, Sergeant Belloc."

Belloc kept eyeing Carter's patient-looking form on the rooftop. If the American's reputation was accurate, he only stood still for the same reason a cobra did.

Sure enough, after a few seconds Carter sprang to action, running in the same direction as the disturbance in the street.

Hoping that Carter wasn't going to get involved, Belloc kept his airborne sloop on an even, casual speed.

Carter now leapt from rooftop to rooftop, crossing distances in a single bound that seemed almost superhuman. Belloc marveled at the man's agility and strength even as he grumbled over his tendency to interfere. After a few seconds of staring through his telescope, Belloc saw the method in Carter's madness. Carter had taken an interest in the disturbance in the marketplace and was running to corral his prey. What he planned to do with that prey was still anybody's guess, and Sergeant Hilaire Belloc ordered the ship to circle in a wide holding pattern to keep an eye on the situation. He wasn't a policeman, but he *was* on patrol to keep the peace!

Belloc now lowered the scope to see the street as a whole, and he saw again the shoppers and hawkers alike yelling and cursing in English or Red Martian as they were shoved aside.

Then a tall person with a shock of wavy blond hair broke from the crowd, running down an open side street that branched from the market street's main artery. The chase had begun at the cross streets named after Kings George and Henry, and now they were at the side streets of Henry and Richard.

Looking through the telescope again, Belloc was almost blinded by the flash of light reflected by the tall person's glasses. *Blast!* Hilaire dropped the scope for a second while he wiped the water that had gathered in his eye.

When he brought the 'scope back up, he almost yelped at what he saw.

The tall fellow with glasses had company. Another man, one a bit too well dressed for this city, was chasing the tall one.

And Carter, sticking to the rooftops, was chasing the well-dressed man who was chasing the tall blond one with the glasses. Belloc swung the telescope back to the tall one. He was blond, lanky, over six feet tall, and as he looked over his shoulder, Belloc got a good look at his face.

"Well, now," said Belloc, "how interesting."

Even at this distance, it was impossible for Belloc to mistake him for anyone but...

"Chesterton," he whispered. "Gilbert Keith Chesterton."

He paused for only a second, and then swung into action. "Lads! Hook up! Full speed and drop altitude to a quarter full! We're on a rescue mission now!"

Chapter 16

"How, for instance, do we as a matter of fact create peace in one single community? We do not do it by vaguely telling every one to avoid fighting and to submit to anything that is done to him. We do it by definitely defining his rights and then undertaking to avenge his wrongs."

—All Things Considered

Herb regretted the words *"scrag him,"* soon as he'd said them. They'd jumped out of his mouth without thought, much as an exasperated child would mumble a curse word under his breath at an annoying parent.

Unfortunately, the agents heard and gave chase as soon as Herb spoke. To change his mind and stop them would be to look weak. And to look weak in the game Herb was playing these days was to take the short route to your own *removal*, post-haste.

Herb thought for a minute about what he'd done. *Scrag* could mean a number of things to an Englishman, from "capture" to "beat severely" to . . .

He shoved away the thought. He'd been carefully taught over the past year about how to "move on" after a job. He swallowed, turned his back and marched off, back to the small apartment that would act as their base for the next few days.

Yes, Herb thought. *Time to move on.* Time to leave behind old friendships, and old ways of doing things. Leave behind the weak, enter the realm of the strong.

The *strong*. It was surprisingly easy when he thought in those terms.

Herb sighed as he walked away, trying to both hold back tears and ignore the irrational sense that he was being watched.

****

"Your attention, please. Your attention please!"

At the sound of the captain's voice, both Frances and her opponent

93

dropped their guard and looked at the gramophone-shaped speaker in the corner of the ceiling. The people gathered around them in the makeshift boxing ring in the recreation area had stopped moving as well, hearkening to the voice of authority above.

"This is your captain speaking. I have truly wonderful news. There is apparently a sizeable asteroid that has been spotted on an intercept course with our vessel. Normally this would be a cause for concern, but . . ." the captain's voice paused while the frightened whispers of the passengers swelled and died. "But," he continued, "thanks to our capable navigator, helmsman, and difference-engine operator, it appears we will not only avoid collision, but use the gravity of this sizable body in space to "sling" our vessel with increased speed to our destination, shaving several days off our journey. This should result in no more than a slight lurch for our passengers when the ship is suddenly seized by the asteroid's gravitational pull. That is all."

There was quiet for a moment. Then someone shouted and the fight was on again. Frances' boxing opponent, slick with sweat and stripped to the waist, looked back and gave a knowing smile to his friends as if he were about to win this fight. In truth he'd been losing ground for the last two rounds, but the short respite had changed all that. He felt invigorated! Enabled! Ready to win the purse of nearly ten pounds that he'd been told would be his if he could just knock this skinny little girl on her . . .

The blow hit his jaw just as he turned back to face her, the smile wiped from his face like a grease spot from a windowpane.

He yelped like a kicked dog. Like almost every steerage class passenger, he'd no qualms about fighting a lady. He'd laughed at Frances's stepping into the ring while wearing her dress with the leather straps on her fists. He'd laughed even harder when, just before the fight, she'd consulted a very thick book with pictures of a couple of boxers on the front cover, and then said a prayer while looking at a holy card of a fellow looking up at the sky with arrows sticking out of his gut.

****

The greatest joke, of course, was the one that he wasn't in on: her unorthodox preparations apparently always worked. She'd won each of her last three fights, and the crowd let out a collective sound of awe as Frances's latest blow spun her opponent in place, his eyes rolling to the ceiling in a stunned daze.

Frances, her face keeping the calm look of a chess player calculating her next move, leapt forward one step and one more to the right. Her leather-strapped fists flashed twice as she connected with his fleshy face. He staggered, each of her arms taking turns guarding her own face as the other struck.

The audience cheered once, then twice, roaring louder with each *smack* when her closed fists made against his chin.

He swayed for two more seconds like a tree with a sawed-through trunk, then fell and hit the wooden-planked floor with a decisive *thud*.

Frances stood, tucked a lock of dark, sweat-slicked hair behind her ear, and smiled. The crowd roared its approval, clapping, cheering, whistling, and exchanging betting slips for money as she removed the leather straps from her hands and smiled wider, showing her two rows of perfect teeth.

After it was over and she had changed her clothes for a looser skirt and blouse, Frances settled into a comfortable chair in the recreation room with yet another book—this one on aspects of human anatomy and healing various forms of wounds and injuries.

"Miss?" said a small voice beside her.

Frances raised her eyes. It was a small boy, looking at her with a nervous expression on his face. Frances had seen him a number of times on the journey, but this was the first time she'd ever heard his voice.

"Good evening, young man," she said, "how may I help you?" She was tired, certainly. Had the boy been ten or fifteen years older, she would have politely dismissed him from her presence. But there was no chance a boy who couldn't be more than six had any kind of agenda, was there?

"Miss, I was wonderin'. Well, I get bullied in me neighbor'ood. Me Da says I needs to get tough by fightin', but I'd rather learn from the likes a' you. Could you show me 'ow you beat up me brother?"

She smiled, closed her book, put it on the small table nearby, and then stood up. The room became very quiet as she moved, and she knew her chair would still be waiting for her when she returned.

"The trick to winning a fight," she said, "is to see it as a very fast game of chess or checkers. Here," she said, going down on one knee behind him and holding his arms by the elbows. "Which arm do you favor, and what's your name, my fine young lad?"

"This one, Ma'am," he answered, holding up his left arm, "an' me name is Jimmy. Jimmy Sweeny."

"Well, Jimmy, you need then to keep this arm, your right one, raised before your face like this. That's the guard that keeps the villains at bay. Next, keep this arm at waist level. Think of it like a deadly snake, ready to strike your opponents if they cross into its lair."

A few practice shots in the air, and little Jimmy was doing well indeed, to the point that several others in the clubroom gave small taps of applause as they watched the boy's efforts.

"Excellent, Jimmy! Now, when you strike, think of someone you are terribly angry at, and then pretend it's *that person* you are pummeling. Good! Just like that. Now, remember: One fight alone is usually not enough. You may have to fight the same bully more than once. I suspect the boys your age will think twice before bothering you again after they see what you can do."

After Jimmy had left, she sat again in her chair, reading about the treatment of a bullet wound to the chest.

"Out of curiosity, dear Frances," said a now-familiar voice behind her, "I can't help but wonder whose face *you* see when you're fighting?"

"A lady, Mister Jaggers," Frances said without looking up from the illustration. "A lady a tad older than myself, with a head of bright, red hair."

****

Running down the alley, Gilbert tore through an open doorway and up a set of creaking stairs. There must be a vacant apartment in here, or at least access to the roof! Someplace he could hide until . . .

His satchel. Where was it? He must have dropped it when he ran from those two goons with Herb!

"Fine kettle of fish you've got yourself into this time, Chesterton," he said to himself, his voice barely above a mumble. He was millions of miles from anyplace he could reasonably call home. No money, not even a spare change of clothes, and the only face he'd recognized since he'd stepped off the ship was that of a dear friend who'd shot him last year.

The hallway was lined with doors, like an apartment building or a hotel. No time to wonder if the place was truly deserted or not! There was a window next to him, one with a view of the street he'd just left behind. He risked a peek and guessed by the position of the sun that it was noon, or whatever they called it on Mars. The research he'd done back on Earth said that the Martian day was about the same length as Earth's, with maybe a few minutes difference. The planet took nearly twice as long to circle the sun as Earth did, though, which made a Martian year twice as long as one on Earth, and played havoc with calendars. How did people know when it was Christmas, Easter, or New Year's Day with a calendar that messed up?

No time to worry about that now. Even if John Carter of Mars *had* stepped into Gilbert's corner, he still had at least one more pursuer to elude! Gilbert found a differently painted door next to the window, and when he tried the doorknob it opened to another set of stairs upward. He followed it until he found what must have been the trapdoor to the roof.

The trapdoor wasn't locked. Gilbert reached up, opened it, and climbed through. The sun was still hot, but the breeze was softer and cooler than at street level. Was he safe? No one seemed to be coming. Gilbert looked over the small forest of small-building roofs, broken ancient Martian buildings that dotted the landscape, past where the red-sanded desert took over again, and further back into the crimson-colored mountains.

He tried to focus, but it was difficult. On the street below, one of the weird Martian beasts that looked like a cross between a rhino and an elephant plodded forward down the main road. It was surrounded by another group of crimson-skinned Martians, larger than the singing group he'd seen before. They were banging even larger tambourines and crying out an odd, sing-songy hymn in another language. The noise of the Martians mixed with the calls of street sellers and the everyday chatter among shoppers and gawkers alike.

Fascinating, thought Gilbert. Change the Martians to dark-skinned natives and the dinosaur to a camel, and the marketplace below could have been any one of a dozen exotic locales back on Earth. He wished he had time to explore. He'd heard some chatter on the ship about a lost city to the north, along one of the large canal routes. But first he needed to find the local offices of the *London Times* here in Syrtis Major and get an advance on his salary to replace the money in his stolen wallet. If he failed at that, he needed to at least find a sympathetic couch to sleep on tonight, and start his official job of reporting on the conditions of the miners in the morning.

And, somewhere in all that, he still needed to find the Doctor, the street urchin who just might be his little brother, and the girl who could be his sister.

Finally having blocked out the sound of the odd cultists below, he relaxed a bit. Somewhere behind him, an engine started *chuff-chuff-chuffing* rhythmically. Leaning against the waist-high wall on the rooftop and sighing deeply, a happy little fantasy slid into his mind as he looked down into the street. Wouldn't it be wonderful, if his sister and brother moved in together with him, back into his old house on the Minnesota prairie...

He felt a pair of gloved hands close around his throat. They begin to squeeze. Hard.

Then a slam from behind knocked him off the roof.

****

Belloc knew instinctively Gilbert was in some sort of trouble when he saw the tall, skinny boy run into the building. Unfortunately, Belloc knew Gilbert had ducked into precisely the kind of building that bred crooks like little Cecil as easily as bacteria in a Petri dish.

He got even more worried when he saw the fellow chasing Gilbert follow him into the building.

"Sergeant Belloc!" shouted one of the crew, "Quarter height reached!"

"Hook up!" Belloc shouted, "We'll move fast when we get our boy down there, and I don't want any of you wogs going over the side!"

"Aye, Sergeant!"

The five crew members on the deck each pulled out ropes and pulleys that ended in clipped hooks, which they attached to a metal loop each had in their belt.

"Any chance for a fight, sir?"

"Itching for combat, Private Freisner?"

"Yes, sir," the private said. Belloc looked in his face for a second and saw a familiar expression: the aching for adventure mixed with the fear of inexperience. He was young for a soldier. Younger than Belloc, anyway, who'd just entered his twentieth year. Maybe even younger than Chesterton below.

"Good," Hilaire said briskly as he looped, tied, and secured one of the cables from the onboard winch to his waist belt. "All young men long for combat, Private Freisner. At least, all *healthy* young men do. But don't let it make you stupid. You two stay on board unless I call out for you. Otherwise I may have too many cooks in the kitchen down there, and that fellow will be dead. Now, helmsman," he said, turning to the building and raising his voice so that it could be heard by the whole crew, "head for the roof of that building, that sagging one third from the corner on King George street. I want a tight circle ready to light out soon as we're out from the rooftop. Freisner, Budd, you two will jump with me. Bring pistols and dirks from the armory in the next fifteen seconds. Make sure you've got enough slack on your lines to reach across the roof. We jump on my mark . . ." Gilbert suddenly emerged from the trapdoor to the roof. He did something incredibly stupid from a military perspective: he walked over to the ledge and looked over it while still standing up.

The fool! Hilaire thought! He was exposing himself to any watching eyes that might be on the street! And he left the trapdoor *open* behind him! Hilaire wanted to reach out and strangle him for his stupidity. He'd heard the fellow had survived tramping about in that sewer with the mollusks a few years back. Hadn't he learned *anything* from that?

Could it actually be that the skinny fool didn't know he was still being pursued?

Hilaire saw the agent emerge from the open door behind Gilbert. The agent's face was both happy for finding his quarry and angry at the chase he'd had to endure.

"Sergeant!" It was Thomasvery this time, shouting over the sound of the engine and the cultists' music and chanting below. The lad was getting better at disguising the fear in his voice. "Below, is that . . ."

"Not now, Private!" Hilaire was getting ready to jump. He'd already checked his harness for sturdiness; all was ready. In five . . .

Four . . .

Hilaire Belloc had not been *formally* trained in leaping from the side of a flying boat with only a length of cord to save him from certain doom. But Belloc's adventures on Mars had long ago erased any irrational fear of heights, bullets, or anything else that could keep him from saving a very important life like Gilbert Chesterton's.

As his ship *chuffed* up from behind, Hilaire tried hard to focus on Gilbert, who was still leaning on the rooftop's waist-high wall and looking past the city and into the mountains. The noise from those blasted Worm cultists! Their tambourine slapping and hymn chanting kept Gilbert from hearing the threat of the agent, who was now only a few feet behind him!

Three . . .

Sergeant Hilaire Belloc analyzed the situation and saw three options:

a) Grabbing only Gilbert with both hands and pulling him off the roof, then having his men reel them both up to the deck of the *Locust*,

b) Grabbing just the *agent* with both hands, pulling him off the roof and dropping him to his death in the streets below, or

c) Jumping and hitting Gilbert and his antagonist *both*, pulling them *both* off the roof while hanging on to Gilbert, and hopefully bringing Gilbert to safety and *then* dropping the agent to his doom.

He dismissed option A as impractical in the first half-second. Though life in the Army and Martian Navy had made him strong and nimble, even he couldn't guarantee he'd swing like a pendulum and snag only Gilbert with the agent in the way.

Option B was even worse. If he didn't hit the agent spot on, Gilbert could be dropped or knocked off the roof by accident.

Thus, by the time the ship was only a few feet from Gilbert and his assailant, Belloc, the ship looming from behind, made his decision:

The agent reaching for Gilbert had his back to Belloc. Belloc would have to try and reach *around* or *past* the agent, grab Gilbert by the shoulders, then pull Gilbert up to safety into the *Locust*.

And, if they were lucky, they'd drop the agent from a great height to his death below.

He knew it would have seemed crazy to a layperson. But he'd been successful at crazier ideas, and carried them out under more improbable circumstances. He continued the countdown in his head.

Two . . .

One!

At the moment he finished saying *One!* in his head, Hilaire leapt from the prow of the ship, his belt tied securely to the deck's cable. No time to wait for Freisner and Budd—Gilbert's life was at stake!

Belloc was swinging in midair like Tarzan on a vine when he saw the agent's hands closed around Gilbert's throat.

Belloc's plan this time was only partly successful.

Stray winds and other factors twisted Belloc up as he swung toward his targets. Instead of grabbing Gilbert, Belloc slammed into *both* the agent *and* Gilbert. Belloc's *right* hand grabbed Gilbert's shoulder. But his left hand missed Gilbert, grabbing a handful of the *agent's* shirt instead.

All three went over the side of the building. Gilbert stayed up in the air, held at his neck by the agent and by Belloc's gripping fist at his shoulder.

The agent, now airborne, was held only by *Belloc's* hand on *his* shoulder.

The agent, better known to colleagues and victims as the Painter, suddenly found himself not only fifty feet in the air, but also now the middle part of a kind of human sandwich, with Gilbert in front and that annoying Sergeant Belloc behind him, holding the shoulder of his shirt in a tight grip!

But even dangling high in the air, the Painter still held to his training. And that training had been very, very clear on this point: when you had a target in your hands you never let it go as long as the target was still alive and you had hands to grip it with. And as he saw the ground drop away, he held on to dear life by gripping Gilbert's neck even tighter.

The ship continued chuffing forward, dragging the three of them. Painter's hands never left Gilbert's neck, but made no progress in choking the skinny boy. In the sudden confusion it was all he could do to keep his grip, much less find the spot on Gilbert's neck that would completely cut off his air.

The Painter looked down. His feet dangled at least fifty feet in the air, and the market goers below were screaming and pointing at them in the sky.

Time to reposition.

The Painter let go of Gilbert's neck, instead grabbing the arms of the soldier that held the Painter and Chesterton by their shoulders. *Cripes*, but the soldier was strong! If only he could somehow break his hold on the boy's shoulders, he could make Gilbert drop to his death, then kill the strong, wiry soldier and escape.

Shouldn't be too hard. He'd gotten out of worse scrapes in his life.

****

Gilbert had just paused to catch his breath when the gloved hands wrapped around his neck. When another hand grabbed his shoulder and he was swept off the roof, his fear shifted into panic almost immediately.

He'd tried to spin around and fight his attacker, but by then his feet couldn't find the ground!

While he poked his feet down, trying to find the roof of the building, the fingers around his neck were digging and searching, trying to find his Adam's apple. Little black dots were sprouting at the edge of his vision within seconds as he tried to struggle and scream.

Have I been grabbed by an angel? he wondered sluggishly while the black dots got bigger. If he was dead and flying in the arms of an angel, then why did he still feel the ugly hands at his neck? Why did he still smell the bad breath of his assailant on his neck, and smell cheap coffee in the air he breathed. Why did he . . .

The hands were off his neck! Gilbert turned his head and looked around.

A hand had gripped his shoulder. A hand attached to an arm dressed in a red military jacket.

What the?!? There were *two* people in the air with him! His assailant was still behind him, and a *third* man who held Gilbert's shoulder with one hand and gripped the attacker's neck in the crook of his other arm.

The man in a soldier's uniform who was a little older than Gilbert himself, but with a thick jaw, fierce blue eyes, wearing a soldier's uniform and sporting a short, military haircut.

The soldier was also attached to a flying patrol boat by a long cable.

And between Gilbert and his rescuer was his assailant. Still gripping the soldier's right hand with both of his own, Gilbert looked back. His would-be strangler was a man in his thirties in need of a shave.

Gilbert's attacker had released Gilbert's neck and now hung on to the soldier's arm, trying to twist, bend, or break the hold that kept Gilbert in the air.

Gilbert gulped and restrained the urge to scream and start flailing about like a rag doll.

Gilbert gripped Belloc's right hand tighter with his own left arm as the Painter tried to pry off Gilbert's hands from Belloc's wrist. All three men swung on the end of the soldier's dragline like the clapper at the bottom of a pendulum. In the background, he heard a whirring sound mixed with the *chuff! chuff! chuff!* of the flying scout ship's boiler engine.

Gilbert tried to move himself away from the Painter, and Belloc's hand almost lost its hold. "No!" Belloc barked, "Chesterton, stay still, blast it!"

He knows who I am? Gilbert thought.

Suddenly, someone slipped. Gilbert couldn't tell who, but he didn't care. He moved without thinking, doing a hand-over-hand maneuver around the Painter, across Belloc's right arm, and all the way to the soldier's back.

Now the places had changed! *Gilbert* was at *Belloc's* back, *Belloc* was in the middle, and the Painter was facing Belloc, with both Gilbert and the Painter both holding on to Belloc for dear life!

But the Painter was still holding on to Gilbert's wrist with one hand, and the soldier's arm with the other.

Now it was the Painter's turn. With a similar hand-over–hand motion, he broke Belloc's hold on his shoulder, twisted his body, and finished by hanging on to *Gilbert's* back!

Things had changed again; now Gilbert was in the middle, *Belloc* in the center, and the *Painter* hung behind *Gilbert!*

Belloc was still in front of Gilbert, facing away from both Gilbert and the Painter. "Gilbert!" the soldier barked, a matter-of-fact edge to his voice as his hands started to fiddle with something at his chest.

"What?" Gilbert yelled over the sound of the engine, the whirring noise, the wind blasting by the three of them, and his own terrified heartbeat blasting in his ears.

"Duck."

Gilbert was just about to ask why when Belloc brought up a pistol and pointed it behind him. It was a single-barreled model, held by the soldier's right hand, pointed directly at Gilbert.

And Belloc's head still faced front, with no apparent desire to actually aim his weapon.

"Whoa!" Gilbert yelled, and bobbed his head to his right, just as he felt the cold leather of the strangler's gloved hand slide past his face and down to his throat for a second try at crushing his windpipe.

A thunderclap blasted in Gilbert's left ear. The hand around his throat disappeared like a bad dream in the morning.

Gilbert still yelled, but he hung on to Belloc. His ear rang in pain, but not so much that he was going to let go! His other ear could still hear the sound of the ship's engine and a whirring, winding noise that started up and mixed with it.

"Gilbert, hang on!" the soldier shouted over all the noise that had become literally deafening.

"Doing that!" Gilbert said back. A witty comeback wasn't going to be on his lips anytime soon. He just wanted to find a safe place now, and hide until all this strangeness calmed down and he could hunt for his siblings.

"Gilbert!"

"What now?" Gilbert barked.

"Look down."

"Wh—?"

Gilbert looked down and froze mid-word. They were now at least a hundred feet in the air; the few remaining buildings and streets spread out below like a toy village.

"Oh, okay," Gilbert said, clutching the cable with one hand and the soldier's neck with the other.

Something gently bumped his head from behind. Gilbert realized the engine noise was louder, and a whirring noise in the background had stopped.

Gilbert looked up. The whirring noise must have been a winch of some kind. Now instead of swinging on the cable like a spider on a silk line, both Gilbert and his rescuer hung at rest against the hull of the flying ship.

Hands reached down and grabbed Gilbert's arms, pulling him up and over. Once over the side, they dropped Gilbert without ceremony onto the hard wooden deck, paying far more attention to the soldier who'd saved him.

Gilbert looked around, irked that he was now ignored.

Once the soldier who'd rescued him was pulled over the side, Gilbert saw him full on for the first time. He had bright blue eyes, close cropped hair like all the military men, and a thick jaw, the kind they called a "lantern jaw" back in the States. His coat was the deep red of all Martian soldiers, with dark pants and a set of crossed white straps in the shape of a letter X across his chest. His shoulders were broad. His arm muscles had felt immovable as rocks but didn't seem particularly large through the sleeves of the coat. He'd carried two people, Gilbert and his attacker, without letting either of them go.

But there was one detail that Gilbert spied which he was particularly glad to see, one hanging out of the soldier's side pockets on his coat.

It was a dark string of beads linked by a shiny, small-linked chain, and a small dark crucifix hung on the end of it.

The beads were called a *rosary*, a set of Catholic prayers in the form of a beaded necklace. Gilbert hadn't ever seen one until a few years ago. Then, he'd been in the company of Father Brown, and the young man holding the rosary in his pocket had been Chang, a Chinese porter.

Chang was another young man whom Father Brown had mentored. After the priest's death, Chang had become good friends with Gilbert, more so now that Gilbert had entered the Church and Chang was in the Seminary to be a priest.

Now, Gilbert's rescuer was sporting, not only a rosary, but one that looked just like Chang's…

"Right, lads!" the soldier said, his close-shaved head and alert eyes darting everywhere as it inspected four, five, six points to be sure that all was set to sail. "Let's get this tub moving proper again!"

"Sergeant Belloc?" said a smaller sailor who looked about Gilbert's age. He was just as skinny, but about a foot shorter. "Shouldn't we drop this 'ere civvie back on the shore first?"

"No, Aspenall. I think the *Locust* has just found its first *bona fide* passenger on this run." He stopped to straighten his coat and looked for a moment at Gilbert as if he knew him already. "Welcome aboard, Mister Chesterton," he said as he straightened his jacket, sticking out his right hand once he was finished. "Sergeant Hilaire Belloc, Commander *pro-tempore* of His Majesty's Ship the *Red Locust,* at your service."

"I—I'm... Oh, sorry," Gilbert said, trying to get his bearings. After an embarrassing few seconds, he stuck out his own hand and shook Hilaire's. "I'm . . . Well, it seems you know who I am already. Thank you for saving me back there! I thought I was a goner for sure. Matter of fact—"

"Would you excuse me, please?" Hilaire cut him off suddenly, turning to the semi-circle of sailors and soldiers that surrounded them. "Well?" he roared at the men, "Don't stand there gawping! What's the matter? Haven't you ever seen a reporter before? Budd!"

"Yes, Sergeant!"

"Hoist sail! I want our coal to last all the way to Mons Olympus and back!"

"Aye aye, Sergeant!"

"Zeppieri!"

"Yes, Sergeant!"

"Forward observer! I want this leaky excuse for a sloop to make it there and back again, and it won't if we're surprised by a bunch of slimy green bugs like the Tharks, now will it?"

"Aye aye, Sergeant!"

"Darcy!"

"Yes, Sergeant!"

"You will give your bunk to our guest until we can drop him at the next safe outpost!"

"Aye, Sergeant!"

Gilbert couldn't help but be impressed with the confidence, competence, and surety that Belloc used with the men, a couple of whom were older than he was. Ex-convicts made up much of the rank-and-file of the British armed forces, and they often had difficulty following orders. Still, if the older soldiers were convicts, it didn't matter. All onboard obeyed Belloc with promptness and loyalty, the kind rarely accorded to officers, much less a Sergeant. Belloc strode off, giving more orders. Gilbert looked and saw the town's small buildings were receding in the distance, as the ship's smokestack chuffed in the air and the winds propelled them toward the open desert.

"You sure I couldn't get a lift back to the city?" Gilbert asked a nearby sailor, the one Belloc had called Budd. "I dropped my bag back there, and I'd like to go get it before something happens to it."

"Sorry, friend," the sailor said, giving Gilbert a hearty slap on the back. He was shorter than Gilbert, but had a smile so happy and infectious it lightened Gilbert's mood instantly. "I saw your bag go over the edge of that building's roof when that bloke decided to try and twist your head off like a cork in a bottle of champagne. Some little dirt rat's already turned it inside out and picked over it six ways to Sunday. You're better off with us here."

Later, Gilbert sat down on a bench jutting out from beneath the gunwale and looked over the edge of the ship. Fifty feet or more below, the landscape sped by at a rate that would have been the envy of most steam engines. The sight made his stomach jumble a few times.

"Feeling better?"

Gilbert looked up. Belloc was standing over him, his back straight and his arms folded in front.

"No," Gilbert said, "but I guess I could be worse."

"For a man who's just had his life saved," Belloc said, taking a seat near Gilbert with a soft grunt, "you're pretty morose."

"Sorry. I don't want to seem ungrateful. It's just that the last few people who've saved my life have either died or tried to kill me."

"And here I thought *my* life was interesting. Here, Chesterton— do you smoke?"

"No, thank you. The occasional cigar is nice, but cigarettes aren't something I enjoy all that that much."

Belloc nodded, put away the tin of thin cigarettes, and took out a flask instead. "You've had quite a scare, Gilbert. Even for one with your history. When that fellow—I think they call him the Painter, come to think—got his hands around your neck, I thought you were done for. And on my watch, no less."

"The *Painter*?" Gilbert said, watching Belloc's face.

After a few seconds, Belloc nodded. "Yes, I know about the Special Branch, and the names their agents use. I know a fair bit, Gilbert," said Belloc, his voice dropping to a low whisper while keeping the same smile on his face. Something about the gesture calmed Gilbert's fragile nerves.

"How did... How did you know that *I* knew? About them and their names?"

"I've known about you for a while, Gilbert, and about *them* much longer. I've known about the Painter and his handiwork ever since he arrived, though I never got a good look at him until today. He preferred to push his prey off a building, make it look like an accident. But if he had time on his hands, he'd crack your windpipe like a dry twig.

"I also saw you eyeing my rosary back there. Yes, Father Brown was a mentor of mine, too. Saved my life on Earth. He was quite good at finding folks like you, Chang, and myself and helping them into the light if we chose to go. Sad about your friend, Herb. From what I heard, he could have been one of the great ones if he'd chosen differently. But that's something for another day."

"I'd like to hear about Father Brown," Gilbert said. "And what you know about the Special Branch, and a few other things, too. I'm sorry, by the way, for flailing around when you were trying to save my life."

"Not to worry, Gilbert. You'd be surprised how many people actually get upset when I save their lives, battlefields excepted. I know you'd rather go back to the city. But in truth, for you right now this boat is the safest place in all of civilized Mars."

"Fair enough," Gilbert said, "what do I do now?"

"Now, you rest. Fresh off the boat from Earth, and you've lost your gear and nearly had your neck broken."

"Yes, and my billfold stolen, too."

"Really? Do you know by whom?"

"My brother. I think."

Hilaire paused, looking at Gilbert. "Right, well, that's for later. Right now I'll have Private Budd take you down to the bunks and you can rest a bit."

"I feel tired, but not very sleepy."

"Trust me. When your head hits the pillow after you've fought for your life, sleep will come."

Belloc called for Budd, who led Gilbert down below deck and into a section with bunk beds lined up precisely beside each other. All were immaculately made, with hospital corners on the sheets and perfectly folded covers on top.

Gilbert lay down and closed his eyes, but contrary to what Belloc said he didn't sleep instantly.

It took nearly half a minute. And when he slept, he dreamed about a Tug of War game where he was both the rope and the puller on both sides.

****

The Painter's body lay on the rooftop where it had fallen. His glazed eyes stared straight up, his right leg bent at an impossible angle, his body leaking blood where the bullet had entered.

No one had come to investigate. The majority of the people in Syrtis Major were British, with a smattering of Canadians. As a culture they held the ability to ignore unpleasant realities as one of the highest of all virtues, right after drinking tea, paying taxes on time, and getting along with the-powers-that-be. There was no stirring below, no one wondering at the spectacle of men swinging on ropes above them, no one coming to search and see if the Painter was alright.

Still alive while wincing and grunting in pain, the Painter reached into his pocket and pulled out a syringe.

The glass tube held a viscous, greenish-yellow liquid. He reached into another pocket and pulled out a set of needles from a leather pouch. He took the longest of the needles and attached it to the end of the syringe's glass tube.

After a few more pain-filled breaths, he sat up and plunged the needle into his leg through the fabric of his torn pants.

After a very long minute, the dark spots on his pant legs stopped spreading as the blood stopped flowing from the now-closing wounds, and the leg straightened out with a series of small bends and clicks.

After his leg had stopped healing, he stood up and put both hands to the small of his back and pushed as he leaned back with his eyes closed.

He leaned on his now straightened leg, testing it to be sure. Satisfied, he flexed his hands and arms, then poked and prodded his torso in several places.

After a few seconds, his face took on an odd expression. His jaw moved and rolled against itself, as if he were trying to remove a piece of food stuck in between his teeth.

He finally reached into his mouth with his fingers, grabbed something and pulled. The loose tooth came out of his mouth with barely a whisper of pain. He pocketed the tooth, reminding himself to visit the dentist before the day was through.

He would not return to the Cleaner, or Herb, or whatever that ridiculously young agent was named. The Painter had failed, and reporting failure to a fellow like the Cleaner was a certain means to an unexpected and unpleasant death.

Covering up wouldn't work either. This wasn't London. Someone was bound to see the lanky kid whom Belloc had saved.

Belloc.

That must have been the soldier who'd interfered. The Painter hadn't gotten a good look at him, but no one else would do something so crazy as to do what that soldier had done. Thinking about that twenty-year old, granite-headed grunt with the bellowing-thunder voice made him seethe with rage.

"That was the last time, Young Thunder," the Painter said. The sarcasm sounded through his voice as he used the name that some of the red Martians had given to Belloc a year ago, after he'd played the hero for the fourth or fifth time.

Couldn't think too much on it, though. Work to be done. He breathed in, straightened up, and within a second or two he was no longer the angry-looking, hate-filled agent who taken more lives than most professional soldiers could ever hope to take. He was once again a nondescript, calm British subject minding his own business.

Yes, the Painter thought as he broke open the lock to the stairwell and gingerly put his weight on his left leg, which was still quite sore. *Yes, I have work to do.*

****

"Is this usual?" Beatrice asked, placing by her bags on the ground. Tresses of her blond hair wafted in the breeze, and looked quite fetching in the afternoon sun.

The Doctor looked at her and smiled. Something in her hair and voice awoke a primal and powerful memory deep in his past, the kind he'd long thought safely extinguished.

But there'd be time to indulge such things later.

"My dear Beatrice," he said, "as I stated earlier, unexpected developments have moved our schedule up a tad. Rest assured, this archeological expedition is quite well funded by generous people, and our journey will prove quite lucrative to us both. Besides this, imagine how this experience will benefit young Cecil! Speaking of which . . ."

"He ought to be here by now," she said nervously and half to herself. Her own traveling bag was packed with a neat, smart air with a perfectly centered belt buckle at the top. It sat alongside a hastily filled duffle bag with a red shirtsleeve and a brown pant leg spilling out of the opening, which was half-drawn closed by a now tangled rope.

"I am certain he will be here," said the Doctor. "In the meantime, I should love to hear about your lives in Canada. Did you, indeed, run a farm completely by yourself? I should think that a nigh impossible task for a young woman alone."

"Well, Cecil wasn't quite the handful then that he is now," Beatrice said, still looking around for her brother with a nervous air. If he derailed this chance for the both of them, she'd thrash him with a broomstick at first light! "It was quite challenging, though. I tried my hardest, but eventually I had to sell it to a local farmer."

"Such a shame! Had you no family to turn to? No family that you were, ah, *aware* of at all?"

"Well, there was an aunt Marie and uncle Edward, and their son, my cousin. They lived in Minnesota, over in the Americas. But my parents left us no contact information for them, and they only visited once, years ago. I barely remember my cousin's name. They called him Gilford, or something. After we greeted him he straightened his glasses and spent the entire weekend visit sequestered in my father's library. I've no other family that my parents ever spoke of."

"Indeed," said the Doctor, looking away from her. Beatrice kept looking around, hoping for a glimpse of her younger brother. She was so wrapped up in her thoughts that she didn't hear the boyish shouts and jeers from the rooftops behind. Nor did she hear the grunts and heavy *thud* of bodies on the metal rooftops and nearby dirt ground.

When young Cecil finally emerged from one of the alleys, he had a cut above his eye, dry rooftop dirt mixed with street refuse covering his pants, and a long, jagged tear along his left shirtsleeve.

Beatrice had just turned to see him when he began an involved explanation for his lateness and appearance that most strangers would have believed.

Beatrice, having heard far too many of his excuse-sagas, wouldn't listen.

The Doctor watched Cecil receive his latest tongue-lashing with a smile on his face. Although they were clearly exasperated and annoyed with one another, it was quite obvious they truly *did* love and care for each another. He had no doubt that Beatrice would fight like a tigress to protect Cecil from harm. And he was certain Cecil would lie down in front of a herd of stampeding sloats if it kept her from crying.

Yes, he thought, *this pair could prove useful, indeed.* Their infantile, outdated familial love for each other would be the ideal leash with which to control them.

Yes. *Control.*

He only hoped Gilbert hadn't yet managed to break the bonds between himself and his fairy-tale belief system just yet. It, too, could be useful. When the time came, he would use Gilbert's siblings as leverage.

And, once broken, Gilbert would be a powerful asset to the Doctor's ambitions, far greater than Herbert, or even the Doctor's former masters.

Chapter 17

"It is customary to remark that modern problems cannot easily be attacked because they are so complex. In many cases I believe it is really because they are so simple. Nobody would believe in such simplicity of scoundrelism even if it were pointed out. People would say that the truth was a charge of mere melodramatic villainy; forgetting that nearly all villains really are melodramatic."

–All Things Considered

"Wakey Wakey, Sunshine!" said a cheerful voice, rousing Gilbert from the latest in a series of murky, disturbing dreams. He looked around with half-open eyes and saw the dark silhouette of a man.

"Wha—?" said Gilbert, still feeling as if his mind were full of cobwebs and fog.

"It's morning, Gilbert!" said the cheerful sailor, the one they called Budd. "Hope you enjoyed your rest. I had to spend the night on the deck, but I didn't mind a bit, not under these stars. My shift is just ending, and yours is just beginning!"

Gilbert, still wearing the clothes he'd put on the morning of his ship's arrival on Mars, felt all rummy and sore just about everywhere. His neck hurt the most, and he could barely turn his head from side to side. His arms and legs felt as if someone was jabbing a knife into them each time he moved.

"Are you ill?" asked Budd.

"Ow!" said Gilbert, as he swung out of the bunk, pain shooting throughout his sore muscles. "No, I . . . Well, not exactly. Yesterday was the first time I had to run for my life in quite a while, and I guess I'm out of practice."

Gilbert swung out of the bunk and stood up. Ignoring the pain in his limbs, he drew himself up to his full height and looked down at Budd. He was a few years older than Gilbert, but shorter and spry, with quick eyes and a smile like something out of a missionary's handbook on how to put people at ease.

"Come on," Budd said, "up to the deck. And don't be put off by Sergeant Belloc. He can seem a little rough at times, but he's a good soul and he's never done a man wrong that I've seen."

As Gilbert followed Budd down the aisle of the lower deck of the gently rocking ship, a thought took sudden and hard shape in his head. Not truly painful, but present and unavoidable as the sound of the wind outside.

God played favorites.

And Gilbert? Well, Gilbert just wasn't one of them.

Good people like Father Brown died, while bad people like the Doctor lived. Good people like Anne, the rogue agent of the Special Branch, disappeared forever trying to save lives, while cruel people like Luther, Gilbert's childhood nemesis, lived and prospered with the county under his family's thumb and their own reserved pew in the county's little Baptist church.

God played favorites. And if you weren't one of them, you had to fend for yourself.

These thoughts and memories pulsed through Gilbert's head. Rather than thrust them away and label them as so much silliness, the day's newness and strangeness somehow made them seem more plausible, the way a tree's shadow will look comforting in the daylight but become a fearful monster at night on the wall of a little boy's room.

They soon reached a small ladder that led to the upper deck. Budd went up first and Gilbert followed. The sun was out, and Gilbert's eyes hurt as they adjusted to the bright morning light.

" 'Lo, Budd," said a large, husky sailor nearby as he scrubbed the decks with a stiff, wire brush. The dirt on the deck looked ground into the fiber of the wooden planks, but the large sailor scrubbed hard enough that the planks gleamed where he scoured them, cleaned as if by magic.

" 'Morning, Barnes," said Budd with an infectious grin, "where's the Sergeant? Oh, never mind."

Budd hadn't finished his question before an angry man's roar blasted across the deck. It was the kind of furious bellowing that gives sweet relief to all military men and schoolchildren alike, because the roar was directed at someone *else*.

"Arias, you call *this* a knot?" Belloc was dressed in a dusty longcoat with three stripes emblazoned on his shoulder. He was bellowing at a sailor, who was standing at full attention and staring straight ahead.

"I thought so, sir . . ."

"What? Did you say you *thought*, Arias? That was your first mistake! Your second mistake was calling me sir! I'm a Sergeant, Arias, not an officer! I *work* for a living! Now remember, Arias: you don't *think* on my boat! Is that clear? You are *not* to think when you're on duty! While on *my* boat, your job is to *do* whatever the duty roster says for that morning! *Not* think! *Do*! Now fix this knot or by gum I'll have you keelhauled! And I'll do it when we pass Mons Olympus! And I'll fly *low* enough that you and the mountaintop will be *close* enough to have a deeply moving love affair! Now fix this so-called knot! You have thirty seconds! *Move!*"

"Yes, Sergeant!" said Arias, quickly trying to fix the thick-roped knot into a form that would keep him out of trouble.

"Now," said Belloc, turning and focusing on Budd and Gilbert. "Private Budd, you will immediately tell me why you are wasting *my* precious time!"

"Sergeant!" shouted Budd, coming to attention and looking straight ahead, "you instructed me to bring you the civilian immediately when he awoke!"

Belloc seemed completely unaware of Chesterton's presence as he started walking around the seaman, looking intently at his uniform. "Your boots need shining, Private Budd!"

"Yes, Sergeant!"

"And your shirt needs ironing."

"Yes, Sergeant!"

"I see stubble on your face and your cap has dirt on it!"

"Yes, Sergeant!"

"Fix all that and get to your morning duty before I keelhaul you along with Arias! Get out of my sight! Now!"

Budd didn't answer. He ran down the deck and below the staircase without fear but with quite a bit of speed.

"Mister Chesterton!" said Belloc, looking dead-on at Gilbert, "Follow me. I'll need to explain the expectations of passengers while you're on board my ship."

"Yes, sir."

"And don't call me sir," he said, turning and heading for the front of the ship, his voice tinged with a hint of sarcasm. "As I said before, I'm not an officer! I work for a living!" This last was yelled over his shoulder to the shipmen busy at their deck jobs.

At the front of the ship, Belloc raised another trap door and walked down another set of stairs. Gilbert was glad to be out of the sun. It was as bright as on Earth, but something in the air or the pink-orange sky hurt his eyes a little when he was outside.

They walked to the back of the ship, and Gilbert could hear the engine boiler beneath him. Another trapdoor must have led down to it. A dozen steps past the loudest sounds of the engine, and Belloc opened another door into what must have been his private quarters.

It wasn't very spacious at all, really. Just enough room for a bed, chair, and a small table with a Bible and a few more books on it. An immaculately pressed dress uniform hung on a hanger that rested on a hook on the wall. A small cabinet was set into the wall, its corner peeking out from behind the uniform. Gilbert could just see the doors of the cabinet were closed.

"Well, Mister Chesterton," said Belloc, taking a seat on the chair and indicating Gilbert should sit at the foot of the bed. Gilbert sat. The bed felt as hard as the wooden deck of the ship. "I'd been hoping to meet you for some time, but I never would have guessed it would be this way. After I was transferred out here, I thought meeting you or doing my specialized work for the Church would be impossible for at least another year or two. Happily I've found myself wrong on both counts."

"You sound pretty happy to be wrong."

"You're quite relaxed for someone who nearly died."

"I think I'm getting used to it."

"That can be a very, very good thing out here, Gilbert. But now, on to other business. Water?" He reached below the table and found another small door in the wall Gilbert had missed. Belloc opened it, and he produced a corked wine bottle filled with a clear liquid and two teacups.

Gilbert suddenly felt very, very thirsty. "Yes, please, now that you mention it."

Belloc poured two teacups half full. "Sip, don't guzzle. We can make alcohol here on Mars from almost anything that grows, but you'll find water is something strictly rationed. Not as bad as if we had to traipse about in the desert like a squad of sand-stamping grunts, but enough to let you know we live in the largest desert ever inhabited by man."

Gilbert took a sip and looked at Belloc. "I'll keep that in mind. Could you answer a question no one seems to know back on Earth? What keeps us alive out here? I was taught in school Mars was too far from the sun for anything to live."

"The mollusks, it seems, were able to live here quite handily. But other races like the two-legged otter-men and some spindly, stick-figure fellows shared it with the Red Men you saw in the market Square. The canals we live in here on Mars are thousands of miles long, and hundreds of miles wide at their thickest point. There are a number of ancient, castle-like forts out here with machines inside that somehow maintain the atmosphere, air pressure, weather, everything to keep all non-mollusk life functional. They haven't broken down in millennia, and, please God, they won't ever. The Red Men won't let us in the places to tinker with them for fear that we'll break something. And they're probably right."

Gilbert waited a second. In the silence his eye crept to the rosary at Belloc's pocket, now only the low bar of the cross peeking out.

"Did you know Father Brown well?" Gilbert asked.

"He and I made our acquaintance a year before the Tripods attacked," Belloc said, relaxing in his chair. "He was a good man, and he and Chang found me after I'd gotten myself into a spot of trouble in a tavern fight."

Gilbert's eyes flicked open. He'd also met Chang and Father Brown almost at the same moment.

Belloc seemed to guess the reason for Gilbert's reaction and stifled a chuckle. "Father Brown had a knack for knowing who needed him and being there at just the right time," Belloc continued. "In your case, you were on the train and had just met that blighter Wells. Wells might have turned you to his side, if Father had not intervened."

"How did you know about that?"

"Chang told me, Gilbert. He's a good friend of mine, too. We had our own share of adventures together after Father Brown brought us in. As I said before, shame about Herb Wells; we had such high hopes for him. But there you have it. No matter how good you are or what you're chosen for, God doesn't take away your free will. You can always choose to do something stupid, or become something terrible."

"Wait, you said, 'brought us in.' What do you mean, exactly?"

"You mean you haven't figured it out yet, Gilbert?"

"It's a funny little quirk of mine. I'm never quite up to snuff after I've nearly been strangled and swept off a roof."

"I'm disappointed. I thought you'd at least do better with a bit of sleep. And feel free to call me Hilaire, at least when the other men are out of earshot. Well, you're already *in*, so to speak, so there's no harm in telling you. Father Brown loved being a country priest. And he solved more than one crime just by knowing how human hearts worked, which is more than you could say about that violin player back in London they're all reading and talking about these days.

"But that wasn't all there was to Father John Paul Brown," continued Hilaire. "He proved quite successful at uncovering truths, so much so that he came to the attention of some very good and powerful people. And when he began to travel in *their* circles . . ."

There was a shout above. Belloc stopped talking, leapt to his feet, opened the door to his cabin, and then ran down the wooden floor back to the trapdoor. Gilbert watched as his new host didn't even bother to climb the steps, but somehow leaped straight up, his hands on the trapdoor frame giving him the only push needed to launch himself up onto the top deck.

Gilbert took a few seconds to react, then followed. He tried leaping up as Belloc had. But even though Gilbert was taller, he couldn't heft himself as quickly and had to bring his knee up to help lift him up over the lip of the door and onto the deck.

The dozen-man crew, including Budd and Belloc, were running everywhere. They tightened and loosened ropes, dropped sails, and fitted guns into the . . .

Guns?

The two largest crewmembers ran with Maxim machine-powered guns in their hands to the rim of the deck and began fitting the large weapons to posts on the sides, front, and rear of the ship. They moved quickly, with the kind of sure-footed movements borne by repeated military drill. Everyone knew without question what needed to be done, and when all was finished, they took their positions.

Except, of course, Gilbert. He stood with a blank stare on his face, watching the hustle and bustle whirl around him. He felt as if he were in the middle of a dust devil in a windstorm, completely ignorant of what needed doing, let alone how to do it.

"Make yourself useful, boy," said the wide-eyed, tall sailor with a large Adam's apple and rolled-up sleeves as he slapped something large and clunky into Gilbert's hands.

He looked down.

It was a large pistol made of cold, gray metal.

"Get to cover, fool!" shouted another voice behind him. "Why's the fop got a gun?" he heard someone else yell as he crouched behind some barrels. "I thought paperboys were non-combatants!"

"Ain't no such thing today," shouted another voice to Gilbert's left.

"Gilbert! Here! Over here!" he heard a cheerful voice chirp. Gilbert looked and saw Private Budd waving to him, his smile wide as if they'd just spied each other in the stands at a baseball game. Keeping his head low and his knees bent, Gilbert walked in a careful crouch from a stack of secured barrels toward Budd and dropped beside him next to the rim of the ship.

"Alright if I hide here?" Gilbert asked.

"Just stay down until Sergeant Belloc says to jump out," Budd said, checking a rope secured around his waist and hooking it to a metal ring behind him. "He's survived several fights with the Tharks. They say he even beat one in hand-to-hand combat, but he's far too modest to talk about it."

"Ready, lads!"

Belloc's voice carried clear over the top deck of the ship. Gilbert could feel rather than hear nearly a dozen men tense up and readying for the fight.

Gilbert, still a punchcard clacker at heart, counted heads. Budd and Gilbert were in the prow of the ship, crouching behind the gunwale. Budd held a sharp saber in one hand and a pistol in the other. To their left and right two men stood, stationed at the Maxim machine guns ready to fire while another man crouched beside the gun, his hands on the belts of ammunition carefully laid out in an open box nearby, ready to feed the deadly belts of bullets into the Maxim's chambers. Another sailor manned a smaller Maxim gun in the rear of the boat, while two men loaded a small lead ball a bit bigger than a man's fist into the back of a post-mounted cannon in the front of the ship.

"Chesterton! Get down and stay down!" Belloc roared. Gilbert dropped to all fours and crawled over to the rim of the boat. "Budd! Keep an eye on him! We need his gun as much as anyone's, but I don't want a dead civvy on my record when we get back to Syrtis Major!"

"Yes, Sergeant!" yelled, Budd, almost in Gilbert's ear.

"What's a civvy?" Gilbert whispered when he got within earshot. Belloc was still shouting orders as the last few men scurried about the deck, preparing for the battle.

"A civilian," Budd whispered in a sharp, quiet voice. "It looks bad if you let one die under your arm. Normally, you'd be below decks for your own safety."

"So why give me a gun?"

"*Tharks* are attacking. You know, the big green fellows with four arms and tusks? When they win, they torture prisoners to death. Then they're skinned and dismembered, their hides used as coats, their limbs as decorative trophies."

Gilbert gulped. "What if you're an *unlucky* prisoner?"

"They skin you *first*. Either way, the last thing you'll hear is their laughter. Nothing makes Tharks laugh harder than seeing pain and suffering."

"Budd!" roared Belloc, "ready?"

"Aye, sir!" returned Budd in a loud voice. Belloc moved on, shouting and checking the readiness of each in turn from his position, crouched in the prow of the boat.

"Now look, Gilbert," said Budd once again, his voice dropping to a whisper and deadly serious, "I won't be able to nursemaid you when the bullets start flying. Do you know how to use a pistol?"

Gilbert nodded.

"Have you ever killed before?"

"Do Martian squids count?"

"Close enough. Ever use a sword?"

Gilbert recalled the one time he'd tried to threaten a man with a blade; he'd ended up having to do field surgery on the beautiful girl who'd gotten impaled on his sword by accident.

"Not so good, there."

"Well, we'll make do, then, won't we? Just hang back and pepper 'em while we take them down at close quarters."

"Lads," said Belloc, his voice rising over the sound of their own ship's boiler. A distant noise that could only be the engine of the enemy vessel started getting louder as Belloc spoke. Suddenly Gilbert could hear a series of screeching, clicking noises that made the hairs on his neck stand up.

"Lads," shouted Belloc, a saber in one hand and a multi-barreled, pepperbox pistol in the other, "the Tharks are chasing the *Locust*, and this may be it for some of us. We're not going to run anymore! The last thing a Thark expects is for an Earthman to turn and fight, but they've obviously never fought Englishmen before! I've ordered the black gang below to increase the engine's output to ramming speed.

"If they evade, we're going to sweep their decks clean as we pass. But if we hit, I'm going over first. Give me a three count and follow. We'll have a few seconds to sell our lives dear! Gunners, when we're in range, don't stop shooting 'til the river of hot lead runs dry! We may not live the day, but, by the God that made us and His Blessed Mother, we'll see to it today that they'll think again before they attack an English vessel! Savvy? Good! Ready, Lads? Who's with me?"

The men cheered!

Gilbert, carried away by the moment, roared too, his pistol high in the air.

A loud *boom!* cut off the cheer. Something black the size of a man's head flew over them in a blur, and missed them by a dozen feet or so.

They were silent for only a second.

"Trimsman!" roared Belloc, "bring us up another hundred feet! Rear, Port, and Starboard gunners, fire at will!"

"Aye aye, sir!" came several shouts from behind, followed by what sounded like several loud typewriters all clacking at once.

"Helmsman!" Belloc shouted over the sound of the machine guns, "hard about! Point us at them, *now!*"

"Aye, aye, sir!"

"Engine room," Belloc yelled, not even waiting for the Helmsman to finish, "increase speed ten knots and cut power when we're at a forty-five! When we ram them, I want a hole in their rotten hull big enough to drive a steam engine through!"

"Aye, sir!" came the muffled yell from below deck. "Speed increased to—"

"All you wogs fire, *now!*" Belloc said. Gilbert saw the helmsman do something to the wheel to lock it in place once they'd turned about. He ran to the prow of the ship with Gilbert and Budd, as did the Trimsman and the three members of the engine crew, who emerged from the lower deck with weapons in hand and grim looks on their faces.

Belloc readied his sword and looked over the pistol in his hand. Gilbert saw that Sergeant Belloc in the King's Navy had a second pistol strapped to his gunbelt, and that each of the pistols also had a thick rubber hose that ran up toward his back and disappeared in the folds of his coat.

"Steady . . ." said Hilaire, drawing out the last sound in the word as if he could sense the men's tension. "Steady . . ."

Gilbert looked forward and saw the Thark vessel bob down as the *Locust* closed in. The sight of the ship turned his insides cold. It looked like a drawing he'd seen years ago of a ghostly pirate vessel, with filth and grime so thick Gilbert imagined he could smell it even from this distance. It had bones arranged in decorative patterns in the rigging and on the enemy's hull, making the ship look even more despicable and frightening.

And he could see the Tharks.

Gilbert had first heard about them two years ago, when trapped in a subterranean maze with the Doctor. The Doctor had mentioned their green skin, four arms, and the horns and tusks. But now he could see them running back and forth on a ship deck like a bunch of green spiders, screaming and screeching while waving heavy swords and the occasional gun in each of their four arms.

Gilbert only saw and heard for a few seconds. The gunners kept firing, pouring hundreds of rounds into the enemy ship and crew.

Three seconds later, a cannonball from the Thark ship blasted the starboard side of the ship. The gunner, gun, and the entire platform disappeared in a flash of splinters, smoke, and pink mist.

Chapter 18

"...inconvenience, as I have said, is only one aspect, and that the most unimaginative and accidental aspect of a really romantic situation. "

–All Things Considered

"Ladies and Gentlemen," said the loudspeaker, "we have begun our descent into the atmosphere of Mars. Thanks to the unanticipated gravity sling of the asteroid we encountered, we will be arriving nearly a full week earlier than our original manifest anticipated. We trust you have enjoyed your flight with us and will avail yourself of our services in the future."

"Wot if we didn't? Can we *swim* back to Earth, then?" shouted someone from the back. The passengers in earshot all laughed. Spirits were high, especially among those seated near Frances' chair.

As the ship descended and gravity began tugging at her arms and legs, Frances mused on how she'd changed in the past few months.

In addition to enjoying her newfound powers of self-defense, Frances realized that finding Gilbert had become almost secondary in importance. Tasting victory in the improvised boxing matches had awakened something in her, a desire for adventure and danger. Even now, buckled securely into her seat by her safety harness, she'd come to *expect* that excitement, to look forward to it more than she ever had a garden party or a croquet match. Gilbert had talked about such a feeling during his adventures, but nothing had prepared her to experience it herself. Yes, she admitted as the ship shuddered to its landing place. It was the *search* for Gilbert she now looked forward to, more than actually finding him.

And, in the back of her mind, so far back in fact that she could almost silence it, was a small, nagging worry:

What would she do once she found him?

Could she go back to the life she'd led, having seen and tasted this one?

And, most of all, what would she do if Gilbert didn't *like* her the way she was now? She no longer dressed purely for visual effect—more for comfort and practicality. How would Gilbert react if she didn't look as pretty as she used to?

The ship shuddered slightly and stopped her train of thought for the moment, as did more announcements through the speaker phone. They were near landing, the speaker announced, and it would be only an hour or so before they could disembark and see the surface of a whole new world.

A new world.

Possibly a new life.

The thought gave her prickles inside.

****

On the ground, many thousands of miles away from Frances' airborne ship, another young lady sat on an outcropping of rock, staring out at the Martian desert.

A dozen feet away was the entrance to a small cave. *Her* cave. It was a cave like thousands that dotted the mountains outside the human cities, but it was *hers*.

She'd decided to move to the caves a few months ago. After she'd arrived on Mars, she'd found life in the British colony unpleasant. Life was no better in the French, Belgian, and German settlements. In each place, she'd made a promising start that was quickly foiled by a corrupt local trying to grab land, power, or another man's wife. She would intervene and win justice for the good people in the town. Much rejoicing would follow.

But in each place without fail, after she'd won, she'd receive subtle hints that she should move on. People were fearful of her skill at killing. Despite her appearance, men were smitten and wives were jealous. Once a group of unhappy women had formed a small mob and pointed pistols at her.

She could have killed the lot of them, but didn't. They all had husbands and children. Besides, what would it prove? What could she gain? Each time she'd turned, left, and walked for many miles.

When she found the cave she'd moved in immediately, hanging a few curtains over a rock window opening and placing her bedroll on a natural shelf in the wall. She spent her first few days hunting and tinkering with a long-barreled rifle, a gift from a grateful farmer that she'd since refurbished with pieces of brass, iron, and steam fittings she'd stolen from shops or blacksmiths from other outlying colonies.

She'd never been caught while "borrowing." She'd been trained too well. But she did wonder how much longer this life could last. Odds were she'd make a mistake sooner or later, through either carelessness or weariness. And that might well be the end of her.

Well, enough about that! She'd survived, escaped, and settled. And finally settled in a place where no one was likely to give her grief, because she was alone.

Now she needed a new goal to focus on, to give her purpose.

Marriage? No. That was a castle built in the air without Cavorite. Not when she had only half a face and a hand made of steel and brass that could break rocks.

Vengeance? Again, no. True, she knew the Doctor was somewhere on the planet. But killing him would be like burning the boot of the man who'd kicked you. The real perpetrators who'd broken her life were literally worlds away, and that suited her fine so long as they stayed there.

What, then, could be her goal? For the first time in her life she was *truly* independent. But it had come at a terrible price, and now that her needs were taken care of she really didn't know what to do.

She was just reaching for her rifle to see if she could spot some game through the scope when she heard the engine of the air boat above her, and the sound of a cannon firing.

In less than a second she'd hid behind the rocks. She closed her remaining fleshly eye, then turned the brass half of her face to the cloudless sky. She touched a small dial on the mechanical brass side of her face, moved it up and then down, then held it in place with her finger.

Her artificial eye stared intently, red lights inside the brass iris glowing like bright embers as more power went to the magnifier.

She could clearly see now that the noisy speck in the sky was a Thark gunboat, flying at full height and chasing another ship through the air.

She spun the dial again, enlarging the boat and its crew until she could see the creatures' pale, green eyes and insectile tusks. They were excited about something, running about the deck of their craft like ants with a newly discovered piece of candy.

Just to be sure, she also checked the flags flying from the mast. The colors consisted of crude shape drawings on yellow burlap denim. No, they definitely were *not* the civilized Tharks from Carter's lot. These were savages, plain and simple. Killing one of them would save someone's life down the road, but did she want to draw attention to herself by sniping at them?

She was weighing the options in her mind when she heard *another* motor.

She searched the sky again and saw a second ship. Its occupants were human, certainly. The flag was British, beyond a doubt. She magnified further, and she saw a handsome sailor leaning with one bent leg on the prow of the ship, looking at the Thark ship through a telescope.

She looked closer. It was that *Belloc* fellow at the prow, now folding up his telescope, giving orders, and looking dashing as ever with a pepperbox pistol in each of his hands and an officer's saber in its sheath at his waist. He was running back and forth on the deck, giving orders as the ship swung around and pointed itself at the Thark ship! Maxim guns mounted on the prow of the British vessel fired at the Tharks, bullets largely missing the enemy crew but chopping the ship's hull and sails to splinters and rags.

She couldn't believe it! Now Belloc had them charging the Thark ship at *full speed*! He was going to ram them!

She looked closer at the British ship. The ship was steaming lopsided through the air, a wood-and-metal crater left where its Starboard gunport had been. The rest of the crew was...

She gasped, so shocked she let go of the dial on the side of her head and let the telescopic eye snap back to normal vision.

No! No, it couldn't be!

She focused again. It cost her precious time to do so, but she didn't care!

Three more seconds and she was certain.

Crouched behind Belloc was a crewmember very obviously out of uniform. He was wearing the brown coat and pants more common to a journalist than a member of His Majesty's Martian Armed Forces.

And with his lanky body, wispy blond hair and thick-lensed glasses, that crewmember could only be one person. The one person whom she'd hoped would stay on Earth and out of trouble for the rest of his life.

"Gilbert," she whispered, half in joy, and half in frustration.

Didn't he realize how *dangerous* it was up here?

She flipped a small latch on her brass faceplate to hold the magnification in place. Looking now at the Thark vessel, she took a deep breath and held it, counting heartbeats as she whispered one of the few songs anyone had sung to her during her childhood in a Canadian orphanage:

> *Little Tommy Tucker,*
> *Sing for your supper.*
> *What shall he sing for?*
> *White bread and butter.*
> *How shall he cut it,*
> *Without any knife?*
> *How shall he marry,*
> *Without any wife?*

After she sang the verse once, she paused, held up her rifle, and adjusted its scope until one of the bigger Tharks was very nearly lined up in the crosshairs she'd painstakingly etched into the scope weeks ago.

And she began to sing again. Squeezing the trigger on the last syllable of every second line, watching a Thark drop one second after each squeeze, and reloading right after.

She might never have the chance to talk to Gilbert again, but by gum, she was going to give him the best fighting chance any girl gave her man!

Her man...

No, she said, as she lined up another target, right after they lobbed a cannon ball that connected with the British airboat in a puff of smoke. *Gilbert is* not *your man*, she told herself between heartbeats and shots. *Gilbert deserves a live woman, one with a full face to touch his soul and two hands to hold his own. You're dead, Anne. Long dead. And it's better he keeps thinking that way.*

Chapter 19

"It is perfectly obvious that in any decent occupation (such as bricklaying or writing books) there are only two ways (in any special sense) of succeeding. One is by doing very good work, the other is by cheating."

–All Things Considered

B ack in Syrtis Major, the largest city on Mars and the flagship settlement of the human colonies, James Matthew Arnold Richardson was forty, balding, and bored. He was quite well-to-do by most standards, but that didn't stop him from being jaded about the banking business. Nothing new crossed his desk, and the money he made from his tasks no longer thrilled him as it once did.

He looked again at the bit of business on his desk right now. It was an odd one, consisting of several accounts in English banks and in countries in Spain, Holland, Switzerland, and Canada. All were linked by one cryptic phrase brought in to his office every Friday, no more than three minutes before teatime at four o'clock.

He had the agreement in front of him, the one that said what the passphrase would be, and the actions to follow if it was not delivered.

Sure enough, as he stood and stretched, there was a knock at the door.

He opened the door, and his secretary handed him an envelope without a word.

He opened the envelope as she closed the door, read the paper, and tossed it casually onto his desk. He lit his cigar and began to suck the wood-smelling smoke back into his lungs for a good pull, heedless of what the smell would do to his jacket and office for the next few days.

It was *quite* an odd bit of business, really. If the passphrase failed to show, he was instructed to make a series of telephone calls and make equally cryptic statements to whoever answered.

As it did every Friday when he received the message, thoughts ran through his head of what he could do with the money. The amount of money that hinged on his delivering that passphrase was phenomenal really. If pooled from all the accounts it affected around the world, it could buy an army or navy rivaling that of Britain herself. Even a fraction of that money could change the life of a very, very bored man...

He shook his head to clear it. Such thoughts had been more invasive, lately, but he had control over them, just as he believed he had control over his habits of smoking and gambling.

"ARCHIBALD IS MY BROTHER" screamed the paper in large, dark, unfriendly letters across the page. He mumbled it to himself as he tore it into two, then four, then eight pieces and threw it into the dustbin that was emptied every night into the furnace. He picked up his speaker tube, spoke the words into it, and closed it when he heard the single word "right" on the other side.

One day, he thought, as he gathered up his teacup without looking at or acknowledging the servant who'd brought it to him, *one day, whoever owns this little batch of accounts will forget to give me this passphrase. And when they do...*

A new client at the door interrupted his reverie. James breathed and readied himself, all the while wishing he was back in the cosmopolitan vibrancy of the city of London back on Earth.

The *Locust* closed the gap. As the ship shuddered under the latest cannon hit, Belloc shouted once more to rally the men. "Steady, lads!" he roared over the sound of the Maxim guns, belching fire and pouring streams of hot, leaden death at the Thark ship now just thirty feet away. Belloc's hand held his drawn pistol while his other hand drew the saber strapped securely to his side. "Steady! A few more seconds, then . . ."

The Thark ship roared as a cannon ball hurtled toward them, hitting the hull beneath Belloc's field of vision and making the ship heave to the Port side with a violent lurch.

"Sergeant!" yelled a voice from the back. "Sergeant Belloc! There's trouble in the engine room!"

"What kind of trouble, Negri?" Belloc said, more than a little annoyed that his speech had been interrupted.

"It's gone, sir! Along with most of the engine! The black gang's gone, too. The ship is lost!"

Belloc looked for only a second at the Thark ship in front of them, getting closer every moment.

"Well," Belloc said, "then it's time to get a new one! Trimsman!"

"Aye, Sergeant!"

"Use wind power! Keep us climbing and drop sails when I give the order!"

"Aye, aye, Sergeant!"

"Lads, the Cavorite's growing dim, but when it quits, we'll be right above them and ready to pounce. Remember, follow me, and leap three seconds after me unless you want to be flat as pancakes when we hit!"

"Hit?" Gilbert whispered to Budd, "Hit? We don't have anything other than Maxim guns! What are we going to hit another ship with?"

"Ourselves, Gilbert!" Budd whispered back. "He's using the Thunder Child maneuver. We're going to ram and board them, then…Wait, that's odd! I just saw one of the Tharks fall down. In fact—"

"Climbing to five hundred feet, Sergeant!" yelled the trimsman as he pulled lever and rope, catching wind currents to ride as their primary source of elevation faded.

"Cavorite's faded to half, Sergeant!"

"Steady, Lads!"

"Altitude dropping, Sergeant! We're at four-seventy-five!"

"Steady! Trimsman, steer so we're above them!"

"They're reloading cannon, Sergeant!"

"Steady!"

"They're aiming…wot? One of their cannon crew just dropped—"

"Trimsman! Drop us on their heads!"

"Aye, aye, Sergeant!" he yelled, banging on the delicate levers with both fists!

Gilbert was standing near one of the glowing green rocks at the corners of the ship. *Cavorite*, they'd called it. It suddenly winked out and went dark. At the same time, the sails dropped from the mast, the ropes that held them unreeling on their winches with lightning speed as the sails blew backward off the ship and into the desert.

When the sails flew away, Gilbert felt the ship drop down like an elevator, his stomach rushing up into his chest.

"This is it, lads! Ready in three…two…"

Belloc, looking over the prow of the *Locust*, ran forward three steps and leaped off. His arms were outstretched as if performing a high dive, the eight-barreled pepperbox pistol and saber in his hands pointed outward.

Gilbert looked over the side of the boat which Budd had called the "gunnel," and he saw the deck of the opposing ship.

Gilbert had seen aliens. He'd been up close to the squid-like creatures that had invaded Earth a few years before and lived to tell the tale. The squids had moved slowly, creeping like octopi, unless plugged into the machines they wore as a man might wear a suit of clothes.

But the monsters on the deck of the ship below were nothing like anything Gilbert had seen. They had bald heads with bulging, pupil-less, insect-like eyes and a mouth full of mandibles and tusks. Gilbert had heard about them before, but that hadn't prepared him for actually *seeing* them. They moved quickly, running around on two, powerful, man-like legs, along with four thick-muscled arms.

As Belloc leaped through the air and spun gracefully toward the Thark shipdeck, the creatures screamed as one with angry bloodlust. It reminded Gilbert of the war whoop of an Indian warrior who'd passed through town with a circus when Gilbert had been a small boy.

Belloc blasted his pistol while spinning gently in midair like a trapeze-trained acrobat. The eight barrels of the pepperbox fired rapidly one after the other, carving a lethal, bullet-holed arc on the enemy deck. Two Tharks dropped from Belloc's deadly aim, leaving a rough circle of open space to land in. Still falling, Belloc turned a somersault in the air, landed on his feet like a cat, bent his knees, and rolled like a baseball on a line drive to first base.

He stopped his roll at the talon-toed foot of a Thark. The green-skinned creature screamed through its opened mandibles and raised a pair of two-handed, giant scimitars in each pair of its hands, fully intending to chop the young Sergeant into quarters with them.

Gilbert watched with a kind of horrible fascination as Belloc, still flat on his back, thrust his own British-made saber up and into the unprotected belly of the Thark. The sword punched through with so much force that the blade popped out of its victim's green-skinned back quick as through a patch of emerald colored fog.

The Thark standing above Belloc stopped. The other Tharks stopped too. The creature that Belloc had just impaled was the largest on the deck. He also had the most decorative rings and bones fastened to piercings in his body, and Gilbert realized in a flash that Belloc had quite possibly killed the Tharks' leader.

For two long seconds while the *Locust* dropped downward, neither human nor Thark moved as Belloc's first victim paused to look at Belloc and then at the yard of British steel growing out of his stomach.

Sergeant Belloc broke the spell after less than a second, twisting his sword sideway while bringing his second pepperbox pistol out of its holster in a quick, deft movement to aim at the Thark leader's head.

BOOM! went Belloc's second, fully loaded pistol, all eight barrels firing at once with enough force to catch the Thark on its thick-boned forehead, flip its body backward off Belloc's sword, and make it flop onto its back on the gray-wooded deck.

Just then, the *Locust* landed on the Thark's body, crunching the monster's still twitching corpse while crushing a good portion of the alien ship's deck beneath it as well.

"CHARGE, LADS! CHARRRRRRRGE!" yelled Budd, leaping forward over the front of the ship as soon as the *thud* of the ship gave way to the sound of wood breaking.

The men had been transfixed by Belloc's performance. Budd's war cry broke the spell and they lunged forward, roaring and leaping over the prow of the ship with sabers waving and pistols blasting.

Gilbert followed them, barely a second behind the last sailor, the skinny fellow they called Negri. Gilbert roared too, holding his pistol with both hands, while the chittering shriek of angered Tharks mixed with the throaty shouts of men pounded in his ears. Somewhere behind him he heard the bellowing snaps of a still-firing Maxim gun as it poured leaden death onto its victims.

"FIGHT LADS!" Belloc bellowed as his sword flashed and flew. He stabbed another Thark through the belly, twisting the sword and withdrawing like a knife through soft butter as green fluid frothed over the deck. Gilbert watched for just a second while the creature stared down at his organs as they sagged and spilled out through the neat seam Belloc's sword had sliced in his midsection.

And then, the dying Thark started to laugh.

The creature's laugh was a chilling, freakish cackle that made the prickles stand up on Gilbert's neck, frightening him more than anything else he'd experienced since coming to Mars.

"GILBERT! LOOK OUT!" Belloc yelled, bringing a dagger up from his belt and flinging it over Gilbert's head. Gilbert turned and saw a Thark, four deadly looking swords in its hands, and a knife hilt growing from the place where it's left eye used to be.

Light green fluid flowed down its face as it staggered back for a second, then blinked its remaining eye and focused on Gilbert. The Thark's tusk-filled mouth shrieked, its head wound ignored as it raised its swords, stomped its feet on the broken, creaking deck and charged.

Chapter 20

"Turning over a popular magazine, I find a queer and amusing example. There is an article called 'The Instinct that Makes People Rich.' It is decorated in front with a formidable portrait of Lord Rothschild. There are many definite methods, honest and dishonest, which make people rich; the only 'instinct' I know of which does it is that instinct which theological Christianity crudely describes as 'the sin of avarice.'"

–All Things Considered

Captain Fortescue Williamson sat in the café and looked out at the masses of humanity as they wafted like living streams past his window.

Even here on Mars, his allowance was hefty enough he could afford this luxury of a private booth and a line of credit for anything he wanted in his favorite restaurant. He was thus spared having to deal with the smells and noises of common men and Martians alike, though unlike back home in Britain he could not be shielded from having to see them as well.

He sighed, looked at his watch and then at the calendar on the wall. Each day scratched off with a jagged line, as if drawn by a child with a crayon ticking off the school days before summer vacation.

He felt rather than heard the person behind him. Then he heard the faint, raspy breath and the dragging footfalls. By the time the shadow fell across his small table, he had no doubt who his visitor was.

"Hello, Daddy," Fortescue said without looking up.

"Fortescue," the voice said from behind, "we need to have a discussion."

Fortescue sighed again. As he'd been taught in etiquette class, he stood and looked at his father while gesturing him to take the seat opposite himself. He looked into his father's tired, sunken eyes, and wondered how long it was going to be before the old goat finally died and left him his share of the family fortune to squander.

"I've no time for trivialities, Fortescue," his father said while he took his seat. "Your past has caught up with you in ways both disturbing and fortunate, and I mean for you to make the most of both."

Fortescue tried to hide the pained look on his face as he sat down and faced the window again. "What now, father? Another need to teach a lesson to the magnates of the Belgian steel industry? Or perhaps you have another heiress you want me to marry?"

"Fortescue—"

"Or perhaps," Fortescue said, years of repressed rage began seeping into his speech, "perhaps buying me a commission in the Army and sending me thirty-five *million* miles from home wasn't far enough? Do you plan to send me *further* away to forget what an embarrassment I am to you? To Jupiter, perhaps? Or are there secret colonies on the ringed planet, now, too?"

"That you have been an embarrassment to me is a gross understatement," his father said, "akin to suggesting that the Crimean war was *loud*. It would be true, but the statement hardly does justice to the reality. Fortescue, I had you sent here to grow a spine, though it appears this method has failed like all the others. Now, *you will look at me* as I speak to you, boy," said the elder Williamson, using the commanding voice that Fortescue had never quite been able to bring himself to ignore.

Reluctantly, Williamson turned to face his father.

"That's better. Now, you were made quite the fool as a result of your pathetic conduct in Berlin last year. Allowing that Chesterton rube to gain the upper hand was completely unacceptable."

"The thugs I hired turned on me, Daddy!"

"They wouldn't have if you'd paid them on time! And you would have been able to do so if you'd kept your money in your pockets instead of using it to fill the purses of gamblers and women. Now, back to the matter at hand: I have an important venture to conclude here, after which I shall return to Earth permanently. You will join me, Fortescue, and then shall live the life of luxury and dissolute pleasure you've craved since you exited your mother's womb over two decades ago."

"There's always a condition attached to anything you offer, Daddy."

"I'm glad you are at last realizing the indisputable nature of reality, Fortescue. There are *two* prices, to be exact. First, Gilbert Chesterton is here on Mars as we speak. He must be eliminated. Second, you've already met with another rather annoying pebble in the shoe of my circle, a cretin by the name of Hilaire Belloc. Eliminate them both, and your commission in the armed forces will be cut short, allowing you to return to Earth."

"And just what business venture are you conducting this time, Daddy?" Fortescue said with an absentminded air, opening a snuffbox and stuffing two thumbfuls of the dark dust into his right nostril.

Fortescue Williamson Senior stared at his son and marveled at the capricious nature of power. He could affect the lives of millions with a gesture and a word, yet he could not make his own flesh-and-blood see his duty to the world with half the seriousness seen in the sons of butchers and blacksmiths.

"My business, dear boy, is *my business*. And mine alone. Never forget that."

Fortescue junior shrugged and took another thumbful of snuff.

"Fortescue," his father said, as he stood in the doorway, suddenly acting on impulse with his son in a way he'd never act in his other, more worldly affairs. "Fortescue, I have tried my utmost to mold you into the kind of person who could take over from me when I pass from this world into the next. I see now that I have failed."

Fortescue kept his eyes closed. "I've heard before how disappointed you are in me, Daddy. Is there anything else, or may I finish my brunch?"

"There is always more. Fortescue, it is time you accepted your responsibilities as a man of your lineage and breeding. You will succeed in your removal of these two individuals, and do so with all available speed, or I will no longer support you in any way, shape, or form."

Fortescue paused in mid sniff. The only thing that moved for a very long second was his left eye, as it opened and glared at his father.

He was just straightening himself and debating whether his father was bluffing when a street urchin, still dusty from the road outside, entered the room, and handed his father a note.

"What does it say, Daddy?" Fortescue asked, as his father unfolded and read the note, eager to change his father's focus and possibly forget his threat.

"Fortescue," he replied, as he finished reading the message, folded it into his pocket, and dropped a few coins into the happy little urchin's hands, "it would appear that fortune has decided to smile upon you even further. I will add one more task to your list of duties to be performed."

"Daddy, for your information, I already have ensured that this Belloc fellow will be taken care of on his next patrol. These green creatures are surprisingly easy to bribe with sparkly things, unlike those giant spidery men, or those slurring cat-things to the Southeast. As for that Chesterton fellow, I'm not sure I can pencil him in. I do have a job to do, you know! I am an officer in his Majesty's Armed Forces!"

"Yes, and I can well see the strain dear King Edward's demands were putting on you just now. Fortescue, you are a failure. My hope must now lie in the generation after yours. As such, after both Belloc and Chesterton are removed as threats, you will ensure our bloodline will not stop with you."

"And how do you propose I do that exactly, Daddy?"

"Frances Blogg," he said, holding up the note, "has landed on Mars. She disembarked from port not a half hour ago. You must win her heart, or at least her willingness to marry you and bear your children before you may return to Earth.

"Further to that, my dear son, it's come to my attention that you've been clumsily planning to engineer my demise, then resign your commission and hop aboard a steam-rocket home. I would strongly advise against it. I have several agents in place who are watching you close as hungry hawks in a winter field, and the minute you attempt to leave here without both young Chesterton and Belloc dead and Miss Blogg as your affianced, they will ensure that your blood will mingle, not with hers, but only with the red dirt of this forsaken place. Do I make myself clear?"

Fortescue now stood straight, his snuffbox placed on the café table and his eyes glaring at his father like two black chips of hate.

"Crystal, Father."

Chapter 21

"... as long as one is loyal to something one can never be a worshipper of mere force. For mere force, violence in the abstract, is the enemy of anything we love. To love anything is to see it at once under lowering skies of danger. Loyalty implies loyalty in misfortune; and when a soldier has accepted any nation's uniform he has already accepted its defeat."

–All Things Considered

1914 A.D.
Mars. German Colony of Wilhelm, Two Hours West of British Colony of Syrtis Major.

The trees waved slowly in the breeze, crowns of gentle green leaves whispering atop regal brown scepters that seemed to deign their gracing the forest with their solemn, yet benign presence.

Silence filled every pore of this part of the forest, in fact. It was a silence that seemed to gather all other sounds into its soft, leafy cushions.

It was a silence so complete that when the man's screams tore through the blood-spattered, now broken windowpane of the doctor's office on the forest floor, the forest itself seemed jarred by the intrusion. The trees seemed to shake their leafy heads in surprise, sending several flocks of birds soaring in feathered blobs of motion towards the pink sky.

"Tighten the restraints!" shouted a woman's voice.

" 'E's broken them, Miss!"

"Hold him down then, man!" she barked over her shoulder.

" 'E's too strong!"

On the table in the doctor's office, four men struggled to hold still the limbs of a man much larger than any of them. The large man screamed, lunged and thrashed, broken leather buckle-straps hanging from his wrists and ankles, all useless as torn party streamers.

139

And his screams only increased when his left arm wavered in front of his face and he saw the ruin his hand had become.

"Miss!" yelped one of the other men, trying to get her attention. If he'd been close enough he'd probably try pulling on her white lab coat like the children sometimes did. "Miss, what do we – oof!" The large man's remaining good hand cut the speaker off as a wild swing caught him on the nose.

"It's Doctor," she grumbled for what seemed the ten-thousandth time. She'd been the only kind of medical caregiver in the town for a decade now, and yet millworkers with wives and children who'd only been children themselves when she'd arrived still called her 'miss' instead of Doctor.

She put it out of her mind as best she could. She had to, now that she'd finished mixing and boiling the morphic powder in the mortar. The last dose should have been enough, but the big fellow on the table, the one they called Hercules, apparently had a reputation for rapidly shrugging off the effects of virtually any chemical in his system, be it alcohol or aspirin. Such a condition was quite the curse when your hand had been mashed by a millstone into so many twigs in a sack of flesh, and a chemical like morphine was the only thing that could block the pain as they cut off your hand to save your life.

Unfortunately she'd never learned this until five minutes ago. He'd only been a patient of hers once before the mill accident today. She wasn't sure if the 'treatment' she'd used to cure Hercules' insomnia back then still held sway in his head, hence the reliance on the concoction she was about to inject in his vein.

"Hold him still!" she barked over her shoulder as she poured the mixture from its glass tube. She poured with her right hand, holding the tube with her left. Her right hand would have undoubtedly been steadier, but its brass fingers had already broken far too many important pieces of glass in the past ten years. Expensive mistakes to make in a little one-sloat-town like this one, one too small to have its own glassblower.

There! The last drop was in, and this new dose was twice the strength of the last batch. If he floated back to earth before the operation was completed, she'd eat one of Mrs. Burgher's expensive hats for tomorrow's breakfast!

"Almost ready!" she said as the men continued to struggle and shout. She fitted the tube into the small steel syringe frame, with a plunger at one end and the needle in the other. Now, she thought, focus. He's too strong

and frenzied for you to do this without any chemical aids, and if you were
to use your last resort it would mean...could mean...

"Doktor! Fräulein Doktor!"

She looked up from flicking the syringe. She'd been tapping it with her
left index finger while holding it with the same left hand—no easy feat, but
far safer under the circumstances than using both hands when one of them
was made of brass and steel. As she looked she saw young Johann, seventeen,
tall and awkward, with a heart of gold and a schoolboy's adoration towards
her. In his latest bid to impress her he'd grabbed a nearby cord, secured
Hercules' arm to the table again and tied a new tourniquet on the soon-to-
be stump with a complicated knot, probably one his father had learned in
the Danish Navy.

Her eyes widened just a bit. With a German mother and a Danish
father, the boy had grown up with an accent thicker than Thames River
mud. Besides that, as an only child on a farm alone with his parents he
was more awkward around the female of the species than a sloat on skates.
But, by gum, for a change he'd just succeeded where the others had failed,
instead of the other way around! Maybe the boy could be a 'doktor' himself
someday.

Most importantly, he'd just called her Doctor. "Johann!" she said,
"Johann! Halten sie seinen arm, und ziehen sie die schnur fest!"

"Ja, Doktor!" he said, putting his knee in the bend of Hercules' elbow
and using both his hands to twist the cord tighter around the un-mangled
part of the big man's wrist. The action wasn't elegant, but it did make the
vein on Hercules' arm bulge out plump as the mayor's belly over his belt
buckle.

The remaining men piled on Hercules' other arm and feet. Even Mr.
Simmons managed to ignore his dislocated nose for a few seconds and join
in.

"Hold," she said, trying to aim the needle into the squirming, wormlike
vein, "Griff, Johann, griff! Hold him!"

She took her final aim, then launched the needle like a dart.

"Won't he need somthin' to bite on?"

The question came from one of the men holding Hercules, and at just
the moment needed to distract her and everyone else. And that moment
of distraction was just long enough for Hercules to buck his body like a
Midwestern bronco and throw Johann off the table. His body slammed her

in the side of the head hard enough that she dropped the syringe on the floor, where it broke with the sound of ice over air bubbles being stepped on in winter.

"Blast!" she yelled, seeing the last dose of morphine spread in a widening puddle on the floor, already contaminated by minuscule shards of glass and dirt from the boot steps of several confused workingmen.

Her patient began a new series of flailing spasms, screeches and wails, acting worse than children she'd seen suffer similar injuries with far greater bravery. Masking her disgust with professionalism, she leaped onto the operating table and straddled his chest, her knees pinning his arms down tightly as she grabbed his ears and stared into his eyes.

"Thomas!" she said, using her reluctant patient's Christian name, "Thomas, look at me now! Thomas, if you know what's good for you, you'll hold still and feel nothing until I've finished!" Thomas Atkins, known to his lifelong friends as Hercules for his girth and strength, went slack in all his limbs and fell silent. His eyes remained open with a peaceful look on his face.

As she climbed down from the operating table, she tried to ignore the stares the men were giving her. Young Johann alone looked at her without fear, but instead with an even deeper degree of love and adulation almost as annoying and unsettling as the reactions of the other men.

"Right," she said, trying to sound casual as she tucked a lock of red hair behind her ear, and grabbed a wooden bite-stick to put between his teeth just in case. She then tested the bonesaw on a nearby dowel of wood with one hand, and with the other grabbed the long-handled metal hooks she was going to need to pull arteries and veins out of the way as she cut into the flesh. "Now comes the easy part."

Long after it was over she sat alone in the back room of her office, nursing a glass of clear liquid. She looked out her open window as the pink sky faded to darkness, and wondered how long it would take for a mob to form outside her house with torches and pitchforks. Perhaps silencing a large, panicking man with a simple phrase wouldn't automatically lead to accusations of witchcraft, but who could be sure? The days of burning witches at the stake were long gone both on the British Isles and in America, true. But she didn't live there these days, did she? Nor had she for nearly twenty years. And though the town was usually calm, it had become an unexpectedly wild place on occasion, with a mob's bloody-minded rampage substituting for the word of law.

When the knock came at the door she darted to her hiding space, disappearing from her chair into the secret spot in the wall with less time or noise than it took to rustle the folds of her long, brown dress. She had a small, well-oiled pistol in her left hand, while her right hand flexed into a deadly, four-fingered fist of brass and steel.

The knock sounded again. It was polite, almost timid. She clicked over train schedules in her head and looked at the darkness outside. The last train had chugged away perhaps twenty minutes ago, and though it was an eight-minute walk from the train station to her office, the traveler could have come after a delay to ask for directions.

Perhaps it was an assassin.

But more likely, someone needed help.

"Come in," she called, looking from her hiding place at the mirror she'd set up on her first day in the building, the one that looked right at the front door.

She heard the doorknob give a clunky jiggle, and the door swung open soundlessly on hinges that Johann had oiled constantly. And for a fleeting moment she thought of all the other odd jobs young Johann had performed out of his misdirected affection, his wish for Anne to be something more to him than the local town girls could be. Such a shame she'd turned forty last month. If indeed Johann had been twenty years older, or even ten...

A man was in the doorway. A man older than Johann. And as he stepped into the office, she saw he was a man who, with those glasses and that gait, he was a man who could only be...

"Good, ah, evening," he said hesitantly, looking for another human being, "Good evening, Miss..."

"Chesterton!" she said, and launched herself from the hidden alcove, out of her room and into his surprised arms.

After spending a full minute in a blissful hug, they'd looked at each other through an awkward air filled with memories. Talk began and ended on clumsy notes several times, and after many such self-conscious moments they now sat, having a drink from the bottle of the same liquid she'd used to clean the bonesaw that hung in the case behind Gilbert's head.

"It wasn't as hard to find you as I thought it would be," he said. "On Mars, at least, people tend to remember a red-haired woman skilled in the *medical profession with an artificial right hand."*

"I'll accept that as flattery, for now," she said, smiling.

He was older, too. His once wavy blond hair was darker, and thinning. And the lenses on his glasses were thicker, along with his waistline. And his...

"Your heel," she said. "It's no longer bleeding."

"It usually doesn't, provided I behave myself." She smiled. He was different, yes. And yet, and yet. And yet he was Gilbert, still. The tilt of his head, the inflections in his voice as he summed up his life in the past twenty years they'd been apart, all of it reminded her of the boy she'd fallen in love with long ago, and hadn't seen since his wedding day.

"Now, I understand you've become quite the pillar of this community," Gilbert said, taking a polite sip of the strong alcohol while trying not to wince.

"Pillar isn't quite the word," she said. "More like the rusty doorframe on a house old before its time."

"You demean yourself unnecessarily, Anne."

"It's only unnecessary because everyone else has demeaned me enough already. Accurate nonetheless. A female doctor is unusual enough for them. One with a steamhand and even the faintest of inexplicable scars around her face tends to be whispered about in the same sentences as Maria Monk and other boogeymen."

"There seems to be some thankfulness on the part of a large fellow's family for a service you provided him today. He might very well have bled to death in less competent hands."

"You've already heard about that? You've only been in town a half hour."

"Perceptive as always. Well, thanks to the local heliograph gossips, I heard about it perhaps an hour after you completed the operation and shooed the menfolk out of your operating theater. More accurately, I overheard it on the platform from two fellows before I ever left Syrtis Major."

She chuckled. He chuckled too. He made a comment on how well the terraforming was going in this area of Mars, how earthlike the trees and grass had become in the decades since his last visit.

Then there was an awkward pause.

"Anne," he said. To her, twenty years of tenderness and thought sounded through that single syllable.

"Yes, Gilbert."

"Anne, I..."

"I said, yes, Gilbert."

"I haven't asked the question, yet."

"Gilbert, I've read every one of the stories you've published, from your accounts of Father Brown's adventures to Mr. Pond's little turns of phrase. You're the most prolific writer on either side of the Great Dark Divide, so for now, I'd like you to listen to one of mine."

She waited for his nod, and then continued. "I hoped and prayed for you to walk through my door for ten years after we parted. I never wished Frances ill, of course. But if, indeed, you found yourself able to love me lawfully, well, then, perhaps.

"After the war I felt it prudent to be where a person can be easily lost. And so, to Mars once again, where an honest person good at a trade can practice it unimpeded by unions, licenses or other bothersome regulations. I began a new life, and tried to give up hope of you actually seeing me as anything other than a phantom, the kind of woman who would appear and disappear at will, in and out of your novels and stories as I once did in your life. Even though I knew I'd never see you again, I began to go to bed at night asking God to at least let me dream of you. For Him to let me be, just for a little while, part of a world with you. Even if it was one that disappeared when I awoke.

"So, Gilbert, when you appear here, I can and must hope that you are now, in some way, free. And that you have a question to ask me, one that I've been hoping to hear, I will say 'yes' to your every entreaty, however awkwardly it may be spoken to me."

"I..." Gilbert began. "Anne I don't know what to say. I should say that, in truth, I do very much love Frances, still. However it would be an untruth to say that – well, I have often hoped for a glimpse of you, as you appeared when we were younger. I'd wake up some mornings, thinking to myself: perhaps this is the day I'll see her. Maybe she'll be on a random street corner, buying flowers. Or maybe I'll see her on a train ride. Or she might even pop out of a cave on the side of the road, rifle in hand and ready for action.

"But, Anne, the reason I am here is not to ask for you to join me in anything other than a last, necessary mission of travel alongside. And I am here to ask you to join me as a comrade only. Do you recall of what I speak?"

Anne took a drink, trying with everything in heart and head not to cry. "I do," she said, after the swallow lit up her throat and burned into her gut.

"I remember all too well. I had hoped what we'd seen that day when we were young was only a dream, a figment of our shared imagination. But as the years have passed I've had to try harder and harder each time I've looked in a mirror to lie to myself enough to convince me of that."

"We haven't much time, Anne. A few days at most."

"I can leave. I have no difficulty doing so."

"Anne, I'm so…so sorry. Sorry for everything."

She looked at his eyes, two brown orbs pleading for forgiveness that she'd given in her heart long ago.

"Gilbert, you and I were young, and working with the only tools our years had given us. Besides, who knows what the future might bring?" She tried to sound hopeful in this last sentence but her voice broke on the last two words, sobs starting slow at first then quickly becoming a torrent.

Gilbert set his drink down and rushed to her side, removing his glasses to his pocket and holding her in a fluid motion, his right hand holding her remaining flesh-and-blood left, his other hand cradling her head with its beautiful swath of red hair brighter than any sunset seen on Mars by man, even though it was by now shorter than he remembered it.

She sobbed for a long time, and eventually fell asleep on his shoulder. Before making himself comfortable with a pillow and blanket on her operating table (he'd truly slept in odder and more uncomfortable places), he placed her in her bed in her apartment behind the office, giving her one, quick kiss upon her forehead as she slept.

As she slept, she at last dreamed the dream of love and union she'd wished, hoped and prayed to have for so very long. It came in the form of a long walk through a park on a summer's day, with her man and two small red haired children with thick-lensed glasses playing ball with a dog.

Chapter 22

"The elements that make Europe upon the whole the most humanitarian civilization are precisely the elements that make it upon the whole the strongest. For the power which makes a man able to entertain a good impulse is the same as that which enables him to make a good gun; it is imagination. It is imagination that makes a man outwit his enemy, and it is imagination that makes him spare his enemy. It is precisely because this picturing of the other man's point of view is in the main a thing in which Christians and Europeans specialize that Christians and Europeans, with all their faults, have carried to such perfection both the arts of peace and war."

–All Things Considered

1892 A.D.
MARS. THE THARKIAN DESERT.

When the bloodied, frenzied Thark charged at Gilbert, he knew with mathematical certainty that he couldn't possibly defend himself against such a threat.

His life might very well be over, but he *could* go down fighting, and maybe buy some time for his new comrades.

He'd just brought his pistol halfway up to the charging monster when the thing's left knee buckled beneath it, spurting green blood and sending it crashing to the floor with peals of laughter.

Gilbert saw his assailant's knee had disappeared, the lower half of its left leg hanging on by a thread of flesh. There was no doubt that it would never walk again.

"Gilbert! Pay attention, man!" screamed a voice to his right. It was Budd, running around the deck like a small white comet while he stabbed and shot and dodged. Gilbert tried to run to him, both to back him up and to add a layer of protection in the crazy, shipboard battle. He took a step and almost fell, slipping in the thick pools and streams of red and green blood running freely now on the deck. Men screamed and Tharks laughed as crew from both sides fell in gory battle, with smaller, plucky humans blasting and gutting Tharks with strategic precision and Tharks falling on their victims and chopping them to death with hideous, rusty swords stained with red blood.

Gilbert heard another Thark scream behind him. He turned, trying to keep his balance while holding his pistol level. A Thark was charging at Gilbert, a small, bloody-bladed sword in each of his four green hands.

Suddenly, the Thark's gut exploded. It looked down at its ruined belly, organs hanging out like a series of distended jump ropes. Gilbert watched, horrified as the creature started laughing just before his head exploded.

The impact knocked the creature's newly headless body backward. Gilbert looked around. *Who had fired those shots?* But there was no way to know—there was simply too much chaos! Gilbert looked around for some kind of cover, someplace where he could be safe and take shots at the enemy while protecting those brave and skilled enough to fight in the open. Where was Budd? Where was Belloc? It was too difficult to tell anyone apart in the smoke, noise, metal clashes, and gunfire.

Another scream to his right, and another charging Thark fell, his neck exploding in a shower of green blood. *Who did that?* The shooter couldn't be on the deck. There was a ton of noise already, but the only bullets flying now came from the remaining Maxim gun in the rear. No single-shots to the head coming from those!

Yet another Thark dropped to the deck, a huge green hole in its chest. Whoever the shooter was, their bullets were chewing up any Thark unlucky enough to be on deck and in Gilbert's eyesight!

Gilbert spotted Budd again and ran to him, picking up a sword from the deck as he ran.

The smaller, spry Budd was holding his own surprisingly well against one of the smaller, squatter Tharks who nonetheless was swinging its swords with its four arms with deadly, savage ferocity. Budd blocked parry after parry with skill, though he was plainly tiring. Gilbert came up to the fight, flanking Budd's opponent and pointing his pistol at the gut of the Thark. He took a second to try and line up the shot, which was difficult considering how fast his target was bobbing and weaving in an effort to kill Budd.

Something caught Budd's eye. "Gilbert!" he yelled, "look to the Sergeant! Behind you—"

Gilbert fired at the Thark and missed.

The Thark, seeing Budd was distracted, lunged at Budd with its lower right arm and *didn't* miss.

Budd gasped.

"No!" Gilbert yelled as Budd dropped to his knees, his Thark opponent already laughing with his tusk-filled mouth opened wide.

Gilbert ran forward, screaming now with his own sword swinging wild, fury at the death of a comrade taking the place of skill or accuracy. The Thark paused, its other three arms raised to deliver a devastating killing blow on Budd when it heard Gilbert's battle cry. The creature turned to look at Gilbert and flipped over backward as a red mark appeared on its chest with a soft *smack*.

Gilbert turned to look again. He couldn't for the life of him figure out where those blasted bullets were coming from.

No time for that now! He ran to Budd. The shipman had fallen to the ground when his assailant had fallen, but the sword still stuck out of his front left side of his torso while he gasped for breath.

"Budd! Budd! Don't worry! I can help you here! I've done... I've done field surgery before. Do you have any silver nitrate?"

"Gilbert," Budd said, blood in his mouth and teeth, "Gil—Gilbert. I'm hurt... *Dear God, it hurts!*"

Budd's sudden screams mixed with the already chaotic battle around them, though the sounds of fighting on the ship deck were becoming sparser.

Suddenly a pair of filthy boots stood in front of Gilbert, caked with red and green blood.

"Gilbert," said a voice.

Gilbert looked up. It was Belloc. He looked stern, but not angry.

"Help me with him!" Gilbert said while Budd gasped. "He's wounded, but I think I can do something for him if we stabilize the ship, and..."

"This ship is lost, too, Gilbert," Belloc said, kneeling by them both. "We're going to hit the desert floor soon. Here." He tossed Gilbert a grimy, slippery rope that was attached to one of the masts of the ship.

"What's this for?" Gilbert asked.

Belloc looked behind Gilbert. Whatever he saw made him go pale as a bedsheet. "Brace for impact!" Belloc shouted, "Brace for—"

They crashed.

Chapter 23

"...I would make a law, if there is none such at present, by which an editor, proved to have published false news without reasonable verification, should simply go to prison...Two or three good rich editors and proprietors properly locked up would take the sting out of the Yellow Press better than centuries of Dr. Horton."

                                                    –All Things Considered

The bar in Syrtis Major hadn't seen much excitement in the last few weeks. There were the usual brawls on Saturday night, but for the most part the bar was a quiet place to get drunk fast and lose your money even faster at cards, darts, or shuffleboard.

As such, when Frances Blogg entered the place it caused a stir, the kind that sent ripples of gossip throughout the bar, the colony, and out far as the Belgian research teams at the base of Mons Olympus.

For it was unusual enough for a truly pretty and well-dressed woman to enter a bar in the Martian colonies. Such a woman usually had no reason to travel to the red planet, much less one of the colony's ill-reputed watering holes.

But while Frances was *both* a beautiful girl *and* well dressed, a few months of self-educated fighting had developed something in her. A facet to her personality had emerged that, while already a part of her temperament and emotional makeup, had been given no reason to bloom until this point in her mid-youth.

She gave little care now for the appearance of her clothes or hands. She was still obviously a lady of means and poise, but the fingers of her right hand had now been bandaged several times over. Her sleeves were worn and ripping in the elbows, and she walked with a calm, easy gait of a woman who wore only a single layer of underwear and leggings beneath her dress rather than the multiple garment layers typically worn by a woman of the upper class.

But most of all it was her *confidence* that made the heads in the bar turn. She didn't so much as *storm* into the drinking house as she *strode* into it with an air that she had a right to be in the place, and any who disagreed would be best advised to keep their mouths sealed tight.

"I require assistance," she said, once the room had silenced and she had the attention of all those present. She spoke from the center of the room, as she surveyed the fifty or so people at the bar, the tables, and the upper landing.

"What kind, my dear?" said the bartender, a man of fifty winters with the calm smile of a happily married man.

"I'm seeking a young man," she began.

"Lots a' them about, Miss!" shouted a voice from above. Guffaws sounded throughout the bar, and she had to wait nearly five seconds before she used the trick she'd learned in the book on public speaking to regain their attention.

She stood straight, arched her back, and surveyed the room with an air of business to be done. With an air of quick efficiency, she pulled out a small locket Gilbert had given her last year with his picture inside.

"His name is Gilbert Keith Chesterton," she said with a clear, firm voice, holding the picture up for all to see, "and I am willing to provide a good payout to the man who can bring me to him."

There was a pause in the room. Everyone had the same rough idea, but no one could really articulate it.

"Miss," said another voice near the bartender, a young man with wolf-like blue eyes and a curve-topped bowler hat, "your man, 'as 'e got a brother?"

"He has mentioned long-lost siblings to me, yes. A younger brother and older sister."

The wolf-eyed man smiled and looked around the room. Several of the patrons chuckled as if all in on the same joke. "Miss," he said, his eyes steady on her, "there's quite a few young men in this colony what could lead you by the nose and takes your flashy tin money without giving you what you ask. But I can say, I think I know who you could be lookin' for. There's a street urchin about what looks the spittin' image of your man there, an' 'e's got an older sister, too. My guess? If you was to find little Cecil, I'd say that 'e could lead you to the fella you seek."

Frances inhaled deeply and looked at the young man. According to one of the fiction books she'd read on her voyage, the black vest he wore over his long-sleeved white shirt marked him as having a high rank among the riff-raff types in the bar.

"Where, then, might I find this Cecil?"

"Well now, Miss," the man said, pushing back his black bowler hat and smiling, showing the gap of a missing tooth, "normally he'd find *you*, along with your purse and anything else you 'ad valuable. But I can take you to the docks where he's about to light out for the desert fringes, with his sister and that strange bloke who lives in the caves out West."

"I know nothing about 'strange blokes,' my good man. I care only about finding Mister Gilbert Chesterton. If you'll take me to this particular dock, I will be more than happy to compensate you for your trouble."

"This way, Miss," he said, offering his arm. She continued to stand straight, not responding to him except to continue looking in his eyes.

"Right," he said, still speaking in a happy tone, apparently unconcerned about the snub. He walked toward the door of the bar and held its swinging portal wide for her.

"Thank you," she said, as she exited, ignoring the chuckles and eyes of the men that followed her as she left. "Thank you very much, Mister . . . ?"

"Jimmy," he said, "just Jimmy, for now, love. Follow me, an' don't get left behind," he said as he started leading her through the crowded, jostling people and livestock in the streets of the city. "This part of town ain't the London Rookery, but it can get plenty rough for someone who don't know their way around a fight."

"Indeed," she said, as she followed him. She made a mental note to look up slang for "the Rookery" in her book on modern language. If she needed his services as a guide later, she'd have to gain his respect or he'd try to take advantage.

And she'd much rather gain that respect by speaking his language and dialect than by having to thrash him.

Chapter 24

*"A society is in decay, final or transitional, when common sense
really becomes uncommon."*

–GKC

"How much further is it, Doctor?" Beatrice shouted over the loud,
beating wings of the ornithopter.

"Another hour, perhaps," he said with a casual air. He, Beatrice, Cecil
and a few other passengers faced each other on two long cushioned
benches in the passenger section of the flying machine.

Beatrice was uncomfortable, but wouldn't say so. Like the other
passengers she wore a pair of clunky tinted goggles to shield her eyes
from the bright sun and flying specks of dust that the 'thopter's wings
kicked up. She also didn't particularly like their traveling companions
yet. The man opposite her was older and had peculiar, sunken eyes in his
head, almost as if the eyes had grown too heavy for his face to hold them
properly.

On either side of the man with the sunken eyes sat a pair of
unsmiling, dark-haired guards. Beatrice didn't even try to engage them
in conversation.

Through it all, Cecil sat quietly next to his sister. And though he seemed
to be looking out the window, he'd made a few judgments of his own by
the time the ornithopter had risen from the ground. Though he was a
cutpurse, Cecil did steal according to a personal code. He generally would
only steal if a) he and Beatrice needed the money, and/or b) his victim
could afford to lose the item, or c) his mark was a decidedly unpleasant
person.

Cecil had to mull his rules for stealing on the 'thopter ride to the site.
For now, he and Beatrice had no real *need* for money, though many of
their *wants* went unfulfilled. On the other hand, he was certain that their
fellow travelers didn't lack for funds and could afford to lose anything

Cecil would lift from them. His fellow travelers weren't dressed for a royal ball, but he figured he could dip into their pockets without fear of their going hungry later.

But tipping the balance was the snobby *attitude* of the folks traveling with them. The man with the sunken eyes seemed quite full of himself, uninterested in any conversation with Cecil or Beatrice. Cecil had no trouble dipping his hand into his pocket as they'd boarded the 'thopter without being noticed.

Unfortunately, his pockets were empty. He either had nothing or was so wealthy he had other people carry his money for him.

"What's the nature of the site?" Beatrice asked, hoping to make conversation as much as anything. They had been flying in this contraption for nearly a half-hour, and hardly anyone had said a word the entire time, giving the distinct impression that the young woman and the old man didn't give a care about anyone on board, and the Doctor seemed consumed by his own thoughts. She barely saw the pilot at all, a man in his thirties who kept his mouth closed, a cap over his head, and a set of tinted goggles over his eyes.

"It is a city," said the older man with the sunken eyes, his speech slow and distinct, with a relatively quiet authority that still carried over the sound of the engines. "A phenomenally *old* city that thrived when our civilization consisted of monkey-like creatures living in caves and mud huts."

"How very fascinating!" Beatrice said. "What have you discovered about it thus far?"

"We've found a ceremonial site," said the Doctor, his eyes looking forward, "one where we hope to harness certain…*resources*."

"One resource in particular," said the man with the sunken eyes, who turned from her and looked out the window again.

For the first time, Beatrice felt that coming out here hadn't been the best decision she'd made.

****

Hilaire Belloc's mouth was full of powder. Filthy-tasting powder, like the bottom of a sewer that had been drained, dried, sifted, and baked to a burnt crisp in the sun for a thousand years. He spit, spluttered, and then remembered why he was face down in a sand dune to begin with. He scrambled to his feet and looked around.

All was very, very quiet.

The Thark ship, masts broken and hull smashed in several places, looked like a ship on Earth frozen in the act of sinking beneath a red sea made of sand and rocks.

Belloc stood and staggered a little. It was difficult to breathe; he had to work to get the air into his lungs, inhaling deeply each time. Each breath felt like trying to satisfy hunger by drinking water, or satisfying thirst by looking at a picture of melting ice.

Nearby he saw another indentation in the sand the size of a person. One pair of shoeprints led away from it toward the broken hull of the Thark ship.

Belloc took slow, hesitant steps around broken wreckage and broken bodies, looking both at the tilted deck and inside the hold. Not a single human breathed, not a Thark stirred at his approach.

Once he reached the Thark ship, he scrounged and scavenged what he could, finding some foodstuffs in a cupboard and pieces of equipment.

Each time he found one of his dead shipmates, he put his hand on their shoulder for a few moments, shut his eyes tight and moved his lips silently in prayer.

When he was done, he took stock of his situation. Breathing was still difficult, not so much from the lack of oxygen as the stench of death, blood, and excrement.

In between his own efforts to breathe, he heard a single, small sound. Something between a gasp and a sob.

He heard it a second time, and then a third. Then multiple times in a rhythmic pattern, somewhere on the other side of the broken ship.

Belloc tried to move quickly but without noise through the piles of red dust, following the same shoeprints he'd seen earlier through sand that was thick and sticky as talcum powder in some spots and grainy as mountain dirt in others.

It took him a full minute to stomp-slide around the wreckage of the ship and find out what had been making the noise.

Gilbert was on his knees, bent over the body of Private Budd, who was lying flat on his back. Blood still flowed out of Budd's mouth and the wound in his side. Some blood had dried and caked on his cheeks, chin, and on his clothes, hands and feet, all from the sun's heat. Gilbert was leaning forward, his folded hands pressing over and over with full force on Budd's chest, nearly three times each second. Budd lay still and unmoving with each shove, the wound in his side still leaking blood around the wadded cloth Gilbert had folded up and pressed against it.

But Gilbert gasped and heaved with each press he made, pushing so hard on Budd's chest that Belloc heard the crack of the injured Navy man's breastbone after a few more presses.

Belloc stood, watching Gilbert, remembering a time not too long ago when he himself had been in Gilbert's place. He sat cross-legged in the dirt, lit up a battered cigarette he found in his pocket, and waited.

Gilbert seemed to take no notice of Belloc but continued shoving his weight onto Budd's chest. After a few minutes he lifted his closed fist nearly five feet into the air and slammed Budd's chest with full force.

"Come *back*, come *back*, come *back*, come *back*," Gilbert chanted, his eyes looking near wild as his closed fist flew into the air on the first word of his rhythmic chant and thumping onto Budd's chest at the second word. His speech was slurred, words escaping in hisses through gritted teeth and tears.

Budd's eyes stayed half-open and unseeing.

"Gilbert?" Belloc said quietly, more to make him aware that another person was present rather than to start a conversation.

"Don't *die*," Gilbert said without appearing to take any notice of Belloc, changing the words of the chant, but not its speed, intensity, or rhythm. "Don't *die*, don't *die*, don't *die*, don't... Sergeant Belloc!" Gilbert said, suddenly noticing Belloc, "do you have a Franklin rod? I mean, a Shocking Nancy? I saw someone's heart get started up again once with one!"

"No, Gilbert." Belloc said. "Gilbert, I think you need to..."

"Don't *die*," Gilbert said through clenched teeth, once again ignoring Belloc behind him, still looking intently at Budd while pounding the smaller man's broken chest with a closed fist.

"Gilbert," Belloc said, his voice now stern.

"Don't *die*, don't *die*, don't *die*, don't *die*. Belloc, shut up, shut up, shut up!" Gilbert said, his speech desperate.

Gilbert went on pounding Budd's chest with an unstoppable energy and focus that bordered on mania. Belloc, doing as he'd been told, waited while sitting cross-legged in the sand, kept nursing the cigarette that barely caught flame, and waited for Gilbert to run out of energy.

****

While trying to revive the downed sailor, Gilbert began to pray. He closed his eyes and prayed fervently, as much wanting his own sanity to stay intact as he wanted the friendly Englishman Budd to live, to do whatever it was God had made him for.

Something, though, felt different in Gilbert as he tried to pray. It felt awkward, *alien*. Like trying to open a door that had rusted on its hinges, and the resistance was fierce.

He'd felt something similar a year ago, after the floating city had crashed and Herb had shot him. But this was worse; then, he'd felt all the good his faith had brought was simply gone. Now, he felt actively pushed *against*, like he was trying to enter a house and the door was locked against him.

Gilbert kept trying though, in between the slams of his fist against Budd's chest.

Finally, Gilbert let out a small cry and collapsed into a curled-up position on his side next to the unmoving form of Private William "Billy" Budd.

Gilbert sobbed for several minutes, until he felt Belloc's hand on his shoulder.

Gilbert looked up. As if a veil had been lifted, he saw now that Budd had only been the last to die. The other sailors were strewn about like bundles of discarded clothes, bodies leaking red blood onto the red sand, limbs twisted into impossible shapes and contortions.

Thark bodies were everywhere, too. Rope-muscled arms and powerful legs lay twisted like tossed-aside marionettes. In some cases green jaws had been torn off heads, leaving strewn mandibles in grotesque parodies of the laughter they'd roared at others' sufferings.

Weapons lay scattered around the crash site, stained with both colors of blood. Thark swords mingled with English sabers, rifles, and pistols both single and multi-barreled.

Gilbert stood and backed away from Budd's still body. He'd quieted now, breathing deep and scrunching his eyes shut. He stood, still breathing. After a few seconds he swallowed, shook his head, and looked back at Belloc.

"Right," Belloc said, still standing over Gilbert. He flicked his cigarette to the ground while looking into Gilbert's eyes, as if taking stock of the taller boy, "you ready to move out?"

"What?" Gilbert said, tears streaming down his face. His voice was both angry and fearful. "Shouldn't we look for more survivors?"

"I did. There aren't."

Gilbert blinked. "Because we held that strap?"

"No. You and I lived because we hit big, red piles of soft powder when we were thrown from the ship. Everyone else was either killed in the fight or got broken on the rocks when the Thark ship hit the ground."

Gilbert looked at the base of the wreckage. Just as Belloc had said, the red shading at the base of the broken Thark vessel they'd boarded was darker, more solid looking than the lighter-colored grainy powder his feet were slowly sinking in.

Gilbert looked back at Budd, then off into the distance. "He died, Belloc. He seemed a good, good guy. It's just—there should have *been* something! I don't know, a bell, like they had at sunset where I went to boarding school at St. Albans! The bell went off at sunset, and you looked at the West and sang the school song, and then the whole sky looked like some kind of beautiful sapphire, and the ground looked like a giant emerald, and everything was beautiful! This isn't *right*! Their deaths— *his* death shouldn't have come like this! Not like this! Not so sudden, no warning, no chance for last words, a speech, a smoke, a kiss from your gal, something! How can a fella go on when he knows it could end *that* quick! Did *any* of them know when they woke up this morning that this'd be the end? The limit? If your life was a painting, then the brush was gonna hit the frame and you'd be over, hung up on the wall? A wall with—"

Belloc sat again and let Gilbert ramble for a little while. After a short time, he stood up and gripped Gilbert's shoulder gently but firmly and turned him around.

Then he slapped Gilbert on the cheek. Just enough to sting.

Then he grabbed Gilbert by his vest and pulled him in, their noses now less than six inches apart.

"Listen to me, Gilbert. Are you listening?"

Gilbert, off balance physically and otherwise, nodded his head.

Belloc turned him around again. "See that boat?"

Another nod.

"We're all on a boat, Gilbert. All of us. Rich, poor, strong, weak. And eventually the boat takes us home. We all get there, wherever we're going to be. Some sooner, some later, but all of us will go. And *that's* why life is precious. Not just because we die, but because we *know* we're going to die. We only get one, and that's why it's *infinitely* valuable. We have the shadow of death over us, even while we enjoy the sun.

"Now I've got to know, *right now*, are you the sort who's going to give up and die, or *live* one more day in the sun? Because if you're not, you need to stay here while I try to make it back and maybe send help. I might make it alone. Two *just* might make it. But I can't make it if I have to carry you, too, in any way. What say you?"

Gilbert thought for a few seconds.

"I made it through the sewers during the Invasion. I can walk across a little bit of sand and rocks."

Belloc smiled. "Right. Good answer. Gather up anything useful. We move out in the quarter hour."

Gilbert found a knapsack and a few pieces of the engine that could double as a club in an emergency. Belloc had already found most things that could be of use, including a rolled-up survival tent. All of it was folded neatly and packed tight into Gilbert's knapsack. While tightening his pack, Gilbert bumped a small pile of rotten-looking wood, which fell over and revealed a small pistol. It looked like hardly more than a decoration, and had just enough room in the trigger-loop for Gilbert's index finger and six small barrels in a miniature, pepperbox pattern.

"Not much more than a wealthy lady's conversation piece," Belloc said, "plunder from some other victim ship. But it might serve if the time comes. Ready to move out?" Belloc said, the sun on his right.

"Don't you need a pistol?"

"I'm armed, don't worry about that."

"You know where you're going?"

"Our patrol started North. We'll head due South. I have the compass from the navigator in my pocket. We should be fine. We were traveling for half a day and a night before we were attacked. We traveled at quarter speed—twenty-five knots, standard for a patrol around a colony's borders—for twelve hours. That means we've got a good three-hundred fifty miles of sand to eat before we get back to a warm bed and a roof."

"Kinda far in a desert, isn't it?"

"This desert is dry, but not hot like the Sahara. If we keep to a good pace of four miles an hour and walk twelve hours a day, we could make it in a week. Maybe less, really. According to this map I took from the *Red Locust*, we'll be walking mainly over a lot of flatlands. Heat in the day shouldn't bother us near as much as the cold at night."

"Fine. Last thing. What do we do about . . . um—" Gilbert looked back at Budd's corpse on the sand.

"Them? We have to leave them, Gilbert."

"Shouldn't we honor them somehow? After all, Budd, he died because of—well,"

"Because of you?"

Gilbert closed his eyes, swallowed, and then nodded his head.

"That's what he was paid to do, Gilbert. It's what he was *trained* to do. Understand? *You're* the civilian, *he* was the soldier. Honor him and remember him, and if you made an error today, you can redeem yourself. Don't make it again. It's what he would have wanted, right?"

Gilbert didn't answer, turning again toward Budd's body. "But can't we do something? Keep the critters away at least?"

"If you mean, 'how will we bury him?', the answer is we won't. We've got only a little food, and we'll need to conserve our energy. I already let you waste enough energy as it is trying to bring Budd back."

"Why'd you do that, then?"

"Easier than trying to wrestle you from Budd. Now stand up. Good. Everything working? Bend your limbs. Good, nothing seems broken on you, though those bruises will smart for a month if we get back to civilization. We're more distant from the terra-formed lands now, and you'll start feeling the lack of oxygen as soon as we start walking."

"I saw some pretty big dinosaurs back in Syrtis Major, Belloc. Will we have to worry about one of them eating us?"

"No, not at all. Our bodies are actually poisonous to the local fauna for some reason. Even Martian bacteria won't break down dead humans. Our comrades will still be here when we return— drier, but intact."

Gilbert tried to breathe, and, finding it was more difficult than usual, panicked just a little. "Breathing. It's—"

"Here," Belloc said, pulling something from the pouch at his side and handing it to Gilbert.

Gilbert looked at it, turning it over and around. It appeared to be a brass cylinder, with a screen at the bottom, straps on top, and a hollow triangular prism with one side missing attached to it.

"That's a *rebreather*, Gilbert," Belloc said, taking another out from his own pouch of scavenged items. Unbuckling the straps, he secured the rebreather snugly on his face. The hollow triangle covered his nose and mouth, and the cylinder dangled below the triangle, parallel to the ground. "See?" Belloc said, his voice made tinny from the hollow metal surrounding his mouth, "you can still talk, but be sure your straps are tight. It'll kick the sand out of the air that could get into your lungs and clog them up. It also sucks air into the filter and recycles it, so you don't have to waste energy pulling in air with enough oxygen in it to keep yourself alive."

Gilbert held the rebreather, turning it over in his hands. He felt a little silly putting it on his face, and Belloc had to help him adjust the straps and buckles behind his head so the brass facepiece fit securely. The triangle-shaped facepiece had a puffy, rubber lining that pressed onto his face and felt a little uncomfortable.

"You're lucky they packed these models," Belloc assured him as he patted Gilbert's head roughly. "When we first trained with rebreathers a few years back, it was straight metal and it cut into our faces. Hurt quite a bit."

"*Lucky*?" Gilbert said. The words were quiet, and they sounded ominous from behind the tinny sound of the mask.

"Gilbert," Belloc said, pulling a pair of brass goggles from his pack and stretching them over the back of his head, "you may not believe this, but as the world understands luck, you're a very lucky man indeed."

"What in the blazes can you mean?" Gilbert said through the mask, suddenly animated with the fresh filtered oxygen. "You call *this* lucky?" he shouted, waving his hands at the wreckage and dead bodies surrounding them. "I've had so many bad breaks in my life that I don't even know where to begin! Look at this, Sergeant Belloc! Look where we are!"

Belloc, his face hard to read behind the breathing mask and the goggles, handed a pair of goggles to Gilbert. "And where are we, then?" he said as Gilbert took the goggles and stretched them over his face.

"I'm surrounded by dead bodies, one of whom was one of the nicest fellas I ever thought I'd meet! And I think he died taking a gut wound *for me*! I'm stuck in a desert, tens of *millions* of miles from home!"

"Gilbert," said Belloc, shrugging his pack onto his shoulders, "you are missing the forest by looking too close at a few, sickly trees. *I* know where you are, Gilbert. You're in the land of the living. And after a fight like this, that makes you very, very lucky indeed."

"I wonder," Gilbert said ruefully as he adjusted the straps at the back of his head, trying to keep the goggles from cutting into his flesh as much as the mask's straps had been a few minutes ago.

"Would you mind being in England, *right now,* if you were in the Rookery, Gilbert? Or would you complain about the dirt and the smell?"

"What kind've question is that?"

"Right," said Belloc, who turned on his heel and started walking away.

"Hey!" Gilbert said, quickening his pace to follow Belloc. "Where're you going?"

"Someplace safe."

"Where's that?"

"A place more wretched than the Rookery. But at least any foes there have fewer arms than our last batch did, and they don't complain as much as you."

Chapter 25

"England is really ruled by priestcraft, but not by priests. We have in this country all that has ever been alleged against the evil side of religion; the peculiar class with privileges, the sacred words that are unpronounceable; the important things known only to the few. In fact we lack nothing except the religion."

–All Things Considered

1914 A.D.
MARS. GERMAN COLONY OF WILHELM, TWO HOURS WEST OF BRITISH COLONY OF SYRTIS MAJOR.

"*You brought Flambeau up here?*"

Anne, now fully awake, very nearly dropped the strong cup of tea she'd been drinking with her eggs and bacon. Now over forty years old, she was frequently more concerned about the quality of the food on her plate than the state of the greater world. But today was different. Today, she didn't care if the eggs and meat Gilbert had cooked for breakfast came from a chicken, pig, or a sloat. She was only bowled over by what Gilbert had just told her, though granted it wasn't nearly as odd as waking up and seeing a man cooking. Gilbert had even tucked a dishtowel neatly into his waistband, and was using it as an improvised apron.

"Yes, Anne. I felt it prudent to bring the holiest priest I knew on this little venture. That he's also a good friend, godson of Father Brown and tough as nails from serving as a military chaplain during the War are all little added bonuses, I must admit."

"During the War . . . tough as nails . . . he wasn't at . . . ?"

" 'By God, they shall not pass'. Yes, he was at that bloody business at Verdun. One of my old fans was there too, in fact. Did you ever meet that little boy in the floating city? Little John Tolkien? The one they called Tollers?"

"I . . . yes, yes I remember him. Did he live?"

Gilbert looked at Anne for a moment while she stared at her tea. "Yes, yes he did. Wounded, but he lived. He's readying himself for a career teaching literature, now, I believe. He and his stepbrother, Jack made a good chunk of tin with their fictions, and now both seem to be Oxford bound as professors."

Anne stared out the window.

"Tollers...actually, Captain Tolkien now," continued Gilbert, "distinguished himself for bravery, apparently holding some kind of stone bridge with his men against a rather enormous and infamous land ironclad named the Cruel Demon, or 'Baal-Rog.' Jack didn't get quite so many medals, but he got his share of fighting done in the trenches over in..."

"May we please discuss something else?"

Gilbert finished scooping the last of the bacon from the cooking pan onto a plate, mopped up the excess grease with a blotting towel, and served them on the table in the awkward silence.

"As you wish," he said with a curt tone, sitting opposite her, then taking the dishtowel from his waistband and turning it into a napkin at his neck.

"How . . . how is your brother doing?" Anne asked, trying to change the subject.

"He volunteered his services as a soldier in the War, after he published the fourth of his popular histories. He was wounded three times in France, reenlisted after each recovery," Gilbert said, stuffing a forkful of eggs into his mouth, "and died at Verdun."

1892 A.D.
MARS. BRITISH COLONY OF SYRTIS MAJOR.

"And this is where they left from?" asked Frances, looking at the gray dock. It was only ten years old, but the desert winds had made it look weathered long before its time.

"Yes, M'lady," Jimmy said. He looked with an uncaring attitude into the distance, but his natural head for languages had also given him an ear for deciphering tones of voice.

Most recently that talent had saved his life. It had helped him hear the disdain his captors held him in, and from that he'd discerned their plans to kill him once they were done with him.

Jimmy wondered if they'd found the bodies yet.

The only survivor would have been the creepy bloke that had left Jimmy for dead after trying to strangle Jimmy with his tentacle.

Jimmy shuddered a bit. That same piece of walking slime had always called himself the Doctor. Jimmy had never trusted him, even back on Earth. He'd been very relieved when the Doctor had stopped coming around, and that sweet little redheaded treat had started giving Jimmy his assignments instead.

But the last assignment Jimmy had gotten from that crew had been directly before the Martian mollusks started turning London into a giant ash heap with their death rays. Jimmy had no doubt the job and the Invasion had been related; the redhead had told him to spend his pay from the odd translation job as quickly as he could. And it was only because he'd bought a train ticket to the countryside in a drunken stupor that he hadn't been burned alive like everyone else in his neighborhood.

Now the Doctor was mixed up with the Chestertons. Who were somehow connected to this obviously wealthy but not-so-easily hoodwinked young lady, who wasn't that much younger than himself.

"Ma'am," he said, "they all left from 'ere. Young Cecil, his sister, the Doctor an' a few others I didn't know from a 'ole in the wall. This is the only dock out to the wildlands."

"And you're certain they aren't in town?"

"If they were, Miss, young Cecil would've lifted your purse from your shoulder without you even feeling it. An' maybe your petticoat, too, if you wasn't looking too close."

"There's no need to be vulgar, Jimmy."

"'Ere, now, who's being vulgar? I'm just tellin' the truth. I seen him once swindle the shoes off a man's feet in a card trick. Another time, he got a sober man to hand over his billfold, just by askin' him and acting like 'e had a right to it. The boy's got a gift with words, Miss, an' if young Cecil were in town, he'd have had your money by now, guaranteed."

"Lovely. Where could they have departed to?"

Jimmy hesitated. Frances's eyes grew sharp.

"Answer me, Jimmy."

"Miss, I, well, I know this is about your man, an' all, but, well, there's people involved in this wot tried to kill me, more than once. Makes a man a tad reluctant, savvy?"

"Jimmy, the more I listen, the more I learn this is certainly not *only* about my man. It's also about people who have worked rather tirelessly to gum up Gilbert's life, which means they have sabotaged my life as well.

"But I certainly understand if a man needs more *rewards* offered when a job becomes hazardous to complete. I have money for your expenses now, Mister Jimmy," she said, digging into her purse and then handing over his exact payment, "and I should like to retain you in my employ as I leave these docks and search for my man. But I need you to tell me *where they have gone* before I give you a red penny more."

Jimmy knew to say yes. He'd be getting more money, and possibly a chance for revenge on his old employers. Moreover, please God, if he manipulated little Miss Frances here he stood to make enough flash to go home to Earth and get very, very drunk.

Although, of course, not necessarily in that order.

"Well, Miss," he said, inhaling deeply, "I might 'ave a good idea as to where they went. But we'd have to charter ourselves a vessel to get there, now."

"Money isn't the issue," she said. "I'll pay you double what I just did, but not until I'm holding Gilbert's hand in mine. Is this a suitable arrangeme— I mean," she cleared her throat and stuck out her hand, "do we have a *deal*?"

She said the last word like a student of a foreign language trying out a new phrase for the first time. Jimmy almost had to laugh. It was obvious that where she was from they would have talked about *arrangements* instead of *deals*.

Still, at least she was *trying* to respect him. That was more than the Doctor's crowd ever did.

Plus, she'd offered to pay him extra.

"There's a city, Miss," he said after shaking her hand and trying hard to look reluctant to speak, "a very old one, old even as Martian cities go. Most of it is beneath the sands, but they've got one part dug out. I 'ave to say I was almost killed for finding it, but I'll still help you get there, if your word is good and I get paid right enough. While a sand sloop ain't near as quick as the ornithopter that young Cecil and comp'ny left in, they'll get us there right quick enough, I'll wager."

"You will commandeer a vessel for me," she said, looking out at the red sands dancing in the wind, "small enough for a crew of two. Ideally a flying machine, but a sand ship will do in a pinch. And then you will give me the heading as to where they would have gone, the nature of this city you say they've gone to, and the nature of our adversaries in general. And," she continued with an air of near regal self-assuredness, "you will do all this in one hour, if indeed you hope to secure terms of employment that are—oh, excuse me, *if you want to make as much flash for this leg of the jump as you have so far.* Is that clear?"

"Crystal, Ma'am."

Chapter 26

"...the two things that a healthy person hates most between heaven and hell are a woman who is not dignified and a man who is."

–All Things Considered

The young man's face wasn't its usual placid self. No matter what disaster was about to strike—surprise army attack, sloat stampede, impending starvation, the list went on—he'd always annoyed the daylights out of John Carter and anyone else with him by tilting his head so slightly he thought no one else could notice, listening to that little voice no one else could hear, and coming up with an idea that, insane as it sounded, always, always brought the group to success in their mission and safety afterward.

Well, brought the *survivors* to safety, anyway.

"John, what are you saying to me, here?" Emrys said.

"I'm saying, Ambrose—"

"Emrys."

"Picayunish. Have it your way. I'm saying that they've gone off into the belly of the beast, and that's where we need to follow them."

John Carter, former confederate soldier of Earth, who hadn't looked older than thirty since the Civil War (or the War of Northern Aggression, as he insisted on calling it), seemed to be working very hard to suppress a smirk.

Emrys looked again at Carter. He tried again to blow and shake the lengthening locks of dirty blond hair out of his eyes while struggling to carry the seven or eight scrolls and parchments he'd rolled into cylinders and not look like a total buffoon in the process.

"Look, John," Emrys said, trying fruitlessly to get a better grip on the scrolls, "it's one thing to casually dispatch one of their operatives. Goodness knows you're proficient at *that*. But I don't think you appreciate the gravity of the situation here."

"Oh, Ambrose," John said, turning from his scholarly roommate while twirling his sword and fighting an imaginary opponent in the middle of the dingy apartment's living room, "if there's one thing I *do* appreciate here, it's the gravity of the whole *planet*. Mars' gravity and the added strength it gives me is precisely the reason I didn't end up food for a Thark raiding party my first week out here."

"Yes, well, your added strength isn't something any other earthling enjoys, along with your odd eternal youth and memory lapses. As for the Tharks, they're a petty threat compared to what those evil creatures from the Special Branch or the Circle or whatever they're calling themselves now, are dickering with. Have you even the slightest clue what I'm discussing? Have you learned *nothing*, in all your decades here, of the *real* power that rules here on Mars? The power that's *always* ruled here since this planet was a ball of unsettled red dust circling the sun?"

Carter paused in mid-sword thrust. "My dear man, you know as well as I do who the power groups are. The Red Men fight the Green Tharks, and until recently those ghost-white Martians actually fed on both groups from time to time. And the Black Martians, in turn, fed on the White ones, until *I*, of course, exposed the whole silly game, and—"

"John," said Emrys, setting the rolled scrolls down on the nearby table and then waving his hands in a dismissive air, "you are an extraordinary warrior, one who cares deeply for those who love you. But in all the battles you've fought, you've never effectively learned *what the real power is* behind Mars. Have you never wondered *why* the seabeds dried up? Or just *why* the old cities died and are just refuges for white Martian apes now?"

"Hmmm...," Carter said, now stretched out on the couch with his hands folded behind his head and the toes of his boots pointing at the ceiling. "No, dear professor Emrys, I cannot truthfully say the concern has crossed my mind. I've been too busy kicking low and evil creatures off this world."

"John," said Emrys, speaking as one would to a foolish child who'd been allowed to believe in Santa Claus far too long, "what kind of conditions can cause the changing of climate and geography on a planetary scale?"

"Too many people? Or too many factories? Perhaps too many cows excreting on the same landmass?"

"John, be serious, would you? Even billions of people couldn't affect a planet billions of years older than they, not when they've only been about the place a few tens of thousands of years. Only an idiot would try to pass that off as science."

"Your scientists in England believe in eugenics and other evil, idiotic things, Emrys."

"Be that as it may, Mars would have healed *itself* long ago if its humanoids were the problem. Try again."

"Perhaps the sun? Something affecting Mars's orbit?"

"Better, but still wrong. If something about the Sun had changed, wouldn't *Earth's* climate and orbit have been significantly altered as well?"

"Oh, true. I hadn't considered that. Well, then, Emrys, I give up. What's the answer?"

"You are the worst kind of student. If you were in any of the classrooms *I'd* been schooled in, the schoolmaster would've given you a dozen lashes for giving up. But I've no time to engage in the futile exercise of expanding your knowledge. Now, consider this: No matter how much a child loves his father, he's often reluctant to wake said father early in the morning. Why?"

" 'Cause a pappy don't like to be disturbed during his rest," John said, exaggerating his Virginia accent. "Of course! No matter how beloved a son may be, a boy has to learn that such conduct typically results in the tanning of one's hide."

"Good, John. A few cells of gray matter remain between your ears yet. Now, what if that father were asleep, and some foolish *stranger* of a child came into his bedchamber. And this child not only *woke* the father, but thought they were powerful enough to *control* and *command* him, too? What then?"

"I'd say a boy like that would be a complete idiot! Any man woken by a stranger would throw such an intruder out the door, with a good stiff boot to the backside besides."

Emrys realized he needed to set down his load, and set his scrolls gently on the nearby table. He pulled out one of the parchments and unraveled it on the floor of the apartment, adjusting his thick-lensed glasses and pointing at various locations on the crude map drawn on the scroll. "You've thus far maintained your perfect score on your oral examinations, John. Now, answer me this for the prize ribbon: What if that father was powerful enough to destroy life on a world of teeming billions? And what if that father never slept to begin with?"

John looked at the scroll and broke out in a sweat.

"I know that place," John said, pointing to a section on the map. "I've been there. It's ancient and it keeps the air going. The last time it broke down, the whole planet nearly suffocated in three days. I barely got it working again, but that was only because—"

"Because-you-*nothing*. You had help, I'll wager. A lot of things went right at just the right time, didn't they? And you probably credited it to your superior strength, or how the Red Martians can't read your mind like they do each other's, or your phenomenal luck, hmm? I'll tell you why, John Carter: That facility is far, far older than you suppose. It's just on the farthest outskirts of a city beneath the sands that not even your princess wife knows about. There's an entire metropolis under those flying red sands that's older than anything Martians of *any* color can fathom, and in the center of that city is the closest thing to God that you will ever see on this rock aside of the holy Sacrament itself!"

"Emrys," John said, now sitting up with a serious face, "Discussion of religion aside, I was here on the Red planet long before you, Edison and his little group, or even Professor Cavor ever set foot on Martian soil. How do *you* know about this place? And where did you get this map?"

"John, where I got this map isn't important. As to how I know about the city, the answer is that I've *been* there. I went on *my* first visit to this place. I *saw* what happened when men tried to tangle with beings more powerful than Olympian gods. And I've spoken to men who *know* what it is to stand in the presence of something terrifying, not because it can kill you, not because it hates you, but because it truly *is* greater than you, the way a massive waterfall or an earthquake can destroy you without a qualm or thought if you forget to respect its power."

John Carter still looked skeptical.

"John," Emrys said, now looking the warlord in the face, "have I ever lied to you? Have I *ever* given you reason to mistrust me?"

"Emrys, your strategy brought down the Mollusks. I did the fighting and Thomas Edison made the machines, but you were the one who knew where they'd be, when to strike and when to retreat. We'd have been dead several times over had it not been for your insights. But still, Emrys! You're talking about a place that *Martians* steer clear of. And something powerful as you describe, why doesn't *everyone* know of its existence?

Why don't the Reds, Blacks, or Whites talk of it?"

"Why indeed. If you live next to a waterfall all your life, you cease to hear it roar, don't you? That place is camouflaged *precisely* because it's been here and a part of everything so long, no one even thinks to question its existence unless they're new here, like us. Or like me."

"Or they have lots of spare time on their hands like you do."

"Don't be caustic, John. It doesn't suit you."

"Better than being the kind of man who stares at pictures all day."

"Goading me because you're jealous of my intellect suits you even less. And it's less effective besides. Where were we?"

"The races."

"Oh, yes. Them. Aside of our cousins here, do you ever do business with the...what do you call the....?" Emrys' tongue formed a word in Martian that John could never quite speak accurately.

"Those eight-foot tall fish hunters? The ones who look like two-legged otters? They are indeed a peculiar sort; never bothered with them much. We've got nothing they want."

"And the [Martian word again—how the devil did he do that?], John. The ones with the long, spindly arms and legs you call the Spider-men?"

"Same thing with that bunch. We've got nothing they..."

John waited, the sentence in the air hovering for a second.

"Wait—wait a second Emrys, now, let me see if I have this straight..."

"Have you noticed, John, that the races *you've* befriended here and *can* trade with are *all* human-like? Have you wondered *why* the otters and the spider-men and the races so *un*-like men are so self-sufficient?"

John, his voice tinged with the slight fear of realization, looked out the window. "No, Emrys. I was always more worried about making sure our tribe of Reds beat out the other tribes of Reds. Then to deal with the Tharks, then the Yellow men by the polar caps, then the Whites down by the river Iss, then the Blacks who were feeding on the Whites..."

"Return to the otters and the spider-men, John. You had *nothing* that lot wanted. The humanoid tribes were so busy all fighting each other, none of you never looked behind the curtain to see who was pulling the strings. The Mollusks have been here longer than you think. And farming humans for a much longer time than the Special Branch have had their arrangements with them."

"The humanlike races here on Mars...they're so humanlike because they're..."

"Because *they are human*, John. Why do you think they took to Christianity so easily when you showed them what their religion of the river Iss was really all about? Why do you think you and a red Martian Princess can have children together? Pure chance? No, John. The Mollusks took humans from earth thousands of years ago, adapted them to this terraformed place, and later, when Edison came here, decided to take more pure strain humans from Earth for their experiments."

"What about the Tharks?"

"If they pulled the humans here, perhaps they pulled other races, too? I've not deciphered their language enough. But look here, John. The whole reason the otters, the spider-men and the rest of them don't trade with you isn't because of a language or culture barrier; I met them my first time up here. They're *unfallen*, John. They can see the spirit world as easily as you or I can see clouds in the sky back home. And since they *are* native to this place, it's not hostile to them the way mother nature is to us back home. Hence their not needing or wanting *anything* we make or offer."

"Why is that so important? Don't misunderstand, it's interesting, to be sure. But what's that got to do with what your English friends are digging about in the desert near the air filter?"

"Because *that's* where—oh, hang it all! Look how far the sun's gone! I'm going there right now, and you can either join me and I'll explain on the way, or you can stay here and harass purse-snatchers like little Cecil. What's it to be, John?"

John stood and sheathed his sword and smiled wide. "Another adventure, Ambrose? With enemies of heretofore-unknown power, perhaps awakening a slumbering giant who can destroy my adopted world and all I hold dear in it? Why are we still here?"

"Stop calling me Ambrose, put your shirt on, and charter a few sloats for the Northeastern desert. And do you think we could *please* leave this city *without* getting into another brawl?"

"Doubtful," John said with a smile.

Chapter 27

"The morals of a matter like this are exactly like the morals of anything else; they are concerned with mutual contract, or with the rights of independent human lives. But the whole modern world, or at any rate the whole modern Press, has a perpetual and consuming terror of plain morals."

–All Things Considered

Gilbert looked at the expanse of red, powdered desert sand around him and wondered just how Sergeant Belloc could stand to live here for as long as he had. The fellow didn't seem all that older than Gilbert was, but whatever charm Mars could have had for Gilbert evaporated with its seas millions of years ago. Gilbert quickly figured out why Belloc didn't complain— the fellow seemed to have a stubborn streak, the kind Gilbert had only ever seen in a child throwing a tantrum or an elderly military man.

"Where are we bound for again, and how much further?" he said between breaths, his voice made tinny-sounding by the brass-and-rubber triangle that covered his nose and mouth.

"I took a closer look at the map. There's a settlement a number of miles from here on this heading," Belloc said without turning his head. The rebreather mask muffled his voice and Gilbert barely heard him. "If we maintain this and don't waste our filters with unnecessary conversation, we should make it in a few days instead of a week."

"How long can these rebreather things last?"

"That depends on the make and model of your rebreather. If you have a Mark-Two, you'll be dead before the next sunrise, clawing your throat and trying to keep your eyeballs from bursting. If you have a Mark-Four, then you could follow me for a month and be fine."

Gilbert stopped walking, held his breath, slipped the rebreather off his face, and started frantically searching its surface. Finding something, he slipped it back on and began sucking air in again, trotting to catch up to Belloc who had never slackened in his pace.

"The bottom of the cylinder said that I've got a Mark-*Three*! What's that mean?"

"It means," said Belloc, without a trace of concern, "that you have a chance to make it, Gilbert. A slim chance, but it's a chance nonetheless. The only way a Mark-Three can make it as far as the town of Danton's Folly before the rebreather runs out is if you keep to a very strict regimen. Can you do that?"

"Sure!"

"Fine. The only way you'll make it is if you keep pace with me, *and don't speak at all*. Understand? Not unless I speak to you. Not a single word, Gilbert. Each word you say drops a second from your time with your rebreather. Every sentence shortens your life by a minute, every conversation like this by an hour. And you *will* need all the hours you can get, I promise you."

"But . . . but how come *you're* talking then?" Gilbert fell back into step beside Belloc, almost having to jog to keep up with the soldier, despite having longer legs.

Belloc, his eyes still forward, shrugged. "I'm the ranking NCO on this mission. Ergo, I've got the Mark-Six. I can talk until Christmas, if I have to."

"But . . . but I . . ."

Belloc kept moving. "Talk or live, Gilbert. The choice is yours. *I'm* going to get there. It's up to you if *you* want to come with me."

Gilbert stood in place, his hands balled into fists, frustration at being silenced when he felt he had a *right* to speak fighting with his sense of self-preservation and...

Independence.

That was it. He was *independent*! He was an *American*, by golly! He had a *right* to speak! He had a *right* to turn his every opinion into an editorial, beloved by thousands! He had a *right* to say just how angry he was about this situation, and how unfair it was! How *dare* that soldier treat a civilian this way, when Belloc's very *reason* for working, his *job*, was to defend civilians like Gilbert!

And, more to the point, Gilbert thought, silently following Belloc's lead, this sergeant's flagrant refusal to give Gilbert the better model of rebreather was doubtless a violation of . . . of *some* law, *some*where! He was sure of it!

Gilbert kept on ruminating about the scathing story he was going to write about one Sergeant Belloc, and got quickly wrapped so thoroughly in his thoughts of dire vengeance that he never noticed the smile in Belloc's eyes, or the chuckles he barely stifled as they rounded the crest of the hill.

****

She'd watched them crash, the bodies flying from the deck of the Thark ship like dust from a slapped saddle. She'd bit her lip and said the most desperate prayer for his safety since she'd landed on Mars.

She'd watched through her eyescope for nearly ten minutes. When the slightest movement danced across her field of vision, she brought up her riflescope to augment her sight even further.

First, she saw Belloc stir in the wreckage, then rise and begin inspecting fellow crewmen for signs of life. Finding none, he walked around to the back of the ship. She was just about to disassemble her rifle and start the journey toward him when he emerged from behind with...

Her heart jumped.

Twice.

It was Gilbert!

After seeing he was alive, she thanked God. He'd been getting better and better at answering her prayers as of late. Whether this meant she was getting holier or He was softening to her entreaties was a question she'd have to ponder later.

There was no question in her mind where they were headed: the French settlement of Danton's Folly. No other place was less than a month away.

And there was also no question in her mind that they'd never make it without a guardian angel looking over their shoulders.

Chapter 28

"For who shall guess the good riddle
Or speak of the Holiest,
Save in faint figures and failing words,
Who loves, yet laughs among the swords,
Labours, and is at rest?"

–The Ballad of the White Horse

The ornithopter chopped air, its three sets of bladed "wings" flapping faster than any earthly eye could follow. It sped over the rocky red terrain like a gray flea over the back of a great, red, rocky-skinned giant, swerving here and there around mountains and stony towers that reached too far into the already thinning atmosphere to be flown over.

"…and to the right, ladies and gentlemen," said the Doctor, "you can see the peak of Mons Olympus, the highest confirmed mountain in the *entire* solar system, just breaching the cloud cover. The Belgians really want something there, we've guessed, since this is the third geological study team they've sent in the past eighteen months, several previous teams having disappeared at the hands of both natural disasters or angry natives. Over to our left, you can see the dried riverbed of what once was—"

"What do the Belgians want over there?" Cecil asked. He'd found that he tended to get what he was after more often when he played the part of the innocent child who never stopped asking questions or begging for treats. Women and most men were likely to indulge him if he didn't push the act too hard. Experience had taught him never to try it on a gunslinger or a woman with a short temper and quick hand.

"Mars is rich in minerals," said the Doctor, almost to himself. "It's believed that there were once lush forests here and that coal-like substances beneath the surface have been compacting possibly twice as long as coal has been forming on Earth. In theory, one lump of the stuff, properly treated, could heat a house for a week."

"Then why don't we take it from them?" Cecil asked.

"We don't need to. We already have it. We ensured the Belgians received bad information, and they've been chasing geological phantoms ever since, digging in the wrong place while we sit on the lion's share of the minerals. Furthermore—"

"Here, the city's coming up," said the man with the sunken eyes.

Cecil looked out the side window.

A large kind of dome-shaped building came into view first, its surface scratched and pocked. To Cecil it looked like the giant stone dome had faced the wind, sand, and sun of Mars for thousands of years and had won, but at great cost.

As they drew near, Cecil could see the dome-shaped building was really the top level of a tower, still partly buried in the sand. And the tower rose from the center of a large crater, a crater whose sides didn't bear the gentle slopes of other craters that had been hit by meteorites. This crater was enormous, several hundred yards across at least, and looked very recently dug by the many workers who currently toiled in its depths.

Their flying craft dipped and flew lower into the crater. Cecil saw a number of other surprising sights. The crater itself was far deeper than he thought initially. What he thought was a thirty-foot depth was more likely a depth of at least a hundred, maybe *two* hundred feet, and several thousand feet wide at its radius. The floor of the crater had been flattened, with ancient stone buildings uncovered and streets dug in the dirt wide enough for people to walk in and small, wheeled vehicles to drive in and loaded-down sloats to plod in.

As the ornithopter lowered down into the ancient city, Cecil saw several smaller towers surrounding the major tower in the center of the crater floor. Five towers, in fact, surrounded the main one. They were shaped like enormous scepters, only half as tall as the main tower in the center, each with a huge, oblong-shaped roof with a flat top that was tens of yards wide.

Other buildings were also scattered about. From the dug-out crater's edge to the center, two-story buildings made of red stone gave way to four, ten, and twenty story high ziggurats nearer the center.

"This was the greatest city of Mars in its prime," said the Doctor, his voice filled with awe. "There were eventually only five factions remaining among the natives, each seeking control of the planet. When they realized that they were too evenly matched and victory was impossible, they built these towers as bases and sanctuaries for their group if a great, final war ever broke out in the city."

"Why did they have that funny building in the center?" Cecil asked. He'd found the Doctor's greatest weakness: he liked to hear himself talk.

"They built it as a place to do business and to hold machines that regulate the air," said the Doctor, "and as a place to conduct certain… rituals, we think, to communicate with the primary power on this planet."

"What's that?"

"Cecil," said Beatrice, "perhaps the Doctor is tired now, and needs a rest from our questions."

"Oh, far from it, my dear," said the Doctor as he stared at the huge tower. "Something about this place is so very, very energizing I need hardly sleep or even rest the entire time I am here. Which is precisely why I like to visit so very often, if I can."

"A little too often to suit the rest of us," said one of the guards, smirking.

"Your insolence will *not* be tolerated!" said the Doctor. His voice carried so much venom and the younger man looked at him with such a lack of fear that the Doctor looked all the more foolish because of it.

"Bea," Cecil said, leaning over and whispering in her ear, "the Doctor isn't quite himself."

"I know that, Cecil," she said. "He's undergone a very, very odd change since we boarded here. Stay close to me, and—and if anything goes amiss, I promise I'll protect you."

Cecil nodded his head, and made a mental note: When under extreme stress, his sister became mildly delusional. Obviously, it was *he* who was going to have to protect *her.*

Chapter 29

"Because our expression is imperfect we need friendship to fill up the imperfections."

– Illustrated London News, June 6, 1931

1914 A.D.

"*A re we all assembled, then?*"

Gilbert spoke to Father Flambeau's back. *The large priest didn't respond but stood still, his six-foot seven inches tall frame and a good two hundred and fifty pounds of packed muscle supporting a head tilted to look firmly at the deep blue Martian sky through tinted glasses.*

Father Flambeau was fifty, and thus a good ten years older than Gil. Still, he was in superb physical condition. Even now, after all the adventures they'd shared, Gilbert still felt mildly nervous approaching the priest. It was the kind of disquiet you'd feel stepping in front of a loose bull, however tame you were told it was. Gilbert had no doubt whatsoever that the large priest could rip Gilbert apart like a dog with a half-chewed rag doll if he wanted to. He looked at Flambeau and once again marveled that this man had turned down the lucrative life of an athlete for a life spent in service of the Church. More surprising was that Father Flambeau had managed to make that choice at an age when most men, Gilbert included, would have been far more interested in Earthly delights than spiritual ones.

Father was standing beside the autofloater, sitting comfortably on the hood of the open-topped vehicle that had been designed to look like an ocean stingray, and hovered a good three feet off the ground when going at full speed. Father Flambeau was also wearing the specialized clerical garb developed by the Vatican for men selected for jobs in the Martian mission fields. The outfit was still colored all black, with a standard, long-sleeved shirt and dark trousers finished off by the white collar of a priest of Rome.

A closer look revealed his outfit to be a sophisticated weave of fabrics and polymers in a pattern similar to knight's armor. It had proven surprisingly resistant to both blades and bullets alike, and saved Father's skin more than once.

A man would only wear garb like this if he expected trouble in his travels. And if someone with Flambeau's training and experience were wearing it, it followed that Gilbert could expect trouble, too.

Gilbert walked closer. The large priest hadn't given any sign he'd heard Gilbert's approach, but kept his eyes focused on the blue sky as Gilbert neared.

"Not quite," the priest said, "I think we have one more coming, don't we?"

"You don't have to pretend, you know," Gilbert said once he reached the other side of the floater. "I know you know who we're waiting for."

"Is that a fact?" Father Flambeau said. "Then I shall have to do better at playing dumb next time." His accent was high British today, but Gil had heard it be many others on their adventures. In truth, he still wondered exactly what kind of accent the priest would have if left alone now. Would it be the French highlands he'd been raised in, or some British-controlled region he'd spent time doing mission or espionage work in for the Vatican?

"I take it our last passenger is due soon, then?" Flambeau said, now doffing tinted glasses and sliding into the driver's seat of the floater.

"I should hope so," Gilbert said, placing his umbrella into the front row passenger seat and reaching to unlock the door...though it had no top, the floater's door wouldn't open.

"Jean-Paul..." Gilbert said, a tired tone in his voice.

"Back seat this time, mon ami," the priest said with a smile, then a wink from behind his glasses. His long-unused French accent had seeped into his words. "You and our red-headed friend have much to catch up on, no?"

"Jean-Paul, I appreciate your attempts here, but there are two very real obstacles. First, she doesn't know about what happened to Frances."

"Oh, and I almost forgot, Gilles," the priest said using the French version and pronunciation of Gilbert's name, "stop trying so hard to sound British. Even if you were born there, you weren't raised British and it doesn't suit you."

"Second," Gilbert continued, pretending he hadn't heard, but his own voice slipping ever-so-slightly into its own Minnesota drawl, "where I was

raised, they say you can put lipstick on a pig, but that don't make it kissable."

Flambeau wrinkled his forehead. Most of his hair had long ago either fallen out or been shaved off, and the wrinkles showed halfway across his scalp. "What's that to do with us, then, eh?"

"Because even if you did dress up in a diaper and picked up a set of bow and arrows, it wouldn't make you Cupid!"

"Ah, Gilles? Si vous savez ce qui est bon pour vous, donc vous voulez être silencieux maintenant..."

"Whaddya mean? I'll decide what's good for me thank you! And why would I wanna be quiet..."

"Hello," said a female voice familiar to them both.

The voice behind him shut his mouth better than Father Jean-Paul Flambeau ever could.

"Hello, Anne," Gilbert said, turning around suddenly with a smile and a calm voice. "We were just discussing you."

"Indeed," she said.

1892 A.D.
MARS. SYRTIS MAJOR. DOCK DISTRICT.

Frances looked at the ship in front of her. Sitting on the sand by the dock, it looked like nothing so much as a sailboat on four sets of skis and with no rudder.

"You surely jest; that is . . . you must be 'aving a *larf*, gov!"

Jimmy was having a laugh, all right. Laughing *inside*, glad for the fiftieth time that he'd been the one to find her in the bar. Not only was she pretty, spirited, and quite rich, she was entertaining in a sweet and innocent way, too.

Plus, Jimmy had discerned, she was a chance for him to reach the Doctor.

Jimmy knew who Gilbert Keith Chesterton was. Had known for over two years, in fact. He'd heard how the Special Branch had *selected* his onetime handler, the redhead Anne, for the skinny boy with large glasses and infamous parents. Plus, Anne the redhead had taken over for the Doctor as Jimmy's contact with the Special Branch shortly before the Invasion.

Trying to puzzle out the connections was enough to make even a head as well wired as Jimmy's hurt with the effort. But what was important was that Frances' boyfriend Gilbert *was* connected to the Doctor somehow, and Jimmy needed to be sure *that* tentacle-armed bloke was six feet underground, for the sake of Jimmy's own safety as much as good old-fashioned revenge.

"Well, Miss, a sand skiff like this is truly the best a man can get on such short notice. It may not look like much, but it can get us there, right sure enough. If you know how to run a sailboat, my friend who supplied it assured me the principle is pretty much the same."

"Pretty much, hmm?" Frances said, walking around the craft.

Jimmy spoke again, fairly reading her mind. "Is it a sale then, Miss?"

Her brow furrowed. "Sail?" she said. "I can think of little else that would look like this when attached to the mast."

"No, no, Miss. I mean, will you buy it for the week? My associate assured me the price will be quite, um *reasonable*."

"It'll do, Jimmy," she said. "Now, I'm going to send you to the market for a few more items while I ensure this craft is ready to transport us."

"Yes, Lo—I mean, yes *Miss*." She was pretty. And she was nice. But she really, truly had no idea just how frustrating she could be. Jimmy wanted to get going, and she was going to send him to buy from the ragpickers in the marketplace.

Price of doing business, Jimmy said to himself, pocketing the wad of bills she'd just handed him. He knew just the place to pick up proper costumes for their trip across the desert. There was a lovely, quirky family who operated one of the stalls in town, selling old clothes to the Earthborn whose bodies couldn't quite take the sun like the Red-skinned Martians or the Green-skinned Tharks did.

Well, no matter. Off to get some clothes more appropriate to the desert, then hopefully off to the desert itself before anyone noticed the empty spot where Emrys's sand skiff used to be. That odd, skinny youth hadn't left his little apartment for weeks, anyway, so there was little risk that Emrys or Carter would get upset with Jimmy for "borrowing" the craft and pocketing the money for its rental.

****

Of course, Jimmy's timing was off. Just an hour later, Emrys stood at the dock, staring helplessly where his skiff had been moored.

"But I *left* it here!" he insisted, rubbing the polished lenses of his glasses for the fourth time.

"And it would seem someone else knew that, didn't they Ambrose?" Carter said, his eyes twinkling.

"But oh. Blast! I've walked by the sand skiff virtually every day over the course of the past year. And it's always been *there*, every day for the last year. Ready for me to use at a moment's notice if an escape were needed or an adventure beckoned!"

"And it disappears *just* when you need it, Ambrose? Hmm? It would seem that the gods of Mars take their marching orders from Loki himself. Such a devilish coincidence, and right when the direst of circumstances arises."

Emrys turned and looked at Carter, his glare at the Virginian a combination of annoyance and puzzlement.

"You think, then, this is no coincidence, John?"

"Whether it is or not is utterly unimportant," Carter said, his Southern accent more pronounced than usual. "In truth, I think you actually have much to celebrate. It appears your earlier plan of obtaining a few sloats instead of riding in the skiff was the proper course after all, and I was wrong to talk you out of it. If we return to the marketplace quickly, I would truly wager the week's pay of a Kentucky wrangler we could still close that deal."

Fifteen minutes later, Emrys was patting the side of his new friend, a large, lizard-like creature about the size of a horse with a name unpronounceable by most human tongues, yet referred to as a *sloat* by most of the colonists for the sound it made when hungry or thirsty.

"Ready to saddle up, Sir Emrys?" Carter said, swinging his leg over the saddle set on his sloat.

"Ready as I'll ever be. How ever *did* you get these things for us on such short notice?" Emrys was trying to sound casual, but mounting the sloat made him suddenly and acutely aware of how long it had been since he'd ridden one of the beasts.

"Easy enough, when I told their owners *I* needed them. They saw themselves as getting the better end of the deal really. Sorry that I couldn't get one that was easier to ride, Sir Ambrose."

"I do wish," said Emrys as he tried righting himself on the restless beast, "for the thousandth time that—Ouch! That you wouldn't call me that!"

"I truly thought all knights across the pond had 'Sir' in front of their names. And could ride horses. Sloats aren't that much different, really, once you get to know them."

"I'm not a knight, John, I'm the...whoa... John, being who I am doesn't automatically get you a... *Whoa*, sloat! John, will you *please* help me out here?"

John Carter looked at Emrys and had to chuckle again.

"Easy, there, boy," John said, petting the creature on its reptilian nose. "Give your new master a little respect, and you'll receive love back from him tenfold."

The sloat calmed. Emrys looked at John. "How on *Mars* do you *do* that, John?"

"I like to think that my natural ability with horses helps a bit. Being king of a nation of mind-readers has its advantages, too. Now, are you ready to find that city?"

Chapter 30

"Women are the only realists; their whole object in life is to pit their realism against the extravagant, excessive, and occasionally drunken idealism of men."

– *"Louisa Alcott," A Handful of Authors*

How much further? Gilbert thought in his head for the hundredth time that hour. The sand stretched out in front of him in a crimson vista far as he could see. Landmarks that appeared to be only a few hundred yards were deceptively farther away.

Walking was awful. Gilbert wore the sensible shoes he'd been wearing when he'd first landed on Mars, and they definitely were better suited to walking on paved city streets than through a desert of red sand. Worse, the wound in his ankle he'd gotten a couple of years back from fighting a Martian seemed to have opened up again somehow. Even though there was no blood, the pain had gone from dull to stinging to just short of unbearable.

On top of the old wound, his ankles started getting tired the first few minutes after he started following Belloc through the sands. The soldier seemed to be immune to every pain and sore muscle that attacked Gilbert's legs, then crept up his waist and back. He was sore in places the he'd forgotten he *could* get sore in. When Belloc finally stopped moving, Gilbert gave a small prayer of thanks for the rest.

"Here," Belloc said, slipping the pack off his shoulders, pulling out a crinkling, tightly wrapped bundle and throwing it to Gilbert. "Get the shelter set up while I set about getting supper together." Gilbert caught the bundle. To him, it looked as alien as the landscape. It took a few minutes to understand he'd been given a tent, and he would have to figure out how to unwrap *and* construct it besides.

"Get a move-on!" barked Belloc through his breathing mask. Gilbert had spent a full minute turning the bundle over in his hands, trying to find where the rigidly wrapped twine began and ended.

Remembering Belloc's warning earlier, Gilbert didn't speak back. Even though he'd thought up many choice words for the young Sergeant during the last few hours of brisk, painful walking.

Finally, Gilbert found a point in the twine where he could begin to unravel it. In a few seconds he'd unwrapped the tent. Folds in the material popped out along with several tent pegs and a small hammer all clattering to the ground.

"I'll give you just five minutes to get that tent up, Chesterton," Belloc said. Somehow he'd started a fire—or was it a fire? It looked like a red glow, rather than flames, and Belloc was cooking something in a pan. It smelled awful, and yet it made Gilbert's stomach growl!

"Smell that, do you?" Belloc said through his metal mask, his eyes focused on the food, not even looking at Gilbert. "Well, you get not a single bite until that shelter's up. Get to it. I've seen you brag enough in your articles about life on a prairie, and how many mollusks you killed during the Invasion. A man *that* capable should have no problem getting a tent up in five minutes, eh?"

Wishing mightily that he could chew out Belloc, Gilbert struggled as best he could with the tent. It took longer than five minutes—closer to a half-hour, really. But when it was finally up and stayed up without falling over at the first breeze, Gilbert stood beside it proudly and looked at Belloc through both his thick glasses and the goggles strapped uncomfortably over them.

Belloc scooped the food onto two plates and entered the tent with them without a sound. The smell made Gilbert follow. Once inside, Belloc sealed the entryway shut and removed his mask, taking in a big gulp of air.

"The filter above," said Belloc, pointing to a white screen set in the roof of the tent, "makes it so we can breathe and speak freely here."

Gilbert happily tore off his own mask and breathed deeply himself, then grabbed the plate and began scooping food into his mouth. "Well, that's a whole lot better!" he said in between bites shoveled into his face. "Now, I want to register an official complaint! About the mask, the walk, and everything! I want to know why you couldn't have at least told me about what it'd be like stomping around in the desert with a set of penny-loafers, when I could've maybe at least taken a good pair of sandals off a smaller Thark! I want to know why it's so long to the nearest settlement, and why you can't just send smoke signals to get them to find us, or something, while we wait in a warm, comfortable wreck of a ship that we don't have to worry about folding in on us or blowing away in a good windstorm! I want to talk about saddling the civilian, *me*, with a piece of inferior equipment that may lead to my death when you get to breathe all free-and-easy! And, most of all," Gilbert stopped to inhale for a second. His face was red and his eyes blazed with barely restrained anger that had been building for the better part of their four-hour trek.

Belloc didn't answer, but just stared at Gilbert. Gilbert fell silent, stopped chewing and felt very self-conscious. Belloc suddenly looked down at his food and closed his eyes. Belloc touched his forehead, chest, then his left and right shoulders, and began saying grace.

Gilbert felt more than a little foolish. Here he was supposed to be the good Catholic, and he'd forgotten to give thanks before his meal. Belloc instead had waited patiently for a break in the conversation to say grace! Gilbert followed suit and after a few seconds finished the rest of his food in a few more bites, using his hands as utensils. There had been some form of sliced meat, and a kind of toasted bread. Gilbert wondered if there was more food after this, but he felt it would be wiser to let Belloc speak the next words.

"So, what are you trying to say?" Belloc asked as he began chewing his food quietly.

"What I'm . . . how much clearer do I have to make it? I've spent the last couple of hours walking, when we could've been maybe holed up in a warm ship's hold. I could've been looking for my...well, looking for some people I have to find, and instead, I get chased after by agents, even on Mars! And you yank me off a building top, and then we're attacked by Tharks! And then I'm kept from even so much as *talking* when I want to talk the most, because talking could end my life! And since we're talking about asking, I want to ask about Father Brown and those agents! How do you know 'em so well?"

Belloc watched Gilbert rant and rave, sitting on his knees in the cramped space of the tent while he sat cross-legged and ate his food. Eventually, Gilbert finally stopped his loud, rambling speech and sat, huffing and puffing as the stress of the day finally rolled off him.

A few more seconds, and Belloc could sense that Gilbert was holding in tears.

Good, Belloc thought. Gilbert was normal enough to *want* to cry after seeing so much death, but man enough to hold it in until they were well and safe.

And once Gilbert was quiet, Belloc began to speak. His words sounded all the pithier in the silence.

"I knew Father Brown the same way you and Chang did," Belloc said, eating his bites slowly and deliberately, as if willing himself not to give in and devour the food with all the grace of a starving stray dog. "Father Brown and I ended up on a little adventure together a few weeks before the Tripods started dancing the Rhumba all over the country from Woking to London. It was there I met an agent from the Special Branch for the first time."

"Have you had to go up against the Doctor?"

"No. But I heard you did a decent job against him before he came out here. I've got a longstanding feud with the Special Branch agent who almost turned you into a pile of bone and meat off the side of the building today. He's called the Painter, and he's a slippery character who's every bit as dangerous as the Doctor. Kills for the fun of it when he can, but at least he's spared me all the long, boring speeches the Doctor's so infamous for."

"What—what about the Actress? Have you ever seen her? She's got bright red hair."

Belloc's eyes widened for a second, then narrowed again. Gilbert realized he seemed to have made Belloc remember something the soldier hadn't wanted to reveal.

"It's time to sleep," Belloc said, stretching out without a bedroll. "The fire canister outside will keep the animals away, and hopefully not give our position away to anything following us."

"You think we're being followed? But don't try to get me off topic! I want you to tell me what you know about *her!*"

"And *I* want to get some sleep. We've talked too much already, and we've got at least two more days of walking. And yes, I think it's perfectly possible we're being followed, and not by rescuers. Now, get some sleep. We'll be up and hopefully moving at first light."

✳✳✳✳

While Gilbert struggled to calm down enough to sleep, he had no idea that their sealed tent was under observation, just as Belloc had suspected. Not precisely a rescuer, Anne had been marking their progress and keeping up with them ever since they'd left the wreckage site. She grumbled to herself as she'd stomped through the piles of sand in her dress and petticoat, (no mean feat, that!) wondering why the blazes that Belloc didn't make camp at the wreckage site.? They could have waited there for days, likely, and sent up flares when a rescue ship came!

She'd thought several times to shout out to the both of them, or at least to Gilbert, as she followed from a distance. Her drab, ruddy clothes acted as excellent cover against the sand and rocks of the desert. But in the end she remained hidden. As far as Gilbert knew she was dead, and that was best for both of them. Aside of the layer of safety this gave her, it freed him to have a stable, reliable love with that kind [if rather vapid] little British heiress back on Earth.

So, she decided, better to remain hidden and keep using her long-range rifle to be his guardian angel.

She fingered the telescopic dial next to her eye again. Belloc and Gilbert had made camp for the night and would likely rise after perhaps six hours of sleep. She considered taking out and pitching her own small tent, but decided against it. Too much work, too great a chance she might sleep through their disembarking tomorrow. Instead, she took her all-weather blanket out from her small backpack, wrapped herself securely inside it, and laid down in the sand with her Mark-2 Rebreather still strapped firmly to her face.

Chapter 31

"The whole pleasure of marriage is that it is a perpetual crisis."
– *"David Copperfield," Chesterton on Dickens*

1914 A.D.
MARS. ONE HOUR WEST OF WILHELM.

*T*he floater covered ground quickly, far more quickly than Gilbert remembered his trek on this land over two decades ago. He adjusted his goggles for the fourth or fifth time that hour, wondering at how much scientific advancement had been made since his last visit. Over twenty years, he thought. Now they could grow trees on Mars, and French missionaries had converted enough of the locals to have a cathedral started in their colony past the Dune Sea. Crimony, the Belgians had even figured out how to mass-produce Cavorite. And yet no one could make a pair of goggles that were actually comfortable to wear for more than five minutes at a time. What was their use in keeping sand, grit and bugs out of your eyes if they only made the sweat pour that much quicker, and the soreness on your cheekbones that much more annoying?

Plus, truth be told, the glass discs kept clouding up on the inside, obstructing his vision of Anne sitting next to him. He snuck a peek at her again—just to confirm for the report later, of course—and saw she really hadn't gotten appreciably older. More than one person he'd known in his younger days hadn't aged well. Of course, there were those who'd say he had no business noticing Anne's figure, eyes, or her perfect, shapely hands... well, hand anyway...

Blast! There he went again. Noticing her when he wasn't supposed to. And noticing her in a way he had no business, no right to. Especially when he'd heard through the channels of communication that she was...

Now, there *was a* way to remove the awkwardness from the moment!

Talk about her current state. He almost wished that the floater was as noisy as motorcars tended to be on earth. That way there was an excuse not to talk if subjects to discuss ran dry in any conversation. But the floater was yet another wonder of alien technology that the Germans had managed to adapt to their purposes through the twin motivations of necessity and profit. The craft glided over the red desert floor with only the barest whisper of noise, Father Flambeau acting as their chauffeur while he drove from the front seat while Gilbert and Anne sat in the back.

Yes . . . the conversation. Best to get to that, so Anne wouldn't be embarrassed by the blocks of silence.

"I, er, I understand you got married a while back, Anne," Gilbert said.

"Yes," she said. "He was a good man, too. A doctor."

"Was? Well, I . . . I am sorry for your loss, Anne," Gilbert answered. *He was instantly ashamed that he felt even the smallest elation over her use of the past tense in describing her husband.*

"He died doing something worthwhile," she said. "He was a patriot, and when Canada entered the war he signed up right away, knowing his skills would be needed at the front lines. They dropped him in with a group of soldiers using parachutes. Unfortunately, the pilot had been poorly trained at his job and let the entire group out behind enemy lines instead of at the front. As an officer, he was given better treatment than the rest. I went to look for him as soon as I heard the news but all I found was his gravesite. He'd refused to cooperate, and the German prisoner camps were rather notorious at that point in the war for their lack of sanitation. He caught the consumption and he died."

"He sounds like he was a wonderful man, Anne. Quite selfless and thoughtful." *Gilbert paused again. The sadness in her voice had been unmistakable, and Gilbert knew he needed to bring her mood and morale up.*

"Wherever did you meet him?" Gilbert said. "Young men aren't particularly well-known for their depth of character at that age, Canadian or otherwise."

"I met him at . . . at a social function in England, and after a short courtship he was willing to marry me, despite my deformities. His depth of character was perhaps aided by his own difficulties, as Gilbert had a steam-leg of his own to cart about."

"Excuse me, Anne? I don't have a . . ."

"Gilbert, my Gilbert, had a steam leg. Gilbert was my husband's name. Gilbert Blythe."

"Ah."

They drove in silence for a few more minutes.

"I hope you won't be assuming anything," she said. "It was pure coincidence that your names were so close to being the same."

"They were the same," Gilbert said.

"I said it was just a coincidence!"

"I never said it was otherwise."

"Are you two fighting again?" said the large priest from the seat in front. Gilbert could hear the smile in his voice.

"Fighting? We haven't . . . that is, she never . . ."

"No, you never, Gilbert. The last fight we had, Father, he ended up on the floor, near dead from a broken nose."

"Well, Anne, if you hadn't brought my family into things . . ."

"Really, you two. Can't you just kiss and make up?" As the youngest child in a large family, Father Flambeau knew exactly what to say to make any situation worse.

"Kiss?" they both shouted at the same time. "Father!" continued Gilbert, "we haven't . . . that is, we've only . . ."

"We've only kissed each other once," said Anne, finishing his sentence.

Gilbert looked at her. "Twice! I know it's been over twenty years, Anne, but I'd hoped your memory was better than that!"

"The first time, Gilbert, I kissed you, right before I broke your nose for the second time. As for the second...well, you can't really say that..."

"Mes amis," said Father, "this little tete-a-tete you are having is most enjoyable, but I suddenly see we have a little obstacle my maps did not prepare us for. What to do: around or through?"

The floater drifted to a halt. Before them lay the ruins of a very old town, large enough to have once been a city. Buildings that had once been nobly built structures of one to three stories still stood, facing down the relentless forces of entropy and erosion. Still, nature had had its way with the town, and virtually every building was missing a roof, wall, or more.

It was very, very quiet, and both Gilbert and Anne watched carefully, recalling more than one painful and frightening memory.

Chapter 32

"The past is not what it was."

– *"The Age of Legends," A Short History of England*

1892 A.D.
MARS. SYRTIS MAJOR. DOCK DISTRICT.

Herbert George Wells stood at the dock in the lost city's early morning light and looked over the ship he would command.

By the standards of the day and planet, it was the ultimate rich-boy's toy. Painted a sleek black with runners waxed to a thickness of nearly six inches, the vessel could sport a crew of six: four junior members and two spoiled wealthy passengers. The four lower members of the crew were bunked in a single room with a long table and kitchen in the style familiar to any member of His Majesty's Armed Forces, whereas the more important members had their own staterooms and could receive their daily sustenance from either a miniature gourmet kitchen or a bar well-stocked with several different kinds of liquor.

Herb didn't care about the liquor. He didn't care about most worldly pleasures these days, only about finishing his next assignment and getting on to the next one.

He looked over his crew, lined up in front of him somewhat at attention, and immediately he felt a wave of repugnance.

The Painter was unshaven, with a moustache and a common workingman's scarf around his neck.

The Woodsman wore dark goggles and a top hat. He'd had some type of eye injury recently, and there hadn't been enough tissue left there for even the aliens' regenerator technology to bring them both back. His hands weren't at their sides, but instead were playing with a rather large knife.

The Driver wasn't much older than Herb, but now he sported a newly fitted artificial hand.

The last was the one Herb had to smirk over. "Fortescue Williamson," he said, looking over the young officer, dressed in a dress-white uniform covered in medals. "It's been a while."

"Not long enough," Fortescue said, glaring at Herb. "I have to follow your orders here, *Cleaner*. But never forget that I will be addressed by my name *and rank* during this venture."

"Good show," said Herb. "Now, if you're through waving your family crest in the air, get on board the ship and await my orders. Gentlemen," Herb said, now turning to the remaining three men in front of him, pointedly ignoring Williamson as he walked up the gangplank onto the skiff. "We have a relatively simple job ahead of us: Find Gilbert Chesterton, and *remove* him with all available speed. If we find any attached to him in any way, in particular his *paramour*, Frances Blogg, or his siblings, they are to be captured to be used as leverage against him. Blogg is to be spared and released, but the siblings will be, *ahem, processed* after Chesterton has been *removed*. Any questions?"

The men were silent, taking their cues from the Painter.

"Right," Herb said, "And remember our secondary order: make some kind of man out of Williamson. Our first task is to follow the vector of the *Locust* until we find something interesting. I'm told you lot know how to pilot one of these overgrown canoes, and each second we wait lets them get farther away. So . . . dismissed!"

The men turned and walked up the gangplank, following the Painter with a pace and cadence that was quick, but not precise.

Herb watched them go, prioritizing his objectives.

First: Complete his official mission to find and eliminate Gil. It took an enormous amount of effort, but at some point he'd felt his last bits of resistance to the idea slip away. Something smooth and efficient had taken the place of his reluctance. And while he didn't exactly *like* it, life *was* easier now.

Second: Watch Williamson. The spoiled rich fop wouldn't likely try to harm Herb, but he would be thinking about it.

Third: Remove the Painter at the first opportunity, preferably in front of the other agents. The Painter saw himself as the real leader on this mission, and he *would* try to harm Herb at the first opportunity. Such men tolerated no sharing of power, and never surrendered it willingly.

Herb would know. Over the last year, bit by bit, he'd become just such a man himself.

****

"Are you certain it's this way?" Frances asked as their skiff dropped over another large sand dune. Sailing on desert sands was similar in many ways to sailing on water. *Easier, in some ways, really*, she thought as she adjusted the ropes that steered the sail. The waves didn't move in a desert. Of course, paddling wouldn't be an option if the wind died down. But one took one's chances. The book about desert survival she'd read on the trip was very clear on that point. One took chances, but one did not allow a mistake. The desert was a most unforgiving host, and a desert millions of miles from home even more so.

"Yes, Mum," Jimmy said in a clear voice from behind his goggles as he looked at the sun and then at a small compass in his hand. "If we keep to this heading, we should reach the deserted town by nightfall. After that, we can go on to a French settlement called Danton's Folly and replenish any supplies we may need. From there it's on to the Martian city where Cecil and his sister have travelled."

"And, presumably, Gilbert."

"Presumably, Ma'am. 'Ow'd you meet him, if you don't mind my asking?"

"We met on a June night in Paris and spent the evening discussing history and philosophy."

Jimmy stared at her for a second or two, then shrugged his shoulders and focused forward while she continued the more difficult job of steering.

****

Beatrice had changed much since she'd been orphaned. She had to rely on herself, her wits and work ethic to survive. Her parents had raised her and Cecil as adopted children in Canada, and despite the lack of blood ties, there had been no shortage of love between them. Extended family hadn't played much of a factor in her life; she only had one Uncle she'd known about. He'd visited with his wife and son six or seven years before. Moreover, her young cousin seemed much more content to be in the library, looking at books through his thick lenses, rather than actually *doing* things on the farm.

203

Plus, he didn't even like playing chess all that much. Not after she'd beaten him anyway.

After the deaths of her adoptive parents, Beatrice had seen survival of her and her brother as a new and challenging puzzle to solve. Though she hadn't been able to effectively manage the farm herself, she had been able to carve a life of sorts for them here on Mars. Along the way she'd realized that if you assumed that every problem came with a solution, it was just a matter of hard work and creative thinking until you solved it.

This new alien city, though, was a different story. Just walking through its streets made her feel she was interfering in the life of someone special. The city was a puzzle wrapped in riddle after riddle, so old and complex that she couldn't even begin to try unraveling it.

And it was the kind of puzzle she knew she would have difficulty solving on her own.

"Doctor?" she said, spotting him walking slowly down one of the many stone corridors in the large central building. "Doctor, may I speak to you a moment?"

"Why of course, my dear!" he said happily. His face had looked preoccupied, but it brightened substantially at the sight of the young lady before him.

In fact, his face changed so completely and suddenly that she was taken aback just a bit. *"Watch him, Beatrice,"* Cecil had said to her last night in a rare moment of seriousness, *"watch him carefully! This whole place isn't what he told you it was. I can feel it. And I don't trust him."*

"Doctor, I was curious as to my role in this operation. We've been here well over a day, and . . ."

"Are your accommodations adequate, my dear?"

"The accommodations are lovely, doctor, truly. But . . ."

"And the food is to your liking then?"

"It, too, is wonderful. But in truth, I am curious that though you said this would be an archeological dig, I have yet to see any actual *digging* taking place."

"My dear," said the Doctor, laughing and extending his arm toward the doorway in front of him, through which Beatrice entered, "Do you believe this enormous metropolis unearthed *itself*? There has been a truly momentous degree of digging here!" He had a point: the buildings had been dug from under literal mountains of red dirt. Thousands of workers would have been required for the job, but Beatrice hadn't seen a single shovel raised since their arrival the day before. Archeological sites she'd seen were often a flurry of activity, with workers, scholars, and onlookers coming and going.

Yet, aside from the burly, leather-jacketed guards and the occasional person dressed like a member of the upper class, this ancient city was empty and silent.

"But it would seem no digging is going on *at present*, Doctor," she said. "As your assistant on this venture, I had hoped to learn more about Martian history and culture. However, it would seem that there is little in the way of instruction or investigation available to me. Guards hold every exit point from this building, and they are most unforgiving in their application of duty. I fear more for Cecil, as he tends to get into trouble when there is little for him to do."

"Your happiness is paramount in my mind, Beatrice. I regret I have been occupied. We will be having a momentous occasion in two days, at which point we expect to free an *artifact* of significant age. If you can be patient until then, I assure you that you and Cecil shall not be disappointed."

****

Cecil was, in fact, far from disappointed. He'd taken the liberty of sneaking out of his room and exploring the city at will. The place was fascinating, and sneaking about was quite easy since most of the guards were actually quite negligent and paid no attention to him.

The city the Doctor's people had unearthed was mostly made up of the broken one-and two-story buildings Cecil had spied from the air. The center of the town was a very tall pillar at least thirty stories high, with a dome-shaped stone roof on top. Surrounding the central pillar were five smaller but still substantial towers, each a smaller replica of the main tower. There was no visible way to reach the top of the main tower. Cecil presumed that it could only be reached by a secret entrance or by ornithopter.

Most of the buildings in the area were open and easy to slip in and out of. But occasionally he found a metal door secured onto securely fastened hinges that had been drilled and bolted into the ancient stone.

The locks could be picked. But they were certainly beyond his ability to even attempt without better tools.

He was just considering where he might be able to "borrow" some when a spot of ground made a hollow sound as his foot trod over it.

Interesting.

A little more walking, and he found more hollow spots. Then a line of them, all of which ran from the central tower to a pile of rocks.

Cecil tugged at the pile, and he found it surprisingly resistant to being pulled to pieces.

He quickly realized the pile of rocks wasn't a pile at all.

It was a *door* made to *look* like a rock pile. He tried to open it, but he only succeeded in finding the hidden hinges and latch that held the door fast.

After some creative work with other rocks and a nearby stick, he reached in and pushed up the feeble latch. The door swung open inward without any more resistance, and the hot pink midday sun shone on a stairway that wound down deep under the Martian surface.

Easy, thought Cecil. Whoever had put this in place wanted this place hidden from others here but was confident enough in their ability to hide it that they held it shut with the flimsiest of locks.

In a second, Cecil was through the door and descending the steps, his mind jumping even quicker than his feet. Would he find the treasures of Ali Baba and the Forty Thieves? Or perhaps there'd be some hideous horror, like a monster guarding . . . still *more* treasure?

Cecil didn't know, couldn't yet know, what would await him at the bottom of the steps as they wound round the central column. The light from the open door above faded away after the third turn in the stairs, and he was soon in the pitch black of a dark cave, his only sure contacts and direction coming from his hands against the walls and his feet touching the next step.

As the light disappeared, Cecil moved with more caution. He now stepped slowly while bending his knees and feeling outward with his hand.

It wasn't necessary for long. A few more turns and the narrow stairwell turned into a wider, open room lit by a series of lights mounted on the walls.

Cecil looked around in the room, and he wished he'd stayed in the dark.

The stone floor was dry and dusty, with a new set of footprints leading across to the other side of the room. The rock walls to his left and right were made of darker stone than the floor and towered at least twenty feet above Cecil's head.

But what made Cecil wish for the safety of darkness was the long table against the wall. It was waist high, made of metal, and long enough that a very tall man could lie down on it.

The metal table also had manacles and straps, which could bind a captive at the ankles, wrists, neck, and torso.

There were several other smaller tables nearby, and as Cecil approached them he saw the wicked gleam of scalpels, scissors, saws, and other tools of the surgical trade laid out neatly in trays.

A few steps closer, and Cecil saw the red-lined stains of blood on the large table, where the victim's wrists, neck, and forehead would have rested.

Cecil felt cold prickles at the back of his neck. Had he been back in Syrtis Major, he wouldn't have hesitated to grab as many of the shiny objects he could, then try to sell them as tools to the tanner or make a present of them to a family who had been good to him.

But something about the sparkling clean instruments set next to the bloodied table made Cecil feel more than queasy. Some kind of surgery had been performed here, of a kind neither voluntary nor for healing. And it had been most definitely performed on human beings.

There were sounds down the hall of dark stone. Cecil looked and saw the lit outline of a door in the rock wall opposite him.

He crept up to the door, despite everything in him suddenly screaming that he should turn, run, and sneak back up into his room and hide under the bed for a week. He stepped quietly, even though there wasn't another human being to be seen.

A noise came from behind the door, a cross between a bee droning on a humid summer day and a dentist's drill. Cecil still crept forward, remembering more and more fairy tales about what horrors awaited those who opened dungeon doors that should have stayed shut.

His shoes crunched softly on the grit on the stone floor. He was ten steps away, eight by the time he finished the thought. Now six. Now four. Now...

When he was a step away, he had second thoughts. He ignored them as best he could. He had to see beyond. He had an insatiable curiosity. He had an empty pocket that needed to be filled. He had…

He *had* to see what was beyond that door.

He saw no hinges, which meant that this door must swing *inward*.

Cecil pushed the door gently. It swung away from him with only the slightest creak, one that only Cecil could hear over the buzzing of the tools inside.

Cecil saw something that haunted his dreams for years.

A slender man sat in a chair with his back to Cecil. His head was bald—recently so, Cecil guessed, based upon the pile of gray hair next to his chair.

Cecil could see the man's face in the mirror, and what Cecil saw so shocked him that he, the most streetwise and cunning urchin in the Martian colonies, was left speechless and stunned.

The man sitting in the chair was stripped to the waist, revealing a back that sagged in folds off a boney frame all too visible beneath the sick-looking flesh.

The man was staring into a mirror, his reflection lit by a yellow electric light. He held a pencil-shaped tool in his liver-spotted hands and was using it to draw something on his forehead. His eyes were so dark that Cecil could see no color or white—all seemed to be the darkness of a pupil. The old man was so focused on his own reflection that he didn't even notice Cecil's opening of the door or the young boy staring at the old man's reflection in the mirror.

In the background Cecil heard a gramophone playing, the kind that used etched wax cylinders rather than playing records. It had a voice speaking in a language Cecil couldn't understand, speaking one sentence at a time, and then pausing. And during each pause, Cecil heard the man repeat the words to himself.

"*Eh ma I*" said the gramophone in a crisp, military-like voice.

"Eh, ma, I." said the man in a voice raspy as sandpaper against deadwood.

Knowing he should run, but still fascinated, Cecil had already ducked out of the doorway and was watching the scene from a corner.

The old man's tool wasn't exactly a drawing pen, but more of a tattoo artist's inscriber. It hummed, buzzed, and growled like a large, angry insect, powered by a smaller steam engine rather than a foot pump.

Something about the man's recitation of the words from the

gramophone chilled Cecil, making his brain and soul scream louder in his head than his throat and mouth could even have done from his body. Word after word came out of the gramophone's wide, flower-mouthed speaker, and was repeated by the old man in a soft, gravelly voice.

Backward, Cecil realized. *They're a bunch of normal sentences, but they're being said backward, over and over again.*

Just as his soul had made its scream of silent terror, the old man started in his chair, as if he'd heard something loud and obnoxious crash behind him.

With all the cruel and terrifying logic of a dream, Cecil knew that despite their differences in age, speed, and strength, he would never be able to defeat the man who now stood from his chair and faced him, displaying what kind of permanent picture he'd been etching onto his face.

Cecil screamed.

Chapter 33

"Poets have been mysteriously silent on the subject of cheese."

–Alarms and Discursions

John Carter had lived a soldier's life. He could will himself to fall into the deep and dreamless sleep of the dead at a moment's notice when needed, and wake at the slightest noise. Early in the morning he'd heard the creak of timbers and the shouts of men while both were still far, far away from their camp. In seconds he was awake and watching the sand ship with his spyglass.

John peered through the lens carefully as the skiff sped by, cresting a dune while catching another gust of Martian desert wind. Several shadowy figures pulled ropes or manned the tiller, working and talking with the ease of inexperienced sailors unafraid of listening ears.

Of course, they were still too far away for John to hear their words exactly. But when he saw that large fellow with the waxed mustache, the one that some called the Painter for his ability to cover things up and make them disappear, Carter knew there was mischief afoot. He saw the miscreant he'd maimed in the alley on the ship too. The hand Carter had chopped was gone, replaced by one of those new steam hands they'd brought from Earth a few months back.

"What's going on, John?" Emrys whispered behind him.

Carter turned. "We've got a skiff running in the same direction we are," he said. "I'll wager they're headed to the same place. There's a few bad fellows on board, but nothing I couldn't handle."

"Do you realize how many times you said that, and then had to rely on one of Edison's inventions to get us *out* of trouble?"

"If you're referring to the incident with the spidery fellows and the Tripod, I had the situation well under control."

"Yes, about as much as you ever do," Emrys answered dryly. "Well, we'd best saddle up and begin following them. This whole enterprise won't solve itself, after all."

****

Gilbert woke with the smell of eggs in his nose, and he hoped he was back at his beloved childhood home in Minnesota.

But before he'd even sat up, he remembered where he was. He rose to a crawl, sighed, and pulled apart the flaps of the tent.

He stuck his head outside and gave a quick, cautious sniff. The air smelled a bit like cooking eggs mixed with a dusty room. Dawn hadn't broken yet, but he could see a pink line against the horizon where he knew the sun would rise. The horizon gave enough light that he could see where the smell of eggs had come from. Belloc had set up a small cook stove and pan. Steam and friendly crackling sounds rose up from it, tickling Gilbert's nostrils and ears. He was suddenly ravenously hungry.

"Good morning," Belloc said without looking up. "Do you know how to make an omelet?"

"Uh, no," Gilbert said. He'd travelled a bit, but he wasn't exactly sure what an "omelet" was.

"Good," said Belloc, still quiet and looking at the eggs in the pan as if they were clumps of lead about to turn into gold. "I'm glad of that. The last travelling companion I had was very, very good at making omelets, but terrible at virtually everything else except wooing girls with bad poetry."

"Not too many poems about omelets, I'll wager," said Gilbert, walking stiffly in the morning chill and sitting down cross-legged by the small cook fire. He could see the eggs had been stirred into a hard yellow disk. Belloc took a yellow lump of cheese from his pocket and began crumbling it onto the large, hardened egg concoction.

Gilbert tried to ignore his gnawing stomach, wishing he could eat right then. But Belloc cooked like an artist who would not be rushed.

"Even less poetry about cheese, come to think," Gilbert said, trying to make conversation. "How long until it's ready?"

Without a word, Belloc folded over the omelet, sliced it in half with the spatula, slipped it onto a plate with a deft movement and handed it to Gilbert. Gilbert scooped the half-omelet into his mouth with his hand and swallowed it in two, large gulping bites before Belloc even had time to hand him a fork.

Seeing Gilbert had already finished, Belloc made the sign of the cross, said grace, and ate his own breakfast. He ate quickly too, though not as quickly as Gilbert. He finished in a minute or so, cleaned his utensils and plate with a white rag, then scooped it all into his pack with a fast and efficient air that suggested he'd done this many, many times.

Gilbert did the best he could, though his breakfast started to disagree with him almost as soon as it hit his stomach.

Over a very short while, the sour feeling moved from his gut to his heart and eventually his attitude. By the time they had broken camp and were prepared to leave, the dawn was breaking and Gilbert had readied himself for their journey with the brass-rimmed goggles over his eyes and a scowl on his face. He worked hard but complained and grumbled at virtually every direction he received from Belloc.

"Gilbert," Belloc said once their packs were assembled and he had his own goggles and rebreather set securely on his face, "did you relieve nature?"

"Did I what?"

"Did you—oh, hang it all. Never mind. I guess we'll just have to stop and make camp each time you're taken short."

Gilbert finally understood, but before he could say or do anything, Belloc started walking.

"Are you sure that's the right way?" Gilbert asked, struggling to get his rebreather on comfortably.

Belloc stopped. He waited for five seconds and turned around. "What did you say to me?" he asked through the mask.

"I said, 'Are you sure you know where you're going?' It doesn't look like the same direction we were headed yesterday."

"Gilbert, do you realize that if you were a soldier instead of a civilian right now, I'd be perfectly within my rights to pound you within an inch of your life?"

"Well, I'm *not* a soldier. I think that's been pretty well established, hasn't it? You'd actually *respect* a soldier if they just made it through the most basic training, wouldn't you? A lot more than a civilian, anyway!"

"Gilbert, you need to be quiet and—"

"Why? Because I'm no soldier? I did what the great British Army bumbled at doing! I'm a civilian who killed..."

"Three Martians, Gilbert. I know. I read all about it." Belloc's voice had gotten very quiet.

"Yes! And don't you forget it! I was swimming in filth and dodging Martian tentacles while you so-called *soldiers* were scratching your—"

"CHESTERTON!" Hilaire shouted, using the kind of voice Gilbert hadn't even heard his most abusive boss use when he was a lowly clacker drudge in London.

The effect was odd and electric. Gilbert suddenly snapped his body straight. He hadn't actually *seen* Hilaire change in any way, but now the young man who was barely any older than Gilbert himself stood tall, his shoulders bristling, the heavy pack looking like it would be no more a handicap to Belloc doing anything he wanted than a load of tissue paper.

Belloc stood, looked as if he wanted to say more. He looked first at Gilbert, then past him. Gilbert couldn't be certain, but it looked like he might be tearing up behind the goggles he was wearing. Though he stood ramrod straight, Gilbert also saw his body tremble slightly, just twice, as if he were suppressing a sob.

"Let's get moving. And remember, *no talking*. Not unless you want to die with red dust choking the life out of you because your filter's full. Soon, there'll be dust thick enough that you'll have to put a plug in your mouth, and not just cover it with the mask." He turned and began walking.

That's another question I've got, Gilbert said, though now the words were safely tucked inside his head. *You kept saying that my filter just might clog up. Well, I tried breathing out here this morning, and it didn't seem to be too hard at all! Not a lot of dust out here. No worse than the chalk dust in the classrooms I was in back in the States. Were you just pulling my leg? Did you just tell me that to keep me quiet? Did you think I'd fall for something as stupid as that? Huh? It'd make a cat laugh! You lied, didn't you? You had no right to lie to me! I should have been allowed to speak! I have a voice! I am a journalist! I have rights! Do you understand that, Sergeant Belloc? I have...*

****

Anne had been watching them since she'd awoken near dawn, her telescopic eye keeping a close watch on Gilbert's new guardian as he left the tent, stretched, and began to fix breakfast.

Eggs—an army breakfast, she noted. With just a touch of luxury in the form of making it an omelet to keep morale up during a difficult march.

214

What she would give for a man who could fix a decent omelet! No matter. Soon enough, Gilbert emerged, ate, and they broke camp.

But then something went wrong. While she was nibbling on pieces of biscuit, she saw Gilbert start to put on his mask again. Why, she wondered, had Belloc been making them wear the things so long? True, the dust in the lowlands was so fine it could get into your lungs and stay for weeks or months, eventually clogging your pipes and suffocating you without a rebreather filter. But they were out of that region now, and quite safe. As she watched, Gilbert yelled at Belloc, and Belloc shouted back at Gilbert. Gilbert stiffened at the chastening, then fell into line behind the shorter, stockier young soldier.

This lasted for a full minute, until Gilbert pulled the rebreather from his mouth and began yelling at Belloc, using the voice of a man so focused on his goal that reason would not enter into the discussion.

And she knew how British Army men tended to react to that kind of approach. "Gilbert," she said as she retracted her eye and grabbed her small rucksack, "I hope you haven't started something you can't finish!" She grabbed her rifle in her other hand and ran across the plain, no longer even trying to stay hidden.

****

Gilbert's internal monologue had lasted only about a minute before all the anger and rage bottled inside screamed for release and prompted him to yank out the rebreather and start yelling again.

Belloc kept walking at first, his face showing no emotion as Gilbert trotted alongside him. Then, after a few more steps he stopped, took the rebreather off of his face and looked off into the distance, a faraway look on his face.

"Who do you think you are, huh?" Gilbert said, walking sideways now, while he tried to get Belloc to pay attention. "Who do you think you are? You know what *I've* had to go through? You know what *I've* had to deal with in my life?"

Belloc didn't answer. He'd reached into one of the many pockets of his shirt, pulled out a cigarette and stuck it into his mouth.

"I've been orphaned!" Gilbert continued. "I've seen good people *die*! I've had people who I *thought* were my friends betray me! I've had my girl drop me!"

Belloc reached into another pocket, found what he was looking for and flicked his thumb. The match in his hand bloomed into flame, and he covered the fire as he lit the battered cigarette.

"I've kept on trying to do the right thing! I fought, and I get someone like *you* helping me, and all God keeps doing is…"

"Watch your step," Belloc said, his words barely muffled by the cigarette. He could have been telling Gilbert to be careful on a rickety staircase.

"What do you *mean*?" Gilbert shrieked. "I'm walking just *fine*!"

"When faced with an acquaintance's existential crisis, most men hesitate to resort to symbolism. But…"

He sucked on his cigarette and blew the smoke in Gilbert's face.

"What the blazes was that?"

"The exact worth of everything you've been saying for the last hour, *civvie*. All your pain, anger, bile and ire count *just* that much in the grand scheme of things—the exact weight of a mouthful of smoke blown in the breeze."

"You're…you're…you've no *idea* what I've been through!"

"You're right. And I don't care, either. Neither does anyone else. Unless you're the one buying the drink."

"You're—you're a…"

"Spit it out or suck it up and soldier on. No third choice, civvie."

"Civvie? You're gonna call me names? When you're so…inept that every man under your command…"

"Careful civvie. Don't open doors you can't close!" Belloc's teeth were gritted shut, chomped tight on the cigarette in his mouth.

"What, did I hit a sore spot? That every man who trusted you…"

"Doorknob's turning, civvie. Latch is lifted…"

"…is dead, and you don't even *care*?"

"*RIGHT*," said Belloc, spinning his body around and cuffing a surprised Gilbert on the side of his head.

Gilbert, at a loss for words, was off balance for several seconds, cursing Belloc and every decision he'd made. Finally, he got his balance. Now, time to turn and face that short little fireplug and tell him—

Gilbert had just turned to face Belloc when Belloc's haymaker fist connected with Gilbert's jaw, making Gilbert's jaw sing with a level of pain to equal a Beethoven symphony as Gilbert spun into the opposite direction he'd gone before, this time landing with a thud on the red, powdery sand that sounded both soft and final.

Gilbert, dazed, inhaled the powdery sand and then spat it out. Rage blazed in his head and heart. Raw hatred coursed through him, blasting through every pore with such undeniable strength and vigor that he jumped to his feet and ran at the shorter, stockier young man, all the while gibbering like an incoherent maniac while totally focused upon his goal of destroying the calm, unruffled sergant in front of him.

Belloc stood, his hands fastened behind his back, cigarette still glowing patiently as Belloc waited for Gilbert to arrive at just the right moment.

Belloc's move was sudden and impossible for Gilbert to dodge. Belloc stepped sideways, then turned his back to Gilbert and bent low. Gilbert had no idea what Belloc was doing until the young Sergeant's booted foot swung in a quick, heavy arc at the side of Gilbert's head.

To Gilbert it sounded like a mallet hitting a wooden floor. His right ear began to sing in a high-pitched whine, and the red-pebbled ground rushed up to meet him as he fell with a cry.

Chapter 34

"Comradeship is quite a different thing from friendship. . ."

– Illustrated London News, May 19, 1906

The skiff jumped over the sand ahead of the rising sun like a black dart flying over a rolling red canvas. Herb held his stomach in check as best he could and tried hard not to be sick.

Williamson had long since retreated into his personal cabin and hadn't been seen since.

"Painter," Herb said, "if they have a day's head start on us, how long 'til we reach them?"

"That depends on how far they got before they were ambushed, and if any made it out to walk on foot. If there are more than a few survivors or if they make it to the town of Danton's Folly, or both, things could get sticky if we try to take them out. But knowing what I do about wild Tharks, they'd have to be quite lucky for even one or two to live through such a fight."

"How far, then, to Danton's Folly?"

"It's a wretched place, Cleaner. Think of the Rookery, and drop it down a dozen feet deeper into a pit of despair. Plus, I've checked the maps. If the Tharks attacked where Williamson said his daddy paid them to attack Belloc and his crew, there's a deserted Martian town that lies smack in between where the ship crashed and the French."

"How do you know the ship crashed?"

"They're late," the Painter said. "I checked by heliograph before we left. He hadn't checked in to the first outpost. I've dealt indirectly enough with Belloc to know he's never late, ergo he must be delayed. And the only way he'd let himself be delayed is if something pounded his ship so badly that it wouldn't fly anymore."

The Painter stopped speaking. Up ahead, the shimmering desert tried to hide the sight of the broken ship in the sand.

"Wreck ahead! Aphid class!" yelled the Postman, his eye glued for the moment to a spyglass.

"Anything else?" Herb said, moving closer to the prow of the boat.

"Another wreck further up, but I can't make out much. Could be Thark."

"Right," Herb said with a crisp air. "Prepare to stop and investigate. Postman, stow that glass and issue weapons. Woodsman, rouse the fearless Captain Fortescue Williamson from the water closet. And Painter," Herb looked at the older man who now sported several days' worth of stubble on his face.

"Yes?"

"Drop any thoughts of supplanting me. It won't happen on this trip."

****

Gilbert hit the ground and gasped in pain. He'd once been nearly blown apart in a sewer by an alien bomb, and while being clouted on the side of the head by Belloc's well-aimed army boot wasn't near as bad, it hurt quite a bit just the same.

Gilbert blinked. The blow had knocked off both his glasses and his rebreather. There were pebbles and rocks digging into his cheek. A flack of grit got into his eye and caused exquisite pain, almost like a needle jabbing into his eyeball.

He breathed just a little.

Belloc had kicked him!

Gilbert had only demanded his *rights*, and Belloc had *hit* him over it!

Snarling, Gilbert jumped to his feet, ready to fight. "Do you *know* just how *stupid* that was, *Belloc*?" Gilbert yelled. He charged without waiting for an answer, making a guttural roar as he ran with both arms outstretched in an effort to grab Belloc and wrestle him to the ground.

Belloc didn't answer. With a face devoid of expression or effort, he leaned to one side, bending his right knee and extending his left leg out.

His timing was perfect. By the time Gilbert realized he was charging at Belloc's leg instead of Belloc himself, Gil had slammed into Belloc's calf. He tried to stop, but that threw him off balance even further. He spun like a top, sailing in the air and landing on his back with a *thud* in a cloud of red dust.

Gil scrambled to his feet, ready for another attack. He quickly got himself into a ready fighting stance in case Belloc decided to press the advantage.

Belloc, though, didn't move.

Ever since he'd learned a few martial arts moves, Gil had felt himself the equal of most fighting men. But now he stood feeling foolish; instead of counter-attacking, Belloc stood watching Gil with his hands in his pockets and a blank expression on his face.

"Come on!" roared Gil. "Come on! You think you're tough? Huh? You think you're tough? Let's see what you've got!"

"Are you finished?" Belloc said quietly.

Something in his calm, cool voice infuriated Gil even more. Months of anger and resentment blew out of his mouth as he cussed for the first time in over a year and lunged at Belloc again, this time ready for the little trick with the leg.

Of course, Belloc didn't use the trick with the leg. Instead he stepped to the other side, reached up and grabbed the back of Gil's head with his right hand. Belloc then swung the taller boy in an arc to the left. Gil, off balance again, screamed in frustration and fell for the third time into the dirt.

Belloc bent his knees and hopped backward out of Gil's reach. Gil was gibbering in frustration, pounding the red sand over and over as he'd pounded Budd's chest the day before.

Gil's angry gibberish became sobs, and salty drops of his tears began soaking the dirt below his face.

"You know, Gilbert," said Belloc, once Gilbert's sobs had become quieter, "people I respect have praised you quite highly. But I'm beginning to seriously wonder why."

"I was beginning to wonder why myself," said another voice.

Gilbert, still on all fours, raised his head to answer.

He saw a brown skirt with two booted toes pointing out at the bottom.

And as his eyes traveled up, he forgot all about Belloc. For the skirt gave way to a woman's white blouse with lacy sleeves caked with red dirt stains. One of the arms ended in a bulky metal steam hand, like the one a Pinkerton detective had used to bash down a door last year while chasing Gilbert. The other hand was whole and human, and it held a long-barreled rifle stood on end.

Atop the torso that held the arms was a woman's shapely neck and head.

The woman's face was half-covered by a veil. And the uncovered portion of the face was unmistakably . . .

"Anne?"

"Gilbert," she said, disappointment in her voice.

Belloc stood motionless. His hand hovered over the pistol in his holster, and his booted feet were firmly planted shoulder-width apart.

"You two know each other, then?" he asked.

Anne had made no move that Gilbert could see, other than to blink the eye that wasn't covered by her veil. Gilbert looked at her, then jumped to his feet.

"Anne!" he yelled, joyfully embracing her! He held her for nearly a full minute, holding her close with his cheek next to hers.

"You're *alive*," he said, pulling back for a second to look again at the veiled half of her face. "How?"

Now he looked down, his eyes drawn to the bulky, three-fingered hand made of iron and brass. "Anne, what's—what's wrong? I knew your hand had been . . . well, hurt, but . . ."

That was an understatement. After Herb had shot Gil in the ribs last year, he'd tossed Gilbert a hand wrapped in cloth that could only have been Anne's.

"Gilbert," she said, "you need to see something else before you go any further."

Before he could respond, she reached up with her left hand and pulled off her veil.

Gilbert blinked and started. Anne's face had always been beautiful. He'd seen her for the first time two years ago in the head office of the London building where he'd worked. The memory of her porcelain skin, sunset-red hair, and her calm demeanor had branded itself into his brain, a happy memory that still gave him gooseflesh when he thought of it.

Now, though, even with the veil off, half her face was still hidden behind a mask. It was a half-mask shaped like her face, but made of brass. And at its edges Gilbert saw on her skin the smallest wrinkles and pink discolorations of a burn victim's skin. But her eye was the worst. Her eyes had always been the deepest china blue he could imagine. Even after he'd reunited with Frances, he'd see those eyes in peaceful dreams. Dreams where he'd walk along a river with his hands behind his back and Anne would be . . .

The memory fled, all steam and ashes. Her right eye was gone, in its place was a circle of dark red glass set in her mask that looked like the business end of a telescope.

"Anne," he said, voicing the name she'd given him a year ago for the first time. "Anne, what happened?"

"I had a fight with an old colleague. She left me for dead. I didn't die. There are times when I wish I had."

"I'm glad you didn't, m'lady," Hilaire said, his right hand still resting on the handle of his pistol, "for if you died, I think I'd be dead, too. As would many more of my men, without their guardian angel from the hills shooting at our enemies."

Anne was about to answer when they all felt the rumbling beneath their feet.

"What's that?" said Gilbert. Hilaire had already dropped to the ground and motioned for silence.

"Gas pockets, underneath the surface. Agitated by the fight you two were in and the skimmer chasing you. They're over at the wreckage site now where you crashed."

"Chasing us?" said Gilbert. "Why should we worry? We've got over a day's march on them."

"It's a skimmer, not a sloat," Belloc said. "A two *weeks* march could be covered by a skimmer in a few hours, if the wind is high enough. We've got to move, and fast."

"More accurately," said Anne, facing away from them, her steam hand held at ear level, "it's a class three skimmer, designed by the White Star line. More often used for private functions and pleasure cruises than government business like war or exploration. Typically dark in color, four pontoons, a crew of between four and six adult male . . ."

Hilaire had already raised his head to look at her. "You can tell all that from listening?"

She turned to face him. Her telescopic eye had fully extended from her face. Without any other explanation, she released the small wheel on the side of her mask and the eye retracted back into her head.

Gilbert stared.

"Right," said Hilaire, standing erect while trying not to look nonplussed, "Well, we've got a job to do, don't we?"

"There's a small, deserted Martian town nearby we could reach if we move quickly," she said, "but you'll have to leave the packs behind."

"Run across a desert? Without supplies?" Hilaire said. "It'd be better to hide. Running across the sand would be like leaving a trail of breadcrumbs for them to follow us with!"

"How do you know they're following us? What if they're trying to rescue us?" Gilbert said.

"A private sand schooner is a rich boy's toy. No one would send it on a rescue mission," Hilaire said. "And I—well, I've got some well-heeled folks upset with me these days."

"I know how that feels," said Gilbert, "but I think Anne's right! We need to move, and fast."

"About time you came to your senses," she grumbled, turning to face the empty desert again and spinning her eye wheel.

****

"This was them, then?" Fortescue was doing his best to keep the famous stiff upper lip of a British officer, but still had to breathe through his mouth and hold a small kerchief up to his face every now and again to keep from retching. He stalked around the wrecked Thark ship inspecting the human and Thark bodies surrounding it.

"This was them," the Painter said, brushing red dirt out of his thick mustache. "These bodies haven't got more than two days' worth of sand blown over them."

"And, er, there were no survivors?"

"Two," said Herb, his hands in his pockets as he looked over at the sets of prints tracking into the desert. "Two people walked away from the wreck."

"Human?" said Williamson. He already knew the answer, but it was the best question he could ask in order to make himself look important.

"Yes, by the look of the prints," said Herb, "unless the Tharks have taken to clipping their toenails enough to wear human army boots."

"Right, then!" said Williamson, giving a crisp smile and walking with long strides back to the skiff. "What are we waiting for, then?"

A chance for you to have a terrible accident, Herb thought, but held his tongue.

Chapter 35

". . . I don't set up to be good; but even a rascal sometimes has to fight the world in the same way as a saint."

– The Flying Inn

"Jimmy!" Frances yelled, her voice carried over the morning chill and sweeping wind. The little valley they'd made camp in overnight had suffered a windstorm, delaying their departure.

"What, Love?" he said from inside his sealed tent. Cripes, but she could be irritating. If the little minx couldn't learn to silence that tongue of hers . . .

"Jimmy, I've been waiting patiently for you to arise, but I can wait no longer! I'd heartily suggest that we resume our trip immediately! Another skiff passed us this morning; it was going roughly in the same direction as we're headed! If we hadn't been camped behind this sand dune, they would have seen us!"

The flap to Jimmy's tent popped open and Jimmy's head peeked through it, squinting in the pink morning sun. "What'd the skiff look like, Love? Tell me quick."

"A black ship, manned by a crew of five or six men. One of them looked familiar—someone I knew back on Earth. A horrible, useless creature named Fortescue Williamson!"

Jimmy smiled. He'd played enough cards with the British soldiers to know Fortescue's reputation.

"Right," he said. "I wouldn't worry too much now, dearie. If Williamson's hunting your man Gilbert, then your man's safe as a coin in a cast-iron chest."

"What?" she said. "How can you say that? Fortescue hates Gilbert, ever since Gilbert bested him last year in Berlin!"

"Miss Blogg," continued Jimmy as he found his round-topped hat inside the tent and began to pull on his boots, "Unless it can be solved by flashing a big wad o' tin and notes, Fortescue Williamson wrecks anything he puts his hand to sure as sand in a steam engine. Now," he said, emerging from the tent and then pulling up the pegs, "let's you an' me break camp. We'll skip breakfast, an' eat some jerky on the run as we give chase."

"Indeed," Frances said.

****

"How much further?" Gilbert gasped.

"A few hundred yards, maybe," said Belloc crisply. Still, even with leaving his pack behind, Belloc was sounding like the morning's sprint was starting to wear him down.

Anne alone among the three of them had said nothing, still running with her rifle in one hand while holding her skirt and petticoat in the other. Though by appearances she ought to have been slower than the other two, both Gilbert and Hilaire had to struggle to keep up with her.

"They'll arrive at your camp," she said, puffing slightly, "and try to pursue us. But there's a windstorm coming up from the Southern valley behind us. If they aren't chasing us, they might leave off when the storm hits. And if they *are* chasing us, we can hope that our tracks will be obscured in the wind."

"Lovely girl," Hilaire said to Gilbert, as his boots clomped in the red dirt. "Where'd you find her?"

"I didn't," Gilbert said between huffing breaths. "She found me. Last time I saw her, she broke my nose. And I found out she'd hypnotized me in Paris."

Hilaire jogged on in silence for a moment, watching Anne's form in front of them. "Does she have a sister?"

"We're almost there," she panted, interrupting them. She must be in tremendous shape, but the air was thinner than any of them were used to. Gilbert had been a runner in school years ago, but even he was developing a stitch in his side.

He wanted to ask what exactly "there" was, but he was too tired. As they reached the top of one of the largest sand dunes, Gilbert saw it.

Anne had called it a town. It was far closer to being a set of ancient ruins.

As they neared it, Gilbert saw several remains of broken buildings outside of a wide stone corral. A few steps closer, and what he'd thought

226

was a corral was really the base of what must have been an enormous tower, now worn down by time and the elements.

"Keep jogging!" she said. "I've no idea how close they are. We can lose them in the ruins, but only if we make it to the paved streets. We can't relax until then."

Soon Gilbert realized the broken tower's walls were still a good eight feet tall.

Past the wall and the small number of broken buildings on either side of it, the ground sloped down toward what had once been a mighty river. But the riverbed now was a wide, dry, and dusty furrow in the ground at least a hundred yards wide and twenty feet below ground level at its deepest point.

He'd seen a ghost town or two in his life, but the lifeless place standing before Gilbert dwarfed anything he'd seen in Minnesota. Buildings torn asunder and worn down by untold centuries of wind and elements, majestic towers that might have touched the skies of Mars were broken like children's toys, lying on the ground in pieces when their tired foundations had given out and allowed them to crumble.

"What *was* this?" Gilbert asked as he slowed enough to look at the remains of a wall three stories high with odd writing etched on them, the individual symbols each the size of his hand.

"Come on! Play archaeology later!" Belloc barked, snapping Gilbert out of his reverie. Seeing Anne alive had given him a surge of energy, even if she did look different. It had helped him keep up with her and the fit young sergeant in their run across the desert floor and into the ruins. But now he was tiring, and badly enough that he knew he was going to embarrass himself by running out of steam before either of his companions.

"Do you know where we're going?" Gilbert asked in a whisper. The city, though deserted, still had an eerie sense of presence about it. Gilbert felt as though their little group was running across the aisle at a high Mass, or at a royal function where nobles were politely pretending not to notice them.

"I'm following her," Belloc said, panting a little at last.

Anne was too far ahead to hear a whisper, so both Gilbert and Hilaire kept pace with her until she ducked into a broken building that still had its walls and most of its roof intact.

Gilbert hesitated for just a second. When the Martian tripods had invaded Earth, he, Herb and Father Brown had all tried to take refuge in a building that looked a bit like this one. It had provided no shelter at all, since the tripod had ripped the roof off and captured them with the ease of a boy kicking an anthill and plucking a stick out of the sand.

"Down here," she said. Stairs led downward, through a doorway and into a dark, stone-floored room. The room's coolness reminded Gilbert of how hot the outside was on its way to becoming. What time was it? Was it even nine o'clock yet?

They piled through the doorway and down into the dimly lit basement.

"Do you think they'll find us?" Gilbert asked as his feet padded on the stone steps.

"It's possible," said Anne, leaning against the wall and examining her long rifle. She fiddled with the barrel of her gun, removing it and handing it to Gilbert. "Here," she said, "see that panel in the corner? Belloc, hold it up against the opening, and Gilbert, use the rifle barrel I just gave you to brace the door. If our new friends pursuing us manage to get this far, I won't need range."

Still sucking in air and trying to seem like the sprint hadn't taken much out of him, Gilbert walked to the top of the stairs and knelt beside Hilaire, who had grabbed what looked like a long wooden board and was trying to hold it up against the opening in the floor they'd just traveled through.

"Reminds me of a prank we used to do when I was in school," Gilbert said, twisting the long barrel into the side of the wide, solid plank. The plank didn't seem to be made of wood, but it wasn't stone either.

Hilaire gave no indication that he'd even heard.

"We used to take pennies," Gilbert continued, still pushing the detached gun barrel between the plank on one of the steps on the staircase, "and shove them in the space between the door and the frame. And the poor fellow inside would get all frustrated because the door had no room to swing op—."

"Do you have another gun?" Belloc cut off Gilbert's anecdote, throwing the question over his shoulder to Anne like a rugby pass.

"I—I do," Gilbert said, pulling out the tiny pistol he'd found in the wreckage of the ships.

Both Hilaire and Anne looked at the tiny pistol for one second, and then ignored it. "No," said Anne, "none that I could hand to you. But I do have a blade or two. Here."

She passed her now barrel-less rifle into her mechanical right hand. It creaked and hissed slightly, like a cat mumbling in its sleep. Gilbert, having done all he could with the long barrel, looked at the hand with a slow fascination as her remaining, shapely hand snuck into the many folds of her dress and produced a knife, which made a wicked *snick* sound as she pulled it from an invisible sheath. She handed it to Belloc, the knife's handle pointed toward him while she held the foot-long blade. "I have one for you, too, Gilbert," she said, "though not nearly so deadly. I hope you've gotten better at hand-to-hand combat since our last encounter."

"Excuse me?" Gilbert said. "Last time I remember it was *me* who saved *you* when that crazy pilot from the floating city tried to turn you into a pincushion!"

"Yes. And he did it by throwing me on *your* sword, and I had to talk you through the whole process of field surgery in order to save my life! You were in such shock at seeing an actual, wounded person in front of you, I don't think you even noticed when I put the stick of silver nitrate in your hand!"

"Talk me through *what*? You *couldn't* talk! You had my cummerbund in your mouth! And you were mumbling some weird thing to yourself over and over to keep from going mad with the pain!"

"You remember that?"

"You don't forget your first operation on a live body," Gilbert said, holding her gaze while he holstered the small pistol and sticking the knife in his boot. "A friend of mine who'd been in medical school told me that. It's like your first kiss."

Her right blue eye flashed in anger at him, and he held her gaze.

"Look, you two," Belloc countered, waving a hand slowly between them, "I don't know what's gone on between you, and I don't care. All I care about is getting out of here alive and making it to Danton's Folly. Savvy?"

They still glared at each other, each reluctant to drop their gaze.

"Gilbert," Belloc said, shoving the taller boy to the door and speaking in the kind of tone a kindergarten teacher might speak to a young charge with, "take out your little pistol and your knife, and guard the door for now. And you, Miss—"

"My name is Anne," she said.

"Spelled with an *e*," Gilbert mumbled.

"Gilbert!" she said, exasperated.

"Door, Gilbert! You hear anything, *then* speak. Otherwise, *you keep quiet!*" Belloc whispered angrily.

"Shouldn't *I* be at the door?" Anne asked. "I have more firepower."

"If we *are* being chased, the last thing any experienced commander's going to do is make a frontal assault on a narrow space like a doorway. If they tried that, Gilbert would hear them." Belloc paused. Gilbert's head had been inclined toward them just a bit, but when Belloc had stopped speaking, Gil had turned more to face the doorway again. Belloc continued. "Just like he's listening to us now, pretending he can't hear a blessed thing. Right, Gilbert?"

"Sorry, did you say something?" Gilbert asked.

"You're a good writer, Chesterton, but a terrible liar. You just listen for anything at the top of the stairs but don't shout to alert us. Stamp your foot a bit if anything moves up there. Savvy? Good. Anne, you keep your eye on *that* little porthole up top." He pointed to a corner of the room where the brick had fallen away, letting a pink sunbeam shine through the gloomy basement. "You see anything up there that looks bigger than a rat, blast it into next week."

"What if they're friends or rescuers?"

"Though we've missed check-in, it usually takes much more time than this for the brass to decide to organize and send out a search party. Someone set up that ambush on my ship, someone who knew our flight plan and just where to hit us. Anyone we see this soon is coming to tie up loose ends, meaning us. Now, *this* is a fairly defensible position," he said, standing straighter as his confidence returned, though his voice remained at a whisper, "and I expect you both to do your jobs and save our lives. If all goes well, we'll stay here until the danger passes, and by this time tomorrow—"

Belloc was not used to being interrupted. When the long white arm reached out of the gloom and wrapped its thick, gray, black-knuckled fingers around his neck, it caught all of them by surprise.

Chapter 36

*"There is at the back of all our lives an abyss of light, more
blinding and unfathomable than any abyss of darkness; and it
is the abyss of actuality, of existence, of the fact that things truly
are, and that we ourselves are incredibly and sometimes almost
incredulously real."*

–GKC, Chaucer

"So, we're lost?"

John Carter was a former Confederate soldier and the first Earth
born warlord of the planet Mars. He'd seen death and sights that would
make an ordinary man's bowels turn into ice water. As such, it took a lot
to make him upset.

But he was getting there.

"I asked you a question, Emrys," he said to the blond, younger-looking
man studying the ancient-looking scroll while sitting on a pile of sand.

"I'm only checking navigation, John," Emrys answered, shoving some
of his long, unkempt locks of hair behind his ear and adjusting his glasses.
"At least try to be patient, would you? I'm trying to use a map whose
language is near indecipherable to us and was written on treated animal
skins back when our ancestors lived in caves on the British Isles."

"We're lost," Carter said. "Lost in a Martian desert." He stomped off
with a frown on his face.

"Sulking didn't work for Achilles," Emrys called after John, "and
it won't work for you. Sometimes you have to let the *scholar* have his
moments, Mister Warlord of Mars," said Emrys.

"Are any words appearing yet?" John asked, facing the sun. "Are there
any of those photo-photo-cannic—"

"Photo-*chronic*, John," Emrys said, still looking intently at the map
and using the distant voice of a parent who'd explained a concept many
times to an easily distracted child. "The Martians knew the difficult

trick of writing letters with a kind of ink that only becomes visible with certain degrees of light. Some of it is only visible by the light of a full, or even a quarter moon. But our particular location is marked, such that it's only visible when the *sun* is at..." Emrys checked his pocketwatch. He remembered again the thrill he'd felt when seeing the ancient Martian script appear like a ghost on the page of the manuscript months ago when a chance beam of sunlight strayed from the window, illuminating half-completed letters on the page.

"There!" Emrys said, feeling a sense of triumph as he pulled a crumpled and many-times folded piece of paper from his pocket. As the sun touched the map, different letter strokes appeared. *Genius*, Emrys thought. Sheer genius, not only to hide a message that could only be read by the light of the moon or the sun, but in separate *portions*, so that only half of it could be read at any one time. The ancient Martians who predated John Carter's red-skinned companions had not only been a noble race for most of their history, but a patient one as well!

Emrys dropped to his knees and began scribbling furiously on the scrap of paper, working with quick efficiency in case the lettering disappeared as quickly as it had arrived. Translating it afterward would prove to be quite a trick in and of itself. He wished his father could see him now. He couldn't recall much about his early life for some reason, but he did remember all those disappointed mutterings his mentors had made about Emrys studying something as impractical as ancient languages, rather than business or a trade. Well, it was certainly paying off now! Because of his studies, Emrys could now read a script that no other living being from Earth could have possibly deciphered! The letters could be quite random, which made it a greater challenge. Oddly, the process might be sped up if he could find something that could randomly generate numbers, but he'd never even heard of dice that worked in multiples of four, eight, ten or twenty rather than six, and ...

Emrys's pencil flew across the spare scraps of paper as he indulged his favorite passion. Languages, especially ancient ones, were so intoxicating to him he'd missed social events in order to either translate old ones or have fun inventing new ones. He had just finished the last relevant word when he stopped, his eyes widening with sudden realization.

"Dear Lord in Heaven," he said, as he crossed himself.

"What's wrong now?" Carter said. "Are we lost after all?"

"Worse," mumbled Emrys. "I know now exactly why the Branch is so interested in the dig to the North."

"What kind of weapon are they after?"

"It's not a weapon John. We've been going at this all wrong. It's not a gun or a plague or anything else they could bring back to Earth and blackmail the nations into compliance with. It's something of far greater consequence."

John was silent. Normally he loved to tweak Emrys' sensibilities, the way a fun-loving schoolboy might pester a friend who took life too seriously. But something in Emrys's face precluded all humor.

"What is it?" John said, cold prickles starting at the back of his neck. "Are they after my wife? Is Deja in trouble again?"

"No, John," said Emrys quietly, looking intently at the ancient words on the paper. "They're after..." Emrys paused, and used a Martian word unrecognizable to most human ears. But it chilled the soul of John Carter to hear it

Carter paused, words nearly failing him for the first time in a long, long time. "We've—" he finally said, "we've got a lot of work to do."

****

Cecil screamed as he ran from the old man who'd reached for him. A rational part of his brain told him he was being ridiculous, that he sounded like the boy who cried wolf. After all, what could be more ridiculous than running from a bald, chubby old man who was talking backwards along with a gramophone?

Yet the fear that gripped him was as complete and total as it was nameless. It was the fear one found only in a nightmare, where something as ordinary as a shadow or a person staring at you could make you wake up gasping in terror.

And so Cecil ran. He ran without looking back and kept running as he passed one of the surprised guards he'd snuck past earlier. He ran even after an authoritative voice boomed behind him, telling him to stop. He ran up stone stairs and back to the little apartment that he and Beatrice shared, ran until he was under the bed with a piece of sharpened stone in his hand he'd secreted there earlier, holding it as a pathetic dagger to defend himself if the old man came after him.

And he remained there until dinner, and past dinner until the shadows began to lengthen through the window. He remained there when Beatrice came into the room, looking for him and calling his name, leaving again to look for him elsewhere. He remained in place until she returned to the apartment some time later, made a more thorough search of their quarters, and finally found him under the bed.

Cecil had been ready for another tongue-lashing. But Beatrice saw his distress and wisely left Cecil instead to his improvised lair.

When he emerged after the sun had set, she made him some Ovaltine on the hot plate cooker in their room. He held the steaming mug, sipping it occasionally while staring at the wall for a long time.

"They're not after you, Cecil," she said after a long silence. "You apparently disturbed one of the gentlemen who is funding the expedition while he was getting dressed for the day. Now that I've told them that you are . . . well, *secure* was the word the chief guard preferred to use, they are largely unconcerned. Is there anything you need to tell me, Cecil?"

Cecil waited a full two minutes, and then he sipped his Ovaltine again. The chocolate taste brought him to his senses, and he began to speak. He meant to say only a sentence or two, but the words came tumbling out and he was crying for the first time in years by the time it was over.

Beatrice stood from her chair and hugged him. It had been a long, long time since she'd done so.

"Beatrice," he said, leaning back and wiping his nose, "he didn't do anything to me. Not the kind of thing you're worried about, no. But I . . . it was like for a while he was in my *head*, grabbing and routing around inside. He wanted to know how much I knew, and I could *feel* how much he hated me. And you. And . . . someone else. He hated Mother and Father, although they were different in his head than how we think of them. Never mind. I sound like a fool."

"Is everything all right?"

Beatrice and Cecil looked up. The Doctor stood in the doorway, his longcoat covering the right half of his body, his left arm visible through his sleeve, carrying his hat.

"Everything's fine, Doctor," Beatrice said, smiling while standing up and straightening her dress. Unconsciously, she stood between Cecil and the Doctor at the doorway.

"Jolly good," the Doctor said quietly with a smile and a slow nod. "I had heard that Cecil had something of an adventure recently while exploring the ruins. You do know better now, don't you, Cecil?"

"Yes," Cecil said quietly, sitting and staring at the floor.

"Jolly good," the Doctor said again, looking thoughtful and thoroughly unconvinced. "Jolly good. Well, Beatrice," he said, his voice raising as he swept his hat through the room to point out the door. "I must truly thank you for your patience. It seems that I am now authorized to show you some of the more interesting wonders that we've discovered during our dig here at the site. Would you and young Cecil care to join me in inspecting some of the artifacts we've unearthed? I'll need you to catalog them tomorrow morning."

"Of course, Doctor. I have a little discussion to finish with Cecil here, and I'll be right down."

"Excellent! Well, I'll, ah, jaunt downstairs and see you in a moment, then."

The Doctor left. When the sound of his feet scuffing the stone had faded, Beatrice leaned down and grabbed Cecil's ear, making him jump and yelp with surprise.

"We have a *chance* here, Cecil," she shouted in his ear. "A chance for something better, do you understand?" Her voice suddenly dropped to a whisper. "*Yell when I slap my hand,*" she said in her new, quiet voice.

"And *you*," she now said, her voice again rising to a roar, "you, boy, *will, not, ruin, it!*" She let go of Cecil's ear and slapped her right hand with her left several times. Cecil, unsure what she was doing but willing to play along, yelled in pretended pain each time Beatrice hit herself.

What in blazes?

"Now!" she roared, tyrant-like, "get in that bed and stay there! If you stir from this room again, so help me, I'll thrash you like mother used to when she was alive! Now, get going! *Cecil,*" here her voice dropped to a whisper again, speaking into his ear while he pretended to sob in pain, "*Cecil,*" she whispered, "*I don't trust these men either, and now you've confirmed what I felt. You'll need to escape. You know how to drive a sand skiff?*"

He nodded his head, still pretending to blubber loudly. "Good," she said, her voice still low. "You'll need to steal one—don't play innocent, I know you know how to do that, and right now I don't care. Steal it, drive it to the nearest settlement, and get help. *Any* help. Get the army, the French, the Belgians, I don't care, *someone!* They've talked when they thought I wasn't listening; there's at least one town a day's sailing away; it's called Danton's Folly. Follow the setting sun from here and you should be able to spot it in daylight. Wait until after I leave, and then go. Do you understand?"

Still giving his fake blubbering, Cecil nodded his head vigorously.

"Now *get to bed!*" she yelled, giving her hand one last, hard slap.

Cecil yelped and ran for the covers.

Beatrice left the room, sweeping up her skirts. As she did so, she heard a faint rustle outside their apartment door.

Someone had been listening.

Good.

Whoever the spy was, they'd report Cecil was now cowering in his room. Hopefully, the guard would be dropped or at least relaxed.

Cecil was resourceful. He'd be able to go. How *she* would escape was going to be quite another matter, but she could only focus on one life-threatening crisis at a time.

Chapter 37

"Even a bad shot is dignified when he accepts a duel."

–Orthodoxy

Herb looked down through his brass goggles at the three sets of footprints, made without any attempt to conceal their numbers. The runners were either inexperienced or rushed; either way, they'd gotten sloppy and were going to pay for it if Herb had any say in the matter.

One set of prints was obviously made by a set of army boots. The next appeared to be some kind of shoe with a swishing, broom-like motion sweeping around them. Perhaps a skirt? The third set was the most interesting. The feet were wide and the prints were far apart, indicating a tall runner. To Herb's trained eye they obviously the kind of cheap penny-loafers that Gil chose to wear whenever he had the chance.

Herb, still in the crouch he'd made while looking at the prints, stifled a chuckle as his finger traced the footprint in the dirt. Gil had found a *girl* willing to adventure with him! Timid, skinny, easily beaten Gil, who stayed with that same weak, wealthy little wallflower of a lady friend no matter what opportunities were dropped in his path.

Herb stifled a snarl at the goody-goody life Gil had chosen. Admitting he was jealous of his old friend was about as likely as the Confederate States of America admitting personhood to its slaves.

Possible? Yes.

But not bloody likely. No, not at all.

"Not at all," Herb said.

"Wot?" said the Woodsman, his own goggles glinting in the light. "Wot did you say?"

"We'll follow them into the city," Herb said as he stood, the footprints standing out to him like lit beacons on a dark winter's night.

"I say," said Williamson, straightening the epaulets on his shoulder, "nobody asked *my* permission on this venture!"

"There's a reason for that," Herb said, brushing the dirt off his hands. "It's because you aren't in charge anymore."

Williamson paused. "Excuse me?" he said. "What did you say to me?"

"I said you aren't in charge anymore, fop. Now, get back on the ship, or I'll forget why I kept Gil from maiming you in Berlin last year with your own shocking-nancy wand."

"What . . . you! You vile little—"

Fortescue Williamson never finished the thought. Herb moved so quickly he surprised even himself as he buried his fist in Williamson's face.

Williamson screamed like a little girl who'd just seen her favorite doll sawed in half. He fell to hands and knees in the red sand, covering his damaged nose with both hands while he was propped up on his elbows. After a few seconds, his muffled screams softened, replaced by a fresh batch of high-pitched shrieks and wails.

When Williamson's booted feet began kicking down into the dirt, Herb's lips curled into a sneer. He stepped over Williamson's prone, writhing body and walked up the ladder into the ship. "Painter," Herb said without looking back, "grab some help and bring that shrieking sack of offal on board. And then," he said, now seating himself in the forward observer's chair a few feet back from the wheel, "raise the sails and get us into the ruined city."

****

"You're quite sure that's the town on our map, Jimmy? I don't fancy spending another night lost and out in the open."

Jimmy breathed and decided to tell the truth. Last night he'd misread the map, stranded them in the desert overnight. He'd slept in the tent, and she'd slept in the boat. And though she hadn't screamed at him, she *had* been disappointed.

"I truly do think we're on the right path and should hit the deserted city soon, Miss."

"Excellent," Frances said, adjusting her goggles. Jimmy was very much like the business associates her Father described to his family at the supper table; a propensity to be conniving, but willing to be honest for those who saw through their guise yet respected them anyway.

Hopefully, once they reached the deserted city, she could end his employment there. Business was business, after all.

238

****

At the touch of the oversized fingers around his neck, Hilaire's eyes had bulged in horror, instinctively knowing just what had grabbed him. It was one of the dreaded white apes of Mars, a creature often discussed but so rarely glimpsed they were half-believed to be myths.

As the large hand lifted him up by the neck and turned him around, Hilaire no longer half-believed. He now stared a white ape in the face, and the creature snarled as Hilaire looked in silent terror, clawing at the ape's digits with his own much smaller fingers. It was at least a head taller than any gorilla to be found on Earth, with pointed tusks where most other primates would only have corner-canine teeth, and *four*, large, muscular arms ending in thick, black fingers poking out of the white fur.

It had snuck up on the little group with no sound they'd heard. Perhaps it had been in the room the whole time, hiding in the shadows without their knowledge. What none of them missed was the creature grabbing Hilaire by the throat and squeezing, its thick fingers making the flesh of Belloc's neck turn purple and black with bruises almost instantly.

Gilbert, shocked by the sudden attack, stared uselessly at both young man and ape for several crucial seconds. Anne swung her metal fist at the beast, who caught it with one of its lower free hands without even turning its head from Hilaire in its right upper hand.

"Blast!" she said, bringing up her boot, with its pointed, metal-covered toe, into the shin of the Martian gorilla.

It hit with a *thunk* that brought a painful memory to Gilbert; he'd seen her try that once before on someone, right before she'd been terribly wounded. The ape, though, stopped in mid-snarl at Belloc and turned to face her, now growling quietly as its bright yellow eyes glared at her with unconcealed fury. Though there wasn't even a spot of blood on the creature's leg where she'd kicked it, the creature let Hilaire go and swung at Anne with its lower left hand.

Seeing the threat to Anne, Gilbert finally snapped out of his own shock and pointed his weapon at the monster in front of him. He fired and missed, slamming a small, neat, dusty hole several inches away from the white ape's head as it squeezed Anne's metal hand in the dark colored fingers of its own.

"Bother," Gilbert heard her grumble over the ape's rumbling grunts and the incoherent gurglings of Belloc, holding his throat as he crawled on all fours. Anne stepped back from the ape, poking and pulling something on the metal wrist of her hand and . . .

She slipped away! Now her right arm ended in a metal stump, while the creature still held her metal hand. The light from the window glinted off the knife she pulled from the folds of her dress with her remaining left hand.

Gilbert aimed again at the head of the ape, hoping this time his aim would find its mark. Or, as old Mr. McGinty would have said back in Minnesota, "He kin shoot *straight!*"

Anne's knife flashed, whipping back and forth in her left hand. Gilbert saw it drag a line along the ape's arm, leaving a trail of bright, green blood behind it. The furry white arm went slack and Hilaire dropped to the floor, gasping and holding his neck for only a second before scuttling away from the fray and trying to regain his feet.

"Kill it, Gilbert!" Anne yelled as the ape's other three arms all swung at Anne, while Anne herself dodged, bobbed and weaved.

Gilbert fired. The bullet's retort made a second *snap!*ing sound in the room, filling it with acrid smelling smoke. The bullet grazed one of the creature's shoulders, making it roar in pain. It spun in place, sniffing the air. It suddenly spied Gilbert, and by the light of the pink sunbeam Gilbert saw its eyes flood with a dark, rich green as its lip made an angry curl over the tusks in the corner of its mouth.

Gilbert brought up his pistol, pointed it at the creature's chest, and almost laughed as the hammer clicked on an empty chamber.

Almost.

The snarling beast threw Anne's mechanical hand to the side and stomped toward Gilbert, who frantically spun the small, six-barreled chamber on the pistol, hoping this time when he pulled the trigger the hammer would come down on a live round instead of misfire. He brought his pistol up and pulled the trigger again.

It did! The pistol blasted with a flash, and instead of a small snap it unloaded its round with a retort that deafened all of them for a moment.

The ape's head snapped back and the rest of his body followed, reeling backward and staggering like a drunken man. The smell of smoke and black powder brought Gilbert back to a memory nearly two years ago when he'd used a pistol to fight another Martian creature in the sewers below the English town of Woking.

Gilbert let out a shuddering sigh, glad that it was over. He was totally unprepared when the ape's bloodied head appeared out of the smoke like an apparition in a ghost story, green blood dripping down its face, its sharp-toothed mouth roaring with twice as much rage and fury as before.

Gilbert screamed and brought his pistol up for what he knew would be the last shot fired in this little adventure, whether he killed this monster or not. But his finger was fumbling! The trigger wouldn't pull! The hammer wouldn't go back! The chamber wouldn't spin! He was going to die! He was . . .

Something shiny clapped down on the ape's head from behind.

The ape stopped in its roar at Gilbert and blinked, confused.

There was a meaty crack in the room, dull but no harder to hear than the pistol retort had been.

The top of the white ape's head exploded in a shower of green liquid and white fur.

Gilbert yelped again, shielding his face and body with his hand instinctively as the warm shower of green blood splattered across him and the walls of the stone room.

The body of the white ape stood still before realizing it was dead. It fell to its knees on the ground with a crunch, and then rolled on to its side.

Belloc, finally recovered, stared in awe at Anne.

The white ape's eyes stared, unseeing, at the ceiling. It lay flat on its back with its head gone from its eyebrows up. A puddle of green blood mixed with a gray paste was growing around it.

"Blast," Anne muttered, drawing the attention of both Gilbert and Hilaire. Her steam hand was reattached to her metal wrist and coated in the same, gooey, green-and-gray paste. "I don't suppose either of you know where a girl could find a tap or a water hose around this place, would you?"

Gilbert looked at Hilaire, who shook his head. Anne muttered something under her breath about amateurs, then grabbed her steamhand with her normal, left hand. She pushed a button in her wrist with her left thumb, her hand made a clicking noise, and then a hiss of steam escaped it. Her steamhand came away again, and she fumbled with it using her left hand alone for a moment with its sudden weight.

Gilbert's eyes grew wide. The stump of her right arm was covered with a kind of brass cap, designed to interlock with her mechanical hand at its base. It had several small rods and nubs sticking out where the steamhand could lock in and be controlled by her as well.

Amazing, he thought. Amazing. Nearly a year previously, when he'd thought her dead, his once best friend Herb had tossed him Anne's hand in a bundle of rags. He'd held her lifeless hand in his own, and now she was alive and well in front of him with. . .

With a Martian monster's brains drying between her metal fingers.

"Could one of you brave sir knights help me clean this off?" she said, frustrated that the folds of her dress weren't doing the job. "I really need two hands for this."

"What? Oh! Uh, sure!" Gilbert said, jumping forward and cradling the prosthesis in his hands. "Sergeant Belloc," Gilbert said, "do you have a handkerchief or something here?"

Belloc nodded his head, reached into his pocket, and produced a rag, which he wadded up into a ball and tossed to Gilbert. "Here," Belloc said, still looking at the two young people in front of him with an odd look on his face. "Sorry, Miss that, ah, it's so dirty. It was clean, earlier, before we were attacked by Tharks, and we had to make camp and all."

"Here, Gilbert, just hold the thing in place while I scrub it. There are key places that need cleaning which I couldn't reach if it were still attached. You don't know the places where dried blood and brains make the most difference. There." As she finished using the rag to dislodge a large clump of ape-brain and splat it on the floor, her left pinky finger brushed against Gilbert's hand. She stopped for a moment and looked into his eyes.

Gilbert felt very warm, and even in the dim light it wasn't hard to see his blush.

"I'll . . . I'll go do a little scouting," Belloc said, touching his neck and wincing.

"Are you sure that's a good idea, Sergeant?" Anne said, her eyes still locked on Gilbert's. "If there's more of these things about, they could do away with you, and we'd never know it."

"One thing about me you need to learn, Miss," he said, checking his pepperbox pistol, "is that I'm never surprised the same way twice. I'll see if I can find a supply of water, and I'll be back in about twenty minutes. Besides, you two apparently have a bit of catching up to do. Stay safe."

Gilbert tried to protest, but Belloc was already out of the room and up the stairs. Gilbert and Anne looked at each other for a few seconds in the room that was suddenly very, very quiet.

"How did you . . ." Gilbert asked.

"You're likely wondering . . ." she said at the same time.

They both stopped and waited a few more seconds. "You first," they both said at the same time.

They paused again, and then they laughed. The stress of the last few minutes coming out first in a few hesitant chuckles, then a few bursts of genuine, relaxed laughter.

"I thought you were dead," he said. "What happened?"

She started, stopped, then started again. "After I . . . well, after I *helped* you leave the floating city, I ran to Norton's control center. I destroyed the false evidence that would have plunged the Americas into war again, and I was about to leave when one of the more evil agents surprised me."

"Long black hair?" Gilbert asked.

Anne nodded and sat down in the dust and dirt. "We call her the 'Farmer.' Her job was to promote the healthy breeding of the 'right' kind of people, making the next generation of laborers. Unfortunately, she's since learned that the easiest way to do that is to treat the 'wrong' kind of people like human weeds, killing them at birth or even earlier."

Gilbert swallowed as he sat cross-legged across from her. "Monstrous," he said. "How could anyone be that sick inside?"

"You'd be surprised what people would accept, Gilbert, if they're told it's their *right* to do so."

"Just 'cause you've got a right to do something doesn't mean it's right to do. Any slave from my country'll tell you that. Sorry, I'm getting preachy."

"Not to worry. In any case, we fought, the Farmer and I. A sharp piece of debris fell down on me from the ceiling, pinning my arm to the ground. The metal was hot—very hot. The last thing I heard as I lost consciousness was the sound of my own flesh sizzling against it. When I awoke, I was in a hospital in Richmond. I'd been rescued somehow. They'd fitted me with a new hand and this," she said, touching the plate on her face with a sad look. "It's not altogether terrible. The mechanical eye lets me see and magnify things far away, which is how I was able to help you with my rifle here."

"You've gotten quite a reputation among Belloc and his men, Anne. They call you the guardian angel. You saved his life at least once. Mine, too, back there, when the Tharks attacked us in the air."

"Yes, well—"

A footstep crunched softly on the gravel outside the doorframe. Anne pulled her knife into a throwing stance with her left hand, and Gilbert raised his pistol, pointing it at the door and hoping a split second later that it was loaded.

Belloc's voice sounded without them seeing his face. "I . . . er . . . hope I'm not interrupting anything," he said from behind the ajar door, "but it looks like we're going to have some company, and soon."

****

"...so it was true, then?" Father Flambeau said, the floater humming softly as he drove it through the deserted streets, kicking up small clouds of red dust wherever it moved. "Not just a story from the penny dreadfuls? You literally pulped the brains of a white ape in the ruins?"

"That's rather tame, considering some of the exploits during the war I've heard about, Father Flambeau," Anne said. "And those are just the ones I've heard about. But to answer your question, yes, it is true. That particular hand was very adept at crushing objects when needed. My current model, though, is not nearly as useful in a fight. But it does allow for a bit more dexterity." She flexed it twice—it was smaller than her first prosthesis had been, but still looked formidable.

"Really?" said Gilbert.

"Well, I wouldn't use this hand to remove an appendix, but I can at least write with it and open doors and the like."

"So," Father Flambeau said, "there's no more danger of apes in the city, then?"

"They were exterminated by big game hunters," said Anne. "Men bored of hunting tigers in Darkest Africa started coming on safaris up here to hunt White Apes in the lost cities of Mars. The local restaurants and hotels loved them, but I was the one who had to patch up the unsuccessful hunters and the locals they hired as porters when the apes and other beasts took exception to their little outings."

"So, the city is deserted, then?" Gilbert said, his voice quiet. Something in the deserted city made him want to be quiet, more out of the kind of reverence you'd have in a room with a dead body in it than anything else.

"Cleared of Apes, yes. Now they're all on some preserve by the river Iss. The greatest danger comes from desert raiders who make these places their base of operations."

"You know, Anne, you might have told us that before we entered."

"It hardly seemed relevant at the time," she said, using a tone that could have been used to adress street beggars or lazy workmen. *"Besides, you said time was of the essence. Driving through here was the quickest route, and I know how to deal with that kind of scum."*

"I'll bet you d—"

Gilbert stopped speaking suddenly, as they heard a small slap, like a hand against flesh. Gilbert jerked in his seat, his eyes wide open. *"I . . . I think that I . . ."*

"Father!" Anne yelled.

"Fra...Fra..." Gilbert muttered, his speech slurring and his eyes going into a glassy state Anne had seen all too many times. She checked his head, his neck and chest with her left hand while feebly trying to shield them both with her right. Who was on that holy card that Johann had given her on her last birthday?

"Saint Raphael," she said, *"if you can hear me at all, I need your help now."*

"Is he hit?" Father Flambeau yelled back to her as he swerved the floater to avoid a pile of rubble in the ancient street. A sound like a hummingbird whizzed past his, then Anne's head.

"I think so, but I can't find where . . . ah . . ." she stopped as she looked on his right side.

"How badly?" Father said, bobbing and weaving the floater as more hums and whines began sailing and singing in the air around them.

"We'll need to get to shelter," she said, *"and quickly! I have to stop the bleeding, perhaps operate to get the bullet out. Hang on,"* she pulled Gilbert down to the seat on his side, looking at his back. The exit wound, like all exit wounds, wasn't pretty in the least. But it did suggest by its width and mess that whatever had hit Gilbert had gone clean through. A quick look at the seat he'd been sitting in confirmed it. The huge red spot on the back of the cushioned seat had a furrowed hole in its center.

"Keep moving forward! Agh!" she barked as another bullet screeched by her ear. She ducked down next to Gilbert. He was mumbling again, this time about chess and baseball.

"Is he still with us?" said Flambeau as the buildings whizzed by.

"Yes, but not for much longer if we don't stop and I take a look at his wounds in a stable environment!"

"There are supplies underneath the seat," he grunted as spun the steering wheel. "Have you ever operated on someone, Anne?"

"Yes," she said, pulling out bandages and tools from under the seat.

"In a moving vehicle?"

"No."

"Then today God will expand your horizons! Hold on!"

Chapter 38

"The whole object of travel is not to set foot on foreign land; it is at last to set foot on one's own country as a foreign land."

–*Tremendous Trifles*

"You want to go to the ruins of the Great City, then? Where the temple of Iss used to be?" said Emrys, the wind whipping his stringy, dirty-blond hair.

"Not immediately, unless that ghost who likes to haunt you now and again says we should."

"Calling an *ousiarch* a ghost is like calling a Viking warcraft a rowboat, John. It's only vaguely accurate and does no justice at all to the reality of the situation."

Carter smiled, happy that he'd gotten the old-souled fellow's goat again. He was having more fun this trip than he'd had since . . .

The smile on John Carter's face faltered, as a terrible memory flitted through his mind.

"Emrys," said Carter, "I may be the Warlord of Mars, but even *I* would consider it foolish to go to that place with just the two of us. There's talk that the Special Branch and their masters have been digging things up at a furious pace, and uncovering much of what should have stayed hidden. Even the Warhoons are a tad shy about going there. I've got a fellow over at Danton's Folly who owes me a few favors. Perhaps we can rally a few troops to better our odds when we arrive?"

Emrys closed his eyes and tilted his head slightly. "Yes," he said. "To Danton's Folly, then. But we'll find something there we're neither looking for nor expecting." Emrys looked off into the distance. Carter smiled again and stayed silent. He'd learned long ago that asking about his friend's cryptic pronouncements was asking for an even more puzzling answer.

****

"Have you been here before?" Herb asked as they slid over the border of the ruined city, the bottom of the ship scraping roughly on the broken stone road as it left the desert sands.

"No, Cleaner," the Painter said to Herb, rubbing his moustache with a nervous air. "I've only heard the stories. People entering and never leaving, or leaving with fewer of their parts than they came with."

"Indeed," said Herb as their ship came to a stop. "Let's go find our quarry, then. Or at least their remains. With the exception of Fortescue Williamson, make sure our men are armed with weapons drawn. But no one kills Chesterton without my say so. Savvy?"

The Painter nodded, then looked back at the other agents gathered behind him on the deck.

The Driver nodded, his new metal hand finally fitted snugly to his wrist where Carter had chopped off the original.

The Woodsman nodded too, but slowly. His pistol was already drawn, and the goggles he wore made his eyes glint in the sun.

The Postman, his hand twitching more than ever, gave a quick, curt nod. His eyes darted back and forth, looking at every empty window and doorway in front of them, scanning for threats.

"Where's Williamson?" Herb asked.

"He's down in the hold," the Postman said, his voice quiet and gravelly. "He tried getting sympathy from me by telling me how awfully he was being mistreated. I told 'im about *my* childhood, an' it shut 'im up good. Can we get goin' now?"

"No," said Herb. "Get him up and out of the hold. I want him with us as we make our way. And give him a knife so he won't blubber so much. He may draw predators out of hiding, and if we can toss him to them as a snack, then I'll be able to truthfully tell his father that his son died sacrificing himself to help us complete our mission."

After a minute, Williamson emerged from below deck. He still wore his full dress uniform with a combat knife at his belt, looking around with a confused air while the Postman guided him from behind.

Suddenly, a muffled blast shook the air around them. The men all looked at each other.

"That way," Herb growled, looking in the direction the gunshot had come from amid the ruins.

Everyone started in the direction Herb had pointed, including

Fortescue Williamson. "Are you sure it's safe?" Fortescue asked as he walked quickly, giving furtive glances at every open door and window in the broken buildings around him.

"Shaddap, fop," said the Postman, his skinny arms already pulling his pistol out of its holster, "or you'll have yourself an accident before we get fifty feet into this ghost town."

Chapter 39

*"I wonder that no one has written a wild romance about the
adventures of such an alien, seeking the great English aristocrats,
and only guided by the names; looking for the Duke of Bedford
in the town of that name, seeking for some trace of the Duke of
Norfolk in Norfolk. He might sail for Wellington in New Zealand
to find the ancient seat of the Wellingtons. The last scene might
show him trying to learn Welsh in order to converse with the
Prince of Wales."*

–All Things Considered

Cecil pulled the rope on the sail as best he could. He'd become something of a jack-of-all-trades in the past year. While he'd gotten the most experience in taking things that weren't his, he'd also learned the basics of cooking from spying on housewives until they'd left their homes empty and vulnerable, police procedures from being arrested multiple times, and the basics of sand-sailing from stealing the occasional sloop.

Taking the sand-sloop this time had been easy. A simple, one-man craft, it had been one of the least difficult pinches in his career.

He'd set up some rickety wood behind a wall a dozen yards or so from the bigger boats and then tossed a rock at it from a safe distance. The single lummox of a guard watching the boats had investigated immediately, leaving Cecil to take the smallest of the dozen now-unguarded vessels without trouble, or even much of a rush.

Cecil had unmoored it, then gave the small ship a strong push and slid it out through a gate, left open during the workday. The noise of the workmen digging and shouting at each other covered the noise of the sloop on the stone ground. Cecil guessed that by the time the slow-witted guard returned, even the sloop's tracks would have been swept away and covered by the Martian winds. With a little luck, he'd be halfway to Danton's Folly before he was missed. Once there he'd begin the real work of finding help for Beatrice. Even if it meant trying to free her with

251

nothing more than a stolen flintlock pistol, he'd be back for her.

He sailed without incident for several hours or more. Suddenly in the distance, he saw something that made his heart jump—something dark on the horizon! Something coming from the direction of Danton's Folly! Each minute he sailed brought the vision into sharper focus. What first appeared to be a single, dark blob on the line between the red sand and the pink sky soon separated into several blobs. Another minute and he could count four of them. Two more minutes, and he saw the blobs were ships very similar to his own craft—single-seater sand sloops, made for fast transport of goods, delivering messages, or (as in Cecil's case) a speedy escape.

Cecil smiled, then adjusted his goggles. The day had started out awful, and gotten worse with his lunchtime encounter with the crazy old man talking backwards to himself. *But now*, Cecil thought, *now things are looking up!*

The other sailors were so good at their profession that Cecil had no idea they were sand pirates until they rammed his ship and sent him flying into the air.

****

"Where are we off to, then?" Gilbert said. He'd adjusted his belt, tightening it in the hopes it would stave off hunger the way it did for the cowboy heroes in the nickel novels he'd read as a child. It had never worked for him yet, but maybe today . . .

"I'm for continuing onward to Danton's Folly," Belloc said, looking out over the red dunes from the ruined balcony he stood on, his right hand shading his eyes. "It's a wretched place, a hive full of miscreants and villainous scum who chose a life on Mars over prison. But it's our best hope right now."

"How do you know we'll be safe there?" Gilbert asked as they trudged down a nearby set of stone steps and back out into the streets of the lost city. "Are there a lot of police, with all those criminals?"

"Yes," Belloc said, "but policemen in a place like Danton's Folly are only bigger thugs with badges. We'll only be safe if we make ourselves look poor and not worth accosting."

"Fine," Gilbert said. "The other thing I was worried about: are you sure it's a good idea to go hiking in the city through these ruins in broad daylight? What if those things come at us again?"

"In truth, Gilbert? I don't know. I only thought of white apes as pubfire myths until today. What of you, Miss Anne? Do you know anything about white apes, or anything else that can threaten us out here?"

"I've seen the apes scurry around in both day and nighttime; they don't seem to have a preference. The only things that seem to attract them are noises in the daytime, or lights and fire at night."

"Right, then," said Belloc, drawing his pistol and moving toward the stairs, "let's keep on the move. We'll be out of this crazy place within the hour, if we can avoid being attacked again. Once at Danton's Folly, we'll figure out our next move."

The three of them walked down, Belloc first, Gilbert second, and Anne bringing up the rear. After a few seconds of walking down the deserted street, Gilbert had the uncomfortable thought that they'd sandwiched him between them because he was the least able in combat.

He pushed away the thought. Though he had credentials as a Martian killer and a semi-able martial artist, this wasn't the time to make an issue about them.

You didn't kill a Martian on your own. You had help and you know it. And the last time you fought someone with your Martial Arts . . .

The thought had jumped into his head unbidden. Well, the Martial arts thing might be pushing it, true. But he *could* take care of himself! After all, it wasn't *he* who'd needed rescuing down in that little basement from the white ape . . .

Without Anne, you and Belloc both would be dead.

Though still moving, Gilbert paused in his thoughts. He hated it when something interrupted a good, youthful rant in his head. But what was wrong with thinking he could take care of himself? How was that different from good old-fashioned independence? His country'd been built on the idea that a man could run his own private affairs, and—

There are no private affairs.

Shut it! He thought back strongly. Besides, there was nothing wrong with being able to take care of yourself! That gave one a right to certain privileges! No more treating him like he was some silly little China porcelain doll! That's it! No more!

Resentment blistering in his head, Gilbert turned to Anne behind him. "Anne, you go in the middle position. *I'll* bring up the rear and cover you if there's trouble."

She stopped and looked at him with a serious expression on her face. "Gilbert, do you recall how I reacted the last time you used that tone of voice with me? Can you really afford to get into another argument, or do you fancy me breaking your nose a second time? Or is it a third? I'm having a hard time keeping count these days."

"Fine," Gilbert said, "would you *please* walk in front of me? I'd much prefer you were between Sergeant Belloc and I if there was trouble."

She shrugged, then stepped in front of him. "Fine, if it'll get us going faster. But really Gilbert, arguing over a place in line here is like fighting over who gets the best deck chairs on the *Titanic*. If God Himself wants to sink the ship, all your efforts are going to be in vain. And if another one of those apes jumps on us, then the marching order isn't going to matter, much."

"Then just humor a silly American boy who wants to be chivalrous."

"Chivalry is dead, Gilbert. At least that's what they're proclaiming in the universities these days."

"And why's that, do you think?" Gilbert said, already enjoying the view of Anne from behind.

"Maybe too few people know what chivalry really is," she said primly, following Belloc.

"She's right, Gilbert," said Belloc from the front of their little line.

"You? As an honorable Army Sergeant? Agreeing with this?" Gilbert said, trying to keep his voice low despite the argument they were having.

"I never said it was a good thing, or not. It's just a fact: Only the girls worth dying *for* have love for chivalry any *more*." Here he turned back a bit with a wince as he moved his bruised neck, and his eyes flicked over to Anne.

"You're a bit of a poet, Sergeant Belloc," Anne said with a smile.

"Couplets are the easiest rhyme," Belloc said with a small smile, "Children love them, to pass the time."

Gilbert blinked. For a second, there seemed to be more of Anne's hair at the back of her head. Then he realized that her ears had just gone very, very red, and she'd slowed down her pace.

Right after Belloc had mentioned . . . mentioned *couples*, and *children* . . . to Anne . . .

"Um, are we still trying to leave this place?" Gilbert asked, his voice rising a bit.

Belloc picked up the pace, his feet crunching on the gravel beneath. "Fine, but keep your voice *down*, will you? I don't know if those apes are asleep, or if they have equally ugly neighbors in this rubble."

"Me keep *my* voice down? What about—?"

"Gilbert, he's right," Anne said. "You are getting a bit loud, don't you think?"

Gilbert spluttered a little, but then he silenced himself. Once they were out of this place, he was going to have to have a serious chat about them both taking him seriously!

He spent a second forming the answer when part of the pillar next to his head exploded.

Chapter 40

"All the mystery of the white man, all the fearful poetry of the white man, so far as it exists in the eyes of these savages, consists in the fact that we do not do such things. . . the cannibals say, 'The austere and terrible race, the race that denies itself even boiled missionary, is upon us: let us flee.'"

–All Things Considered

"No!" Herb yelled, "I said *don't* shoot Chesterton, you dolts! *Bring* him to me! I don't care about the others, but *don't kill Gilbert!*"

The Painter blew a disgusted sound through his moustache and stood up. He'd dropped to one knee when they'd caught sight of Chesterton, then the annoying, unbribable Sergeant Belloc and some girl with red hair all walking in the ruins.

Red hair?

The Painter stopped for a moment and looked more closely. "Actress?" he mumbled under his breath, standing tall and starting to run towards them.

The Woodsman and the Postman were behind him, jogging with their pepperbox pistols in hand. "Why can't we kill Chesterton?" the Postman yelled in his high, screechy voice.

"Because I *said* so, *that's* why, you worse-than-useless dolt!" Herb said in an angry whisper, grabbing the Postman's pistol and speaking an inch from his face. "Do you need any other reason? Do you?" his voice raised in volume and grew louder as he became more upset. "Didn't the Branch weed out cretins like you at birth when they found out that you have a capfull of dromedary droppings between your ears?"

"Shut yer gob, Cleaner," the Woodsman whispered, fear making his voice shake slightly. "Ye don't know what could jump out at—"

The Woodsman never finished his speech.

A white ape leaped down out of the shadows cast by the buildings, grabbed the Woodsman's head in a giant white-furred hand, and twisted it at an angle impossible to find in nature.

The ape then grabbed the Woodsman's limp body in its two lower hands and proceeded to pull and rip the goggled man's arms off easily as if they belonged to a tattered rag doll, without any need to pause or even pull very hard. The Woodsman had become an armless, near-headless corpse in less than three seconds. The body bounced and rolled away behind the ape, who gnawed the arms with such total focus that it didn't even notice the Postman. To his credit, the Postman had kept his composure while his colleague was dismembered beside him. He now brought his own pistol to a slow aim at the beast's head. He squeezed the trigger, and—

He never knew what hit him; while he was aiming, another white ape leapt at him unseen from behind. In less than a second, the white monster brought down its upper two, incredibly powerful fists onto the Postman's head. The blow hit with so much force that the smaller man's skull cracked, snapping loud enough for the sound of his breaking bones to echo through the city.

Not quite as discriminating as its brother ape, it began devouring the Postman's still-twitching body instantly, consuming bone and meat alike in great, grinding gulps and chomps.

Herb had fallen still when the first ape had killed the Woodsman, and then he had slowly gone into a crouch behind a pile of rubble with a broken wall at his back when other, smaller apes had crawled out of the ruins to feast on the Woodsman's armless, headless corpse. With the Postman dead, too, Herb knew that his chances of surviving this encounter had gone down by at least a factor of ten.

Options and assets, Herb thought, remembering one of the more benign parts of his training as an agent for the Special Branch. *When in a fix, always look at your options and your assets.* He looked first at the Painter, who'd already taken cover, with his weapon drawn. Herb felt more confident. And all that new confidence vanished instantly when he saw Williamson, wearing his once well-ironed and polished uniform, standing out in the open with his eyes wide and his hands at his sides, too frightened to even twitch.

"Oh, blast," said Herb.

****

After the agent had fired at Gilbert and missed, Belloc, Anne, and Gilbert had sprinted toward the nearest building for shelter. "I'm not sure what this was, but it looks important," Belloc rasped as he ran up the stairs of the Martian building, trying to keep his steps silent. The stairway was perhaps a dozen feet wide and worn down in many places by the erosion of wind and sand. "And big enough for us all to get cover in."

As the screams began echoing down the street, they began to move even more quickly. The deaths of a number of their pursuers did nothing to make them feel secure. Looking back as they ran, Gilbert had recognized Herb leading the little group, all of whom had drawn weapons in their hands. Even if the fellows who'd shot at them were all eaten by white apes, that didn't mean more of the creatures wouldn't come to feed on Gilbert & Co., too!

"So, it's hide and hold position, then?" Anne said, turning around and spinning the dial on the side of her head as she tried to gain a closer look at the apes feasting on the corpses of the two agents.

"For the moment," Belloc said, now halfway up the long set of outdoor stairs.

Gilbert turned too, but he didn't see more than a flash of white fur in the distance before he urged Anne to move even more quickly up the stairs. The three of them moved single file through the open doorway into the stone building. The doorway and walls were thick, carved out of the deep red colored rock that almost all the buildings appeared to be made of here in the city.

The inside of the building was cool and dimly lit by pink beams of light from the doorway and through chinks in the wall. Slow-moving spirals of red dust made leisurely, elegant movements in the beams of rosy light.

"How do we close this?" said Gilbert, ineffectively pushing and pulling on the slab of rock they'd just moved past as they'd entered. "Or should we barricade it somehow?"

"Wait," Belloc said, "I've seen these before. There should be a beam over . . ."

He moved to a space beside the door. A small hole was set into the stone wall beside the doorway, through which a narrow beam of light shone through. While the other beams in the room all pointed in to the West wall, this beam pointed straight down into a small crater dug into the floor.

"Let's see if this works," Hilaire said. He waved his hand, palm up, splitting the beam and letting the shadow of his hand play on the floor for a few seconds.

There was a small rumble, the kind you'd hear from a reluctant piece of furniture moving across the floor. The three of them looked up and saw a heavy, flat slab of stone emerge from inside the doorway and move without any apparent machinery or other aid.

In seconds it had blocked the doorway. The room was darker now, but not entirely unlit; there were still cracks in the wall that let sunlight in from outside.

"What now?" Gilbert asked.

"What now indeed," said Anne, rummaging about inside the pack she'd carried on her back all this time. Gilbert was impressed; she'd packed everything so tightly and well that none of her gear had made a sound while she moved. Gilbert had seen men with twenty years in the armed forces whose gear would jingle like Santa's sleigh in an earthquake on Christmas Eve, especially if they ran with it. "Now, I think," she said, after a few seconds, "we see if we can find a light in this very dark room and get it working, and then we move deeper into this place. After that, we hold position for a bit until things cool down outside."

She struck something against the stone floor, and a small stick in her hands bloomed into flame.

"Is that the . . . uh . . ." Gilbert asked. During their last meeting, Gilbert had needed to burn closed a wound Anne had received from a sword to her gut. Fortunately, none of her major organs had been speared, and she'd at least been able to hobble with him and force him to escape.

"No," she said as she started to lead them down the nearest corridor, "it's not the silver nitrate you used on me. You did a very nice job on my wound, by the by. I didn't have the slightest bit of infection."

"Infection?" said Belloc looking at Gilbert. "*You* performed field surgery? On *her*?"

"You'll find I'm full of surprises," Gilbert said, in what he hoped was a manly sounding voice. "If you were really in contact with Chang . . . well, *Father* Chang, now, you'd have known that."

"I'd heard a few things about you. But I was beginning to think that Chang's praises were just kindness and wishful thinking."

"Well, real is what's there, no matter *what* you or I think," Gilbert said, remembering the philosophy he'd been reading in his spare time. "And if you want *real* proof, I'll bet her scar can speak to that louder than I."

"Is that so?" Belloc said, his face coloring. "I find it hard to believe that a jumble-fingered fellow like you could make a surgical incision any straighter than the mouth of a jack-o-lantern."

"Gentlemen, if you *please*," said Anne, not even trying to conceal the annoyance in her voice, "I'm rather uncomfortable with two strong, healthy young men discussing the exposure of my midriff to settle a wager about the strength of Gilbert's manliness!"

Gilbert and Hilaire stared at each other for a few more seconds. Then, as if by an unspoken agreement, they broke their gaze at the same time and both pretended to look for more doors in the wall. While his fingers began searching crannies in the wall, Gilbert beamed inwardly, his thoughts perfectly logical for one of his age and mind:

She thinks I'm strong! And manly, too!

****

"Do you think this is truly wise, Miss?" Jimmy said for the fourth or fifth time since they'd entered the outskirts of the ruins in their sand skiff. He held on to the ropes of the skiff and pulled hard, in an effort to keep moving at the snail's pace they'd been keeping since they'd entered the city limits.

"No, Jimmy," Frances said, "but it *is* what I *have* to do. Keep going at this pace, won't you? I truly think we've little to fear. Every book I've read on survival in hostile environments has said that signs of a recent meal ought to give an explorer a sense of security, as whatever has recently eaten won't be coming after the explorer herself."

But Jimmy looked around warily. Something had feasted recently, and done so on human flesh. Bones littered the ground, which had been painted bright crimson with human blood. Another sand skiff pointed towards the West, and had apparently left a number of crew members behind to be dinner for something very large and strong.

"Er, if you don't mind me askin', Miss," Jimmy said, looking at Frances. She was in the prow of the boat, looking intently at the ground in front of them, pointing like a figurehead in the direction she wanted the ship to travel in.

"Yes, Jimmy? I can talk while I'm following footprints. The other ship left recently, but there's another party on foot leading away from this fracas. Pray, ask your question."

"Well, just 'ow many books did you read about how to survive here on Mars?"

"Only one, Jimmy. But I read it several times and quite thoroughly. Thus far it's proven quite reliable."

Jimmy sighed and kept steering the ship, driving it slowly over the sands. This job was beginning to take twists both strange and dangerous. If this kept up, it'd be hard for the Queen of England to make it worth his while to stay on.

"Hold!" she said suddenly, her pointed hand suddenly raised to a fist. Jimmy pulled hard on the ropes, and the sails rose all the way up, the wind now flowing around the mast without the slightest bit of catch against the ship.

After she'd raised her fist they'd stopped the ship, and she jumped from the bow of the boat. A pair of rugged hiking boots purchased in a local shop before their trip on the skiff had replaced her dainty pointed indoor shoes. The new boots made a hefty *thud* as she landed on the ancient stone of the broken street, and they left much larger prints in the fine sand than her older shoes would have.

"Miss?" said Jimmy. His voice shook a little as he looked around at the ruins and the human remains on the ground.

"Shh," she said. She'd gone into a crouch, staring intently at the ground. Now she held up her hand while turning slowly in a circle on her booted toes. "There was a very one-sided conflict here," she said, "and quite recently, too. The blood over there has pooled, but not fully congealed. Furthermore, several sets of tracks lead over there," she said, pointing, "then they circle back here to the set of tracks where the last ship was. What type of creature here has hands for feet, Jimmy? There are several tracks like those around here."

"White Martian apes, Miss," Jimmy answered, looking about with a nervous air. "The yearlings are bad enough; they's only about seven feet tall and maybe sixty stone. But the big ones, the ones full grown could be twice that, easy."

"Quite a job for any mother, to have an eight-hundred-pound gorilla for a son. Well!" she said, standing and straightening the folds in her dress. "I'd suggest my dear beau is not on the ship that left, but instead on foot."

"Wot's that, then?"

"Because there were three sets of footprints leaving from the crash site we spotted earlier. And there are . . ." she said, now more to herself than to Jimmy, "still *three* sets of prints—a set of sensible, men's walking shoes, a set of army boots, and . . ." her eyes closed for a moment, then opened again as she regained her composure, "a pair of women's walking boots."

"You can tell all that, miss?"

"Jimmy, girls of my station in life know *everything* about shoes by the time we're old enough to hold a dinner fork."

Something tapped her toe. Frances looked down and saw a battered, black top hat that had been blown by the wind. It had a set of goggles strapped around it, and a small dark stain across its brim.

Not long ago, an accessory stained by the blood of its previous owner would have made Frances Blogg turn away in terror and disgust. But several months of travel with a rough crowd combined with her recent journey through a harsh and unforgiving desert millions of miles from home had made her into a very different kind of person indeed.

She picked up the hat and placed it on her head, turning the bloodied part away from her eyes. Though not a perfect fit, it worked quite nicely as a sun visor. And who knew what use the goggles might be put to later on?

Within a minute or so, they'd reached the stairway to the red stone building.

Frances motioned Jimmy to follow her as she climbed the stairs. Jimmy looked around nervously, but then he straightened his round-top bowler hat and followed her.

"Can you read these at all, Jimmy?" she asked, looking at a set of ancient words carved in the stone wall.

"Not too much trouble there, Miss," Jimmy said. "I may very well 'ave been the first person on Earth to do so, in fact. 'Ere," he pulled out several dirty, wrinkled pieces of paper from an inner pocket in his worn suit jacket. "Looks like . . . could you remember these words for me as I say 'em, Miss? Thankee . . . *To . . . get . . . gain? To gain* . . . inside? No, no, *entrance. To gain entrance, block light.*"

Frances waited. "Is there anything else?"

"Well, Miss, this is a mark I 'aven't seen before. It's right here, and . . ."

Frances looked at it. "That's an arrow, Jimmy," she said quietly.

"Um, yes, well, I don't see any light, there, Miss. As you can see, the building's in shadow right now, at least our half of it, and—"

Frances' hand jumped to a small stone construct jutting out beneath the arrowhead carved in the rock. It looked like half a small stone dish turned upside-down, held about a foot above another dish.

Her hand moved in between both dishes, palm up.

"Are you sure you want to do that, Miss? Are you sure that this is—"

For the second time in untold centuries, the stone door beside them began to move. This time the stone moved smoothly and without noise, having cleared away the small bits of rubble and dirt from the doorway when it had opened a half hour ago.

Jimmy looked at Frances, but her eyes were on the doorway. "They went in there," she said, flexing her leather-strapped hands several times as she stepped over the threshold.

****

Cecil woke up with sand in his mouth, a headache in his temples, and the smell of stale beer in his nostrils.

He tried to shake his head, but the pain was just too great. Where was he?

He sat up and sneezed, making his head hurt even worse. Sawdust in his nose, too, from lying on the wooden floor of the...

He looked around the room. It was fairly quiet in here, and in the silence the memories came back, slowly but surely.

Despite trying to dodge the larger craft, Cecil's tiny vessel had been rammed by the very sand-ship he'd hoped would give him aid. After flying from the small, one-man sand sloop, Cecil had ended up head first in a red dune of sand. He vaguely remembered being dragged up by rough hands and swarthy, laughing voices nearby, but nothing else afterward, nothing until awakening here in this—

The room had swinging doors, open to the outside.

He was in a bar?

Cecil leaped to his feet, just as several large men entered the swinging doors, shouting with the loud but tired voices of men just leaving a hard workday behind. They stopped when they saw him.

"Awake, huh, kid?" one of them said, smiling. "The bossman wants to see ya."

Cecil's instincts to fight or run rose up, but he pushed them back. There was only one way out of this place, and several very large men blocked it. No, neither fighting nor running would be in Cecil's best interests right

264

now. His job wasn't to pick a pocket and escape, but instead to get help for Beatrice. And he'd be more likely to find that from someone whom the workers nicknamed "Bossman" than any of the lowlifes he knew back in Syrtis Major.

"Fine. Where is he?" Cecil asked, standing with his fists planted at his hips and his chin stuck out in a defiant pose. Whenever he faced huge odds, doing this either got the men laughing good-naturedly, or clouting him on the ear. Hopefully, today he'd get the former.

His hope was rewarded. A number of the men chuckled at his bravado despite being tired from a long day's work. Several of them spoke with accents that sounded French, but there was also a British cockney tone or two lifting up from the cacophony of voices quickly filling the room.

More rough hands grabbed him, then propelled him from the barroom and out to the dusty main street of the town.

Rickety buildings lined the street. Many looked to once have been trimmed and well kept, but time and the elements had quickly worn them down until they looked like weathered sets of old men's teeth.

The largest of the sagging houses was at the end of the street, and it was here the small mob of five grizzled men shoved Cecil, his rumpled and dirty shirt picking up still more dust and dirt as the men around him kicked it up and pushed him forward.

After a few minutes, they reached the stairway leading up to the large house's door. During his unwilling walk, Cecil's sharp ears picked up from stray conversations several important facts:

a) half the workers here had been "rescued" the way Cecil had been by the town's patrols from the desert and pressed into service,

b) the town's Bossman was easy to get along with, if you were a good worker; and

c) the last fellow who wasn't a good worker had disappeared into the desert sands, and not of his own free will.

Ouch.

The workers pushed Cecil up the front steps and to the door. It opened with a creaky, screechy noise, and a fairly pretty young woman stood in the doorway, wearing rumpled servants' clothes, the kind Cecil had seen British maids wear in picture books his sister had read to him when he was little.

"This one's awake," said the only voice without the slur of whiskey in it as another rough hand shoved him through the doorway. The door, which had opened outward, slammed shut behind him.

"The Lord of the Manor is upstairs," the girl said. Cecil realized as she spoke that she wasn't much older than Cecil himself was. She started walking upstairs, more creaking noises sounding with each step she took.

Cecil followed. The wall of the house sagged in places, especially where the portraits of several people weighted down the walls themselves, splitting paint and bending wood to the cracking point beneath the nails or wires that held the heavy frames in place.

Most of the portraits had unsmiling faces in them. A few had even been defaced with mustaches, devil's horns, or eye patches. One portrait was that of a married couple, and had the names "Fitzwilliam and Elizabeth" engraved at the bottom. But the tall, handsome groom on the left had a pair of crude glasses drawn onto his face, while his smiling bride had been given a pair of horns and a blacked-out, missing front tooth.

The girl took a right when the stairs bent, and she stopped at the top of the stairway, which ended at a closed wooden door.

She tapped softly at the door. "Lord Wickham," she said, "someone here to see you."

"Come," said a voice behind the door. The girl opened the door. "Go in," the girl mouthed, sweeping her hand into the room impatiently.

Cecil went in striding with as much confidence as he could muster. Whoever "Bossman" Wickham was, he commanded enough respect that even the rough characters in town didn't want to enter his house, and his lone servant seemed like she was afraid someone was going to pounce on her.

The man she'd called Lord Wickham sat at his desk, an open bottle of cheap whiskey at his right hand and a stack of papers in front of him. He held an ink pen in his left hand, which rested next to a minuscule ink pot set on the desk.

Lord Wickham wrote for a minute or two, apparently completely ignoring Cecil. Cecil, in turn, fidgeted on the carpeted floor, which did its share of creaking beneath him.

Mr. Wickham looked up.

Cecil took a step back. He'd been frightened before by nameless qualities about a person—most recently, by the old, wrinkled man in the basement of the lost Martian city the previous day.

But when Lord Wickham looked up from his desk, Cecil saw a face that was only maybe early to mid-thirties. But his eyes looked like those of a far older man, one who had seen things more interesting than Cecil before, and knew that his best days as a man were behind him.

"You are the lad they brought in from the Western desert," Wickham said. It was a statement, not a question.

Cecil nodded his head.

"I have never received a new recruit for this town from the Western desert. Do you know why?"

Cecil shook his head.

"It is because no one ever leaves that particular lost city. I have sent several emissaries to that particular location, but none have returned. Do you know why?"

"I . . . I think it's because they have very, very effective ways of eliminating anyone who wants to enter the place."

"Indeed."

Wickham stood. He had a slight paunch, but he was otherwise in visibly good shape. "Young man," he continued as he walked to the large window that took up most of the wall behind him, "do you know how old I am?"

"No, sir."

Still looking out the window, he tapped the pane several times. "I am over twice my apparent age. When Edison returned from here to Earth the first time, he brought back a number of trinkets he had not had the time yet to use."

"*Thomas* Edison?" Cecil said. His name had been bandied about as the First Man to reach Mars, and Americans and British subjects would quarrel for hours as to who had 'really' landed on Mars first, Edison or Mr. Cavor, the Belgian that had discovered Cavorite.

"The very same," Wickham said quietly as he looked out the pane. "Edison returned with a number of technological wonders he'd pilfered while here. Radium pistols and an oxygen producer or two. But the most interesting one he had was the one that he never got to show the American government. One that made its way to me, thanks to a servant with a terribly misplaced sense of loyalty."

Wickham turned to face Cecil, his hands behind his back in the semi-ready pose Cecil had seen many upper-class men take when they'd spent some time in the military.

"Young man," Wickham said, "I'll not beat about the bush. Before her death years ago, my servant learned that Edison got a hold of the greatest bounty of Martian technology in the city you were fleeing from, and she managed to steal the most important trinket for my own personal use. But now, it's used up. Since then, year by year, I've felt the need, the overwhelming *need* for the kind of rejuvenation that that technology *alone* can provide. Do you understand?"

Cecil nodded his head. He understood perfectly. He understood the man was crazy. A quiet kind of crazy, but still mad as a hatter, and batty as a bedbug.

But, as a character in one of Beatrice's books had noted, poor men had no time to go mad. If Wickham was crazy, he must also be rich.

"And," said Cecil, realizing the method in his new captor's madness, "since I apparently got *out* undetected, you need *me* to show you how to get *in* to the city undetected, where you think more of those little treasures can be found, and keep you looking and feeling young."

"I had a feeling you were a lad of singular intelligence when they brought you in, Mister . . . ?"

"Chesterton," Cecil said, smiling. Now was the time to play the neophyte, the gullible child whom fate had tapped with a golden wand of good fortune. At least until this crazy man could help him spring Beatrice from captivity.

"Chesterton?" said Wickham. "Now where have I heard that name before? Well, no matter." He pulled a bell, and the maid returned to the room. "Anna, would you kindly bring up a glass of milk for the lad, and a brandy for me? He and I have much to discuss."

"Yes, m'lud," she said, as she left them alone. The door creaked shut slowly, closing behind her with an audible thud.

Chapter 41

"Gored on the Norman gonfalon
The Golden Dragon died:
We shall not wake with ballad strings
The good time of the smaller things,
We shall not see the holy kings
Ride down by Severn side."

                             –The Ballad of the White Horse

1914 A.D.
MARS. THE RUINS OF AN UNNAMED CITY.

"Keep driving!" Anne yelled, cradling Gilbert's head in her arms. "He doesn't have much time!"

"Do you have even the faintest idea where I'm supposed to go to, Mademoiselle?"

"Yes! At this speed you'll be through the city in two minutes! After that, you'll hit the settlement! They'll be able to help!"

Flambeau drove like a man possessed, but managed to avoid all the piles of rubble that would have flipped over the car of a lesser driver. Somehow he managed to keep his composure as well. "You want to deal with those silly, English-friendly pig-frogs? What good will they be here?" he shouted as another stray bullet dinged and bounced off the car frame.

"Just keep driving, Father!" Anne shouted over the roar of the floater's revving engine, all the while keeping her head low to protect both her and Gilbert. "And don't even slow down until you get out of the city! Gilbert? Gilbert, listen to me. Gilbert? Can you see my finger?" Her right thumb suddenly flicked, and a small flame leaped out of a tiny nozzle in the metal thumb. Gilbert's eyes were open, and following her flame back and forth.

"That's it, Gilbert. Good. No, don't try to talk. We'll be safe soon. Soon."

Flambeau looked back at her. "I'd heard of those, but never seen one before."

"What?" Anne snapped while still looking at Gilbert, "A thumb lighter or a woman who'll cuff you one in the back of the head with a brass hand when you ought to be silent?"

Flambeau shrugged his shoulders and focused again on the road. He'd heard much worse from both criminals and comrades in his day. He would have kept driving, too, had not a line of at least a dozen armed youths appeared a few tens of feet in front of them to block their way. The tallest one, likely the leader, sported one of those new top hats that had clock on it with several sets of visible gears. Considered a frivolity by all adults, the fashion seemed to exist for the sole purpose of looking silly as a form of intimidation to others.

It failed miserably, though. All the yob's intimidation came from the long-barreled rifle in his hand. Smiling, he raised and pointed it at the floater, and the other boys followed suit.

Moral considerations aside, Father knew he'd never stand a chance of running them over and breaking their line before they put more holes in him than one of the punchards Gilbert had worked with in his youth. Stifling a curse, Father Flambeau spun the steering wheel hard to the left, then the right and down a different path as more bullets began flying around him. The lads were truly awful shots; how had they managed to hit poor Gilbert?

"What do you remember about this place, Mademoiselle?" he barked over his shoulder.

"Keep on this path," she said. "We have one other option, but it's a risk. Look for a temple-like building on our right. We can't leave the city now; if they operate like the scuttlegangs who trap people in the ruins of London, those boys have likely blocked off all exit routes. Didn't you know about this before, Father?"

"I am sorry, Mademoiselle, but I'm trained to filch secrets and defend the innocent from ruthlessly organized adults. Escorting pilgrims through lost cities and running from youthful gangs of thieves was the work of my ancestors during the crusades. Still, if you . . ."

"There!" Anne shouted, pointing at an unblocked straightaway that suddenly caught her eye. "That direction!"

Flambeau floored the accelerator so suddenly the floater leaned backward with the recoil. Gilbert grunted in his unconscious pain as he and Anne leaned back at a near forty-five degree angle.

"Faster," she said under her breath, still holding Gilbert's head in her bloodstained left hand. "we've got a few minutes at most. Can you get us to the settlement?"

Flambeau didn't answer, focusing his eyes on the road. "How far?" he said quietly, just loud enough for her to hear.

"At this speed? If you can keep from bumping him like beans in a baby rattle, and the poor creatures haven't been exterminated? We might just make i-oof!"

She stopped speaking suddenly as they bounced over a hellishly well-hidden mound of earth. Gilbert groaned again from the back seat, mumbling something about his mother and hedgehogs.

"Sorry, mon ami," Father Flambeau said, more to himself than to his critically injured passenger, "but you are a magnet for trouble these days, it would seem. And I have to go all the faster to outrun your trouble, even as you pull it behind you."

"Some things never change," Anne mumbled as she pulled a small pistol from the folds of her dress, firing a few random shots at movements she spotted in the rubble.

1892 A.D.

"So what do you know about this place, Anne?" Gilbert said, remembering with a mixture of joy and pain the last time he'd followed her through a darkened tunnel.

"Only as much as you, really," Anne said, who was herself following Belloc. The fellow had gotten a torch going somehow with the small bits of equipment in his belt and a stick of wood from the rubble. Or what passed for wood around here, anyway. The important thing was that it burned—and could keep burning.

"This was, I think, a temple of some kind," Hilaire said. "We had to know basic Martian architecture when I was training for work in the field."

"They trained you in Martian architecture in the British Army?"

"No . . . in the Vatican."

"Wot?"

"What?" It was Anne's turn to sound surprised.

Then Gilbert could hear the smile in Belloc's voice. "Your group is not as perfect as they'd like us to think, m'lady. A few years ago, I was recuperating after I'd survived a battle I'd no right to live through, a most unusual priest paid me a visit and made me an offer. Since then, I've been both doing my job here for the British Army and working to foil the plans of your old masters."

"What do you mean by my 'old masters'?"

"I mean the Special Branch, Anne. By-the-by, you've managed to fool them into thinking you're dead, but it won't last forever. They aren't perfect, but they aren't stupid either."

"So, you heard from Father Brown too, back then?" said Gilbert.

"Father Brown . . . well, he claimed later it wasn't so much that he recognized a talent in me—more like he happened upon people like me when we needed to be found. The same way he did with Chang after he lived through a fight with a nasty bunch from a Tong gang, or with you and Herb Wells when the Tripods landed."

"But wait, wait," Anne said, "back to the Special Branch. How do you know they think I'm dead? Are you in contact with them?"

"No. But I still hear the things they say through my own contacts who monitor what the Special Branch do and say."

"Fine," she said, looking at the tunnel walls by the light of the torch Belloc carried. "Did your contacts give any insight on those ruffians back there with the expensive sand skiff?"

"You misunderstand, Anne. My group—we aren't a spy organization. Our main job is to counter people like the Special Branch. For rescue missions, well, we tend to ask someone higher up for that."

Anne sighed. "If you're going to go that route, Hilaire, I'd rather we just stop talking. I won't join the Church of Rome. I like my independence these days, and I'd prefer not to have it interrupted so I could wear a nun's habit and have to say five rosaries each day before breakfast."

"Then, m'lady, your bigotry aside, what *do* you believe in? What keeps you going?"

"I'm not a bigot. I just don't like the Catholics, that's all. I haven't cared much for God Himself, really, since I found out He's to blame for giving me red hair."

"Anne," Gilbert said, "Hilaire and I are both Catholic. And if you think you have to be a nun and pray an hour before you eat, that *is* bigotry."

"Just to have an opinion? *My* opinion?"

"There's nothing wrong with having an opinion, Anne," said Gilbert. His voice had regained some of the jaunty character it always took on when he was beginning a debate. "Nor is there anything wrong with believing it's right, even when it's wrong. But to refuse to admit you *could* be wrong? That's not an opinion, or honesty, or being intellectual. That's *bigotry*. Pseudo intellectual opinions are the first refuge for bigotry these days."

"I . . .," Anne started. "I'm not—well, I have too much to do with to secure my day-to-day survival to consider such things, Gilbert."

"Most of humanity has been a day away from extinction, Anne," Gilbert said, the gravel in the passage crunching under his feet. "Right from birth, death has always been around the corner. A missed meal, getting in the way of the wrong person's cough or sneeze, all these could have been the beginning of the end for most people since the beginning of the world. And yet, even the starving medieval peasant found time to think about what his life meant, and where it was going. Even an Egyptian slave could make a silly drawing of his fat master, and begin the art of written language. The fear of death, the work for survival has, in fact, been the cause of the greatest advancements in society. It's when you know a party is only minutes from ending that you begin the most frenzied fun and madness. The most revelry in anyone's life in America, in fact, is in the last ten seconds before the old year ends and the new year begins."

Anne sighed. "Fine, Gilbert. I've used my life's chaotic nature as an excuse not to think about the greater things. I've said for the last year that I needed to focus on survival. But I'm getting rather tired of that, I must admit. I used to think that the Special Branch was making a better world. But when I learned that it wasn't so, my life became focused on escaping it. And now that I have escaped, my life's been focused on getting enough food to eat and clean water to drink each day."

"There's worse things you could be doing."

"I'm glad we agree. And in between that, I save the occasional Tommy like Belloc here from those ravaging Tharks. Or I try to get the more hirsute natives to stay still long enough to teach me a few words of their language. But the greater questions of why I'm here are things I just don't feel capable of discussing or thinking about, so I don't bother."

"It's funny you should say that," said Belloc, stepping carefully down a circular stairwell. "because your former masters want most of us to have the same attitude. The less we ask the question, or the more ridiculous the answer, the less likely we are to ask why we should follow them, or fight the world they are trying to make. There was a funny group of folks who went that route, you know . . ."

Gilbert now realized that Belloc had ceased talking to either him or Anne. They were descending further into the building, one that had been in place before man had built the pyramids of Egypt, and Sergeant Hilaire Belloc dealt with this kind of fear by talking and telling stories. Belloc continued what seemed like a self-soothing ramble. ". . . called the *Manicheans*. Bit of a scary bunch. Thought the world was made up of a good god and a bad god, and they decided that the way to go was to say all matter was evil."

"But we're stuck *in* matter. How could someone seriously believe that?"

"Maybe someone who doesn't like what they see when they look in the mirror? Anyways, for them the *worst* sin wasn't murder, but having children, since you took a perfectly good soul and put it in a perfectly bad body. And some of them believed that we were only the tools or the chess pieces that the good and evil god used to fight each other with, and appealing to them was as useless as talking to the universe itself. No one was responsible for anything—it's all the gods' doing. A nice thought for lazy people, to say free will doesn't exist. Of course, teachers who push that bunk still grade late papers as though you had free will if you turn them in late. And some went off and believed in . . ."

Belloc quieted his near-monologue when they passed through a stone doorway at the bottom of the stairs. It opened to a large chamber of clean, red stone, without so much as a pile of red dust littering the floor. A soft pink light lit the chamber, and the room looked cozy and inviting.

". . . magic," he finished his sentence.

****

"What do *these* things say, Jimmy?" Frances asked, looking at the latest batch of scratches on the stone.

"Hmmm . . ." Jimmy said, looking intently at the drawings on the wall.

"These 'ere are a little more difficult, Miss. I'd need some time to do these up right."

"How much time?"

"Last time I saw symbols like these, it took me a good 'arf hour."

"The quicker the better, Jimmy, even if it means . . .Oh, bother!" she said as the light burned out, leaving them in darkness.

"Allow me, Miss," Jimmy said, reaching into his pockets and rustling about for a few seconds. Suddenly, a small puff of flame erupted from his left hand and then came to rest on the wick of a candle he held in his right.

"You're wonderful Jimmy. If we survive this, I'll talk to my father about getting you a job as a guide for one of his ivory expeditions to Darkest Africa."

"Thank ye kindly, Miss, but for now, let's stay on Gilbert's trail."

"Yes!" she said, taking his candle from his hand and stomping down the hallway in her explorer boots. "Gilbert! *Gilbert!*" she began shouting down the hall, "Gilbert, if you're there, dear, it's me, Frances, looking for you! Please come back, dear Gi—"

Frances's voice stopped as she suddenly collapsed to the floor and lay still with her eyes closed, the candle rolling away from her slackened hand to rest against the stone wall. A heartbeat later, a very surprised Jimmy closed his eyes and did the same.

Chapter 42

"Joan of Arc... put her dreams and her sentiment into her aims, where they ought to be; she put her practicality into her practice. In modern Imperial wars, the case is reversed. Our dreams, our aims are always, we insist, quite practical. It is our practice that is dreamy."

—All Things Considered

"This is Danton's Folly?"

Emrys had expected to see something like the mining villages that had grown up around the coal industry in England. But the town of Danton's Folly looked nothing like the soot-covered two story homes squashed into a single set or two of streets. Here, a grid of streets in the shape of a spoked wheel radiated out from a huge hole in the ground, around which a wall and many layers of brick and steel scaffolding had been erected.

"This is the place," Carter said, smiling. "I reckon you'd have to look very hard to find a sadder, more depressed blemish on the face of two worlds. Wretched little town, fulla' the kinda folks who'd cut your throat for the laces on your boots."

"It sounds like the kind of place you and Deja spent many a quiet evening in as a couple," Emrys said.

"It was only quiet after the locals tried to start a fight, making comments about a Bluesider like me and a Red woman tying the proverbial knot. Deja, being the lovely warrior woman of Mars that she is, never took much to talk like that. Why, there was this one place where we had a number of Belgians *and* a few Tharks giving us grief, but she pulled out her sword and—"

"John, you told me about this."

"Just listen, Emrys. She pulled out her sword, and—"

"I'm not going to listen to this for a fourth time," Emrys said, kicking his heels into the sides of his reptilian mount. The sloat muttered and started toward the town.

Carter smiled. Despite the life he'd lived, Emrys was still a skittish bookworm at heart, and he was nervous about visiting anyplace where a fight could break out. But the threat of another one of John Carter's stories seemed enough to push even Emrys into the arms of another potential adventure.

****

Cecil pulled out another box of cups and mugs, hefted it up in his skinny arms, and grunted as he backed out of the storeroom. As he pushed the door open with his back, a sea of noisy men, a man playing a mandolin over the din of loud conversation, the smell of beer, and the click of ivory balls on a pool table assaulted Cecil's senses. He'd seen drinkers in the bars at Syrtis Major, but nothing compared to this. The men seemed to work only so they could come to this nameless bar between their shifts.

Cecil himself was unsure exactly what was mined or how the men pulled it from the ground, but at this point he really didn't care. Governor Wickham, who claimed to be twice as old as he looked, had talked to Cecil for a half hour about what conditions were like inside the dig site where Beatrice was still being held. Once Wickham seemed satisfied, he had Cecil escorted back to the bar.

Cecil had then been shoved into the bar without introduction or apology. The barkeep, a man with a handlebar mustache and arms thick as tree trunks, told Cecil to start hauling glasses for beer from the back room in preparation for the incoming wave of customers. Once the glasses were all out, Cecil was to roll barrels of beer in from the same place.

An hour after the latest wave of off-duty workers rolled in, alcohol flowed so freely in the place that Cecil began to seriously wonder if he was in danger of becoming drunk just from the smell of evaporated beer. While he was hefting the latest box of glasses in the storeroom, the bar behind him suddenly fell silent. Cecil paused. In Cecil's experience only two things could stop a rollicking, drunken carousal of several dozen men in an enclosed space: An insanely pretty girl, *or* a ridiculously huge threat.

Cecil hadn't been in town long, but he'd seen enough to believe that the second choice was more likely than first. Still, since he was a thirteen-year-old healthy male of the species, he peeked out through the door to see if a pretty girl was, indeed, present.

The storeroom door creaked quietly in the silence. Cecil crept out hunched over. The men on the bar, smelling of sweat, dust and beer and the dust, in their jackets and workpants had all stood up. Peering between the standing men, Cecil spotted what had captured their attention.

It wasn't a pretty girl.

It was the largest, ugliest man he'd ever seen.

He had a wrinkled bald spot on his head, a huge lantern jaw, and a broad, bright smile with several teeth missing. His fists were balled at his sides, and his smile was so wide that his eyes were crinkled shut. One of those eyes looked like it had somehow melted, slid down the left side of his face and re-hardened.

Cecil had heard about this man in Syrtis Major but never seen him. He'd been a pilot or guard of some kind, and since the injuries that had deformed him, he was a kind of boogeyman. *"Don't turn tail and run, or they'll send Strock after you,"* a guard had told Cecil. *"He stays in his room in the dungeon all day, talking to dead friends and getting ready to hurt people who think about leaving."*

And this must have been Strock. No one else could have fit the description Cecil had been given. For a change, the legend of the hideousness of the boogeyman didn't do justice to the real thing; Strock actually looked worse than Cecil had imagined.

Strock's feet were planted firmly on the ground, in thick workman's boots. They were scuffed in the right places for a sand skimmer pilot, Cecil thought, though his jacket was the brown leather preferred by ornithopter pilots in the valley.

"So, where's the boy?" Strock, the smiling gargoyle, asked. His voice sounded like a man who'd been gargling with acid and then tried speaking with a tongue coated in sandpaper.

"This ain't the place for you, Strock," said another voice. It came from one of the larger workmen in the room, and Cecil knew it was from one of their leaders, a bearded fellow with hands so calloused he'd let kittens play by sinking their claws into his calloused fingertips and pulling the mewing critters across the table.

"My place is where I want to be," Strock said, stepping forward with a left leg that dragged a bit. Cecil heard the door open again and several more pairs of booted feet entered the room behind the twisted man. "And I'll ask again only once more, my friends: Where is the boy?"

The door swung open once more. Cecil knew the smart thing to do was to run right away, but he couldn't just yet. He'd need these men if he wanted to free Beatrice.

"There aren't many children on Mars," said a new voice. Cecil recognized it immediately. Cocky and brazen, it didn't have the strong-but-tired quality of the workingmen in the bar, nor the quiet confidence of the career soldier.

It was the voice of a man who could survive just about any kind of adventure and knew it.

"John Carter," Cecil breathed. His hero!

Still smiling, Strock turned faster than anyone could see and pounded Carter in the face.

Carter dropped to the floor and lay still.

****

"Look!" Gilbert said suddenly as they reached the end of the staircase. They were in a large room lit by Belloc's small torch, and something had caught Gilbert's eye to their left. He took an extra step in that direction, and small clouds of red and yellow flecks kicked up from his feet.

"Don't get too far ahead," Hilaire said, drawing his pistol and following close behind Gilbert. "You don't know what could jump out at you here in the dark."

"But it's not dark," Anne said, falling into line behind Gilbert. "Don't you see it?" She held her hand up above her head, looking at the glow that surrounded her hand and fingers like a white corona.

"I see it, but I don't really know where it's coming from, or why it's there to begin with," Hilaire said. His right hand, which glowed like Anne's, held his pistol readied and pointed in the air in case a threat showed itself. "And having something that close to me makes me nervous until I know what side it's on."

"But . . . I don't think there's anything here out to hurt us," she said. Now that they could stand apart enough from each other, each could see that the soft glow covered each one of them fully. "Can you feel it? It's like there's something comforting here."

"A combination of experience and training has taught me not to always trust feelings, m'lady. Even if someone like the great Gilbert K. Chesterton is running in front, and likely to take any bullets or fall into any holes waiting in the ground ahead of me!"

Belloc had said this last part louder, intending for Gilbert to hear. Gilbert *was* ahead of them, moving into one of the darker corners of the large stone room on his own. He slowed at the warning tone in Hilaire's voice, but would have done so even if Hilaire hadn't spoken.

For Gilbert had come to something he'd never seen before.

There were rows and rows of stone platforms, the size, shape, and height of beds for people the size of humans.

Gilbert looked at the rows—there were at least five in each row . . . twenty-five stone 'beds' in this room alone.

"This is . . ." Gilbert started, searching for the words.

"A place of healing," Anne said, looking around the room.

"Do you have a reason for believing this? Besides your intuition, that is." Hilaire said, his pistol still drawn, looking around the room, his eyes flicking from stone bed to stone bed, checking for threats.

"Women usually have a reason for their intuitions," Gilbert said softly, "or at least, most of 'em are smart enough to figure the reasons out, eventually. I've found it's good to listen."

"Fine," said Hilaire, yawning suddenly, "*you* listen, while *I* stand guard."

"You're coiled a little tight, don't you think?" Gilbert said while rubbing his eyes, the wonder leaving his voice as he turned to face Hilaire. "Usually you don't see a military man get that stuck in one direction until he gets a little older."

"Getting shot does that to a person," Hilaire said.

"Hmm," Gilbert said. "Well, Anne, what d'you . . ."

Gilbert looked.

Anne was stretched out on the slab of red stone, fast asleep. "Anne?" Gilbert said, his voice quiet. "Anne, are you..."

The world became very odd at that moment for Gilbert. He wasn't *tired*, but it was truly difficult to keep his eyes open. He put his hand out to steady himself, and the touch of the empty stone slab next to him suddenly made him think of every soft bed he'd ever laid in.

"Stand...*up*...," Hilaire gasped, still standing on both feet as Gilbert reeled over backward and fell onto the stone he'd touched.

Chapter 43

"It is not the business of the doctor to say that we must go to a watering-place; it is his affair to say that certain results of health will follow if we do go to a watering-place. After that, obviously, it is for us to judge."

—All Things Considered

"Ere, Bill, why'd you sign up for this lot, now?"

"Same as *you* did, Ernst. Easier than doing time on Earth, or working in the Wickham mines."

Guard duty for the Special Branch in the deserted city wasn't the most difficult job Ernst or Bill had ever had. But Ernst was more of a talker, while Bill was the kind of person that could stare contentedly at a wall for hours if need be.

The pay was good, no doubt about that. But the bosses could be strict.

"What," said Ernst after several more minutes of silence looking at the desert, "What d'you think happened to Frank an' Victor? After the Cecil lad got away in the skiff? I 'aven't seen 'em since then."

"They got a lousy duty, prob'ly. Maybe peelin' taters. All I know is I don't care much."

"No, Bill, you wouldn't," Ernst said.

A few more very long minutes dragged by. A cloud of dust plumed in the distance.

"Ship coming in, Bill."

"Yep."

A few more minutes passed.

"Be here soon. What kind you think it is, Bill?"

"Looks black."

"I can *see* that, Bill! But 'oo's on it, you think? Civvies, or maybe someone important?"

"I dunno, Ernst. Just wish you'd be quiet an' leave me to my thoughts."

"Fine, then."

Nearly five minutes later, the black sand ship swerved to a stop very near to Bill and Ernst. Both guards tried valiantly to seem unconcerned, but they had to scamper at the last second to avoid being clipped by the ship's runners or the red dust it kicked up.

A large gangplank lowered from the side of the ship. Herb, his eyes shaded by tinted brass goggles, strode down it to the sand. The Painter, dressed in his trousers and shirt, followed close behind while holstering his pistol. Williamson, taking quick, timid steps, scurried behind them both. His eyes darted about, making him look like a mouse fearful of a hawk diving down on him at any moment.

"Tell Mister Williamson I've arrived. Williamson the elder, that is." Herb said, taking off his goggles and tapping them against his shoulder, then brushing the dust off his jacket.

Bill, hoping that his last conversation hadn't somehow been overheard, kept his eyes on Herb as he spoke. "Who may I say is calling, sir?" Bill asked.

"The Cleaner, the Painter, and his idiot son. You've got exactly two minutes to find him, get back here, and then bring us *to* him. Now *move*."

Bill and Ernst snapped their heels together and moved, jogging with their rifles at attention, their boots making soft chuffing noises in the red sand as they ran.

The three men now stood in silence.

"My allergies are acting up again!" said Fortescue Williamson, snuffling again and wiping his nose on a jacket sleeve now stiff with dried mucus.

Herb made another mental note: Idiot sons may be considered genetically superior, but they were still quite annoying. Each one Herb had met still thought himself immune to the punishments typically meted out to those of lower stations.

Such allowances caused them to become even stupider as their lives progressed. Until they met terrible, terrible accidents that removed them from the gene pool.

Herb looked up. One of the two guards had already returned. "Mister Williamson, *senior*, is now available to see you gentlemen," said the guard, standing at attention in front of them and looking straight to the front. "Will you all follow me, please?"

Herb smiled. "Of course," he said quietly.

They followed the sweating guard up the stairs toward the largest of the spires in the lost city, and in through a wooden door. They continued through a number of alcoves, tunnels, and other doorways over the next few minutes until they emerged in a large underground chamber.

The ceiling of the room they'd entered was at least fifty feet high, with the dark, blood red walls made of very ancient stone. The floor of the chamber was circular, at least fifty feet in diameter, and made of lighter colored stone than usually found in the area.

Herb followed the guard to the center of the disc-shaped, stone floor. Several workmen with jeweler's goggles were carefully measuring sections of the floor, etching deep lines with metal styluses and consulting notebooks for other symbols they were drawing next to the lines. Herb noted with mild interest that the symbols of one workman resembled Egyptian hieroglyphics, while those of another looked like Sumerian cuneiform, a type of writing Gil had shown him back when they'd still been friends.

Herb shuddered. He and Gil *had* been best friends. That was all *past*, now. All in the past. He couldn't live in the past anymore. He had to move on to the *future*.

"Mister Williamson?" the guard said, once he reached a group of men who were talking to each other in low voices.

The shortest of the men turned to face Herb, the Painter, and the younger Williamson, ignoring the guard as one would a horse that had brought a carriage of people to him.

"Ah, yes. The Cleaner and the Painter. And . . . Fortescue."

Fortescue sniffled and tried to stand somewhat at attention under his father's withering, sunken-eyed gaze. "Good afternoon, Father," he said, in between sniffs, "I trust you're doing well?"

"Quite," he said. Turning his attention to the two agents standing in front of his son, the elder Williamson now ignored Fortescue as much as he did the guard, who still stood in place with a worried expression on his face. "Report," he said to Herb.

"Sir," said Herb, "I arrived on Mars and met the Painter and the Driver. They were briefing me when I saw Gilbert Chesterton in the city of Syrtis Major. The agents gave chase, but they were unable to catch Gilbert. Their efforts would have been successful, but they were foiled by two locals, a soldier named Hilaire Belloc and a Confederate American who's gone native named John Carter.

"After failing to catch Chesterton, we regrouped and learned Gilbert had escaped onto a Navy flier. We pursued. Later we found evidence in the desert that the ship was attacked by Tharks and lost with all hands on board, except for Chesterton and Belloc. We tracked them to a lost city, where they apparently picked up a third person, a young lady with red hair who has evidently been living in the hill country on her own. I believe she is an agent who went missing last year, the one we called the *Actress*.

"Though we had Gilbert in our sights, our party was attacked by a tribe of white Martian apes. Three agents died in the attack, including the Driver. We escaped, circled back while the apes were feeding on the corpses of our comrades, and made our way here. It is unlikely that Chesterton, Belloc, or the Actress survived the encounter."

Williamson blinked his sunken eyes, twice.

"Unlikely," he said. "By that, you mean you did not *see* Chesterton or his companions dispatched by the apes?"

"No, sir."

"Fortescue," the elder Williamson said, approaching his sniffling son and now ignoring both Herb and the Painter, "walk with me."

The two walked away from the agents, exiting through the door Herb and the others had come through.

The air grew very quiet.

"What do you think we do now?" Herb said in a whisper after a very long five minutes passed. The only noise was the steady scraping of the workmen, cutting very straight lines and symbols into the rock floor.

"I don't think," the Painter said, "I act. Which is why I'm still alive. And right now, until I hear otherwise or have extremely good cause to do so, I'll be standing right here where that bloke remembers me standing, just in case he might be needing my services."

"Which is," said a wheezing voice behind them, "*precisely* why men like yourselves will continue to have a job in the future."

Herb turned at the voice, his stomach churning inside at the memory of the last time he heard it.

Approaching them now from the door they'd entered was Lord Musgrave, a man who, like the elder Williamson, was a member of the circle of five men who conspired to rule the world. Musgrave had weighed at least four hundred pounds when Herb had first met him, and he seemed even heavier now. He waddled with a heavy, ponderous air, and no fewer than four attendants sought to fulfill his needs, one hovering with a parasol, another waving a fan to blow air on his enormous, triple-chinned head, and the other two carrying books and a small chair.

"Walk with *me*, lad," he said to Herb. "Painter?" he continued, "go and amuse yourself for a while. Perhaps you can reminisce with the Doctor on one of the upper levels."

"Perhaps," the Painter said, turning and leaving.

Lord Musgrave was not a man to waste time on pleasantries. "The beauty of our age, Cleaner," began Lord Musgrave, his triple chins bobbing and almost becoming six chins with each word, waved a large ham-fisted hand to the expansive ceiling as if the universe itself was already under his command as his assistants dodged and cringed. "is that our very strength is in our elusiveness. If indeed the commoner wants to rebel against our benevolence, who shall he fight against? The king? A dottering figurehead. Parliament? Too many to kill. Change from within our own group? Perhaps. But rock the boat and you'll be found dead in the most embarrassing position possible.

"No, *Cleaner*. As I told you when we first met, we can only move our race forward if the people are properly manipulated. And they may only be properly manipulated when they are convinced that they are *not* being manipulated, but are, in fact, commandeering their own fates. All the while, we gain more control over them as a mass, as a cattle driver controls his herd."

"Yes, well. I'm here, now," said Herb, "and Chesterton has, apparently, been reduced to fodder for some very large, multi-limbed primates. What is my next assignment?"

Musgrave smiled. "To the point, and impatient, as always. Well done. Remain vigilant, and you'll soon see. You have promise, Cleaner. Don't squander it."

****

Far away, in a stone chamber and stairwell far below ground, five young people from Earth slept the dreamless sleep of the heavily drugged.

Gilbert, Anne, and Hilaire had fallen asleep in the large room with stone slabs the size of beds, and when the last of them had closed their eyes, the room's lights had dimmed and the low glowing around their bodies vanished.

After a few minutes, an interesting display began to form on the walls beside the three of them who slept on the stone slabs. Were any of them awake to see it, they would have found it most intriguing, though Jimmy who slept in the stairwell next to Frances would have enjoyed it most of all.

First, a glowing white dot appeared on the wall next to Anne's head.

The dot lengthened from both ends, extending to become a vertical line. The line began to branch in a series of ninety-degree bends, making three, then nine, then more and more lines. They moved slowly, perhaps a half-inch every second, spreading out from Anne's head.

The front portion of each line glowed, leaving a white, chalk-like color in its wake as it drew its pictures on the stone wall. After a quarter hour, the space in the wall directly above her and the floor surrounding was nearly covered with a large tree-shaped, chaotic-looking grid of white lines etched in the stone.

The glowing lines moved slowly but ever more surely, gradually drawing a rough picture of a humanoid.

The lines first drew a picture that looked like an eight-foot tall otter, with the natural curves around its body done by many tiny right-and-left turns. When finished, the glowing beads in the wall paused, a small pulse of light riding back in a flash over the tracks on the wall. The beam of light buzzed on the lines drawn on the wall like a small toy train on a track. It waited, moved, and hovered on the lines around Anne's head, then on the lines on the ground surrounding her stone bed. Satisfied after a few moments, it shot back along the whitened tracks drawn into the wall, tapping each of the glowing white dots and causing them to resume drawing.

The glowing dots on the wall began drawing again on a new blank space on the wall. This one was taller and spindly, with a triangular head and long, thin spider-like arms and legs. At its conclusion another small touch of light ran to Anne, buzzed around her on the circuitry written in the stone, and returned. This, too was left behind as the dots and lines began etching a third drawing next to the spindle-creature.

The third drawing was oddest of all, looking like a large frog with an anteater's head. This time the rejection took half the time of the others.

The fourth drawing, though, took longer and had more promise than the others. Looking decidedly human in fashion, it was first in the form of a male (rejected, but not nearly as quick), but then the dots on the ancient stone wall of the temple drew a final picture, the first of its kind in over ten centuries:

The drawing was the rough outline of a human female.

The light, clearly excited, buzzed back on its drawn line-track to and around Anne and back to its brothers again. The tiny glowing dots added more details to the figure. After another minute the small dots converged on the last drawing and began drawing in new colors and shapes. First one, then many smaller *red circles* were drawn about the figure's right hand. After this, the process was repeated on the right side of the figure's face.

More lines travelled out to crevasses and nooks in the vast room. Until finally, one of the now dozens of glowing, drawing white dots on the wall drove itself into a hole in the wall and stayed there.

What emerged was very interesting.

It was a small mechanical creature. Were any of them awake, Gilbert, Anne or Hilaire would have likened it to a five-legged mechanical spider, apparently built from the cast-off pieces of brass pipes and clockworks, with miniature telescopes for eyes.

It sprouted from the home it had slept in for millennia and looked about once, then twice. Spotting the network of white lines in the stonework, it scrambled along the wall without respect for gravity or any other logical obstacle, and within less than a minute it had reached the sleeping form of Anne.

Her left, flesh eye was shut in a dreamless sleep, the red-glass orb on the mechanical plated, right side of her face remained dark.

And when the little creature reached her, it paused, its telescopic eyes focusing, extending and retracting, checking to see if it had found the right subject.

Satisfied, it paused. Keeping its 'eyes' on Anne's right temple, still covered by the bolted-in-place brass cover that hid half her face, the small mechanical creature shook slightly as several more spindly 'arms' unfolded from its back.

Were she awake when it was finished, Anne would have been horrified to see four tiny metal arms pointed at her face.

Meanwhile, Gilbert and Hilaire still slept soundly. The events of the last few days had left both of them far more exhausted than they knew, and when the room's hidden mechanisms had sensed their exhaustion they hadn't nearly enough inside them to marshal a real resistance.

Gilbert was dreaming again, trying to fight a pair of giants that bore more than a passing resemblance to Frances' parents. They'd never been overtly cruel to him, but it seemed in more than one way that they had tried to obstruct their relationship.

In his dream he'd just saddled up on a missile that used a windup key rather than rocket fuel. His armor was made of paper with ancient writing on it, and his lance was a giant fountain pen. He was already feeling a bit too much like Don Quixote getting ready to tilt against the windmill when he opened his eyes.

He thought at first that he was still dreaming; then he realized that every time in his life that he'd *thought* he was dreaming, he actually *wasn't*. He looked up at the rock of the ceiling above him, red stone illuminated by a glowing soft white light tinged with gold.

Gilbert sighed. Though still sad over the lost crew of the *Red Locust*, he did feel better. Rather than feeling tormented or guilty, he instead felt the kind of sadness one had at friends who had moved on, graduated early from school, and wouldn't be seen again anytime soon.

Gilbert was just inhaling deep and contentedly once again when he heard the quiet scrape of a point of metal against stone. Reluctant to sit all the way up and see what had disturbed the comfortable ambiance of the healing room, he turned his head to the left and saw something that moved so quickly and decisively he had no real power to stop it until it was too late.

A weird, metal, spider-like creature, only a little larger than a man's hand, stood on Anne's left shoulder with several spindly, pointed, and jointed mechanical legs. Four small arms had sprouted from its back and were pointing at various spots on the half of her face covered by the brass shield, as if looking for something.

No! Gilbert thought, *What is that thing? I've got to stop it before—*

But it moved fast, faster than he ever would have believed possible. He tried to raise himself up, but it felt like he was moving through a sea of mud. In the time he sat up from the stone slab, the spider had launched three of its four arms at the nearly invisible screws that held the metal plate to Anne's face.

Chapter 44

"'I'm afraid I'm a practical man,' said the doctor with gruff humour, 'and I don't bother much about religion and philosophy.'

'You'll never be a practical man till you do,' said Father Brown."
— *The Dagger With Wings*

****

1914 A. D.
Mars. Outside the Ruined City.

G ilbert blinked.

He hurt. He'd been hurt before, of course. When she'd been alive, Frances berated him when injured. "You're waking up in the hospital too often after your missions, Gil!" she said, visiting him for the tenth or eleventh time with a business-suited and tinted-spectacled member of the Swiss Guard standing discretely behind her.

"Where should I be, then, my dear lady?" he'd asked that time, the most recent explosion having given him a case of partial amnesia that took him several days to recover from.

"Home," she'd said, tapping him on his chest while she wore a stern expression that was not at all like her soft and gentle voice.

That had been long ago, this much he knew. Now, instead of lying on a starched hospital pillow, his head rested on a pile of fine gravel. He could hear running water—not like a faucet, but a brook or a healthy stream. There was also a quiet rhythmic sound in his ears like a steam-powered water pump. He was looking straight up into the pink-orange sky, with the slightest trace of blue in the direction of his toes.

He heard a splash next to him. He turned and saw a very odd looking creature resting on its skinny, almost bony elbows, staring at him with a set

291

of brass goggles set in its pale face over its narrow, elf-like eyes as it sat next to the small stream beside Gilbert.

Gilbert's mind searched, but he couldn't find the right word. Or was it words? What language did these guys speak, again? He couldn't quite recall from the three or four different ones they sported on this world.

"Heh...hello..." Gilbert said. His mouth felt dry; not overly so, but enough that he couldn't quite muster up anything more right away.

The thing's narrow mouth smiled, and Gilbert's new 'friend' stood up, it's skinny legs extending its frame to a nearly seven-foot height. It looked Gilbert over for a moment, smiled again and strode away with long, silent steps.

Gilbert turned back to look at the sky. It was daytime, that much he knew. But the sun was invisible right now; hidden behind either the branches of the thick-leaved trees or the dark red mountains. Still, he felt warm, and the air was easy to breathe. They couldn't have strayed far from their path—

The path! The city! The sun! The time! He tried to sit up, but a rude pain jabbed him in the armpit and wrenched his insides. There was also a heavy feeling on his chest. He laid back down again, silently gasping for breath and offering up his pain. Looking down he saw a device had been strapped to his chest. It was a bizarre pastiche of small brass rods, gears, wheels and a few small lights. A set of tubes stretched from the device to his right armpit, and another set reached down to below his left set of ribs.

And then he felt the call of nature.

Blast.

"Awake, mon ami?" said a familiar voice behind him.

"Yes, Father," Gilbert said, his face still looking up. "Alive, but I feel a tad damaged. What happened?"

"A bunch of local voyous decided to shoot at us. One of them got a lucky shot at you. Not too lucky, I'm glad to say."

"And you brought me to a native settlement?"

"There were too many bullets flying around to try and find that temple you two and Belloc took a nap in, Gilles. Anne knows where the nice locals are far better."

"I see."

"Lovely little gadget they had here for you," Flambeau said, leaning in and seeing the small pump attached to his comrade. Its quiet rhythm

soothed Gilbert even as it presumably patched him up. "I halfway believe they cobbled it together on the spot, based on some rough drawings Anne made of your innards."

"The—hum, can't recall or pronounce their name in their own tongue, but some call them the spider-men for their skinny limbs. They're quite clever," Gilbert said. "The red men don't exactly trade with them, but they have a lovely relationship of needs and gadgets being exchanged for a good story or two."

"Excellent way to divide the labor. Best of all in this part of the place is the fish—the things almost seem to want to jump into the nets and be a meal for us."

"Yes, well..." Gilbert was about to give a short lecture on the nature of unfallen nature, but he suddenly felt very, very tired. He closed his eyes, but a thought jumped him out of the nap he was about to take.

"Where's Anne?" Gilbert asked. "Is she safe?"

"Calm yourself. Becoming agitated over a paramour hardly befits an avant le dragon like yourself."

"I hardly feel the part these days, Jean-Paul. More like an after than a before. But is she well? My feelings aside, you know how vital she is to this little venture of ours."

"I know, Gilles. I know. She is fine. She's had a rough . . . well, I think seeing you has brought back many memories. When she was certain you would be well, she went off by herself into the woods for a bit. I haven't followed her, but there are a few of our hosts watching her from a distance."

"Fair enough. Do you know when I can stand? I assume this thing on my chest saved my life, and I wouldn't want to dislodge it."

"They haven't said anything to me, Gilles, and my Martian is rusty. Plus, you may recall these boys aren't very big talkers, even by Martian standards."

"Yes, well aware. How much more time do we have, Jean-Paul?"

"Judging by the stars and the charts? Two days at most. But that should be more than enough time if you can avoid people putting holes in you between now and then. We're only a handful of hours away by floater, and they've filled it with that amazing fuel they squeeze from the coalite and the gold in the ground."

"Lovely. And, er, has Anne asked anything about . . . well, about . . ."

"About Frances? Non, mon ami. She has not. I think she accepts, for *now. Why the deception, though?"*

"I'm not deceiving her, Jean-Paul. Just . . . well, misleading her a little. If I'm wrong (and we both know I have been before), I wouldn't want . . . wouldn't want her to be disappointed."

Father Flambeau began chuckling, poking at the nearby campfire with a stick.

"What?" Gilbert said, suddenly aware of the smell of dried blood. He brought his hand up and realized it was flecked into his mustache.

"You, Gilles," said the priest. "You are so transparent! You make a much better window than a door, despite your best efforts. I find it funny that in our younger days with the fate of the world at stake you could bluff the best agents of evil the world threw at us. And since that gift the draggle-haired fellow gave you, you have amassed a veritable legion of readers who follow every word of your gifted pen. But when it comes to a single woman from your past, well . . ."

"Hello, gentlemen," said Anne from behind them.

Father Flambeau stood, his powerful body sweeping up to a respectful pose in a single fluid motion.

"Bonjour, Mademoiselle. We were just discussing our options for the rest of our travel and ascent."

"Indeed," she said, turning to face Gilbert on the ground. "How are you feeling, Gilbert?"

"Been better, to be honest. But well, considering the circumstances. How on earth—or, rather, how on Mars—did you ever manage to find these fellows? They're not especially good at conversation, but they are quite good at not being found."

"I won their trust a while back when I saved a few of them from a big game hunter, and they've got long memories. Good for us, and bad for the hunter if he ever gets up the gumption to return here. Well, on my little walk just now I stopped by one of their huts and got them to start cooking up a spot of fish. You stay there, and tell me if the sky does anything odd. I'll get you some . . . ah . . . 'grub' as you call it on your side of the pond, and be back forthwith."

She swept up her skirt, now starting to tatter in their travels, and started walking towards the sound of muttered speech over the hill. Gilbert smelled the scent of cooking fish, and his mouth began to water.

"She is quite a lovely lady, wouldn't you say, Gilles?"

"Jean-Paul, I appreciate what you're doing. Really, I do. But we have a job to do and I can't let a little thing like . . . like . . . well, like this interfere with it. You know, though . . . all this does make me think about a few things."

"Like what?"

"Well . . . Frances. She was such a wonderful wife, Jean-Paul. So wonderful. I felt so awful so often that we could never have kids. The look on her face every Christmas, when the nieces and nephews all left and the house was silent again . . . it tore me up. And when I had to leave her for my little adventures, as you called them? Well, did I ever tell you that she showed up on one of my jobs?"

Father Flambeau shook his head. Even though he'd heard the story over a dozen times, it was important now for Gilbert to talk.

"I . . . I was in this little fix in Chinatown. Don't ask me why the Cardinal sent me there instead of Chang. It never made complete sense to me. But Frances had been getting more and more alarmed with each job that landed me in the hospital, or had me waking up with nightmares afterwards, or a host of other things.

"I was on the trail of this . . . well, you could hardly call him human anymore. He was a Chinese crimelord operating out of the London slums. I thought I'd avoided detection, and I was just patting myself on the back for my discretion when several thugs surrounded me in an alleyway. One pulled out a set of ivory sticks connected by a chain, another pointed a knife at me, after flinging it around his head and clicking it a few times. You know how the young ones do that? To scare folks before they rob them and beat them senseless?"

Flambeau nodded again, smiling. Gilbert turned back to the sky and closed his eyes, telling the story while he was lost in memory.

"The third one had one of those odd little sticks shaped like a letter 'L'. I'd never seen one of them before. Somehow, seeing something you know is intended to do you harm, and not even knowing exactly what it is to begin with makes things ten times worse. The anticipation, you know? That things are going to go very, very wrong?

"I had my whole routine set out—that I was a tourist, lost in town. It often worked among genuine rapscallions like that. Usually they'd just rob me of what money I'd had and that'd be the end of it, but this bunch weren't buying it. They'd been following me for a while, were ready to fight, *and kill me. I knew a few tricks thanks to Chang, but . . . well, I knew they'd win the day.*

"Then, suddenly, around the corner came this skinny little fellow. Small, even for a Chinaman. Suddenly, he whipped off his hat, and Frances' beautiful, brown hair spilled out. She snarled something at them, and just started takin' them apart."

"She'd kept up with her fighting, then?"

"Huh! Had she ever," Gilbert said, closing his eyes as he re-lived the memory. "I couldn't believe how well she'd done. She beat them all, even with them armed and her with just her hands. She swept one guy's feet out from under him, then jumped up and stomped his head with both her boots. Then she leaped up and punched the knife-boy in the throat, then dropped to her knees and punched the last one in the . . . well, let's just say he didn't get the chance to yell too loud or low as he sank to the ground.

"And Jean-Paul, I couldn't speak, I was so shocked! I mean, here I'm supposed to be this secret agent of the Vatican, and I just had my wife pull my fat out of the fire. And she looked lovely, absolutely lovely, while doing it!"

Father Flambeau nodded his head as Gilbert remembered. Having counseled too many victims of tragedy to count in his career, he knew well the difference between a person who needed healing, and who had healed and moved on. Many nights he had spent with Gilbert himself, trying hard to lift his spirits and bring him back to being the man he'd been before Frances had been lost.

Today, though, Gilbert had recounted the entire episode without a quiver in his voice, or the shedding of a tear. He remembered Frances as she'd been, and his life now was full again. Part of his heart and life had been cut away, but the place had healed over, causing little if any genuine pain.

In another minute Anne returned, several strips of the most delicious-smelling fish Gilbert could remember on a rough, baked-clay plate.

"Lunch is served," she said, going down on one knee next to Gilbert, the small machine on his chest still humming and pumping clear liquid into Gilbert's wounds.

"Is it advisable for him to eat?" Jean-Paul asked.

"Our gracious hosts made this repast specifically for Gilbert. They've had a bit more experience being shot at than I guessed. Eating fish gives

the healer machine more raw materials to work with, and speeds things along. Here, Gilbert," she said, lifting a piece of fish to his mouth, "when they learned it was you, they cooked this specifically to a human's palate. I sampled some, and it's quite lovely."

Gilbert tried to be polite and sit up, but she gently pushed him back to a prone position with her brass fingertips on his collarbone. Resigned, he opened his mouth as she fed him fish with her left hand. "Delicious," he said. "I never tried local cuisine, you know. Not even when we were here with Belloc."

"You said, Mademoiselle, that they knew who he was," said Flambeau. "Does his reputation as a journalist stretch this far? Or are they privy to his work for our group?"

"Neither," she said. "They can see things on a very different spectrum than we can. And they can apparently see that thing that Emrys gave him years back, hanging over his head like a glowing geissler tube-sign."

"Indeed," said Flambeau. "Perhaps that explains why they kept sending you places that didn't make sense to the rest of us, Gilles." Gilbert, still chewing and in a state of semi-ecstasy over the taste of the fish, frowned slightly. "What Emrys gave to me was an honor, Jean-Paul," he said, his mouth still half-full. "And for men in our line of work," he paused to swallow, "an honor is not necessarily a pleasure."

"Well," said Anne, her voice immediately lightening the mood, "the reverse can be true as well. There's no real honor in eating, but if it's done right, there certainly is a pleasure. Eat, Gilbert. If you finish this, you might be ready to travel by nightfall."

Chapter 45

"Great poets are obscure for two opposite reasons; now, because they are talking about something too large for any one to understand, and now again because they are talking about something too small for any one to see. Francis Thompson possessed both these infinities. He escaped by being too small, as the microbe escapes; or he escaped by being too large, as the universe escapes."

–All Things Considered

1892 A.D.

Before a blast of artificial lightning had turned John Strock into a hideous, gargoyle-like creature, he'd been a handsome, formidable, and dangerous person. Due to a number of untreated traumatic events in his life, he was now insane as a Lewis Carol daydream.

However insane he was, he was still quite dangerous, as John Carter had discovered. Strock had just slammed the Earthborn Warlord of Mars into a wall and knocked him unconscious, a feat no ten men on two worlds could have accomplished. That this was due more to Carter's carelessness than Strock's ability made little difference to the men in the bar. The bigger, deformed man had sealed his status among the humans of the red planet as a folk tale boogeyman. For generations to come, Strock would be known as The Man Who Beat John Carter. As his tale would be told and re-told, Strock would gain deeds and inches in height and breadth, and be a phenomenal speaker of high, epic poetry in every newer version of the tale.

None of this made a difference to Strock now, of course. He was quite a bit more unbalanced than he'd been when he'd worked for a would-be American dictator a year ago. He'd now been given a job to do by his new employer, and that was find young Cecil and drag him back to the city

299

that the Doctor and others were digging out of the red sands to the North.

Seeing Carter laid out unconscious on the floor, Strock shook his hand a bit to loosen the muscle and shake the smarting pain. He smiled with half his face, the other half remaining still, looking like the visage of a melted wax doll. "Now, where's the boy? Can't be too many of them in this town."

Cecil was already outside, the back door banging in the breeze as the wind began to pick up.

He ran around from the back of the bar to the front, making for the line of sand skiffs parked at the hitching post. The night had come quickly and the sky was dark, but one of the moons was high. Cecil could see several skiffs lined up and tied to the long post in the manner of horses at an old West watering hole.

There was enough light for his practiced eye to spot the easiest knot to untie. Maybe while he was casting off, the other bar patrons would start a fight and either delay or (hope against hope) kill the hideous thing that had once been John Strock.

"It's not going to work, you know."

Cecil had been frantically fiddling with a knot that suddenly wanted more than anything to remain tied, despite looking easy to loosen. At the sound of the voice, he looked up and saw a young man with a few days' growth of whiskers on his face and long, stringy, dirty-blond hair in his saddle on top of a sloat.

After his comment, both man and sloat looked at Cecil quietly.

Cecil had paused for a full precious second, then got back to fiddling with the knot. "If you've got a better idea, buster, I'm open to suggestions," Cecil said, frustration bubbling through his voice.

"I have a ride for you, right here with me," the fellow answered. "And I know just where you're headed. I'm going there too, in fact."

More noises rose from the bar through the night air. Cecil, no stranger to bars or drunks, had no trouble interpreting the rising and falling of the slurred shouts and sounds of breaking glass as the bar patrons' cheering of a renewed fistfight.

"Yeah?" Cecil said, still struggling with the knot, "Well, I know where I'm going too. Straight outta town—any direction. And hopefully ugly-face in there finds someone else to chase after."

"He'll never stop pursuing you, lad. I've seen his kind before. I can help you, but only if you let me."

The sound of metal clashing, like swords crossing with pipes, echoed in the darkness. Silence followed.

A few beads of sweat formed on Cecil's forehead as he focused on the hitching post.

"Ugly back there laid out someone a minute ago," he said. "The fella who got soaked a good one, across the jaw? He looked like John Carter of Mars. If Carter didn't stand a chance, how could—"

The sound of gunfire peppered the air from back at the bar. Cecil looked up, and then he doubled his efforts on the knot, now made surprisingly complicated by Cecil's own stress.

"Is there any help I could offer you that you *would* accept, lad?" The young man spoke with the calm air of a lighthouse on a reef in the path of a battleship.

"My name isn't *lad*, buddy! And right now the only help I want from you might be a knife to cut this Gordian knot with!"

A thud sounded at Cecil's hands. He looked down and saw the tattered remnants of the knot's ropes in his fingers. A knife, obviously not of human make, lay simple and mute sticking out of the middle of the hitching post where the knot had been.

Cecil looked up at his new aquaintance, who regarded him without any expression other than a slight twinkle in his eyes.

"You're pretty good with a knife, for someone who looks like a university scholar."

"I've had good teachers. I make one last offer to you, to ride with someone who knows where he's going."

"Thanks for the offer," said Cecil, already adjusting the sails of his latest soon-to-be-stolen skiff in preparation for his escape, "but I've got a boat to catch."

With a loud crash of sound and a huge belch of flame, the back wall of the bar suddenly collapsed as the windows shattered outwards, covering the rear ground with glass blasted to melted powder.

Sitting now in the pilot's seat of the one-man sand skimmer, Cecil's hand had just reached down to where he knew most pilots would keep the goggles. He stopped at the sound and the flare of light.

The swinging doors of the bar opened as the giant, ugly man staggered out, stepping over several bodies of other men who had also been in the path of the explosion but not weathered it nearly so well.

"You!" said the dark shape, stomping like a wounded bear in Cecil's direction, one of its feet dragging behind him, "you can't . . . you . . . *won't* leave . . ."

"Poor, shattered creature," Cecil heard the mounted man say to Strock, as he eased his sloat in between Cecil and his grievously injured pursuer. His voice sounded like one decades older as he addressed the broken man. "Will you even now, so close to the end, accept what is offered you?"

Under normal circumstances, Cecil would have taken off in the ship without a second thought to anyone. But Cecil had just seen the back wall of the building explode and a phenomenally tough man not only survive, but walk out of the ruined building toward him. The sight held Cecil's fascination like nothing he'd ever seen before. A mouse in the gaze of a cobra could not have been more hypnotized, even when the young man and his mount blocked his view.

"Can't . . . *leave* . . ." Cecil heard the big man wheeze, the smell of burning hair and meat in the air. He was less than six feet from the old man's mount now.

"*John*," Cecil heard the young man whisper, "John *Strock*, are you listening? It's almost over. The door is unlocked. The knob is turning. Will you at last accept what you're offered, and be at peace?"

The young man and the large lizard he was mounted on now blocked Cecil's view of the broken man.

The shuffling steps in front of the young man stopped. Cecil heard a gentle thud, and he knew the big man had fallen to his knees. The young man still sat in his saddle, his body relaxed, his hands holding the reins of his sloat.

"I . . . Fa . . . *Faaaaaaaa* . . ."

A final *thud* sounded on the porch of the bar, as the young man leaped from his sloat and ran forward.

Cecil, no longer afraid, now leaped from the skiff for reasons he could not and would not ever be able to explain, other than to say he knew he was safe, and he needed to see what the young man was about to do.

"Strock? It's me, Emrys. Do you remember me, Strock? You tried to kill me last year, but I forgave you for it, instantly. Do you understand? Do you understand? You are from Wales, too, I know. *Mae'n Iseu*, John. When you see Him, accept Him! Accept what He gives you, what He's always offered you, *now!*"

Emrys held the deformed head and broad shoulders of his one-time assailant cradled in his arms. Strock's only working eye was cold and bright, first looking at the old man with hate, then behind him with a look of puzzlement.

"Fa . . . Bru . . . Fah . . . Brahhhhhnnn . . ." he said.

Then the light went out of his eye, and his body went slack. A breath—and then he breathed no more.

More talk, and Cecil realized that Emrys was saying something under his breath in Latin, or maybe some other weird language. His voice broke several times, as if he were holding back sobs.

Cecil hadn't seen anything like this in his life. It took a great deal to render him speechless, and Emrys's forgiveness of the hideous creature who'd tried to kill him had done it. He was so entranced by the scene in front of him that he didn't even notice John Carter until he was standing over all three of them.

"He sure could give a punch," Carter said softly, his Confederate accent slipping through the awe in his voice and his swelled lip. "I've been 'round awhile, and I have yet to see another man outside of the tall tales who could keep walking after a grenade blew up a wall behind him."

"It was because he had a great deal of help, John," Emrys said, standing after he gently placed John Strock's body on the ground. "The kind of help that wasn't interested in his welfare."

Carter looked at the lifeless form on the ground, and then back at Emrys. Cecil saw the warlord's face swollen where Strock had hit him. "Well, Emrys, what do we do now?"

"This young fellow," Emrys said, walking over to Cecil and clapping his hand on the boy's shoulder, "needs our help. He will be the means by which we will discuss an alliance with the leader of this little colony. And it is through *him* we will build our army to attack the evil forces back at the lost city."

Cecil looked up at Emrys, not at all sure he liked what he'd just heard. "I don't mind going to get my sister, Mister. And I appreciate you helping me just now. But are you sure you understand what you're saying when you say you want to go back there and actually *attack* those guys?"

"Indeed, I do," Emrys said. "By-the-by, there's no need to call me 'Mister.' My name is Emrys..."

"But we all call him Ambrose," Carter said, smiling again under his fat lip.

"Quiet John," Emrys said with a brisk tone that suggested they'd had this discussion many times. "Emrys will do just fine. Young man, John Carter here and I have fought in and led armies of more than one kind into battle before this, young Cecil, just as you will lead armies *after* this, ergo we do know what it is we are engaging in. In the meantime, though, I believe we will have to convince our local hosts that the destruction of their meeting place and drinking establishment was indeed not our fault."

Following Carter's lead and the dragging footprints of the late John Strock, a crowd of angry survivors from the bar battle and the few miners who hadn't been in the drinking establishment to begin with had gathered into a small but angry mob.

John Carter smiled at Emrys, then at Cecil as the crowd started toward the three of them in the light of the small fires around the tavern. The smile was just a tad crooked from his swelled lip, but his eyes still twinkled merrily. "Leave them to me," he said. "I'm good with crowds." He sauntered off in their direction, leaving Emrys and Cecil alone again.

"Oh, dear," said Emrys, as Carter walked into the middle of the group, which became louder and more hostile as he approached. "I do believe he's overstepped again."

Chapter 46

"All science, even the divine science, is a sublime detective story. Only it is not set to detect why a man is dead; but the darker secret of why he is alive."

–*The Thing*

1892 A.D.
Mars, Beneath the Ruined City.

Gilbert lunged at the mechanical spider-thing that rested on Anne's face.

He wasn't fast enough. Still sluggish from sleep, he staggered around several stone slabs on his way toward her still sleeping form.

"G'wan, get away! *Git!*" he yelled, trying to run even though his legs felt like rubber and the room tilted like a dangerously listing ship. Between his drunken gait and scraping his legs against the raised stone rectangles, it took him a good half-minute to navigate his way to Anne's side.

By that time, three of the small mechanical arms from the back of the mechanized creature found the bolts that had been used to attach the brass metal plate into Anne's skull and jaw. The tiny arms gripped the small bolts on Anne's metal mask tightly, and started spinning them with speed and fury. The bolts were out in less than three seconds, and the metal mask fell to the floor with a clang.

Approaching her from her left side, Gilbert was spared the sight of the terrible burn scars on the right side of her face. Her artificial red eye had stayed in place once the plate was gone. It looked wide open, with many colored wires attached within the flesh around her eye socket.

Heedless of Gilbert's yelling, the creature's three bolt-arms retracted into its body, and a new arm popped out.

On the end of the new arm was a medical device known and dreaded by young children of Gilbert's generation and all generations to come.

It was a syringe, filled with a viscous, glowing blue liquid, and ended at a wicked needle's point.

Gilbert saw it when he was only eight feet away, but he was still too far to stop it. Anne's face no longer had the brass half-mask to protect it. The mechanical spider poked in the air around Anne's right temple with its syringe, and then stabbed her through the skin just to the right of her right eye socket.

It took Gilbert only a second more to reach Anne's side, but that second was everything. He punched the machine with all the strength he could muster, hitting it with a sweeping arc that knocked it off the table and left a drop or two of the cool-blue colored liquid on the floor.

"G'wan! Get outta here!" Gilbert shouted, still wobbly on his feet. He felt more like one of the Minnesota farmers he'd grown up with swatting at a varmint in the fields than anything else right now. Except the "varmint" in this case was a crazy looking mechanical bug, scurrying away from Anne after stabbing her in the side of the face.

He could hear the small metal legs chittering against the stone floor as it ran off. Gilbert was about to give chase when he heard Anne sigh and stir in her sleep.

He turned back to look at her. And for a moment, he couldn't breathe.

He had seen people with injuries and handicaps, of course. Growing up among farmers on a prairie, one saw people with burns, the occasional missing limb, deformities from birth, and the like.

But the left side of Anne's face was twisted, wrinkled, and scarred. The last time he'd seen her face in its entirety, she'd just kissed him as the floating city fell apart around them both.

And yet for him Anne's face had been the stuff his dreams were made of. Now, not only had a clunky, three-fingered brass-and-steam prosthesis contraption replaced her shapely right hand, but the left side of her face was a scarred mess like something from a nightmare. Her eyes—one of them was gone, replaced by a red glass bulb. Gilbert walked slowly back to her, sat halfway on the slab beside her head, and awkwardly cradled her head in his arm. He could see her ear appeared to have . . . well, *melted* was the only word that made sense here. He turned her face slightly so he could speak into her good ear, and also so he could see the undamaged side of her face better.

"Anne," he whispered, "Anne, are you alright? Anne, *Anne*! C'mon, Anne! Wake up!"

Gilbert had been in tough spots before. His life had been threatened more than once, and in the last two years he'd lost more people he'd loved to death and terrible choices than some people lost in a lifetime.

But through it all Gilbert realized that there was one, common thread that had woven its way through almost every trial and difficulty he'd faced. Nearly always, he'd believed *his* victory and abilities had carried the day.

He'd bragged and convinced himself that *he'd* killed Martians during the invasion. The reality was he'd had last-minute bursts of inspiration while being chased in the sewers, killing aliens that were only near their own deaths anyway. He'd convinced himself he was a good fistfighter after a few encounters in which he'd used a couple of fighting moves on surprised men who'd thought he would be easy prey.

But when he'd found himself having to fight Belloc in the desert, he'd realized he wasn't so strong after all. Last year in the floating city, the tiniest taste of popularity had made him throw away half his beliefs and nearly all of his promises to Frances.

But even then, he'd always had a choice. An action was always there, waiting for him to take it so he could set things right.

Now, things were different. Anne was *maimed* and unconscious in his arms. Her hand was gone, and half her face was burned and horribly scarred. And all at least in part because of choices Gilbert had made. Now an alien robot had stabbed her in the face, and there wasn't a thing he could do about it. Anne might die, and there was *nothing he could do*.

"Dear God," he said, the words sounding hollow and useless as a child tapping a tin drum in a deserted parade square. "Please, help. Anne, please, please wake up."

He heard more skittering noises around him. Still holding Anne, he looked and saw dim shadows of what could only be the legs and bodies of more of the Martian mechanical creatures.

He shook Anne, repeating her name again and again and feeling worse than helpless. Still cradling her head while murmuring to her, he checked her pulse with his two forefingers on her—what had Doc Johnson called it? The carotid artery, that was it! He checked the artery on her neck, and he found her pulse to be steady. And then he looked where the thing had stuck Anne, and . . .

And . . .

What the . . . ?

Her face!

The spot where the mechanical spider had injected her face was looking very different indeed.

He could see the small spot, about the size of a dime, where the blue liquid had been injected.

And in a circle around that spot, Anne's skin had become smooth again.

"Je-*hosephat*," Gilbert said, as the spot of smooth skin widened.

He was happy, but conflicted. If the spider had done this, could they be trusted? If they were on their side, why were they coming in greater numbers?

"Anne," he said, a desperate edge creeping into his voice as he heard the skittering of the spiders coming closer. "Anne, Anne! C'mon, Anne! Wake up! You gotta wake up! Wake up!" He thought about, but couldn't bring himself to give her a tap on the face with his palm the way he'd seen farmhands sober each other up after a round of drinks.

While he was thinking about it, he felt a small breeze on his neck.

Gilbert gulped and looked to his left, fully expecting to see that one of the spiders had crept up on him.

It wasn't a spider.

It was much worse.

Next to his head there was a shapely hand, curled into a fist, with several straps of leather pulled tight over the first two sets of knuckles.

The shapely hand was attached to the puffed sleeves of a very attractive dress, the kind that a number of seamstresses likely spent weeks pulling, cutting, and shaping the materials for.

The puffed sleeve was attached to a shoulder, which was in turn just below the very, very unhappy-looking face of Frances Blogg.

"Frances?" Gilbert whispered.

Chapter 47

"It isn't that they can't see the solution. It is that they can't see the problem."

                         –The Scandal of Father Brown

"Gilbert?" Frances whispered back, the fury in her voice barely under control, "Who is this?"

"This? Well, this is . . . Oh, Frances, I know how this might look, but—"

"Please step back," she said, nudging him aside, "I know what to do."

"Frances," Gilbert said, standing as Frances began to take the pulse and lay the back of her hand against Anne's forehead. Anne now laid flat on her back. "Frances, let me assure y—"

"Shh," Frances said suddenly, holding the back of her hand to Anne's mouth. "What's her name?"

"Uh . . . Anne."

"Anne?" Frances said in a louder voice, tapping her sharply on the collarbone. "Anne? My name is Frances, and I'm trained to give aid to those in need. Do you need assistance?"

Anne blinked her eyes and . . . Gilbert looked a second time. She'd blinked *both* her eyes!

The spider had removed her faceplate. Now, the place where where the red glass eye had been was as whole as the rest of her face. And that face was slowly but visibly changing, scarred skin un-wrinkling like a smoothing-out sheet, radiating from the point of her injection out to the rest of her now healing visage.

Her eyelid had grown back, too. Gilbert looked around, on the table, on the floor. Had her artificial eye been extracted somehow, or had it melted away, too, like the deformities in Anne's face?

Anne's eyes twitched over to Frances. She then opened her mouth slightly, as if unsure whether she was asleep or awake, and then she gazed at Frances for a second with a puzzled expression.

"I . . ." she said. "You, you are . . ."

"My name is Frances," she said, "and you have apparently been injured. Does anything—," Frances looked at Anne's face, as the last few bits of flesh wrinkled by scar tissue smoothed out and healed, seemingly by magic. "Does anything *hurt* at the moment?"

"No," Anne said, "but I'm thirsty. Have you any water?"

"I can help there," said a now familiar voice. Hilaire was now awake and already removing his canteen from his belt. Gilbert looked at the one on his own belt that had belonged to the late Private Negri and felt two kinds of guilt: one for not moving more quickly to offer water, and another, irrational guilt for taking the property of a dead boy.

Belloc, though only a Sergeant, moved with the speed and grace of a stereotypical British officer. Before Gilbert was halfway through his own thoughts, Belloc had untied the small leather laces that held his canteen to his belt, unscrewed its cap, and raised the precious liquid to Anne's lips.

"Careful, not too much or too quickly," Belloc said as Anne began to drink, "We've still got a long journey ahead of us."

"You're very kind and able," Frances said, looking at Belloc while Anne drank. "Mister—?"

She let the sentence hang in the air while looking at him.

"Belloc. Sergeant Hilaire Belloc, 43rd Regular Hussars of Her Majesty's Rifles, at your service, m'lady." Belloc answered while still looking at Anne, obviously amazed that her face had been completely healed. As such, he did not appear to notice at all the lingering gaze that Anne gave him...

Oh, no, thought Gilbert. *That's not happening here.*

"Um, Frances, just how did you—"

"Gilbert," Frances said, checking Anne's pulse, her eyes reacting to the soft light in the room, and several other physical checks. "This girl is well enough. Do you know what that now means?"

"Well, I . . . well, that is, I'm not altogether certain if you want it to mean that I, or that she, or that—"

"Gilbert," Frances said, reaching up to the tall boy and placing her hand on his cheek.

"Yes," he said in a whisper.

Frances suddenly punched him in the face. Hard.

Gilbert yelped, more in surprise than pain, though it *did* unmistakably hurt. He'd been hit harder, but never hurt more.

"What was *that* for?" he yelped, holding his hand to his throbbing cheekbone, his other hand brought up to defend against any further blows.

"We'll settle our other differences later, Gilbert," she said, standing straight and brushing clean the strap across her knuckles as if cleaning a recently used dust mop.

Belloc looked at Gilbert with an odd expression. "She's a live one, isn't she?" he muttered and stepped away from Frances.

Then something caught Belloc's attention.

"Jimmy?" he barked, striding toward the way that Gil and the rest of them had entered.

Gilbert looked in the direction Hilaire strode. There was a man there, a bit older than Gil or Hilaire, staring at the scribblings on the wall. He'd pushed back his bowler hat a few inches to scratch at his dark hair, and the thumb of his other hand had hooked into his belt loop.

"Jimmy! I'm *talking* to you!" Hilaire said, now just a few inches from Jimmy, and looking angrier by the second.

Jimmy, still focused on the wall, held up his hand and said something in a language Gilbert didn't recognize at first. Maybe it was Greek?

"Oh, I'll disturb it, you skinny little miscreant," Belloc said, coming closer, "and quoting Archimedes won't help you, here! And don't think your knife's gonna scare me! You *know* who *I've* been trained by! What's your game this time? And why'd you drag some innocent girl into the Martian wastes? Did you pick her purse already, and now you're going to bury her somewhere in the sands?"

Jimmy stopped trying to read the wall, looked at Hilaire, and straightened out the black vest he wore over his white, long-sleeved shirt. "'Ere, now, I resent that!" Jimmy said, the cockney seeping through his words. "I've got me a code, Sergeant! The lady's never done me wrong, not a once. She pays me on time and treats me right. I generally don't kill ladies, anyways, not 'less they're serious-like about endin' my life, too."

"Spare me the details of your professional life, thief," Belloc said, his fist suddenly materializing under Jimmy's chin and bunching up a handful of his shirt collar. "Tell me what you're doing here, before I start using that bony jaw of yours for a shuttlecock."

"Careful, *Sergeant*. I killed three men for threatening me a few months back, an' they were all better than you."

"And likely none of them were able to get as close to you as me. Last chance, before I—"

A female voice moaned nearby. Hilaire, Gilbert, and Jimmy all turned to see Anne struggling to wake up, while Frances waved a small white tube under her nose.

Gilbert walked closer to the pair of them, unsure of how he should act. "Frances," he said while standing behind her, "this wasn't—"

"As I said, we'll have our things to discuss later," Frances said, checking Anne's pulse again, "but for now, I finally get to put some of my charitable training to use. Are there any more injured in the vicinity?"

"No. We were chased by a group, but they're all either gone or dead. And one of them was my old friend, Herbert."

Frances looked up at Gilbert. "Herbert's on Mars?"

"He's joined with *them*," Anne muttered, her eyelids fluttering. "He's called the *Cleaner*, now, by his new masters. I found it out through a little subterfuge months ago."

"Anne?" Gilbert said, moving from behind Frances to Anne at the stone bedside. "Anne, are you alright?"

"What happened to her?" Frances asked.

"We . . . we came down here, all of us. When we got to these stone beds, something came over us and we all fell asleep. When I came to, there was this weird spider-thing that was near Anne, and it was sticking a needle in her left temple, there, an inch or two above her ear."

Frances moved back a lock of Anne's red hair to examine her eye more closely, and Gilbert marveled even more. Anne's *hair* had grown back over the spot that had been injected! The area had been burned bald above the left, ruined side of her face, but it had grown as lush and bright red as the rest of her hair.

"Anne, do you know what this place is?"

"We're in a city that's over ten-thousand years old," Anne said, trying to sit up. Frances moved back and away, standing between Gilbert and the red-hired girl. Anne sat up, shook her head, and ran her left hand through her hair, not apparently realizing how much of it had now been restored. "I'm afraid I don't know much else, though. I've been far too busy surviving and keeping out of the sight of the locals to be much of an archaeologist."

"This is a hospital," Jimmy said, his eyes once again entranced with the pictures on the wall. His collar was wrinkled where Hilaire had released it. "And you, m'lady, have been fixed by a machine designed by the local natives, better known as the—" Belloc spoke the name of the race in the Martian tongue, alien in more than one way to their ear.

"The who?" Gilbert asked, beginning to take an interest in the pictures. A lot of them looked like pictures of Egyptian hieroglyphics his mother had shown him when he'd been schooled at home. Some of the stylized drawings looked like people, but there were other ones that looked like the Martian squids who'd invaded Earth nearly two years ago.

Still other drawings were of beings taller than men, creatures that were skinny with spindly arms and legs. In one such engraving, one of the skinny-spindle men was passing some kind of box on a figure that looked vaguely human, with jagged-edged drawings of broken arms and legs. In the next panel of pictures, the broken arms and legs were healed and whole, and the box appeared to have unfolded itself into a hieroglyphic version of the spider–thing Gilbert had seen on Anne.

"Them spider things you saw," Jimmy said, more to himself than to anyone else, tracing the pictures with his finger as he spoke, "they was thought up by them tall lanky fellows what live in the mountain caves. Nice enough chaps, though they won't talk to us much. Poor blokes prob'ly couldn't stand more than a minute on Earth if'n they hadda be there. And . . . Well, this is even *more* interesting!"

Gilbert was standing behind Jimmy now, looking at the picture writing on the wall with almost as much intensity as Jimmy himself.

The scene depicted members of the tall, spindly race. There were other line drawings as well—animals, he guessed; a group of the spindly fellows and other figures, all in a line looking up as the Squids descended on Mars in the same large cylinders they'd used to invade Earth.

The next row of pictures below depicted the Squids traveling to a blue circle and then gathering up humanoid stick figures that could only be representative of humans.

In the third row of pictures, some of the stick figures lay prone with a large Squid hovering over them, its tentacles turning them red, yellow, white, and red.

In the last row, several of the stick figures had somehow broken free from their confines, running to be with the Martian natives and their animal companions while the Squids pursued them in their giant, tripod machines.

"The Red Men of Mars," breathed Belloc. "They aren't native to this world. They aren't from here at all. Do you know what this means?"

"If you think *that's* interesting," said Jimmy, "look over 'ere. I spotted this'n right after Miss Blogg and I awoke on the stairs."

The next set of pictographs took up the far wall, and most of the ceiling. Gilbert wondered how they'd missed it before. It loomed above them, ominous and intimidating, frightening Gilbert and the others even before they fully understood its meaning.

They were all quiet for a very long minute while they took in the latest pictograph.

"Mother of God preserve us," Belloc said, when he understood.

Chapter 48

****

1914 A.D.
THE NATIVE SETTLEMENT.

"*R*eady, folks?" *Gilbert said, trying to keep a jaunty air.*

Father Flambeau looked Gilbert up and down like a broken car that a slick salesman was trying to pawn off on him. "I am," said Flambeau, "but I'm not altogether certain about you."

"Our gracious hosts have proclaimed me ready to roll on," Gilbert said, his hands casually in his pockets as he looked around, smiling. Where was Anne?

"Our hosts are, indeed, gracious, generous and kind. But they know less about human anatomy than we do about an angel's," Flambeau said. "Do you really think they're qualified to make that kind of judgment about your innards, Gilles?"

"First, my name is Gilbert. The last time I went by the name Gil, I ended up blinding myself to the world around me so badly that it took a broken nose and a bullet wound to wake me up. Second, thanks to their little translator gadget I've been able to have a decent conversation with those skinny fellows. It turns out I'm not the first person these folks have patched up. There were a few soldiers who passed through here a while back, and before them a number of prospectors looking for ice deposits."

"Have it your way, mon ami. But I know how important this job is, and

I don't think it will hurt it much if we give your battered body a while more to heal."

"And I don't *know if it* will *hurt things, Jean-Paul. That's why we need to keep moving. Is the floater in good working order?"*

"It's in excellent working order," *said Anne, her voice carrying out from behind him, making him turn and smile.* "But," *she continued,* "we'll have to go at it on foot unless we can find some mounts. The terrain from here to the lost city is far too rocky to support the floater. We'd bounce around like grease spots in a frypan, and perhaps jog loose the stitches I put into you yesterday."

"You stitched me up? I thought it was the magic box they had on my chest."

"That extracted the impurities from your system, and accelerated the healing process. I had to make sure none of your cleaned-up insides spilled out after they took you off of the box while you were anesthetized. Pity they couldn't cobble together one of those healer spiders we found back then. It would have been useful, but someone lost the plans. You can walk, but you'd better leave off running for a while."

"What about mounts?"

"If we could find sloats," *Flambeau said, gently, not wanting to spoil the moment he saw forming between the two,* "we could go at it much easier, I think. I've yet to hear of even the most delicate stitch job coming loose while the patient was on a calm mount. Just don't kick it into a gallop."

"You sound as if you know where our mounts are coming from already," *Gilbert said.*

"I've an idea or two," *Flambeau said, standing from the small cooking fire and pushing the small of his back with both hands and a grunt.* "I've been at this a while. Almost as long as you two, in fact."

Gilbert looked over at Anne, who looked back at him.

"He's not thinking about stealing them from the Tharks, is he?" *Anne said, looking at Gilbert.* "Gilbert, please tell me you told him how that turned out when you tried it back then!"

"I . . . well, I maybe left out a few things."

"He tried to steal a pair of sloats for our trip back to Syrtis Major, after the dust settled. The Tharks caught him, beat him senseless, and would have skinned him alive for the sport of it if a French regiment hadn't happened upon us, purely by chance."

"Nice to know my people can do something besides surrender these days," Father Flambeau said with a smile. Anne and Gilbert, too focused on each other, ignored both the priest's comment and the smile.

"I wouldn't say I was senseless, Anne."

"You were trying to order those greenskins about like Americans always do when they feel threatened, demanding your rights as a citizen, warning that a steam-Lincoln or an ironclad would mow over their village, or some such rot. Really, Gilbert! There's a significant difference between courage and a simple stupidity that would terminate your life! And all to impress a girl! Your girl . . . rather, Frances, would have ended up the bride of a Thark if I hadn't fired that flare gun. It was only because they didn't think it would be any trouble to make you scream that they felt you weren't worth skinning before the soldiers came on the scene."

"How did you know this, anyway? I don't recall you being with . . ."

Anne had been caught up in the moment, retelling the story with more and more agitation as the memories flooded back to her. At Gilbert's question, though, she was suddenly silenced, and looked down at the red dirt while she tried to think of something new to say.

Gilbert blinked, then looked at Anne sharply. "You were watching us? After the adventure was over, you followed us? That flare gun was you? I always thought it was the French, calling for reinforcements! And you never told me?"

"Um, children, can we focus on the issue at hand?" said Father Flambeau.

"NO!" they both shouted, their eyes locked on each other. "You know what we call a person in the States who follows you around without you knowing about it? You know what kind of person does that?"

"The kind that saves your life?"

"Well, that's beside the point!"

"The kind that made your life with Frances possible? Marrying a corpse really isn't an enjoyable experience, I've heard."

"Don't you go changing the subject! How long were you stalking us?"

"Until I met a man of my own who could love me the way you wouldn't!"

"PEOPLE!" shouted Father Flambeau, his voice suddenly changing tone and commanding their attention. "I know this is a difficult time for you, but you need to put that all aside for now and complete the task before us, no?"

They were silent for a few moments. They heard the sound of thin feet *scraping on rocks and dirt around them, and thin, alien heads with dark eyes peeped at them over piles of rocks like scared children looking at parents in a fight.* "Which direction do we need to go in, Anne?" *Gilbert said quietly.*

"North. As we always do," *she said.* "If Father Flambeau can get us those mounts he was talking about, we can start and be there in a relatively short time—perhaps a day or two."

"We might just make it, then," *said Flambeau, and without having to resort to theft, either.* "But, if we do, Gilbert, I will be the light fingered one, and you shall stay here and protect the person of the lady with us, understood?"

"As if she needs protecting," *Gilbert grumbled.*

Chapter 49

"What we call emancipation is always and of necessity simply the free choice of the soul between one set of limitations and another."

– Daily News, Dec. 21, 1905

1892 A.D.

"Jolly good to see you, Cleaner," said the large man from his seat at the circular table. "Sorry to hear about your team."

Herb stood as he faced the table, set in the middle of the large meeting room, where four men and an empty chair sat quietly. All four of the masters of the Special Branch and god knew what else in the world, were assembled here in a meeting room in a lost city on a planet far from home. He tried not to think about what would happen if a bomb went off in here; wouldn't the world be a better place?

He gave a wan smile. He'd learned from the mistakes of others to never appear too eager, and never appear resentful. *You're a tool to be used*, he reminded himself. No tool ever profited from being loyal, joyful, or bitter. Only by being *useful*.

"Thank you. It was unfortunate, but those are the risks we took when we signed up, aren't they? I am curious, of course, what's motivated you to bring me up to Mars in the first place. I find it interesting that Chesterton is here, too."

"Yes. That was surprising, was it not?" said the youngest man at the table, next to the empty chair. He was fifty and a tad bulky, with thick arms filling a white sport coat. "We sent for you," he continued in a voice that sounded like pouring milk, "and you almost immediately encounter Mister Chesterton on the streets of Syrtis Major. A shame you weren't able to remove him."

The Fourth Man looked like he was going to say more, but the first, oldest man interrupted him. Herb noted the oldest man had large dark spots on his throat, the kind that grew with age. "Well," the oldest man said, the spots pulsing on his throat as he spoke, "your next assignment won't be nearly as intriguing. We had one for you that deals with an event taking place in a few days from now. However, with these new . . . *developments* with Mister Chesterton, we've felt it prudent to give you a different assignment. This will be one you can complete on your own, and still may involve finding a different member of the Chesterton family."

Herb's eyes widened slightly. "Do tell."

The Second Man turned to face Herb, his sunken eyes focusing on him in a way that made Herb quake a little inside. This was Fortescue Williamson's father, and Herb had a poor history at best with the Second Man's son. "First," the Second Man said, "we have a little mining settlement nearby. Quite profitable. Unfortunately, the self-declared Governor, a fellow named Wickham, has forgotten who the real power is here on Mars, and has gotten a rather nasty case of the *arrogants* in his system. You've proven very able in encouraging men like him to return to the reality of the situation. Moreover for you, we have reason to believe that the younger sibling of your . . . acquaintance, a young fellow named *Cecil* Chesterton, is with this governor."

Herb paused. "What do you mean, 'younger sibling'? Gilbert Chesterton is an only child. What's his relation to Gil?"

"The young boy is Gilbert's long-lost sibling. He believes himself to be a scion of the Oldershaw clan. However, records show he was indeed born with the name Chesterton. And, though Chesterton is not a wholly *un*common name in the British Empire, this lad of thirteen summers has given many indications of his connection to your acquaintance, Mister Gilbert Chesterton."

Herb waited for a few more seconds before he spoke.

"Might I ask," he said, "why you brought me here for this? Persuading some dunghill-king and grabbing a little boy is something you could have had a few local steam-monkeys do, without waiting months for me to arrive from earth."

"Perceptive as always," said the Third Man, ponderously tapping the ashes of his cigar into a small ashtray with a large ham-hand. "My dear boy, this latest assignment comes just recently to our table. As you are the most able agent available, we've handed it to you. The real reason we've brought you here is perhaps more . . . delicately put."

There was another heavy pause in the room. Herb noticed that each of the four men made a subtle glance at the sole, empty seat in the room.

Dare he hope...?

Still, that empty seat looked inviting...

"How are things back on Earth for you these days, dear boy?" asked the Fourth Man, his voice still soft and silky. "How is that lovely young lady whose company you were keeping?"

"Margaret? I've really no idea. She dropped out of sight in the Americas—or, rather, in America, now that the five American countries signed their treaty and reunited. She stopped off to campaign against some law or other in a town called Comstock, then got into a tussle with that aged Pinkerton fellow who gave me trouble last year in New York. She dropped off the map soon after. Haven't heard from the Pinkerton since, either. Finn, I think was his name."

"Yes, well, we've reasons to suspect we'll not hear from her for some time, dear boy, if ever," said the First Man, the liver spots on his face pulsating as he spoke.

He rose stiffly. "Walk with *me* now, Herbert," he said, "and I will show you why we called you to deal with Mister Wickham." He escorted Herbert out of the room. He felt a distinct level of tension in the air as soon as the Second Man stood, but made no issue about it. "How old are you, Herbert?" the First Man asked, as they descended the stairway, down to the lab Cecil had visited earlier.

"Eighteen. Almost nineteen."

"Too young to be worrying about the end, then. When you are a youth, you believe yourself to be an *ubermench*, a superlative person whom no disasters will touch. 'Others die, but *I* go on.' Is that how you think these days, Herbert?"

"I've seen my share of death," Herb said.

"Excellent. Knowing your own vulnerabilities is the beginning of most kinds of wisdom."

As they neared the stone doorway, a guard opened the door that had been added and bolted onto the rocky door frame since Cecil's escape. The door swung open without the First Man having to pause in his steps or slow his gait, and this impressed Herbert greatly.

"May I ask where we are going?" Herb said.

"To a place where you will see something quite new," the man replied. "Ah, here."

They were in a room made of the same red and yellow stone bricks for walls, and a number of steam-powered contraptions lined the walls around them. A stone table was in the room's center, long and wide enough for a man to lie down on, if need be. A man in a white lab coat was busy in one corner, chatting softly to something in a small cage the size of a fish tank.

"Doctor Moreau? May we have a word?"

The man in the lab coat straightened up, swept a sweaty blob of gray hair out of his eyes, and looked at the both of them with an expression halfway between fear and blank misunderstanding.

"What do you want?" he said with a hunted air. "I *am* making progress, but the sample was so small. I'm never, ever given enough to work with. I've produced *miracles* for your people, yet I feel as though I am a prisoner here! When will you let me leave?"

"Doctor Moreau," said the First Man, his liver-spotted skin almost pulsing in the pale gaslight of the lab, "this is one of our associates, one Herbert Wells. We desire that he see a demonstration of your work."

Moreau looked at Herb, then scurried back to his table. The First Man followed without taking his eyes off him.

"This," said Moreau, waving his hand at the table, on which sat a small jumble of rods, wires and tubes all twisting, winding and ending at a large, empty but still severe-looking syringe, "is what I have been working on. I have been able to synthesize the mollusk formula to a degree. Their formula protected them from most forms of disease and injury and prolonged their lives by many ages. I've modified a number of native-created machines to administer it, but it was the mollusks themselves who created the concoction."

Moreau's face darted back and forth like a rat trapped in a cage. He moved with quick, scurrying steps into a back room, and emerged carrying a small wire cage the size of a man's chest in his arms. The cage wobbled in Moreau's hands, and as he came closer to him Herb could see there was a rabbit inside the cage with a black number "8" painted on its mostly gray fur.

Moreau's body language made no secret he felt he was being intruded upon, but he reached under the lab table and pulled out a small kit of instruments. He pushed a number of buttons on his bizarre looking machine, flicked a few switches and stood back as machine began to hum, huff, puff and spin parts of itself.

After a minute of activity Herb saw the syringe fill itself with a viscous green liquid. Dr. Moreau gently detached the syringe from the machine that held it and inspected its sides for a moment. Holding the point of the needle up to the light, he flicked it several times with his finger and moved the plunger with his thumb just enough that he could be sure no stray air bubbles were left in the tube.

Now holding the syringe in his right hand, Moreau flicked open opened the cage. He reached in with a practiced hand and put a firm grip on the scruff of the rabbit's neck, holding him down as he plunged the needle into the suddenly animated rabbit's back.

"Now," said Moreau, resealing the cage shut and stepping back, "Watch this grandfather rabbit closely. He is close to the end of his life, you know."

Herb watched with the kind of practiced boredom common to youth the world over at demonstrations of excitement by their elders. But after a few seconds, his fascination was undeniable.

And this was because the rabbit was changing.

Gray fur became brown, and already dull brown fur became dark and sleek. Boney haunches with little muscle left on them became powerful and full again. Eyes that looked like a pair of dull black beads with tiny cataracts became jet black and sparkly, quick and alive with possibility. Intrigued, Herb moved in for a closer look. He even saw several new whiskers sprout on the small creature's face.

"Thus far," Moreau said, taking off his glasses and polishing them with a smile of pride, "the subjects have proven quite able in terms of their ability to metabolize and process the material. But I have been thus far unable to synthesize a sample well enough to avoid . . ."

A loud bang went off in the rabbit's cage. Blood and mess spattered on Herb, who hadn't realized how close he'd stood. Herb howled in surprise and anger, then looked back at the First Man and Moreau. Both of them had already moved discreetly to a safe distance, leaving Herb to take the brunt of the exploding rabbit on his person.

"As you can see," said the First Man, discretely offering Herb a handkerchief from a pocket in his waistcoat, "we have, in essence, found the fabled fountain of youth. The Mollusks used it as a form of tissue-regeneration, but they modified it to keep their human slaves and test subjects healthy and alive for longer periods of time. We have, ah, yet to fully synthesize our *own* formula from it, however. And virtually all the expeditions we have sent into the deserted Martian cities have been decimated by the White Apes that inhabit the place."

"I still don't see what this has to do with *me*," Herb said. He'd grabbed the handkerchief and angrily began mopping his face and then his ruined black longcoat. A bit of irony jumped into his head: this time last year, a murderous gang called the Dead Rabbits had chased him through downtown New York, but never caught him. Now, an *actual* dead rabbit had managed to stink up his best coat and embarrass him besides.

The First Man looked at Herb with a cool smile. "Your friend Gilbert has apparently made contact with the Martian warlord John Carter, one of the few *Earth*-born humans to have received a dose of the original version of this formula concocted by the mollusks themselves. There is another human whom we believe to have received a dose of the elixir as well, the governor of the mining colony to the East. His name is George Wickham, a man well in excess of a century old, but whose apparent age is not yet forty.

"It would appear Carter somehow had his memory erased, for though he fought in the American Civil War near a half-century ago at the age of thirty, he has no recollection of being any other age, which is consistent with those kidnapped by the mollusks for their studies. Perhaps they visited Earth unobserved, or perhaps they had human agents to do their bidding. We will likely never know, since Carter has been most unwilling to divulge information to any of our undercover agents who have befriended him, and he has proven nigh impossible to capture and interrogate properly.

"But Mister Wickham, now. *He* is ageless, as Carter is, and has nowhere near the material or mental resources to evade us. It should be a simple matter for one of your talents, Cleaner, to obtain him for our purposes. Even if he cannot himself provide us anything useful, his vivisected carcass could reveal very interesting information on the subject of eternal youth."

"You want me to bring this Wickham fellow to you?"

"Indeed, we would be most grateful if you could acquire Wickham.

More so grateful if you can acquire young Chesterton's brother from him too. You may have noticed that there is an empty chair in our circle that wants filling."

Herb stood as dignified as he could with bunny guts drying on his sleeve and in his hair. He hated this part of the job—the men of the circle always had to make sure you knew they were your superiors. "You can count on me for this, sir," Herb said. *And first chance I get,* he thought, *I'll slide a knife though those brittle, old ribs of yours, and see if the elixir of life protects you from* that!

Chapter 50

"It is the main earthly business of a human being to make his home, and the immediate surroundings of his home, as symbolic and significant to his own imagination as he can."

– "The Artistic Side," *The Coloured Lands*

1892 A.D.
THE ARCHEOLOGICAL SITE.

"Beatrice, my dear, wonderful girl! Would you have time for a spot of tea?"

Beatrice looked up from the desk in her room. The stone-walled apartment had the feeling of old things, and the British-made furniture felt decidedly out of place.

The Doctor had entered with a large-muscled and elegantly dressed manservant behind him, who held a metal tray decorated with gold-colored flourishes. On the tray were a teapot and two steaming cups, along with two small bowls with silver spoons.

"I'd love some tea, Doctor. Thank you. Please sit down."

The Doctor, ever the gentleman, held his top hat under his good arm and placed it on Beatrice's nightstand as he sat beside her. The manservant set down the tray and arranged teacups, kettle, and the small bowls of sugar and cream on the table for them. When this was finished, the Doctor dismissed him. and he waited outside the door without a word.

"I thought you would like to hear the update regarding our search for your brother," the Doctor said. "It would seem he is not as easy to locate as we thought."

"He *is* a clever one, I'll give you that," said Beatrice. "Many's the time he managed to slip out of school, chores, and punishments, even when our parents were alive."

"Yes, I had wished to discuss that, if I may. Your parents. What do you recall of them, Beatrice? By that, I mean, what were your earliest memories of them?"

Beatrice paused. Something in the Doctor's demeanor had changed. It was very subtle, yet spoke of danger and unhealthy interest on the Doctor's part. He had leaned in just a little, his eyes widening just a bit more with the question.

Beatrice pushed a ringlet of her honey-blond hair behind her ear. Remembering an event in a penny-dreadful novel Cecil had brought home one day, she looked at the steaming teapot for just a second and then briefly at the Doctor's face.

"I wouldn't," the Doctor said, his voice full of quiet menace.

"Wouldn't what?" she said innocently.

"I wouldn't take the pot of boiling tea and try to either splash it in my face, or bash me across the head with it in the hopes of knocking me unconscious. My manservant Horace is outside, and he can hear every word. You wouldn't get six feet from this room before he captured you and bent you to his will. Now, as you and Cecil have, shall we say, *escalated* the level of urgency to our trip, I will be blunt about what it is I want of you."

Beatrice looked down and away, horrified, though her hands remained folded in her lap. "Though Canadians are not known for our willingness to fight," she said, "you ought to know that I was raised to protect my family name, my own reputation, and my personal virtue at all costs, Doctor."

Fear raced through her mind, and a stolen glance at the Doctor and the table caused her to see things in ways she hadn't seen them before. Whereas a few days earlier she would have seen the teapot, table, and window as ordinary things, she now saw them in a very different light.

Very much like a game of chess, in her mind the table and plates became more than simple surfaces to place food and drink upon. She saw a line from her hand to the plate. She could break the plate, and then lunge at the Doctor's throat with a shard. A sweeping kick to the table's wooden legs would tip it on its side and form a barrier between herself and Horace when he re-entered the apartment to investigate. She could then leap out the window and into the dust-covered and deserted street, slipping in between deserted buildings and other structures until she could . . .

The Doctor was looking at her again.

"Plotting my demise and your own escape," the Doctor said, looking at her intently. "Your response to stress is neither quiet surrender nor brute force, but a planned and ruthless attack. You are, indeed, a Chesterton," he said.

"My last name is Oldershaw," she said.

"No, it isn't. Your last name is Chesterton. The Oldershaws, the people who raised you are not your birth parents, for your adoptive mother was a minor functionary of the Special Branch. Your adoptive father, Mister Oldershaw, had no idea of your real parents' actual status, believing your mother and his own wife to be sisters. You are not from Canada, but were born in Minnesota, though your roots are in England. And your brother Cecil is not your only brother; you have a second younger brother named Gilbert, who is now here on Mars."

Beatrice looked at the Doctor. Normally she would have laughed off such comments as drivel. But coming from the Doctor, here in a strange land after so many changes in her life? Had Beatrice not been taught repeatedly that panicking and sobbing in hysteria never helped anything, she might have broken down then and there.

At the Doctor's comments about her parents, she felt several parts of her world break away into tiny pieces and fly in the wind. Whereas a lesser person *would* have become very upset, Beatrice settled for quietly gripping the table in a viselike hold in her right fingers and thumb while holding the Doctor's gaze.

"Yes," the Doctor whispered as he stood, now looking more towering and menacing than Beatrice could ever remember seeing him. The jovial and generous man she'd met her first day on Mars was gone now, if indeed he'd ever existed. "Yes," he said again, looking deep into Beatrice's eyes, "so very, very much like your mother. Meeting adversity straight on, with eyes level and perfect poise. She would be quite proud of you, I think, dear Beatrice. I wish your foster-mother hadn't tried to imitate her mentor, Marie Chesterton, and married your poor, unsuspecting foster-father and run off. Made things quite challenging and awkward for me. To say nothing, I suspect, of the shock your foster-father must have has when he learned the true heritage and earlier profession of his bride."

"Stay back from me, Doctor, if you please," she said. Still sitting, she'd noticed the Doctor inching toward her with almost imperceptible movements. Her mind raced in a way she'd never known it to do before. Even when trying to keep up in an argument with Cecil, she'd never seen the world as she did now as a series of paths and choices, many of which ended with her still in the Doctor's clutches, or worse.

"You need not fear me, dear young Beatrice," said the Doctor, "for if I'd planned to do you or Cecil harm, I would have done so long ago, as I did to your adoptive parents when I arranged the accident that took their lives."

"You're *not* a good man. You're not a man at all! You're a filthy, insane creature who needs to be locked away where you won't be a danger to yourself or others!"

"What do you think this entire planet is, Beatrice dear?" he said, now standing and taking a full step toward her. She pushed on the table while still sitting and shoved her chair a full pace away from him while keeping the table between them.

"This planet, Beatrice, is a place for people like me. People too dangerous to others—people who need to be locked away from the affairs of those on our home world. But since I could not leave to get you and Cecil and Gilbert, I arranged to have you two, and then Gilbert, come here to me."

"I am not your assistant!" She said, more to herself than the Doctor, "I see now. I am only a hostage!"

"Clever girl. And now, I grow tired of this charade. I have decided to do some, ahem, *selecting* of my own. And I have selected—"

No more paths or options crowded her thoughts. Now, the way she should go was clear. Clear as a well-lit corridor leading to an open door.

She flicked her right hand, the one that had been holding onto the table, as if she were going to toss something at the Doctor. His eyes darted toward the sudden movement for only a split second, but that was all she needed.

While his eyes were busy with her right hand, her left hand grabbed the tray and spun it across the table at his midsection.

She leaped up from the table, hoping her efforts at misdirection had worked. Now, she saw the Doctor's right arm erupt from his coat and she was stunned.

Horrified.

Odd enough that his *right* limb, the arm he'd always said was crippled and useless, had leaped from his jacket and grabbed the serving tray in midair as it had flown at him.

His arm wasn't crippled. In truth it wasn't an arm at all. What he had was a thick, ropy *tentacle*, at least five feet from shoulder to tip. The tentacle was three-quarters of a foot thick at the shoulder and had at least a half-dozen slimy smaller tentacles sprouting from it along the way, like tributaries from a river.

And as she watched, horrified, one of the smaller tentacles took the tray from the main tentacle, then passed the tray to another smaller tentacle further up the Doctor's arm.

The Doctor's smaller tentacles passed the tray twice more up his arm, until the tray was now near his shoulder. Taking the tray into his left hand from the smaller, sprouted tentacle closest to his shoulder, the Doctor looked approvingly at his own reflection in it as he laid the main portion of his tentacle on the table. "Quite amateurish, my dear. Trying to strike me with a flung tray. Your brothers are worth ten of you. Still," he continued, dropping the tray to the floor with a loud clang, "as I cannot torture and kill either of them, I can think of no better way to spit upon the memories of your troublesome parents than to. . ."

The Doctor paused.

Beatrice had gotten hold of the teapot while he was looking at his reflection in the tray.

He ducked and brought up his good arm to block, expecting her to fling the teapot at his head.

But she didn't do that.

Beatrice had learned something from her younger brother, Cecil. He was successful as a scamp because he could come up with a new ruse each time he needed it, one that she never expected.

Knowing that he'd expect something flung at his head again, Beatrice took the teapot and did the first thing that came to mind.

She tipped the teapot, pouring the scalding hot tea through the spout and open lid onto the tentacle on the table.

The Doctor's shriek reverberated throughout the small room, out through the open stone-framed window, and into the open courtyard nearly ten stories below. Hellish tricks of acoustics made his voice bounce and play even further, down to a long staircase where Herb and the First Man stood.

Herb paused, still trying to brush the sticky, slimy innards of the dead rabbit off his coat and his hands. He and the First Man looked up at the sound of the Doctor's yell. Dr. Moreau moved not a whit, already wrapped back up into his studies, with his thoughts and delicate cooings focused on to the caged animals next slated for death in the name of science.

Back up in the room, the Doctor looked in pain at his suddenly disobedient limb. Scalded a bright red with blisters already filling with yellowish-white pus, it flailed around the Doctor with a will nearly all its own, sweeping crockery from the walls and tried to batter the plaster-covered stone.

Beatrice edged toward the doorway. Her movement caught the Doctor's eye as he tried to grab his whipping arm. "Oh, no, pretty. We can't have you running about, can we?"

Faster than she would have thought, he ignored his tentacle and lunged at her, grabbing her by the throat with his remaining good hand, holding her against the wall. "Clever girl," he said again, "but not clever enough! I'll just have to *select* another after I'm done with your lovely little—"

A rude, cold finger poked the Doctor in the back of the head at the base of his scalp. The sensation made him stiffen a bit, and the well-oiled *click* afterward made him stiffen his back even more and cease all movement.

His hand remained on Beatrice's neck.

"Horace," said the Doctor, barely keeping his body still as his alien limb continued to thrash about, "you will immediately holster your weapon and cease threatening me with it."

"I concur," said Horace, his voice surprisingly cultured for one who looked to be such a brute. "I will cease all potential for hostilities to your skull and upper vertebrae, immediately upon your release of the young lady's windpipe without further attempts to compress it."

The Doctor looked at Beatrice and then gave a sidelong glance back to Horace. The Doctor's gloved left hand opened wide, and Beatrice jumped sideways along the wall, away from the Doctor with her hands raised in defense.

"I'll remember this, brute," the Doctor said, his eyes still fixed on Beatrice while his tentacle whipped back and forth against the wall.

"I sincerely hope so," Horace said, stepping back with his pistol still raised. "I truly do hope you remember I needed only one bullet and a few words to make you obey my employers' wishes that the young lady remain unharmed."

"*I* am your employer, you oafish simpleton! You are supposed to obey *me*!"

"I left your employment this morning, Doctor, and accepted a new job from *your* employers. My duties thus far include, but are not limited to, ensuring you do not jeopardize any leverage they have against the Chesterton brothers which this young lady represents."

The Doctor stared at Horace's chiseled features for three long seconds, then looked at the floor. His eyes fell on Beatrice, who now held a very large iron cooking pan in her slender hands.

"Next time, I won't harm your tentacle," she said in a quiet voice.

The Doctor looked back at Horace and then let his shoulders slope slightly.

In the next few seconds, Herb, the First Man, and a series of very large guards entered the spacious apartment.

"What seems to be the trouble, m'lady?" said the First Man, his liver-spotted face pulsing with either anger or some kind of excitement.

"He . . ." said Beatrice, suddenly breathing quickly as the stress of the encounter began to settle. Her body began to shake a little, though both her hands were gripped tightly onto the heavy iron handle of the skillet.

"The Doctor unfortunately attempted to take unlawful liberties with the young lady," said Horace. "I found it necessary to enter the room and quell the disturbance."

"Who is this?" Herb asked. His eyes had grown wide. There was something so familiar about her in the face, chin, and eyes . . .

"This," said the First Man, "is Miss Beatrice Chesterton, elder sister of your one-time associate, Gilbert Chesterton."

"My brother's name is *Cecil*!"

"My dear," said the First Man, "perhaps we should expel the remaining members of this group, and explain things to you over a cup of tea."

"I am most *emphatically* not your 'dear,' nor do I wish any more tea from anyone associated with that . . . that . . . I can't rightly call him a *man*," she said, pointing to the Doctor, "and not only because of whatever bizarre circumstance gave him the limb of a giant octopus! I wish only to leave here, collect my brother, and return to Canada. Being a washerwoman, a seamstress, or a scullery maid would be preferable to life here!"

The First Man was silent. He looked for a few seconds at Beatrice with the expression of a man adding sums in his head, then turned to go. Without a word spoken or even needed, Herb, the Doctor, the guards, and Horace all followed him out. The door was shut behind them, and clicked as it was locked.

Beatrice swallowed, looked around the room, and then at the skillet in her hands.

This is heavy, she thought suddenly, *and I would have used it to bash in the skull of another human being, without a second thought.*

The thought was frightening, and she dropped the pan on the floor with a clang.

Chapter 51

"Business, especially big business, is now organized like an army. It is, as some would say, a sort of mild militarism without bloodshed; as I say, a militarism without the military virtues."

– "The Drift From Domesticity," *The Thing*

"What does it mean?"

Frances's question echoed through the hollow yet still well-lit room. The glow that had spotted on Gilbert, Anne, and Hilaire now alighted on Frances and Jimmy as well.

"Take a look, Frances," Gilbert said quietly. "Imagine it was a picture drawn by a child, rather than trying to look at it like a language."

The panel picture was larger than the rest and showed more stylized pictures of the Squid-like creatures striking out even further than Mars and Earth, their odd-shaped ships leaving a series of concentric circles that could only be representative of the solar system itself.

"But there are only five or six planets in our solar system," Frances said, "why do they have *ten* orbits drawn around the sun?"

"Why indeed," said Jimmy. "Maybe they know some things we don't, hey? Look, there's . . . just a minute, that's—"

As they looked, things became odd indeed. For the pictures on the wall did something drawings were not supposed to do.

They began to move.

"I thought the drawings were doing this when I first looked at them," Belloc said. "Keep watching. When you all came here, they set themselves back to their original positions."

They watched quietly, as the indentation in the wall shaped like a mollusk's yellow cylinder left Mars, following a dotted-line arc toward another star.

The picture of Mars suddenly enlarged, filling more than half the wall. Small red-skinned humanoid figures were fighting the squid-like mollusks, driving them from land after land.

The surface of Mars on the wall seemed to spin to a different location, where the red humans were waving weapons over their heads, while the squids were building a fleet of yellow cylinders and cannon-like devices to launch them.

Then the picture shifted again. Mars shrank in size on the wall, and the view moved to another section of the Martian world.

"I know those mountains," Hilaire said suddenly. "That rocky outcrop looks like the nose of one of our officers and we named it after him. They've been doing some kind of archeological dig out there for months now."

"Look at what they found," Anne said, now behind them, her voice sounding like she felt she was in a dream.

"Anne!" said Gilbert happily, "You're fully awake!" But he cut his jubilation short when Frances shot him a dark look.

"They've poured a phenomenal amount of money and resources into uncovering this place," Anne said. "I haven't been able to get near enough to it without putting myself too much at risk."

"But what's it for?" Gilbert asked.

"I'm not sure," Anne said, "but there's been a great deal of activity there over the past few months. A lot of folks coming and going . . . mostly coming, not going."

"Glad to meet you at last awake," Frances said, looking Anne up and down. "Now that you're feeling better, Gilbert, could you please introduce us?"

"Ummm . . ." Gilbert started. "Well, uh, Frances, this is . . . this is . . ."

"My name is Anne. And you are?"

"My name is Frances Blogg. And I have the great fortune of being Gilbert's intended. At least, this is what he's told me thus far."

"Intended?" said Anne. "Does that mean the same thing on her side of the pond as it does on ours, Gilbert?"

Anne and Frances had both begun to stare at Gilbert. Gilbert felt quite uncomfortable. Looking around, he saw that both Hilaire and the fellow called Jimmy had instinctively relocated to a farther section of the underground hospital, all the while giving the occasional wary look at the skinny, befuddled American.

Gilbert swallowed, said a prayer, and got ready to try and talk himself through the verbal equivalent of walking through a mine-laden field at midnight.

"Well," Gilbert said, trying to smile, "it seems there's a lot to be explained!"

****

"Can you please explain to me," Herb said as they left Beatrice's apartment, "just what happened back there?"

"Nothing you need concern yourself with," said the First Man as they walked back to the large chambers from which he'd originally departed to give Herb his tour of the lower laboratories. The spots on his skin had begun to pulse and nearly glow when he'd seen the young blond girl in the room above.

"Nothing to concern myself with? That was the *Doctor*! He tried to kill me! More than once! He's half a monster now, and he tried to—to take liberties with that girl! Doesn't that anger you in the slightest?"

"I am only angered, Herbert, by three things in this world: the thwarting of my ambitions, servants who will not mind their place, and a cold cup of tea."

"Right, then, let's get something straight: I've done everything you've asked me to. I've betrayed friends, I've lied, I've killed those who've gotten in my way, all for *you* lot. But I draw the line at harming the innocent! Especially an innocent . . . innocent—"

"Especially if the honor and virtue of an attractive, *innocent girl* is at stake, Mister Wells?"

"Well, maybe. Yes."

"Am I to take it that you'd be *less* concerned, if it were an *unattractive* girl that the Doctor had attempted to assault?"

"Look, please don't twist my words like that. I know what he did was wrong *now*, and I won't have you doing any kind of shell game on me to hide it!" A small thought in Herb's head said that continuing this discussion could only bring him pain, but he didn't care. Something in the girl's face had frightened him, awakened something in him he hadn't known was there anymore, and he knew it was worth pursuing. "Isn't the Doctor going to be made to answer for that?"

"Herbert Wells, you are indeed a youth. I had high hopes you had outgrown your schoolboy desires for vaporous ideals, but it seems I was mistaken. If you wish to make the Doctor 'pay' for what you perceive as his 'crime,' by all means, do so. *After* you have completed your assignment, of course."

Herb stopped. They were at the large double doors of the conference hall that the men of the circle used on a regular basis. "You mean . . . if I get this Wickham chap here on board with us, then I can do what I wish with the Doctor?"

The First Man smiled, revealing perfect rows of well cared for teeth nestled between his spotted lips.

"Mister Wells," he said as the doors swung open, "You may recall that at one point you were assigned to liquidate the Doctor, though circumstances have since changed. If you perform adequately on this assignment, if you deliver George Wickham to us alive or dead, with most of his bodily fluids intact and uncontaminated by poisons or other chemicals, then I shall be moved not only to stand aside while you mete out whatever punishments you see fit to the Doctor. I shall allow you to decide the fate of that damsel he nearly assaulted as well. Now," he said, stepping into a new doorway and facing Herb on the other side, "be off with you. You have been selected for this mission not only because of your demonstrable moral flexibility, but also because you and Mister Wickham have a similar history of a willingness to exploit the fair sex for your own personal gain."

"Exploit the . . . ? Now just what do you mean by—?"

The door swung closed as if by an unseen hand. A lock clicked with quiet finality.

Herb was alone.

****

"So, what's the plan of attack?" Cecil had had a good sleep after the bar blew up the night before. He now sat at a table with Mr. Wickham, John Carter, Emrys, and a couple of large-bodied, roughly dressed men whom he assumed were leaders of the miners.

Cecil's question went ignored. It was Carter who'd won them all over last night with his charm, and now they virtually hung on his every word, the mayor (or governor, or whatever he called himself) included.

"The sandhogs can make it, Mister Carter, sir," said one of the men. "They've been kept in good repair; the deals we made wit' them skinny folk in the valley've seen to that. But it's a question of 'ow many men we can fit in each of 'em."

"How many men currently?" The question came from Wickham, who'd subtly pushed his way in between Carter and the miner leader.

"Twenty comfortable," said another miner, "thirty each if we squeeze. That's a force of a hundred eighty in the six working hogs we got."

"For a place the size of the city they've unearthed? You'll need at least two hundred," said Carter. "Remember, you'll need to do more than just conquer. It's holding it when they counterattack that's the trick."

"We can't fit that many in a sandhog!"

"I never said you needed to, my good sir," said Carter, his Southern twang coming back with his impish smile. "One-hundred eighty in the sandhogs will do just fine, since I'm worth twenty."

"What are the numbers of our adversaries?" asked Emrys, ignoring Carter's bragging. He looked as if he'd been distracted until the question had popped into his head.

"According to our intrepid informant here," said Wickham, "there are a few dozen men that the prisoners can see. As this is primarily an archeological dig, I doubt they've got a force sizable enough to be a concern. I've already had our fine gentlemen spread the rumor that the boy here died in the fire last night, to ensure that the men on the dig are not in a state of alert."

"Dead in the fire?" Cecil said, his voice going up in pitch as his indignant voice bloomed out. "My poor sister's gonna be upset about that!"

"Young man," said Wickham with a politeness that held no small amount of force behind it, "this is a place for adults. You are here to give information and nothing else, and even then only when you are spoken to. Is that clear?"

Cecil bristled. "You wouldn't have gotten this far without me. I managed to escape from that place, no one else has done *that* so far. *And* I'm the one who convinced these two fine and experienced fighting gentlemen to join up with you and your miners, Mayor Wickham. I'd suggest that earns me a speaking place at this table, and a few steps up in your respect from that mynah bird over your shoulder."

Cecil pointed to the black bird over in the corner. It cawed twice dutifully. The miners chuckled a bit, and Carter gave Cecil a smile and a wink. "I truly think," said Carter, "that this lad has earned not only a seat at the table, but one beside me on the sandhog as well. He's got firsthand knowledge of the place, from the basement to the courtyard to the towers and beyond. Guided by a dashing warrior like myself, he could only be an asset to this little mission."

"And what, precisely," said Emrys, jumping into the conversation while looking at Wickham, "*is* your understanding of the mission, here? I know why *I'm* going, but do you? Are you mobilizing all this material and men in an effort to save a young girl, or do you have other motives?"

"My motives," said Wickham, "are simple. The men digging out that temple city only get their hands dirty when finding ancient technology. I have need of that. Moreover, I have evidence they think I have something *they* need as well, and they're not above cutting me up into drippy little pieces to get it. It's simply a question of hitting them first. Having a guide in the form of the boy and you two accomplished war heroes is a stroke of luck I intend to take full advantage of. Having my men and resources is a stroke of luck I hope *you* will see fit to take advantage of, Mister Emrys."

****

"Well, what do you think, Emrys?" said Carter once the meeting was over and they were in one of the many 'guest rooms' in the hive-like miners' quarters. These were hewn out of the rock untold centuries ago and now inhabited by earthmen who come to take treasure from the Martian soil.

"I think he means to use us as long as we are of use to him. I don't think him foolish enough to try and assassinate us at the end of the mission; he seems a tad too well informed to know how useless a gesture that would be, particularly against you."

"And you, too, dear fellow," Carter said, unsheathing his sword and doing practice swipes with it in the air. "Especially with you and that wonderful brain of yours in your primes."

"You can be very kind when you want to be, John. No, I know that my end in this story is, in fact, approaching with relative rapidity, and I'll be handing the torch onto another soon."

"What?" said Cecil, his head popping out from under the bed. "What do you mean, 'handing on the torch'? And what do you mean your end is coming? You're talking like an old man, and I don't think you've gone past twenty winters!"

"Cecil," said Carter, "this is hardly the time for—and just what were you doing under there?"

"He was listening in, John," Emrys said matter-of-factly. "It's what he does, and he does it well. In time he'll be an excellent spy for the forces of good in the world, if he continues to make the right choices. Won't you, Cecil?"

"Please don't change the subject," Cecil said as he came out from under the bed. "What do you mean, your end is coming?"

"Yes, the boy is right. As such I'll spank him with the flat of my sword later for being a snoop. Now look here, Emrys," Carter said, sheathing his sword, "why don't you enlighten me as to what's been upsetting you as of late? I've seen generals who've lost a thousand men in a day display less melancholia than you're showing right now."

Emrys sighed again. "John, did you graduate from school?"

"I assume so. I have a difficult time at best remembering much before my adulthood."

"Graduation is a bittersweet time for most, because while you have achieved your goal, you will be leaving many you care about behind for a time, and some, perhaps, never to be seen again. It has been made clear to me that I'll soon be graduating, and that many of the things I wished to do will not be done. At least not by me."

Carter was silent. "Are you saying you're going to die, Emrys? Have you got a case of the red death, or something worse?"

"John, you've been a good, if at times exasperating, comrade and friend to me. Do you remember what that traveler from Earth called me when he stepped off the rocket last year?"

"Some kind of dragon, or something. I thought it quite rude, but you wouldn't let me teach him any manners."

"He was working for the *Pendragon*, John. The latest in a long, usually invisible line of men whose job it is to keep the boundaries of darkness pushed back from our world. I've been an assistant, guide and confidant to the leader of the resistance. Much like Belle Boyd and her spy ring was for you Confederates, and I've been such for quite a long time now. It brings with it some perquisites but a number of burdens as well. My anointing to this position has allowed me to communicate with certain persons you are wholly unaware of, and said persons are aware of forces and events near and far I literally cannot dream of. What I *do* know is that the most recent holder of that honor, of being the *Pendragon*, has passed on. And whether we win or lose this little gambit we're taking with Wickham, I shall have to pass the office on to a successor."

"Well, I— Emrys, thank you! Thank you *sir*, so very *much*!" Carter said, pumping Emrys's hand mightily. "I knew you held me in high esteem, sir, but to be promoted to head of a secret society for good, *and* be Warlord of Mars in the same lifetime is nearly more honor than any man could stand! I, however, will endeavor to make you proud of this choice of me! Clever, how you got me to start this conversation—"

"John," said Emrys.

". . . after all, I would make the most logical choice—"

"John—"

". . . not only due to my stellar skills in combat, but my peerless abilities at stealth and infiltration—"

"John—"

"All of course, tempered by the delicate sense of humility und understanding of my own limitations which this life has imposed upon me,"

"It's not you, John."

"Needless to say, I shall . . . *What?*"

"It's not you. You aren't the one. You've got a different purpose, one that will set you against Wickham eventually, if he survives."

"What? I'm expected to waste my talents on that whisky-mop excuse for a man? Are you certain of that?"

"Oh, yes. I have been privileged to see certain events prior to their happening," Emrys said. "For many years, I was what was called the . . ." Here he used a word in a language that neither Cecil nor John Carter had ever heard before. "I am not the Pendragon, nor will I ever be him. I *anoint* the Pendragon, one chosen to lead the good against the bad."

"Back when we lived in Canada," Cecil piped up, "I heard a minister say once over at the United Church that there ain't really no good nor bad people, Mister Emrys."

"People who say that are usually in the thralls of the bad and are trying desperately to hide that fact. No, I'm called to help a long, long line of men called to lead. Some have been kings, some have been popes, a great many have been ordinary men of the world and workbench. The seat's been vacant for a bit, but I'll soon find the next, and then I'll be off to fight in the Boer Wa-."

"That's another question I have, Mister Emrys: Why do you keep talking in the future tense?"

"Yes, Emrys," Carter threw in, "you've been doing that more and more lately. Can you foresee anything useful to our victory? Information is always valuable at a job like this, isn't it?"

Emrys looked at the boy and the man in his room and sighed. "John," he began, "you've been both a good ally and a good friend. And one of the things that bonded us initially was that we *both* had things done to us by the mollusks that have affected our ability to age."

"I hope you're not complaining. I know quite a few older men who wish they looked twenty when they were fifty."

"Indeed, John. No, it's—you know, John, how the Mollusks captured you, injected you with their serums, and tried to wipe your memory of the event?"

"Of course! They wanted their slaves to be more durable and long lasting. Gave me quite a bit of strength, too. I wouldn't have known it had we not invaded one of their bases and found their records. Dear Deja was invaluable at deciphering their–"

"Well, John," Emrys continued, cutting him off gently, "they did much the same to me. Except I was an old man when they experimented on me. Nearly a thousand years ago, in a little fishing village in Wales."

Both John Carter and Cecil were silent.

"I realize it sounds quite improbable, but it is the truth. My er— *treatments* were a tad different than yours, John. I received no great strength, and it would appear that I have—well, that I age, not only quite slowly, but *in reverse.*"

John looked at Emrys. The expression on the soldier's face was a cross between a desire to laugh irreverently and incredulity at what he was being told.

"But—well, that still doesn't explain how you seem to know future events now and then. Or what's happening *now*, when no one else does."

Emrys smiled. "I never understood it myself, really. Not until I— well, it seems that since they first did what they did to me, they put me in a lighted chamber after they injected that substance into me. And it-it seems that since then, I've been *unstuck* in time."

"Unstuck?"

"Yes, Cecil. You see, most of us are *stuck* in time, on the road that moves forward. Somehow, I've been taken off that road and I—I just skip about as needed. I've done it three or four times already during this conversation. I'll suddenly be in the fourteenth century, then the tenth, and then—here again. I've had the devil of a time trying to understand what happened to me, until I met up with a fellow named Werner Heisenberg. Very clever chap—said what I was experiencing was a confirmation of some branch of science or physics he'd been toying about with."

"Physics?"

"A branch of science that deals with the physical world."

"Ah, well, Mr. Emrys, sir..."

"Just Emrys, please, will be fine. Anything except Ambrose or 'hawk' as John over there sometimes likes to call me."

"Ah, certainly. Well, I wonder, then, if you can travel to the past..."

"Why not go to the future, and find out how we can best succeed in our little adventure? And get the names of a few winning horseraces and sporting events besides, and become wealthy in the process?"

Cecil nodded his head. Eagerly.

Emrys chuckled. "First, I have no control over the process whatsoever. Second, I can only go to *my* life, at different points. I'll move at what first seems to be an utterly random pattern, but in the end, after a time, I'll see that-that it's all part of my job. My mission."

"Which is?"

"I—I have to find a person. I know who it is, but getting to them is a devil of a difficult business when you're skipping about as much as I do."

"It happens a lot, then?" John said.

"Only when something crucial is going to happen," Emrys said. "And it's been happening a lot; I can't seem to stay here more than a few—a few words at a time. As for the fellow I am looking for, I have to keep my eye out for them, and strike when the iron is hot."

"You must have had some thrilling adventures!" Cecil said, the wonder and admiration in his voice genuine for a change, rather than faked as a manipulation tool.

"That certainly *is* a way of saying it. Sometimes they are thrilling. Sometimes they are boring. Frequently, the more thrilling ones are just the result of poor planning."

"You ought to write them down or something. I bet they'd sell a bundle!"

"Yes, Emrys," John said, unusually serious. "Not only for the monetary value; methinks there are many who'd benefit from seeing and hearing history from the perspective of one who's actually *been* there."

"One of my colleagues has written the adventures down, and a lad who is being trained to join us will publish them as his own one day, if he stays on the side of the *glain*. And when I have to pass on the blessing of—"

The door to their room opened without a knock. One of the larger and younger workmen with a slack jaw and little to say looked at them with a dull expression.

"Time, gentlemen," he said, shutting the door as quickly as he opened it.

****

"So, what now?" Jimmy said. The large underground room was starting to smell a bit musty, and the lights were beginning to dim.

"I'd wager that we need to get moving," Hilaire said, "unless we want to start camping out here. There's very little food in our packs, now. We'll need to start soon if we want to make Danton's Folly."

"How far is it?" Gilbert asked. He was still staring intently at the pictographs on the wall. They kept trying to shift and change, but Gilbert had learned that tapping the wall made the lines re-set themselves and begin again at the start of their storytelling dance in the lines of the rock.

"At least another day or two," Hilaire said, "depending on whether we have to run, hide, skulk, or are otherwise delayed by our charming new friends in the area. I'm not really thrilled about traveling through the ruins above with those white apes lolling about, but I see our options as being rather limited."

"Yeah," said Gilbert, "well, in my experience, this is a good time to look at life and say 'is that the best you've got?' Your options are only as limited as your imagination. Have you scouted the walls to see if we have any other exits out of here?"

"What do you mean, Gilbert?" said Frances. Gilbert liked how she sounded—he couldn't hear any anger in voice, at least for now.

"Most places, especially a hospital, have more than one way in or out. In the Slave Wars they'd often turn ordinary buildings into hospitals *if* they had tunnels or other kinds of hidden entrances and exits. It's a way of escape if suddenly they had a bunch of folks all get sick at once or some disaster hit or something like that."

"And you think something like that could be here?" Anne said, already up from her stone couch and moving toward the walls.

"Couldn't 'urt to check," Jimmy said, pointing to a new place on the wall, one where the lines did not move no matter how often they were touched. "This picture looks a bit like it's meant to be this place we're in now. An' there's a fair bit of lines moving from it to the outside."

"Then it seems we should be on our way," said Frances, tucking a lock of dark brown hair under her stylized top hat. Somehow, it had held its shape through all the actions of the day since she'd scooped it up. "But how shall we—"

She stopped.

Very, very slightly, but unmistakably, the room was vibrating, shaking *just* enough to be perceived. She looked at Gilbert and the others; they felt it too.

"What's happening?" Anne asked.

"I don't know," Hilaire said, "But we need to move, *now!* The way we came isn't an option. We'll be food for apes in an hour. Fan out, start sliding your hands along the walls, see if you can find a crack in the stone, a hollow sounding space, anything that could—"

The sound of grinding rock echoed in the large room, mixed with the scuttling sounds of the medical mechanical spiders on the floor. Dirt and dust dropped from the ceiling as a section of the wall slid to the side and opened.

Hilaire, Gil, Frances, and Jimmy looked up and saw Anne standing by the newly opened door. The soft light that still had no readily visible source shone all around her, giving her already bright head of hair a beautiful corona.

"How did you do that?" Hilaire whispered.

Anne pointed to another part of the wall, where an outlined map of their large basement-room showed a hidden place above a thinner line.

"Clever girl you've got there, Gilbert," Hilaire said, as the vibrations slowed and ceased. "You sure she hasn't got a sister?"

"She's . . . she's not . . . *my* girl," Gilbert said, glancing quickly at Frances. If she'd heard the question, she'd given no sign as they moved to the exit. "And I don't know if she has a sister, or anything about her family, or even her last name."

"Well, all right then," Hilaire mumbled as they charged through the doorway, followed by Frances and Jimmy.

****

1914 A.D.
THE ARCHEOLOGICAL SITE.

"Here it is," Father Flambeau said, as he slowed and then stopped the floater neared the entrance. It was a large, natural gateway of rock, formed over millennia, with a very human-made paved road that had been placed decades before, but now sported cracks and discolored spots where the sun and sand had scoured it clean and nearly white, and even the occasional blade of green grass peeking through.

"Why are we stopping?" Anne asked.

"It's a good idea," Gilbert said, hopping out of the vehicle by jumping over the unopened door, "to take a short look around the entrance, and see if anything twitches up ahead. Sometimes predators of the animal or human variety will take up residence in a spot like that."

"Standard procedure, Mademoiselle," agreed Father Flambeau.

They hopped out and started walking, Gilbert doing so more spryly than he'd moved before. The sun was high, the breeze was dry, and for reasons he couldn't explain he felt exhilarated.

"What was here?" Anne asked. "Who built this place, anyway?"

"It was a temple of some sort," Gilbert said, "and it housed a great warrior of the Tharks. The fella became something like Paul Bunyan back home, for being too tough even for the Warhoons."

"War-whats?" said Flambeau.

"Warhoons," said Anne with a crisp tone in her voice, "are a branch of Tharks so vicious, even the mainstream Tharks consider them savages."

Looking high up, Gilbert saw the many-stepped tower rising from the base of the valley, ending at a red-stone dome with a large bite taken from its West side. "My sister's little apartment, the one they held her captive in—it was right there. I remember it, about halfway up the tower, under that metal prong jutting out to the North."

"Is that where the Doctor . . ."

"Yep," Gilbert said, cutting Anne's question off. "Let's get walking again." He started towards the tower, walking and winding his path around the half-dozen large holes in the ground, whose edges had been worn away by *time, wind, and sand.*

"You don't like to talk about it," Anne said as they approached the tower's base.

"No, no I don't, Anne. I lost someone that day—remember?"

"I remember."

They'd come to the center of the holes in the ground. They were large— bigger than Gilbert and Anne remembered, in fact. And when they heard the throaty chuckles coming from deep inside the wells of darkness, all three of them knew to run without need of word or gesture.

It was pointless, though, and they knew it. Before they'd cleared the dug-out area, over a dozen green-skinned creatures had surrounded them. Each of them nearly a dozen feet high, with four arms carrying evil, rusty- looking blades in their hands and yellow untrimmed tusks sprouting from their mouths.

"Uh-oh," said Father Flambeau. "Would these be the Warhoons you told me about?"

"Unfortunately . . ." began Anne.

"Yep," finished Gilbert.

****

1892
MARS. TOWN OF DANTON'S FOLLY

"So how do these things work?" Cecil asked.

"Ever so glad you asked," said Wickham. His voice sounded much more serene than it had when he'd been ordering the men around this morning. "The steam that powers many machines today," Wickham continued, "simply wouldn't be enough to move *these* mechanical beasts. Thus, while we use steam for some of its systems, another device called a *coal-gassificator* transforms oil and local coal into a new type of fuel with higher-energy properties. Some call it *gasoline*."

Cecil looked again at the machines in their underground hangar. They were large, squat cylinders at least three stories high, lying on their sides with huge drill heads on the front and caterpillar treads on the sides.

There were no windows anywhere on them, only large, heavily armored doors in the rear of the machine.

"In mining operations, the drill pulls the sandhog, while the treaded wheels push forward, digging a tunnel for the miners to follow. We cannot look for anything visual underground, hence the need for expert navigators like my team over there," Wickham pointed to a group of men dressed in the grungy overalls of the working miners who were murmuring and bent low over a table with drawings, maps, and measuring instruments on it.

Behind them, the miners began to board one of the half-dozen sandhogs lined up in the underground bay.

The men carried an unusual array of weapons; some held pistols, others rifles, others had hand weapons that looked like modified picks or shovels, and still others held instruments that Cecil couldn't have guessed the nature of had he a week to consider it.

"How do you keep everything in order here?" Cecil asked. "These men don't really look like miners, much less an invading army."

"They aren't," said Wickham. "My workers are men from England, America, and a few other countries. They were given the choice of living out their lives in prisons, workhouses, or other unpleasant places, or instead coming here and working for me. Many are quite grateful and work hard, others less so. Such men who cannot fit in or decline my directives are released from my service, and encouraged to find their own way—elsewhere." He said this last part casually, looking out over the desert.

Cecil gulped. He'd had enough experience in his short life to recognize a subtle threat.

"Well," said Wickham, suddenly strutting forward, "we shall be leaving within the hour. Head down to the outfitters, Cecil, and get what you need in terms of accouterments. I have other business to attend to. You'll be travelling in the largest sandhog, tagging alongside John Carter while he leads the troops. Good luck, and all that."

Cecil felt a cold rush in his gut as Wickham walked off. Like most boys, he yearned for adventure. Up until now he'd satisfied that instinct by leaping from rooftop to rooftop to escape bullies or the law, or stealing from those who could afford it. Now, though, he realized he would be travelling in close quarters with genuinely tough and dangerous men. Men who would be firing real bullets and swinging truly sharp and heavy blunt objects, and who would be on the receiving end of the same.

He realized he might truly be harmed, even *dead* before the next sunrise, if they left on schedule.

"You look concerned, Cecil. Whatever is the matter?"

Cecil turned. It was Carter. The leather straps of his X-shaped Martian battle harness fit snug over his shoulders and chest, while his sword and odd-looking pistol were strapped comfortably into their holders at his belt. His smile was wide as ever, as if he were getting ready to play a championship baseball game instead of risk his life in an assault on a fortress.

"Why are you so cheerful?" Cecil said. "Aren't you scared at all?"

"A little," Carter nodded. "But there's something that keeps me going when I do things like this, Cecil. Want to know what it is?"

Cecil nodded, turning to look at another column of miners filing into another of the sandhogs.

"I fought in the War of Northern Aggression, Cecil, what my brothers to the North called the Civil War, or sometimes the Slave Wars. I know I don't look it, but I can only remember being thirty. I can't remember ever having been younger, and I've never looked older. On more than one occasion I've considered that whatever was done to make Wickham live so long was perhaps done to me at some point, but that's neither here nor there.

"One of my commanders, General Jackson, was a phenomenal man. Most of us in my regiment didn't care one way or the other about slavery like our leaders did. But for him as for us, it was about keeping the gov'ment out of our backyards while we lived our lives, hey?"

Cecil nodded. Wickham's servant girl, the one Cecil had met the night he'd arrived, was moving back and forth among the men and giving them each a small glass bottle of water from a wooden box she carried.

Carter seemed not to notice Cecil's distraction. "And then the shells started falling around us, screaming through the sky while the bullets started whining and humming through the air. And men started getting blown into pieces, or scurrying under rocks like lizards hiding from the noonday sun.

"Well, while this happened, General Jackson was just there on his horse, steady as a stone wall, watching everything. And when I asked him later why he didn't run when the action started, he didn't even break a smile. 'Sir,' he said to me, 'if God almighty wills that I die today, no amount of running and hiding will change that. And if He wills that I am to live, no amount of lead or powder fired by man will change that, either.' I never forgot that, Cecil. Not even when old Stonewall lost his left arm and died of infection a few days later. If I'm to die, then that'll be it. My wife and son are taken care of in their city of Helium on the other side of the planet, and jaunts like this are sometimes necessary to help my fellow earthmen. Besides, this is a special case: I've got no love for those evil fellows who've taken up in the Temple of Gorath."

"Temple of what?"

"Gorath. He was an evil fellow, considered so even by his own, green-skinned race. He spent his life in that place, doing terrible things there to the few victims he left alive. I've only visited once, and seeing what was left of the folks there were was enough for this Confederate man."

"Hopefully, this will be the last visit you make in your own lifetime," said a familiar voice behind them. It was Emrys, dressed casually in the work overalls of the miners, his scraggly, dirty-blond hair now cut shorter, but his round-lensed glasses were still in place.

"Gentlemen," Emrys continued, "it's high time we made off. They are ready and waiting for us."

The three of them turned and walked up the gangplank. "Are you ready for this?" Cecil asked Emrys suddenly. "Mr. Carter here acts like he's going to the fair or something, but you look more than a little worried."

"I can see a few things ahead of me, Cecil, because of the company I keep. My worries are not so much for me, or even you, but for someone I'm fairly certain I'm going to meet on our journey there."

Cecil wanted to ask for more details, but the next second they were crowded into the sandhog and conversation was impossible. Men smelling of sweat and red dirt jostled each other with rough shoves and rougher words, and within seconds all were seated in two rows, facing each other.

The door closed, shrouding them in darkness. The massive engine started like the sound of a waking giant, and dim electric lights sprang to life above their heads. A pounding, whirring noise sounded from the front of the machine, and they began to move.

Chapter 52

"There are two ways of being bloodless—by the avoidance of blood without, and by the absence of blood within."

– Illustrated London News, *Aug. 3, 1918*

1914 A.D.
THE ARCHEOLOGICAL SITE

"So, what happens now?" asked Anne.

Anne, Gilbert and Father Flambeau stood in the center of the arena and gazed around at the dirt floor littered with bones and drying feces. In the crude stands were a number of Tharks, but even by Thark standards they were disheveled, unkempt creatures. Their tusks grew in wild, curved angles, dark green, open sores festered on their faces and the green skin of their limbs, and the stench from the screaming, hundred or so of them on the stone benches almost overpowered the three captives at the center of their attention.

"Now," said Gilbert, "we fight. We either win, or we die."

"As they saw fit to relieve us of or weapons, I'm not particularly liking our odds, Gilbert," said Father.

"Nor I. But I know a thing or two about these folks that might even the odds just a little."

As he finished, the largest of the Warhoon Tharks stood up. Wearing nothing but a tattered, furry loincloth, he stretched out all four of his snaggly-taloned arms and looked around for any who'd dare to talk when he was about to speak.

He began to grunt, cough, and slaver, speaking in a tongue most Tharks would have had difficulty with, but Gilbert seemed to follow with relative ease.

"He's telling everybody how pathetic we are, and what pathetic creatures

353

Earthmen are in general," Gilbert said at the first pause. Another minute of Tharkish grunting followed, with a few hisses thrown in for good measure. "Now," Gilbert said, "he just explained what an incredible war chief he is for having so easily captured three of the race who killed the mollusks and have subjugated Mars."

"But I thought he said humans were . . ."

"I never said he was rational. Anarchists never are. Just listen."

Fully a minute ensued of the Thark leader's next verbal volley. This time including finger pointing, fist pounding, and gestures whose meanings Anne could only guess at.

Gilbert paled. "He is explaining what he plans to do with our corpses once his pets have disposed of us."

"Charming," said Anne. "Are we to be a meal for a rabid sloat, then?"

"No," said Gilbert, "he has a bunch of wild calots that he's going to release on us."

"I thought they were tame as dogs," said Father, his muscles already tensing instinctively as he readied himself for the fight.

"If trained, or even they are left in the wild, yes, they aren't much more dangerous than a dog pack. But if you feed them a high-protein diet on a regular basis for a few years, they not only grow quite large but become quite mad as well. Something in vegetables calms their spirit, and . . ."

"Understood," Anne said. She readied her right mechanical hand, twisting the metal with the human fingers of her left hand until something clicked. There was a flash of light on metal, and now Anne's human left hand held the knife blade that had been secreted in her right.

"Where did you get such an amazing piece of work as that?" Gilbert asked.

"I saved the leg of a Swiss clockmaker's son two years ago. He was so grateful I got this" she waggled the metal fingers "in the mail a few months later. Here," she said, tossing the knife to Gilbert, who promptly tossed it to Father.

"Sure you won't be needing this, Gilbert?" said Father, "I have my fists, you know."

"I can get a blade, Father," said Gilbert. "Watch."

Gilbert stood with his fists at his sides, looking at the Warhoon chief. His face suddenly twisted into a sneering, angry visage, and he began to snarl, hiss, spit, and grope the air in a way that would have seemed comical and pathetic at a party, but was viewed with deadly seriousness by their Warhoon audience.

After two full minutes of Gilbert's ranting, the Warhoon chief cut him off, bellowing in so much anger that strings of yellow-tinged saliva flung from the warped tusks of his mouth into the arena, splatting on Gilbert's shoes and the lower legs of his trousers. The chief barked out a command and reached behind with an open hand while staying focused on the three captives in front of him.

A minion passed a sword that had seen better days to the chief, who then flung it down to the arena floor.

The sword spun wildly through the air, landing with a clang at Gilbert's unmoving feet.

"Still not what I'd hoped for," Gilbert grumbled, retrieving the weapon from the ground and giving it a few swings to test its balance. "The last Thark chieftain I tried that on gave me two swords. And they were good enough that they stuck out in the dirt. And there wasn't any rust or dried muck on the blade!" Gilbert yelled this last at the chief, who glared at Gilbert with malevolent eyes.

"What did he . . ." started Anne to Father Flambeau. She stopped when she saw the priest was already kneeling in prayer with his hands folded and his eyes closed. "Gilbert," she said, "what did you say to him?"

Gilbert was already focused on the large door to the arena, where their opponents were presumably going to be entering the ring with them. "I thanked the chief in advance for sending us to our deaths unarmed. The poets of Earth and the Red Men of Mars, and even the Tharks would sing the praises of the man from Earth so feared by the Warhoons that they had to have him die without weapons. The chief was so angered that those 'wimps' in civilization might see him as a coward he gave me a sword. Best I could do. I don't know any other good insults in Warhoon."

"Well," said Father, jumping up suddenly into the air like a spring and landing soundlessly with both feet on the sandy ground, "I should go in front. I have the size, the armor, and while I soak up their attention you two can hack and stab the things to . . ."

The portcullis opened. The calots ran out at them.

They'd all seen calots before, of course. John Carter's author cousin had once described them as being like puffs of white cloud and cream the size of a large wolf, only with four stumpy-yet-agile legs. They also had a pair *of baleful, staring yellow eyes and a mouthful of needle and razor sharp teeth. When tame, they were as kind and faithful as a beloved dog in a story written for English schoolboys. When wild, they were dangerous as a wave in a seastorm, and as deadly in a pack as a group of freight trains with fangs.*

And now a half-dozen of them were charging Gilbert's little group, roars of hungry pain screaming from their canine throats, their mouths fully opened to reveal row after row of sharpened teeth. Gilbert stood with his feet planted firmly on the red sandy ground, his eyes twitching over several locations on the lead dog-creature as the pack roared and screamed towards them. Unconsciously, noticed only by Anne, he spun the battered sword in his hand twice in a quick arc as the creatures moved towards them, now twenty feet away, now ten . . .

"NOW!" Gilbert shouted, and all three moved as if they'd fought together a dozen times across both worlds.

Though Gilbert was in the lead, Father Flambeau passed him with three bounding steps, reaching the first calot and leaping forward, planting the heel of his hiking boot squarely in the creature's eye.

The lead calot screamed in rage, the volume jumping up a notch as a hidden blade in the heel of the priest's boot shot out and stabbed into the soft flesh of the creature's eye and into its brain. Green blood gushed from the creature's ruined eye socket, and it fell with a heavy thud against the floor, twitching and still screaming, unaware it was dead.

That's one, Gilbert thought with a calm part of his brain as Father Flambeau withdrew his boot blade and picked his next target.

But this was no time to look around! Now, with Anne matching him step for step on his left, Gilbert ran past the dying monster and focused on the second beast in front of him. At the last second, he leaned back and slid on his back in the dirt, aiming for the space between the calot's front paws like a baseball player trying to steal home.

Had Gilbert been alone and tried this maneuver, the creature may have easily scooped him up in its powerful jaws and broken Gilbert's spine in a single chomp.

But Gilbert knew he wasn't alone. And he knew that Anne knew what to do when your fighting partner tried something this dangerous. Yelling with a screech loud as a Celtic warrior woman, she leaped forward and punched the calot as hard as she could on its bulbous green nose with her brass and steel hand. *Worse for the creature, in the last split second before impact Anne's mechanical thumb twitched, and her artificial hand popped forward six inches with a pneumatic, air driven hiss, pounding the monster's face with even more force.*

Thus the second creature met its end quickly after Anne connected, its nose crumpling like cheap wax paper while splinters of bone blasted through its brain with such force that some exited through the back of its head, embedding themselves like small darts in the wall behind it.

While Anne was punching the creature's face into pudding, Gilbert had continued his slide. He ended up under the huge dog-like thing, stabbing up and at an angle into its ribcage while his inertia and the calot's speed made them pass like speeding horse-drawn cabs on a London street. Green blood sprayed over Gilbert as the calot passed over him, and once it was no longer above him Gilbert rolled to the side.

Though the second calot was dead, the rest of its body hadn't quite heard the news. It kept running forward with blind, unseeing eyes as Anne dove out of its way, and slammed itself headfirst into the curved wall of the little coliseum. The creature laid almost still, a single back leg still twitching in a bizarre parody of running motion.

Now two more calots charged. Gilbert, on the ground and still on his back, rolled towards the creatures, counting on the calots' speed and frenzied bloodlust to keep them from noticing him until it was too late.

It turned out to be a good bet. Both calots were used to their prey either retreating from them or standing and fighting. They leaped over Gilbert, giving him another opportunity to slash at their legs. Two expertly delivered cuts in a half second, and they were howling on the ground, using their front paws to drag their heavy bodies with the tendons of a leg cut and bleeding on the ground.

That made four creatures in the arena dead or disabled, and none of them were Gilbert, Anne, or Father Flambeau. The two remaining uninjured calots, crazed at the sight of blood and not caring what color it was, attacked their wounded comrades. In their maddened feeding frenzy, they ignored the three humans who now crept up behind them . . .

In seconds, the last two calots lay dead, bloated and bleeding on the floor of red sand.

Gilbert wiped the blood off the lenses of his glasses and his forehead with the back of his hand. He then stretched out his arms, puffing out his chest and roaring loud as he could, the blood of the calot on his face and shirt making him look almost frightening.

Almost. Anne and Flambeau had to stifle a chuckle.

"What?" Gilbert said after the roar was done.

"It's just always a little too hard to see you as a vicious warrior, mon ami," said Flambeau, wiping the blood off his retrieved knife and tapping the heel of his boot a few times to get the sand out. "After you're done, you go back to being the gentle person God made you."

"Yes, well, in the next few minutes, our lives may depend just a little on our being perceived as a mighty threat," Gilbert said, "so if you don't mind, for now at least pretend I'm just that."

The Warhoon leader suddenly stood, his four powerful arms rippling with muscle as he extended them and made a roar of his own. His four unkempt tusks were splayed in wild curvy angles, and his yellow and black inner teeth glinted in the dim light as he bellowed word after word in the rough language of the Warhoons.

Gilbert nodded as the leader spoke, looking back and forth at his companions and giving a slow wink as the speech progressed.

"What's he say—" Anne started, but Gilbert shushed her with a small sound and a gesture.

After nearly a minute, the Thark chieftain finished his speech. Several guards walked towards them, thankfully with their hands empty of weapons.

"What's happening, Gilles?" said Flambeau. "Do we fight?"

"No," said Gilbert as one of the Warhoons scooped him up in a powerful sweep, carrying him like a sack of potatoes towards the exit. "The chief thinks we're a threat, so he's sending us precisely where we want to be."

"And where—oof!" said Anne, as she was scooped and carried by a large Warhoon female. "Where is that, precisely?"

"The place where they make the sacrifices to their gods!" Gilbert said happily, as their new captors began to climb the stairs.

Chapter 53

"There are only two kinds of ballads. There are sad ballads about broken hearts and cheerful ballads about broken heads."

– "The Voice of Shelley," *Apostle and the Wild Ducks*

1892 A.D.
THE TUNNELS UNDER THE MARTIAN DESERT

Gilbert, Anne, Hilaire, Francis, and Jimmy pressed forward. The stone walls of their underground tunnel gave them room to walk side by twos, but little else. Several times they happened on a long ancient cave which had spilled red dirt and bricks into the already narrow walkway, and they were either forced to move in single file or wait until they'd dug enough of a pathway first.

It took what seemed like hours. The small tinderbox Hilaire had in his belt and a few candle stubs Jimmy found in his pockets helped light the way during their trek, and Frances assured them that they'd not been under the ground for longer than an hour or so. She had a timepiece she'd hidden in the folds of her dress.

"How far d'you think this goes?" Jimmy said. He was leading the way, since he had made it clear that he was unwilling to part with his candle.

"I've no idea," said Anne from the middle of the line, walking beside Belloc. "For the past few months I've been living in a cave above the ground, rather than trying to map catacombs beneath it."

"These definitely were made on purpose, though," Gilbert said, looking at the walls while he and Frances brought up the rear of the line. "You can see where they cut the stone and made bricks."

"Yes, and if you're not careful," Frances said, "one of those could bean you. Between the tremors we felt as we left and the cracks this place is sporting, I seriously doubt this place is all that stable."

"Don't worry, Frances," Gilbert said. "I'll protect you from whatever might come after us here."

"Come after us?" Jimmy said, a tinge of fear in his voice. "You know something I don't about this place, gov?"

"Nope," Gilbert answered. "It's just that the last time I was in a tunnel with a bunch of other people, I ended up stuck in a deep hole in the ground and had to fight a squid or two to get out. But after it was all done," he paused to look at Frances and take her hand, "I got to meet the best . . . Hey!" he said with a small amount of annoyance, for she'd twisted her hand out of his gentle grip, then pushed his hand away with more force than he'd ever seen her use before.

"Gilbert Chesterton, I don't want you lay a finger of yours on my hand or any other part of me until we've finished this little adventure and you've explained a few things. Is that clear?"

"Frances, what's . . . ? Look, if this is about what you saw back there, let me assure you, there's nothing, *nothing* you have to worry about."

Anne gave a rather loud sniff. Hilaire gave Gilbert a glance that suggested silence would be a better idea right now.

Gilbert, however, was in no mood for subtlety. "No, really Frances. What's wrong? Why did you break my heart, and then show up here on Mars?"

"Break your heart? Oh, you . . . you arrogant, self-centered, skinny . . . man-child! Break *your* . . . Ooh!" she gasped in anger, and then she stopped while turning to face him with her fists hovering in front of her chest, staring up at him with fury in her eyes.

"I wouldn't press the issue, Mister Yank," Jimmy said, clearly amused. "I've 'eard what she can do in a fight, I 'ave. The ship she came in on, the blokes nicknamed her fists 'thunder an' lightning.' She's sent a few lads into a dreamy conversation with Queen Mab in less time than it takes to bowl a game o' nine pins."

Gilbert looked from Jimmy and then to Frances. Her hands and legs had tensed up almost imperceptibly, as if she were a coiled spring ready to fly at a false move. "Is it true?" Gilbert said, his voice holding no small amount of awe. "Is . . . is that why you decided to give me the heave-ho?"

"What on *Earth* are you talking about?" Frances yelled. "I never *gave* you any 'heave-ho,' or whatever it is you Americans call it! It's *you* who betrayed *me*," she said, searching in a fold in her dress. "Here!" she finally shouted, pulling out a many-times folded piece of paper. With a single motion, she opened it and shocked Gilbert and everyone else in the narrow corridor.

"That's . . . that's—," said Gilbert, stammering.

"That's not Gilbert," Anne said. "It is me, but that's not him."

Gilbert looked at Anne. "It's not?"

"Of course it *isn't*, you idiot! When have I ever kissed you? Frances, *Gilbert* hasn't ever kissed *me*. The only time we were ever close enough for that to happen was in Norton's city, last year. Look at the background of that picture! What building is stipplographed in the window?"

None of them could resist looking.

Over the shoulder of the two young lovers engaged in their kiss was a large window. And in the window was plainly visible the outline of . . .

"The Leaning Tower of Pisa?" Gilbert said. "I've never been there!"

"You're quite sure about that?" Frances said, not altogether convinced.

"Frances, I sent you letters from every place they sent me on assignment. I've only been to Italy once, and, well, that was in *Rome*. Besides, I thought you wanted nothing more to do with me. Here." Gilbert pulled the crumpled letter from his pocket and thrust it into Frances' hands.

She read it for a few seconds, her eyes growing large. "I *never* wrote this!" she said. "Who could have . . . Father or Mother would rather I looked elsewhere, but they'd never stoop to . . . the Williamsons, perhaps?"

"As in the late Captain Fortescue Williamson?" said Belloc looking over Frances' shoulder. "There's nothing I'd put past him or his crooked family. They've no more morals than a bag of black adders. I'm just glad Fortescue's not nearly as clever as he ought to be, considering his parentage."

"So," said Anne between Gilbert and Frances, gently gripping Gilbert's hand and placing it gently into Frances's own while she took both offensive pieces of paper, "can you two make up now, and we can continue? I'd hate to have a fight here underground. Who knows who, or even *what*, might hear and come investigate."

"She 'as a point, folks," Jimmy said, his latest candle nearly burned down. "I'd sure not wish to be under 'ere when the last of our lights go."

Even Frances, still visibly unhappy, agreed. They began moving again, though Frances decisively moved her hand away from Gilbert's when he tried to hold it again.

Gilbert thought to protest, but then he thought better of it and they kept moving.

Another hour passed underground. Several of them grew hungry, but no one spoke up.

Then Gilbert felt something against his face.

"It's cooler here," he said. "I feel a bit of a breeze."

"We must be near the surface!" Frances said.

A few more steps, and light began to shimmer in the stone corridor. Soon Jimmy no longer needed the candle, and blew his out.

"Where's this light coming from, I wonder?" Gilbert said. "It's coming from the walls itself," Belloc said, "a lot like how those spotlights trained on us in the underground hospital we came from. I'd wager that . . ."

And then they saw the city.

The tunnel they'd been walking through suddenly opened up into a vast, underground cavern. The light came from a small hole in the cavern's rock ceiling. A few more steps and the path they'd followed through the underground corridor became a descending stone staircase broken in parts by time and wear.

The spot of light in the ceiling illuminated a series of broken buildings in the cavern, along with an underground river that wound through a carved stone channel carved into the rock floor.

"Is this a sewer, Gilbert," Frances whispered, "like the one you were in two years past?"

"No, Frances," Gilbert answered, his voice also in an awed whisper. The buildings, if he counted correctly, had dozens of floors to them. These things were hundreds of feet high, bigger than the biggest buildings of the New York City skyline, or even the giant Steam-Lincoln he'd had an adventure on last year! "No, I think this is an honest-to-goodness, full-blown underground city."

"Wonder what they've got worth taking, then!" Jimmy said happily, jumping toward the stone steps and taking them down two and three at a time.

"Jimmy! Wait!" Belloc yelled, taking off after him.

Anne, Frances, and Gilbert took the steps much more gingerly, one step at a time and in single file. By the time they reached the bottom, both Jimmy and Belloc were vague shadows in the murky gloom of the lost city. "C'mon," Gilbert said, "we need to catch up with them. Belloc's a good fighter, and Jimmy's the only one who can read anything from here to Syrtis Major!"

Anne and Frances didn't need to be told twice. Both took a long fold of dress in their hand and began running after the two young men. The shoes of the three young people in pursuit echoed through the dead city streets, the smell of old stone and spoiled water permeating the air.

"Jimmy! Belloc!" Gilbert yelled in the lead, running fast but not sprinting his hardest—no way did he want to lose Anne *or* Frances a second time!

Gilbert caught up with them perhaps a hundred yards ahead. The city had been constructed on either side of the underground river. The large buildings had been built to last, evidently more so than the inhabitants!

Belloc and Jimmy were standing in front of a large wall, one of the few ones on the sides of the buildings that had no windows at all.

"Did you find anything worth stealing?" Gilbert gasped as he stopped, leaning with his hands on his knees. He'd let himself go too long without exercise in the last year!

"Shh," said Belloc, pointing at the wall as the girls caught up. Gilbert looked too, adjusting his glasses.

It was more of the moving picture writing that they'd seen on the wall of the hospital.

It was similar to what they'd seen on the wall of the hospital, only larger and with more detail.

In the moving image on the wall, a large hand reached out and destroyed the line-drawn ships that left Mars. It then reached into a different direction, waving its fingers slowly over the spires of the Martian cities. Crowds of stick people fled to crudely drawn underground cities like the one Gilbert and Co. currently stood in. But the hand slowly lowered itself until they, too, laid down and disappeared. The tops of the drawn buildings in the picture cities above and below the ground became broken and shabby while the hand retreated, retreating into a large tower, and then quickly changed from bright red to a sickly green as multi-limbed creatures scurried about inside it—and the top of the tower became broken and ragged as well.

The pictures all disappeared, replaced by writing.

"Can you read it, Jimmy?" Anne whispered. "You were the only person on Earth who could ever read their writing, I think."

"It'd be easier with me dice, love," Jimmy answered, "but I've had a little more experience since then. Once you get past the vowels, it's not too tough to see this says . . ."

Jimmy was already walking towards the huge, living mural, lost in thought and calculation. "Baa . . . Baaarrr-ruh . . ." he said, trying to sound out the word. "Bar-sum?; Bar-*soom*! It's a name I've seen now and again, but it's usually so stylized I couldn't quite make it out before. Right, *Barsoom*, that's it! It says that this Barsoom . . ."

Jimmy was quiet again as his face grew very serious.

"Barsoom has stayed his hand, and fallen silent. He . . . no, not *sleeps*, but he . . . *waits*. And woe to all, should they rouse him through action or . . . I think it's *trickery*."

"You mean," said Gilbert, getting close and looking at the picture on the wall, which had now fallen still, "that all we've seen since men have landed on Mars—the broken cities, the struggling tribesmen where there used to be a thriving civilization—all that has been because of this Barsoom character?"

"It would appear so," said Jimmy. "I don't know if this Barsoom fellow was a warlord, or something else. But he's credited here with breaking all the civilization of Mars, right enough."

"Ridiculous," Belloc said. "Impossible for anyone, man or Martian, to do that much damage to a whole civilization. Napoleon, Alexander the Great, even they could only conquer a region, and their empires never lasted after their deaths."

"I don't know if you're looking at it right," Anne said. "I doubt if this Barsoom is a man at all."

"Wot?" Jimmy said, irritated. "You doubtin' my translation, dearie?"

"Not in the least. I just know that when I've done trading of any sort, be it with the red men or the spindly fellows, Barsoom is the name they give to the *world*, to Mars itself."

Everyone paused. Gilbert spoke first.

"We named Mars after a god. A thing that we believed was self-aware, unimaginably powerful, and in possession of virtually none of the virtues to any degree."

"Except none of the Greek gods were able to destroy an entire civilization, much less snuff out almost all life in the world."

"This is the god of Mars then?" Anne asked, looking at the mural. The large figure stretching his hand over the red circle of the world they were on took on a more frightening aspect every second. "This Barsoom, character? He's their version of Zeus?"

"I don't think so, love," Jimmy said. "This bloke don't seem to be like that. I don't even think he was a god, now 'ow we unnerstan' gods today, ennyways."

"I don't agree with him much, but Jimmy's right," Belloc said. "Man-made gods demand worship, and they're none-too tactful when they don't get it. But there's not a statue or a temple to this 'Barsoom' anywhere on the planet that I've seen."

"Good point, Belloc," Gilbert said. "Moreover, a man-made god usually ends up reflecting the worst aspects of the people who create it. Zeus was a skirt-chaser, and tossed down thunderbolts when he was having a tantrum. But look at this fellow, won't you?" he said, pointing at the figure's dispassionate, straight face.

"That's not the expression of someone angered or displeased by a behavior," Frances said. "That's the face our servants wear when they're doing their job. He's not out to hurt people—he's just…"

"Takin' out th' trash," Jimmy finished, "or maybe doin' the dishes."

"And now he's sleeping, or waiting or whatever, and we'd better not wake him up."

"Precisely," Jimmy said, tipping back his bowler hat. "The problem is, mate, that I recognize that little spike-shaped building back there in the picture. That's a place that I've 'eard described again and again by a few of the fellows what held me captive. They 'ad me translating a bunch of stuff for 'em, then they was recording it on their little wax cylinders, then movin' those over to that place, I'm sure of it. They talked about the big platform on top, exposed to the air, and all the little apartments with windows on the side, like they're showin' here."

"What kinds of things did they have you translate?" Belloc asked, his voice unusually sharp, even for him. "What were some of the words you remember? Think especially about words that were repeated. Anything that is repeated is important in ancient writing."

Jimmy put one hand to his eyes and thought. "A lot'f it was just odd," he said. "Lots of big words, names of people an' places no one's ever 'eard of. But there were words I saw a lot, words like 'binding,' 'control,' an' the like. It were all on these little paper discs inside a metal container, half the size of a man's hand wit' little spinny things on top."

Gilbert suddenly couldn't move. He looked around the group: only Belloc's and Anne's faces showed the same spark of quiet terror that had just jumped into his own soul.

"You figured it out, mate?" Belloc said.

Gilbert nodded. "Anne gave me a disc-shaped container in Berlin. I managed to open it with some help on the way to the Floating City last year. It had a bunch of those little paper-disc things inside. Herb got it from the kid that helped me, though. Johnny Brainerd was his name, and he told me the whole story. Jimmy, the things you translated; did they sound like oaths at all? Did they come out with things like 'by the power of *this*,' or 'I invoke *this*,' stuff like that?"

"Chock full of it, gov. Like those things you'd hear at a séance, when they try to call up the ghosts of dead people. Only there were hours and hours of speech from start to finish. What I got done, it'd take a man a month of Sundays to repeat it all."

"Whatever are you discussing, Gilbert?" Frances said.

"Frances," said Gilbert, "don't you see? Whoever this Barsoom guy is, he's the one that turned Mars from a place like Earth to what it is today. *Barsoom* destroyed Mars. When those squids tried to move their craziness out of the solar system, *Barsoom* reached out and turned the whole planet into a desert. The only life left were the races that lived relatively peaceful-like in the canals, the human-like folks the squids had made to live here, and whatever squids who escaped into the canals and these caves beneath the ground."

"But if anyone were to wake something like that . . ."

"They aren't trying just to *wake* him at all, are they?" Anne said, as understanding lit up her face. "That's not what that crew is digging about for at all."

They looked at Anne, waiting. "Don't you see?" she continued. "They don't just want to *wake* him. They want to control him, turn him into a pet monkey who'll destroy things at their bidding. He's a spirit or something, so they want to use Earth magic and perhaps even Martian sorcery to control him, like mediums claim they can do in London."

"But why would they care?" Gilbert asked. "They already dominate the

British Empire, and it rules the world."

"Folks like that, mate," Jimmy said, "they're never happy with enough, 'cause for them enough's *never* enough. When they won the Empire, they prob'ly set their sights on a planet, maybe two. An' just maybe they think *this* bloke is their ticket to taking over a whole *bunch* of planets."

"Planets," Frances said, her voice a whisper. "But, if the mollusks themselves couldn't keep this thing from wiping out most of life on Mars, and this Barsoom decided to destroy most of Mars when the Mollusks pushed its boundaries, what could be the consequences if these *men* tried to wake him? Or worse, what could happen to us, or even to *Earth*, if these men tried to *capture*, or *control* him?"

"What indeed?" said a new voice. Before they could react, the five of them heard the hammer pulled back on a firearm.

Chapter 54

"If you really read the fairy-tales, you will observe that one idea runs from one end of them to the other— the idea that peace and happiness can only exist on some condition. This idea, which is the core of ethics, is the core of the nursery-tales. The whole happiness of fairyland hangs upon a thread, upon one thread. Cinderella may have a dress woven on supernatural looms and blazing with unearthly brilliance; but she must be back when the clock strikes twelve. The king may invite fairies to the christening, but he must invite all the fairies or frightful results will follow."

–"Fairy Tales," All Things Considered

It waited. Waited as it had for decades, ever since the humans had stood in its center room and told it about the silent blue planet, and the dealings of its brother there. It waited without boredom or anticipation or any other feeling that would have been familiar to a human in such a situation. It only waited. It knew what to do when things changed; it had its orders, and would carry them out when needed, without excessive joy or any animosity.

For now, it waited. Aware, but waiting.

****

"How much longer will we be in here?" Cecil asked, squished between two large workers. "It feels like we've been travelling for hours."

"We're digging through solid ground, lad," said Emrys, quietly, leaning across the aisle and speaking directly into Cecil's ear in a normal voice. "It's not like the trip you took on the sand sloop. Digging beneath the ground, we could take an entire day below the surface to make a trip you could take in an hour above. Methinks they'll be bringing us up to the surface soon to refill the air tanks and give the men the opportunity to walk about a bit."

Almost as Emrys spoke, they felt the slightest upward tilt in the direction of the tunneler. Several other passengers felt it, too, and a cheer went up.

After a few more minutes, the tunneler craft straightened out and the rear door opened again. Fresh air flooded the compartment, air that smelled of dirt but was still welcome by the men who'd been underground for the last couple of hours.

"How much longer to the destination?" Emrys asked once they were all out and stretching their legs. His tone of voice sounded odd to Cecil, as if he weren't really looking forward to the journey's end.

"Hanged if I know," said Carter, adjusting the leather straps on his chest for a better fit and then practicing his sword strokes in the air. "All I am certain of is that it can't come soon enough. I'm quite impatient for a decent tussle these days. Maybe if I take on a few of those guards your English friends have hired, they'll give me more of a challenge than the last batch of Martian miscreants I had to dispatch."

"There will be challenges enough for us both," Emrys said, looking off into the distance.

"You mean—" Carter looked around and then spoke in a low voice only Emrys and Cecil could hear. "You mean Wickham? You're saying I'll be dueling that puffed-up fop? Where's the challenge in that? Who've you got in mind instead of me for your spot on the top shelf, then?"

"That's for me alone to know for now. I've likely said too much already. As for Wickham, you and he have more in common than you might surmise. Have you ever wondered why you don't recall anything before you turned thirty? Or why you *and he* have apparently not aged over a period of more than two generations? You've fought alongside Edison and I against the Mollusks, but you owe *them* the long life you had, thanks to their experiments on you, if I understand my friend correctly."

"What friend? Those ghosts that keep talking to you?"

"Not ghosts, John. *Glain.* That's their name in Welsh, anyway. They're akin to angels, but not the kind you paint pretty, soft-edged pictures of. They know things, can wait literally forever for anything, and can destroy a world without a trace of regret if it's necessary. And when they go bad . . . well, it becomes quite terrible."

"Have you seen it happen before?" Cecil said, having drifted over and eavesdropping on the conversation.

"Yes," Emrys said. "The—well, *son*, in a sense, of the first Pendragon. His mother was very, very evil, so much so that—well, one of the worser *glain* got into him. After that things went very, very badly. About a century after that, the same *glain* got into a queen over in Scotland. The poor, foolish lady actually *asked* the thing, invited it into her soul in an effort to make her cruel enough to push her husband into—"

"Time, gentlemen!" said one of the workingmen. Everyone began filing back into the tunneler machines.

"So, this *glain* that you're talking to? It'll help us win, then?" Cecil asked hopefully.

"I know who will win at the *very* end, Cecil," Emrys said in a tried voice, "but I've no idea who will win or lose in between now and then. Which is what makes things sad, exciting and fearful all at once."

****

Brigadier Brackenbury looked out the window again for the fourth or fifth time that day and gave a deep sigh. He was in his mid-forties, balding, and wishing he could have gone into either business or the service of the Church as his elder brothers did. He'd comforted himself time and again with the knowledge that his army commission had allowed him to travel farther and see greater sights than anyone in the history of his family, however well-to-do they'd been. And yet, he still felt galled when he woke up in the morning, upset at the nagging sense that his life was not his own. That he was only allowed a certain degree of freedom, and beyond that there would forever be an invisible leash tugging on his neck.

And the holder of that leash was a man who no longer even tried to hide his identity. The wealthy industrialist Williamson and his idiot son Fortescue saw the Brigadier and his men as little more than field beasts, chess pieces or raw material. Their lives were not to be frivolously wasted, but were not reverenced in the least either.

"Sir?" said a voice behind him, interrupting his reverie.

"Speak, lad," he said, sipping his whiskey.

"Sir, we've received word regarding Sergeant Belloc's patrol. A lone sand skimmer found the wreck of the *Red Locust*, along with a number of the dead. They were attacked by Tharks, sir."

The Brigadier closed his eyes, his hand tightening around his glass. "Are the bodies in transit, lad?"

"Yes, sir. They just arrived. However, not all of them are accounted for.

The American journalist who allegedly left with them, Gilbert Chesterton, was not discovered. Sergeant Belloc's body was also not among the dead. There are several sets of tracks leading from the wreck of the *Red Locust*, though the skimmer did not attempt a rescue."

The Brigadier turned, setting his glass down on his Martian-wood desk. "Why did they not attempt a rescue?"

The soldier, no more than a private, really, broke into a sweat and kept facing to the front. "Sir, they were a civilian craft and fearful of Thark attack. Shall I order a rescue mission to be mounted? The passengers of the skimmer said the tracks were leading toward the town of Danton's Folly."

Brigadier Brackenbury turned again to face the window. Brutal self-interest fought with comradely instincts in his soul, his eyes moving back and forth like small, trapped animals in his skull for ten *very* long seconds.

Until his eyes landed on his bookcase, and he saw the title of his father's favorite book of poetry.

The Charge of the Light Brigade, and Other Works of Prosaic Verse.

Another full five seconds passed before turned to face the young soldier.

"What's your name, lad?"

"Private Salisbury, sir!"

"You will *not* order the rescue of Sergeant Belloc and the American journalist, Private Salisbury."

"Yes Sir. However—"

"No, Private. You will not. *I* will."

The young man's face brightened at the last two words of his commander.

"Yes, sir!" Salisbury said.

"Follow me," the Brigadier said, his glass of alcohol now forgotten as he launched himself down the hallway with crisp, military steps that boomed to all in earshot. "Salisbury, inform your duty officer that I want a squadron of no fewer than four cruisers outfitted with full crews within the hour. I want the location of the *Red Locust*, for it shall be our first destination. I shall command this venture personally. And," he stopped and turned to Salisbury, who snapped again to attention, "you shall accompany me on my ship. I may be in need of an attaché, and the good Lord has seen fit to put you in my path. Is that clear?"

"Yes *sir!*" said Salisbury. "I shall see to it personally, *sir!*" with that, he ran to find the duty officer.

Brigadier Brackenbury strode with purposeful steps toward the outfitter's station. *Yes,* he realized, *this will likely be my last action as commander of the colony. But, by gum, even if they trump up a charge and put me in front of a firing squad for crossing Williamson, I'll sleep well for whatever nights I'll have left.*

****

When the click of the pistol sounded behind Gilbert and his little crew, he froze up and raised his hands instinctively.

"My, my, my," said the voice behind them, "this is almost enough to make me attend services willingly at the cathedral where my cousin is the vicar. Think of it; in one place, I've gathered all the members of my latest quest from Daddy," here they heard the crunch of gravel underfoot as the speaker approached them, circling from behind, "and a few more besides. This is a truly lovely situation, wouldn't you say, Frances darling?"

"Fortescue," Frances grumbled under her breath. "Why couldn't you have died in a fight with a Martian?"

"Captain Williamson," said Belloc, dropping his arms and assuming a position of military attention while turning to face Williamson, "good to see you. I'd informed our guests here that His Majesty's intrepid forces would rescue us, much to their personal honor, and here you are. Now, we can—"

"Step back, Sergeant Belloc," Williamson said, waving his ugly-looking eight-barreled pistol. "You won't be able to tempt me with any thoughts of receiving honors. Not after that little performance at the inquest. Bad enough my toady died at the fort; I lost my best source of laudanum in the process. But you had to go and convince that troublesome Brigadier that I was a coward, and upset my Daddy in the bargain. No," he said, "I was left behind by the men I traveled with, but since then I've been exploring. Some of *Daddy's* men found this city, and I've been looking to scavenge something I can use to get a bit of power for myself. Now, methinks after listening to you five, I think I now have the last piece in a very confusing puzzle. My only remaining question is: What to do with the rest of you?"

"Did your Daddy give you instructions, Fortescue?" Frances said. "He's rather good at that, although I understand you're less than able at carrying them out."

"My *dear girl*," Fortescue Williamson said. His white Captain's uniform nearly glowed in the faint sunlight beaming down from overhead, despite the dirt he'd encountered in his travels. He walked slowly over to Frances, his pistol nearly touching her chin. Gilbert tensed, wanting more than anything to jump and rip the gun out of his hands, but he was too afraid Frances could be hurt or killed in the process.

"My dear, *dear* girl," Fortescue continued, now standing in front of her, "I fear you have misunderstood the nature of this little *tete-a-tete*. I'm going to bring you back alive to my Daddy, so that we can, ahem, *complete* a few longstanding arrangements he had with *your* father, dating back to our childhoods. That is my only instruction here. Obtain *you* so *my* line will continue.

"As for the rest of you, we're going to march back to the stone spire that Daddy and his friends have set up as their base of operations. I've heard tell that this river," here he tilted his head, indicating the river still flowing behind him, "leads out of the underground city to within eyesight of the place, and now we're going to walk along its banks until we reach the end. Shall we?" he finished, his right hand still training the gun on their little group while his left hand waved them forward.

"Ah, gov," Jimmy said, looking at Fortescue's leg, "there's somethin' you should look at below at your ankle."

"My dear primitive, do you truly think I'd ever fall for so simple a ru—"

Fortescue stopped speaking, fell flat on the ground screaming for all of one second until his body slid over the edge of the stone banks of the underground river.

A quick *plop*! sounded in the water, followed by complete silence.

Everyone stood still, their hands still over their heads. "Jimmy," Gilbert said quietly, "what did you just do?"

"I didn't do nuffin'!" Jimmy said defensively. "I just saw something white an' slimy wiggling at his ankle, an' when I warned 'im, 'e got all untrustful. Most unkind, if you ask me."

"Well, we *didn't* ask you," Belloc said. "I know just what that was, and we want to move away from the river's edge, very quietly, until we're out of reach of its tentacles."

"Tentacles?" Gilbert asked.

"They call it Jenny Greenteeth," Anne said, "after a boogey-man creature in England that supposedly grabbed children who strayed too close to the water's edge."

"Very good, m'lady," said Belloc, slowly moving away from the river towards the buildings. "So now, if you'd kindly begin following my lead, we can get to the . . ."

Gilbert had already begun to move. His toe hit a rock. When he tried to brush it aside, it moved back in place and touched his shoe again.

Oh, no.

He looked down and was only mildly surprised to see the tentacle searching in the dirt for prey, pausing for a second each time it touched one of his shoes.

"Belloc," he said quietly, "it's here. It's about to grab me. What do I do?"

"Hold still, friend," Belloc said, carefully stepping on his tiptoes toward the spot where Fortescue had disappeared. "It's deaf, Gilbert," Belloc said, his voice still talking in a quiet, soothing, even tone, "but it can hear the vibrations of your shoe against the ground. It could also conceivably hear if you screamed or yelled. So, if you'll just stay calm, I can reach the fop's gun where he dropped it, and—"

Frances drew something out of the folds in her skirt. There was a snap and the pungent smell of gunpowder as fire blasted from her small weapon. The tentacle exploded in a white and green mess about three feet from Gilbert, and then it slid suddenly back into the water, recoiling faster than a fishing line into its winder.

Everyone was silent.

"Well, *that* was unexpected!" Hilaire said happily, scooping up Fortescue's dropped pistol and putting it in his belt.

"We better get moving," Gilbert said. "The last time something like this happened to me, the tentacle's owner showed up and started making even more trouble."

The ground rumbled.

"Go!" Belloc yelled. Jimmy was already halfway to the nearest building. Gilbert grabbed Frances' hand, then grabbed Anne's left hand in his other and began pulling them in the same direction Jimmy had gone.

Belloc raised his new pistol to chest level as he ran backward, pointing it at the river while he pulled back the weapon's master safety catch.

There was a flash of ghost white in the gloom, a hump of pale movement in the darkness. Belloc pointed the weapon but didn't fire, waiting for a clearer shot.

The ground rumbled again. Still moving backwards while pointing his pistol, Belloc steadied himself. The ground then bucked beneath him like an errant wave on the beach, and he had to wave his arms on both sides with a surprised yelp while he kept his balance.

For just a moment it seemed he'd gotten taller, but once he stopped moving, he looked down and saw that something very different had happened.

The ground had risen in a large mound beneath his feet. And the mound wasn't just in a single place like a molehill, but a long raised line of dirt, like he'd seen a rabbit dig in a kinotropic cartoon years ago on Earth.

Something had tunneled beneath him, and it was still moving, and fast, toward the group as they neared the city.

"Blast," Belloc muttered under his breath. He pointed his pistol at the front of the burrowed line and pulled the trigger.

The pepperbox pistol thundered in the underground chamber, the air smelled instantly thick with the acrid smell of gunpowder. The rumbling stopped for a moment after the bullet hit the dirt harmlessly. But now the line of disturbed earth turned and began burrowing toward Belloc at a frightening pace.

Like most combat soldiers, Belloc had accepted the idea that he would one day be called to give his life for God, King, country, or comrades. He stood his ground now, his feet shoulder-width apart as he fired one, two, then three bullets into the raised piece of ground where he hoped the thing's head was. Now it was twenty feet away, now ten, now five . . .

****

"What is making those blasted tremors?" shouted Dr. Moreau. He'd just spilled a drop out of a flask for the third time that day.

The First Man, Williamson Senior, looked at Moreau with a blank stare, as if it was beneath his Williamson's dignity to answer a question posed to the air by someone of a lower station. Moreau knew Williamson Senior believed this, and continued to work.

"When will you be ready, Moreau?" the First Man said, the liver spots on his face flaring red as he controlled his anger. Moreau never had fully appreciated the kind of pain that the First Man could have visited upon his frail, scientist's body, and that made the First Man angrier than anything had since he'd left earth.

Moreau kept pouring, drop by drop, holding one flask over the other with a pair of tongs, pausing between drops as the chemicals mixed and got used to each other.

Another tremor, and this time a precious drop almost, but not quite, missed the destination flask. Moreau was ready this time, and he compensated just enough that the drop hit the mixture anyway, despite the infernally perfect timing of the latest tremor.

"I'm asking the question, Moreau!" said Williamson.

"If you want this mixed properly, Williamson, you'll close that silly orifice of yours and leave me to my work."

"We've tried that, Moreau. And you have yet to produce a satisfactory result."

"If you could just manage to capture a subject that the aliens had been successful with, like that walking bag of swords they call Carter, or that lecherous lothario Wickham, perhaps you and your rivals would be immortal already, hmm? But *you* can't, so *I* haven't. I have to resort to synthesizing the secret to undying, eternal life using the scientific equivalent of Stone Age knives and bear skins."

"I am phenomenally unconcerned about the quality of equipment you find yourself using, Moreau. You have until this time tomorrow to produce a tangible result, otherwise I will be forced to use a more . . . physical form of motivation to encourage your progress."

"A beating? Oh, my *dear* Mister Williamson!" said Moreau in mock horror and fear. "Please! Please, not a *beating!* You're the masters of the world, Williamson, and that's the best you can do? Evidently you didn't get there by using your imagination."

Williamson looked blankly at the slightly rotund scientist in front of him. "Tomorrow, Moreau. Or you'll find out what the Warhoons like to do to fat, balding scientists who are dropped off in their desert territories."

Moreau looked at Williamson. "I have seen men like you, Mister Williamson. Do you genuinely think I don't know what fate awaits those who are no longer useful to you? I already know I am a dead man. My only hope lies in creating something long enough to outlast me."

"Assuming I am the monster you make me out to be, Moreau—"

"You are. And it's *Doctor* Moreau."

"Quiet! Even if I *am* the kind of amoral creature you make me out to be, completing my tasks in a timely fashion is all that stands between a quick and painless end for you, and a long, slow, drawn out one, dangling at the end of a gibbet while slow-roasting over an open fire while a bunch of Thark savages parade around you, salivating while the flesh peels off your musculo-skeletal structure. Is that clear?"

Moreau smiled, turned, and went back to work. "Crystal, Mister Williamson. Now, if I may be left to my tasks?"

Williamson turned and left the room, his expensive black shoes tapping against the ancient red stone and grinding the sand beneath their soles as the two thugs at the doorway soundlessly fell into step behind him.

****

Belloc kept firing on the mound of earth. Two bullets blasted and slammed into the ground, they but didn't slow the tunneling menace by so much as a whit.

Blast, Belloc had just enough time to think the word as the thing reached him.

As the creature passed underneath, Belloc stumbled, thrown off balance as the mound of earth raised him nearly a foot in the air. He felt something slap his foot, and when he looked down he saw that a white, ropy thing had emerged from the freshly dug earth and wrapped itself around his army boot.

In less than a second, he had his knife out of its sheath. The flesh of the tentacle cut easily, thankfully. *Very much like the skin of a deer*, Belloc thought with the calm part of his brain.

As he finished the thought, two more tentacles wrapped around each of his boots, and the mound of earth launched him another foot into the air. The dirt sloughed off, and Belloc found himself standing on the head of a giant, white worm with a snout that extended several feet from the nose of the creature, and ended in a number of starfish-like, wriggling arms.

Belloc sliced off both the tentacles that held his right leg, but more took their place. As the creature moved, it dragged Belloc beside it, the tentacles which sprouted from the crown pulling him toward its mouth like a fisherman reeling in a catch.

Belloc, keeping his head as best he could, saved his bullets and stabbed the creature in its side with his knife. There were hundreds of tiny plate-shaped pieces of armor on the surface, hard to pierce but soft enough that the sharp blade could slice *beneath* them. As the dirt fell into the exposed worm-flesh, the creature turned slowly, moving both its wound and Belloc up and away from the irritating dirt.

Mother of God, Belloc thought as he watched, perhaps I can ride this thing like a horse!

That dream died quickly.

The giant white worm surged forward, inhaling the dirt in front of it while burrowing. Belloc, still holding on to the knife in the creature's back, whooped nonetheless as it turned in the column of dirt, moving forward while rotating toward more of the buildings of the lost underground city.

The irritation of the sand under its scales caused the worm to release Belloc's foot. Instead of jumping off the worm, though, Belloc held on to the knife he'd stuck in its backside. *I may die in the next few minutes,* Belloc thought to himself as he held on to the knife, *but at least I'll go in a way that would be good for a song or two!*

****

When the worm had risen from the underground river, Gilbert, Anne, Frances, and Jimmy ran. All but Jimmy looked back when they heard Belloc's pistol shots, but Gilbert urged them on. "He said *run*," Gilbert shouted. "He held off armies of Tharks; he'll be alright against that! We'll just get in the way."

"Has that 'appened before? You getting in the way of a fight?" Jimmy asked once they'd caught up to him.

Gilbert looked back over to Anne, who returned his glance. "Yes. And someone I knew ended up hurt and needing field surgery because I thought I was a better fighter than I was. So keep running! Hey! Hey! Up here!"

The building they'd stopped by was built like a fortress. It looked out of place among the tall, elegant, and stately buildings with ornate, stained-glass windows. The building Gilbert now entered through its open doorway was squat, thick-walled and had a stone spire rising up out of a sturdy rock dome on top.

"Are you certain a building is a safe place to be right now? Couldn't that creature dig under and cause it to collapse?" Anne asked, her metallic right hand scraping alongside the wall as they ran up the stone steps. The darkness was almost total—occasional windows along their stairway

WHERE THE RED SANDS FLY

allowed only a fraction of the light in from outside, which was already thin enough.

"We're still safer here there than out in the open. And this building looks better designed than most to withstand some kind of attack."

Another rumbling. More pistol shots. "I *do* hope he's alright!" said Frances, running just behind Gilbert.

"Oh, *do* you now?" Gilbert said, more than a little sarcastically.

"I *hope* you aren't the least bit jealous, Gilbert Chesterton! You've got no business snipping at me! Not after what brought me here!"

"Look, Frances, now isn't the ti—Whoa!"

Gilbert had almost tumbled off into space, for the stairway suddenly ended, becoming no more than a hunk of broken stone and twisted railing which led to a long drop into darkness. The building was hollow inside, with circular walkways surrounding a central, empty space. The empty shaft circled and spiraled downward. Winking, glowing lights sparkled at the bottom in a darkness that seemed to go down forever.

"Blimey...," Jimmy whispered. "This ain't no fortress. It's a library."

"Yes," Anne said, "they had a Martian book on display over at the little museum at Syrtis Major. I've heard it glows like those lights down there, but only when certain levels of sun or moonlight play on the pages."

"How'd you know that?" Gilbert asked, steadying himself again against the back of the wall, his hands still shaking at the near fall he'd taken as he wiped the nervous sweat from his brow.

"I stole it from them," she said matter-of-factly. "Jimmy subcontracted me."

"That wasn't wise, Miss," Jimmy said darkly.

"What? Stealing for you, telling these folks about it, or trusting you to pay me on time?"

"Hey!" Jimmy said.

"Hey what?" she said. "You were lucky I didn't take interest for my late payment in a pound of flesh from your hide. And we both know I could do it, too."

More tremors tabled the argument. "Let's keep moving to get to higher ground," Gilbert said, looking up at the spiral staircase that hugged the inside of the stone spire. "I don't think it'd be safe to be underground with a giant worm running around!"

"But the *books!*" Jimmy said. "I got a good *thirty pounds* for the *one* she stole for me, and now there's *thousands* down there! Thousands, mate!"

"Jimmy, are you coming, or aren't you?"

Jimmy didn't answer. He looked up at the three young people, then down at the sparkling bookshelves.

"I'll catch up, mate. Down there is my ticket back to Earth, the Rookery, and many other dreams besides."

Another rumble hit the building. Sounds of flying dirt and large rocks thudded against the outside wall.

"Jimmy, if you don't get to higher ground, that thing's gonna tunnel right through here, and you won't make a dime! Now c'mon!"

But Gilbert's speech was lost on Jimmy, who ran down the stairs two and three at a time towards the quiet, glowing lights surrounding the shaft.

"Up!" barked Gilbert, grabbing Frances' hand and pulling her behind him.

Anne followed quickly behind Frances, gathering up the folds of her dress as Frances did to keep from tripping on the staircase, lit now by the eerie green glow let off by several of the books as they passed.

A howling call sounded outside, stopping Gilbert and the girls from their ascent. Gilbert saw that Jimmy had heard it too—and stopped. It sounded haunting and made them fearful inside . . . until Gilbert recognized it.

"It's a cowboy, riding a bronco!"

"What?" both Anne and Frances said.

The worm pounded through the wall and into the library.

✳✳✳✳

1914 A.D.
THE ARCHEOLOGICAL SITE, TOP FLOOR
OF THE TEMPLE'S CENTRAL TOWER

"So, you had to dodge one of the white worms, eh mon amie?" Flambeau was smiling as he spoke, sitting in the dirt with his back leaning against a wall of the ancient, dirty cell they'd been thrust into. A small window in the ceiling let a thin beam of light into the place, and several wooden beams had been crudely propped and sealed over a large, smooth-edged,

381

man-sized circular hole that had been dug into the wall of their cell a long time past.

"There's more of them?" Gilbert asked, but with little focus to his words. His hands were flitting over the walls, searching with movements that were quick yet methodical.

"There have been several sightings of them over the past few years," Anne said, her tone similar to Gilbert's as she tapped the wall with her metal finger, listening intently to every sound her searching made. "But our sighting was the first one recorded in the modern age. Those members of our party who were eaten by it must have been tasty treats; others came up out of the depths in the next few years and started looking for bipedal, earthborn meals. Gave the big game hunter types something new to traipse after, once they cleaned out the ruins of the white apes. In fact," she continued, "there's a contingent of humans and humanoid Martians that have begun a cult to the beasts of some sort. I've even heard some folks have turned to human sacrifice again. Hard to believe, isn't it?"

"Not really, Anne," Gilbert again, now with his fingers dancing over the wall in a series of circles and taps. "Whenever men worship animals, they eventually sacrifice humans. It's crazy, but sad and true and can always get worse. When men won't believe in God, they'll believe any cockamamie thing that comes down the tube. Ah, here!" he said in a triumphant whisper.

"I am truly amazed you found anything, Gilles," said Fr. Flambeau, still sitting in a relaxed position. His own head had twitched just before Gilbert had sounded his victory. "With the chatter you two are keeping up, how could you hear anything resembling a hollow spot?"

"We're not chattering that much," Anne snapped. She then gave a quick look at Gilbert, who was trying to hide his hurt expression. "Mathematically speaking," Anne continued with a calmer tone of voice. She walked over to Gilbert and peered over his shoulder, her chin resting on his deltoid muscle, "in a jail cell tens of thousands of years old, it's highly improbable there hasn't been some kind of escape route completed here, or at least attempted in secret at some point. Here," she said, noting a hole in the wall just slightly thicker than a human finger.

"Hang on," Gilbert said. His face had brightened considerably since Anne had rested her chin, and he now tried to hook his index finger inside and pull. It was no use, though; if indeed Gilbert had found a door to a secret compartment, it wasn't going to be opened by his relatively un-muscled digit.

"Here, Gilbert," Anne said, reaching her arm under his, and gently moving his hand aside.

She then balled her hand into a fist, pointed the knuckles at the stone, braced herself and let fly. A pneumatic whoosh! fired from tiny jets in her wrist as her fist suddenly leapt forward from the rest of her wrist, blasting the rock into pieces and powder.

Gilbert spluttered and sneezed as dirt invaded his nose and tickled his nostrils. "Was that necessary, Anne?"

"Oh, excuse me, Gilbert. Did you think I was flirting with you? I just needed you to ensure my frock wasn't dirtied up worse by ten-millennia old thick layers of dust. Now, what's in that compartment?"

Gilbert, looking more than a little non-plussed at Anne, turned and looked instead at the alcove Anne's pneumatic punch had managed to uncover. He had to work to ignore Father Flambeau's silent, barely suppressed chuckles behind them.

"It looks like . . . hang on . . ."

He drew out an oddly shaped pistol. It had a handle and trigger like a revolver, but it was brass colored and the muzzle had several knobs and concentric disks on it.

Flambeau, his chuckles instantly gone, was already on his feet with an all-business expression on his face. "What's that," he asked with a sharp, direct edge in his voice.

"Our ticket out of here, and straight to the top floor," Gilbert said. He turned to look at Anne with an expression of mock seriousness, "Though I'm not sure if it's a male-only club up there. We may need Anne to bat her eyes a bit in order to—ow!"

Anne had just flicked Gilbert's collarbone with one of her metal fingers. "Do you remember how I had to shut you up back on the floating city? The one in Berlin, not over Richmond."

"All too well," Gilbert replied, looking ruefully at the small pistol, and now at the door. "We've got a nice little key, now. The trick is gonna be finding the right lock. I'll come clean, though: I knew this thing was here earlier."

"How?"

"I put it here, Anne. The last time I was in this cell."

****

1892 A.D.
MARS. UNDERGROUND, IN THE RUINED CITY.

"Whoa!" Gilbert yelled. The walls of the library exploded inward as the giant white worm blasted through the wall of the hollow shaft-space. The sound of bricks grinding and clinking together nearly deafened him, and sand was spraying everywhere. Jimmy's screams of terror sounded up the shaft as the freight-train-sized monster exploded into the area above him and below Gilbert's group.

Gilbert flew backward, the floor beneath him shoved as if by an invisible hand. He slammed against an ancient wall and for a second or two he laid senseless, the sound of a girl's scream resounding through his head and dust flying up his nostrils, in his eyes, and virtually everywhere else around him.

He sneezed, looked, and saw Belloc, holding on for dear life with both hands to a knife handle he'd embedded into the back of the worm, where several cut strands of the worm's smaller tentacles were trailing from his boots as he swung to and fro from the worm's movements. Belloc was still whooping like a Comanche warrior to keep his courage up while the creature slid forward in huge, shifting shunts, slithering forward ten or fifteen feet, stopping, then moving the same distance forward again.

"Belloc!" Gilbert yelled, jumping to his feet. Belloc looked up, saw Gilbert, and tried to wiggle the knife in order to free it.

"Jump off, Belloc! Quick!"

As the creature moved forward again, it decimated dozens of stone shelves, knocking hundreds of ancient books into a glowing green cascading waterfall of papyrus-colored pages and covers towards the unseen floor below. Gilbert watched as Belloc jumped, pulling his knife extra hard and leaving a jagged tear in the white worm's flesh as he leaped off the creature's back towards Gilbert.

Gilbert tried clumsily to grab him. His hands slipped over Belloc, who fell and hung on to the lip of the broken stairwell.

"You idiot!" Belloc yelled, along with some other words Gilbert had gotten his mouth washed out with soap over when he was a kid. His one hand held on to the broken stairway for dear life, his other gripped the hilt of his knife.

"Hang on!" Gilbert yelled back, scrambling toward the hanging soldier.

Gilbert could hear the body of the worm beneath Belloc. Propelled by its own bulk and inertia, it still kept moving into the room. He watched as its head bumped the wall of the vertical tunnel, and tried to find something solid to grip onto. Failing that, its nose with tentacles waving in front of it, first pointed and then fell down the empty shaft, armored scales and tentacles scraping the sides of the walls, crushing and toppling the books on the side.

"Knickers," Belloc grumbled. Gilbert suddenly remembered he'd left Belloc hanging. Belloc holstered his knife with his free hand and then used it to grab Gilbert's.

Gilbert pulled him up, though he realized quickly he was more of an anchor for the stronger boy to pull *himself* up with.

"Where are the girls?" Belloc gasped once on the platform.

"On the other side, I think. I got knocked over here."

"Where's the language chap? Where's Jimmy?"

A scream sounded from below, answering Belloc's question with a long, terrified shriek. It stopped suddenly, leaving only the sound of the worm's grinding away at the walls.

"Frances?" Gilbert called out. "Anne? Are you there?"

He heard no answer.

****

Cecil tried to stretch again inside the cramped tunneler, but he failed. "How long are we going to be in here again?" he asked.

"Ten minutes less than the last time you asked," Emrys answered, almost absentmindedly.

Two hours and fifty minutes, then, Cecil grumbled inwardly. He wished he at least had a gun or a smaller steamhammer to fiddle with. As it was, he only could twiddle his thumbs and think about someone *else* bashing the Doctor's head in.

Cecil amused himself in the dim light by looking at the faces of each of the hard-looking men who'd joined the mining colony and tried to attach a life story to each of them. *Which one, he wondered, had spent life as a hard-working miner, and which one had the face of a thieving jammy?*

" 'Ere," said one, noticing Cecil's wandering eyes, "the little sandsnake's taking it all in. Wot're you doing, lad?"

"Nuffin'!" Cecil shouted back over the grinding, hissing sound of the engines. Though Canadian by upbringing, Cecil was careful to use the accent of a cockney street urchin. He'd found more than once it could spare him a fair bit of difficulty at the hands of a large, bruising hulk like the one that had just spoken. "Jest lookin' about!"

"Well, keep yer eyes in yer 'ead. Things is going to get hot as 'tis. We don't need some lit'le chap gettin' underfoot."

"Jest do yer job, mate, an' I'll do moine, see?" Cecil hollered back. This time he was loud enough that the whole transport heard him, and everyone fell silent.

"You're quite the leader, young man," John Carter piped up in the awkward silence. "Have you ever considered a military career?"

" 'Course I have," Cecil replied, his voice normal again, "who hasn't had nightmares?"

Carter gave a hearty laugh, one infectious enough to start the whole transport chuckling. "What say for a song, boys? Hey?" And with that, Carter began to shout out a marching song.

> *Oh, I wish I was in the land of cotton,*
> *Old times they are not forgotten;*
> *Look away! Look away! Look away! Dixie Land.*
> *In Dixie Land where I was born,*
> *Early on one frosty mornin,*
> *Look away! Look away! Look away! Dixie Land.*

Thanks to the lessons his sister had tried to teach him in history, Cecil quickly picked out a number of key words and phrases and realized it was a song from Carter's days as a soldier in the American Civil War. Or the War of Northern Aggression. Or the Slave Wars, or the War of the Right to Choose. All were different names of the war the Northern and Southern United States had fought over slavery, and the happy, romanticized songs came from the white men who'd won the war for the South.

Carter's voice, mingled with that of the criminals-turned-miners-turned-soldiers, echoed throughout the transport. Somehow, the men knew the words already, at least of the chorus. This likely hadn't been Carter's first time singing this song with this bunch. *History*, Cecil mused, *was usually written by the winners, but what happened when there was no clear winner, only huge losses on both sides before they decided to quit and go home?* And, more important, who would write the history of *this* little conflict he was going to be fighting in a matter of hours? Would anyone? Would anyone bother? Or would all those who wrote the histories pretend this was an incident that never happened? *To arms! To arms! And conquer peace for Dixie!*

"You will, Cecil," said Emrys, his quiet voice carrying to the young boy's ears through and over the sounds of the engines and din of the transport, and the raucous song which bellowed and echoed off the walls of the vessel. "You will write the histories, if you make the right choices."

Cecil pretended he hadn't heard, but the young man's voice chilled a part of him in a way he could not truly describe.

****

Brigadier Brackenbury strode toward the dock where four of the largest ships of the British airborne vessels on Mars were docked, decked, and ready for flight. Salisbury tried as he could to keep up the pace with the older man before him, but thankfully the Brigadier was too focused on the ships and the men scurrying on them to notice Salisbury's missteps and fumbling attempts to keep his commander's pistols, maps, and other sundries properly balanced in his arms.

"Private Salisbury!" boomed the Brigadier.

"Sir! Yes, *sir!*" shouted Salisbury through the pile of objects in his hands.

"Which ships have been appropriated for this venture?"

"Sir, they are the . . . uh," here Salisbury tried to pull out a scrap of paper from the pile, wishing yet again that he had a third hand to work with. "Sir, the *Nemean Lion*, the *Golden Eagle*, the *Minotaur*, and the *Andros*. Each has a crew of forty, ready for duty."

"Excellent," said the Brigadier, his thick black polished boots not even breaking their pace as he neared the largest of the ships. "The *Golden Eagle* is best suited for a flagship on this venture. We shall make it our command vessel."

"Sir, *yes sir!*"

"All vessels are to be combat ready within the hour."

"Sir, *yes sir!*"

"And Salisbury," said Brigadier Brackenbury, stopping suddenly and turning to face his nervous, recently promoted attaché.

"Sir, *yes sir!*" bellowed Salisbury, suddenly still as he stared forward while in his hands he precariously balanced two pistols, four rolled-up maps, a snuff box, an ammunition belt, and the manifest of each of the four ships.

"Salisbury, calm down a bit. You're coiled a bit too tight, lad. You'll do much better if you stay focused, yet relaxed. Clear?"

"*Sir* . . . I mean, sir, yes sir."

"Better, Salisbury," said Brackenbury, turning and resuming his pace, Salisbury only two steps behind. As he neared the *Golden Eagle*, sailors began to snap to attention and salute. "But if the bullets begin flying, you get as savage and excited as you need to. Savvy?"

"*SIR, YES, SIR!*"

****

The Doctor stood outside the door of Beatrice's apartment. He'd recently been evicted from it at gunpoint, but in his experience there were very few places he could be kept out of if he truly wanted access.

He tapped on the doorframe gingerly. "Ahem, ah, Beatrice? Are you there?"

There was no answer.

He spoke up. "I, uh, I am willing to offer a bit of an olive branch, in reparation for the beastly way I behaved earlier. It's this limb, you see, my right arm. It hasn't, *ahem*, agreed with me much these past couple of years. If you could be so kind as to let me in, I could perhaps ensure that you'll be released after the great to-do that the men of the circle will be conducting tonight. In fact, I can guarantee that . . ."

He heard a creak. Looking down, he saw that the door had swung inward by a few inches.

"Why, thank you, Beatrice!" said the Doctor, stepping into the room and looking around.

The apartment was empty. The bed was made, the dishes done, the carpet straightened, and the floor immaculately swept.

And the broom was in the window, used as a crossbar, holding a long curtain rope that had been wound and knotted around it.

The Doctor ran to the window and look down. The rope was thin— too thin to support a grown man like himself or one of the guards, but perhaps slim enough to hold a small, slender girl for a few seconds, at least.

The rope ended a good dozen feet above the ground.

And there was no prone or injured body at the bottom.

The girl had escaped.

The Doctor's human hand slowly curled around his walking stick, and the lower portion of his tentacle whipped back and forth like a fish caught on a long line.

The Doctor had been rather frustrated in the past year. He'd once wanted Anne to be his own, and before that he'd wanted Marie Chesterton. He'd lost both women, and then he'd lost his right arm in a way that no man in this or any other time could understand.

After his arrival on Mars, he'd dodged or killed one miscreant or fool after another who'd wanted to settle a score with him.

He'd had a measure of success on Earth and survived on Mars, all against incalculable odds. And for what? To be merely tolerated, like an insane uncle at a family reunion? He now faced his waning years without so much as a screaming whelp as evidence that he'd passed through this world.

He looked out the window, hoping for a glimpse of the escaped girl. Why *did* that name keep arising in his life ever since the invasion of the mollusks two years ago? A name kept floating to the surface of his mind, each time he'd been thwarted, each time he'd thought on every failure of the past two years:

Chesterton.

True, the Doctor fumed as he stormed down the stairs from Beatrice's apartment, the boy hadn't *directly* thwarted the Doctor's chances at reproducing with a suitably fit female. But the boy's mother *had* escaped the Doctor's embrace, years back. Worse, he'd heard that a certain tenderness had developed between Gilbert and Anne. Yet *another* potential conquest lost because of the Chesterton family.

And now, the boy's *sister* had decided to spurn his advances as well. And escape besides! He walked briskly out of the apartment and down the walkway towards where Beatrice Chesterton must have gone.

"You!" the Doctor boomed at a hapless guard once he'd exited the tower.

"Yes sir?" the guard shouted back.

"The prisoner in the North tower has escaped! Grab a contingent of your similarly apelike fellows, and go get her! There's a cord that's dropped down from her window, and . . ."

He paused suddenly. A thought appeared in his head and a smile on his face in roughly the same amount of time.

"And what, sir?"

"Well, go find her, you frivolous waste of evolutionary energy! Head north! She's not going to go further *into* this fortress, not when freedom could be on the other side of a single wall! Now *move*! And keep this quiet! You *know* what is supposed to happen tonight! No one else of consequence needs to know that there is *anything* awry! If she's found in the next ten minutes, I'll bring your name to the attention of the *number one man in the circle*. Do you know what that could mean for you?"

"Y-yes sir! But . . . what if I take longer than ten minutes, sir?"

"Then," said the Doctor with a voice that had suddenly gone icy, "I'll still bring your name to the attention of the number one man in the circle. But *you*, sirrah, will receive attention of a very different sort. Am I making myself clear?"

"Yes sir!" the guard shouted, bringing the volume of his voice down just in time for the last sound to escape his mouth in a whisper. He ran north, along the floor of the fortress, already signaling frantically with a whistle and a gesture to a comrade on a stone balcony two floors up.

Good, thought the Doctor. *Jolly good*. Without a further sound, he made a jaunty step or two, almost dancing while his tentacle whipped back and forth, almost in time with his happy, jumping feet.

After the guard ran off, the Doctor began to walk away, but stopped. After a second of thought, he looked back up to the cell window. Once the guard was gone from view, the Doctor suddenly ran *back* up the stairs to the outside of the apartment. He parked himself outside of Beatrice's apartment door, and waited for a few more seconds as the soft sounds of booted guards' feet moved a few floors down and ever further away from his location.

Within five minutes, the door opened wide.

Beatrice Chesterton appeared in the doorway.

Clever girl, thought the Doctor. She'd never left the apartment, but had hidden inside it and *staged* an escape. A classic move, she would have waited until the base was in turmoil looking for her, and *then* escaped during the confusion. If he were truly capable of love, he might feel it for this young lady, in time.

She was looking so furtively over her shoulder that she didn't see the Doctor right outside her doorway until she literally had bumped into him.

"Hello pretty," he said, his left hand covering her mouth and stifling her startled scream as his tentacle wrapped around her wrist.

"You *are* a clever one," he said, pulling her towards him, "just like your mother, father, and brothers. Unfortunately for you, I know their tricks. Otherwise you *might* have stood a chance against me!"

Trying hard to scream behind his hand over her mouth, she stomped her heel against the toe of his boot three times.

He chuckled. "Time was, that too would have worked, dearest," he said as he dragged her down the stone floored hall. "But now I live in a much more hazardous place, one where boots with steel toes are *de rigueur*, you see?"

He dragged her down from the tower apartment, across the courtyard over to a new doorway and down a new flight of steps, and past a series of red and yellow stone doorways.

She struggled the entire way, all in vain. "Your little imp of a brother Cecil was down here last," the Doctor grunted. "Managed to see a bit too much, I'm afraid. Heard a bit, too, but it seems not enough to go mad. Not entirely. Would you like to know what he saw here? Would you?"

He cast her to the ground. She looked around and saw that the room had chairs, comfortable ones. Toward the back wall, there were also a number of metal tables in the long room, tables made of metal with large heavy "skirts" of material around them, more akin to workshop benches than those used for eating dinner. She saw that several of the dirty, grey-white skirts around the tables had stains the color of rust on them, and she shuddered.

Closer to her, one chair was next to what appeared to be a large mechanical stand, with joints, sockets, and needles that would have been more at home in a dentist's office. A wide-mouthed gramophone sat on a stand next to a comfortable chair. Wires and flexible tubes hooked the gramophone to a bizarre-looking contraption about the size of a coffee table, which looked to be made almost entirely of gears, pistons, and delicate needles.

"Would you like to see, just what your dear *other* brother has tried so hard to prevent? And why his feeble attempts to depose us are doomed?"

Beatrice made no answer, but she still sat on the floor. Her eyes darted back and forth, looking for an opening anywhere it could be found. *He's mad*, she thought. *Truly mad. I have only one brother, and he's younger than I.*

"Here," said the Doctor, walking to the gramophone contraption. "Cecil walked in on my master as he was preparing himself for tonight's festivities." He turned its crank, and rather than its turntable moving, a disk smaller than the palm of a human hand began to spin at a slow, then increasing rate, until it began to whiz at a speed so quick its edges became a blur.

The voice from the gramophone began to speak, first in English, then in Latin, then in other languages she couldn't understand. This went on for several minutes, until . . .

The speech slowed down.

The disk on the gramophone slowed as well, matching the speech. Eventually, it stopped, and it began to spin in the *opposite* direction.

The words on the disk filled the room again. But this time, the voice spoke *backward*. The other languages were more muddled than before, but where the voice had spoken English, where the voice had said '*I am he*,' she now heard the same, distinctive gravelly voice say "Eh ma *aye*."

Then, the speech quickened again, speeding up to a chipmunk-like chattering. Beatrice felt the very air . . . no, not the air, but the *atmosphere*, in the room begin to, change. Something seemed to hint at madness and evil. A depressing insistence that madness would rule the day, and that resistance would be futile. Worse than futile, resistance would be dangerous. After a few seconds of crazy gibberish, Beatrice found herself plugging her ears. It helped, but not enough. If she had to describe the sensation that the sound made to her, it could best be described as a wet, angry cat trying to get inside her brain and claw it to pieces.

"Beautiful, isn't it?" bellowed the Doctor over the cacophony.

"What did you say?" said Beatrice.

"I SAID . . . Oh, hang it all!" he flicked a switch and the noise ended.

Beatrice sighed. She'd hoped that feigning an inability to hear would have made him shut off the sound.

"Beautiful, wasn't it?" the Doctor said.

"I've heard more agreeable typhoons."

"In time, I think you'll learn to appreciate it. You see, dear girl, what you've heard is just a taste of the strength of my masters. They scoured the whole of the world, found every scrap of magical pronouncement, every mystical word that could be spoken in the service of binding the will of sentient mystical energies, and placed them upon a stack of *these*." Here the Doctor pressed the disk, which popped open with a click. With a move worthy of the deftest card player, his left hand flipped a small circle of paper from it and held it up to one of the glowing lights set into the ceiling.

"Every spell, every word of power, young Beatrice, every means known to man of compelling the gods of the ages to the wills of their minions, all of them, gathered, here in one place. There was a little vixen, an *actress* who tried to steal this, then play both ends against the middle with that floating city business last year. But now, *now*—"

He paused, looking at Beatrice again. Her face held none of the admiration or fear he'd hoped to see.

He saw nothing but revulsion—revulsion and rejection. Throughout his life, from the Doctor's early days as a schoolboy who'd known too much and been made to suffer for it on the playground, rejection had been his constant companion.

Rejection. The sting of it, the curling of lips when he asked to join games, the sneering voices filled with disdain when he'd begged for inclusion. It burned his soul yet again. The vengeances he'd taken over the years against those who hurt him were sweet at the time. But afterward he'd felt as hollow as a wine bottle ready for the candles.

And now, on the eve of his greatest triumph, a kneeling, twenty-three-year-old girl looked at him with disgust and loathing. He could not command respect or admiration, even from a girl who by rights should have been desperate for a man—*any* man.

He could make her kneel. But he could not make her love.

And that angered him more than anything had in a long, long time.

"Don't you, see, Beatrice?" he said quietly. "Don't you see? How beautiful this can be? How wondrous it is, to have something more powerful than Aladdin's genie to do your will? Imagine having a genie, not offering three wishes, but thirty. Thirty-*thousand*. A never-ending parade of power, with the seas, the sand, and the air itself at your command. Zeus, Poseidon, and Hades, all bound to *your* will and *yours* alone. Would you not be willing to share that, with me?"

"You think you can tame a god, Doctor?" her voice was quiet, trying to reason as she once had with Cecil when he'd found a stick of dynamite as a toddler.

"We've—" the Doctor had to close his eyes, both hands against his closed lids as he tried to control the swirling in his brain. "Beatrice, we've . . . we've *already* won on Earth. We won this fight against the greatest of all spirits there a long time ago. I was present when we bent the great Being of Light to our will, and then set our sights almost immediately on Barsoom, the spirit who rules here on Mars."

"You mean to say, Doctor, that you've conquered *God* Himself? That would be quite the achievement, were it true."

"No, the Light told me that there is no God, Beatrice. That's the funniest thing of all, isn't it!" He giggled a bit, then regained his composure, trying very hard to become again the polished, British gentleman. "The Light, he's . . . it's so unimaginably powerful and admits *no* greater power than itself! None at all! It said so to me. Isn't it silly? All those men and women throughout the ages, calling the Light silly names like 'Lucifer' and 'Satan,' fighting him on behalf of a non-existent God! Isn't that the biggest joke of all? All those martyrs, burned at the stake and thrown to lions, suffering and dying for no reason at all! None, but a vaporous concept of emotion and chemicals called *love*! When all the while, true power consisted not in fighting the White Light, but in *controlling* him, knowing him, and then subjugating him through guile and subterfuge."

"Could it be, Doctor, that all the while you've thought you were controlling this 'Light,' *it* has been, in fact, controlling *you*? Lying to you? About God, about itself, about *everything*?"

The Doctor paused.

Nearby was an earlier version of Moreau's creations, a squat, twisted piece of metal, gears, and tubes. The Doctor felt suddenly very much like that device in front of him. Something that had been twisted, shaped, and warped into something no average man would recognize, and all to suit men who cared no more for him than they would for a piston on a steam-train.

And like a tire or this machine, he'd be completely discarded when no longer *useful*.

For a second, Beatrice's words helped him see clearly the path he'd taken. The way he'd chosen had left him battered, twisted, and very nearly discarded on the refuse heap. He was not a god— he was a man, but one holding on to the last scrap of his humanity by a thread so thin the metaphysical equivalent of a strong breeze could shatter it, sending him falling for ever into an abyss where the tormentors he'd known in school had unknowingly learned their trades. It was an abyss where there was no bottom to be found, where suffering and grief awaited him in forms even his considerable imagination could not conceive.

And the final, supreme irony of the whole of his wasted life would be this: he'd entered into such a place willingly. His desire for power had sprung from feeling powerless against the bullies of his life, and his solution was to become a bully, and would of course land him in the hands of bullies who would bully him forever.

His insight lasted only a second.

"I...It...such...such a thing simply could...could be...," he said, his voice sounding more still, more in control.

The Doctor, for his part, had been quietly offered a new thought, one that hadn't bubbled up in a very long time. Assignments or threats to his life had occupied literally his every waking moment for years, leaving no time for reflection.

And now that single phrase of Beatrice's had become the verbal equivalent of a crowbar, popping the lid and releasing thoughts held captive for far too long. Thoughts of a world where the strong did not control the weak, but left them to their affairs and assisted where helpful or necessary. Where those in power saw it as their duty to *serve*, rather than control others like cattle. Where the individual's allegiance to God made him a better and wiser person, rather than an ignorant field beast.

And for just a moment, he saw the fragile beauty of such a world, one so much more worth fighting for than the one he'd been serving. It appeared in his mind without coercion, hatred, or any attempt to manipulate him, freely and without condition, all in hardly more than a second.

He looked down with unseeing eyes. In a few more seconds he looked up again, his eyes wide and the corners of his mouth tugging gently upwards.

"Y—Ye—Yes-"

A pop sounded in the room. The Doctor's body had jerked a little, as if he'd been rudely bumped. He looked down and saw a large red stain appearing on his chest.

"Th-thank ... Thank ..." he said, lowering himself slowly to his knees as his eyes began to look less like eyes and more like glass marbles.

Beatrice had been kneeling, but only for the briefest moment. When she heard the bullet strike the wall behind her head after it passed through the Doctor's body, she scurried under the nearest operating table in the center of the odd workshop, hiding under the thick, dark blue material that surrounded the table like a mother's protective skirt.

"Hello, Doctor," she heard a man's voice say. Peeking through the gap in the small curtain around her, she saw the voice's owner enter the room through the door, a pepperbox pistol in his hand and a thick rubber lab apron covering his chest and lower half of his body down to his ankles.

Beatrice recognized him after a few seconds from the shock of white hair on his head. He was the one the guards called Dr. Moreau, and when they spoke of him they did so with hushed whispers and shifting eyes.

Moreau brought the pistol up to his lips and blew into the single, smoking barrel. "It's been a while, hasn't it?" he said to the Doctor's prone, bleeding form, sliding the pistol into a large holster set on his hip. "That's an upper torso shot, so five points to me."

She heard the Doctor say something, garbled by the blood in his throat.

"Why haven't you bothered to revive yourself? Did I make too lucky a shot? Have no fear, Doctor. I have the vial here, and I've no intention of breaking the rules of our little game. You will have no worries regarding our wager." The new speaker snapped his fingers, and two guards appeared around the corner, booted feet tramping the floor as they sprang quietly into action. They lifted the Doctor, still moaning and speaking garbled tongues, and brought him closer to Beatrice.

Though every instinct told her to be silent, quiet, and still, something had awakened in Beatrice since her fight with the Doctor. She now had a willingness to fight for what she felt was hers, rather than try to flatter or reason with those who held her against her will.

And, most of all, she had an insatiable curiosity.

She peeked out again through the folds of her new, small alcove, to see what was about to happen to the Doctor.

Two large guards had brought the Doctor to a table on the other side of the room and laid him out upon it, in the fashion of a cadaver about to be dissected.

Beatrice gulped. She could clearly hear the Doctor still gasping for breath, though she couldn't see if his eyes were open or closed. "Leave us," said the man standing over the Doctor. "da Vinci didn't suffer little children to point at him while he was painting the *Mona Lisa*, and I don't like having fools watching me work, either."

The men left without a sound tramping on the tile stones of the floor and crunching softly in the gravel.

"Now, Doctor," he said, as he drew out a syringe and a small glass vial from a buttoned pack near his belt, "let us see just what it is you were doing down here before I scored my latest little victory against you."

He took the syringe and pulled back the plunger, filling the syringe with the glowing, green liquid from the vial. Even at her distance of a dozen feet away, she could see the liquid seemed to quiver when he held it up to the dim light of the oil lamps. He flicked it with his finger several times, then gave the smallest tap to the liquid through the narrow needle.

"N-no..." she heard the Doctor mumble, as if in a deep sleep. "Don't..."

"What?" said the man. He pulled open the Doctor's holed shirt and looking quickly for the exit wound in the Doctor's chest. "Why, I don't even think I hit your lung this time. Why are you being such a baby about this? You've killed me far worse in our little game, hmm? Here, ready?"

The Doctor made no answer. From her small alcove, Beatrice saw the man inject the viscous fluid into the Doctor.

The Doctor gasped almost as soon as the man was finished. "Do you know, Doctor," said the man as the Doctor gasped for breath, "have you any *idea* just where this little formula came from? Your precious mollusks, that's who! They'd been planning on making us live longer and healthier for quite a while. Not because of any altruistic streak, of course, but to make us more durable, healthy, and long-lived livestock for them.

"But they just couldn't get it right. They managed to succeed on just three humans before you made that rather one-sided deal with them, Doctor. They first jabbed an old man, back in the Middle Ages, and did a few other things to him besides, if I've deciphered their records aright. More recently they managed to abduct and give George Wickham quite a dose, and it's left him well-preserved for quite a few years now.

"Later, they did the same to John Carter, and *that* dose blanked out any of his memories before the age of thirty. Quite the inoculation, if they had succeeded. Bring humans here from Earth, give them a shot that will triple their lifespan, and leave them no memories of a free life on their home world. Very much like what those Bolsheviks are planning, with everything from healthcare to re-education, hmm?

"Indeed, thus far all I've been able to do is make this little concoction that heals and very nearly brings you back from death itself. It has rather odd effects the more it is used, but thus far the Painter hasn't displayed any significant side effects. Ah! Are you awake, now? I should say that—"

The Doctor's tentacle wrapped around the man's neck, cutting off his speech. He gurgled, then pulled at the fleshy noose around his neck.

The Doctor slowly sat up on the operating table, his face unreadable as Moreau dropped to his knees, his face turning from bring deep red to a pale blue.

"You really, really shouldn't have done that, Moreau," the Doctor said. His voice sounded different now, as if something were speaking *through* his mouth from a long way off. "I've been living in here for quite some time, and now, now that one of my more exquisite little patients has gotten away, I'm going to be quite upset and difficult to live with. Especially when I *have* to be *here* in *this!*"

Here, the Doctor's human hand plucked at his clothes and skin and worked his jaws several times, as if trying them out for the first time.

Moreau slapped the Doctor's tentacled arm ineffectively. "Not much like Mordred," the Doctor grumbled, looking at Moreau like he was some specimen of frog or pond scum. "And you're even weaker than Emrys was." The Doctor grimaced as his tentacle flexed and squeezed. Beatrice put her fingers in her ears as Moreau's neck began making sounds like stiff paper crackling, then dry sticks breaking.

Beatrice now realized that, awful as the Doctor had been, the entity who now help held Moreau's neck was now no longer really the Doctor in any more sense than a suit of clothes was the man who'd worn them an hour before. After a few seconds, it unwrapped the tentacle and let go of Moreau's lifeless body, which slumped onto the floor like a sack of rotten potatoes. The thing that had been the Doctor watched cynically as the dead body slumped to the grainy stone floor.

"Pathetic worm," she heard the Doctor's voice mumble, shoving Moreau's corpse with a foot. "We've had laugh after laugh about you and your ilk, thinking you were masters of the world. And *none laugh more than our master himself!* Now," it said, his voice sounding like someone talking to himself who had no idea how loud his voice sounded. "Now, to the meeting room, or the church, or whatever those worn-out little Adamites call the place where they're going to try and trap Barsoom."

The Doctor's laugh cackled through the laboratory as his feet shuffled towards the doorway. Beatrice found it more unsettling than the sound of Moreau's death, or even the recordings the Doctor had played for her. Fear ran through her like a winter chill, and the animated corpse of the Doctor suddenly stopped its shuffling walk to the door.

"Well," it said. She heard it lick its lips and spit a little, speaking without turning to face her as it hobbled away. "This is interesting. I'll not worry you now, little girl. There'll be time enough to drink your despair after I'm done."

****

Brigadier Brackenbury looked over the red sands as a distant wind blew the dunes into new patterns. They'd landed a half hour ago, and they had seen no movement. They all knew what that meant, but he landed anyway. *My career will be over as soon as it's learned I left to help Belloc,* the Brigadier thought to himself. *If I'm to be destroyed on the altar of some fop's spite, I might as well be the right kind of soldier all the way to the end.*

Salisbury interrupted his thoughts by running up to him and snapping to attention. "Sir!" he said in a clear voice, "No survivors among the wreckage!"

The voice behind him was Salisbury's. He closed his eyes and waited until he had complete control of his voice before he answered.

"Transport the bodies aboard ship. What is the condition of Sergeant Belloc's body?"

"Sir, the reports were accurate. Alone among the crew, Sergeant Belloc is not accounted for, nor is the American who reportedly joined as a passenger at the last minute!"

The Brigadier opened his eyes slightly, a small, hopeful smile barely playing on the corners of his mouth. "Indeed?" he said.

"Yes sir!" answered Salisbury. "Furthermore, there are two sets of tracks leaving the wreckage. Further from the debris the wind has obscured them, but initial reports said the tracks led in the direction of Danton's Folly."

"Excellent, Salisbury. Carry on. Once the last of our comrades are safely aboard ship, we shall make for the colony at all available speed. Inform the other captains."

"Yes *sir!*"

Salisbury, enthusiastic at his commanding officer's approval, ran to dispatch his orders while the bodies of the crew were brought aboard with reverence by their fellow British sailors.

Alone in his tiny cabin, the Brigadier chuckled to himself. *I'll see you again, Belloc. You and I will show those Williamsons that there's yet a trick or two a couple of honorable men can show even the most wealthy and cunning predators in this world.*

399

✳✳✳✳

When the worm blasted its way into the library, the impact flung Frances and Anne backward against one of the library tower's stone walls. Several of the glowing books fell from their alcoves and shelves. Some opened up and began to speak or sing in voices either beautiful and haunting or harsh and direct.

"Hang on!" Anne shouted over the din, gripping one of the shelves as sludge from the worm's skin sloughed off on the bricks less than a dozen feet from them both.

"Where's Gilbert?" Frances yelled back as she heard a very humanlike, deep voice begin to shriek in terror from below. In a second or two, the screaming stopped.

"They're on the other side of this thing," Anne said. "Come on, this place isn't safe! We've got to— Ooh!"

Anne thought at first she'd only slipped or tripped. But she quickly realized the brick in the floor she'd been standing on had broken off and fallen. Worse, more and more bricks in the floor near the giant worm's body were doing the same! Each brick she stepped on to try and gain better footing broke away, falling down and into the abyss like a short line of dominoes, followed by more glowing Martian books whose pages jabbered as they fell open.

Anne reached out her left hand and tried to grab a shelf, but what she thought was a sturdy plank of wood gave way as the wall snapped and broke! Still leaping forward, she kept her head and grabbed at anything solid with her mechanized right-hand, and then with her left as more of the bookcase fell. The floor fell away faster than she could run, and suddenly her legs were dangling in midair. Grabbing at the shelves, she pulled her body forward in a herky-jerky fashion as more ancient works fell out of the bookcase onto her head.

Frances, she thought suddenly! Where was she? No time to worry, now! She reached out, tried to grab a brick in the wall, and it broke off in her hand.

Anne began a slow backward fall.

Still not giving up, Anne readied herself to make a last-ditch effort to save her own life, this time using the worm itself to break her fall. Anne reached for her knife with her left hand, all the while keeping an eye on the skin of the worm below, looking for a place to stab . . .

Her left hand wouldn't move.

In fact, her body wouldn't move either. And when she tried to move, the rest of her moved upward just slightly.

She looked up. Frances held her, from a ledge just below that one Anne had fallen from. The straps Frances had bound around her knuckles were now a kind of crude, small lasso she gripped in both hands, and the straps now secure around Anne's left wrist.

"Climb up," Frances gasped, holding either side of the strap in each of her hands and pushing back toward the slowly buckling stairwell with each of her booted feet. Anne gripped the straps in her hand and pulled.

For just a moment, their eyes locked. Something fearful and angry in Frances' eyes almost made Anne freeze in place.

Almost. The slimy skin of the worm brushed her boot and she pulled harder, scampering up onto the still crumbling platform beside Frances.

The roaring, grinding noise continued as the worm travelled, then suddenly it was over. The hind end of the creature sailed through the wall and down into the long space below. Long trails of brown and green slime and feces spurted out behind it as it travelled down the stone shaft of the library.

The worm was gone.

In the silence, Anne felt her heart beating. Her breathing now sounded quite loud.

"I wouldn't have dropped you, you know," said Frances, wrapping her hands back in the leather straps.

"That's extremely comforting," Anne said, already standing. "But you thought about it."

"And what if I did?" Frances asked.

"Do you love him?"

"Do *you* love him?" Frances answered, "Love him enough to give up *everything*, every*one* who is important to you?"

Anne looked at Frances and held up her right, artificial hand.

"That's not fair," Frances said.

"Isn't it? I wonder if part of his appeal to you is that your family could *never* approve of him, yet the rest of the world does."

"You'll want to watch yourself, young lady!" Frances said, her voice dropping an octave.

"*You*, Frances, you want to . . . to—"

Anne stopped as Gilbert's head suddenly popped over the top of the ridge. "Ladies?" he said, utterly unaware of their simmering conflict, "time to get moving!"

Gilbert's head disappeared again, and Anne dropped her voice to a whisper. "Frances, I'd *suggest* we table this conversation for now. Once we get some place civilized and things are calmer, we can have this discussion. Agreed?"

"Agreed," said Frances, glaring at Anne while tightening the strap on her left hand. "But don't think that clever metal hand of yours will save you if things take a more *pugilistic* turn. And for the record," she said as Belloc gathered his strength to jump to their platform, "I *did* think about dropping you down to the worm. But being a Christian woman, I fear God's wrath just a *hair* more than I hate you."

Chapter 55

"A stiff apology is a second insult . . . The injured party does not want to be compensated because he has been wronged; he wants to be healed because he has been hurt."

– *"The Real Dr. Johnson" in The Common Man*

The room had been redecorated in an effort to make it more like the conference room they had enjoyed on Earth in the old house on the outskirts of London.

The efforts had been fairly successful. Ancient coats of arms hung on the wall, bolted in place by drillers and stonemasons. Weapons and trophy cases filled with the remains of various deadly animals shared space with works of art, parchments, sections of bark, framed pieces of rock, and metal all with designs esoteric and arcane drawn on them.

Most important was the conference table in the center of the room. It was the exact one that had been used on Earth. The cost would have seemed horrendous to any person of normal means in the British Empire, but the men at the table had long since passed the point of worrying about expenses in their quest for total and absolute power.

There were now four men at the table. The youngest man in the circle, a robust-limbed and gray-haired man in his fifties with a surprisingly soft voice, now held the Fourth Man's traditional seat.

The fifth seat was now empty, as it had been since the youngest man had moved up a notch on the totem pole by taking the slender Fourth Man's place when he'd been removed a year ago.

The First Man spoke, his sunken eyes pulsing as he opened his mouth.

"Tonight the event will take place." His voice had the tone of stating a fact rather than of asking a question.

"The device is in place and prepared," said the Second Man, the liver spots on his face turning bright red in anticipation of the evening's event. He had been the First Man until recently, though a few setbacks had caused him to lose his seat. Though known to the rest of the world as Henry Williamson, father to the late Fortescue, here he had no name or societal rank. For now, here he was only the Second Man.

"Young Chesterton remains unaccounted for," said the Third Man, his bulk and rolls of fat jiggling slightly and with great dignity as he spoke. "But it is unlikely at best that he is even aware of our existence on Mars, much less poses a threat to the event."

"Once we have successfully brought this 'Barsoom' entity 'on board', as it were," said the Fourth Man, his voice sounding softer than usual, "we may have no further need of the other arrangements we've had in place. I move that at the conclusion of the event, we remove with all available speed the Chesterton girl, Doctor Moreau, and any and all other agents nearby, beginning with the Doctor and the Cleaner."

"Your point is well taken," said the First Man, looking into the distance while blinking his sunken eyes.

The First Man was about to say more when the double doors to the conference room burst open. "And fully ignored," said the Doctor's now scratchy voice as he barged in. "Move your worthless hide, Marconi," the Doctor said to the First Man, "your seat is mine, now. I don't care about your silly little pretend games of rank and wealth, but I like upsetting and angering you. This body's already started decaying, and I mean to use it fully before it rots away around its own ankles."

"I say," said the youngest man, a slight edge perceptible in his voice. "Doctor, we are in conference here. At this point, you need to—"

"Marconi," bellowed the grating new version of the Doctor's voice, "tell Rothchild here that I am not the Doctor, and that you all need to move a seat *down*. Otherwise, the men here get to hear about your sister, Marconi, and *your* cousin, Williamson, and *your*—"

The other three older men were already ceding their seats, and encouraging the youngest man to move with the most baleful stares they could muster.

In the end, the Doctor's posterior plunked into the First Man's place at the table, while the rest watched and seethed from seats one notch lower than they'd previously enjoyed.

"Good, honest hatred," the Doctor's new voice cackled, looking around the table with eyes blurred by white film. "Good. Good. Oh, stop trying to shield it from me. You're all as obvious to one of my kind as a guilty little boy in front of a broken vase. Now, listen carefully you bunch of fools. The Doctor is gone. I speak now, as one *literally* far more knowledgeable than you can imagine. Your little ceremony tonight will have repercussions far beyond simply getting you power—they have foreseen this. I, of course, as undersecretary of the Department of Precognition, foresaw it sooner than most. But I won't be able to get my job done if you bumbling dolts continue to treat this as a grubbling little money concern like those you kept hatching back on Earth. Now, to continue—"

"I think," said the milk-soft voice of the youngest man, ignoring the frightened stares of the other, older three men at the table, "that the Second Man has the floor after your comment. Our agreed rules are—"

"They are *not* in force when *I* sit here, dolt! The sooner you gain greater cognizance than a cucumber, the sooner you'll realize that! Otherwise, you'll meet the fate of their old colleague, *Archibald*. They never *told* you about *Archibald*, did they, *Mister* Rothchild? No? A terrible, terrible thing. He thought he could outwit me. Argued for hours until I grew tired of him. Then he went mad. Quite *mad*, thinking first his clothes were full of bees, and then that cats were trying to claw their way out of his brain. He tried every medication and beseeched every god and spirit under the sun (and a few beyond—we all had a good laugh at that one!) to save him, beseeched all *but* the one who might have actually *done* something. Sad and pathetic creatures, you, one and all! And now? *'Archbald is my brother! Archibald is my brother!'* Ever since then, you all have had to use Archibald's name in greeting and identifying those in your venture. Because *each one of you* could go just as mad, and certainly are as close to that kind of madness as that human, Archibald, if you cross me. Is that clear, Rothchild? Or do I have to bring your dog into this?"

"My...my..."

"Yes. Racer. Remember him? When you were twelve? Need I go on? Speak with that milk-blooded voice of yours or be silent."

Rothchild, who had caused men's deaths without so much as a twinge of conscience for years, suddenly had a painful-looking spasm sweep across his face. It spoke of a memory in Rothchild's past that was both shameful and painful beyond measure.

"No...," Rothchild said in a voice that had gone several notes higher, "that...that will *not* be necessary."

"Good," snapped the creature. "Now, it's time for—"

The Doctor's voice stopped suddenly, as Rothchild fired a small revolver and hit the Doctor three times in the chest and once in the face. He was halfway through pulling the trigger a fifth time when the Doctor's smile stopped him.

Rothchild, aka the Fourth (now possibly the Fifth man—that would need to be sorted out later), looked at his companions at the table. His small pistol now looked almost comical in his large hands. All avoided his gaze, looking purposefully at the table.

The First Man, Marconi, had closed his eyes in apparent painful knowledge of what was to come.

The Second Man, Williamson, looked fearfully *around* the table. It seemed clear that he hoped he would not share in what he knew would be Rothchild's dreadful fate.

The Third Man's eyes were riveted to a few stray specks of red dust on the table in front of his ponderous, inflated belly. Known as Lord Musgrave to the rest of the world, his eyes were inscrutable. But there was a slight smile playing at the corners of his lips, like a schoolboy who knew punishments were about to be doled out to an annoying classmate, though he himself was safe.

The Doctor's face now wore an abnormally large smile. One of Rothchild's bullets had torn a furrow into his face, lengthening the already unnerving smirk until the left side of his face looked as if it had been carved into an obscene jack-o-lantern's grin. Red blood leaked rather than pumped from it, and holes in the Doctor's torso and chest leaked blood as well.

"Oh, dear," said the Doctor, his tongue flipping and flicking, visible between the molars of the torn-open, left side of his smile. "It appears Archibald is going to have a *new* brother to keep him company."

****

"What are these?"

Now safely out of the Martian library tower, Frances looked at the five tunnels dug into the side of the wall, all of which were smaller in diameter than the one left by the giant white worm. Her voice sounded very, very loud and lonely in the near darkness and near total silence.

"These," said Belloc, running his hand along a groove in the dirt, "were made by *tunnelers*, mining vehicles that bore underground, carrying their crews inside them."

"No wonder we felt those vibrations back at the Martian hospital!" Frances said. "Perhaps that's why the worm attacked— those machines frightened it from its hiding place!"

"Frightened?" said Gilbert. "What's something that big got to be frightened of?"

"I'm surprised at you, Gilbert," Belloc's voice chimed in. "Don't you Yanks all have forests outside your home? Bears, bulls and the like are startled by something crashing through the underbrush, aren't they? Just so. Now I know why the worm, er, can't think of the word—"

"Stampeded," Gilbert finished. "And look! Those tunnels go up to the surface. I bet if we follow them, we'll make it up in no time. C'mon, who's up for a hike?"

Anne stepped up to Gilbert's left, her now stocking-clad foot stepping just a hair more gingerly than her booted right foot. Frances, giving Anne a short glare, stepped up to the other side of the lanky boy and gripped his right hand firmly in her own. Gilbert looked at her and gulped. Holding her hand still had the power to make him feel just a little tingly inside, especially considering the crazy near-death many of them had just—

"Fortescue," he said. "Fortescue, and Jimmy! They're both—"

"Mourn the dead later," Belloc said, stepping in front of the three of them and starting the ascent.

"Yes," Anne finished, as she walked forward, limping slightly in her stocking foot, her mechanical right hand swinging free. Fortunately, the powdery dirt had been ground up further and then packed down by the drill heads, so the walking was easier than it normally could have been. "The living have to make sure they stay alive. No distractions."

"We just saw two people...die," said Frances. "Doesn't that affect you? Any of you? Fortescue is . . . he was—"

"Frances," Gilbert said, falling into step behind Anne while still holding Frances' hand, "you weren't in England when the Tripods landed. Those of us who were there, well, a lot of us saw death. A *lot* of death."

Frances was quiet for a few seconds. "Does that make it easier?" she asked.

"No," chimed in Belloc. "You still see them. But when you are in the middle of it, you have to close the door on that part of you. Some men think too much at the time, and they either end up dead for lack of focus or go mad after the fighting's over."

"It sounds horrible," Frances said. "How do you live with it?"

Gilbert shrugged his shoulders. "The way I figure, you could say Father Brown didn't deserve to die, but that's only if you think dying is a punishment. For some people it is, like getting expelled from school. For others it's more like starting summer vacation earlier than the rest of us. Thinking about it that way helps me, anyway. The other part is that seeing dead folks is bad, but it doesn't mean the rest of your life has to be about that. It doesn't mean the rest of your life has to all be about one week out of thousands in your life."

"Well said, Gilbert," Hilaire said. "If you'd taken a different turn, you might've made a passable soldier. Now, look up. I'll wager by the smell of the air that this tunnel isn't as long as I thought it was. We should be up and out in the light again in about an hour or two, at this rate."

"And then," said Frances, "perhaps, we'll have time for a rest. Along with some . . . conversation."

Gilbert tried not to swallow too hard as Frances gripped his hand tightly. Anne, walking a little ahead now, didn't look back. But Gilbert wondered if she could feel Frances' eyes boring into the back of her head as she kept ascending.

****

The skiff sped across the sands with a speed Herb found more than enjoyable. It was exhilarating! Enthralling! The wind in his hair, the grains of sand bouncing off the lenses of his goggles, all of it made him feel freer than he'd felt for quite some time. *Free*, he thought. *Free from the prying eyes of the Special Branch, the circle, or their toadying little minions. Free! Free to enjoy the sun, the sand, the air... If this weren't a desert, I'd almost swear this was the beach!*

The sand skiff was surprisingly easy to steer as well. A long rope looped behind his back connected the sails, and the rest was simply pulling in one direction or another. The ship itself was obviously of British make, but he wondered as he tugged the line how much of it was based on Martian design, either inspired or outright stolen.

The large ship was a surprisingly quick traveler. It was a sub-mission of Herb's to bring Cecil to the tower as well as Gilbert—alive if possible. If it were up to Herb, though, he'd leave Cecil to his fate as a dirt-urchin in a mining town of miscreants who'd barely escaped the hangman's noose by becoming colonists out here.

The town was in sight. *Good.* He'd enter it in minutes, find the local watering hole, buy a round of alcohol for the house, and wait until the tongues loosened and loyalties were changed. Wickham and Cecil would be snatched by nightfall by the men of his town, in exchange for liquor, money, or whatever else Herb could provide.

Easy. If Herb played his cards right, he could be back at the main base by dark.

****

The afternoon sun shone brightly and cheerfully through the windows of the hangar as Anne's little group emerged from the tunnel and into the middle of the building in Danton's Folly, illuminating the dirt and grime that had fallen and caked on their clothes and in their skin.

Anne, having emerged from the tunnels first, surveyed the town through a nearby window. Within seconds, her instincts told her something was wrong—or at least different.

"What, ho?" said Belloc as he came up behind her with a jaunty step, obviously happy to be out of the tunnel and back on open, level ground again.

The hangar was quiet and empty as the streets outside, its only significant features being a few benches, a stack of lockers against one wall, and a set of metal circular steps curling up to a lookout point in the ceiling.

"Things are quiet. Is it Sunday or something?" Belloc asked as Frances and Gilbert emerged.

Frances chuckled. "It *is* quiet," she said, "but I doubt it's because everyone's in Church."

"True," said Anne, "at Danton's Folly they'd be more likely sleeping off a good party from Saturday night than in a place of worship. But still, it's a bit eerie that it's this deserted."

"They took those tunnels someplace then, I'd wager," Gilbert said. "But what would empty a whole town?"

"Either they were running from something, or heard of something better," Belloc said. "We won't know for a while, at least. Meantime, if the place *is* truly deserted, we can at last relax a bit."

They stepped away from the window and took in their surroundings.

The building they'd stepped up into was extremely spacious, big enough to store a small airship in, if needed. So much so that it reminded Gilbert of an airship hangar more than a place to begin a downward journey.

"What's this?" Frances whispered. "What are those things over there?"

Belloc looked over in the direction of Frances's question-filled gaze and chuckled. "You're quite well-to-do, aren't you?" he said, barely holding in a sarcastic chuckle. "M'lady, these are called 'lockers.' When you went to play lawn tennis with your family and their friends? The servants or attendants stored your goods in *those*."

Frances looked doubtful, as if wondering if she were being lied to. "My things never smelled bad as *this* place when they were returned to me!"

"That's because this isn't a country club, Frances," said Gilbert, letting go of her hand and approaching the lockers. "This is a workman's station. Some kind of mining operation, too, from the looks of it. And," he said, suddenly walking over to a rack next to a glass window pane where outlines in the grime suggested a number of tools and other weapons had hung in place. "They left all at once, in a big group. Not just the day's shift, either, or we'd see more evidence of other activity here."

"What would make miners leave in such a hurry?" said Anne. "Were there a bunch of Tharks attacking? Or Americans, maybe? They've been known to 'accidentally' attack outposts and then occupy them afterward."

"Nope. They weren't responding to a threat," said Gilbert. "Nothing's been left undone. No dropped tools, no half-eaten lunches—" Gilbert's voice drifted off.

"Gilbert's right," Belloc said. "Look at the floor. See these footprints? All in a row? Too orderly for a panicked exit, like you'd have if workers were under attack. Besides, if you wanted to leave in a hurry, a digger isn't the way to go. Miners would know that."

"So," said Anne, "if they weren't all running *from* something, and they were carrying guns and heavy handtools to use as clubs in melee, then the miners were going in an ordered fashion—"

"To *attack* something," finished Belloc. "And whatever they're going after would have to have enough potential value to suspend their operations for at least a few days. Wickham isn't above hiring out a few yobs to knock some compliance into someone. But this...," he said, looking at the five holes in the ground, each as tall and wide as two horse-drawn hansom cabs, "even with his history on Mars and his long reputation in England, this is beyond anything I've heard about him."

Gilbert said, "He's been doing this a while, then? How old did you say this fellow was again?"

"I didn't. That's the real trick, you see. There're men in my regiment who remember him serving quite long ago in the Crimean. One older fellow claims to remember him trying to hide from bullets as far back as the war at Trafalgar. Something stopped him from aging past thirty summers, and he's been fresh as a sunborn daisy since."

"If he's old enough to have been at Trafalgar, it explains a few things." Gilbert started walking around, speaking and thinking at once. "Military men I interviewed had different ideas about a lot of things, but there was *one* thing they all did agree on: once they got older, their opinions didn't change. Americans like their black coffee, Brits like their tea. American officers want to be left alone, and British officers wanted to expand the Empire."

"Gilbert," Frances said, "where are you going with this?"

"Here's my point: Wickham may *look* like he's thirty, but he's much older. And he certainly didn't 'go native' the way some officers do, taking a local wife and worshiping Martian gods, or whatnot. He may be a cad, but he's still got the mind-set of a British military man, one who's very, old *inside* if not outside. Is he single? Thought so. A mistress doesn't count as a wife or family; she can be discarded quite easily. Religious? No, I didn't think he was. Without a religion, family, or some sort of creed to guide him and check his appetites, a man that old and fit will either go mad with boredom, or he might just sit in whatever house or apartment, or manor, brooding over injuries he believes others have perpetrated against him, hating people who've been dust for decades. And then . . ."

"Then," said Belloc, understanding, "like most British officers, he'll be thinking about an empire. Either expanding the *empire* of the King, or more likely getting one of his own. But," Belloc continued, walking back and forth just like Gilbert had, "he's had a *long* time to think. And he's had a long time to get tired of being king of a little dunghill of a mining town."

"And," continued Gilbert, "if he somehow heard about the Doctor, with the kinds of plans he and his masters have been hatching—."

"Or if our—I mean, the *Doctor's* masters are *here*," said Anne, "there's been a great deal of traffic in the desert, most of it sand skiffs which end up pointed back, but it keeps going to that old temple, the one with the stone tower in the center of it! Look, even the tunnels are pointed in that direction!"

"So, if I'm understanding you aright," said Frances, "this Wickham fellow's gone off with the mineworkers to attack the Doctor and his masters at an ancient Martian tower? Or temple, or whatever it actually is?"

Gilbert looked around at Belloc and Anne. Each of them nodded their heads almost imperceptibly. "Yep," Gilbert said, "that looks about the size of it."

Frances blinked her eyes and shook her head as if trying to clear it. "Are you three listening to yourselves? Do you hear how ridiculous you sound? Just based on some footprints, four holes in the ground and—and a wall that needs washing, you're saying—saying all of this? Immortal lotharios attacking ancient temples, with an army of yobs and diggers?"

"It's not hard to believe if you've known enough of the right kind of people, dear girl," Belloc said, clearly annoyed at the train of thought being interrupted. "I bet your man here can tell you quite a few stories about the crazy things that people will start believing when they stop believing in God."

Frances let that one sink in. "Well, assuming you're right, what do we do now?"

"I say," said Belloc, "we keep our original missions in mind. I have to return to Syrtis Major, to report on the fate of my patrol. Gilbert has enough material to write a number of articles about life in the Martian colonies. And your goal, I'd imagine," he pointed to Frances, "was to find him," he said, now pointing to Gilbert. "And, well, Anne—"

"I've had no goal for a long time beyond my own survival," Anne said "I've already benefitted more from this trip than I thought I would. It's time for me to return to the company of other people, starting with a return trip to Syrtis Major, and then possibly back to Earth as well."

"Well, then, we are in agreement. I think it would be prudent for us to find a transport, supplies for the journey back, and then leave this place. Or, how is it you Americans put it, Gilbert?"

"Get the heck outta Dodge," Gilbert said. "Fine. I saw what looked like a general store when I looked out the window. I can head over there and grab food, and anything else we'll need. How about the rest of you?"

"I can guess where the skiffs are kept in a place like this," Belloc said. "This hangar was where they kept the tunneler transports for the miners. The skiffs would be kept in a different place. If there are guards left in this little one-sloat-town, we're more likely to encounter them in the town garage than in the general store. Anne, from what I've seen and heard, you'd be useful if a lock needed to be picked or a guard needed to be dispatched discretely. Am I correct?"

Anne didn't answer. She scooped up a small rock from the ground, and it disappeared in her left hand. The small rock then appeared suddenly between the finger and thumb of her right brass hand where she instantly crushed it to powder.

"Right," said Belloc. "Frances, would you be willing to hold the fort here? I know it seems we're abandoning you, but if you get higher on that scaffold, you'll be able to see most of the town. We'll need you for a lookout, and you could just break the glass if you need to alert us—"

"And you'll keep the rich girl out of your hair, hmm?"

"Frances, this isn't the time." Gilbert's face was unusually stern. "Belloc's right. We *do* need a lookout, and you have less experience than most of us at handling just about everything that could go wrong out there. This is both safest for you *and* needed by us."

Frances inhaled once. "Fine," she said, "but you must be *certain* you'll return, Gilbert Keith Chesterton," she gently but firmly grabbed his collar and glared into his eyes. "I'll never forgive myself *or you* if you let yourself come to harm. Am I clear?"

"Crystal," he said, smiling.

"Right, then, let's go!" Anne's voice echoed through the deserted hall, as she suddenly marched off toward the door.

Belloc shrugged his shoulders and followed Anne out of the building.

Gilbert watched Anne leave, but then saw Frances was watching *him* watching *Anne*. He started to speak, but Frances cut him off. "No, Gilbert," she said, "just go and see if you can find those supplies."

"Now, wait just a minute, Frances," Gilbert said, "do you think that Anne has some kind of hold on me?"

"Mother always told me not to ask questions I don't want the answers to."

"Well, maybe I *do* want an answer to this one, Frances!"

"Well, maybe *I don't, Gilbert!*"

"Frances, what's that supposed to mean? Here I've been torn up inside over you for months over that letter I thought you'd written me. You've been on my mind every minute of the day since *before* my rocket took off. But just because Anne's here you think I'm all twitterpated over her, and it just ain't so!"

"I've thought of you every minute of the day too, Gilbert. So much so that I left everyone behind I've ever known to find you. And yet, when I finally find you, you're doubled over, hovering atop the very girl in that photograph! Faked or not, there you were. And on top of it all—"

Gilbert stood quietly as she paused. "What?" he said. "What else, Frances?" His voice, though still quiet, sounded loud and hollow in the deserted building.

Belloc looked at the closed door behind him. "Shouldn't we, ah..."

"No, Mister Belloc," Anne said primly, her eyes focused intently on an invisible spot on the horizon as far away from the hangar door as possible, "We most certainly should *not*, 'ah'. Not in the least."

"Fortescue is dead, Gilbert!" said Frances, "and so is Jimmy! Jimmy wasn't a dear friend or anything, but . . . but I'd gotten to know him. And now he's *dead*! And Fortescue—"

"I thought you hated him."

"I did! But, well, even though he was a horrid, cretinous lout, he was always there. He was a part of my life since our childhoods and now he's *gone*."

"I thought you'd be happy about that."

"I'm—well, relieved, perhaps? But it's a different kind of relief. I'd rather Fortescue had turned his attentions elsewhere, not been eaten by a giant worm! I've never seen another person *die*, Gilbert! Much less someone who played such a large part in my life as he did, however unwelcome the part may have been."

She sat on a nearby bench and began to cry softly. Gilbert stood behind her and put his hands on her shoulders. "I'm sorry, Frances," he said in a gentle voice. "I get it. Losing someone you don't care for is still a loss. It's like getting a tooth pulled. Even if the tooth was hurting you, you still feel the sting when it's pulled out and there's a gap when it's gone. I keep forgetting you were on holiday when the Tripods first hit England. You didn't return from that vacation in France until things were rebuilt and cleaned up. You've never had to face death before, or had someone taken from you."

Frances put her hand on one of his. "What do I do, Gilbert? Hilaire was wise to put me as a lookout. I'm useless doing anything else right now."

"Well, my dear lady, I can think of two things. First, you're British. And the Brits are famous for more than tea. You folks keep a stiff upper lip when things go bad. I don't know how good the tea is out here, but I *do* know a British gal who's got enough spunk and pluck she can jump on a rocket without hesitation when there's something in the sky that she's after. Plus, have you taken up boxing? I've been meaning to ask about those leather straps on your knuckles."

"A long story for another day, dear Gilbert. You said there were two things. What was the second?"

She called me dear! Gilbert thought. *I'm making progress!* "Frances, The second thing is this: When I feel overwhelmed about those who've passed on, for people I saw who died in London, Richmond, or even just Father Brown, I say a little prayer for them, then I do what I need to do. I do just what I'd want *them* to do if I was dead."

"How?"

Gilbert reflected for just a second on the latest irony in his life. He'd met Fortescue Williamson when the spoiled brat had tried to have Gilbert and Herb beaten by hired thugs, all in an effort to make Gilbert give up his relationship with Frances. Gilbert had responded by freeing himself and nearly disfiguring Williamson with an electric rod. Back then his hatred for the wealthy, amoral child-man burned white hot and knew nearly no bounds. But now? Now Gilbert was teaching Frances how to pray for the fool's soul. Life was strange—stranger than fiction, sometimes.

"It goes like this," he said, having her repeat each line as he spoke it:

> *'Eternal rest, grant unto him, O Lord,*
> *May your perpetual light shine upon him,*
> *may he rest in peace.*
> *May his soul and the souls of all the faithful departed,*
> *through the mercy of God,*
> *rest in peace,*
> *Amen.'*

"You say that every time you think of Father Brown?"

"Most times. Also, whenever I pass a graveyard. I like to think one of those folks will think of me when I need help, if I happen to be the one who prays them into Heaven."

Frances smiled. "Stiff upper lip, then? And prayer?"

Gilbert picked up the top hat that she'd dropped on the floor, then spun it by the brim a few times on his fingers. "Those two things've been getting British subjects through tough times since Augustine came to Kent. Here, take your hat. It's a bit battered, but it still has a kind of draggle-tail elegance about it. You make it look good. Are you hungry?"

Frances nodded, placing her hat firmly back on her head. "Then I'm going to get dinner," he shouted as he ran to the exit, blowing her a kiss before he ran through the door.

When he was gone and she was alone, Frances sat and thought a while. Nearly five minutes, in fact. When tears came, she let them flow freely for five minutes more. After she was done, she mounted the stairs at the side wall of the hangar to the top of the building.

"Stiff upper lip," she said as she climbed, then said the lines of the prayer Gilbert had taught her, as best she could remember them. Though a good student by nature, the stress of the day had made it difficult and she didn't recall it well past the first few lines. She kept trying to get it right, gazing out the paneled glass in the lookout station as she spoke.

A grinning, goggled face appeared in the windowpane in front of her, stopping her speech in surprise. Then a gloved hand grabbed her mouth from behind, stifling her scream.

Chapter 56

*"...the truth is that the difficulty of all the creeds of the earth
is not...that they agree in meaning, but differ in machinery. It
is exactly the opposite. They agree in machinery; almost every
great religion on earth works with the same external methods,
with priests, scriptures, altars, sworn brotherhoods, special
feasts.*
*... what they differ about is the thing to be taught... Creeds that
exist to destroy each other both have scriptures, just as armies
that exist to destroy each other both have guns."*

–Orthodoxy

When Beatrice saw the Doctor's body suddenly re-animated after
its death, she'd felt more afraid than she'd ever felt in the twenty-
three years of her young life. Once he'd left the room, she'd waited a good
fifteen minutes before even peeking out from behind the curtain under
the operation table.

It took only a second to spot Doctor Moreau's stiffening corpse. The
surprised expression on his face coupled with the impossibly twisted
angle of his head and neck made her duck back in fear and hide for
another fifteen minutes.

And then, once she had calmed down, she started to think of options.

"If you assume every problem has a solution," a kind teacher had once
said to her, "then you're far more likely to find it."

She hadn't really looked much at her surroundings when she'd first
arrived. But ever since the Doctor's last visit to her cell, her senses had all
been in a state of high alert. She thought about her mad run through the
lost city from her apartment to this twisted, evil excuse for a labratory. As
she calmed, she recalled small details of the place as she'd moved through
it. She'd smelled onions—food cooking had been in one corner—and
heard the sounds of rocks breaking in another.

More important, she remembered her eyes stinging from the fumes of detergent around the corner from the vivisection lab. Beatrice had cleaned enough houses and loads of laundry to know that detergent meant *clothes*.

Here, clothes likely meant *uniforms*.

And uniforms meant *camouflage* and the chance to escape.

Yes, she said to herself, *the odds are terribly against me finding, getting onto, and escaping in a transport. But I can't just wait to be captured. Cecil may return, and yet he may not. I'll just have to risk it, come what may.*

Breathing deeply, she emerged from her hiding place. Dr. Moreau's warped body still lay on the ground gazing at nothing. The sight made her wince, and she was reluctant to step over or around it.

Still, she thought, *I am a Canadian. Canadians are British at heart, and the British are famous for their stiff upper lips.* Setting her mouth firmly, she edged around Moreau's body and left the lab. Carefully peeking around a corner and making sure the way was clear, she crept forward in the dimming afternoon light.

Odd, she thought. Despite a prisoner (herself) having escaped, a shot being fired, and the Doctor walking about like a badly driven marionette, there weren't any visibly watchful eyes around the compound. She didn't see a single guard face-to-face, all the way to what she believed was the laundry. The only visible guards were at a distance, staring off into the desert from a high vantage point or having conversations with each other in low tones about football or somesuch.

Her instincts paid off, and her plan to steal a uniform even more so. She not only had correctly identified the compound's laundry, but seconds after entering through its open-arched doorway she saw it was devoid of people, and had several racks full of the simple uniforms the guards all sported.

Using quick fingers and quicker thoughts, she assembled the pieces of a guard's attire. When she finished dressing it wasn't a perfect fit, but it would likely do.

She also palmed a pair of scissors, and in a few more minutes she shed most of her blond locks of hair and more than a few silent tears. When finished she was shorn enough that she could pass for a boy, and jamming the pillbox cap down hard enough on her head hid most of her face from would-be prying eyes.

Cecil, she thought as she examined her work in the free-hanging mirror, the tears still drying on her face, *I may not be as devious as you. I can't leap rooftops or send my adversaries into self-destructive rages. But it would appear I can succeed in the game of subterfuge quite handily, thank you.*

She looked in the mirror one last time, pulled down her hat brim, and swept her cuttings into the trash.

****

Gilbert, Belloc and Anne split up to look for supplies. After crossing a couple of streets, Gilbert found himself facing the town's second largest building. As he pushed on the door he heard a scuffling sound behind him in the street. Whipping around, though, he only saw what passed for tumbleweed among the local flora.

Sighing with relief, Gilbert tried to turn the knob. With a little force it popped open easily and he walked into the building, a place which he'd correctly guessed was the company store.

The smell of sawdust, stale air and rotting garbage assaulted his nostrils, bringing back a host of unhappy memories of the time he'd spent living in the London Rookery. The poorest part of London, it had stunk of trash and human waste during the day and cheap beer and vomit each night as poor workers tried to escape the pain of their crushing, fourteen-hour workdays.

Pain.

The word seized him with surprising force. Much of his life had been marked by pain, but he'd kept those memories from wrecking him by focusing on the happiness he'd experienced as well.

Still, he knew he had a job to do first. Thankfully that job took him all of about ten minutes, as there wasn't much in the way of provisions here in the store. Gilbert suspected the workers were fed from large cafeterias in the mines. He'd seen things like that in England where a cart or permanent underground cook room had served workers in an effort to squeeze more productivity out of them.

Well, no matter! Behind the bar he found a package of salted beef, a block of cheese, and a few jugs that smelled of sour beer. Gilbert piled them all on the table. If Belloc managed to rustle up a skiff, this meager feast would only have to feed the four of them for a day or two instead of the couple of weeks a walk would have taken.

He was just about to take a short break and peek at the desert outside when he spied the bottle marked "Cola" near the end of the bar.

Surprised that such a luxury would be found so far from Earth, and in such a poor town at that, he drew closer. *Hooray*! Fortuna's wheel was spinning upward! There was even a small bottle of vanilla flavoring next to the cola bottle.

Well, why not? What difference would five, or even ten minutes make, in the end? The fate of the world wasn't at stake as far as he knew. True, Gilbert felt a little odd taking things without permission, but they were already taking supplies, so why not a swallow of cola?

Gilbert emptied the small cola bottle into a tall glass. He then squirted a bit of the vanilla flavoring into it, stirred it with his finger and took a seat at an empty table. As he sipped his treat, he thought about his life for a few minutes—where he'd been, what he could hope for in the future. Things were still a bit tense between him and Frances, but if she'd taken a rocket for several months to chase after him, that was something positive, wasn't it? Still, she seemed to have . . . changed, somehow. Not necessarily for the worse. Maybe it was her top hat, or the leather boxing straps on her knuckles. Or the assertive way she'd commanded the situation when she'd walked in on him and Anne at the bottom of the Martian temple-hospital.

"So, what comes next?" Gilbert said to his transparent reflection in the glass, twisted by the glass's curve. His voice sounded very loud in the empty air. Anne, he knew, was exciting. But Frances was, well, *real*. He'd *talked* with Frances, both in letters and speech, for over a year now, even before he'd left Earth. They'd discussed everything from history to family to religion and their futures together. He knew Frances' facial expressions and nuances, her handwriting, her favorite composers and writers. He knew what things in life made her happy, sad, moody, and ecstatic.

But he had to be honest with himself: he could count on the fingers of one hand the number of actual conversations he'd had with Anne.

Anne was exciting, true. Technically she'd been his first kiss. And she saved his life, likely more than once. But did he know, truly *know* her, like he did Frances? Did he know if Anne would be a good wife? Or a good mother? Besides (and this made him wince), the kiss they'd shared had been more used to distract him than an actual expression of love or emotional bonding.

But, on the other hand, if she'd saved his life, didn't that prove *she* loved him?

But, on the other hand, could a love borne of a stressful situation be trusted? Would a love like that still be there once life calmed down?

And, most important, should you marry someone just because *they* loved *you*? Did he truly love *either* of them? Could he know that now? If he didn't, would that be fair to Frances? Or to Anne? "Not really," he said to himself, rubbing his eyes. "What happens next?"

"Next, you take a little jaunt with me, old bean," said a familiar voice behind Gilbert.

Before the sentence was finished, Gilbert had spit out his drink, dropped his glass with a crash, grabbed the empty cola bottle, jumped up and whipped around, brandishing the bottle like a small club.

Herb stood at the open door.

Herb had always been slim, but now Herb looked even thinner than Gilbert remembered. "Rail-thin" was what old farmer McGinty would have called Herb back in Minnesota. Herb's black longcoat and dark-tinted goggles tilted up on his forehead worsened the gaunt effect. The sun blazed behind him, but in a second or two Gilbert's eyes adjusted and Gilbert could see the shadowy outlines of several more men behind Herb, all of whom were outside beyond the open door.

Stay calm, Gilbert thought. Herb was the kind of person who played to win. He wouldn't have shown himself unless he was already certain of victory.

And that meant Gilbert had to be very, very careful of his next move, because chances were Herb already had plans in advance for anything Gilbert could think of.

Not to mention the last time they met, Herb's idea of helping Gilbert had been to shoot him in the chest.

Herb pushed through the creaking door and walked over to Gilbert's table, his silhouetted entourage staying outside. As he approached Gilbert, Herb's steps were relaxed, but perfectly timed and measured.

"Is this seat taken, Gil? Hmm? Well, I'll just take it anyway." Herb sat in the vacant chair opposite Gilbert. The silence hung in the air for a very uncomfortable few seconds.

"I do hope you're not still upset over that little incident in Richmond, Gil."

"Herb, you shot me," Gilbert said, still standing with his bottle at the ready.

"I was trying to help you."

"Then you tossed me Anne's hand."

"I *could* make a terrible pun here, of course. Look, Gil, I was *trying* to *help*."

"You couldn't have come up with something better than putting holes in me?"

"Gil, I'd just fallen."

"You can say that again."

"I *mean* I'd fallen out of the *city*. Remember? The city that floated in the air, where you helped start a revolution? Margaret was watching me, little bits of sky dropping on people's heads, people running about everywhere, screaming. I was under a bit of pressure, and people rarely make the best choices under that kind of situation. I'd hoped *you'd* understand."

Gilbert looked back at the door. His eyes were now adjusted, and he counted four large men in dirt-red uniforms with rifles in their hands and holstered knives at their belts. Winning an argument with Herb here might be satisfying, but it would serve no other real point.

"Sure," Gilbert said, still nodding warily. "You didn't hit anything important, and Anne's doing alright, considering. We can let bygones be bygones. But what happens now?"

"You come back with me to my new little place. I think you'll be very interested in the family members you'll meet there."

Gilbert tried not to react, but Herb picked up the small shot of scare that went through Gilbert's face. "You look scared, Gil, and I'm not surprised. I guess you already know about your siblings, then? Beatrice is quite a fetching young lady, but your little brother Cecil is quite a challenge for his handlers. Was it the Doctor who told you? I thought as much. It makes sense. He's been acting quite erratically as of late. Soon we'll likely remove him—"

"With all available speed," Gilbert finished. "Herb," Gilbert continued, "doesn't it bother you just a bit that you're talking, even *dressing* like the Doctor now? Has it occurred to you that if someone like the Doctor is going to get himself 'removed,' then it's only a matter of time before the same thing happens to you, too?"

Herb smiled. "After tonight, every agent will be a king, and every member of the Circle will be a god. No one need be removed, Gil. We'll have an ordered, tidy pair of worlds here, and there'll be no further need for 'removing' anyone. All will be equal, want for nothing. All under me will receive justice, dignity, and a clear sense of self-worth from the gifts I'll dispense."

"Do you really believe that? Dying old men with an appetite for power don't usually share it, Herb. Not with their servants, anyway. They're more prone to squashing anyone who gets in their way or annoys them."

"How right you are, Gil old boy. So it's best I don't annoy them by being tardy, *hmm*? Let's be off," Herb said, standing and walking to the door without bothering to look back at Gilbert.

Gilbert looked at Herb's back, then through the shop windows at the burly, goggled guards at the door. All four of them had rifles in their hands, and they watched Gilbert closely.

Sighing, Gilbert rose and followed. Once outside the sun blinded him for a second, and he saw Frances, Hilaire, and Anne kneeling on the ground with their hands bound in front of them about a hundred yards away, on the other side of the small outpost town.

No wonder he managed to sneak up on us, Gilbert thought. The skiffs were known for being silent in the red sands, and the red sand in the town streets must have muffled the footsteps of Herb and his goons until they'd been at the bar/store.

Blast.

****

1914 A. D.
MARS. THE TOP OF THE TOWER TEMPLE.

As the savage Tharks ran screaming from their latest attempt to attack, Father Flambeau and Anne looked at Gilbert and the pile of rocks at his feet with a newfound degree of wonder and respect. "Nice trick, Gilles," said Father Flambeau. "Now can you magic us up a floater? Or perhaps an ornithopter? Or perhaps you have a magic carpet in your pocket that'll take us back to Syrtis Major?"

"I'd be deliriously happy at this point if he could get us to Danton's Folly with a fingersnap, as easily as he made that boulder collapse into powder." Anne said. "Where'd you learn that little parlor trick anyway, Gilbert?"

"A long time back, Aldonza the Magnificent graduated from juggling on

street corners to vaudeville on stage. She stepped up her game, which meant she had more to barter with when she needed me to help her out of a tight spot, or free publicity in an article for the Times. So, she taught me a few tricks like that one when I had a sudden need to impress someone."

"But Gilles, to make a rock split open with a touch of your finger? How did you ever? How could it be done? And why that instead of your new toy?"

"I realized this nifty little pistol we picked up in the cell could take out half-a-dozen of the greenskins in one shot, but there were at least four times that number rushing us. A parlor trick like that impressed them all at once, and sent them running. As to how I did it? The trick is told when the trick is sold, old friend. That's what Aldonza always used to say. I wish I could do it again and get us out of here, but the misdirection and preparation involved is—well, let's just say I owe a lot of thanks to Saint Genesius. A lot of things went right back there that didn't need to, or usually wouldn't."

"Well and good," said Anne, "but even though our gracious hosts have been scared back down the stairway we used to run up here, I'd guess we've only an hour at most to make our escape before the Warhoon chieftain gathers enough courage and reinforcements to make another go at us."

"An hour is what it usually takes," Father Flambeau said. "Enough time for...a...oh, mere..."

The priest had been walking across the large room's stone floor, yet when he passed the center he stopped and wavered, as if in a daze.

Gilbert and Anne both ran to Father Flambeau, steadying him and helping him sit down slowly.

"Gilbert," Anne whispered, her voice small in the near darkness, "I've just realized something. Do you know where we..."

"Yes, yes I do. It just occurred to me. Here, look." He ran his hand across the floor. "I didn't recognize it with the roof blown off and opened to the stars, the way it is now. But, see, run your hand along here and you can feel the etchings in the floor. You can even..." he stopped. Anne was beside him, her pinky finger resting gently against his.

"Er, yes," he finished. "Well, I think I can shed a little light on this situation, but I can only make a little flash and poof with the powder in my pocket that Aldonza gave me."

"I can do that," she said. In a second, Gilbert heard her slide something out of her boot. A strike on the floor, and the room bloomed into a soft, red light from a tiny flare in her hand the size of a cigarette.

"*Much improved over silver nitrate,*" Gilbert said.

Anne smiled. "*Hopefully you won't have to use this to burn a wound closed on me this time.*"

"*What...what is this?*" said Flambeau, looking around.

All three of them could clearly see that the room they were in was the ancient, broken high auditorium of the Martian Temple of the Red Men of Mars. It had been a victim of neglect or other occupying races, and the roof had long since either caved in or been blown away bit by bit. It had been one of these broken roof pieces that had been broken in two by Gilbert's magic trick a few minutes before, which had scared their captors away.

The stars and both moons hung in the sky, looking down on them with infinite patience.

And on the floor, a bit ragged from the wear of two decades, was the still unmistakably etched outline of a five-pointed star.

And Father Flambeau had walked through the pentagon at the center of the pentagram, right before he'd felt faint.

"*It's here,*" Father said. "*We all thought it was further away, but the Warhoons have brought us to it. It's here.*"

Gilbert looked at Anne. "*I have something to tell you,*" he said.

"*Yes, Gilbert.*"

"*It's about Frances. You see, the truth of the matter is . . .*" he paused, searching for words.

"*Yes, Gilbert?*"

"*The truth is...my brother, Cecil. He didn't die in the War. He was only eighteen when it stopped. He died in Verdun, but from a heart attack a few years ago while he was on a book tour, promoting his latest histories there. I wanted to tell you more, but you seemed upset and agitated.*"

"*I—I see. Gilbert, is there...anything else you wish to make me aware of?*"

"*Frances has been dead for over a year now,*" he blurted out. "*I've no doubt she's in Heaven, for she died the afternoon after a morning Mass and Confession, at the hands of bloodthirsty thugs at the end of the Mexican civil war.*"

"*Yes, Gilbert.*"

"*No, not that. I mean, well, first things first. Please, please believe me when I say that I didn't mean to deceive you. I truly did not.*"

"*I know, Gilbert.*"

"*Blast it, Anne! Don't you see? You should be angry with me, and you aren't! Frances died because they pointed a gun at her, and she said 'Viva Chirsto Rey,' which meant 'Long Live Christ the King,' and they hated that, because men who abolish God from government won't stand for any god but their own government. Do you see? They shot her. And—they did it in the name of human rights and dignity, of all things! She went to save them, and they shot her. Men who thought that killing the Church would somehow be good for humanity. And Catholics who believe someone who dies like that, they . . .*"

"'*I am not the God of the dead, but of the living.*'" Anne said, a hint of sadness as she quoted the Bible verse. "Yes, Gilbert. I know. My late husband was a devout Anglican. Read the Bible aloud every night."

"*Anne, you're . . . you're not angry? Truly?*"

"Gilbert, I can read you like one of your books. You might as well be a street sign in broad daylight, written with large, black letters on a broad white background. You know I loved you. I even fought her for you; one of only two women I ever fought in my life. And to keep me from being distracted on our journey, you had to keep me focused."

"*Well, I . . . you know Anne, I . . . wait, wait just a minute!*"

"Yes, Gilbert?"

"*You fought* Frances?"

****

"How much longer?" Cecil asked over the roar of the engines.

"No more than another hour and a half," Carter said with a jovial air. "Now do you see why they can't eat or drink a full two hours before we board? Are you itching for a fight, lad?"

"No. I just don't need another leg cramp before I get there."

****

James Effortson the Fourth sat in his ornate chair in his plush banker's office and looked impatiently at his watch. Almost time to go.

He wished for the millionth time or so that the client, identified in their ledgers only as a series of numbers, wasn't so lucrative.

But the client *was* lucrative, and so insanely rich that the fee made up about a third of the firm's annual income. As a result, anything the client wanted, the client got. And one thing the client wanted was for Effortson to wait every Friday until seven o'clock to receive a call from the client

426

over the Edison telephonic device.

Staying in the office late on a Friday when he'd rather be enjoying one of the few comforts available in Syrtis Major was not a terrible chore, but still an annoyance—like a pebble in his shoe. He wished he could foist this one duty onto an underling, but the terms were very specific . . .

There! The telephonic. Effortson picked it up before it had finished its first ring. "Archibald is my brother," said the raspy voice on the other end. It had begun speaking as soon as Effortson had raised the receiver.

"Very good sir," Effortson began. But as always, the line was dead before he could finish the sentence. No matter. His leisure time had officially begun, and it would not officially end until Monday morning. As he stood to put on his round-topped bowler hat, his eyes fell on the small drawer in the upper right hand corner of his desk.

In a strange way, he felt the drawer was watching him, like the closed eye of a dragon pretending to be asleep. He shuddered, adjusted his hat, and left his office, hoping the day would never come when he had to open that drawer and post the dark-papered envelope inside.

****

Beatrice strode through the area with a bearing she hoped appeared manly enough. Though raised on a farm, her mother had nonetheless taught her by word and example how to move like a lady until it had become near habitual, and acting like a man did not come easily to her. Fortunately, she did find that walking with a confident heel-toe stride seemed to work. The shapeless gray coveralls hid her womanly figure neck to wrist to ankle, her shorn hair kept away any attention that might once have been paid to her beautiful, blond locks, and she'd found a set of tinted brass goggles in one of the uniform's pockets that she hoped would distract any unfriendly eyes from her girlish face.

So far, it seemed to be working. She'd steered clear of the men when she could. But the few times she'd had someone walk close by, they'd been too busy to take close notice. Dressed as a low-ranked employee, everyone treated her as a piece of furniture. And as long as she'd kept reminding herself that her hair would grow back, she was fine.

Now all she had to do was keep looking like she belonged here, and eventually she'd find the hangar where they kept the large ornithopters and the sand skiffs. After that freedom was practically hers, she told herself. How hard could it be? After all, if her little brother got clean away, then—

"You! Trooper!" yelled a voice above her. "Yes, you!"

Beatrice looked up, careful to keep her face blank and expressionless. "Yes, sir!" she said in her deepest voice.

It didn't sound deep to her at all, but the man above seemed in too great a hurry to care. "Get your worthless hide up to the temple floor, *now*! I don't care where you've been posted! I need a replacement for a fool of a guard who just disabled himself by juggling his lunch and a bayonet, and *you're* it! Now *move*! Go! Go! Go!"

Beatrice began a salute, but her new commander had already run off to shout at someone else. Perhaps now that he was gone she could run off and—

The loud commander appeared again. "What're you waiting for?" he shouted, "Judgment Day? Get moving, or you'll be feeding sloats with one hand and shoveling their refuse with the other for a month! Move!"

Beatrice ran. She was running before the commander had even finished his sentence. Unused to being yelled at, she had to stifle tears as she ran toward her new destination.

Fine, she thought. *I'll just do this last duty, and then* slink off. *The sun is nearing the horizon. It'll be dark soon. Everyone's so busy I doubt I'll be noticed missing for at least a day. Security here isn't terribly tight, since this place wasn't designed to be a prison. Cecil said it's more of a laboratory of some kind. It'll be dark soon, and when this little bit of to-do is finished, I'll slip away all the easier afterward.*

But as she ran, she felt her rifle chuffing against her back, and the trooper knife slapping against her leg as it swung on her belt. She wondered if she could use it if it became necessary.

****

"How long 'til we get there?" Gilbert asked, shouting over the loud droning hum of the ornithopter's flapping wings above them. The huge craft had landed after Herb had fired a flare into the sky, and their sand-sloops had been left abandoned as the entire crew climbed into the sizable airborne craft.

"Another quarter hour at most, Gil," Herb shouted back, his eyes still hidden behind the brass-rimmed goggles with the dark lenses. "What's your hurry, anyway? I thought you Yanks didn't care if you missed afternoon tea?"

"I'm just wondering how much longer I have to listen to that annoying engine out there," Gilbert yelled back. "It's almost as bad as hearing you back on Earth when you tried to talk your way out of all the trouble you'd get us into!"

Herb raised his goggles. His pupils were large, black, and deep. "Oh, really?" he said. His eyes were animated in a way Gilbert had learned both to delight in and fear when they were best friends back on Earth. "And how many times did I get you out of trouble, old chum? Remember who distracted your girlfriend's gorilla squad in the sky palace, while you went off on your first dance?"

"I remember, Herb."

Herb was about to speak, but then he paused. He stood shakily, walked to the other side of the passenger compartment of the 'thopter, and closed the door which opened to the outside. The space was quieter now, the loud engines reduced to a dull, constant hum. Herb sat back down and continued. "How about telling me just who managed to get you two," he pointed to Gilbert and Frances, "to meet up in the first place, back in Paris after the alien invasion? You, Frances, and that little blond friend of yours?"

"Madeline," said Frances.

"Yes, whatever her name was. If it weren't for me, you two wouldn't have even met."

"Herb, old buddy, you're getting a little defensive there, don't you think?"

"Herbert," Frances said, "whatever has happened to you? Even after you shot poor Gilbert here, he's never said an unkind word about you. Not once. How can you do this to someone who was your best friend?"

Herb paused. "I damned myself," he said simply, leaning back and putting his goggles back on. "In a moment of anger and foolishness, I destroyed any chance of redemption."

"What?" Frances said, "That's perhaps the silliest things I've ever heard! And *I* live in a houseful of girls! Gilbert, didn't you tell him there's nothing that bars you from Heaven? That you can— what's that thing you Catholics say to the priest?"

"Confession," said Gilbert, "and Penance. I learned about them in Catechism classes. The ones Herb was *supposed* to—"

"Penance," Herb sneered. His voice was bored, but his body language was suddenly agitated. "What's that, except for a lot more Catholic mumbo-jumbo?"

"When my room was untidy as a child," Belloc said, speaking up for the first time, "my father stormed in on me. Not only had I left clothes and toys about, but I'd gotten carried away painting the walls and melting several of my tin soldiers as prisoners of war. They were making nice, smoking holes in the wood of the floor.

"My father's voice roared like thunder through the room, and in an instant I looked about and saw what I'd done, how much damage I'd wrought to my room in such a short time. Remembering our parish priest's homily on the Prodigal Son, I fell on my knees and begged for forgiveness."

"Did it work?" asked Herb.

"Yes, but I still had to spend the day cleaning the mess. And that's what penance is: cleaning the mess after you've been forgiven, and spared the striping on your back you so richly deserve. Greater love hath no man, than he who gives his life for his friends. That's why penance works, Herbert. Someone gave His life to make it so."

The little group was quiet for a moment in the large flying craft, whose engines had become muted when they'd flown into a canyon. "Approaching base, Cleaner," said the pilot from his chair in front.

"Cleaner," Gilbert said. "So, they gave you a new name and everything, huh? Do you get to say Archibald is your brother, too?"

"Archibald Campbell was the name of a member of the inner circle who tried and failed to leave the group," Herb snapped. "Member of Parliament, scientist, a baron no less. Came to the Circle's notice through the Masons. But he forgot who he was and who he was dealing with. Agents now use his name as a password to remind themselves and each other that however high up the ladder we climb, a humiliating death is only one failure away."

"Awful place to work," said Belloc. "Makes the military look like a seminary. How's the retirement plan? A little villa in the Alps? A pension with a quiet apartment along the Seine? Or, perhaps, buried without ceremony in an unmarked grave with worms as your only mourners?"

"We're here," Herb said. Gilbert, Belloc, Anne, and Frances craned their necks to see out the windows of the craft, even though their hands were still bound.

Outside, Gilbert saw the base growing closer. It was a large, castle-like structure in the middle of the desert, all made of red stone. There were five towers connected by walls, bridges, ropes, and cables, all surrounding a central tower twice as tall and thick as the others around it. As they drew closer, Gilbert could see the towers were weathered and worn, though still sturdy enough to last for many more thousands of years if need be.

"What was that place?" Gilbert asked. As they neared it, they could see it was larger than they initially thought. At a distance it seemed no larger than a small building. But now they were close enough to see small silhouettes of people walking around in it.

"Many things," Herb drawled. "A fortress, a temple, a monastery, and an observatory. It was built when that desert below us was still seashore. Now, though, it'll be used as a beachhead of a different sort. One to conquer a world, then a solar system, then beyond."

"So they were serious," Anne said, her voice barely audible over the ornithopter's engines as they touched down. "They're really going to try and do it. They're going to try and capture Barsoom."

"So, you figured it out, then?" Herb said, giving a few claps of his hands in mock applause.

"Herb, are you people serious?" Gilbert said. "All this for a ghost? How are you even thinking this'll be possible?"

"Wot, you think you can just leave a carrot in a bottle or something and trap it?"

"No, Gilbert," Anne said, looking at the tower. "They're going to use that disk I gave you back in Germany to try and trap the soul of Mars itself, and then bend it to their own twisted wills."

"You've no idea of the power of my masters," Herb said, "or the depth of their motives."

"Barsoom," said Belloc. "It took a while for me to remember, but I do now. A provincial governor who went native with a red wife told me the story. Think you can trap something like that with parlor tricks, mate? You'd have an easier time trying to catch a tornado with a windmill. If you try you get shredded to atoms and scattered."

"Herb," said Gilbert as the ornithopter touched down, "please, tell me Anne and Belloc are wrong about this. You've hitched your wagon to a bunch of fellas who are going to try and trap Barsoom? *Barsoom*? I've heard what the Martians say about him! Barsoom destroyed most of Mars with a *thought*! Your people think they can hogtie him with some mumbled spells and incantations?"

"Not a *few* incantations, Gil. All of them. Recorded onto tiny circular punchcards, and played at such a high rate of speed that it can contain and speak every spell in human history that's been used to summon and bind a spirit to the will of man. Mathematically speaking, the right spell *has* to be in there, somewhere. And before you try to turn me against them, Gil, remember: The Circle today already runs *our* world with the might of the British Empire. Now they'll expand their territory to *this* world as well. Barsoom will make this world bloom again, and it will become the *next* Earth. In time the Empire will move through, then *keep* growing. To the edge of and then past our solar system. Imagine an empire expanding for the rest of eternity, and with us at the helm."

"But what happens when the empire falls, Herb? All empires do, eventually. You *know* that, Herb! You've studied enough history to know it's true! Empires get tired after a certain point. And when the empire falls, who runs the show then? It's not like the British monarchy *or* your masters are going to live forever! They won't be around long enough to see all these ambition be realized!"

"They're working on that, too," Herb said quietly as they rose, prodded by the guards and small bayonets.

"Herb," said Gilbert, as they were led away and Herb stayed in his seat, "Herb, listen to me! You haven't seen the ruins, have you? The underground city, or what's left of it! The squids tried something like this, and it made Barsoom wipe out most of Mars to protect the rest of the planets! Herb, the Circle, whoever they are, they don't get it! With a plan like this, Barsoom may have to destroy the *rest* of life here! You've gotta stop them! Herb! Herb!"

Gilbert's voice suddenly stopped with a thud as one of the guards smacked him in the back of the head with the butt of his rifle.

Gilbert yelped in pain and surprise and went down to the floor of the ornithopter. Belloc glared at the guards but didn't move, keeping his eyes on the half-dozen steam rifles their captors carried.

Each of the women dropped to one knee on either side of him, saying his name. They suddenly stopped, staring at one another.

Gilbert came to quickly and saw both Anne and Frances kneeling over him—they'd both kneeled to help him, but had stopped; their eyes appeared to be locked on each other in a steady battle of wills. "Um, ladies?" he said, struggling to speak even though it felt like the back of his head had been blown out with a stick of dynamite. "I'm, well, I'm going to—look out!"

The guards had already raised their rifle butts again, this time to hit the girls. Gilbert saw Belloc raise his thick-soled army boot to slam down on the foot of the guard behind him when—

"Enough!"

Herb's voice boomed. "Take them to the temple," he said, "without incident."

"Yes, Cleaner," said the biggest of the guard as he pulled Gilbert roughly to his feet. Two other guards pulled up Frances and Anne as well.

"Guard," said Herb, still looking away, "If anything happens to the prisoners, especially the women, I'll see you answer for it." Gilbert couldn't help but notice the disappointed looks on the faces of the biggest guard and several of his underlings. But with a quick look from their leader, the guards hustled the little group out of the aircraft and over towards the large, central tower.

Herb, still sitting in his seat in the ornithopter, waited until they were safely out of earshot before he spoke again.

"You," he said to the pilot as he began leaving through the cockpit's side door.

"Yes, Cleaner," the pilot said with a deep sigh while closing his eyes.

"Before you leave to get drunk, you will show me the basics of how to start, take off, and steer this vessel."

"Yes, Cleaner, sir," said the pilot.

Always, the pilot thought. Always, the younger agents wanted to feel godlike by learning how to fly. "This," said the pilot with a voice and routine he'd used several times before, "is the throttle..."

****

Wiggins sat in the basement of his London house and looked at the scrap of paper in his hands. He'd spent his time since the Martian invasion creating an information network of pneumatic tubes and informants so vast, so very nearly perfect in its scope and breadth of influence and knowledge that he'd made a better living for himself than any member of his family's historical line. Still, intellect alone had not been completely responsible for his success. Though not yet twenty, Wiggins had learned to trust his instincts when they began waving their imaginary antennae in his mind.

They were waving now, wiggling with huge red flags of danger. The paper in front of him confirmed what other papers in similar handwritings had hinted at for the better part of a year.

And it was something that made his blood run cold each time he looked at it.

It spoke of War. Doubleyew-ay-are, War.

Not just conflict. Not a series of battles in a local place like the Crimean, or Tasmania.

War.

The kind that could be triggered by the paper scrap in front of him.

Wiggins had learned long ago what a dead-man's switch was. In such a construct, a man holds a lever. Releasing it causes untold destruction to something important. Ergo, it was important to keep the man holding the switch happy, content, and above all, *alive* so the switch would not be released.

After tracing the paper's origin and then its destination, Wiggins had no doubt that he held a dead-man's switch, one whose progress even he couldn't stop.

The intercepted paper in his lap confirmed that for over a year now, powerful people had been receiving word from an obscure banker on Syrtis Major, the British colony on Mars.

The banker's unnamed and (so far) untraceable employer had made the unwitting banker into a living dead-man's switch.

The banker had a phrase of some kind, one Wiggins still hadn't been able to discover. Were he to fail in its regular delivery each week from Mars, various governments of lesser nations would be ordered to take actions. Actions that would lead first other small nations and then larger ones into...

War.

It meant war, and war on a more epic scale than ever witnessed before in human history, greater than the Martian invasion, which had only touched England. It wouldn't involve a country or two. Or five. Or ten.

A *world*-spanning War. Big enough to cause the death of a generation of men and reshape civilization and cultures into forms untold and unimagined.

He had to talk to the Prime Minister! The American President!

Someone! But how? How to get them to believe him?

He knew, deep down, that it would be useless. Worse than useless, really, since he could be busying himself setting up ways to profit in case the war ever came to pass.

But he couldn't.

He grabbed another paper and wrote swiftly across it, hoping that this time the twelve scribes from various firms whom he held under his sway would somehow get this message to the Prime Minister or a member of his cabinet.

Yes, it was *worse* than useless. It was outright dangerous, if it got into the wrong hands.

But Wiggins knew he had to try!

1914 A.D.
MARS. THE TOP OF THE TEMPLE TOWER.

"Roll that stone over here, Gilles!" said Flambeau, "it'll have to do."

"Can you do this on such short notice?" Anne asked.

"Mademoiselle, I have said mass on a battlefield at midnight, while bullets whizzed around me and the ground shook from American Steam Lincolns and German Eisensoldats. *I can say Mass if a few Warhoons are banging on the door outside."*

As if on cue, a loud crunch sounded from the heavy wooden door. A piece of it the size of a man's head fell inwards, revealing the green, tusked head of a Warhoon behind it.

"Speaking of which," Anne said, reaching into a fold of her skirt, she pulled out a small glass vial with a white substance inside it.

"Anne, what's..." Gilbert's voice stopped as Anne tossed the vial at the door, narrowly missing Gilbert's ducked head and lobbing through the new hole in the door, where it exploded with a loud 'BANG!' and a cacophony of warhoon voices.

The screaming warhoons faded in volume soon after the noise erupted. Gilbert looked at Anne.

"Pure sodium," she said. "Easy to hide, and makes a decent distraction with a surprisingly small amount of material."

"Not bad," Gilbert answered, "but have you tried . . ."

"If you two could stop bonding for a moment," Father Flambeau said as he tossed a small folded cloth from his pocket onto the boulder, his voice just

a tad on edge, "we have an hour's work and perhaps ten minutes at most in which to accomplish it."

"Bonding? But . . . Of course, Father," Gilbert said, standing dutifully in front of the improvised altar. He looked over his shoulder at Anne standing several feet away.

Gilbert extended his hand. "Anne," he said, "Will you . . . ?"

****

1892 A.D.

THE TEMPLE TOWER, LOWER LEVELS

"Well, I've been in worse places," Anne said, looking over the walls, trying to find an exit from the cell she and Frances had been locked into.

"I'm glad *you're* so optimistic," Frances said. "Now, could you please use that wonderful secret-agent expertise I've heard so much about and help me find a way out of here?"

"Frances Blogg, why are you suddenly all thorns-and-prickles?"

"Since I learned you were no longer on the list of the dead or injured. Don't think I don't know you've still got a Gilbert-shaped arrow in your heart, my fire-headed friend! I've seen how you look at him when you think no one's looking at *you*."

"This again? Really, Frances. I thought such pettiness would be beneath one of your station. Hasn't Gilbert told you that the alleged photo of us was doctored? More doctored than a wealthy hypochondriac?"

"No, he didn't," Frances snapped, turning to face Anne with narrowed eyes. "And truth be told, it makes little difference to me. You could have your choice of men in two worlds, and I only want one, perfect, wonderful...well, you just keep your eyes in your head when he's around! I'm better for him anyway, and you know it!"

"Oh, I *do*, do I?" Anne said, her own eyes narrowing. "You might ask him yourself if he prefers girls like me who can fly into his life or the more earthbound type."

"When his world crashed to the ground last year, I didn't see *you* at his bedside in the hospital! But *I* was! *Me! And me alone!*"

"I *couldn't* be there, you silly little twit! I was in the hospital too, just down the hall from him! With my hand gone and half my face burned off!"

"Just down the hall? How on earth did you—?"

"I find things out, Frances. It's what I do. And have you ever wondered why a woman like me would fall for a farmboy like Gilbert, anyway? It's because he's just like me. He found himself alone in a terrible world in a terrible situation. And he's not only survived, but *thrived*. He's a survivor, Frances, like *me*. Drop either of us in a jungle, or a London slum, or a black tie party for a Prime Minister, and we'll make ourselves right at home. Unlike *some* upper-class twits I could name, who only love him because her daddy hates him!"

"That's not true!"

"Isn't it? Then maybe Gilbert is your *escape*! All you wealthy Brits have an intended from the moment of your conceptions, don't you? You girls all read your romance novels and long for a boy who can love something besides himself and his horses. But that's not going to happen for you if Daddy has his way, *is it*?"

"Stop it!"

"That fop who claimed you for his own, Frances? Fortescue? He may be dead, but men like your *daddy* always have a *second* plan, don't they? If you ever get back to Earth, then the next fop in line for your hand will be invited to a little dinner party. Gilbert shall be bought off or threatened, and then—"

"Be quiet!" Frances said between gritted teeth, leaning her head forward, her nose inches from Anne's. "My father can't make me marry anyone! And you just keep your hands off—" she looked down, then looked smug as she continued, "keep your *hand* off *my* man!"

Anne blinked, then glared at Frances through eyes that had become narrow as razor slits as she moved even closer. "It's not my *hands* you should be worried about when Gilbert is near," Anne hissed. She then puckered her lips and made the softest noise with them once, twice, and thrice.

Frances' face fell. "He didn't," she said, her voice a near whimper.

"Oh, no," Anne said, "he didn't kiss me, dear," she said, leaning even closer to her cellmate until there was less than an inch between them.

Frances' face relaxed.

"Oh, no. *I* kissed *him*!" Anne stepped back, closing her eyes as if lost in memory. "And it was the most wonder-filled five seconds of both of our—"

Frances' eyes flashed with anger again. Before Anne had finished the 'd' in the word 'kissed', Frances's eyes had flicked over Anne's head, hands and feet. Frances then she did something Anne hadn't been expecting at all . . .

Frances put her hands over her face and began to cry softly.

Anne waited for what seemed a long and very awkward pause while Frances sobbed. "Look, Frances," she said, approaching the dark-haired girl, "you've every right to be vexed with me, but blubbering is *not* going to help us out of this cell."

Frances said something incoherent under her breath and beneath her hands.

"What? What's that?" Anne said, exasperated. Why on earth had Gilbert ever fallen for a weepy, shallow little heiress like this?

"You . . ." mumbled Frances between sobs, "you should . . ."

"I should what? Really, Frances, I thought you tougher than this. I'm beginning to wonder what Gilbert sees in you."

"You shouldn't . . . shouldn't—"

"Oh, for the love of all that's holy, Frances!" Anne said, grabbing the other girl's shoulders from the front and shaking her, "pull yourself together, girl! Say what you have to say and be done with it!"

"You shouldn't say such things to me!" Frances said. Her voice sounded tired by sobs, her eyes red.

"And why ever not, hmm?" said Anne, still holding Frances's shoulders firmly and looking her straight in the eye like a determined schoolteacher. "Because you're from a rich and powerful family?"

"No," Frances said, her voice suddenly calm, and her eyes focused.

Oh, no, Anne thought. But she was too late and she knew it. Her own eyes grew wide with understanding, and she brought her arms up suddenly.

As Anne tried to pull back, the heels of both Frances' hands shot up and smashed into Anne's chin.

Anne's teeth rattled as she staggered back a step and turned halfway around. She felt something hard like ice chips sliding around on her tongue in the middle of warm liquid. The room spun over her head and toward her feet as her jaw sang out in exquisite pain. *Truly,* thought a more rational portion of her brain, *truly I cannot recall another time I was in this much physical distress. Perhaps when I crashed into that pillar?*

Then the back of her head seemed to explode into matching agony as Frances struck her again, this time from behind. Anne howled and brought her hands to her injured jaw and head.

In her near frenzied state, she'd forgotten that her right hand was made of a shiny, brass alloy. Her metal hand now hit her injured jaw with all the gentleness of a brickbat wielded by a savage Cossack. The pain in her jaw ratcheted up from a singing sting to a screaming symphony of agony, making Anne shriek and drive her into the kind of rage she'd not experienced since she'd begun her training for the Special Branch nearly seven years before.

"You shouldn't have done that," Frances said primly, her earlier distress gone. She now stood above Anne while adjusting the leather straps on her knuckles as if they were ladies' white kid gloves. Then, she shook the hand that had connected with the left side of Anne's jaw while fixing her hair with the other. "After all," Frances continued, "I'm nearly out of straps. I could have broken a knuckle."

Anne paused, breathed deep, said a few words to herself under her breath, and stood up.

"I," she said, flexing her metal fingers as she took a fighting stance, "I have no such concern."

Frances gulped, but she held Anne's gaze, squared her own feet in place, and brought up her fists so their backs faced her opponent.

Frances gave a quick nod of her head.

Anne charged.

****

"So, what's our next move?" Belloc said, looking out the window of their cell door.

"Well," said Gilbert, "first we look around for hidden panels. See if we can find something useful or interesting." Gilbert began tapping the wall with one knuckle while Hilaire Belloc put his hand over his face.

"*Primus*," Belloc said, still looking at the wall and pointing his index finger at the ceiling, "I wasn't talking to you. *Secundus*, you've been reading too much American fiction. Things like that don't happen in real—"

Gilbert held up his hand, silencing Hilaire. He tapped the wall again, and it sounded hollow.

Very, very hollow.

"What the—" Belloc said. Gilbert gave two more experimental raps, then punched the wall. His fist ripped a hole in the stone wall as if it were made of thick paper, exposing a small alcove the size of a man's head.

Gilbert quickly began routing inside for treasures.

"Stranger than fiction," said Hilaire, as he tried to nudge Gilbert out of the way and look inside the alcove himself.

"Sorry, bud. Keep back a bit. To the victor go the spoils, and all that. As for the fiction thing, you'll find, —"

He hissed with glee as his hand closed on something solid and tried to pull it from the hole in the wall.

"You'll find," Gilbert continued, "truth is very often stranger, heck, it's usually *crazier* than fiction. After all, we've—" he paused again and grunted as he gave a determined pull on whatever was lodged in the hiding space, "we've all made fiction to suit ourselves, and truth doesn't give a *darn* about accommodating *us!*"

With one final tug, Gilbert pulled his new find free. "And truth is always more than we can guess," Hilaire said. "Do you know what you've found?"

Gilbert turned it over in his hands. It had a handle and trigger like a revolver, but it was brass colored and the muzzle had several knobs and concentric disks on it.

"It looks like some kind of pistol," he said. Though it was dirty, it was the color of white sand underneath patches of brass-colored grime.

"The Red Men of Mars," whispered Hilaire, clearly wishing he could take the pistol, "once had a flourishing civilization. Now I wonder if they were only allowed one by the mollusks, but that's a question for another day. I've heard tell of weapons like this one. Some of them can turn a full-sized Thark to ashes with a single blast. Others can put a hole in a wall of stone wide enough for a man to walk through. How did you think to do this, Gilbert? To look for a hidden panel, I mean?"

"I—well, this may sound odd, but the thought popped into my head that a place as old as this has had its share of prisoners. Prisoners are always trying to escape, and successful ones usually don't come back to get their tools or toys once they reach the outside. But there's something else, too. This place just seems familiar to me, somehow."

"What, like you've been here before? I highly doubt that."

"No, that's not it. I know I've never been here. More like, I know I'm *going* to be here. I knew this wall when I saw it, except it had that hole in it, right there. And I remembered the gun, here, remembered finding it. And

I remember that I'll be putting it *back* there later. D'you see?"

Hilaire looked at Gilbert with an expression of admiration and the other part incredulity. "No, not really," he said. "But we now have a weapon, and since that betters our odds I'm happy with it. But first we've got to get out of this cell, and stop whatever crazed plan those old goats from Earth are trying before they do something truly stupid and destroy Mars."

"What about saving the girls?"

"Them, too, if we can. But oughtn't we put the fate of two worlds before them?"

"Fine," Gilbert said, now turning the pistol over in his hands. "I'm a little surprised this pistol looks so much like one from Earth, with a grip, a muzzle, and all that."

"It makes sense if the Red Men were really originally transplanted from our home. A number of their ships, both land and air, also look like the kind of thing Earthmen have been making for millenias."

"I guess so. So, let's see. If this works like an Earth pistol, where's the—"

Belloc's eyes widened as Gilbert, focused on the weapon, swung it around and had it pointed in his direction for the briefest second. A shade too far away to grab Gilbert's hand, instinct and training made Belloc dive to the ground.

Not for the first time or the last, it saved his life. For as Gilbert toyed with the pistol, looking for a trigger, his thumb and forefinger touched two of the largest red dots on the smooth white handle.

A small pinhole opened at the tip of the gun's barrel. Purple light flashed out in a cone shape, filling the air where Hilaire had been only a moment before. It fired without any recoil, jumping no more than would a flashlight shining its beam. The flash lasted for only an instant, but after it disappeared an added illumination remained. For the rays of the late afternoon sun were streaming through the man-sized hole in the wall where the locked cell door had been.

Light pink vapor steamed around the hole's edges.

Hilaire looked at the hole, then back at Gilbert.

"Sorry," Gilbert said.

"You know," Hilaire said quietly, "since you found that thing, it may be best if you be the one to use it. But if you so much as come *close* to pointing it at me again? I will break your wrist."

"Fair enough."

A guard's frightened face poked around the still gently steaming edge of the remains of the cell doorway.

Gilbert raised his pistol.

"Boo!" said Belloc.

The guard ran, his retreating steps echoing.

"We make a good team, huh?" Gilbert asked, stepping forward.

"Not yet," said Belloc, keeping an eye on Gilbert's fancy pistol.

"You go first."

****

Brigadier Brackenbury stood on the deck of his ship as it sped toward the horizon. His rekindled interest in his job was infectious; the men behind him performed their duties with a level of efficient vigor they hadn't displayed for years.

The Brigadier looked over the prow of the ship as the sands sped by below. He'd felt invincible at moments like this in his younger days, ready to leap over the side of the ship without a moment's hesitation and take a bullet square in the chest for Queen, King, country and empire, all without a moment's hesitation. In his middle age, he would have been more judicious, waiting for the most opportune moment to leap, hoping that he'd live long enough to command his men and be effective enough not only to win, but also lose as few of their men's lives as possible.

Now, in his sixth decade, Brigadier Brackenbury seemed stoic. He waited for what he knew might be the last battle of a life lived full and moderately well.

"Salisbury," he said, his voice barely a whisper as the first sight of a tower poked up over the horizon in the distance.

"Sir?" Salisbury answered. It was the first answer he'd given to the Brigadier all day that hadn't involved a shout.

"We are likely going to enter combat in the next hour. What's the mood of the men?"

"Some are excited. Some are frightened. All are ready, sir."

"And you?"

"I feel all of that, sir. All at once."

"Good lad. If you were only scared, I'd send you below decks as useless. If you were only excited, I'd likely throw you overboard on the nearest dune, because you'd live longer in the desert than you would in battle.

Keep your saber ready, and your powder dry. If I die, Lieutenant Moseby will be second in command. He knows this, and I'll expect you to obey him as you would me."

"Yes, *sir!*"

****

Herb sat in the cockpit of the parked ornithopter, carefully thinking about as little as possible. Belloc's words had resonated in his head, as had the conversation he'd overheard between Gil and the Actress. He tried to distract himself by going over what he'd just learned. The basics of ornithopter flight weren't difficult to grasp. One turned on the engine with a pull on a long cord. When the engine reached a high enough revving speed, you pulled a lever to open the throttle. This made the engine roar even louder and the machine fly higher and travel faster. With more practice, he'd be able to hover and fly in a straight line.

But he'd definitely need more practice. "Move too quickly with too little knowledge, and you'll pull an Icarus," said his pilot/teacher. "Your engine will stall, and you'll fall like a rock nine-meters-per-second-squared, until you and the rocks below become forcibly acquainted."

"You're point is well taken," Herb had answered as they landed. Now, having dismissed the pilot, he sat alone in the cockpit silently regarding the men scurrying around the base, many ending up at the top of the Temple tower.

Herb realized, and not for the first time, that he'd been tricked and neatly trapped into working for this lot of evil men. His former paramour/girlfriend Margaret had snared him with one kind of temptation, and then he'd convinced himself that his actions, being unforgivable, meant he had to join the other side by default in the hopes that they'd find him useful enough.

Useful enough to do what? Be used some more?

Employees are rungs on the ladder of success, he'd heard a businessman say at a meeting, *so don't hesitate to step on them!*

Herb could see clearly, now. He would have a time, short or long, and at the end of it, he would be discarded, like a machine part that no longer worked. Some parts lasted longer than others, but none were paid any mind when they ceased being useful.

But that little verse he'd heard Belloc say . . . *No greater love.* And *Penance.*

A new plan took hold in Herb's heart.

****

"Hold still, you filthy *witch*!" Anne yelled, as another clumsy swing of her deadly metal hand missed Frances' nimble body.

"Oh, like this?" Frances suddenly stood perfectly, utterly still, standing erect with her hands at her sides like a soldier at attention, her eyes facing forward.

"You little *beast*!" said Anne, leaning back and aiming a vicious kick with the pointed-toe of her right boot at Frances's kidney.

Had it connected, the blow would have been deadly. But Frances had spent several months learning how to be far deadlier. She spun on her heel, deflecting Anne's boot and grabbing her ankle tightly in the process. She used a move she'd witnessed two men use on each other on her flight from Earth, dropping herself to the hard stone floor while gripping Anne's ankle. When Frances hit the ground, Anne's leg hyper-extended in a very wrong direction, dislocating with a sickening crack.

Anne didn't yell or scream, but she inhaled and started saying words to herself. It wasn't effective. She'd never considered that Frances could match her in a fight, let alone actually hurt her. Out of practice, the short litany she used to shut off pain in her body failed. Her mind let the pain flow back into and throughout her in a screaming, angry flood, and her shrieks of anguish echoed throughout the cell.

Frances made a quick decision. The book she'd read on pugilism said she had two real options in a situation like this: First she could continue her hold onto Anne's leg, twisting the limb to do more damage. Second, and recommended if your opponent was deadlier than you in the hand-to-fist arts of fighting, was to get as far from the fight as possible in the hopes your opponent thought you weren't worth pursuing.

Having heard of Anne's abilities from Gilbert before, Frances opted to let go. Rolling away in a flurry of brown dress and lace, she rose to a standing position again once she'd gotten into the corner of the cell. Her hat was at her feet, battered but still serviceable, and she scooped it up and put it on her head with a jaunty air.

"Your leg isn't broken, Anne. I'd know if it was."

Anne's reply was unintelligible, hidden behind a number of angry sobs and hisses as she held her injured leg.

444

"If you think I'm going to come over there and help you, you're quite mistaken," Frances said. "I know that trick all too well. In fact—"

Anne's response was too quick for Frances to react. While she'd been talking, Anne had crawled on the floor to close the distance between herself and Frances. Suddenly, Anne swept the floor with her *good* leg, knocking out both Frances' legs from beneath her and sending her crashing to the ground.

"Oof!" Frances gasped as she hit the stone floor on her back. Instinct and experience merged, and she rolled to the side before the next blow hit.

It was a good choice! Anne had rolled too, swinging her armored hand in a deadly arc, slamming the ground where Frances had been only an instant before with enough force to crack the stone floor down the middle.

In a twirl Frances was on her feet again. "In Gilbert's country," she said, breathing just a little harder than she wanted to, "I believe the proper response is 'Is that the best you have?' "

"Got," growled Anne, still prone on the floor, "is that the best you've *got*," she yelled the last word, this time swinging both her legs, one after the other. Frances was ready for the first sweep.

But Anne's timing was off. The second sweep missed too, and the heels of Frances' boots both fell squarely on Anne's previously uninjured ankle.

Anne yelped, trying to roll away from Frances. There'd be no defending herself if she tried to stand on *two* injured legs! In just a few seconds, her mind had run through a dozen scenarios and possible outcomes to their tussle in which she was the victor, but . . .

No, she couldn't see it. There was no way she could win this fight without killing Frances. With her current injuries Anne could deliver no knockout blow, no nerve pinch, no *anything* that would incapacitate an opponent as dangerous as Frances had become.

And she *couldn't* kill Frances. Frances posed no true *physical* threat to Anne other than superficial injury. Besides, Gilbert loved her. Eliminating her as a romantic rival could be expedient, but it would backfire when Gilbert learned the truth. No, Anne couldn't kill someone with that much love in her heart, even if it was Gilbert she loved. Even if she stood in the way of Gilbert loving *Anne*.

By the time she'd resolved the issue in her head, her rolling body had come to rest against the wall of her cell. She was dimly aware of the sound of cheering coming from the tiny barred window in the cell door—

perhaps the guards had made bets on the outcome?

Though her legs hurt bad enough to feel they were almost on fire, Anne did get to her knees and manage to make her arms into an X that met at her wrists. It was a hand gesture known to honorable fighters the world over.

"Pax?" said Frances. "You've kissed Gilbert, just about eviscerated me, and you have the *gall* to sue for pax?"

"Frances," Anne said quickly while holding her arms steady, "Gilbert's told me everything about you. He loves you more than he ever could love me. I only kissed him to distract him, because he wouldn't leave me to die in the floating city over Richmond. Most of all, he told me you were honorable and merciful."

Frances looked at the kneeling girl in front of her and shook her head, making a disgusted noise through her teeth. Still keeping her fists up, she took two steps back while keeping her eye on Anne.

"So, if I drop my guard, you'll end this fight? I'll not have to worry about you slitting my throat or something equally horrific, just so you could have Gilbert without me as a threat?"

"I gave up all hope of ever seeing Gilbert again when I saw myself in a mirror, with half my face burned off after Norton's floating city fell into the Potomac. I'd had the single most difficult fight of my life against the most evil woman this century will likely produce. She slammed my face against a sheet of burning metal, and then used a jagged metal door to sever my hand as she left. I—I thought no man would want me. And even if my face is healed, there are other issues most men would have difficulty surmounting," she flexed her metal fingers, still held up as part of the X over her face.

"And you expect me to believe you'll just walk away from him?" Frances said, "After your little adventures together? You injured and abandoned him, while I traveled millions of miles to find him after I thought I'd lost him. Yet," she said, now leaning over Anne with her fists planted angrily at her hips, "yet now, you think me so stupid that I'd believe you?"

"Frances, what do you intend to do, then? Kill me? Maim me, *again*?"

"Perhaps. First, I'm going to escape. And then find Gilbert. And then convince him to either escape this place with me or die trying."

"Frances," Anne said, "you are a good fighter—far better than I expected. But I know how to escape from places like this, and you do not.

Moreover, the most able fighter can do next to nothing against a gun or its bullets. If these ruffians catch you, the best fist-fighter in the world will be able to do next to nothing against their weaponry and numbers."

Frances relaxed her stance slightly. Anne began to rise, moving forward on her knees. "I would have little chance at my best," Anne continued, still moving forward until she was only a foot away from Frances. "But you? Frances, you wouldn't last a half-hour out there. Stay your anger, help me escape this place, and you'll see that—"

Anne then launched her body forward, slamming her forehead into Frances' midsection.

Frances gasped, a scream of pain torn from her in surprise as she fell to her own knees and began to hiccup.

"I'm so sorry, Frances," Anne said, struggling to her knees while repeating more words to herself under her breath. She grunted as she slammed her leg and hip into the wall, then shook her leg a few times to make certain it was safely back in its socket. "But I have to try and rescue Gilbert. You're a decent fighter, I'll have enough trouble getting out of this cell and keeping *myself* alive. I can't be watching over you in this place."

Frances didn't answer. She was too busy retching on the stone floor, her last meal turning the ten-millennia old surface into a canvas for improvised, abstract art.

"Guard!" Anne called, "A prisoner is ill! She's vomiting! Quick! We need help!"

The guard, more of a simpleton than the professional mercenaries who'd entrusted him with the keys, began hastily unlocking the cell.

"Don't worry, Miss," said the guard, barely out of his teens by the sound of his voice, "I'll help you out in three shakes of a lamb's tail."

"Indeed," Anne said, flexing the fingers on her steam hand as the door swung inward, careful to stand between it and Frances's now prone form on the floor. "I couldn't agree more."

***

Beatrice had been slinking around the compound, looking for the exit. She'd entered a doorway and mounted some stairs, only to find that instead of the desert or a hangar, she'd stumbled on a series of meeting rooms.

And as she walked past one of them, she heard a voice that made her blood turn to ice water in her veins. The voice of the Doctor, now different, suddenly echoed down the hall. The Doctor's body stiffened. "It's happening again," he said.

Beatrice froze, her eyes wide.

The thing that had taken over the Doctor suddenly started laughing.

"I've been doing this a long, long time, you little, filthy strumpet," the Doctor's voice grated. "I know you're there and I don't care. What I *do* care about and truly hate, is that every time I'm close to completing a project like this, those goody-goody brothers of my masters' family always make a last-second effort to spoil the fun. Fortunately, they nearly always fail. But I *hate* that they always try! And I *hate* that those little tarts down in their cell have failed to kill each other!"

The thing that had been the Doctor paused, as if listening to something only he could hear. "I further hate that something is coming from below, and something else from above. And they are holding the details from me, blocking it from my view, and I hate this! Hate it! And I want to—to—"

His tentacle sprang from the longcoat. It must have grown in length, for it jumped out of the doorway and hovered around Beatrice's head and neck for a few seconds. She winced, but she didn't try to break free or run.

"No matter," he said, suddenly retracting the limb back into the room. "Williamson! Musgrave! Cobden! Rothchild! Where are you, you pathetic bondsmen?"

As Beatrice looked up, she saw four men run around the corner from another meeting room down the hall. In the lead, already short of breath from the minor exertion, was the man with the sunken eyes who had arrived in time to save her from the Doctor's earlier advances. The Second Man in line had wrinkled, spotted skin, the third was ridiculously fat and wheezing even harder than the sunken-eyed First Man. The Fourth Man was muscular and younger than the rest, but with white hair, several healing cuts on his face, a wild, frightened look in his eyes and a white, thinly trimmed moustache. All were oddly well dressed for men in a desert outpost, wearing the kind of outfits she'd seen men in high-society photographs wear to immensely important events.

"Is, ah, is something amiss, Doctor?" said the oldest man, apparently the leader, farthest to the left of the men on the stone balcony, looking at Beatrice and the Doctor on the ground below.

"I'm *not* the Doctor, you pile of near-artificially animated flesh and wormscum! And you know it, too! You're about to be attacked, fool! From two directions at once! And you're such a group of clods that I'm tempted to let all your plans slip through your gnarled and rotting excuses for fingers, except that your failure could become *my* failure as well! Now get to those pathetic giant slugthrowers you installed! Get them operational to meet the threat from the sky, and next get that bunch of hairless apes with sticks you charitably call your guards down here to meet the threat coming from beneath—or you'll see all the power you've been given go to the Americans next century! Move your lazy skins, you idiots!"

The older men looked to their leader, the First Man, whose face showed fear for the first time in the living memory of anyone present.

"But—but the ceremony!" he spluttered.

"The ceremony will be useless to you if the other side interrupts it! Get to carrying out my orders! My masters in the spirit realm all laugh at you idiots when you conduct those things, anyway, wearing the black robes, spouting ponderous phrases, and playing with waggled blades! Move yourselves, or I'll have the kinds of tortures readied for you that you've only *wished* you could have visited upon your worst opponents!"

Without a word, the older men disappeared from the balcony. Beatrice heard their voices rasping and barking out orders, and guards scurried to obey.

"Now, let it work," she heard the Doctor's breaking voice beside her, and she smelled the decay on his breath. "I'll soon have something so wonderful to present to my lord, he'll have to promote me to one of his councils. Perhaps even to the position of underseer, the first fallen human soul with authority over the demons themselves! But, as for *you*," his tentacle had been hovering near her, but now wrapped gently but firmly around her arm, "to the temple. I need only have the foolish toys of the enemy held at bay for another hour, and all will be well. All life on this worthless rock extinguished, success where others failed before, and it will be *mine*, and no one else's!"

"Won't you die too, Doctor?" Beatrice asked.

"Look at me, daughter of Eve." He spun her slightly so she would have to see his face. His face had a ghostly pallor, and the skin had split along his jaw line, as if torn along the seam of an old blanket.

"The Doctor is dead already. *Eh ton ma I!* I am not he. He escaped at the last second, and *you* helped deny him to me, after decades of careful, meticulous work! I will watch *you* die, horrifically, in his place. But first we can enjoy a bit of entertainment as those old fools try to trap my master's one-time brother, Barsoom, and cause him to destroy the last of all life on this world in response. Come," the Doctor's arm shoved her roughly, the tentacle still wrapped firmly around her left arm, even though it had begun to stink and exude a foul substance through its pores. "Come," he said, "up to the tower! The perfect place for a princess to watch as a thousand would-be princes die."

****

Herb lifted off and landed the ornithopter for the second or third time. He was fortunate in that everyone was so busy scurrying about that his three practices at rising and landing the flying machine had gone virtually unnoticed by the guards or anyone else in the compound.

Satisfied, he turned off the engine. He'd learned and practiced enough to have the basics down to . . . what, exactly? He knew, but he didn't want to speak it aloud to himself or anyone else, or even think about it too loudly. Could a thought have volume? He didn't know. And he didn't want to think about that too much, either.

He leaped out of the cockpit and started for the smaller tower that held the apartments for the agents. He suddenly didn't *want* to be at the fancy ceremony, no matter what reward was promised. He'd been promised things before by this lot, and they always—well, they always met their obligations, to the letter. But Herb was always left dissatisfied in the end. Playing truant from the ceremony? Suddenly, *that* was satisfying. To commit disobedience? Today, that seemed its own reward. Even the power he'd been promised—well, really, they *hadn't* promised, had they? Just implied. And they'd very, very rarely followed through on an implied promise.

He reached the guards' barracks in less than a minute. The tower with Herb's designated quarters were in the ancient stone tower right behind it. Like the other human buildings hastily constructed in the tower-compound, the barracks looked quite out of place. Built of local woods and brick and painted white, it looked strange in the red dirt and beside the stone tower, as misplaced as a dog nestled in a Christmas manger.

No matter. The barracks were deserted, and he was a few steps away from the smaller tower and his apartment when he heard the raspy voice of the Doctor screeching something in the distance. Herb felt cold prickles at the back of his neck. In seconds, he heard more feet running and voices shouting as guards ran from place to place.

And then, he heard the hiss of steam and the grinding of gears, noises that came from the four towers in the corners of the fortress.

Something is truly happening, Herb thought. *Not just another silly little test or ceremony, but something truly large. And I am likely the only one that can stop it from happening!*

He knew he faced a choice again:

Disobedience to those who saw him as no more than a chess piece to be moved on a board.

Or *obedience* to them, so as to live another day. Until he was cast aside like a broken machine part.

For the first time in a very, very long while, Herb saw clearly, and he made his choice.

He turned to run, aiming himself in a direct line to the ornithopter.

And it was on the way back to the 'thopter, now a scant fifty feet from him, that he nearly plowed into one of the prisoners he'd helped take from the town of Danton's folly. The fellow they'd called Belloc. And behind him walked a tall, skinny fellow who, despite his the guard uniform he now wore, could be none other than... "Gilbert," Herb whispered, whipping out his pistol and backing up several feet while staring at both Belloc and the best friend he'd shot nearly a year before.

****

Beatrice looked at the Doctor again. His flesh was sagging like dead, rotting meat on a slaughterhouse hook, but his yellowing eyes were bright, alive and angry.

"Now, little whelp," he said, "you'll see how we crush hope, dreams, and belief. Always, always, there are some little vermin who believe that they can defy us. And very nearly always, we prevail and remove them from this cursed plane, with all available speed."

"Why are you telling me this?"

"Because I *despise* you, you worthless little mongrel," he said, pulling her so close she could smell the putrid odor coming from his mouth. "I despise your *stench*. The stink of your accursed brother oozes out of every one of your pores. I know how many he's already convinced to jump over to the side of our enemies with his scribblings, and how many more might swim the accursed Tiber because of him in the future. But *today*, today if we prevail, we'll crush you, him, and all he might accomplish in one, swift stroke. And my masters will *have* to give me the respect I've earned and deserved but never been given for nearly a thousand years now! This way."

The tentacle, surprisingly strong for something that looked weak as a dead fish, propelled her up the nearest stairwell. As she tried to move without tripping, she heard a rumbling sound that made her think of sleeping dragons at the bottom of mountain lairs.

After a few more steps, she saw the source of the sound. The four towers that were at the corners of the fortress-temple were belching smog and steam from openings at their bases. Sounds of machinery, like the large cogs in the machines of a factory that had opened up near her home years ago, began to grind with a sound like sand screaming.

"Up, up, you waste of cellular tissue!" the Doctor said. "See my final triumph before your death!"

Before her death? Beatrice had had enough. There was no doubt what the end to this story would be if she went willingly with the Doctor, or whatever was controlling him! Even so, there was an odd murkiness in her mind, as if she were a horse and he a human pulling her bridle.

But even a horse with a bridle in her mouth could buck!

She fumbled with her free hand at her belt, stomping even more clumsily on the steps as they ascended, pretending to wince with fear and worry as the Doctor's voice raised to shriek, uttering profanity after profanity at her, her brother (why was this creature so obsessed with little Cecil to begin with?), her parents, and a host of others connected to her the Doctor had no real business knowing about.

He knows far too much about me, she thought as she found the knife at her uniform's utility belt.

He was still screaming at her when she pulled out the knife to stab and cut his squishy, fishy tentacle, shearing more than half of it off in the first blow and making his angry tirade suddenly turn into a high-pitched shriek of pain and anger.

****

Brigadier Brackenbury looked at the approaching fortress through his spyglass. Satisfied, he collapsed the small telescope and handed it to Salisbury. "Estimated time of arrival, Mister Salisbury?"

"Five minutes at most, sir," Salisbury said. "The fortress is in sight."

"And, how do we know that our quarry is there?"

"We do not, sir. However, by examining the sand, footprints, and tunnel directions back at Danton's Folly, we were able to discern their heading. And the tower at the center of this dig is the only building on any map within many, many miles of that heading. Ergo, Sergeant Belloc and any other survivors he picked up in his travels are likely there, if they are alive."

"Well done, Mister Salisbury. I might just let you serve in His Majesty's Martian Rifles for a bit longer before I return you to desert patrol duty."

"Yes, sir! Thank you, sir!"

The Brigadier looked through his spyglass for a moment. "Maintain alert status," he said. "There are ornithopters buzzing back and forth at the place. And I don't like ornithopters flying about an operation like this when they don't have British flags on them."

"Yes, sir!" Salisbury said, dutifully opening his own spyglass and watching the tower as the Brigadier put his away.

After a very long minute, Salisbury's eyes widened, though his right eye was still stuck to the telescope's eyepiece.

"Sir?" said Salisbury, "I think you should see this."

"Why? What's happening?"

"The four towers at the *corners* of the fortress, which surround the main tower. There's a carpet of steam flowing out of each of the four smaller tower's windows. And the towers themselves . . . they seem to be . . . getting taller."

"What? Give me that!"

Looking for himself, the Brigadier saw a sight that made his blood run cold.

The towers were not growing. Something was growing *out* of them. And as he watched, the pointed ends of the structures rising from the towers bent a smooth ninety degrees on unseen hinges, and pointed squarely at his little fleet of four ships.

"Blast," said the Brigadier, "they've got some kind of cannons held up there. Salisbury!"

"Sir!"

"They're not going to talk. And they *dare* to point a gun at *us*! Fly the signal flags! Ready cannon and call for evasive maneuvers! We'll have to play it close to the ground, but we've no choice if we want to get within reach of the place."

"Sir? Don't the protocols say we cannot fire unless fired upon first?"

"Hang the protocols! Draw and quarter the protocols! Then tar and feather them, like the Americans do! We're not going to stand by and let the protocols of some university-educated, bureaucrat soldiers tell us how we're going to wage war!"

Salisbury was already giving the message to the signalman. Within seconds, the proper flags flew at the prow of the ship, and the trimsmen of each of the four vessels brought the ships to within a dozen feet of the rocky, sandy surface.

"And *if* they are *so* foolish as to fire on a vessel of the British Navy, I don't care if it's the King himself who inhabits that rotting structure! I want us brought close enough that I'll be able to blast a cannon through its walls like a rifle shot through a garden mole! Trimsman! Did you get that?"

"Aye-Aye, Si-"

The steam cannons on top of the towers fired.

****

When Gilbert and Herb locked eyes, the world seemed to stop for both.

"Gil," said Herb, his voice barely a whisper.

"Herb, I—" Gilbert's voice stopped as a klaxon siren began wailing. Steam began blasting out from the four corner towers as the ground rumbled.

Belloc spun around, grabbed Gilbert's gun by the muzzle with his left hand, and swung at Herb with his right.

Gilbert hardly knew the gun was out of his hands before it had been used to club Herb across the head, followed by Belloc's right fist slamming into the other side of Herb's head with a meaty *smack!*

Herb yelped and went down, his pistol dropped and forgotten in the dirt while he moaned and held his temples.

"Sorry, mate," said Belloc under his breath, handing Gilbert back his Martian weapon while he scooped up Herb's pepperbox pistol. "Come on Gilbert, let's go before he comes to."

"Glad you didn't kill him, at least," Gilbert said as they ran. An alarm sounded and guards suddenly appeared by the dozens, though fortunately all were too busy to notice them. They were instead occupied manning stations and moving equipment to and fro.

"Moral considerations aside," said Belloc as they mounted the wide, circular stairs to the central tower, dodging guard after guard, "a flash from that pistol might have brought too much unwanted attention. If that siren had started just a few seconds earlier, Herb might've been singing in the choir invisible. Now," Belloc slowed down, having rounded a corner, "follow my lead and walk like you have a purpose. That siren says someone's coming to attack this place. If these lunkheads act the way most militaries do, each man will be more concerned about themselves and the job of their own group to check on escaped prisoners."

"Well and good, but where are we going now?"

"Up. To stop a ceremony, save this world and the few living things left on it!"

****

When the alarm sounded, dozens of guards, most of them hired thieves, miscreants and ne'er-do-wells from the streets of Syrtis Major all ran to the positions they'd been told to man if the city was attacked.

One particular squad of unlikely soldiers consisted largely of a number of youths barely old enough to shave. They'd lived in fear of their Sergeant, a burly, brutal, murderous thug they all hated who'd ruled and trained them with terror and violence from the first day without the slightest concern for their well-being.

But for the moment, it was his brutality that had them all formed up at the northeast corner of the main courtyard, in rank and file at attention while other soldiers scurried about and fretted.

"Squad, *number*!" the sergeant shouted. "One!"

"Two!"

"Three!"

And so it went, until the last member of the group shouted "Twenty-one! All present and accounted for, sir!"

"Don't you call me 'sir' private Bridgeman, you maggot!" he yelled with a guttural growl, "I'm not an officer! I *work* for a livin'! Now, I can tell some of you are worried about that jumbling under yer feet! Well, Tha's just the tower guns steaming up now, in't it? Now keep your eyes peeled! We're under attack from the air, and the courtyard's the most likely place them fools'll try to land. And when they do, we get to cover and pop'er pop their heads. Savvy?"

Another few seconds, and the air was thick with steam.

Private Isaac Bridgeman, who'd confirmed 'all present and accounted for' seconds earlier, looked around as a new sensation began to tingle through his feet, then up to his knees.

"Sergeant! What's that? What's that I feel?"

"Bloody 'ell, private! If you open your mouth again, I'll pop you a lead pill in the head, just like I did to that little toffer last week! Now do your job, and—"

The Sergeant's angry speech stopped with his scream, as the ground beneath him erupted and a cone-shaped drill the thickness of a man's leg poked up through the ground and shredded his foot into so much paste. As Bridgeman and the other youthful soldiers on duty watched in fascinated horror, the drill moved up and widened, grabbing the sergeant and spinning him around like a whirling, screaming rag doll, whipping him into the air and tossing him into the courtyard.

"Invasion!" the lad next to Bridgeman babbled. "We're bein' invaded, gov'! Run for it! Every man for himself!"

Bridgeman didn't need to be told twice. He and the other young soldiers broke and ran in a panic before the fellow soldier had finished his sentence.

As they ran, though, the little group suddenly had to stop again. The dirt had begun to swirl about a dozen feet in front of them like water draining from a spout.

A second more, and *another* drill popped up out of the dirt!

The boys screamed again, breaking their run and backpedaling away from the new threat, only to stop *again* as they turned around, fear moving every muscle, and reason having jumped out of the open window of their minds.

Now, the drill that had killed their sergeant had risen further out of the ground, revealing itself as the frontpiece of a long, oval shaped vessel without windows and a single, wide, rectangular door along the port side.

Bridgeman felt more rumblings under his feet. Even *more* drills were popping out of the dirt, all around them!

Another rumble nearly knocked him to the ground, but this one came from a pistol shot that detonated at his feet, kicking up the dirt and making him stop short.

"You, soldier!" barked a voice of command. It was another uniformed guard, this one with the insignia of command on his shoulders. Bridgeman realized quickly: this wasn't one of the quick and expendable street thugs, like himself. The real positions of authority had been given over to former military men, men who wanted better pay and the freedom to kill those who upset or displeased them. Bridgeman looked behind and saw his fellow soldiers had stopped running, and the guard who'd just called him 'gov' was lying dead on the ground.

"Up to those balconies now before you're cut off from escape, you worthless dogs!" shouted the mercenary commander. "Once there, train your rifles down 'ere, and kill anything what stirs from these tunnelers! No tricks, or you'll get a new breathing 'ole!"

Bridgeman ran, out of the circle the tunnelers were making in the courtyard, cursing whatever gods of fate had led him from a very nearly satisfying life of thievery to this awful life of quasi-military discipline.

****

"We've broken through to the surface!"

Cecil had thought the news would bring cheers, but it didn't. All he heard was silence from the men inside and then the sound of sand and dirt falling off their vessel on the outside.

And then more sounds from outside: the popping, blasting noise of fired rifles, the screams of men hurt and dying, and a deep rumbling in the ground, as if something heavier than a freight train was rumbling by them.

"Stay near us, Cecil," said John, his muscles and his voice both tense.

"Stay behind John, but in front of me," said Emrys, adjusting his glasses. "I'll ensure your safety until my own work here is finished."

Cecil nodded his head, but he stayed quiet. He'd spent the last few years of his life melting into the shadows when things got dangerous for him. He knew he wouldn't be able to do that here, and it frightened him.

A grinding noise sounded from the floor up front. A long, glowing horizontal line appeared in the roof of the tunneler. It lengthened and became an upside-down U-shape as the door to the outside world widened. It opened slowly at first like a drawbridge, then suddenly let go and hit the red stone ground with a clanging *thud*.

"CHARGE!" yelled John from the front, pointing his saber forward and raising his pistol in the air. The men behind him roared in voices thick with violence as they followed. Heavy work boots stomped first on the metal floor of the tunneler, then onto the hard stone ground and soft sand outside.

Like most boys, Cecil had dreamed of fighting on a battlefield. But in those dreams of combat he was always the soldier charging forward, untouched by the slaughter around him. He hadn't taken his fourth step out of the digger before he heard a grunt and saw the large man at his right fall down and lay still.

"Come on, boy!" John yelled, grabbing Cecil's arm and urging him onward, while Emrys grabbed the other. "We've got to get to cover!"

Cecil ran, fear screaming in his head. In his daydreams there had been no *smells*. His dreams of battle never had the coppery smell of blood, and no sickening stench of human waste from men ripped open by weapons meant to tear apart trees, ships, or solid rock. Cecil looked around and saw a corpse lying against a wall, its leg torn off and its head and arms thrown about like a puppet thrown in a corner by a careless child.

"Down!" yelled John, and the whole squad of men threw themselves into a small alcove between a broken wall and the ground.

"How many made it?" John yelled.

"Lost Hutch," shouted a voice, "Tyree, too!"

"Acceptable," said John, "but it does present a challenge. Very well. Cecil, wave this flag and get the rest of the men in hiding over here! We'll establish our perimeter. Any sign of Governor Wickham?"

"No, sir!" said a smaller man, unfurling a flag from his pack and waving it energetically. "I heard him say he was going to attend to personal business once we arrived, and leave the fighting in your capable hands."

"That certainly sounds like him. Well, no matter!"

"Right," said Emrys, still ducking down but watching the area with alert eyes. "This is where I go. Cecil, stay with John and the company, and you should be safe."

"You sure you're going to be all right, old friend?" said John, his eyes scanning the courtyard where the last digger had just broken through.

"My mission is already almost done. Two more little tasks, and I can rest a little while from this war."

"Off to it then! As long as this little toy of mine lasts, I'll give you fire cover!" Carter stood up and fired two blasts from his ancient Martian pistol at a cluster of confused-looking guards. Each blast found its mark, leaving a pair of smoking boots where a man had once stood.

"Cecil," said Emrys, shaking the boy's hand, "take care of your brother."

"My...? But I don't have a—" But Emrys was already gone, running across the courtyard with an apparent complete lack of concern for his own safety. He moved quickly, but in a straight line without even seeking cover.

"Now, boys!" shouted Carter, blasting his weapon in the general direction of the enemy, "to me! Get inside the perimeter, and let's set about taking this fortress!"

****

"Sir!" yelled Salisbury, "the men are ready! Orders?"

"Forward full speed. Increase lift just enough to get over that wall, then drop altitude so those big guns don't hit us! If we try evasive action at this distance, they'll pepper us to bits!"

"Yes sir! Moving into position!" Salisbury said. One of the sailors had already heard the order, transmitted it to the helmsman by hand gesture, who'd relayed it the same way to the signalman. The signalman made the same gestures to a member of the steam gang, who'd been looking out of a porthole from the engine room. The whole process was far more efficient than it sounded. Before the Brigadier had even finished speaking, the engines had roared louder and the green stones of Cavorite had glowed an even brighter shade of green as the ship sped up.

"Salisbury, are you still with me?"

"Sir?"

"We're going into the belly of the beast, Salisbury. I've a sense you'll come out of this breathing, unlike some of the others. Are you with me on this?"

"Yes, sir!"

"Remember Salisbury, this isn't just about finding one man, or even a group of men. It's about stopping a whole host of very, very *bad* men! Keep the aim in mind or your men fight and die for nothing!"

The guns from the fortress fired, cutting off the Brigadier's speech. Four very large plumes of white steam blasted from the huge cannons as they fired on their airborne targets.

"Brace for impac-!" Salisbury yelled, his own speech cut off by the loud *boom* of the cannons. Salisbury felt the breath torn from his mouth as a metal ball larger than his head sailed less than four feet above him, miraculously missing everything else on the ship but the tail-end of the rear prow as it fell.

"Faster!" cried the Brigadier, drawing his pistol in one hand and his fighting saber in the other. He leaned forward in the bow of the ship, one foot on the gunwale just above the wooden mermaid at the ship's front, his saber pointing at the central tower. "Faster, engine room! Drive us closer! I want to hit them with my sword before the next cannonball flies!"

****

"What the devil's going on out there?"

The Third Man moved himself with several ponderous steps to one of the five points on the five-pointed star that had been measured out and cut into the dirt and stone of the floor. Dressed in dark pants and a white collared shirt, he impatiently mopped the sweating folds of fat in his neck with a cloth, now very damp after his walk up the steps.

"I suspect someone is attacking," said the quiet voice of the Fourth Man, dressed in his favorite white suit. He looked around with a nervous air and shifted places on his own point in the star. After a few seconds, he began rocking back and forth in place again. The corpse of the Doctor had stared into his eyes for a full five minutes, and he would go to his grave without telling anyone, ever what he'd seen, felt or heard inside. That he had gone just a little bit mad in the head was the unquestioned belief of all present. That he was losing his mind, bit by precious bit, was a secret he hoped to keep from them long enough to finish the ceremony.

"They will fail," said the Second Man with the sunken eyes, who stared at the center of the star. He had opened his shirt to reveal a bizarre set of tattoos on his chest, with designs, pictures, and patterns mixed in an utterly confusing collage of images and pictures.

"Let them come," said the First, oldest man, not caring at all that the group was speaking completely out of turn and order. "We will be finished too soon for them to do anything, and be elevated to the status of *gods* of two worlds before the next half hour is out."

"There is still the last place to fill," said the youngest man, now having to raise his voice over the sound of the massive, hissing steam guns as they powered up for another shot, and the sound of roaring machines and gunfire below. "Where is the—"

"As I said before," said the grating voice of the Doctor's decaying voicebox, "the Doctor himself is permanently indisposed. But I have it on the lowest authority that I will be a suitable replacement."

The creature that the Doctor had become entered the temple hall, dragging Beatrice behind him with his human hand, the tentacle now dragging on the filthy floor. "Now let's get this massive pile of poppycock over with so I can turn my attention to the rest of my agenda."

"Er, yes, Doc— may I continue to call you the Doctor?" said the oldest man, trying hard not to wrinkle up his nose. The smell of the Doctor's animated corpse was now quite overpowering.

"Blast you, you *fool*! Will you begin the farcical ceremony before I pop that miserable excuse for a cranium off that ridiculous joke of a head that sits on your pathetically weak shoulders? I can't tell you how much the very sight of your kind makes me ill, now, despite my having been one of you so long ago. And all those moronic tattoos on your wasting, wrinkled body won't protect you either, despite what you read in the yellowed pages of those books you paid far, far too much for! I might just try to possess a *live* one of you next time, just so that I can properly experience the sensation of vomiting in disgust every time you pretend you are as important as you believe yourself to be! Now get started!"

****

Gilbert and Belloc were halfway up the stairs towards the top of the tower.

"Don't do that," Belloc said when he saw Gilbert looking back. His voice was loud enough to be heard over the ringing in their ears after the first volley of steam cannon had fired at the approaching ships. "We've got to keep our minds on our job. I thought you were a runner?"

"I ran cross country a bit in high school."

"Good enough. Runners never look back. They keep going forward until they cross the finish line."

"Where's ours then?" Gilbert asked, huffing just a little as they rounded yet another curve of stairs on their way up the central tower.

"Our finish line? It's right at the top, where they're holding their latest little shindig."

Gilbert looked up. There was no way to tell how long the stairway was, but it already felt like he'd been climbing it forever. "Why don't we just hunker down and let the Navy take care of things?" Gilbert said.

"Have you ever seen steam cannons like that in action? Whoever's leading that charge is going to have his hands full just keeping his men alive. If I know my brothers, they'll keep these minions busy enough that we'll be able to slip through the net and get to the top. I'm quite glad, really. I doubt we could've done it otherwise."

WHERE THE RED SANDS FLY

Gilbert couldn't believe Belloc was keeping the running pace he was while talking so much. It was all Gilbert could do to keep up the pace Belloc had set, never mind keeping up a conversation! Gilbert suddenly remembered a circus that had passed through town when he was little. *What was it that old showman said? The one named Tom Mix who dressed like a cowpuncher? "Time to Cowboy up."*

Taking a deep breath, he continued mounting the stairs, keeping no more than two paces behind the spry sergeant in front of him.

****

Anne saw Gilbert dressed in the uniform of a local guard, pretending to escort Belloc across the courtyard. *Bold move*, she thought, wondering if it was Gilbert or Belloc who'd decided on that plan.

Probably Belloc. Although Gilbert was good at bluffing, walking into the belly of the beast like they were required the kind of confidence borne of either experience under fire or blind stupidity. And, while Gilbert had shown himself more than once to be quite naïve, he wasn't stupid.

"All the way to the top," she said, looking up and seeing the top of the tower. It looked like a fortress itself, albeit a round one with stone walls and roofing. It was, in fact, a tower with so thick a base there were no fewer than four entrances at its base with four separate circular staircases rising to the tower's apex. Or so the information she'd wheedled out of a drunk guard weeks ago had said.

She checked the pistol she'd acquired by knocking her guard unconscious. She hadn't had the time to steal a uniform and try to make herself look masculine, but a pistol could protect her—a uniform might not.

With the first volley of shot fired from the cannons, the guards of the fortress had taken positions in towers and behind parapets and other forms of cover in the courtyard. Others had knelt behind stone balconies around the courtyard, firing their rifles furiously at the tunneler machines that had risen from under the ground like submarines from water.

"Quite the day," Anne mumbled under her breath as she ran in short bursts from cover to cover, making her way to the central tower. Martian structures like that always had a staircase inside their central pillar and narrower than the outer, more obvious staircase. If she hurried, she could meet or perhaps even beat Gilbert to the top.

As more gunfire erupted from the courtyard, she saw a small group of burly men surrounding a young boy and a slim, handsome fellow dressed in the harness of a Martian warlord run from the enclosure made by the encircled digging machines.

The young boy seemed to be leading them! And in the wrong direction! They were running toward the entrance to the lower levels!

Fools, she thought. *My former masters see themselves as* above *the world, and place themselves there at every opportunity.*

But there was too much danger and too many bullets flying for her to run, yell, or otherwise warn them. Besides, for the work she was going to do, stealth and solitary action would be more effective.

With the mayhem now in full swing in the courtyard, she had little trouble dashing across to the central tower. Though Gilbert and Belloc were likely now nearly halfway up, she spied just what she was looking for: a small alcove door, half hidden in the dirt—a door to the second, *inner* stairway.

She slipped into the alcove, kicked open the few wooden slats that had been crudely propped in place to block it, and quickly found the staircase. *Perfect,* she thought. She'd likely meet Gilbert and Belloc at the top at the same moment, if she kept a decent pace the whole time.

And, if she could end all this, if she could end her one-time masters' lives, *she would be free!* And *Gilbert* could be free, and the *world* could—well . . . well, be *freer,* until the next round of would-be tyrants made their move.

She'd just thought this when the earth shook with the second volley of the steam cannons.

✳✳✳✳

The four huge projectiles fired by the large steam cannons hurtled across the sky, making the British sailors duck and hit the decks.

Three of the four shots missed hitting any of the men directly, though the mast of the *Golden Eagle* was shaved by a cannonball, and the *Minotaur* had a long furrow torn in its side. Splinters, cannon, metal, and men burst and fell from the ship toward earth with a sickening roar of breaking wood and screaming death, and the *Minotaur* began to sag on its right side where one of its Cavorite rocks had been torn away.

"Sir, the *Minotaur's* been hit!" Salisbury said, surprising himself with the calm in his voice.

"Continue the assault!" yelled the Brigadier, his right leg still bent and planted on the rim of the deck, his hands still holding his weapons. "When we're in cannon range, hard to port and let fly!"

"Yes, sir!"

The Brigadier focused his eye on the nearest tower, the one that had crippled the *Minotaur*.

You are mine, he thought. *Blessed Saint George, you died for the truth after slaying a dragon. Though I may die today, help me die in saving men from a beast every bit as evil as the dragon they told me you slayed in the desert back when I was a wee lad in the nursery.*

"In cannon range, sir!" yelled Salisbury, "Moving to port!"

"Steady, lads!" Shouted the Brigadier, "Sell your lives dear! No retreat, no surrender, and *no apologies! FIRE!*"

Cannon erupted from the starboard sides of the *Golden Eagle*, blasting the nearest tower into powdery bits from halfway up its base. The tower's cannon, already extended halfway over the rim of the crenellations, served now as an unbalanced deadweight. The rest of the tower broke under the weight of the huge gun, falling slowly with a roar and rumble of breaking rock, twisting metal, and the screams of dying men, both in and on top of the tower. Huge, ancient chunks of red rock that had stood in place for tens of thousands of years broke to pieces and fell to the surface.

****

1914 A.D.

MARS. TOP ROOM OF THE TEMPLE TOWER

"You feel it, don't you?"

Gilbert looked around, feeling very much like an animal in a trap. Having been caught in traps quite a few times, he was more than fit to judge.

There was nothing immediately visible. They still heard occasional scratching in the walls and some Warhoon calls outside, but they had been left alone for the last few minutes since the walls had last been breached. Then, Father Flambeau had broken one of the creature's necks and Gilbert and Anne had dispatched two more each with their pistols, knives and Anne's splendid, updated clockwork hand.

"Yes," said Father Flambeau, "I've felt like this more than once. But

I usually prefer to think it's my own fear rather than the actual presence of tangible evil, unless I see things flying off the walls by themselves and people's faces changing shape."

Anne looked at Father. "You mean, that actually happens?"

"Mon Cherie, the things I have seen would make even a seasoned woman like yourself turn white and cold. I've seen blood of martyrs, solid for centuries, liquefy and bubble on the anniversary of its owner's death. I've seen the sun dance and decayed noses grow back, and hardened criminals run at the sight of holy little nuns who would not break in the face of evil."

"Fancy that," she said, in a thoughtful voice.

"There's far more, Anne," Gilbert said, "and if we had enough world and time, I'd tell you all. But for now, we need to get this piece rolling to help ourselves, back then."

"Of course," she said.

"Then," said Father Flambeau, "as I've the feeling we're running short on time, let us begin. In Nomine Patris, et Filius et Spiritus Sanctus . . . "

Gilbert made the sign of the cross, and Anne followed as best she could.

" . . . the fellowship of the Holy Spirit be with you all . . ."

"Gilbert," Anne whispered.

"And also with you," Gilbert said to Flambeau. "Anne," he whispered as the priest continued speaking in Latin, "could it wait? I'm trying to focus here."

"Gilbert, I don't know much about your religion, but I do know this part all depends on what he does," she said, pointing to the priest, "not what you hear. Now if what has to happen is going to happen, don't I have to be part of it, or something like that?"

"What do you . . ."

"A reading from the book of . . . well, of Genesis," said Flambeau. "Male and female he created them. Now, a reading from a Psalm of David . . ."

"I mean, Gilbert Chesterton," Anne persisted, "that we may be dead very soon. And we both know what has to happen if this is going to work the way we plan it to."

"Anne, I'm a man of many words and very few understandings. Now will you tell me what this is about? And tell me after he's done with the Mass, please? This is kind've a sacred thing, you know."

"A reading from the book of Corinthians . . ."

"Look, Gilbert, these ceremonies of yours are more powerful if . . . well,

if it's more than just a single thing, aren't they?"

"Anne, it's not like a cake where you get bigger servings if you add more flour!"

"It is best for a man to be unmarried . . . "

"Gilbert, I mean . . . we know what we're up against, back there. We're trying to do this Mass here and now, so it'll shut the door here and then. But what if more's needed to shut the door that they opened back then? Back when they tried to capture Barsoom? What if more's required to make Barsoom stay his hand, and not end life on Mars? What if . . . what if we made this more than just a Mass? What if we made it a . . . well . . . for it to be a wedding, Gilbert? That'll bring God, or goodness, or whatever it is, that'll bring more into it, won't it? And it could be in name only; we could get divorced right after. Frances need never know! But we have to think about the past!"

" . . . yet if one is on fire with passion . . ."

"Frances wouldn't mind at all, I don't think, Anne."

"Wot? Explain that to me!"

"She's . . . she's been dead for nearly two years."

" . . . it is better to be married . . ."

Anne looked at Gilbert, shocked. Then she slapped him in the face with the palm of her real left hand. Hard. Gilbert didn't move, but only looked at her with a sad expression that didn't change, even after the sting of her blow began making the right half of his face turn red.

"Just when," she said, her left hand now balled into a fist, "were you planning on telling me this?"

"Before now. But there was this little adventure in the lost city, recall? I was shot, we had to fight our way past wild woolahs . . ."

" . . . than to be on fire with passion . . ."

They both looked at Father Flambeau, instinctively wishing his silence. Having finished the recitation of the scriptures, he began speaking more words from the Mass in Latin, holding their gaze all the while. Even her slapping of Gilbert hadn't made him pause in his speech.

"Well," Anne went back to whispering in Gilbert's ear while her body still faced the priest, "this is a fine time, isn't it? You told me she was very much alive! Was that the first lie, or were there others?"

"Anne, for believers, those in Heaven truly are alive; more than we are, in fact. So what I told you was true, from a certain viewpoint."

"A certain viewpoint? That has got to be the worst, most ridiculous justification for a barefaced lie that I've ever—"

"Anne, look, that vision we saw here? Back in our youth? I don't know what it meant exactly. Neither did you. But if it is what's needed now . . ."

"Well?" she cut him off.

". . . Sanctus, Sanctus, Sanctus tantum ergo . . ."

"Well what?"

"Well, Gilbert? Do I need to be baptized first, or can that come after?"

"After . . . you mean . . ."

". . . ere Dominus Sancti . . ."

"Gilbert, for a man who writes and speaks as much as you do in your cover job, you really are fumbling this bit. Are you going to ask me or not?"

A loud slam sounded against the heavy wooden door outside.

The sound of wood cracking slowly followed.

Gilbert looked at the door, then at Father. The priest gave Gilbert an urging look while still reciting the Mass in Latin, and Gilbert turned to Anne.

"Anne, will you marry me?"

****

1892 A.D.
MARS. THE TOP ROOM OF THE TEMPLE TOWER

"He's here," the Doctor's voice grated as he entered the room, pulling Beatrice by the wrist now with his human hand. No one but Beatrice heard him over the recording coming out of the paper discs loaded into the gramophone. The other four men were sitting with their eyes closed in comfortable chairs placed at the points in the five-pointed star that had been etched into the ground.

"Come with me," his voice sounded now like sandpaper on metal as he dragged Beatrice through the door and toward the last available chair in the room. "I can't wait until this is over. I'm so sick of looking at these idiots. Their eyes shut in meditation, the gobbledygook oaths and incantations they're spouting, the tattoos on their bodies, all of them thinking it will make them more powerful and respected. None of it means a thing. The only thing that truly matters is results. *Results!*"

He dragged her past the Third Man, who had sat his ponderous bulk in an equally large plush-cushioned chair and was busily inhaling fumes from a pile of smoldering herbs on the ground. Then past the Second, who had stripped to the waist, revealing multiple tattoos of odd pictures and languages stamped on his shoulders, back, and chest. The Third man opened eyes that were nearly submerged in the blubbery flab of sleep deprivation, but popped wide in fear as the Doctor walked by him, the sagging tentacle moved in a tired fashion like seaweed at the bottom of the ocean. The Fourth Man hadn't been passed by at all, and took no notice of the loud rant. He sat crosslegged at the opposite end of the star etched into the floor, and tried hard not to look at the animated corpse dragging Beatrice.

"Why have you brought me to this?" Beatrice asked.

"Because I want you to see your last, greatest hope extinguished before every bit of life on this red chunk of rock and ice is nullified. And that includes you, you worthless waste of muck and protein chains!"

"No," Beatrice said.

"What did you say to me?" he grated, his voice barely audible over the chittering, squeaking noise coming from the flowering gramophone speakers. No one else in the voluminous room acknowledged them.

"I said, no. You can kill me if you want, but I think in your state you won't find it quite as easy as you could have a few hours ago."

"How *dare* you! Do you *realize* who it is you speak to? What I've done throughout history to those who've opposed me with *half* the impudence and insolence you're showing now?"

"Whatever you've done, you won't be doing today. Your left arm is half rotted off. And the tentacle you're toting around in place of your right limb is wilted like a batch of rotten cabbage stalks."

"You—you worthless little *Adamite*! When I was a young woman in this world, I would only have been that insolent when…I'll…"

The Doctor's voice broke, with a sound like toothpicks snapping underwater. He swung clumsily at her with his left, semi-human arm, hefting the blow as if trying to move a weight so heavy and awkward it needed to be carried close to the body.

Beatrice dodged, as easily as she would have a slow-pitched baseball. The Doctor panted, his broken chest creaking as his tentacle thrashed and kicked like a worm in agony on a hook. "I . . . *will* . . . remove you . . ."

he said, the words sounding like a loud whisper on the wind. Beatrice stepped back with a cool, measured air.

As Beatrice moved, she saw a young girl with red hair and a curiously large right hand slip through the door behind the Doctor without noise. Fearful for the girl's safety, Beatrice was careful not to look directly at her.

The Doctor's eyes were locked with such fury on Beatrice, and the cacophony of sound outside so intrusive that he seemed to take no notice of the girl behind him.

"Arthur," Beatrice said suddenly, the word leaping from her lips unbidden, and unexpectedly.

The Doctor's head reeled as if slapped, and he took a halting step backward. "I will *remove* you *later*," he muttered, "you—you can face your doom yourself, then. You worthless, fleshbound, squishy little amphibians aren't worth the effort. Hanged if I know why He loves you so much more than my masters."

The Doctor's body pivoted stiffly on legs that looked as if they were small stilts, and stalked toward the empty place at the last point on the star.

Chapter 57

"The timidity of the child or the savage is entirely reasonable; they are alarmed at this world, because this world is a very alarming place. . . fairy tales do not give the child the idea of the evil or the ugly; that is in the child already, because it is in the world already. Fairy tales do not give the child his first idea of bogey. What fairy tales give the child is his first clear idea of the possible defeat of bogey. The baby has known the dragon intimately ever since he had an imagination. What the fairy tale provides for him is a St. George to kill the dragon.

Exactly what the fairy tale does is this: it accustoms him for a series of clear pictures to the idea that these limitless terrors had a limit, that these shapeless enemies have enemies in the knights of God, that there is something in the universe more mystical than darkness, and stronger than strong fear."

–'The Red Angel' in "Tremendous Trifles"

Emrys ran. Like most men who'd focused their lives on study rather than athletic development, he ran stiffly and inefficiently. As he ran he wished for the ten-thousandth time that he'd spent more time training his body than his mind—but that couldn't be helped right now.

A hail of bullets blasted the wall behind Emrys—someone had hold of a Maxim gun! He ducked and continued crawling on his hands and knees, trying to avoid panic. He *had* to reach the top of that temple tower! He had to, *had* to! "Have to, have to, have to—" he muttered as his hands kicked more and more red sand out of the way.

He stopped suddenly. His hands rested on a pair of black leather boots. He looked up.

There was a young, dark-haired man standing above him. Though they had never met, Emrys recognized him instantly from the files the Vatican had gathered and given him.

And the young, dark-haired man was pointing a pistol with a number of sizable barrels right at Emrys.

"Good afternoon, Mister Wells," Emrys said.

"Good evening, Mister Emrys," Herb said. "You look a trifle concerned. Can I be of assistance?"

"You—" Emrys stood up, his fear of the Maxim gun forgotten. "You dare to offer *me* assistance? You . . . you've committed atrocity after atrocity in the last year, all the while keeping up the front of a respectable intellectual and writer?"

"It's a living, Emrys. Or are you still under the delusion that you're the dispenser of the spiritual office of King Arthur? Yes, I've read your file, and no, please don't try to argue the point. I don't have time to bandy this about. I'm actually trying to get out of this sordid little game I've gotten myself mixed up in and save my friend at the same time. I'm thinking, in fact, of turning over a new leaf, and I'm going to start now by sparing your life," Herb said. He started to holster his pistol, but he had a second thought and instead dropped it to the ground in front of Emrys and took a step back.

"Now, do whatever it was you were going to do," Herb said. "I'm going to be leaving this little pimple of a planet. Leaving it rather spectacularly, in fact, on my first and last piloting job up to that tower. Good day."

"You're *what*?" said Emrys, flabbergasted. Everything he knew about the Cleaner flew in the face of the mercy he'd just been shown.

Herb had already turned his back to Emrys, stalked back to the ornithopter and stepped inside it so swiftly he didn't even bother to draw up the gangplank.

A few seconds later, its engines started.

Emrys picked up the pistol by a corner on the holster, holding it like it was a dead, rotting fish carcass.

Right after that, he tilted his head, as if listening to something.

"You *can't* be serious," Emrys said, seemingly to the open air. "Morgan, *here*? Aren't you one of the ones with a sense of humor?"

****

Gilbert and Belloc mounted the last of the stairs. Emerging through the doorway, Gilbert saw something that would haunt his dreams and nightmares for years to come.

Though it had been light outside, the large temple room was shrouded in darkness. A screeching, chattery noise came from a gramophone against a wall. Five torches stood at the points of a pentagram-star etched deep in the ground. As Gilbert's eyes quickly adjusted, he saw that a man stood by each torch, staring at the center of the star.

Just as they walked into the room, they heard the frantic chittering noise come to a halt, leaving the older men to continue making a different noise, with solemn-sounding chants in a language Gilbert couldn't place or understand in the least.

But it was what was in the center of the room, hovering above the center of the star on the floor that startled Gilbert, and made him cross himself involuntarily. He noticed Belloc do the same.

A large circle hovered a few feet in the air perpendicular to the floor over the center of the five-pointed star. It was perhaps ten feet across, and looked to Gilbert like a giant round doorway. Its edge seemed to be made of white smoke, and the world seen through it looked blurry.

And *above* the circle, Gilbert saw something that left him both terrified and awestruck. Not so much with fear as with pure astonishment, as standing atop a huge cliff would make you queasy and fearful even if you had a railing to hold on to.

What stood *above* the circle was a humanoid figure. It was colored—at first, he would have said it was a deep red all over, but if he looked again, it was a brilliant white, seemingly made of light itself, with a corona of colors that he couldn't exactly name. They were colors that he could *feel* rather than see. They made Gilbert think of cold mornings on the prairie when he'd been a child—bright, clear, cold, almost metallic in strength.

The being held something like a spear in his hand. His bare feet hovered close to the floor, the top of his head brushing the roof of the domed room.

The being turned to face them. Its face was vaguely human, with glowing eyes set in the almost featureless face.

The eyes were . . . they were *different*. They were *alive*, but *alien*, in every way the word could be used. They saw everything around them, all at once, but the eyes were—unreadable? Gilbert couldn't think of any other way to put it. It wasn't that they had *no* emotion behind them; rather, any thoughts or feelings behind those red eyes the size of Gilbert's head were unlike any other emotion Gilbert had seen an alien display, either on Mars *or* Earth.

Gilbert had seen the squids that had invaded Earth two years ago. And he'd seen the Red Men of Mars as they'd passed him by after he'd landed in Syrtis Major. He'd also come face to face with the buglike, green eyes of the Tharks as they'd tried to take his life. The eyes of the squids had been lit by a cold kind of hatred and disdain, while the eyes of the Tharks had been full of the hate and violence that comes with deadly battles and vicious fighting. The Red Men he'd seen had usually been busy, getting on with the tasks of their lives. But for the most part their emotional states were exactly like those of the average earthman.

But the eyes of this giant in front of him surveyed the scene with a different sort of look; they reminded Gilbert just a bit of the kind of focused yet dispassionate look a workingman would give to a job area.

The five men in the room at the points of the star did not, however, see the being as Gilbert did.

"Kneel!" cried one of the men, his ancient, cracking voice carrying in the suddenly silent room. "Kneel before us! The charms and spells have summoned you, and we bind you to our service!"

"Crush them!" called another voice from the opposite end of the room. "Crush all of them now! As you did the others when they tried to leave!"

"I know that voice," Gilbert said, "kinda—"

Gilbert saw and recognized him in the torchlight. The form was bent, twisted somehow, and the limbs were moving more like a stiff marionette than a human, but the face and eyes were unmistakable.

"The Doctor!" Gilbert breathed. And beside him, unmistakably, even if she was wearing a guard's uniform, was the girl in the photo Gilbert had seen long ago. The girl the Doctor had said was Gilbert's sister.

****

Steady, old chap, Herb thought to himself as he kept the ornithopter in the air. *If you're going to give your life today, it had better be for your friends. If you waste this, you throw your only chance away at saving yourself!*

Herb, though new to flying an ornithopter, found it relatively easy to raise the craft from the ground and turn it to face the large tower. Something was going on in there, he knew. He'd been around enough of the strangeness of the men of the circle in the last year to know when something strange, terrible, or both was going on behind their doors. *Which means that either I'm getting closer to how they really are all the time, or that they're falling deeper and deeper into madness. Either way, my little boat of life would be swamped by anyone of that lot if they fell. I have to either run or die. Better to do both!*

Herb took a deep breath and made sure the steering controls were set to propel the craft full speed at the top of the tower. The 'thopter was big enough to hold a dozen men if need be, and could easily smash a nice, big hole in the bulbous room at the top of the tower, reducing a sizable chunk of the ancient roof into so much powder and so many little rocks.

Now, forward, Herb thought, moving the lever to open the throttle, keeping his other hand on the stick that kept the 'thopter at its current altitude, and ignoring all the cannon blasts, popping rifle shots and screams of dead and wounded that seemed to be erupting around him in a cloud of cacophonous sound. *Forward, with all available speed.*

Herbert set the direction and pulled the lever that opened the throttle. He focused on his goal, which was the widest part of the top of the tower. Fully intending to plow into it at the greatest speed his craft could muster, he began to scream in a primeval, guttural voice, the kind of scream men gave to strengthen their resolve in the face of certain death.

And, perhaps, thought a quieter portion of his mind, *perhaps by giving my life for my friends, I'll save it. There's a chance, a reasonable chance that I'll no longer be damned.*

The thought gave him comfort for a few seconds, until a shadow covered Herb and his craft.

Looking back, Herb saw the massive bulk of the Golden Eagle rising behind him, flying directly towards the dome, with Herb the only thing between the sizable cruiser and the dome on top of the tower.

Herb whispered something unprintable.

****

"Ramming speed reached, Brigadier! Contact in ten seconds!"

"Excellent, Salisbury!" the Brigadier replied. Although something inside him— something primal, good, and true— said in a quiet voice in the midst of the mayhem that the greatest threat to Brigadier Brackenbury, his men, and virtually everyone else on the planet lay not in the giant steam cannons, but in the dome at the top of the tallest tower in the middle of the four smaller towers that held the cannons and their deadly payloads.

His men had been trained well. They had disabled three of those tower cannons, either through ramming action or their own well-aimed ordinances from the sides of their ships.

"Ornithopter, dead ahead sir!"

"Ignore it, Mr. Salisbury! Plow through it! Focus on the dome!"

"Aye, sir! Contact in ten seconds, sir!"

One cannon remained.

"Nine!"

Only one cannon left. And the central tower.

"Eight!"

Knowing somehow that time was of the essence, the Brigadier had ordered his ship, the largest of the four he'd brought, to ram the tower.

And they were nearly there.

"Seven... Six... Five...!"

"Going to smash into you," Herb mumbled under his breath. It had taken him only five seconds to raise the 'thopter high enough that he was now pointed directly at the dome on top of it. He could almost tune out the gun and cannon shots blasting around him, along with the sounds of stone breaking, wood splitting, and men screaming and dying.

And now, it looked like one of the Brits flying ships wanted to do the same thing!

"Now!" Herb urged. The ornithopter's wings beat obediently, still charging toward the dome where he knew, *knew*, they were undergoing some new and ridiculous ritual in an effort to cement their hold on a *second* world. "I've perhaps ten seconds until impact," Herb suddenly said in a quiet voice, the voice he'd used time and again on one nefarious mission after another in the last year to calm his nerves or steel his resolve. "Ten seconds, nine, eight . . ." he counted as the dome loomed large, and the even larger flying ship behind him came closer, closer . . .

The last cannon tower fired its shot.

Where the other three towers had been either blown to bits or rammed clean off by the other three ships in Brackenbury's little armada, the remaining cannon had turned and pointed squarely at the *Eagle*.

So focused had the British Admiral been upon smashing the same target Herb had designated for himself, Brackenbury hadn't thought to compensate for a cannon shot too small to destroy his ship, but could still hurt and distract.

The cannon shot blasted into the portside hull of the *Eagle*. It barely punctured the hull, and the hit took not a single crewman's life.

But the shot succeeded in one thing; the *Golden Eagle* was knocked off course.

Flying at a new vector with the superior speed born of Cavorite and a stiff wind, the Golden Eagle passed Herb's much smaller ornithopter by a dozen or so feet instead of crushing it like a fly in the grille of an oncoming steam engine. The *Eagle* also missed—just barely—the dome on top of the tower. Hitting it with a glancing blow, Brackenbury's flagship left an oval-shaped dent in the dome's surface.

"Four," said Herb, barely noticing the much larger *Golden Eagle* in the back-viewing mirror as it neared his ornithopter. Herb's eyes narrowed as he neared the dome, flying his craft with the focus of a first-place runner at the finish line of the race of his life, "three, two…"

Suddenly, Herb saw the flash and heard the huge *boom* of the last cannon from the far side of the dome. Herb instinctively pulled back on the throttle, as a carriage driver would pull back the reins of his horse at the sight of a threat.

The huge, floating cruiser that had been racing Herb to the dome instead jerked off course, missing the tail of his craft by only a dozen feet and smashing the barest *glancing* blow in the *side* of the dome, rather than hitting it head on.

Herb was elated for a second. He'd be able to smash the villains himself after all!

And then he saw the lone remaining cannon on top of its smaller tower, its crew frantically reloading its next shot, turn and point its long barrel straight at Herb.

"No," said Herb, "*No!*"

Still moving with incredible speed, the Eagle passed Herb on the right side then pulled ahead and away from him in less than a second.

Herb, who had been flying toward the dome, now flew toward a weakened spot the large ship had pushed *into* the dome. A spot *just* large enough for him to comfortably fly into, and bash *through*.

"Knickers!" gasped Herb, still moving forward. He leaned on the steering wand, looking back for a second at the floating galleon. The battleship's hull had missed him by only a dozen feet—maybe less!

In seconds he was aimed again at the dome, this time at the weak spot in the dome's roof.

"You know," said a voice behind him, "there are alternatives to throwing your life away."

"Wot?" Herb exclaimed loudly as he looked back.

It was the long-haired fellow from the courtyard, his eyes hidden behind the lenses of glasses that were even bigger than Gil's.

"How the blazes did you get in here? I never noticed you!"

"A fine little feat that my friends have conducted for me more than once. Now, I believe we *both* have an appointment with someone on the floor inside this now-vulnerable tower fortress. If you'd be kind enough to please *nudge* through the weak point in the dome and *land* us inside, instead of trying to *bash* a new hole in and killing us both . . ."

Gilbert didn't want to leave. Even when the large ship had shoved part of the roof inwards and broken several large beams in it, he'd stayed rooted to the spot. His eyes were riveted on the young lady next to the standing but wilted form of the Doctor at the other end of the room.

Dust, dirt, and millennia-old grime churned in the air. The darkness was still thick inside, like smoke, while dim rays of light tried hard to shine through.

Still looking over at the Doctor, or whatever he'd become, he tried hard to ignore the glare that Hilaire Belloc was giving him. "That girl!" Gilbert said, "beside the Doctor! She's—"

"Gilbert! Quiet!" Belloc whispered sharply into Gilbert's ear while pulling him into an alcove.

"But she's—"

"I don't care *who* she is!" Belloc said, looking up at the huge, man-shaped being now hovering in the air. "We've got to think quickly! Those fools have finally stepped in it this time, and we have to both stop them and find a way to protect ourselves from that thing in the air."

"But—"

Suddenly, a huge *BOOM* sounded from above. The bent and damaged beams now broke into pieces, falling in a shower of powdered plaster, splintered wood and twisted metal to the floor as something flew through the dust and filth, humming like a swarm of bees as its wings beat time.

It was the very ornithopter that had brought them as prisoners! Even in the gloom, thanks to the few rays of light Gilbert could see the dark-haired pilot of the craft was...

"Herb!" Gilbert yelled, leaving Belloc and running forward while waving his arms, for the moment ignoring the now forty-foot tall ghostly giant in the domed room. "Herb, over here!"

Herb flew the ornithopter, its wings beating like those of a hummingbird. It hovered unsteadily in the air over the five-pointed star etched in the floor, wobbling like a drunk man trying to keep his balance. Gilbert saw that Herb carried a passenger, a young man about their age with glasses and stringy blond hair.

"Emrys?" Belloc said, as Gilbert saw the older man with glasses and long white hair move out of the seat next to Herb and over to the open side door of the 'thopter.

"You know him?" Gilbert asked.

"We've crossed paths before. Look!"

The great being was still surveying all before him, ignoring the ornithopter and the five people on the points of the star etched in the floor. The being was taking small, soundless steps in the air and turning slowly in a circle. The five men were still finishing up their last round of chanting mysterious incantations, their voices sounding stilted and silly over the squeaking, chattering sounds coming from elsewhere in the room.

The ornithopter flew forward toward the men of the circle. The giant blocked Herb's path, but Gilbert saw the flying craft dive *through* the giant, as if it were a phantom made of light.

The fattest man in the room blinked as his stupor faded. Gilbert had just enough time to see the fat man's mouth open in gaping horror at the sight above him before he disappeared. He looked up with a surprised expression at the craft as it fell on him with a crash of twisting metal and breaking wood, the noise of the flapping wings was so loud no one heard the crunch of bone and squish of tissue beneath the 'thopter's wheel-less undercarriage.

The other four snapped to, though they moved more slowly than Gilbert and Belloc, who were now sprinting towards the 'thopter as its flapping metal wings slowed and stopped.

"Give me your pistol!" Belloc barked. Gilbert handed over the odd gun he'd picked up from the jail cell. Belloc kept running. Gilbert looked around the room as they saw the young man Belloc had called Emrys leap from the open door on the side of the now broken ornithopter, carefully shielding his head from the slowing flap of the blades. As he looked, Gilbert saw one of the men at the pentagram pull a pepperbox pistol from the folds of his white suit, his face twisting into a snarl as the thumb on his thick hand pulled back the hammer on his weapon.

"Belloc! Gun! To your right!" Gilbert yelled.

"Get down!" Belloc yelled back without pause, spinning around to his left while pointing his weapon. Gilbert dropped flat on the ground and closed his eyes. The room burned white as the Martian pistol blasted. When Gilbert opened his eyes, he saw a pair of shoes resting where the Fourth Man had stood. Quite expensive looking white leather shoes, with a pair of smoking ankles growing out of them, ankles ringed by a few inches of pant leg that were immaculately white on the bottom and barbecue-black at the top ring.

"You," said another one of the men, looking at them with eyes that appeared to have sunk far into his head, "you killed the Fourth Man! And the Third is dead too! Do you realize what you've done?"

"No, he doesn't," grated the Doctor's cracking voice as the young men reached the 'thopter wreck. Gilbert noticed a kind of dark fog was swirling out of the portal that still hovered below the giant, and the fog was quickly surrounding them and blocking out the light.

"Nor do you," the Doctor continued, ignoring the fog and speaking to the Second Man of the Circle with a tongue that sagged in the Doctor's mouth like a bloated slug, slurring his words like that of a drunken man. "Do you *really* think your ridiculous chants and spells captured the *glain* of Mars? Do you *really* think that standing on a shape drawn in the ground keeps *him* here? Your silliness just opened a door, and he's here to shut it—and sweep out the entire race of rats that was fool enough to nibble it open!"

Gilbert saw Belloc reach the 'thopter, just as the long-haired fellow was disembarking. Then Gilbert reached the same point a second later.

Upon seeing him, the long-haired young man grabbed the vest of Gilbert's waistcoat and seemed about to speak when he heard the voice coming came from the Doctor's decaying shell.

"Emrys!" it said.

"I know that voice," said Emrys, still holding on to Gilbert but seeming to look past him. "The years have—not been kind."

"Shut up, Emrys," said the Doctor's raspy voice as he started to walk with a staggering gait towards the 'thopter. Gilbert saw the girl in his grasp wriggle free and run behind a pillar.

"True," the Doctor's voice cackled over the sounds of war outside and breaking roof and beating 'thopter blades inside the domed room, "my looks aren't what they were, but I won't *need* them to defeat you, the Pendragon, or anyone else this time!"

"Morhagaine," Emrys said silently, "Morhaghaine *Le Fai*."

"You *know* him?" Gilbert yelled.

"Her, actually. She was—something of a rival, back then. She fooled me and locked me up for a long time. It was a very, very long time, Morhaghiane, but I *did* eventually awaken and escape, albeit with some help."

"You won't succeed this time, by thunder, *baby hawk!*" the Doctor growled in a guttural voice, still limping towards Emrys.

"Let's get out of here!" Gilbert said, looking warily at the giant.

"No one is going *anywhere!*" shouted old Williamson from his place at the first star point. "Doctor, the rest of you, back to your places! Now—"

He was thrown off balance as the tower suddenly rumbled and shook. The sound of cannon fire, dying men shouting, and rifle blasts ripped through the air once again, sounding louder now that the ornithopter's blades had fallen silent. Gilbert realized that the noise had always been there but none of them had noticed.

"Trying it the hard way, are they?" grated the Doctor's voice in the gloom as he stopped to look about. "Fine, then! But first, time to settle accounts!" he lunged forward, taking a clumsy swing at Emrys with his blubbery tentacle.

"Gilbert, quickly! This way!" said Emrys, dodging the blow and dragging Gilbert away from the fray.

Gilbert jumped back as a gun fired in the room. A girl screamed, Belloc shouted, and Herb leaped out of the pilot's seat, his dark coat suddenly animated as he threw one of his fabled punches at a target hidden to Gilbert in the fog.

Gilbert felt something cold on his leg. He looked down and saw a long, ropy tentacle had gripped it. He yelped and tried to kick himself free.

"That won't work now, boy!" the Doctor gasped in his now gravelly voice, ignoring the punches that Herb was landing on his face, even though each new blow scraped skin and muscle, exposing more flesh and even bone. The Doctor's now yellow eyes focused on Gilbert, his voice a high screech. "By ending you, I *will* have my vengeance against Emrys!"

From the other side of the room, a door burst open. Guards in gray uniforms poured into the room, armed with rifles glinting in the dim torchlight.

Oh, no, thought Gilbert.

****

Brigadier Brackenbury wiped the sweat from his face as the helmsman brought the ship around for another pass. Two of his four ships had seen their Cavorite stones stripped off by cannon blasts. Forced to land, they were now aground in the courtyard of the compound below, the *Nemean Lion* making a stand after damage forced it to land beside the wreckage and survivors of the *Andros.*

The Brigadier looked at the back of his hand, and he grimly noted a streak of red on his sleeve he hadn't noticed earlier.

"Orders, sir?" said Salisbury, both fear and adrenaline in his voice. His eyes were wild with the fear and bravado that accompanied combat, a look the Brigadier had seen on too many young men all too many times.

He looked at the badly damaged prow of his own ship, the hole scraped in his hull left by the cannon shot, and then turned to look at the large bite they had helped take out of the central tower dome minutes ago by hitting it. "Bring us about, have the *Minotaur* lay down a barrage of covering fire, and get us up to ramming speed again!" roared the Brigadier, ignoring the blood that dripped into his right eye. "I want that central tower in ruins by the next pass!"

"Aye, sir!" said Salisbury without hesitation, as he ran from the prow of the ship to relay the order.

The Brigadier looked again at the central tower. *I've no real idea what's inside, he thought to himself, but for some reason, I know that Williamson, his cronies, and everything evil in my world has all its chips bet on that place. And now it's time to gamble big and cash them in, win or lose.*

More guards poured into the darkening room through the now broken door, shouting for people to stop moving and put their hands up.

Everyone stopped moving. The Doctor's face pulled into a hideous smile. Seeing the impossible odds, Gilbert raised his hands, and he watched Herb, Belloc, and even Emrys do the same, though Emrys had kept his left hand gripping Gilbert's vest.

The filmy eyes of the Doctor turned their attention away from Gilbert to the old man who still gripped Gilbert's vest.

"Check and mate, gentlemen. Unless you'd like to be fertilizing the local fauna, you'll cease your pointless struggles now. Now, Emrys!" grated the Doctor's voice as he released Gilbert, his tentacle now whipping around the old man's left wrist.

"Stand down, Doctor," Belloc yelled back, drawing his pistol and pointing it at the creature's decaying face.

The dozen guards in the room raised and cocked their rifles. Belloc ignored them.

"I don't think even your minions could kill me before I pull this trigger, Doctor, or whatever you are," Belloc said, the Martian pistol still glowing red from its last discharge.

The Doctor's face kept its half smile. He spoke through the torn cheek on the side of his face.

"I'm a reasonable being, Belloc," the Doctor's voice said. Even considering its decaying state, its pitch had gone higher, sounding more like an angry woman than the evil man they'd all come to know and hate. "And I need this shell a little longer. Guards, put away your guns."

The guards, looking hesitatingly at each other, pointed their rifles at the ground.

"Now," Belloc said, "tell your mutts to let go of long-hair there and step back, or I'll shoot."

"Belloc, dear fool," the Doctor's voice said. "I think I'll snap this idiot's twiggish neck anyway, just to show you I need no guns to protect—"

Belloc fired. The Doctor dodged.

Had he been a few feet further back, the cone of the weapon would have disintegrated the Doctor's body as it had the Fourth Man.

But at point blank range, with the Doctor moving with surprising speed, the gun's spread wasn't quite so wide. Instead, only the Doctor's jaw disappeared in a slimy explosion of green flesh, dried blood and noxious-smelling spittle and vapor.

The Doctor paused in his dodge, eyes wide and face gone below the nose. Everyone else paused, staring in horrified fascination at the even greater ruin the Doctor's face had become.

Several guards began to retch and ran through the thickening fog back to the door they came in through a minute before. Their weapons were left on the floor, forgotten in the face of nameless terror and disgust.

Then a number of other things happened very quickly.

Gilbert heard a rage-filled female voice fill the room, and Anne leaped seemingly out of a patch of the black fog, her metal hand locked in a fist swinging in a deadly arc at the remains of the Doctor's head.

Herb shouted something Gilbert couldn't understand, and made a quick shoulder roll. He ended up *behind* the Doctor, leapt up and spun around, his leg fully extended as he made a roundhouse kick aimed at the Doctor's back.

Moving in a single, fluid motion, Belloc bent into a crouch and rolled forward on *his* right shoulder. Splaying out on his stomach, he was still moving when he fired the Martian pistol into the center of the dozen or so guards who *hadn't* dropped their weapons and run. Belloc's aim was good, and nearly all of them disappeared either in full or in part, leaving smoking remains to drop and splat on the floor. The remaining guards beat a hasty retreat, despite the howling, ineffectual orders of the First Man.

All this happened in the space of a single second. Now Gilbert watched Anne land from her leap between the feet of Belloc's prone body and the Doctor, her brass steamhand still on its course to collide with what remained of her hated adversary's face.

Both Anne and Herb's blows connected simultaneously, making the Doctor's head twist and his now brittle back break with sounds like snapping twigs as he released Emrys.

Belloc stood and pointed his pistol, holding it with both hands while keeping his eyes on the Doctor. Belloc moved closer to the creature, and—

Gilbert remembered something.

The Martian he'd killed in the sewer . . . Martians tended to have a trick up their sleeves when they were beaten and their opponents came too close to examine the body. A Martian had stabbed Gilbert's ankle in the sewers and nearly blown him up afterward for good measure.

"Belloc! Anne! Herb! Don't get closer to it! Don't go near—"

"Hush, lad," said Emrys, placing his hand on Gilbert's head, "they have their own battles to fight. You must finish this one," he said, as he gently pressed on Gilbert's shoulder until the taller boy knelt on both knees. Still standing, Emrys then placed his hand on Gilbert's head.

Gilbert, for reasons he could never later explain, didn't move. He felt something warm on his head, more than could be explained by the presence of the old man's hand alone. A warmth that slowly spread through his body from the top of his head under Emrys' palm.

The old man began speaking, saying words in an ancient language that Gilbert could nonetheless understand:

"Blessed are you O Lord, King of the Universe, for He has brought you forth as the new Pendragon, leader of His armies, scourge of his His foes, bringer of peace in times of war . . ."

****

1914 A.D.
MARS. TOP ROOM OF THE TEMPLE TOWER

Father Flambeau looked warily at the door as another hit slammed against it. "Blessed are you, O Lord, King of the Universe," he said, raising the Host into the air, "who brings forth this wine to offer. Fruit of the vine (SLAM!) and work of human hands, it will become our spiritual drink."

"Blessed be God forever," Gilbert said. Anne followed as best she could.

"Anne?" Gilbert said, "Would you truly do anything for me, if I asked it of you?"

"Provided," she whispered over the Priest's incantations, "it wasn't immoral or too illegal, yes, Gilbert, anything."

"Would you . . . would you trust me, if I said that something would be good for you, would benefit both of us, and even the whole world?"

"Until the sun stopped setting, Gilbert."

"Father?" Gilbert said, "may I be Anne's husband, godfather, and Confirmation sponsor too?"

1892 A.D.

"What's happening?" Gilbert felt odd, odd and yet giddy, fearful and yet energetic as the old man's words continued. Out of the corner of his eye he saw the animated corpse of the Doctor rise, his tentacle now seeming to grow as it whipped around, knocking Belloc, Herb, and Anne all to the floor in a single, violent spin.

"I am the anointer of the Pendragon," said the old man, whispering into Gilbert's ear. "A line of men a thousand years old, who have led armies of *glain* with their prayers and killed demons with their bare hands. The chair has been empty for a long time, and it now falls to you, young Chesterton. But only if you will accept it. You, your wits, your soul, your hands, and your pen, and those you take into your confidence must use it to work for the good and against the evil of this world."

"But King Arthur was the Pendragon! And he died a thousand years ago!"

****

1914 A.D.

Flambeau had brought out the vial before Gilbert had finished the sentence. He motioned Anne to come to him. Anne looked back at Gilbert, swallowed and stepped forward as the battering ram hit the door yet again, this time breaking off a quarter of one of the thick, ancient wood and metal doors.

"I'm ready, Father, for whatever type of torturous papist ritual you have in store for me."

Father Flambeau looked at Gilbert, and both men chuckled. "Anne," said Father Flambeau, "this is Baptism. A sacrament of the Church. It washes away the original break between you and God, and makes your soul clean and new."

"Does it hurt?" she asked.

"I imagine it would if you were a demon. But they don't ever request my services, so I've never had the chance to test that one out. Anne, I must know if you want this before I commence."

"I may be dead in a few moments, and I'd like to shorten the odds of my damnation for all I've done. Does that count?"

"Well and good. Anne, do you reject Satan and all his works and empty promises?"

"Certainly."

"Then, Anne, do you profess faith in God the Blessed Trinity as the rewarder of the just and the punisher of the wicked and in Jesus Christ as God's own Son and our Redeemer? And can you express the willingness to accept all that the Catholic Church teaches?"

"I saw what that faith did twenty years ago, father. And if it can make a good man like Gilbert live and walk the earth, then I'd believe it a thousand ti—"

Yet another thump outside interrupted her, followed by the sound of

ancient wood creaking and cracking.
"*Yes or no, Anne, please! We've not the time!*"
"*Then yes, yes, yes!*"

****

1892 A.D.

"Brace for impact!" shouted the Brigadier as they neared the main tower for their second pass. Out of the corner of his eye, he saw the last of the cannon crew on the last standing cannon tower drop, courtesy of one of the Brigadier's remaining sharpshooters. Salisbury had become the kind of soldier every commander enjoys in a battle: someone befuddled and awed at normal life, who finds his way to become cool, fearless, and focused when bullets fly and bayonets flash.

"Impact in three," Salisbury counted down, his left hand wrapped in a leather strap which was also tied around his waist and the railing, "two, one..."

Stunned and lying on his back, Herb looked at the pink sky through the room's dark haze and the hole in the broken ceiling he'd flown through as the sounds of battle raged from outside and inside their arena. His back hurt, and he could taste blood in his mouth. He might have to call a—*The Doctor!*

Now Herb remembered. After kicking the Doctor, or whatever the Doctor had become, something had struck Herb and his cohorts with the power of an ocean wave and knocked the three of them flat. He couldn't remember if it was the Doctor's tentacle, a piece of debris, or something else. All he knew right now was that he was in pain, and it hurt even to think.

Herb rose to his feet, trying to ignore the pain screaming from four or five places in his body.

He scanned the room, looking for threats and allies.

Gil was in one corner of the room, near an alcove. He was kneeling, and appeared mesmerized by the old man who'd hitched a ride with Herb. The old man had his hand on Gilbert's head, saying some words of blessing or benediction.

The Doctor was near the center of the five-pointed star, the lines of which were glowing in the red rock, either from the twilight sun or from some other source. His jaw was gone, leaving tendons flailing, spittle falling in long, thin snaky threads, and caked blood falling off the top part of his jaw in flakes and chunks. His tentacle had *grown* somehow. Grown longer and changed color from a brown to a sick green with seams and tears all over it. He saw Anne struggle to her feet as well, then get her bearings and take another run at the Doctor. How had that evil creature remained standing, after being shot and then hit by *two* killing blows from different directions?

That Belloc fellow, the one Herb had been briefed on before arriving on Mars, was proving quite brave, too. He'd somehow got ahold of one of the ancient Martian pistols, and pointed it at the Doctor. *Do it*, Herb said silently to himself, *kill that beast . . .*

But when Belloc tried to fire his pistol on the Doctor, nothing happened. Perhaps it had jammed? Run out of power? Or maybe it couldn't fire on a squid; Herb had heard of such protocols built into Martian devices, to keep the Red men from ever using the higher-level technologies to rise up and overthrow their slimy masters, and the Doctor's tentacle would be saving him in this case.

Belloc, however, was unconcerned with any of this at the moment. With the guards gone and the pistol clicking ineffectively at its pulled trigger, Belloc ran at the Doctor. Like Anne, Belloc ran at the Doctor with his back straight and his eyes never leaving his target. In a seemingly single motion, his steady hands scooped up a fallen repeater rifle, aimed and pulled the trigger over and over again while still in motion.

A screeching, hate-filled shriek sounded from the Doctor's ruined throat. The Doctor's eyes opened wide and stared through green-tinted irises at the three young people nearing him.

Suddenly, quicker than anyone would have thought, Herb saw the Doctor's stiff-walking corpse became very limber, its arm-thick tentacle suddenly extending to a huge length, and slamming both Belloc and him like a sick, green wave. Both flew against the stone wall and lay still on the floor.

A second later, Anne reached the Doctor, who whipped his tentacle at her as well.

But when it reached Anne, her metal hand grabbed it, as if it were the bicep of a man taking a swing at her.

The Doctor stopped his attack, startled.

Anne squeezed, little jets of steam blasting from her brass knuckle joints.

The Doctor's Martian arm snapped off like a wilted stalk of celery.

She opened her hand and dropped the dripping, smelling piece of the Doctor's appendage to the ground, where it continued squirming like a landed fish.

Emrys, his words finished, smiled kindly at Gilbert with eyes that seemed so much older and removed his hand. "Now, go," he said, "and do good while you can."

Gilbert, feeling quite odd, mumbled quick thanks. He turned to see Herb and Belloc laid out on the floor, stunned.

Gilbert ran to help Anne, who was closest to the Doctor. Before he could reach her, the Doctor squatted and sprang at her like an agile frog, his snapped tentacle squirming like a bisected worm. She brought up her metal hand to stop him but this time was too slow. The Doctor blasted by her, knocking both her and Gilbert to the ground in one movement.

Both were largely unhurt, and Gilbert quickly realized it was because they had not been the creature's intended targets.

The Doctor's corpse had flown with its full force and fury past Gilbert and Anne, hurtling towards Emrys, who . . . stepped aside neatly, avoiding the Doctor's leap.

The Doctor flew past him, landing in a huddled, squirming heap behind Emrys. "Morgan," said Emrys, pushing his glasses up the bridge of his nose as the creature struggled to extricate itself from the tangle its dying human limbs had become. "You've hardly changed at all. I'm not so old that I can be tricked the same way twice." The twisting corpse paused, suddenly stood, and began a kind of sick, huffing breathing noise that sounded like a pitiful imitation of laughter. It pointed at Emrys's midsection with a broken index finger.

Emrys looked down. His stomach had been sliced open, and he was bleeding freely.

"Oh *bother*," Emrys said, sounding more peeved and perturbed than angry, and he sank to his knees.

Gilbert looked in silence at Emrys, then at the Doctor's still-standing corpse, which was giving its hideous imitation of laughter at the sight of Emrys' demise.

Gilbert realized that the room had fallen silent. The gramophone had stopped playing its infernal, twittering, squeaking racket.

"You see, young Chesterton?" bellowed another voice. It was the last remaining old man who'd been standing at the second of the five points in the star drawn on the ground. This one had gone to the lengths of having several tattoos inked on his face, which sported a sunken pair of eyes. "You see? All your efforts have been for *nothing*! Now, with a final word, I summon the ultimate power on two worlds! Power I *alone* now will wield!"

"What about Williamson?" said Gilbert. He stopped as he looked at the point in the star where the First Man had stood.

Williamson, aka the First Man, laid in a huddled heap on the floor, his face frozen in a twisted snarl of anger and fear, a single, dark hole in his chest had a drying, thin red line trailing down to the floor.

In spite of all that was going on, Gilbert marveled at the irony. The most powerful man in the world had been reduced to a powerless heap by a single, likely accidental shot.

"Gilbert, help us!" shouted Anne, still conscious and now running at the Doctor again, her steamhand flexing into a deadly fist.

But the Doctor's tentacle whipped out again. Though shortened, it was still long enough that it pushed Anne against the nearest wall, and then moved to grab and twist the head of the Second Man so hard across his sunken-eyed face that his tattooed head suddenly turned at a deadly, unnatural angle.

The Second Man fell to the floor without a sound and was still, an unmoving sneer set on his face as his dead eyes looked to the sky.

At seeing Anne hurt and knocked about yet again, Gilbert ran at the Doctor. He was seeing red and not caring what consequences might come from the creature's dying but still deadly arm.

Roaring like a battlefield warrior, Gilbert leaped into the air, fully intending to kick the monster in the creaking, sunken chest.

Gilbert's kick found its mark.

And when he hit, half the room's walls and ceiling were torn away.

No longer threatened with cannon fire, the *Golden Eagle* had turned about and hit the domed roof at the top of the tallest tower square on. The smooth roof had stood since the days of Gilgamesh, but now it broke apart and crumbled inward. Wreckage fell on and around those left inside as the *Golden Eagle* broke through the dome, careened through the room, and sheared away nearly half of the ancient stone floor as it blasted through, carrying several of the bodies of the late members of the Circle with it. Herb's wrecked ornithopter remained on the floor, the fat ham-hand of the Third Man reaching out from under the wreckage in a pool of blood.

Though it connected, Gilbert's heel flew wide by a few crucial inches. Instead of hitting the Doctor's chest, it struck him in the head while the ship continued its deadly parade through the domed room. Gilbert felt rather than heard the creature's skull bones crack with a sound like the breaking of a brittle piece of melba toast, making the Doctor's body stagger back several feet with part of its remaining head caved inward.

Still standing, it spat another curse at Gilbert and ran at him like a staggering, drunken bear, so completely focused on Gilbert that it didn't even notice the ship behind it tearing half the room away.

The cracks in the crumbling floor worked their way toward Gilbert from behind the Doctor.

Herb had been groggily trying to rise after being hit, but woke fully aware when he saw the floor fall away beneath him. He leaped into action, running away from the crumbling side of the domed room, hopping across pieces of floor as they broke away beneath his feet.

Herb's last leap took him off the last falling piece beneath his feet, sailing head-first past the Doctor while his flailing arms found something thin and solid enough to grab on to. Thinking it might be a solid rail, pole or something equally stable, he grabbed hard and didn't let go. Even when he felt the "rail" squirm in his hands and try to jerk loose from whatever it had been attached to, Herb held fast with a strength born of both desperation and fear.

Still flying forward in his jump and holding onto whatever it was he'd grabbed, the 'solid' ground Herb had leapt forward to rushed up and hit Herb in the face, turning his world black with flashing stars. As he opened his eyes slowly, he saw the remains of the Doctor's human arm lying nearby, still clothed in the tattered remains of sleeve of a once expensive longcoat, the hand a grayish-green, and the white nub of the shoulder bone looking like something pulled off a hastily dismembered chicken.

Herb blinked, still stunned. Much of the far wall in front of him had been torn away, too. With the remaining red light coming from the center of the star in the floor, Herb saw a shadow-puppet play of the Doctor, his torn but still functional Martian limb still knocking opponents down left and right, until another shadow stalked up behind him with something large in its hands.

The new shadow-person raised the shadow-rock and smashed it downwards, grunting with a woman's voice as it crushed the Doctor's head. The Doctor's shadow fell to the ground, and the shadow woman continued to grunt and scream as she hit him again and again, shrieking and bashing until long after the unliving corpse and its twitching tentacle had finally stopped moving.

Herb turned over and raised his head to better see what had just happened. He beheld a young woman with short blond hair dressed in a guard's uniform. She was standing over the Doctor's battered corpse, breathing hard with eyes that were wide and wild with the intoxication of the fight. A large bruise, probably from some wreckage earlier, covered half her forehead. Her face was half-crazed with a mixture of fear, anger, and triumph, reminding Herb of a slave he'd seen in an uprising a few months back in the Middle East who'd killed a hated master in the heat of a riot.

Herb blinked again.

Gilbert was standing over Anne, who'd fallen when the ship had hit their large room at the top of the tower. Gil looked first at Anne, going down on both knees to make sure she was well.

And then Gilbert looked at the girl who'd finally killed the Doctor.

She was still breathing hard, when she sensed someone watching her, looked up from the Doctor's body, and locked eyes with Gilbert.

Herb could see so clearly now. Gilbert and this new girl. Their faces, the color of their hair, their cheekbones.

They were the same.

Then Herb saw Anne, who struggled to her feet and began to yell once she saw the fallen body of the Doctor. She yelled something about how it had been *her* right, *her right!* She charged forward, her dress now filthy and dirty around the ruffles, and gave a deadly, pointed-boot kick to the Doctor's body.

There was a *crack* and a *squish* as her boot punctured the Doctor's ribcage. The force carried the Doctor's broken corpse over the side of the broken floor, falling uncounted stories to burst open in an explosion of red and green slime on the stone ground below.

There was silence for a few seconds. Then, as if by an unspoken agreement, everyone remembered what was in the center of the room, and turned to face it.

The enormous spirit still stood. Now forty feet tall, its head rose up higher than the broken roof of the dome, silhouetted against the pink Martian sky. It watched them silently while standing in front of the dark portal that still hovered in the center of the star drawn on the floor.

Emrys, his face and body spattered with blood, gestured to Gilbert with a small gasp.

Gilbert ran to the dying man, while he stared with steady eyes at the giant spirit. Gilbert had always been taller than most, but since the old man's blessing Gilbert now seemed taller still. His face had some of Emrys' blood on his cheek and forehead. His shadow casted long on the floor with the setting sun, covering Belloc, Herb, Beatrice, Frances, and Anne, and all others that remained in a room now half its original size.

The silence was so perfect that it wasn't broken for nearly ten seconds.

"Sir?" said Salisbury, speaking carefully through the blood that kept filling his mouth. The wreckage of the *Eagle* around him crackled with small fires and the moanings of the injured and dying. The base of the tower stood nearby.

"Salisbury," Brigadier Brackenbury said, looking down at his chest. A large wooden spike, splintered from the main mast, seemed to be growing out of the space below his right shoulder and above his lung. "Salisbury, I said we'd likely not return, didn't I?"

"Yes, sir. It didn't matter to me, sir, or the men."

Brackenbury looked around at the ruin of their ship. The impact on the ancient tower had downed their ship in a crash landing.

It meant there were perhaps a dozen men left, with only the wreck to use as cover once the enemy realized what had happened. He touched the pocket that held his St. George medal, the one his father had given him the day he'd received his commission as an officer over a quarter-century ago.

"Lads," he said, his voice strengthening, "I told you to sell your lives dear. But that was when I was sure we'd die. That need not happen now!" He stood again, straightening his back and ignoring the pain in his leg and chest, wincing when the stick that had impaled him below his shoulder moved...

Something new in the Brigadier shifted. Remembering an old copy of the *Iliad* he'd read in his father's library as a child, he reached behind his shoulder, grabbed the spike from the large end behind and pulled with all his might.

The spike slid out without any barbs or other impediments. The pain was still exquisite, and the Brigadier gave a shout of pain that lasted exactly three seconds. "Mister Salisbury!" he gasped after the scream was done.

"Sir!" barked Salisbury, spitting out a loose tooth that had been annoying him.

"Mister Salisbury, get a wog to heat a bayonet to burn this wound shut. I can't die yet—I have too much to do."

"Yes sir!"

"Then Salisbury, take defensive positions with the men! Select the most able and inventory our weaponry assets! After that, move the wounded to safety below our deck—or what's left of our decks, anyway. Once we secure our position, we can attempt to contact the other downed ships in this compound!"

"Yes, sir!"

"Lads! *Don't* sell your lives dear!" the Brigadier roared, his voice carrying throughout the compound to the crews of the other three ships that had landed or crashed. "Buy *their* lives on the cheap! Take positions, and fire at will!"

A roar went out from the healthy and the hurt, the able and the lame, as the Brigadier's order gave strength to every man under his command. Soldiers found cover, pistols and rifles were loaded! Ragged Miners under John Carter's command found common cause with the Queen's soldiers, running to the fallen to give aid, cover, and comradeship to those they would have thought their enemies only a day before.

The Brigadier yelled once, then twice as his wound was burned closed. But his roar, far from upsetting any, invigorated the men under his command. Battle lines were drawn, rifles and pistols blasted forth, and within less than five minutes the few remaining forces of the Circle were quickly routed! The sound of cheers from men young and old sounded and resounded, echoing past walls that had stood thousands of years and seen battle untold times throughout Martian history! *Victory!* came the cries over and over again as grey suited guards ran, died or surrendered, *Victory! Victory! Victory!*

****

In the utter, complete silence of his clean, ordered little office, James Matthew Arnold Richardson looked nervously at the clock on his wall.

It was Friday and the mail was due. The call had not yet come, and was in fact late for the first time in his memory. If the messenger did not arrive, he knew what his instructions were. But something inside caused a black well of fear inside him to turn and churn. Something dark and nameless told him that following the instructions this time would have terrible consequences, but he knew he'd follow them anyway.

Nature had given him a brain, but not a spine.

****

Frances woke. She was prone, lying flat on the ground, looking up at a sky that was the gentle dark of twilight. There was a gentle breeze blowing on her face. She shook her head, breathed deep and sneezed. Her jerking head kicked up a red cloud of dust that shot around her, dancing through the deepening red beams of light cast by the setting sun. She looked around, and she could see little in the red-lit smoke and dust around her. Her face hurt. As she put her hand on her jaw, it hurt worse and she hissed. Her hand came away with a streak of red on it, but a quick self-check revealed no additional injuries, other than . . . *Ouch!* Her leg! Something in her knee hurt worse than anything she'd felt in a long, long time. She looked down, and she saw her cell had been broken nearly in half. The floor was a jagged zig-zag of stone, and half her cell had been torn away, exposing her to the outside. She had guessed that she was near ground level, but she was actually high up in the air. She gasped in fear and moved her body close to the wall and away from the jagged edge as quickly as her hurt leg would allow her.

Looking up again, she saw that another tower, the central one, had suffered the same fate, it's walls broken and torn to where the rooms inside were readily visible.

And on the top floor of the central tower, what looked like a dark, giant, man-shaped creature hovered a little bit above the tower's top floor, gazing neutrally at the world below it. Gilbert and a few others were in a broken-away half-room like her, and everything was suffused in a soft, red glow and a dark, transparent fog. On the ground below, the men of the downed airboats were cheering while fighting a number of the now ragged-looking yobs wearing the grey uniforms of the guards.

Fortunately, the staircase had been spared whatever force had broken the tower. "Right," she said, wincing and trying to hobble quick as she could, hoping she wouldn't draw attention to herself as she did so, "time to . . . *bite the bullet!*" She said, using a phrase she'd heard Gilbert say when he was about to do something unpleasant.

And as she rose, the fog at the top of the central tower cleared a bit. She saw Gilbert, standing tall and brave, staring at the multi-hued transparent giant. Beneath the giant was a hovering black disk that made her think of a portal or doorway, and from which the black fog seemed to emanate. "Dear Lord," she said, as she hobbled towards what was left of the stairs.

"What...what *is* that?" Belloc said while looking with eyes wide as silver dollars at the still unmoving man-shaped spirit hovering in the air. After kicking the Doctor's body off the edge, Anne had fallen to her knees in fear. The girl in the uniform who'd bashed the Doctor's corpse to pudding had done so too. In the silence they had all suddenly realized that the giant and the portal it stood in front of had been hovering over their tiny squabbles, and now with their human conflicts concluded it dominated their attentions.

Though the giant hadn't said a word, both it and the open portal beneath it caused Belloc a particular kind of dread he'd never experienced before.

Though truly fearful in the being's presence, Gilbert nonetheless still did not collapse in front of it. There was a kind of acceptance in his heart—an understanding that he was in the presence of something *greater* than himself in every sense of the word he knew. It was a bit like when a congressman had come to town years ago. Though the man had not been twenty-five feet tall like they'd said he was, nor anywhere in the neighborhood of it, Senator Sawyer had commanded the town square with his smile and speech in such a way that all listening had been enthralled.

Gilbert felt that way now. He somehow *knew* that the thing in front of him had entered creation long, long before him and would continue to do its job long after Gilbert left the stage of this life.

And it now surveyed the remains of the room, looking first at the little group of youths around him, then at the dead tattooed man on the floor beside Gilbert, and the wreckage of the ornithopter next to the corpse of the man with the sunken eyes. The giant then swept its gaze out to the world past them, looking at the walls with constant, unblinking eyes. Despite the calm expression it wore, Gilbert felt the being seemed unhappy with what it saw.

1914 A.D.

Father Flambeau ducked as a chunk of the ceiling flew past him, and continued speaking as if nothing had happened. "Do you reject the glamour of evil and the false promises of the devil?"

"I do!" Anne said.

"Then I baptize you in the name of the Father, and of the Son, and of the Holy Spirit," Father Flambeau said, pouring a few precious drops of water from his vial over her head three times.

****

1892 A.D.

"Gilbert!" Anne whispered in the large room that had suddenly gone silent, her eyes riveted to the giant being above their little group. "What do we *do*? What is that?"

"I—I don't know!" Gilbert said. "I think it's . . ." he looked down at Emrys, whose eyes were now closed even though his body was still breathing, "this fella called it a *glain*."

"Some kind of angel?" Anne asked, checking.

"Maybe," Gilbert said.

"Aren't they supposed to be sweet with fluffy wings?" Anne asked.

"Sometimes," Gilbert said. "And sometimes in the Bible they're given the dirty jobs, like wiping out an army of a hundred thousand bad guys in a single night."

"And, in just a few moments," Beatrice said, "it will finish the job of sterilizing this place, and wiping it clean of all life, just as the Doctor said it would."

****

1914 A.D.

"Anne," said Father Flambeau, "be sealed in the Holy Spirit." He placed his cupped hand upon her head, the scented oil smelling sweet and pungent in the night air as it flowed in from outside the massive gaping hole in what remained of the large room's ceiling.

"Father, am I confirmed now? Can we finish this and save the world yet?"

"Your intended is quite eager, Gilles! Yes, Anne, we can begin the final portion of . . ."

Gilbert heard a whine by his ear, followed by a wet thud. Father Flambeau stiffened, grabbed his neck with his left hand and crumpled to the floor.

"G-gosh darn it!" Gilbert yelled, dropping to his knees. In one smooth motion he'd pulled the small pistol he knew to be secreted in the priest's waistband and began blasting in the direction the dart had come from.

Scurrying noises came from the back of the room as the Warhoon ran from the exploding rocks near its head.

"They don't like guns," Gilbert said. "It's why they won't come in through the big gap over here—too exposed. They'll only enter through the doorway because of the cover it provides."

"What now?" Anne said. "We can't do this without a priest, can we?"

"Actually, we can. We can in a pinch. And if this doesn't count as a pinch, I don't know what would! Anne. . ." he paused. He didn't even know her last name! "Anne, surely as I stand here, I take you as my . . ."

The door, weakened by repeated blows, finally gave way and let a flood of Warhoon fighters into the room.

"Oh, blast it all!" Anne said, spinning around and punching the fastest Warhoon Martian in the throat with her metal fist, cutting off its war-cry and making it go down into a green, four-armed crumple of arms and smelly green flesh.

Gilbert spun round next in a fluid motion, knowing instinctively and

498

correctly that there would be another Warhoon behind him to meet the end
of the blade he'd pulled from his waistband.

"Anne," he said with a grunt, "I take you as my wife," (turn, stab! grunt,
turn, stab! dodge . . .), until death do us part!" He continued to dodge, thrust,
spin and strike as more Warhoons, drunk on bloodlust, entered through the
shattered doorway and charged them.

"Gilbert," Anne replied, firing upwards with two brass fingers into the
face of another Warhoon, then pausing after she impaled his head with her
two forefingers, "I take you as my husband, until death do us part!" She
let loose a final sigh as the Warhoon's caved-in face suddenly let loose and
gushed noxious-smelling green fluid all over her steamhand.

It was suddenly quiet. Five Warhoon bodies lay at Gilbert's feet, two at
Anne's.

They looked at each other in the silence.

****

1892 A.D.

"What's he doing?" Beatrice asked, looking at Gilbert and his little
group. Gilbert, unsurprised by anything at the point waved her over to
join them.

The red giant was now turning in a slow arc, its eyes unblinking,
moving subtly across the field of vision.

"It's looking at the world, I'd warrant," said Belloc. "It's checking
conditions before it acts."

"Shouldn't we be trying to escape?" Anne said.

"My guess is it wouldn't matter where we ran to," Belloc said. "And if
my nose smelled right, killing the Doctor was something of a redundancy.
He was already dead and gone to whatever awaited him long before he
got kicked over the ledge. Whatever was in him was something else,
something Emrys had fought before and beaten, something literally from
the pits of He—"

Belloc interrupted himself by screaming, then gasping silently as he
fell to the ground with his hands around his throat.

Anne, Herb, and Beatrice all began screaming, too. Gilbert had never
felt such agony before. Looking up, he could see the lighted corona around

the giant suddenly deepen and become more intense. He heard the laughter of the thing that had taken the Doctor's body, but heard it laughing in his *head* rather than with his ears. The air was harder to breathe, Gilbert's ears were popping, and he felt his lungs and heart pushing harder and harder against his insides, like balloons with too much air in them. There was no real noise he could hear with his ears anymore, only a loud, tinny whining, like he'd heard when he was littler and a cruel classmate had clipped him a hard one on his ear and knocked him to the ground.

"*I win!*" screamed the voice in Gilbert's head. It was close to the triumphant shriek of Luther, the bully he'd known in childhood, but more like a screechy angry girl. "*I win! The whole of a world, the rest of it! I've got you at last, Emrys! The baby hawk has lost it all! All to me! A whole world, dead because of me, and using one of my masters' unfallen brethren as my pawn! No water or fire needed! This time it will be the air! The air! I'll be rewarded with a kingdom, and undersecrtaryship—perhaps even freedom from Hell! The name of Morgan the Fay will bring terror to-*"

Gilbert, trying to block out the shrieking monologue in his head, tried to extend his hand to the ominous, stoic spirit across from him. Belloc was trying to do the same, but the twenty or so feet between them and the giant might as well have been a thousand miles. Anne, her eyes bulging almost out of her head, reached out with her mechanical hand. A small trigger popped open from her thumb.

Gilbert's eyes, attracted by the movement, saw that what had popped out of her thumb wasn't a trigger.

It was a target sight.

****

1914 A.D.

"*What do we do now?*" Anne said. Father Flambeau's prone and silent form lay in front of them in the middle of a half-dozen Warhoon corpses.

Gilbert looked at Anne. Her perfectly-shaded red hair was askew after their latest combat, the chrism oil Father had used on her evident in a broad backwards streak from her forehead to her hairline. "We have at least a few minutes until the next wave hits," he said. "Until then, we can . . . we can . . ."

"*Gilbert,*" she said quietly.

"Anne, Anne spelled with an e," Gilbert said, straightening his back, looking into her eyes and clasping both her hands in his own. "Anne, let us do this properly. Anne, I take you as my wife. For richer, for poorer, in sickness and in health, forsaking all others, until death do us part. Even if that's only a few minutes from now."

"Gilbert, are you sure this'll work? Father Flambeau is unconscious, and I don't know how strong the drug in that dart was. Shouldn't I try to revive him?"

"This is the only sacrament you don't need a priest for, Anne! We give it to each other! Now please, stop arguing theology with me and work alongside me?"

"Right, then," she said, straightening her hair. Gilbert fumed silently. Why, why, why did every woman he'd ever known insist upon clean hair at the most inconvenient of times? It was the kind of thing that frustrated him enough to start a revolution! More than once he'd told Frances . . .

Frances . . .

No. She had died. She was no longer his wife. It still hurt. But then, as he saw Anne . . .

"I, Anne Shirley, being of sound mind and body . . ."

"Anne, it's a wedding, not a will!"

"Who's arguing theology now? Fine. I take you, Gilbert, as my husband, under all circumstances, until death do we part! Is that right? Can we . . ."

Gilbert kissed her.

In a moment they were both eighteen again. Seventeen. Sixteen. In his mind's eye Gilbert saw her fighting the white ape, then felt her rocking him as a mother rocks her child after his emotional trauma in the floating city, and then he was once again in the offices of Mister Effortson back when he'd been a youthful clacker in the East end of London, before the Martian mollusks had landed.

She stiffened at first, then melted. All time, all her memories of Gilbert had become one, single, unending happy moment. All thoughts of Gilbert had become one beautiful thought. She felt all times, all memories, become one, beautiful instant without beginning or end. Her first glimpse of him from afar, after learning he'd been selected for her by her evil masters. Her first sight of him in the office of the clacking firm in London, her hypnotism of him in Paris when they were seventeen, his breaking of the conditioning she'd locked into his brain, the kiss she'd given him to distract him while she *threw him into the escape pod and . . . And this beautiful, perfect, shining moment. This time, this perfect time, and they two had become one forever.*

This was love, and something more than love as she'd known it. All was around, before and inside of her. All. It was all, and she was within it.

And it was beautiful.

Then they both felt the pain in their lungs.

****

1892 A.D.

He watched as Anne's cocked finger snapped, sparked, and fizzled. What would have been a bullet fired weakly from her pointed index finger, with hardly enough power to move it more than six feet before it hit the dirt.

Gilbert's eyes felt like they were going to explode. The gigantic being loomed over them with neither malice nor pity, no more threatening than a bus driver who seemed intent upon completing his job. But it also moved with no more willingness to pause or stop than a glacier moving forward through a valley, a sun shining on a brilliant summer's day, or a tide sweeping sand before it on a seashore.

Please, he tried to whisper, *please, stop . . .*

But the voice in his head still kept laughing.

"Salisbury!" spat the Brigadier, blood trickling out of both sides of his mouth.

"Sir!" said Salisbury, gasping while trying to reload his pepperbox pistol.

"Status report!"

"All ships down, ten survivors from our crew present. About a half dozen visible from the *Minotaur*, the others not visible at this time."

Brigadier Brackenbury looked around the battlefield. His head hurt, and he had difficulty seeing anything clearly. He'd given Salisbury a battlefield-promotion to the rank of Lieutenant, so the boy could legally act as the Brigadier's eyes.

"Threats, Lieutenant?"

Salisbury peered through a break in the wooden slats of their downed ship's hull. "The main forces of the enemy have been killed or are falling back. I think we only have stragglers and snipers— Wait! I see them!"

"Who?"

"I recognize Private Stevens from the crew of the *Andros*! He's leading the men toward the wreck of the *Minotaur*! We have reinforcements, Brigadier!"

"About time. Signal the men to join us. I can tell from the lack of sounds that we've won for now. We'll need to pursue the blighters before they rally for the—"

Brigadier Brackenbury suddenly gasped and could not speak. He felt almost exactly as he'd felt as a lad of eight, when he'd fallen from a tree branch onto his back and the fall had knocked the wind out of his lungs. There was that same sense of trying so hard to pull air into his body, and the air refusing to enter.

Already sitting, the Brigadier laid back his head and tried to breathe. Salisbury fell to his right. The boy's knees hit the dirt, broken wood and stone and sounded a thousand miles away, rather than right next to him.

Looking around as he lost consciousness, his last thought was how odd all the little blurry forms around him looked as they fell to the ground. Looking so close yet sounding so far away . . .

****

1914 A.D.

Gilbert looked at Anne as they pulled back from each other, their eyes still locked. "Have we . . . are we . . ." Anne asked as they parted. She had no idea how long their kiss had lasted.

"I would say so. Again, I've no idea if they've . . . if we . . . oh, hang it! Wasn't Father in the thing when we saw it? And why does it hurt all of a sudden?"

"Perhaps, mon ami," said a shaky voice behind them. Father Flambeau stood up slowly and surveyed them. "Have I missed much?"

"We just exchanged vows while you were unconscious, Jean-Paul. Is that going to be a problem?"

"Gilles, there is never a problem when one can finish the saying of a holy Mass. Now," he said, reaching into the folds of his belt and taking out

a small white disk. He stood with the uneven block of stone in front of him, his back turned to the pair of adventurers and looked at the chalk cross he'd drawn on the red stone wall.

He spoke Latin for a few seconds. Gilbert felt Anne's hand slip into his own.

He turned to look at her, and their eyes met. Father Flambeau continued to speak the words of the Mass in a language centuries old, and the air itself seemed to tingle around them.

"What's happening, Gilbert?" Anne whispered.

"I don't know, Anne," he said, "but I think . . . I think they . . . we can see us now."

"Then, you know what to do?"

"Haec omnia de te ipso manducaverit," *said Father.*

"I . . . well, yes. It wasn't that long ago, you know."

"HOC EST ENIM CORPUS MEUM," *Father said, focusing on the small circled wafer in front of him while raising it high above his head.*

"Well, then?" Anne said, smiling slightly.

"QUOD PRO VOBIS TRADETUR."

When the host was at its apex, Gilbert leaned down and kissed Anne, gently on the lips. Then then both turned to face Father, who still stood with his large, powerful hands holding a small disk the size of an American silver dollar in the air above him.

****

1892 A.D.

Gilbert gasped for breath. His eyes were ready to burst. Even the voice in his head had stopped cackling, and seemed to be waiting for whatever would come next.

"Gi—" he heard a voice say from a long, long way off. He looked and Anne was staring at him while lying on her side, clutching herself in a curled up position, her face twisted by pain. "Eye—" she said, more in a lunging breath than a word, "Eye . . . lov—"

Then she fell silent.

A distant low noise sounded next to him. Hilaire Belloc was roaring in anger, sounding a million miles away. He struggled to his feet, shouting something, trying to ignore the pain. He stood, still shouting, and took staggering steps toward the red giant that stood impassively above them.

Belloc took step after step, five in all, each one a huge effort. With the last step, though, even he reached his limit and fell face down at the foot of the giant spirit.

The being stopped, folded its hands for a moment, and looked down at the prone form of the young soldier at its feet. It had been moving its hands down toward the floor, but at the sight of Belloc's immense efforts, it stopped and regarded him.

Gilbert thought, *Why bother? It's only prolonging the inevitable.* The dark portal that had opened during the ceremony was still open, and the dark fog was still flowing slowly through it next to the giant.

But then something very strange happened, strange even by the standards of Gilbert and his little army.

As Gilbert watched, another disc appeared in the air, right in front of the dark one.

It was white, and much smaller than the first one. And the white disc grew larger and larger. It grew to be four feet tall, then as tall as a man, now half-again as tall as Gilbert himself, now twice as tall, then tall enough to reach the waist of the red giant.

And then it wasn't a disk at all anymore, but a stretched-thin portal, like a doorway viewed through a bowl of milk.

And through the portal, Gilbert could see . . . a man who looked like him.

He looked older, with a mustache, and he was . . . well, not fat, but a little on the heavy side, anyway.

And the man was standing sideways in profile, holding hands with a girl while looking into her eyes. A girl who looked just a bit like . . .

Oh, my.

And between them he could see a priest with a white collar and stole holding a host aloft, as he would at the consecration point of a Mass.

It's because that dark portal opened, Gilbert realized. Someone opened a bad door, and that giant had to come and close things, and close us along with it. But . . .

But now, with the vision of the portal, Gilbert, Anne and the priest, something very, very odd began to happen.

The fog stopped flowing from the black portal. And then the portal itself began to fizzle and sizzle on its edges.

And then it broke, like a pane of black glass, shards falling to the stone floor with cold, clipped tinkling sounds.

The giant looked at the space where the black door had been, and then back at the rest of the world in front of it.

And just like that, Gilbert could breathe again.

The new portal remained, and looking at it Gilbert could see much more clearly. He could see . . .

The two people in the vision; they didn't look like ghosts at all anymore. But they were . . .

"It that you?" he heard Anne's voice behind him. He turned to look and saw her beautiful blue eyes staring as if hypnotized at the sight. Gilbert turned back after only a split second. The figures before them were no longer transparent, but clear as if they were standing in front of them. They made no sound, and cast no shadows on the ground.

Gilbert saw who the man was.

It was *him*.

And the woman was . . . it was . . . they were . . .

"Married," Belloc whispered behind them. "That's the two of you, only older. I'd bet my honor on it."

Gilbert looked up at the giant. It, too, was looking down, not at Gilbert, Anne, and Belloc, but at the silent tableaux below it of the older Gilbert, Anne, and the priest.

"It's the Mass," Belloc said.

"All time," Gilbert answered. "At that moment in the Mass, all time is one, for anything eternal. It's happening somewhere . . . no, it's happening *here*, but some-*when* else, but affecting things *here*."

Anne looked like she was about to speak, but closed her mouth and said nothing.

And as the air thickened and returned to normal, the clear vision in front of it became even clearer. Gilbert would have thought his older self was truly present in the battered meeting room of stone, if he hadn't seen 'his' feet step on a rock or two and move through them.

And, as he watched, the older Anne's head tilted lovingly up to that of the older Gilbert's, and began to speak.

1914 A.D.

"Are they . . . are we watching us, right now?" she said.

"I think so," Gilbert replied. He swallowed again—there was a bit of the communion host still lodged at the back of his throat. "The pain—it's gone. For me, anyway. And you?"

She nodded her head. "Gilbert, it's happened. It's really happened. We saved the world, but I don't know how we did it."

"The Mass is ended, go in peace." Flambeau finished. He walked without hesitation around the altar and gave them both a large bear hug. "That," he said, "is without all doubt the strangest circumstance under which any priest has said Holy Mass."

"Is It really over?" Gilbert asked. "We still have to get off this rock now, you know. We saw the Mass back then, but we didn't see ourselves escape, Jean-Paul."

As if on cue, they heard the scrabbling of Warhoon feet and hands on the rock outside.

"That's . . . that's a little odd," Anne said.

"What's odd about it?" Gilbert asked. He and Father Flambeau had already dropped into a tense fighting stance, holding up their weapons to point at the sources of noise outside, ready to fight if they broke in again.

"Warhoons," Anne continued, still standing in a normal form, listening hard to the scratchings outside, "aren't complete savages. They're fairly quiet before they attack, and they only make that particular noise when they're on the way out from someplace. If they were going to attack, we wouldn't hear them at all until they thought it didn't matter."

"If they are leaving, then . . . what's getting them to go?"

Outside, the sound of a machine's hum carried into the broken chamber. Gilbert recognized the steady beating sound of an ornithopter. A big one.

****

1892 A.D.

"What happens now?" Gilbert said. The giant had disappeared without any word or trace.

"Well," Hilaire looked around, fists on his hips, "It would appear we are alone in the place. And . . . Gilbert, you're bleeding. Doesn't that hurt?"

Hilaire looked down at Gilbert's feet. Gilbert and Anne did the same. There was a dark stain at his heel.

"Jeepers," said Gilbert.

"That was . . ." said Anne. "The trail, your footprints . . ."

They all looked. Five bloody heel prints traveled backwards from their little group, back to where the young blond man had laid down and become still "Gilbert, do you know what he was?"

"When he put his hand on my head, he said something. Called me something."

"*Pendragon*," Belloc whispered. "Gilbert, do you know what he did? You're the leader now, of all who oppose the darkness in England."

They were silent, in a room that had suddenly become very, very silent. A large, pink sunbeam shone through the huge break in the roof, making their shadows even longer.

"Anne," said Gilbert, "what do you think about . . ."

He turned, but Anne was gone. A gentle breeze, wafting through the large meeting hall, erased the small places where her feet had disturbed the sand on the floor.

"She disappeared—like a summer wind." Belloc said, his voice a little dreamy. "Does she do that often?"

"If you mean jumping in and out of your life without warning, greetings, or farewells, yes." Gilbert said. "Truth is it gets old after a while. She's someone you can fall hard for, but I don't think she's someone I can settle down with."

"Pity," Belloc said, still looking wistfully as the last vestige of the footprints disappeared. After a second or two he sighed, blinked, shrugged his shoulders. "Your friend Herb—he's gone, too. Perhaps he and Anne might be a match, hey?"

"Not likely. I—hey, where did...Emrys, he's gone, too."

"Well, whatever has taken place out there seems to have stopped. This large beast isn't going to be going anywhere, it seems," he said, looking at the wreck of the large ornithopter. The fat hand of the third man could just be seen beneath the twisted metal, snaky trails of blood reaching out from his fingers.

There was a sound at the stairwell. Belloc's hand went to his empty holster, and Gilbert brought his fists up and planted his right foot in the ground in the fighting stance Chang had showed him a long time back. He winced slightly as his now injured foot hit the ground, but held his position. He looked to his right and saw Belloc in an identical pose beside him.

"Come to think of it," Gilbert said, "if they have guns, wouldn't it be smarter to hide?"

"If they have guns, they'll find us and shoot us eventually, Gilbert. I'd rather go down fighting, wouldn't you?"

The door burst open. It was Frances! Her top hat was a bit off kilter and her dress was a bit tattered at the edges, but all else was still in place.

"Gilbert!" Frances shouted, and ran to him.

Something in Gilbert shifted. Yes, Anne had been beautiful. And exciting. But she could never be the woman, wife, or mother that Frances was right now, at this very moment. Anne had been trained to be an agent for over half of the eighteen years of her life. It would take another twenty for her to be the kind of woman Frances was *now*, right now, and in front of him.

He ran to her, and she to him. They embraced each other in a hug that lasted for several very long minutes.

Belloc looked, and saw the girl—girl? It was a girl who'd put on a uniform! What a clever thing she...

He and Beatrice looked at each other across the room.

Beatrice felt her throat get very warm at the sight of the handsome lieutenant.

Belloc, seeing the pretty girl in the uniform of the enemy, bristled for a moment but stopped when he saw the Joan-of-Arc hairstyle she sported. She had lovely blue eyes, and was tall, near as tall as that Gilbert beanpole . . .

Oh, wait . . .

"Gilbert!" Frances said, looking into his eyes, "I have wonderful news! This girl! She's your sister! Your sister, Gilbert! She heard it from the Doctor himself! You have a sister, and a brother, too!"

"I know!" he said, pulling back just enough to pull out the photos the Doctor had sent him. "They were the reason I came here! I kept trying to tell you when we were running around, but never got the chance—we kept being interrupted!"

"Why didn't you tell me when you received these pictures, then?"

"I wasn't sure if it was all a fake—I had to come here to be sure. And now—" he looked at Beatrice, who by now had walked over and stood beside Belloc, smiling, "now, I know."

Gilbert started to walk towards Beatrice, his arms extended to give a hug. But Frances pulled him back. "Gilbert," she said, pulling him aside and whispering in his ear, "When I close my eyes I still see that horrible, false stipplograph of you and that red-haired girl. Before we go any further, Gilbert, before anything else, I must know: is she in your heart? I *must* know!"

"Once," he said, "once, she was. But that's done. She's gone, and something tells me she won't be back."

"And you?"

He smiled. "Well, *I'm* back," he said, and gave her a gentle kiss on the lips that lasted a full minute.

"Umm . . . Gilbert?" Belloc said. "Did you, ah, want to consider our escape from this place anyti-OOF!" he grunted, as Beatrice elbowed him in the gut.

"I've been thinking," Beatrice said, "perhaps it might be best to leave these two alone for a bit? It's quiet outside, now. The thugs have all run off—the ones who weren't captured, anyway. The rest I saw fleeing through a hole in the stairwell wall. We'll be quite safe in the courtyard they have down there, where a bunch of soldiers have gathered."

Belloc looked first at Gilbert and Frances. Their kiss was now finished, and they were locked in a hug, each with closed eyes.

Hilaire Belloc watched the pair of young lovers for a few more seconds, and then back at the girl before him.

"You know, you're very convincing, Miss . . ." he let the pause hang in the air.

"Chesterton," she said, smiling. She turned to go and led him out the ruined doorway, down the stairs into the courtyard.

1914 A.D.

"*What do you think that is?*" Anne shouted. *The sun was rising, but not yet enough to see clearly what was approaching them in the gloom.*

Father Flambeau shrugged. "An ornithopter?" His eyes were fixed on the sky, visible through the empty half of the dome and floor that had stood unrepaired for two decades, as had the wreckage of the ornithopter on the ground near them.

"Well, I guessed that," she said. "I mean whose side is it on?" "Quick," Gilbert said, running to the dusty wreck on the ground and taking a hiding position behind it, grunting a mild curse under his breath as his boot heel crunched the skeletal hand that reached out from underneath the wreckage.

They hid, Gilbert, Anne and Father Flambeau. A few seconds later the ornithopter came into view. It was an opulent flying machine, flying the colors of England and His Majesty, and sporting a very intimidating set of cannons and smaller arms that bristled from its nose, sides and tail.

Despite its encumbrances, it slipped neatly onto the floor and landed gently next to the wreck, on the other side of Gilbert and his companions.

While the blades powered down, Gilbert looked first to Anne, then to Flambeau. They each nodded in turn, tightened their hands on their weapons.

They heard a sound of metal doors opening, and then that of a small staircase unfolding and hitting the stone ground.

Heavy shoes sounded on the steps, with a cadence that suggested no need to be careful, quiet, or to hurry.

Gilbert gulped and prayed. Men who sought his life were almost always more dangerous when they weren't cautious.

After five, meaning-laden steps, the first shoe made a dull thud on the ground, followed by silence.

The pause was infuriating.

"Gilbert Chesterton," called a voice, "you can stop hiding now!"

All three on the other side of the wreck looked at each other. "Is that the Prime Minister?" Father Flambeau said.

"Belloc!" shouted Gilbert and Anne both at once, sheathing their weapons as they rose and ran around the side of the downed ornithopter.

As they rounded the side of the wrecked machine, they beheld a figure familiar in pictures to all in the Western world: A large man, with a square lantern jaw, dressed in a dark suit and covered with a black cloak, carrying a shiny black walking stick. The hair was thinning at the top, but still dark and slick against his head.

And the wide, welcoming smile, seldom seen in photographs, was unmistakable to those like Gilbert who'd seen it before.

"Hilaire!" Gilbert shouted, grabbing the larger and shorter man in a hug. "How'd you get here?"

"Fairly easily," he said as he gave a hug of his own that lifted Gilbert aloft and nearly broke the taller but more slender man's back. "When I heard," he said, after setting Gilbert down "that you lot were on planet, I knew just where you were headed, and thought you might find yourselves in trouble. Glad to see I was right, and now I can play the story to the press as a curiosity trip that turned into a rescue. Oh, and . . . hello, Anne."

Anne smiled and curtseyed. Belloc leaned over to give her a welcoming kiss on the cheek.

"Well, then, Hilaire," Gilbert said, "has my sister tamed you as of yet?"

"Long ago, as you know. She's waiting for us back at the base. She joined me on the rocket and wanted to come out here to the tower, but I forbade it as too dangerous. She's likely on pins and needles waiting for us! Let's get you both aboard, and . . ."

Hilaire Belloc paused, seeing the largest man he'd seen outside of the army in a good, long while emerge from behind the wreck.

"Hello, Prime Minister," the man said, extending a huge hand from his dark clothing.

"Good evening to you, Father," said Belloc, noting the white collar that was still part of the priest's armor. "Gilbert, I take it this is the great Father Flambeau?"

"The very same," said Gilbert. "This priest saved my life—our lives, really—more times than you have fingers. And throw in a few toes for good measure."

"Well, in an official Ministerial ornithopter, there's always room for one more," Belloc said, shaking the priest's hand and smiling. Then he turned to the three of them, pointing to the door of the 'thopter with his walking stick. "Come on, all of you. We've got to eat supper, and then I've got to meet with the delegation of the Yellow Martians to sign the latest treaty. The Reds and Whites are already on board, hopefully after tomorrow the darker fellows south of the river Iss with come along as well."

"What's the holdup?" Gilbert asked as they boarded.

"Apparently there's some dignitary of theirs who's been kidnapped by miscreants of one group or another. Perhaps, if someone were to rescue him, it might make that next round of negotiations go much more smoothly."

"Well, if it helps save lives," Gilbert began.

"After dinner," said Anne. "We just finished one adventure."

"And you've already begun another," finished Father Flambeau, who *winked as they seated themselves in the plush couches.*

Belloc smiled, and whistled through his teeth at the silent pilot. Anne looked at Gilbert lovingly, who leaned over and kissed her.

"Supper, yes," said Belloc as the ornithopter obeyed the pilot's commands and rose from the stone floor into the air, then began the journey back to Syrtis Major. "Supper, and then the next adventure, whatever form it may take."

He smiled at Gilbert, who blushed and chuckled as Anne nuzzled his cheek.

****

James Matthew Arnold Richardson, London banker and amateur gambler, tapped his pencil furtively. It was Friday, and very nearly four o'clock. He wished to be home. He wished to be drinking a tumbler full of strong alcohol, and he wished to be sitting in his favorite chair, anticipating an evening of betting on dogs, rats, sloats, or any other number of animals in competition with one another.

But the call had not come. The one that came every Friday. The one with the cryptic statement inside that he would then relay by phone and telegram to the local heliograph station.

He'd often wondered where the message went. In theory it could have flashed a message through relay stations and ships in the ether all the way back to Earth in a matter of hours. But when four p.m. turned to five, and then five thirty, he made the call with the words listed in the packet to use in such an emergency. He dialed the number, heard the receiver rise on the other end.

"Barsoom is silent," Richardson read carefully to the silent speaker on the other end of the phone.

Instead of a quick hangup, there was a pause. Richardson felt a cold prickle in his back and a sick feeling in his stomach for reasons he could not name.

"Say it again," said a gravelly voice on the other end.

"Barsoom is silent," Richardson said, emphasizing each word and syllable.

Another pause. Then the call ended as the other party hung up.

Richardson looked at the envelope he'd pulled the words from, and swallowed. This was difficult. Perhaps a night of gambling and drink would steady his nerves, perhaps not. Tonight, in any event, he'd go directly to the men's club without a stop home, and begin drinking immediately.

****

The Caller looked at the phone. The message he'd been given dictated that he open a specific envelope, with a message inside to him he had more than simple trouble believing:

Caller, it began, *if you have opened this message, it is because you have received the words "Barsoom is silent" from your contact.*

You have also confirmed that this message is correct.

If you receive these words, it is because you are effectively the last man of consequence among the agents of the Circle here on the red planet. You are to transmit the Heliographic code below to our receptors on Earth. If you fail to do so, or even delay, our network will slowly unravel. Governments will operate independent of our guiding hand, and we can't have that. They have already become dependent upon our benevolence to the point that they might very well begin shooting at each other in unsanctioned conflicts, without us to inform and guide their steps. You must immediately send the code below, else all might be lost. It will set in motion the contingency plan we have in place, calling up those we have been grooming to take our places, albeit earlier and in a larger group than we had planned. If you fail, the civilization we have striven so mightily to form will shatter, and our plans for a world unified under our qualified management may be delayed for generations.

Your words are:

BARSOOM IS SILENT, AND ARCHIBALD IS DEAD.

He never, ever thought he'd have to relay the message he'd just been given, but there it was. After years of punctuality, it had happened.

And the message he'd been given could only have been given if the Circle was totally, utterly in ruins, without a single man left to helm the ship of control over the world, or even their flunkies and sucessors to keep their hands on the wheel.

He took one last bite of the sausage he'd been eating, and walked towards the Heliograph. His knees were shaking, his stomach was churning, and his mouth felt drier from fear than ever before. Maybe the bit of food in his stomach would help quiet his gut a bit, at least.

He swallowed the bite, took the goggles out of his pocket, strapped them onto his head and fired up the gaslight in the giant spotlight.

The bite of sausage stopped.

He closed and opened his throat a bit, in an effort to push it down. He knew that it'd play havoc through an upset stomach later, but as he tested the slats in the heliograph, he suddenly realized that his airway wasn't working either.

He cleared his throat. And did it again. And again. It wouldn't budge!

He looked out the window. He was purposely the only man within a hundred miles of the station. There'd be no outside help today.

He tried to swallow again, and the sausage now blocked his oxygen completely.

He tried to stay calm, to massage his throat and unblock his airway. But it was no use.

No, he thought, *Not like this . . .*

He began to move the slats, but knowing that it would take him perhaps five minutes to relay the message, if he hurried. He was doing the equivalent of holding his breath, that was all, he told himself. Just holding his breath . . .he tried to ignore the little black dots that began collecting at the edges of his field of vision. He began moving the slats, but realized he'd forgotten which letter he'd just flashed to the ship in orbit above the surface of Mars. Had he reached A, R, had he already flashed the S? Should he. . .

Darker now. Trying to breathe. . .

As the darkness claimed him, he fell to the ground and had no more real thoughts. No more wishes, only regrets. In the midst of all his panicked ideas while the room began to tilt and sway, the one thing he could see clearly was that his life had been truly wasted in every sense of the word that was important.

He laid there for a few more minutes, clawing ineffectively at his throat with hands than had become as useless as flippers. When he was finally still, the light stayed on for six full hours. Finally exhausted of fuel, the gaslight burned out and died.

The station and the Caller's rotted body within wasn't discovered for two more years, not until the Great War had spread to Martian colonies. The German scouts who found the station and burned what was left of the body noted the station as a curiosity of British make, burned all irrelevant paperwork found there, and appropriated the great heliograph's spotlight for the war effort.

****

"You can get up now, Hawkeye."

He opened his eye and looked up to the pink-orange sky. He took a deep, shuddering breath and made a point of not looking at the owner of the voice that had woken him. "You know I hate it when you call me that, John." He said, slowly rising and brushing a lock of dirty blond hair out of his eyes.

"And *you* know that I just don't care. How many times have you feigned death now, just to escape saying your goodbyes to people?"

"Far too many. Help me up, would you?"

Still smiling, John rose from his cross-legged position with a quick, single elegant move, and grabbed Emrys' wrist in a manly grasp. "Up, ho!" John said. "Some day you're going to have to show me that trick of putting yourself back together without burning or stitches."

"It's not precisely a trick, John. And it's not magic, either. Not as you understand it, anyway. It's just *help*."

"And are you ever going to *help* me understand it, Emrys?"

"I doubt it."

"Oh, *please*."

"No."

"Please, *hawk*."

"No.

"*Baby* hawk."

"No. And tread lightly, warlord."

"Alright...*merlin*."

Emrys stopped and closed his eyes, then opened them and nodded to something on his right invisible to John Carter.

Carter's smile disappeared and his laugh turned into a yell of surprise as he was lifted several feet into the air and dropped unceremoniously into a heap on the ground.

"Well, that's more the spirit, Emrys! What're we going to do now, hey?"

"*You*, John, are going to go home and get your wife's people ready for a rather protracted conflict that's going to reach here in about two years."

"I? What about you then, old friend?"

"I'm going back to Earth. Alone."

"And why's that?"

"I've got to fight a war."

FOUR MONTHS LATER

****

Gilbert dug a finger down his collar and pulled in a semicircle for the fortieth or fiftieth time that morning.

"Gilbert, will you stop doing that? I've faced down Tharks with naught but peashooters in my hand, and you're making me nervous."

"Easy for you to say, Master Sergeant Belloc. Your bachelorhood won't be ending in the next" he looked at the large clock, "twenty-four minutes!"

"No, you're right. But I wish it was."

Gilbert looked in the long mirror. His dark wedding clothes looked immaculate on him—the Blogg's personal tailor had seen to that. The jacket alone added an inch to each of his shoulders and biceps, making him seem almost muscular.

As he looked at his reflection, a white-gloved hand clapped on his shoulder. "You wish he were here, don't you?"

Gilbert shrugged. "Herb was a good friend, Hilaire. I couldn't exactly ask him to be my best man, but it would've been nice to have him here today."

"Would you have him here, if you could pick anyone?"

"No, not really. If a fairy godmother came down and asked that question, I'd actually pick my folks."

"Sounds like you've got a good head on your shoulders. My father once said, a boy puts friends before family. A man puts his family before all."

"What if your family's evil?" Gilbert asked, still looking at his reflection and fiddling with his tie for the three-hundredth time since he'd put it on that morning.

"I think there are exceptions to almost anything, don't you?"

"Almost. Well, Hilaire, these days there's no other man on earth than yourself I'd rather have watching my back, either in fight or at my wedding."

They heard a knock at the door. Hilaire looked at Gilbert warily, and motioned him to stand back. Two nights previously, a fellow in a long dark coat and hat had offered Gilbert a staggering amount of money to walk away from the marriage, adding two zeros to the end of the amount before he left. After he was gone, some lunkhead accused Gilbert of spilling his drink and started a bar fight Gilbert and Hilaire had barely come out on top of. Hilaire had been there both times, and was invaluable on both occasions.

But, Hilaire had cautioned after the bar fight, folks who tried money first usually tried a beating second. Since both had failed, they might get a little more desperate next time.

Now, less than a half-hour before the wedding, Gilbert and Hilaire got on either side of the door to the changing room and readied themselves. Hilaire's hand was on the doorknob.

Gilbert, his fists up, held out three fingers, then two, then one . . .

Hilaire pulled open the door just as the knocking started again.

An older man stood in the doorway, dressed similarly to Gilbert and Hilaire.

"Fath . . . I mean, Will . . . I mean, Mister Bl . . . I mean,"

"Hello, Gilbert," said the older man. "May I come in? I wish to speak with you."

Hilaire stepped back out of sight and shook his head emphatically, mouthing the word "NO!" three times without any sound while waving his hands in front of him.

Gilbert thought for a second about following Hilaire's advice, but then decided against it. If this was going to be his father-in-law in twenty minutes, it'd be wise to start out on terms as good as possible.

"Certainly, please, come in."

William Blogg was not a tall man. In fact, he was close to the same height as his daughter. As he entered the room that had been reserved for Gilbert and his best man, Gilbert could see he had tucked his sizable top hat underneath his arm.

"Have you found the accommodations adequate, Gilbert?" he said, looking around the room.

"Um, yes. Yes, very much. There's, ah, a lot of light in the windows, and the mirrors are, well, very, very clean."

"Our compliments as well to your tailor, Mister Blogg," said Belloc, his hands at the sides of his military-dress uniform pants while his head tilted just slightly. The perfect model of a British soldier addressing his betters in a formal situation. "The fit and cuts of our suits are excellent. I have truly never found their equals."

"I will let him know, Master Sergeant Belloc. When do you *leave*, to begin Officer's Training?"

"I will be transported to the school in Kensington within the month. God willing, I shall be able to use my time served on Mars, and be commissioned in a month instead of a full year."

"Splendid," said Mister Blogg.

"Yes, quite. I relish the opportunity to serve Her Majesty, either here or on Mars again."

"You'd be willing to, ah, *return* to Mars?"

"Mister Blogg, a good soldier never shies from any duty to his Queen, country *or* comrades."

"A very, very admirable position. Would that more of our own fighting men and officers had your mettle, we would have prevailed in far more conflicts. And been the unquestioned masters of the world far earlier and remain so for quite some time."

Gilbert watched the conversation with a subtle fascination. It really wasn't hard for him to decode the subtext of their speech; Blogg was telling Belloc he didn't care much if he lived or died, and would like to be left alone with Gilbert for a period of time. And Belloc had said in so many words that he didn't plan to let Gilbert out of his sight without Gilbert's say-so.

"You know, Hilaire, it seems I need to talk to Mr. Blogg here. Could you stand sentry for a second and make sure no one disturbs us?"

Hilaire looked at Gilbert, as if to confirm that Gilbert knew what he was getting himself into.

"Oh, no," said Mr. Blogg, "on second thought, Gilbert, I think your friend should be here for the matter I need to discuss."

Hilaire looked again to Gilbert, who nodded his head.

"Now, Gilbert, as I said, a matter has just come to my attention. It would seem you and Master Sergeant Belloc have had a degree of unwanted attention in the past day or so. Is this correct?"

Gilbert made a point of avoiding Hilaire's eyes. He knew he needed to appear the man in front of Blogg now, even if he didn't feel it inside.

"Yes, Sir, you might very well say that. A fellow at a pub offered me enough money to start a small country if I broke the engagement. Another fellow started a fight with me a few minutes later by spilling a drink on me. Fortunately, Hilaire here was able to pounce on him before his knife did a little tapdance on my innards."

"I see. Most regrettable. Gilbert, I have learned who it was that made these crude attempts at bribery and murder. I assure you, I had nothing to do with either of them."

"Who, then? Who wants me gone or dead, or both?"

"Rivals, my boy. As I am sure you know, there is no shortage of people who believe that marriage to my daughter would result in their fortunes being made. You *are* aware of this, aren't you?"

"Where I come from, most men who want a lot of money work for it. Marrying for money is looked at as one step up from thieving it."

Blogg smirked. "Too often here, they are one and the same. Gilbert, I want to believe with all my . . . with all I have that you truly love my daughter, and desire her for *her alone*. Let me explain." He handed his cane to Gilbert, but Hilaire politely took it before it touched Gilbert's hands.

Blogg smiled as he began unbuttoning the tunic of his suit. "You have the makings of a true friend, here, Gilbert. Treasure him; he's one that won't turn on you later. Here, now," he said, unbuttoning his shirt and then his undershirt.

Gilbert now saw why Mr. Blogg was so habitually protective of his chest area. For with his three layers of clothing now exposed, Gilbert saw that the small, stout man had a wind-up box the size of a man's fist in place of where his heart would normally have been.

"This," he said, "is why I agreed to the marriage. I have no idea how much time I have left in this world, even with the extra sand in my hourglass that this little bit of clockworks has bought me. I wish to see my daughter wed, and wed happily. And she seems happier with you than any of the wastrels or idiot sons who've sought her hand since her twelfth year on this earth.

"But, young Gilbert, I wished to make you aware of this: I will resist a man who weds her for her fortune alone as much as I would a man who would beat her and my grandchildren. Do you see this? The elder Williamson thought he could buy me, but I never intended for that quisling son of his to marry Frances, do you understand?"

"Completely. I love your daughter, Mister Blogg. I think I've been clear on this point many a time."

"True. But will it be as clear after this? Gilbert, as I said, I'd rather she be happily wed than richly if I had to choose. This has been a difficult decision for me, but it is one I make now and without falsehood. If you marry my daughter today, she will not have a dowry beyond a hundred pounds. You will not be able to count upon my death as being the means to a life of leisure and ease. In short, you will receive a pittance, but can expect no more in terms of financial support from myself or Frances's mother, sisters or brother, or any other quarter of my family. Is that understood?"

It was Gilbert's turn to smile. "Mister Blogg," he said, suddenly feeling very expansive, "I can truthfully say that your family's money has never been a reason for my attentions to her. Had you been a baker or a costermonger, I still would have pursued and proposed to her. I fully expect for us to move into the modest apartment I've rented for the last year, and to continue my career as a journalist. I've made this clear to Frances on more than one occasion, and she's been most willing to agree."

"Very well, then," said the older man, winding up his heart. After buttoning up his shirts, he then held out his hand to take his stick from Belloc.

Stick in hand, he looked steadily at Gilbert. "Be assured, young man, I will not change my position. This is no simple test. I hope you are truly sincere regarding your affections for my daughter. I am decidedly less than thrilled at my daughter being married in a papist ceremony, but this is irrelevant to the financial considerations I put before you now. I will not donate a single penny to your fortunes beyond her dowry, which I am certain will not last you out the year."

Gilbert smiled and stuck out his chin and his right hand. "I wouldn't have it any other way."

Mr. Blogg looked, nodded, shook Gilbert's hand briefly and left the room. Belloc shut the door behind him. The sound of his expensive shoes tapped and plodded down the wooden steps.

"You have a hard row to hoe with a father-in-law like that, Gilbert."

"Frances is worth it. She's worth ten-thousand father-in-laws. A million. A million million."

"What about her mother?"

"She's not so bad."

"Makes me glad my intended has only two brothers for extended family."

"Your . . . have you . . . you and Beatrice?"

"After officer's school. I proposed last week. Didn't she tell you?"

"No, but it explains why she's had that smile on her face even with Cecil being more of a brat than usual."

"Makes sense. Right after she said yes I tried to get her to say no. Told her all about how hard it was to be married to a man in the military. But she's a difficult person to dissuade when she sets her mind to something."

Gilbert had trouble digesting this last bit, and settled for looking out the window. "Twelve minutes," Hilaire said. "Still time to run, if you wish. I've got a pair of shoes better for running than those."

Gilbert looked at him. "You're serious?"

"Yes. Most assuredly. You're a good fellow, Gilbert. And she's a good lady. No need to see a pair of good people yoked together who really should be with other people."

Gilbert looked him square in the eye. "Belloc, maybe you killed Tharks with a pistol and a saber, but I killed my share of Martians with a six-shooter and a pair of old boots. I know you mean well. But if you try to tempt me like that again, I'll pound you six ways to Sunday. And you may kill me, but I'll leave ya something to remember me by. Now," he said, "having said that, facing down Tharks, Warhoons, white apes, and just about every agent the Circle could throw at me, I think I can handle getting married to the most beautiful, holy, and wonderful woman in the world before she wakes up and figures out she can do better than me. Wouldn't you say?"

Belloc stood tall. "I seriously think that kick to the head I gave you in the desert knocked a bit of sense into you."

"Maybe. Maybe. We made a good team the other night, when I saved you from that brawler in the bar."

"You . . . *you* saved *me*? Just how much *did* you drink?"

"Not so much I didn't see you take that pool cue to the head 'afore I stepped in with a steel beer mug."

"Oh, this is redic—wait! What time is it?"

They looked at the clock. They had three minutes!

The priest looked at his watch. Gilbert had a reputation for being late, but on his wedding day?

Then, Gilbert was there, at the back of the chapel that had been modified and consecrated at Mr. Blogg's specific order.

How the dickens? Did it matter? Father Flambeau, barely a priest for three years now, readied himself for his first wedding outside of his low Church in the Rookery. He raised his hand and the organist struck up the tune.

Gilbert, now at the front of the Church before the altar, gulped and gulped again when he saw the most beautiful girl in the world walking down the aisle in her white wedding dress, her face hidden by a beautiful, intricate veil made of white lace.

There was also another woman wearing a veil in the audience. As the groom had few family present at the wedding, Frances's family, friends, and business associates of her father were packed into pews on both sides of the church. It was easy for a woman with a darkened veil around her face to view the proceedings without interference.

"Lovely couple, aren't they?" said a man's voice next to her on the left.

She turned her head to look. The man who spoke to her wore dark glasses and a black longcoat as he watched the young lovers during the ceremony. His hair had once been brown, but was now dyed a dark black, the color of a jet jewel.

"Why are you here, Cleaner?" she said, leaving the veil in place.

"The same reason, I suspect, you are, Actress. By-the-by, would you be comfortable dispensing with the aliases? With the circle broken and war clouds gathering all over the continent, it seems a bit silly to use those names, don't you think?"

"Certainly. What will you do now, Herbert?"

"I've no idea. I've got a bit of money from some trinkets I stole after that Martian temple-thing fell to pieces. I suspect you did the same? Well, no matter. I'm not their man anymore. Even if I was, they're all gone, and the coming war will likely clean away anything else they've left behind."

They watched the ceremony for a few more minutes. Bible verses were read, the priest spoke, and through it all Gilbert stared at the veiled form of his love. She did the same back to him, her smile visible even through her veil all the way to the back row where Anne and Herbert sat.

"I proved a poor friend to him," Herb whispered, more to himself than to Anne. "Despite my best efforts. I came today because I wanted to see him happy."

"He's happy, Herbert," Anne whispered, her own voice close to breaking. "Happier *without* us than I think he ever could have been *with* us."

They waited a minute more.

"Anne," said Herb, looking at her brown veil, "what do you think about . . ."

"No."

Herb looked as if he were going to say more, but instead shrugged and sat for another minute. When the crowd stood at part of the Mass, he moved to go. "Goodbye, Anne," he said. "With a little luck, you'll never see me again."

"With a little more, you'll never see me, either."

Herb slipped away.

"A bit of a difficulty, was he?" whispered a new voice at her right, after Herb had disappeared from her left.

Anne turned. She knew that tone of voice, and felt no desire to put up with some fool trying to impress her.

"And you are?" she said.

"Gilbert," he replied.

Anne hiccupped.

He turned to face her. He had a pair of brass-rimmed dark glasses, and a small, soft red light glowed from behind one of the lenses. "Gilbert Blythe," he finished, "at your service."

Anne stared at him for three long seconds. She took her right brass hand out from inside the muff she had been hiding it in, and swept away her veil.

It was Gilbert Blythe's turn to hiccup.

"Are you a stranger to red hair, Mister Blythe, or are you ill in some way?"

"If I were ill, I should be glad of it. I'm a medical student, and could cure myself. No, actually, aside of your utterly irresistible blue eyes, milady, what made me jump just now was that right hand you swept your veil aside with. Is that a mark five pincher?" He then touched the edge of the lens of his glasses without the light behind it, and it flipped up on a hinge at the top rim. He looked closely at the hand Anne had just used to sweep aside her veil.

"I . . ." she said, looking at her three-fingered artificial hand, suddenly wishing she could hide it again.

"Oh, I hope I haven't upset you," he said. "Please forgive me, you see, not only am I a medical student, I am, well," he raised his pantleg, revealing a leg made of brass and steel.

"Oh, my," Anne whispered.

"Yes, a medical school prank gone horribly wrong. But it sparked my interest in artificial limbs. How many points of articulation did they give you?"

"Points of . . . you know the terminology?"

"Know it? I worked for the fellow who wrote most of it last year! Look, I'm sorry, I'm certain I'm making a fool of myself here. I don't even know these people getting married. My mentor's research is funded by the bride's father. But . . . well, do you have any connection to these two?"

Anne watched as Father Flambeau gave the last blessing of the Mass; she and many others in the back row had declined to go up for Communion.

"No," she said. "Not any more."

"Well, then, would you be willing to join me after the ceremony? I'd rather not go to a reception where I neither know no one and have nothing in common with anyone present."

Anne looked at him again. His skin was smooth and pale, but not sickly. His hair was black, black as coal . . . or maybe raven wings. He removed the glasses, and . . .

His eyes were normal! Better than normal; they were a pair of two, perfect brown orbs that . . .

"These are some visual enhancers," touching the rims of his spectacles. "I'm testing them out for my mentor."

Anne smiled, truly smiled for the first time since she'd left Mars.

"I'm ready," she said, "for just about anything."

"Quite the spirit," he said. "Oh, look! They've finished!"

Father Flambeau faced the congregation, all of whom had stood when told to.

"Ladies and gentlemen," he said, "I present to you, Mister and Missus Gilbert Keith Chesterton!"

The congregation clapped politely. Flambeau whispered to Gilbert and Frances. Gilbert smiled widely, turned to her and lifted her veil.

Gilbert kissed Frances.

Behind them, Gilbert's best man kissed Beatrice, who looked resplendent in her bridesmaid's dress.

Anne turned to Gilbert Blythe and kissed him on the cheek. He blinked, then turned to look at her. "That's a tad forward, don't you think?" he said, smiling.

"We're at a romantic wedding, war is coming, and I feel that I shall delight in your company this afternoon. Forward is the order of the day, wouldn't you agree?"

He looked at her again, unsure. But after three seconds he broke into a happy smile. "Wholeheartedly," he said.

****

And, at the same moment in another time and place, Gilbert and Anne stood on a balcony and watched a pink sun dip below an orange skyline.

"Well, Mrs. Chesterton," Gilbert said, his arms wrapped around her waist from behind as they both watched the horizon, "yet another day ends, and another night begins."

"And what will our first day tomorrow bring, do you think?" she asked, her voice soft and dreamy.

"Well, Hilaire said there was that nobleman that needs rescuing from the Warhoons. Plus, there's some concern they may try to make an attack on the city . . ."

"Let's think about something else, first," she said, turning around and tilting her head up towards his.

They kissed.

Gilbert was in such a sense of pure joy that he didn't even hear the war horns cry at the city gates warning of an attack. Neither of them heard the defender ships rising from the hangar bay to meet the threat, and they both happily ignored the agonized screams of the vanquished attackers as their ships were blasted from the sky.

And after their kiss was finished, they had only eyes for each other and left the balcony for whatever adventures awaited their futures. The worlds were theirs.

And when Anne found herself with child a month later, it changed everything.

THE END

Post Script...

I began this series in 2003 A.D. during a week when we were snowed in our home in Vancouver, Washington. I have finished the final edits of this, the last book in the Trilogy, twenty years later in Irving, Texas during another week-long series of snow days [it happens, even in the Lonestar state]. My goal was and always has been to re-present Gilbert Keith Chesterton in a way familiar and accessible to an American audience, so that a new generation of readers will grow to appreciate the real man Chesterton was and became.

A lot's happened since then. The Obama presidency, the Trump presidency, the Biden presidency, our family has ruptured and reunited, and we've had one medical emergency after another. Spontaneously and accidentally erased final edits, issues with IPs of long dead great authors, and welcome mentorships from more established authors, births, deaths, postponements, and a hundred other things that could be a series of novels on their own. Through it all, the aim's always been a beacon in front of me, or my old Sergeant from Air Cadets yelling: *Finish! Finish it! Let's go, people! You're not done yet!*

I'm grateful to God for seeing me through and guiding me through all these many trials and tribulations. I am grateful, too, for the many good people God has seen fit to send in my path when I felt like giving up and letting it all die on the vine; it seemed each time I said inside 'I'm done,' that I got a new email from a longtime fan, or someone would approach me after Mass to talk about writing, or a parent would ask: "Are you *that* John McNichol? My son loves your books! When is the next one coming out?" Not the least of these was a poem I received about a little Catholic shrine in India called Our Lady of the Red Sands...

I am thankful, too, for the good people who have encouraged me in their own, immutable and very welcome ways to help me finish this last book in the thirteen years it's taken me to this last finishing at my dining room table.

My parents encouraged my writing from the days when my mother bought me the plastic toy typewriter that I banged out my name and the alphabet on again and again, later graduating to book reports on the ancient model my grandfather Coleman had used, and then to stories and books. Most important, my Mom and Dad gave me the gift of their faith, which has brought me through more storms of life than I can count. My siblings have always been there for me when I have needed them, and I both thank God for and pray for them, too.

Dr. DeOna Bridgeman helped with medical questions in the last volume and this one, and managed the difficult trick of explaining what a person could and could not survive in ways that even an English major like myself could understand. My dear friends Peter Cooney and David McCarthy not only gave me inspiration time and again with this work, they've been the Spock and Dr. McCoy in my life with a number of issues that have arisen in the truly surrealistic adventure that the McNichol family life has been in the last decade.

Steve and Cheryl Acton and their wonderful kids Ted and Ashley were wonderful supports during my most challenging days when I was teaching in Oregon, as has Mike Galvan, the Rodenbeck family, and the host of other wonderful parents who became friends over time after their kids graduated. Lori Lett became a friend and helper time and again after privileging me by using my humble works to teach and form her children. My gaming crew from Portland have never let me down, always been better friends to me than I have been to them, and taught me so much about how a good story can build bridges and bond friendships forever. My students now and past inspire me every day in ways they never suspect. Last here but near first in my life are my McNichol family members, who will always be in my heart no matter how delinquent I have become at communicating with them.

There are many I have forgotten. Please forgive me. It's due to stupidity, not malice.

Thank you God, once again, for all you do...

John D. McNichol
Irving, TX
2/3/23,
2:20 pm

Printed in the USA
CPSIA information can be obtained
at www.ICGtesting.com
LVHW012353021124
795398LV00001B/2

9 781955 402248